The Icon Painter

Derek Beaven lives in Maidenhead, Berkshire. His first novel, *Newton's Niece* (1994), was shortlisted for the Writers' Guild Best Novel Prize and won a Commonwealth Prize. *Acts of Mutiny* (1998) was shortlisted for the Guardian Fiction Prize and Encore Prize. His third novel, *If the Invader Comes* (2001), was longlisted for the Man Booker Prize.

For more information, visit www.derekbeaven.com

Also by Derek Beaven

Newton's Niece
Acts of Mutiny
If the Invader Comes
His Coldest Winter

Pharmakon (Poetry)

The Icon Painter

DEREK BEAVEN

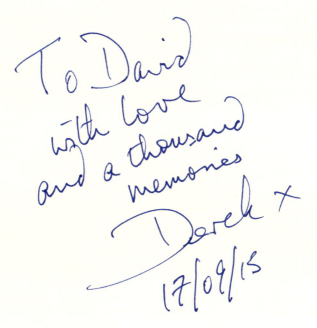

To David
with love
and a thousand
memories
Derek x
17/09/15

Rossendale *Silk Moth* Books

For Adrian

CONTENTS

About the book

by Adrian Blamires

'These are icons of hell'

What is the truth of the 'left hand paintings' produced by the artist, Owen Davy? Why—now that he has moved to a Greek island in order to paint—is his own self-portrait proving so problematic? And what, if cultural and linguistic barriers can be overcome, is to be learned from Spíros Apostolíthis, the local painter of Greek Orthodox icons?

Owen, writing email epistles of supreme literary craft to his gallery owner and friend, Theo, starts to address these questions, looking back on his youth—particularly to an affair with a married woman, Julia, and his subsequent tragicomic exile on the streets of Paris—and to his childhood, with its dark iconography. What emerges is of profound spiritual and artistic consequence, as, with new arrivals on the island and new friendships forged, the novel becomes a remarkable exploration of love.

Hilary Mantel hailed Derek Beaven's astonishing debut, *Newton's Niece*, as a 'wonderfully capacious, generous and vivid book', the work of 'an important and original writer'. Here, in his fifth novel, Beaven's importance and originality become clearer than ever. *The Icon Painter* offers a fierce critique of numerous cultural orthodoxies, whilst probing the very roots of art, memory and relationship in strange and moving ways.

Adrian Blamires is Creative Writing Fellow at Reading University, UK. He is the author of two very well received poetry collections, both published by Two Rivers Press:
The Effect of Coastal Processes (2005)
The Pang Valley (2010)

Acknowledgements & Note on Pronunciation etc.

My very sincere thanks are due to the following people: Sue, Jonathan & Kirstie Beaven for their love, support and editorial advice; Adrian Blamires for his unflagging support and encouragement during the writing of this book, his tireless editorial wisdom and inspired interventions; Derek Johns of A.P Watt, my agent for ten years, for his great and patient structural help and advice; Ian & Lynn Hogg, Nikos Atsiknoudas & Beba Skabilis for the generous hands-on experience of island bee keeping and for Ian's tales of shipwrecks and Aegean local politics; Tom Niven, Josh Lambert for much appreciated help with photographic and web design, Lakis & Shelagh Akrivos for their generous assistance with my Greek, James & Paula Wilson for their friendship and kindly editorial advice; and Peter Lamb for wonderful long walks and discussions.

Any novel set in Greece will necessarily include some snippets of Greek conversation. I've made sure that these are almost always immediately translated. The flavour of Greek speech, nevertheless, is important both to the realism and to the character of the book, and so I've also attempted to render the *sound* of Modern Greek words as nearly as I can into our more familiar alphabet.

One or two surprises show up as a result. Google Maps, books and holiday brochures print the island immediately next to Kálymnos, for example, as 'Télendos'. Certainly, it includes the letter 'δ' — delta — which gave us our own 'd'. But in Modern Greek the delta is pronounced more like 'th' in the English word 'whether', and therefore I've chosen to write the name as it sounds: 'Télenthos'. To give another example, Sýntagma, the name of the famous Square in Athens, is actually pronounced 'Sýndagma', with the 't' (when it comes after 'n') far softer than in UK English and more as in North American — and so I transliterate it as such. I should add that Greeks never make the sound 'ch' as in English 'church' (or 'sh' as in 'shiver' — or 'j' as in 'jar', for that matter). Where I do use the letter combination 'ch' in transliteration it is to represent the Greek letter 'χ', pronounced as the 'ch' in Scottish 'loch'. Greek 'γ' — gamma — is far back in the throat and not like English 'g'. Sometimes a 'y' is best.

All Modern Greek words of two syllables or more carry a simple accent mark to indicate which syllable is to be stressed. Needless to say, I have reproduced these accents, and occasionally an extra one when the syntax demands it at the end of the word. As for Ancient Greek, that is usually written with a much more complex system of accents. On the very rare occasions I use any examples in the original Greek alphabet, I've often kept in any Ancient or New Testament accents for the sake of authenticity. And I've included a translation.

A further decision had to be taken about accenting Ancient Greek names and places. The problem is that many of them are well known in English and already have their own 'English-style' spelling and pronunciation deeply embedded in our literary culture. Arcadia, for example, is written with a 'c' and stressed in English on the second 'a', whereas the Greeks standardised their spelling with a 'k' (*kappa*) and accented the 'i': effectively *Arkadía*. Philoctetes, the name of the poor archer left on the island of Lémnos during the mission to Troy (because no one could stand the smell of his wound), is traditionally stressed in English on the 'o' in the second syllable. In Greek, the accent fell more on the 'e' in the third: Philoktétes. Choosing English letters and accents in these circumstances is all far too complicated, and so I've made a rule and left such ancient names unaccented and, mostly, as they are written in English. I've left them also without italics. The same applies to any other place names, ancient or modern.

All other clearly non-English words — of whatever language — are italicised as is conventional.

In all of my novels I try to stick very closely to known information; I don't like to bend history or alter anything 'on record'. In this book, there may be a few small liberties taken for the sake of the plot with the current built environment on the islands of Léros and Kálymnos, and so I think I should acknowledge the fact here.

A final point: when speaking directly to a Greek male, you lose the 's' on the end of his first name. So 'Spíros' becomes 'Spíro' when you address him, 'Yiórgos' becomes 'Yiórgo', and so on.

Part I

Friendship

1

From: <u>owend@mail.gr</u> **Sent: 14th April 2012**

To: t.l@kuyps.co.uk

Subject: Prospects of an island

Well, Theo, the impossible has happened: Eléni and I have our own house on a Greek island, and what started as the unlikeliest and most magical fantasy has turned into fact. Mind you, once you take into account the prospecting, the permits, guarantees, caveats, contracts… Not to mention the UK sale, conveyancing, insurance, storage, shipping and the rest, then there's nothing the least magical about it. Just a lot of hard work and, occasionally, desperation. When you set your heart on a house… well, those are exactly the deals most likely to fall through. And that's in the best of times. Try relocating to Greece in the middle of the worst financial cataclysm for a generation!

Oh, and then there are the lawyers, who seem happy to let matters teeter on the brink for weeks. I can tell you, once or twice we did consider cutting our losses and giving up; you and Fran are very wise never to think of moving again.

Yet on the one hand there was Lily. And then my mother was either angry or impossibly demanding. My studio space was getting clogged more with paperwork than paintings, and the big multi-panelled project I was desperate to get going had stalled. I felt trapped.

Eléni saw the way out. She reckoned she could actually do most of her work for DCG remotely, from home. Given just a little extra hardware, and so long as she could jet to London, Frankfurt or New York now and then—and occasionally Athens—it really wouldn't matter where she was based.

It meant we could go. She hardly dared put it to her boss. But would you believe he jumped at the idea. I can only presume her occasional flights will be cheaper than London office space.

Of course, they can rely on her.

And so it was that we dared to think the unthinkable. Honestly, who would have imagined such an escape? And to Greece!

Alright, a Greek island is something of a cliché, but that doesn't trouble us. Nor does it trouble my children. Chloe seems settled in

3

Suffolk; Arun, after all the tribulations, has given his blessing. They still have Lily, and nowhere in the world is so very far away, these days.

Our decision to leave the country was made very soon after you and I last walked in the Chilterns. Too long ago. I must apologise for letting these months slip by without keeping you abreast. Everything was still up in the air. Rest assured, though, I've had you and the gallery constantly in mind. And I really do wish I could have seen you before we left, to tell you face to face everything I now have to explain in writing. We could have walked again, Theo, and the beauty of the hills would have provided just the right farewell both to you and to England.

Nevertheless, what's done is done, and I have to keep pinching myself to believe it. And so, today, with our broadband connected at last, my very first thought was to drop you this note. Yes, our running away together, Eléni and me—it's a silly, romantic notion. But there again what else does an artist need except light and peace? She says so herself.

The island? Léros is in a big sprinkle—the Dodecanese, Greek for 'twelve' of them. Imagine some primordial Titan hurling boulders north-east from Crete: Pátmos is furthest, then comes tiny Lípsi—and we're just short of that.

And why have you never heard of Léros? Because we're off the main tourist track, and the economy is mostly subsistence farming and a little fishing. Our great feature is a Byzantine castle towering right over the town, from whose heights you can see the coast of Turkey. Oh, and another claim to fame is our deep-water port, Lakkí, where the ferry comes in. The port was a prize in ancient times—and in modern: Mussolini nabbed the island before the war. Then we British bombed it. Finally, the Luftwaffe took a turn. This poor rock has come in for a pasting!

To be frank, Léros wasn't our first choice. We'd been looking further north where it's a little less arid in summer. We thought we'd found the answer in a captivating house in the Cyclades, all views and bougainvillaea, with an olive tree or two, and the obligatory grapes and pomegranates; can't you just imagine it? But someone broke the chain, and we lost it, and that was only the start of a list, as I said, of disappointments. So when Léros popped up, we took it. And it's fine. Delightful, even. We tell ourselves we've ended up where we were meant to be.

4

There's a small airport; the plane comes direct from Athens. It's better, though, to fly to Kos, for then follows a wonderful sea voyage past rocky Kálymnos and the stumps and crags of Télenthos. Not a difficult journey; and the sea glows with every marine shade imaginable. Naturally, this travel information represents a standing invitation. We have a spare double room. It would be wonderful to see you and Fran.

Our house is tucked into the slope of a hill; well, more a rise. We overlook that glorious sea again, and we're painted white — with a shiny steel water cylinder on our roof just like everyone else's. Roof is a misnomer: it's actually nothing but a reinforced concrete platform through which ugly iron stalks protrude. A common sight, the harvest of some absurd Greek tax law about completed housing. Tax dodging is one of the reasons, as everyone now knows, that the poor Greeks are in their current dire straits. Still, rain's rare, and everything else about the house is beguiling. The garden 'needs attention', but then again our neighbours' yard is nothing to speak of, either: they keep a goat and an old car in it. Fortunately, they're three hundred yards away around the face of the little rise. Anyway, we have no car and walk more or less everywhere. A store half way into town sells provisions, and we can always get a taxi if we need one.

What more should I say? Our downstairs boasts a good-sized sitting room and a rudimentary kitchen; upstairs are the bedrooms, with views. It *is* romantic. A converted outhouse serves me for a studio. I promise I shall be getting down to work once the dust settles: namely on the big project I mentioned above, which I'm very sorry not to have discussed with you earlier.

Theo, artists like me find it easier to speak with our hands than face to face. You know this. Each work begins darkly at the back of my mind, until the first germ thrusts through, sometimes with merely a line, or colour — which I hardly know how to explore, for it may be nothing. I look for a certain condition: that if it won't grow, at least it won't die. Then I might have something. And that seems to be the way of these things. They leaf out into fullness by painful degrees, and I'd be a fool to rush the process. Art waits on its own schemes and scarcely at all upon ours. I've shown you false starts and ill-advised daubs before and always regretted it.

What *shall* I tell you, then, about this big project? Let's call it self-portraiture. It's designed to make sense of all my former pieces and pull them together, so to speak. Don't worry, I'm not mirror-gazing. I

5

shan't be sending you a row of *yours truly*s that you'll have to try selling to dear Rod Hearn, or old Sherrington-Cole, or Jansen International. I'm not Rembrandt. Or Bacon. Or anyone else whose brooding, duplicated phiz they'd all kill for. I know where I stand in the market.

But I *am* myself, and doesn't self-scrutiny have an honourable pedigree? Everything we make is a kind of disclosure, and all the figures I paint—which you and buyers have so far admired—are me and nothing but me. Now I want to come clean about them.

Then imagine a string of panels, canvases, highly worked, whose figures repeat. Think of any sequence of frescoes. The Gozzoli *Magi*? Or imagine those Mantegna *Triumphs*—on their huge stretched cloths. No, I'm not that good! Yet I'm thinking of life as myth. I'm thinking of self-portraiture in an antique, almost forbidden form. You know how the artist's face will suddenly stare back at you from a crowd—at the foot, say, of some Umbrian crucifixion. It's a ploy, a painterly conceit; but your eyes meet and you do *know*; and for a minute it shakes your grasp on everything. Because you suddenly *see* him. That's the nub. I want to make it contemporary. I want to make it uncomfortable. And I want it to come alive with bright enigma.

Now, through the window next to me, the sunset air has a touch of purple. The castle glows on its high promontory, no more than a mile or so off. And there's something else to say to you. Something else needs to be a part of all this. There was a year—a missing year I've never spoken about. It was '76—that burning summer, and a girl, Julia. Lost love sent me packing off to Paris. Four months I wandered the bright streets and boulevards, as though they were the Elysian Fields, the true Champs-Élysées. City of art, city of philosophy, city of street theatre, for that matter, where I actually strutted my stuff for the crowds! Paris was broiling and comical, but the gateway indeed to an underworld. A string of painted panels, Theo. And then there was Lily.

I'm talking in riddles. Paris is a far cry from these goaty wastes. Paris and Greece: comedy and tragedy. In a manner of speaking!

Yes, take no notice of all this. Attached are some snaps of the place, and of us, taken with Eléni's phone.

I do hope all's well with you.

Owen

Subject: A sail

Dear Theo,

You're too generous, and I'm sorry you'd been worried. I wrote with trepidation; it's a genuine relief you haven't abandoned me.

Also sorry to have taken a while replying. So much to do! But I've been buoyed up by your message of support. At least things are more shipshape now. Yesterday, I was fixing blinds — the downstairs is pretty much as we want it. Not counting the kitchen, which remains primitive. Never mind. Life is good. We've even started on the garden, as the new photos show.

Eléni's extended leave is now over, though. To begin putting in the hours, she has a desk upstairs in the spare bedroom, and we've outlined a routine: I'll paint as long as she works — except today I've had to catch up on admin.

But now, with business transacted and bread-and-butter letters done, what better than to write to you? Such a pleasure, and not only because of chatting to a trusted friend. It's more. You are, and always have been, the keystone of my work, the point of reality that keeps me on track. More still, I notice that when I write to you I enjoy the keyboard in itself, finding the act of typing somehow touches my situation. For each hand has something to contribute, doesn't it? And so, too, for all I know, has each finger. That involvement of bone and sinew is bosom-close to art. It's as though one were sculpting language — a medium at once soft and very hard; each line's evocations streaking away beyond the screen, behind the script. Catch them! Why, yes, sitting here, staring through, it's almost as though we can.

You ask for more detail of the project. Of course, you want chapter and verse. But words have that perilous character of telling too much, too soon. Would you mind for the moment if we stick to exteriors and appearances? What's painting, after all, but surfaces. Critics and theorists always try to cut through them, and under that scalpel painting nearly died. So, with your permission, I'll swear off explanations. Let's allow the brushed forms to speak for themselves. When they deign to appear…

Theo, I've a confession to make. I think back over all my finished pieces, detail in place, colours minutely pulled or pushed, figures fleshed uncannily into life — and can hardly remember the hundred layers and stages that went into their achievement. That's the trance of composition. After it's done, I struggle to believe it. Almost

7

straightaway, I can't for the life of me recall how one gets from the blank canvas, or the primed and gessoed panel, to the end product.

That's how you find me now. Suddenly, at the start of things once again, I have almost no idea how one does it. And my confession is that I'm scared.

I sound like a novice. I just need to remind myself it's always like this. There are painters so delirious with their medium they dabble and scratch at it all day. I envy them. Painting's my joy, but it's also a torment, especially at this juncture. So much feels at stake: career, identity, survival…

So let's put it all to one side. Today we're bright with spring. A breeze stirs the patch of new growth I can see through the window, and one or two puffs of cumulus have shown up in the cloudless blue. It might even be England.

Oh, but Greece is always more than a place. That's why I was interested to hear of your schoolboy studies. I'm secretly jealous of your old fashioned education, your ancient declensions and tenses, your tantalising Greek 'aorists' and mysterious 'middles'. You say you remember nothing about it, but I can't believe you. I actually crave such a direct line to all that poetry and philosophy.

Yet, strangely, even to breathe the air here is somehow to take up poetry and philosophy *at source*. 'Oxygen', 'idyll', 'lyric'—pure Greek. Here *is* such an origin! For, when the sun warms up the rock, this same air, so deceptively 'southern counties' only a paragraph ago, soon begins to vibrate and shimmer in the heat. Then, yes, things do seem merely the signatures of what was once firm and concrete, and one feels for a moment as though the prime unknowable were actually present.

I rhapsodise. Forgive me. I *am* learning Greek—the painless way: from CDs. This morning I held a fragment of conversation with a lady in town. She was surprised at my even trying, and broke into the usual Hellenic generosity, praising my command of her language. She asked where I was going. I clutched the bread I'd just bought and managed to say, '*Sto spíti, Kyría*—Home, Ma'am.' It felt odd, and a little emotional.

But other words still quite defeat me: *ksenothochío*, for one. What a mouthful! All it means is 'hotel'—literally a 'box for strangers'!

I've started sketching and making notes. I've stretched that big empty canvas ready—and I do mean big, so large, in fact, that I've had to put reinforcements and struts across the woodwork as though I'm

8

making battens to a great sail. I'm preparing to crayon in some ideas. Here and there I've already dragged a couple of oil washes over it, so that it's no longer quite *tabula rasa*. Sorry, now we're into Latin. But I use the phrase advisedly: *scraped*, as though even a blank space might bear traces of some previous imprint we shall regret to discover...

It will be of me and Julia—the girl I mentioned, in that same year, '76. It will be of England, opening the whole sequence. But not a word more.

Owen

Subject: **Darkness, with reflections**

It's late at night, Theo: that time when thoughts turn back on themselves. Was I out of order in my letter? Too headlong? Have I written too much and so forced you into an exchange?

Therefore this postscript—which I realise can only make things worse, but which I yet feel compelled to add. For I'd no sooner clicked 'Send', earlier today, than I thought how selfish of me to drop all that into your mailbox without so much as a by-your-leave or enquiry as to your health, or Fran's. I tried to intercept, but the wretched thing flew off into cyberspace that very second.

The last thing I want is to overtax or misuse our friendship. Accept my apologies. I was just excited at having got even half an idea going about the damned Next Work. Trouble sleeping, now. Financial worries? Perhaps.

Still, you have good hopes, don't you, of our American friends. They take their time; but they were keen before, and I can see no reason now why they shouldn't buy again. So it's not the money, I think—rather that my artistic impulse feels stifled and resistant.

Now I'm rattling on once more, as I swear I didn't intend to. Theo, I get so locked into these sentences, once I start, that I'm almost reluctant to let them go. Look, it's just that writing was one of the things that got me through my illness, the clinic and so on, and it makes a huge difference to feel I can talk to someone such as you. Do tell me if I'm—what's the word—overstepping the mark. You must. But I do value your opinions—about everything. And I do want to hear how things are.

Well, now Eléni has woken and is calling me to come up to bed. I

9

shall sleep. All's fine here. Completely. Write when you want to.
All best wishes,

Owen

2

Subject: Landscape, with figures

Delighted to hear your news. And a two-page splash on Léros, you say, in one of the Sundays. Didn't know we did fishing holidays. Tuna, I suppose. Which paper? I might have a go, myself!

Eléni and I have just come back from a mighty island trek. Feet hurt, legs hurt, shoulders hurt. But it was good. We swam *en route* and dried quickly in the sun, before getting up into the hills again. By the way, your extraordinary story of Doug Frank! His ruse to get back on TV? I agree; that last series was dire.

To proceed. You, the classical scholar, will be pleased to know this new-found territory is divided, like Gaul, into three parts. The northern end is a hilly, sparsely inhabited region in the shape of a cauliflower. So far as we know, it contains little more than a military base and the airport. Then the land narrows to a waist or 'stalk', before abruptly filling out again for the middle section—ours. More oblong in form, this holds the town, Plátanos (= plane tree), the port, Lakkí, and the administrative offices for the whole island, such as they are. South, and the coastline narrows again to another isthmus of less than half a mile before expanding into the last part of the isle. That reminds me of no familiar object at all, unless perhaps the head of a baby elephant. Down that way there's only one road.

Or maybe two—cartography isn't a strongpoint here. Tourists go places in taxis; islanders either know the terrain like the back of their hand or wouldn't dream of wandering over its interior.

The bay of Goúrnas was the goal for our walk. It's in the central section. We set off with backpacks from the local crossroads, where there's some regular traffic and a couple of shops. Then we began climbing, with our meretricious map at the ready, up past a few attractive houses. The gardens were all afire with blossom. Birds chirped, small lizards basked on the paint-washed walls.

Very soon, though, we were in pastoral Greece. Arcadia? Parnassus? No, there was nothing poetic about it. Life off the beaten track has always been savage in these parts. Now, with the Euro crisis, people get by on what they can grow or sell. The hard earth grudges.

True, as we levelled on a plateau, there were beautiful green shoots

11

to either side and occasional patches of yellow and white spring flowers. But without these one could almost have conjured up the Australian outback. But not even rusty station wagons graced these occasional shacks: only a few chained dogs behind fences that were made from scraps of tin or wire. On someone's veranda, I saw the carcass of a goat hung up next to the cheap plastic chairs, and I made Eléni wait while I dashed down a sketch. She took a snap (attached) on her phone. The inhabitants emerged just as I'd finished — the man in vest and braces, the woman in a long black dress. '*Kaliméra*! — Good morning!' we shouted, as though we were just passing. We hoped they wouldn't set the dogs on us, but they just stared at our pale skins and outlandish shorts.

Then our unmade road dwindled to a mere hint of passage, and we sweltered along on an agricultural plain. Its crop was stiff weeds, and the sun, well up and emerging from high transient cloud, did little to enliven things. A couple of miles, and there were tree-clad clefts in the terrain, and greener folds below us. One or two brightly painted farmhouses dotted the distance, like trinkets dropped by some thieving bird.

Then we got lost. One little church was seemingly abandoned in a dip. We tramped on. An incongruous couple on a motor scooter buzzed past us before simply vanishing across the stone-strewn clay.

No other soul did we see, until, at last, the far crags of neighbouring islands reared out of the heat haze, and expanses of gorgeous sea began to gleam. We steered by the view.

The plateau ended abruptly in a drop. Beyond that had to be our bay, Órmos Góurnas.

We crossed the runnel of a dry stream to peer over the edge. Yes, there was our beach, a strip of white sand down below us about the length of a cricket pitch. Two miniature men lay naked beside a rubber dinghy. Nakedness, Theo, is visible from a height.

The sun was oppressive over our shoulders. It was noon. We wanted our swim.

So by zigzags, goat tracks and natural slopes amid sudden swathes of flowers — poppies, yarrows, teasels — and with our ankles continually scratched by the thorny scrub that was both green with new growth and baked razor sharp from summers past, we blazed a twenty minute trail to the bed of the stream. And from thence to the beach.

Maybe the lovers saw us coming. They were on their feet before we were half way down and began throwing their belongings into the dinghy. They waded to clamber in: Germans, we guessed, too tall, too smoothly tanned, too blonde to be Greek, and still wearing sunglasses while half-immersed. One got the outboard started, the other took the wheel, and they were off in retreat by the time we arrived. We would have shared; though four might have been a crowd!

On the sand lay some old burnt logs. And there was a tall frame, made of ugly, thin tubes, long rusted. We could see no reason for this eyesore until we'd put down our bags and turned around. Then we felt the fierce sun coming down between the cliffs and almost as blindingly up again from the shingle and sea. Our nook was a magnifying glass, and we were ants. Maybe the Germans had simply overheated.

Lacking either canvas or tarp, we hung our towels on the frame and managed to eat our packed lunches in a postage stamp of shadow. Then we swam, which was an instant joy, the water vacant and clean and rinsing away all preoccupations of the land. Coloured fish flickered under the glass of my facemask. The sloping silver bottom was dotted with perfect sea tokens: a star, a shell, a single, scuttling crab.

Bobbing up my head, Theo, I did sense here some intimation of your ancient world. Those nude Germans, quite Theocritan for a moment! Well, not really, but the rock about and above was gnarled and preternaturally twisted. Only the lapping sea and the cliff — hardly a bird. Whichever way I looked, I felt something chimeric just out of vision, perhaps an entity horned, incalculably limbed, or wearing a Gorgon face to scare off the would-be spirit catcher. A description of the artist? I could imagine capricious forces, the blood-ghosts of antique crimes, condemned here to replay once in a while.

Dear friend, I'm learning how to write, and this is a little far-fetched. Yet I swear I did once see, years ago on a trip to Kálymnos or Télenthos, was it, certain figures against the setting sun whose silhouettes still echoed, suddenly and uncannily, those beak-profiled people from the earliest black-figure Greek pottery. Of course, they were simply Cretan holidaymakers at play on the Aegean's edge, afloat in modern pedalos. But nevertheless…

Eléni herself seems sometimes a native here. And it's particularly by the sea, the amorous wave, rolling me over on my back to glimpse the cliff and again those drifts of flowers where we came down, the bursts of new growth… Theo, a glimpse is all that's possible in the

13

sheer intensity of light falling all around us, the blink of an eye—and it's by the sea that I do find myself truly wrested back to some prime… *tópos*. A place for Zeus, Poseidon. I'm in Greece. I live here. Again, I have to pinch myself. Laughing and splashing each other, we made love in the shallows.

Subject: *continuation* **Landscape, with ruins**

Too much information, Theo. I'm sorry. Carried away, you see, by narrative impulse! Narrative a force of its own, I discover; a pleasure at times quite irresistible, as though… Almost as though it had its *own* god.

There again, you see, the thought would never have occurred, but for the sentence demanding completion. Then hurrying on to the next, and then the next, like an addiction. Oh, we must resist the fanciful. This lure of 'and then'.

And then we returned via the coast road: a barren, cliff-edge track. But absolutely no gods here. No fanciful Sciron, either, nor Procrustes to ambush the heroic traveller. One beat-up car passed us. It jolted over rock, over tamped mud and loose stones, going who knew where. Beside us were more views, more flowers, spring orchids of incredible design, anemones, vetches, acanthus… or were they asphodel? Even some lavender. But I remained wary of that brick-red, boulder-strewn drop down to the sea on our right.

It was hot for May, even here. Sensible Northlanders, we wore our hats, slapped on sun tan lotion and drank our bottled water. Sensible Greeks, elsewhere, took their siesta.

We came upon twisted groves and gun emplacements with bunkers. We found the rust-earthed caves where islanders sheltered from wartime bombing raids—as I guess they'd done once upon a time from Barbary pirates and slavers. I took these pictures of Eléni at the mouth of a great cavern; and the one of me she took beside a bunker. Then at last we rounded a headland and were tramping homeward, dropping gradually towards our local port of Lakkí.

It was a sweat. The road goes a little inland on the foothills of a ridge, skirts an abandoned olive farm or two and then, in a long kink of pines, both hides and discloses something quite unexpected. You have to peer down through the trees. An institution—yes, that could be the word for it. Theo, we found ourselves overlooking cement-coloured buildings like low, prefabricated barrack blocks. They were disused and empty around a trashed parade ground. Beyond them lay a sheer drop to a patch of blue sea.

I stood still. Eléni walked on. She called back, 'What are you waiting for?'

'Nothing,' I said. Yet some *atmosphere* about the place had left me suddenly comfortless.

I caught up with her, and we came right down to sea level, swam again at a beach where there was some show of habitation — summer tavernas and so on. Then, eventually, tired and footsore, we slogged the last mile through the port. We got home by late afternoon. In the evening, I wrote the first part of this account to you.

This morning, still conscious of some vague, unaccountable disquiet, I did a little research.

The internet soon gave me back more than I'd bargained for. It seems Léros has a recent history as well as an ancient one, and it's a matter of shame. A scandal. It was only unearthed two or three decades ago by rightly nosy journalists. Athens was furious — it was just when Greece was positioning itself to join the EU.

Do you know, I believe I *had* read something before we arrived. In fact, I'm pretty sure there was a veiled reference in one or two of the travel guides. But when Léros came up with the estate agents and we were growing jaded in our quest for sun and solitude, maybe the last thing we wanted to think about was an extensive Google search for skeletons in its cupboard. One Greek island was surely very much like another.

The truth is quite otherwise. I told you Mussolini had grand designs on Léros because of that deep water port. He'd even built a summer residence here; and consequently the place was heavily garrisoned, which led to an abundance of military accommodation. In fact, there was a whole network of barracks, dotted both around the port and also up in the island's northernmost reaches — the cauliflower sector. Well, after the war, these buildings became vacant. Where better, thought a hard pressed Greek government, to dump the most intractable of its mental patients? And that's when the scandal started.

In truth, the mainland was still barely able to feed itself, let alone look after its needy. So the poor souls remained here. They were uncared for and often treated abominably. Then, in the sixties, during the rule of the Colonels, Léros offered perfect Gulags for dissidents, ready-made Guantánamos, well out of the way of prying eyes and far remote from the emergent tourist traps on other, prettier islands.

These appalling 'hospitals' apparently survived until quite recently, resupplied with mental cases instead of politicals. I suppose they provided much-needed employment for the natives — perhaps our neighbours, even.

Of course, there was a huge to-do once it all came out. When they opened some of the places up, they found — and there is a pictorial record — speechless souls, poor wasted creatures locked quite out of sight, out of mind. Theo, it was a horror. And maybe an emblem. For wasn't Greece itself quite out of mind, politically and psychologically, for both West and East during most of the Cold War?

I'm beginning to understand now that the islands *are* all different. Beautiful Kálymnos, next door southwest, is the traditional home of sponge fishers. Hardship once drove their young men to take ship and dive far off seas, dive too deep and too long — and, worst of all, to be hauled up too quickly by the shipmasters. There are still guys alive at Mýrties who were permanently crippled by it. Little Lípsi, to our north, is quite innocent — simply where the nymph Calypso is said to have detained Odysseus. Pátmos, a mile or so further on, basks in the reflected glow of St John of the Apocalypse.

But our Léros, Theo, in the midst of them all, was once hell on earth. What do you make of that? I gather the place has always been a byword in the Aegean for the unsavoury, because the name means something to do with dirt. It's like another Isle of Muck, you might say. Except here the connotations really stick.

Theo, my glance down at those empty huts has thrown a chilling light on my fancies about gods and spirits. Didn't asphodel mark the entrance to Hades? I saw truer than I knew.

It's also thrown a chilling light on our new home. I don't even know for sure whether the huts I saw were part of the hospital complex. They might just have been some abandoned school with its forlorn, rubble-strewn playground — though I doubt it. I've emerged from my researches the wiser. Whether sadder, I don't know. I'm not sure how to tell Eléni. Or whether to.

My friend, I've tried to walk our ground dispassionately. But there's a sense in which I, too, have been wearing Greek spectacles from childhood. You know I'd nothing of your school experience — mine was a state education, which stretched only to Latin... Yet when I was five, my father bought me Kingsley's *Heroes*, because I'd a terror of ordinary fairy stories. 'You'll like this,' he said in the shop, and I can see the book's jacket now: a soft watercolour, framed as in a window of twining plant stems. And when we came back out into the Reigate sun, deepest Surrey, I kept taking the little volume out of its brown paper bag to look inside and see more and still more of those dewy prints of gods and warriors, Theseus, Orpheus and the rest.

Dad taught me to recite the Greek alphabet, too, showed it printed both in his diary and in some great scientific index he had. And because I had the feeling, Theo, that here was something close to his heart, poor man, I learned the Greek characters almost before the English ones. I think I sensed some imaginative land in which he'd once been able to lose himself as a boy. Or was it perhaps just some place close to my own heart? For haven't I always been here in my imagination? Theo, Dad knew nothing else of Greek, or Greece. He made not the slightest reference to his boyhood ever again. But I had a strange vision, much later, that Greece had once been my home, and it made me weep uncontrollably. Crazy, a grown man weeping for Greece!

So no, then. I'm not put off by the island's past. It's almost a relief: that we *haven't* run away, and that as an artist I find myself rightly at the rim of the pit. Léros, home of Artemis the Virgin, Léros, notorious island of accommodation, the dusty courtyard, the smell still lingering, almost, among those few stunted pines by the road, of hopelessness, humiliation and torture — I need the truth in painting.

Besides, Theo, I discover in passing that Léros, precisely because of its former notoriety, has now become something of a model. I mean for psychiatric good practice. Island of redemption, then.

Subject: From a melodrama

Very well. I admit it. I deliberately ignored your concerns. I chose to prate instead about our island walk. It was because you'd rattled me. Suddenly, you were challenging: you demanded, out of kindness, damn you, to know *the real reason for my leaving England*. My 'voice', you said, came *as if from the bottom of a well*.

At first, I thought what an impression I must have given. Surely you were reading far too much between my lines. I was on the point of replying there and then to say *Really, Theo, things are fine, thanks very much. If we were chatting man to man as usual, or out walking, maybe sitting over a pint together at Checkenden, I'm sure you'd never imagine*

17

anything at all amiss.

Then comes your last. You arrive home from work, but instead of sitting down to Fran's meal, you climb up into your loft. There, in the dark and dust you go to the immense trouble of hunting through all your old boxes and bags, and find—I'm inventing the finer points of these details, of course—the battered Greek lexicon from your schooldays. You thought it was lost. You wedge yourself in an angle of the rafters to read by torchlight the word... the word you say has nagged at the back of your mind ever since my emails started arriving. It's the ancient Greek word for friendship, *Philía*.

Theo, I'm so deeply touched. Thank you. Thank you so much.

I have to say in passing—because any more of these feelings might threaten to overcome me—that I also very much enjoyed your little pen-portrait. I can quite visualise your be-gowned Classics master, Haskell the Ferocious, and his four chalk stabs at the vocab on the blackboard. The four Ancient Greek words for love...

Challenging for ten-year-olds! And we'd expect a teacher to play safe and follow up with St Paul, wouldn't we, 'And the greatest of these is Charity—*Agápe*'. But no, the bold guy sticks to his guns: that for the Greeks the noblest of the four wasn't *Agápe*, nor *Éros*, nor family love, *Stórge*. It was actually this same *Philía*, Friendship. Ah, but then you hide once more behind Haskell's voice '...noblest, because only friends are bound together by a shared concern for something *outside* and *beyond them*.' My dear friend... I do read the transparent code of your seemingly throwaway little scene, and I'm doubly touched—I can't really express how much. You and I are bound together indeed. Yes, by art itself.

The Four Loves... that book by C S Lewis. Do you remember it? Caused a stir in the sixties: a sort of Christian sex chat for chaps—hopelessly innocent, poor fellow, of any world beyond Oxford. Or Narnia...

But at least Lewis offered a genuine vision of friendship. Friendship is two souls standing side by side. Not, like lovers, face to face; no, side by side, because of their shared interest. You see I, too, have dusted off an old volume. And at least Lewis was unabashed in using the word. Poor *Philía*, lately tainted by one particular association. You say you were hesitant even to use it, and I don't blame you. Yes, in Lewis's day you could still say bibliophile, Francophile, cinephile without inadvertently conjuring the word *paedo*phile in the next breath. The echo has become almost unavoidable, now, hasn't it.

Paedophilia—so ubiquitous a term, so often strewn over every front page—yet so rightly brought out into the open, so rightly shocking. The shocking custom of the ancient world, too.

But enough of that monstrousness. You're right; the catalogue of evil shouldn't deter us from a Greek etymology of honest friendship. Theo, I'm delighted at what you remembered—poor inky little morsel in your gothic vault of a schoolroom. And in a foreign alphabet... Yes, you and I are friends. Truly, I'm so glad Fran persuaded you to tell me of your loft expedition.

So I looked back through my 'Sent' folder and reconsidered the circumstances of our leaving England. Alright, an incident did come to mind; but it took place well before we left. My son, Arun; he was always uncontrollable as a child, but now as a young man, suddenly living back at home with Eléni and me, he became chaotic. The life he'd begun to put together had started to fall apart. I spoke to him. As always, I racked my brains to work out what was the matter and what I'd done wrong. Had I been too hard on him as he grew up, or too soft? Had the guard I'd kept over his safety been compromised? Certainly on that point, I thought not.

Yet he'd always seemed so... alien. Even the years I was a single parent with him, I used to wonder was he mine at all? Until one day Chloe was with us. She's the older of the two, you remember— heavens, it's ages since you've seen them... It was warm. Arun and I were both sleeveless, our right arms side by side at the table, and Chloe happened to notice how exactly alike they were. His bones a deal bigger, of course—he's taller than me, as a man, by two or three inches—but the genetic design of our elbows, forearms and wrists was, you might say, mathematically similar. It was striking. And I think he and I were both pleased and somehow relieved at the discovery—that we really were father and son.

Well, not so long ago, an issue arose, and I tackled him about it. I don't know. Lots of little things had started to build up. His mother, Lily, chanced to call in. Eléni was at work in London. Lily and I had just buried the hatchet—for Arun's sake, as much as anything—and I took the opportunity of a witness. I confess I wanted Lily to see just what my life with him had been before, and how it was becoming again. On cue, at the first hint of criticism, he flared up. That was the pattern, so I carried on saying my piece, and pretty soon he was stamping and swearing. I was out of order, too, and told him—as I absolutely shouldn't have—that he'd grown up a bully, trying to

19

intimidate others into letting him do whatever he wanted. Then he went blazing, Theo—a full half hour's worth of the most withering contempt. My God, he hardly broke off. It was as though some dam had burst to release a great torrent of filial hatred. At the peak of it, he pointed directly at me and then turned to enquire of his mother: 'How could you ever have married that?'

He went on to make me out the most worthless of creatures and the most spineless of fathers. 'Your pathetic weakness is the reason I'm like I am,' was one line that has stayed with me. The rest of the rant I don't actually recall; it was too hurtful.

'Don't speak to your father like that,' Lily remonstrated at one point, but he just carried on and on, like someone possessed. And I just stood there and took it. What else could I do? What? At length, there were some self-destructive histrionics with the kitchen implements—which I gently removed from him. Finally, he grabbed his bag and stormed out. Lily called after him from the door, but he ignored her and stalked off down the road, never looking back.

Only when his mother had gone home did I become aware of my physical response. I felt as though I'd been stabbed. I mean there was a burning pain in my stomach, and I started shaking. All my hopes for him were in ruins. And was it somehow my fault all along? The attack had been so disproportionate and, in some senses, so unexpected. Was he actually right in what he'd said, that I was the most despicable, pathetic object that ever crawled out from under a stone? Did I maybe deserve such absolute scorn?

I think there are people—maybe you, Theo, maybe the majority— who have a consistent enough sense of themselves to perceive instantly that such aggression is unfair. My difficulty is that I have an inner voice already at my shoulder, already reciting much that Arun had said—and worse. And, through long conditioning, I'm predisposed to agree with it. The extreme is paranoia, of course. Ideologically, too, I've always sided with the son; for isn't this how we're so often encouraged to see the artist—as a rebel against the patriarch? So, in the moment, I found myself crippled by my own personality, and unable to take my own side in the dispute.

But where was he? The clock crept round. No call. No sound of his key in the door. It was as though he were a teenager again. My anxiety grew; my imagination fermented. He'd killed himself. Already, he'd be dead, his body in a ditch or stretched out chilling in some patch of waste ground. Should I get in my car and search the local parks?

Should I stay at home in case he returned? I tried to busy myself. At such times a parent can only sweat it out, it seems, no matter how old the child.

I rang Lily, once evening came. She was relaxed, and quite sanguine about the situation. She knew where he was — but hadn't yet got around to telling me. Sorry. Apparently he'd gone to a friend, an old schoolmate, and would be staying there the night.

Eléni got home from work, and of course we talked. Yet it was still another few hours before I could think clearly. No, I hadn't cut a pathetic figure in his life. A confusing one, maybe: a single parent who'd occupied the mother role, who'd cooked and cleaned and done the washing, bought the shopping; a parent who'd been diagnosed ill for years — allegedly — and merely painted instead of going out to work like other dads; a parent who remained so isolated he could afford little beyond an old car and the very basics, and who'd constantly tried, and failed, to impose some kind of order and discipline on his growing son, a parent now with a much younger girlfriend, Eléni.

Oh God, Theo, this is suddenly such a rush, a spill. Bear with me. Telling is a relief, even down to the trivial details. For, no matter for the failures, I knew I'd tried to do my duty as a parent. I'd kept him safe. And he'd always been well fed and looked-after. He'd absolutely no business launching into me like that.

So there began to dawn certain glimmerings of freedom. Freedom! *Elevthería*!

The situation as it stood was unacceptable, in so many ways. Whatever he was smoking — skunk, certainly, though I wonder now whether that was the worst... by having it in the house I was an accessory. Then there was the complete lack of any help or financial contribution from him, despite many requests. And he *had* bullied me. Not physically — although he was very strong and intimidating — but via my almost pathological concern for his wellbeing. No, that's still too hard on myself; I should say simply via my *natural* concern for his wellbeing.

I'm painting a picture you'll find hard to credit, you of all people, who come from what has always seemed to me so gilded a world: an honourable, affectionate family, a generous old school and ancient university... You, who, because of those things, I believe, have always looked upon me and upon life itself with all the warmth and kindness you've just demonstrated in your letter. You've had your setbacks, of

21

course, but have ridden them with courage, almost as though they hadn't happened.

My dear friend, I speak not from envy, but distance; and it's you who over the years have tirelessly encouraged my art and often drawn out of me my best work—that otherwise I should most likely have abandoned. And perhaps this explains my reluctance to allude to this subject of my son in the first place. For you'll say to yourself, from your innate good sense, here's simply a rocky marriage—to Lily—that produced a difficult child. It's not so very unusual. It just needs a good dose of reality and a few tough decisions. What it doesn't need is Owen's sudden, hysterical, 'wartime' vocabulary about safety, death, and 'the glimmerings of freedom'. Is he exaggerating for effect, or just trying to compel sympathy?

Yes, you and I meet, and are bound together, in art. I treasure your words about friendship, and my eyes are full at the thought of them. But you come from the wholly good. And art, I think, does not. This is my point: that art begins with the Fall and with Blake's idea of shrinkage—shrinkage into language, maybe, which is our expulsion from paradise. I'm not like you. My case is unusual, my body awash with the residues of evil. How can I possibly explain to you what it is to live forever in a family where life and death, and indeed moral survival, are made day to day issues?

I wouldn't write such things if I didn't know it was to you and to you only, who will take care with my words. Others would not. And about art, too. Our trade is bedevilled with cultural theorists. You may pass them by, but I need to keep up with them, because they engage with matters central to painting: desire, gaze, viewpoint, societal and familial economics and so on. Yet they know nothing of the lives of the artists they purport to chronicle. They speak of art either too reverentially, or too playfully, wickedly, as though it were some game of transgression; art whose true function is to portray, to name and to combat evil—and to *propose* good. There, it isn't fashionable to use such terms.

Let me continue my story just a paragraph or two longer. Arun had walked out, but was safe, and the thought gradually occurred to me over the next few days that it was an opportunity. I'd had enough: I might just not let him come back when it had all blown over. If he couldn't find a place of his own, he could go to his mother's.

We strive for insight. We yearn to interpret powerlessness. Perhaps, as unhappy children ourselves, we even overdevelop the intellect and the intuition, as an athlete pumps up the musculature. We become philosophers. In the pain of the incomprehensible, we clutch at anything.

And, of course, the upshot was that he did go to his mother's, and I did tell her he couldn't come back. And I stuck to that, despite the fact he only lasted a fortnight there before storming out after a similar row with her partner. He went and dossed with the old school friend on a semi-permanent basis.

And I? I noticed after a week or so that I began to feel better. This incident had been a catalyst. In the absence of being defeated and overridden in my own house I was almost beginning to flourish. I had energy and could bear both the fact of people coming to visit and the idea of being able to go out and about myself. You and I took our Chiltern walk. You won't know this, but it was when Eléni and I had just got the place cleaned up. Particularly, I'd emulsioned over his smoker's finger-marks on all the walls. Very soon afterwards, the idea first formed that we might make our bid to cast off.

Theo, I'm tired now, and so will send at once and finish tomorrow. I want to add something about this notion of love. *To be continued…*

Subject: **Section through the womb**

Another bright day. Eléni's at work upstairs.

Me? Perhaps I shouldn't tell you, but I still remain daunted by my large canvas. Stage fright? Pressure, I suppose, that I'm putting on myself. Because, as I've said, much is expected, if I want to hold my place in the market. Although you encourage me to take my time and trust to the process, I delay and procrastinate, and that makes it worse. I've stood for some time in front of my easel without so far making a mark, and that, I'm afraid, is the tale of the morning. I did go out along the road, the strip with the single row of pines that leads to the town. I took my notebook and contented myself with external forms: the trees themselves and the slope of the hill beyond. It would be good to capture the smells, too, the resinous tangs so characteristic of the islands, and the pungent waft of sage or wild thyme underfoot on the slopes!

In the meantime, let me pick up as promised where I left off last night, because that email of yours and my story of Arun has made me think so much about the nature of love. His was a quick birth. There

23

wasn't too much anaesthesia, Lily managing well, I holding her hand and reminding her how to breathe. She was only too glad to get the child out of her, so relentless had he been in there, churning endlessly like some interior turbine. By night, in the later stages, I'd imagined him twisting up all his life support until it kinked and throttled him. 'Does he ever unwind?' I'd asked, and it was a genuine enquiry. She'd no idea, of course, past caring with the discomfort.

He was overdue. She took castor oil, and a mere twelve hours later he was my son. That intense bubble of involvement! Love for our children — the *Stórge* you spoke of — is almost an envelopment by the womb: birth not so much a breaking free as a greater enmeshing by an invisible, psychic membrane, a net, infinitely elastic, that forms and reforms about the family group. Isn't that what compels this extravagant devotion?

Which brings me back to the end of my story. I grew very angry with him, once I knew he was safe. And that was the spur to our decision.

So here I am on my island for another kind of love, *Éros*, the love of Eléni. She loves me. She assures me she does. We're here to make a new life for ourselves. She's set up this whole situation so that I can give myself to painting: I have my dedicated studio and a good supply of materials. Why, then; what should my subject be but love, and The Triumph of Love?

Have I accounted for myself, Theo, by this long confessional? You say I'm calling for help. There is pain. I feel for my son. I've made him out to you as doggedly recalcitrant in all this, but he did come and apologise. And we do love each other. But when he mooted living again in his old room, I just said let's see how things go, shall we, Arun? And he took that as a no, and didn't ask again. And now I ask myself, have I abandoned him? Have I failed him? It eats at me. Did he somehow rely on me to keep him at a distance from his mother, rather than pal up with her again?

Well, now you know. I believe I made the right decision. It's a tough one. Arun must stand and be a son; his mother must have the chance at last to be a mother.

3

Subject: The painter and his model

Eléni? I'm lucky to have such a support. Thank you for asking. You met her that once, didn't you. Oh, she came into my life like a whirlwind. You know she's American; but the name, as you've correctly spotted, is Greek, and she comes from Greek stock. The grandparents managed to emigrate after the war. They maintained the traditions, but most of their experience of the poverty-stricken hills of Évvia they wanted to leave behind. So this adventure is almost as new to her as it is to me, though she does have a little more of the language. And she can't but feel in her blood a certain identification with our new situation.

As to our first meeting there's little more to tell. She'd seen my work. She sought me out, only to find me bogged down with the leftovers of mental illness: poverty, broken family, etc... I was producing nothing. She moved in and took over—young, pretty, a rescuer, a radical. To some extent, I became her project. Maybe I'm *her* artwork!

It did the trick. Kick started things again. Now I swim and walk and feel half my age, which is hardly that advanced in the great scheme of things. I pride myself on keeping pace with her, not least financially. What with my last show and those commissions we had, and my other bits of income, I've probably been bringing in as much as she does, maybe a little more.

Any news, by the way, of our Americans? They sounded so positive. Might you email? Or shall we just let nature take its course. Your call.

Good news on another front! There's a party, and we're invited. Well, there are two parties, but the second is a public celebration down on the quay at Pandéli. That's tomorrow. I saw them setting up a PA system. There'll be dancing; I think it's a birthday. Or some saint's day. The Greeks will celebrate, economic meltdown or no.

But the party of today is to be given by a Dr Markova, and we move into island society. I've identified the address: a substantial house on the street that drops from the centre of town towards the small harbour of Áyia Marína. The invitation came one morning last

25

week, pushed under our door. Eléni was wary. 'It can't be for us,' she showed me the letter. 'It must be for the people before.'

'Written in English?'

'A kind of English. But who's Dr Markova, for heaven's sakes? It's not even a Greek name. He sounds Russian. It's some marketing scam. I thought we'd got away from all that.'

'Wouldn't Markova be a woman?'

She scanned the paper again. 'You actually want to go, then?'

'I think we should make the effort.'

'They'll speak Greek. Or whatever.'

'They've written in English.'

'I won't know what to wear.'

'Wear something nice. It'll be fine.'

She reread the invitation. 'But how do they know us, Owen?'

'A small island. Word about an English couple must have got around.'

'I'm American.'

'A wintry-looking, pale skinned couple, then.'

'I guess.'

Theo, I've slipped into dialogue. How about that!

But last night I woke after a bad dream, and now I'm the one getting cold feet. How strange is the night, when our rearward preoccupations come elbowing to the fore. The waning moon shone through our un-curtained window. It stood just above the cove, still and yellow, its reflection fused on to the flat sea. One or two lesser lights gleamed: on yachts, on the Turkish heights. Eléni was half-snoring, her spectacles and wineglass on the chair beside her. I didn't wake her but weltered instead in my anxieties, sure that the islanders already hated me, older man with his too young mistress, certain they'd been pointing and staring at us behind our backs each time we emerged from our four walls.

Theo, guilt and shame have been my lifelong signature, the *leitmotiv*, so to speak, of my character. Time and again, and especially in the nightmare-ridden dark, old certainties of ruin and damnation do come, like devils. And persist beyond the dawn. All morning, I tried to conceal the panic. After lunch, a siesta without sleep.

Just an hour ago, Eléni was at the mirror putting stuff on her eyes, and I sat frozen on the bed. My clothes were laid out, but all I could hear were voices, suspicious, suddenly hate-filled: the Englishman and his concubine; the painter and his model; father and daughter?

How would I be able to explain myself? How defend — and in Greek?

'I don't think I can go.'

'Hello?'

'Maybe just you could show up,' I said. 'If you still want to.'

She turned to me, the eye-liner held up beside her. 'Go by myself?'

'Yeah. You could.'

She threw the eye-liner against the wall. I watched its flight, almost in slow motion. It made a black mark on the white plaster before clattering to the floor. 'Fuck!' she shouted.

'Look, I...'

She collected herself. 'Owen.'

'Give me a break,' I said.

'Give *me* one!'

Christ! Relationships are like jig-saw pieces. I believe that. People are together for a reason. No matter what we like to think, or how ill-assorted couples might appear, the behind-the-scenes material always neatly locks into place. That's been my experience. And when Eléni came to me she was in a mess. I didn't know it, but she was simply waiting to fall to bits: coming off this; coming out of that; coming down from the other. She didn't know who or what she was. Three thousand miles from American friends and family, she needed someone strong. And that's what I am. They say depression is an illness of the strong, did you know? Panic and agitation fight under the same banner. And so it would be fair to say that there's another way of looking at our relationship, and maybe I'm the rescuer. Eléni would dispute this, of course.

On this occasion, she made sense.

'We're going,' she said. 'I'm not letting you duck out of this one. If you have issues, this is a chance to confront them. No buts. We're leaving in an hour.'

I've got myself ready, Theo. We'll be off shortly. Paranoia profits from a kick in the arse. Paranoia is rage that comes up the spine but can't quite get into the head. That's why it sits on the shoulders, poking hate. A voice. Subliminal. Usually. All feelings are from the past, but infallibly they colour the present, and so now I'm here at my desk with that familiar, equally mocking half-empty expanse of canvas outside in the studio; and I'm trying to deal with this, this still rising, breathless panic — by writing to you.

Subject: **Recumbent nymph**

It's Sunday morning. I'm awake. Eléni's sleeping it off. We had a fine time.

Marta Markova is an accomplished woman, a medical doctor. She speaks English, Greek and, of course, Russian—and probably a host of other languages. She lives on Léros because her husband is an import/export factor. There's a big warehouse in agricultural produce down near Lakkí, which I think might be his.

The invitation was absolutely genuine; a drinks party before dinner, the difference being that here everything starts much later. Our arrival on the island had indeed been noted, and hospitality—that prodigious Greek virtue—was extended. They made us so welcome, Theo. Everyone took immediately to Eléni, because of her name. She only needed to mention her origins to become a long lost daughter. As for me, my anxieties vanished the moment we arrived—of course they did. I even held my own in Greek, I believe; my few words—*merikés léxis*—being much appreciated. And once my small talk ran out, Eléni's better grasp got us by. And there were English speakers who, as everywhere these days, were keen to practise. So we lacked nothing for conversation and came away at about nine-thirty, the others going on to a couple of tavernas, *tou Míltou* and *tou Yiórgou*, which means Míltos's place and Yiórgos's. But at that point we decided to go home and eat.

Until then, the whole group had made about thirty: a very convivial number, not counting the children running in and out. The house is tall—an old-style villa. There are a number of similar ones, quite grand, down that particular street. It was furnished attractively in a blend of traditional and modern, and was charmingly full of flowers and pretty lamps. Our hostess put different colour themes with different platters on each level, while at the back was a courtyard with lights in jars to show off exotic fruit trees, some still in bloom in great earthenware pots. Everyone was from the islands; some had come by ferry that afternoon. One family was visiting from Crete, I believe.

Yes, fine it was—nothing to have been worried about at all. And it feels good to have dipped a toe in the social pool. Eléni and I even talked about how nice it would be to give a celebration ourselves later in the year, once we're more settled and established. When in Greece...

Theo, some time has passed. Eléni's still asleep, and I've thought hard about what I've been writing. Who am I trying to fool? Not you—I know now that I shan't succeed in that.

Myself?

I'm still not quite sure whether I'm allowed to write the truth, or whether doing so is another act of betrayal. The thing is, I need to. I need to open the matter up, to register it. You're miles away, and so it can do no harm. My friend, what is the *right* thing to do, to say? What, in a word, is my duty? I owe a duty to Eléni. But don't I also owe one to myself?

Very well. I said everything at the party was fine. It was, until Eléni keeled over. She just dropped on the spot in mid-sentence. I saw her glass go, and then suddenly there was her crumpled body lying in a pool of wine, glittering with the shards.

Everyone turned. Silence, then consternation, shouting, crying out. Women swooped to tend to her even before I could do so myself. A female voice kept repeating a sentence with '*tou kraníou*' in it. 'Of the skull'—fractured? That was my immediate concern, too, since the floor was marble tiles. It was also now slippery with broken glass; a lady arrested her barefoot daughter just in the nick of time: the look of astonishment on the child's face, one second hurtling in at the door, the next held by her mother's arm at an angle in mid air, her skinny brown legs still going. And Eléni. Fainted? *Epilipsía*? *Apoplixía*? Was it a *katastrophí*?

Someone had already called the ambulance.

She started to come round. She'd probably only been out for less than a minute, but it seemed much longer. She was examined, searched for blood, checked for pain. She was helped to a bedroom and made to lie down, with Dr Markova herself attending. I stood beside them. After some moments, our hostess looked up at me, her expression full of ambiguity. She simply said, 'She is okay. I think she is quite okay.'

If my own tone in sketching this is also mixed, Theo, it's because by this time I, too, recognised what had happened. My lover had simply downed too much white wine—*pára polý levkó krasí*. Bypassing drunkenness by sheer speed, she'd managed to slip her motor neurones; which resulted in collapse.

The trouble is, I've seen her do it before. In fact, it's something of a foible of hers, and we've had words about it, which isn't pleasant. The next day, you put it to the back of your mind and carry on again as though it hasn't happened. Then every so often it comes back to bite you.

She doesn't keep track, Theo. Of the glasses. She doesn't always register the count. There are no outward signs; she doesn't *do* tipsy. And she'll turn up wide-eyed afterwards: 'But I don't understand; I swear I only had a couple.' And she believes it.

Whatever, this incident hastened our exit and was the real reason we didn't go on to the taverna. Our departure was attended by profuse good wishes and genuine concern on the part of the company, and by acute embarrassment on mine — because the last humiliation was being driven home in the ambulance. It had been called out and had nothing better to do. I'm sorry, but I was very angry.

She has in the past asked me to keep an eye on her. She herself says she wants to beat this as much as I want her to. In some ways she does accept responsibility. But I'd thought of the island as a new leaf. Do you see? And now this.

How did it actually happen? We'd been separated at the party for quite a time; our hostess had scooped me up to meet someone, 'Now, Owen, my dear, you must come with me.'

Dr Markova doesn't brook refusal. Besides, I was intrigued. I went downstairs with her from the reception area to a smaller room that looked, through open doors, on to the courtyard. The interior lights down there were lowered to avoid attracting insects, and it took a while for my eyes to adjust. Men stood in knots of three or four, or spilled outside, drinking and talking noisily; and sweet scents from the trees drifted in to mingle with the cigarette smoke. My hostess, holding my hand, found us a space next to a tallish young guy in a linen suit. Then she clapped her hands and waited for attention. The room hushed. She spoke in her broad, swallowed Greek: 'Now listen everybody, here's someone I've been waiting to introduce to you. Please meet our famous local painter.'

That, at least, was the gist of it. *Thiásimo* rang a bell because I'd encountered it in my textbook the previous day about famous Greeks; *topikó* means 'local'; and *zográpho mas* means 'our painter', literally 'life-mark-maker' — a quaint and literal description of our trade.

Marta rattled on a little more, and I was flattered. Upstairs, I'd already overheard someone use that same word *zográphos* and had recognised the mention of *ikónes* — 'images'. I'd jumped to the perfectly reasonable conclusion that my slim reputation had gone before me, and now people were gathering round. I looked down modestly.

It was as well I did, because when I looked up again, the men were all gazing at the fellow next to me, the one in the linen suit. Only just quickly enough did I put two and two together to turn and gaze with them. *He* must the local artist, icon painter or whatever upstairs had been talking about, and a ripple of applause soon demonstrated that his presence at the party was our hostess's particular coup.

As for my inclusion? I guessed at a hasty act of courtesy—Eléni must have said something about us to Marta while I'd been gazing around in the reception room upstairs. Quite! My guess was borne out once the fuss had died down, because Marta went on to present me, with a word to him in Greek about an English artist, *'agglikós kallitéchnis'*, and one to me in English: 'You two should have plenty to talk about.' Then she left us, all smiles, to get on with it. *Pride goeth ever*, my friend, and note the subtle shift of epithet from 'life painter' to the rather vaguer 'artist'. Does that signify, I wonder? Anyway, my fall was a moral lesson. Eléni's more literal one half an hour later carried a teaching I can't for the moment fathom.

My counterpart's name was Spíros Apostolíthis, I should add. We did make a stab at talking to one another—until the onlookers got bored or turned away. It wasn't easy. He spoke no English, and I felt a little crushed. But I must tell you, Theo, the one thing that sticks in my mind as satisfactory about this sorry tale is that we conversed at all. In fact, I found myself more fluent than usual. Well, that was no doubt because we were speaking about art, and I'd taken the trouble to familiarise myself with some of the terms before we came. Yet God knows what it was I actually said to him. Maybe I myself had had a little too much to drink. Yes, he was an icon painter. *N.B.* also *ayiográphos*—painter of the sacred. All credit to him; I've never given icons much thought. He lived on Kálymnos.

And I, he asked?

'Ah yes, *Kýrie*! We live here on Léros. *Kséni*—strangers. *Ággli*—English.'

'You are welcome to Greece.'

'You're very kind.'

'The weather is good.'

'Fine weather for painting.'

'Of course. Global warming.'

Laughter.

Then came more, which I struggled to understand. He was devoted to his work, I gathered that. He sounded quite inspired by it.

Eventually, we lapsed. The doors were shut and the lights turned up, and someone who spoke a bit of English was kind enough to

31

enquire about my own painting. I found myself stumbling about it even in my mother tongue. I stood like a lemon until awkwardness got the better of politeness. Then I slipped away.

That was all there was to it. Back upstairs, the *débâcle* of Eléni followed on, exactly as I've told you. In an otherwise disastrous evening, the only thing I return to with any pleasure is that brief dialogue in a difficult language, with an artist in a different tradition, in a land I've elected to see as my permanent home.

I expect Eléni and I shall carry on once again as normal—after I've 'confronted the issue' and we've had a row. Maybe I'm being unfair to her. Maybe the drinks party was a great success, and we're not social lepers. Maybe some 'scene' is even de rigueur here in the passionate south, and I'm just bad-tempered the morning after. Sometimes I catch a glimpse of myself: uptight and English, as self-righteous, cold and craven as Eléni seems to think me.

Hardly the attributes of an artist! My large canvas is out there behind my back as I type. Its naked glare a reproach: why am I not at work?

4

Subject: **Sgraffito**

Bledlow Cross marks the mid-point of the Chiltern scarp. You and I never walked so far north. It's a lookout, flanked by hanging beech woods. The top juts, tussocky and rabbit-grazed over a prospect of three counties. It leans into a perpetual wind — the same warm westerly that holds up the gliders over Ivinghoe Beacon, a dozen or so miles further along. On Bledlow, in early summer, wild orchids thrust from the turf, and rare gentians stand among vetches, trefoil and scabious. The air from the Vale of Aylesbury tastes of gorse-coconut-dust.

Scratch the surface anywhere and you find chalk. Spiked grasses tell the tale: whitened rabbit trails lead to outcrops just under the edge. They crumble almost visibly. This rock leaches lime, flint, old battles; these hills are a jawbone once fractured, still eroded.

In a circle of trees lies the chalk figure that names the place. It's a 'Greek' cross, as it happens. Two broad equal cuts in the turf blink out over the drop — a genuine antiquity, like the great White Horse on the slopes far to the south; or perhaps not. It used to be scoured, the people of Chinnor and Bledlow and Henton coming up once a year with their spades and hoes, their bottled beer and sandwiches. That custom fell into abeyance. Very recently the cross was restored by the County Council, so I discover online, and its cleaned face was tamped and then shuttered with wooden edging. But, in my memory, grasses encroach once more. The outline blurs, and rose bay and sorrel pock the bright integrity. Maybe, like memory itself, the cross will soon be lost again. It will become as overgrown as the old chalk pits, disused sockets, where transparent creatures hover out of the wind's loom.

At that place, thirty or more years ago, I was robbed — at one stroke and in their full promise — of my love, my hopes, and, in a manner of speaking, my destiny. I was an apprentice then; I'm an artist now. Now I mix my colours like unguents, and my bases are chalks and other earths.

Theo, I made myself write the above. It's self-consciously literary, but I needed to get some distance from what came today in the post. I needed to divert, trick the mind. Like desperately forcing yourself to

33

paint background, maybe, while the main subject sorts itself out.

To no avail. It's evening and I still find myself overwhelmingly surprised and inexpressibly moved, my thoughts awhirl. Do you recall sending this envelope? Clearly, no one at your office opened it, but the original buff cover with my name on has been enclosed in a new one and redirected. Was it perhaps your Jas, or Fiona? Otherwise I thought you might have mentioned it in your last—since I'm not usually deluged with fan mail.

Nothing inside but a photograph: the image of a woman at this very spot, Bledlow. That's the extraordinary thing. No message, no indication as to who sent it. Nor why. The postmark is indecipherable. Theo, I say 'woman'—but that's simply me trying to be dispassionate again, objective, forensic. Why? Because it's only that girl I told you of, Julia.

Julia stands there on the ridge in plain Kodak large format colour, 120 film—the old bellows Zeiss I had, eight shots on a reel. Do you see? It's Julia, and I can only have taken the picture myself!

I'm thunderstruck. What am I to make of it? Of course, it fuels exactly the painting project I'd outlined to you. But it was yesterday that I actually got down to it. I'd sketched in our portraits, Julia and me: so that, effectively, out on the canvas in my studio, we were *already standing in that spot* before I went to collect the mail!

And the overgrown cross just down the slope from our feet, that almost hidden carving in the chalk—some other artist's—was *already* the sign that begins any work, the first essay into substance, the first mark that alters everything. For we know well enough that no piece of art is ever entirely new, nor innocent; nor no blank surface ever quite blank.

But alteration by post? The very next day?

Theo, with that photo, Bledlow Cross becomes an X on a treasure map, an algebraic unknown suddenly forced to burst and spill. Christ, all art comes from the body—but this?

Very well, I'm standing beside Julia at the lip of the ridge. It's the moment before the blow fell. The blow that ended our relationship. I'm 'The Artist as a Young Man', and this writing will…

Indulge me, Theo. Narrative *does* subvert the brain. Narrative, I find, springs almost unasked from the heedless, typing hands. Narrative, with its formality, rules and self-consciousness—surely *because* of them—seems to well up unstoppably, like pure paint from the fingers' ends, born of the body direct. Narrative quite undercuts the head, that slave of time, slave to all rational doubts and censoriousness. Why, if I obeyed my head, I'd surely put down only the threadbare, cropped emails of business or appointments. I'd most likely have nothing to say to you at all!

Allow me, then. It's the May of '76, that year already so dry they said the ground would never fill up again, that Spring—and all Springs to come—unnaturally forfeited. But the view from our high point seems so settled and in a way timeless. Our voices muse into the breeze, into the insect buzz of the grasses behind us. Julia and I gaze out, ordinary lovers.

And so we are. And, yes, the body leaps to representations of itself. High above us, a skylark makes one shrilling point. Far below, sown fields stretch into the distance, to where light coats low hills on the horizon, sun-spokes melting, a sheen racing towards us, switching on greens, duns and ochres as it comes. Roof tiles under the bluff kindle in the gleam, chimneys of the cement factory down there begin to glow, and the Cuttle Brook is suddenly all tinned wire past Ilmer and Aston Sandford.

Theo, I can feel right now the habit of Julia's fingernails against my palm. Her shoulder touches mine. I turn. Her hair flicks my cheek, the collar of her old Afghan fleece sets off the profile I know by heart. There's nothing about her I don't desire.

This photograph. We'd driven out that day from London. The hour we'd snatched in bed in my studio left us scarcely another, now, before she had to return.

Just the previous November I'd asked her to leave her husband and live with me. She'd said she needed 'time' and a chance to 'sort herself out'. I'd taken it as rejection. It had been such a wound, indeed, that I'd tried to scrub her quite from my work, which was all bound up with her. I'd tried to put her out of my mind—to scrape quite blank the sexual space she'd occupied.

I couldn't do it. I couldn't do without her.

Nor she without me, so it seemed; for when she returned with the Spring she spoke only of our life together. She was ready, she said. She'd give up the sad security of her unhappy marriage.

So we'd made plans. Her husband mustn't suspect. He scared her, Miles. He hit her. We took care, covered our traces. We'd find somewhere outside the city—out here at Bledlow, maybe... somewhere obscure, it didn't matter. We'd bury our faces in nature. That's why we'd come. We were naïve, ecstatic. Bledlow Cross looked out over the place where I was born.

'Where, Owen? Show me.'

I pointed: the broad plain was still alight, with Aylesbury just visible as a sepia transparency at its northern end. We were too late to go there now; it wasn't important anyway, didn't seem so. Besides, the field behind the old house would be built over, the brook I used to wade in parched, the town itself spoiled...

'Better to leave on a high note.' I laughed and kissed her neck. 'We can come again...' I held her, and gazed at her.

We stand there, in that illumination, in the mirror of memory, Julia's eyes glistening, her mouth—that fair down on her top lip, the fine, strong, beloved features crossed once again by the blown strands of blonde hair she makes to pluck away...

Theo, I broke this writing off to go out and paint again. My left hand—that is my body—made little childish angels in the sunshafts. I don't know why. You'll see them when you look closely, their trumpets held out, their wings streaked red from stray fibres in my brush. The body sees what the eye can't. And it attunes to feature and posture, to the small print of the face; it reads the bone, the attachment of muscles, their history, their secrets. Julia, her cheeks a hint fuller than ever I'd realised at the time, the skin just that micro-tone brighter. I worked fast. I painted the sheen of hindsight.

That young man beside her, tallish, well favoured enough, his own eyes just moistening to the wind, his longish hair tugged by it. That's me, of course. I'm dressed in the flapping, theatrical, patched-up gear of the decade, a grey denim jacket over my red velvet flares.

But what heightens Julia darkens me. Those are faint circles under my eyes. How abstract, how already 'missing', do I appear; my face, my bearded mask at twenty-seven so starved of its being that the colours won't go on. Simply, they won't. I can't do it.

Instead, the damned canvas shows through—like chalk, like the wretched hillside itself—as though I had no presence in the place. I stand next to my lover, imagining all well, believing my life surrounded by well-wishers and warm associates, so unaware of what's been and what's to come—unaware of what's to happen even in the very next moment—that I might as well be weightless... as weightless as those gliders on the thermals over Dunstable Downs, a spectre, a soul already half snatched behind some metaphysical veil.

Subject: **Bay with swimmer**

You knew nothing of the envelope — nothing of the mysterious photograph.

No surprises, then, but thanks for investigating. There's no point in asking, I suppose, whether Jas remembers anything else. No, of course, there isn't. Just a routine mail redirection, wasn't it. Fingerprints! DNA! Electrostatics! No, I guess it'll have to remain a mystery.

In the interim, Theo, I've plunged from excitement back into... Ah, take no notice. I'm melodramatic again. The dry fact of the matter is that I've worked further on the Bledlow landscape, but I still can't paint my own damn portrait, and the ludicrous problem won't resolve. I was sure it would, given a day or two — during which I've denied myself whingeing to you and have just tried to keep at it.

But now I honestly don't know what to do. I can't paint my*self*. It's bizarre. I'm stumped. I look down at my hand. It's a real enough hand, here in present time, present space, the skin sun-browned, a little hardened with the first meshes of old age. There's a silvering of light upon the knuckle. See, the thumbnail slightly ridged lengthwise.

Solid enough, you'd have thought. And just this morning the same fist held four brushes, sticking upwards like some abortive bouquet, like a little kid's gift to his mother. It also gripped between thumb and index finger the chipped enamel plate on which I mix my colours. And I could have knocked you up a first rate study of it in an hour, like some lovely hand of Dürer's. *And* anything else you might have wanted: grass, sky, Julia. I did all those.

But when I come to my own image, my *historic* skin and bone, some force physically kicks me off and leaves me feeling quite wretched — almost as though a snake uncoils and spits poison at me. Then it takes a few hours for the depression to wear off, before I give it another go.

Now all inspiration has collapsed. I've given up daubing pigment on my big yardage of stretched cloth, pushing the slick of it pointlessly this way, now that. I'm back at my desk, typing this to you — as though typing were some kind of self-medication. You said in your last you don't mind. You were encouraging. You said you looked forward to my reports from the front...

Siesta-time.

Through the window in front of me, the huge Mediterranean sun fires the island. Rock, promontory and castle bake and swelter. I'm a thousand miles from Bledlow, it's the twenty-first century. Two places at once: that's the condition of the artist. Yes, I'm susceptible to trance, able to go down into the past as though it's the present. I possess a tactile eye that can glance about the cave with both greed and insouciance, like Aladdin, like the Tinderbox soldier, like Monte Cristo—an eye to snatch just enough before it fades, just enough to fix it in form and bring it back. That's the gift.

But the bloody curse of it, too: to be cast up against oneself across time and space, clinging to one spar only, at the mercy of winds and currents one has oneself released, having no choice but to choose this...

Forgive me. I'm milking it, aren't I. What's fine art but coloured froth. It's only a decorative craft, only so much synthetic foam upon the surface of reality. We've had too much of artists' lives, their damnable angst and tantrums! Ditch the lot of us!

I've taken a break. I've paced about, telling myself not to be so stupid. Here I am again at the keyboard, and it's the devil of a problem. I can't just skip it. Listen, I try to paint myself, the self of thirty odd years ago, come to his chalk-land cross. What do I find? The wretched colour halts, the brush lifts off, identity gives way. I simply can't account for it.

But of course I can. And the fact that I do know exactly what it's about drove me out of the studio, brushes thrown down, enamel tin plate a-clatter on the floor tiles and still spinning as I lurched into the blinding sun. It sent me out of the house to pace again my accustomed route—the tarmac strip between the pines, the road down by the bay—and then at last by narrow turns, little shops, bars, people, mopeds, towards the wide, whitened steps at one end of a town alley, climbing and climbing the open stair I've taken every day for the last week up to the Byzantine castle set high, massive and impossibly romantic above the glazing streets.

And I stand by its walls hearing random voices from the past and wasting my time, full of the knowledge of my own paralysis and yet quite unable to *tell*, Theo, to tell you or anyone the thing at the heart of it. Theo, I *can't*...

...

'Art's material, Owen. It's stuff on stuff. Forget representation. Mimesis is a bourgeois conjuring trick; cameras do it better than you ever will. All images are images of property. And property, Owen, is theft. So chuck 'em, chum. From now on paintings are pure machines for causing pure emotion.'

38

Random voices from the past: that was George Brede, the abstract expressionist — now the colourist Academician. He was my tutor at Hornsey. Have I told you of him? Freud and Sartre were his prophets. Anyone who was anyone those days was high on McLuhan, stiff with Warhol, busy screwing the surrealist unconscious into Marx.

I do remember those times — in all their monumental irrelevance. Poor George's kit was too industrial even for our radicalised college! He took a panel beater's spray line to the vast blank canvases he'd nail up to a breezeblock baulk. It was in a lock-up over Crouch End Hill. He'd set to work, brutalism the happening thing. George wasn't tall. He'd stand on a wooden rostrum in his jeans and cowboy boots and shoot colour from the hip. Out of his spray-pipe came imitations of Rothko's colour fields, but done with a cold un-Rothko-esque animosity. It was as though he saw firing back at him all the old masters he was so hell bent on rousting out. A little John Wayne of the plastic arts! In those days, George set his sights against connoisseurs and salerooms — he wouldn't have given tuppence for you, Theo! He was gunning for every image nailed up in the National Gallery — images I couldn't help haunting at the time, and which haunted me.

I was secretly in thrall to them. But George I was in awe of. And capitalism *was* robbery. And clearly it *did* patronise art. So once I began at Hornsey, I tried my hardest to forget old masters: dryads and their lovers, to forget tragic eyes staring out and all the rocks of heavenly intervention. I tried to make myself hate those virgins and centaurs, over-designed fauna, the astonishing trees and precise colours of martyrdom. I embraced what I took to be new. Even now, Theo, as I skim through some classic of art history, Panofsky or Baxandall, say, with their choric figures and mysteries, I can still hear that scorn in George's voice, weirdly, paradoxically prohibitive: 'The fucking nymphs, Owen, have fucking departed.'

So far away now, art school, England, and Julia, too. Yet some things — that last moment with her on Bledlow, or George in his posturing, crazy action (those who can, do; those who can't, spray) — are clear as yesterday. Clearer: for the days here are such perpetual summer they bleed one into another. Just today, as I stood at the high point of my island, looking out not over Aylesbury but the Aegean, I thought, 'London's a far cry. Our first hop is Athens. So forget it.'

I'm prevaricating. Maybe I could just get a job down at the boatyard, once my Greek improves. Marta tells me they already call me 'the English', *o Ágglos me to simiomatárió tou* — that fellow with his

39

notebook. They've seen me out sketching, no doubt.

And Julia?

Julia is Julia. O how can I explain to you about *my* condition, *my* secret; how dare I let on to anyone what the matter is?

So I stood up there at the castle trying to fit the present hilltop into an earlier one, staring west into vacancy, as if at the gap in the years, trying to short-circuit the ground between Then and Now — ground, or estranging sea. Yet if I say nothing…

What I *can* tell you is that there was no refuge from the noon. I put my hand to the wall of the old *kástro*, and its stones were already hot enough to bake bread. Sun stung my fingers; burned, too, the tops of my toes, softened earlier by seawater. I gave myself to the heat, wilfully. I couldn't *do* any more. Like some George Brede figure who couldn't even spray; that's how useless I felt. Couldn't paint, I mean. Jesus, don't get the wrong idea. Everything else works!

But my head ached. My neck and shoulders, too. It was intolerable. And I knew, up there in the burning sun, that it was punishment.

For what? You'll think I'm mad. For simply working at my own painting down there in my house beside the rocky cove, with my back to the open window? For having a woman, my lover? For the simple indoor smell of the nymph Eléni's coffee mingling with wild thyme and sage from the path down to the sea's edge — and the waft from my neighbours' goat? Yes, punishment for all that.

Making no sense, am I. Just drawing ever bigger and crazier circles around a most painful and difficult centre.

Okay, as the detectives say, let's try and get this clear from the beginning. First thing, I'd been swimming. The dawn was heavenly, the Med like honey, the yard or two of shingle down at our cove a-glitter in the first light. Musical, too — the chirr from the bank so loud and shrill as I got out. And mathematical, the witty polygonal scrub plant whose name I don't know scratched at my ankles all the way back up the slope: one sweet thorn in this garden of earthly delights.

So I came in, elated, through the low blue door, a hummingbird hawk moth brushing my face like a blessing with its wings, before it nosed the straggle of new-flowering bougainvillaea over the lintel. I put down my beach shoes in the passage. I showered and got dressed. I kissed Eléni, picked up my coffee and padded barefoot out to my studio. I sat in my familiar wooden chair, carefully avoided looking at my canvas. I opened the leather colour-case my son had given me. Deliberately, I made ready to pick up where I'd left off, topping up the oil in the two china pots, mixing the accustomed squirts of pigment against my enamel plate, knifing and nudging the blobs I'd cling-filmed the previous night. I pressed anxiety aside and collected my thoughts.

Well, then. I stood up and took a good fresh look at this *work in progress* clamped up sturdily to its wooden support (I have the mysterious photo of Julia pinned at eye level on the stand). I liked what I'd already done. Close up, I reviewed the broad, taut weft. Brush in hand and holding my breath, almost, I sought stealthily to lose myself in the impasto of my previous days: Julia and my youthful self on Bledlow.

Painting in oils is eternal revising; you don't need me to tell you. Forever going over the same ground — that's the pleasure. No matter how *avant garde*, it really is a matter of coming repeatedly back to the same places, understanding a detail here, now a highlight there, intuitively telling and retelling, until the true image begins to emerge. Today, I gave myself every chance, tuning in to the chalk hills and the vale under them, trying to trick myself with that prime radiance, to keep busy by lifting it out of shadow.

And everything was plain sailing, even those angels, because here was just an abstraction of landscape and cloud forms: pure tones, reflections, absorptions and refractions arising from nature. If we allow painting at all, then marks are just marks, pigments just pigments; they can go either way. I was enjoying myself.

Almost without any shift of emphasis, I began on the figure of Julia. So often I'd painted her, once upon a time, that I still knew her by heart. She'd been my muse. Her face, her planes and proportions, her joints, her movement, her particular liberalities and even her inhibitions were instinct in my mind. I'd finished much of this work yesterday and was still pleased with it. I felt I had only a little more to add, for already she quite leapt out at me, just as I've described, her portrait speaking in this more than I'd ever known. Maybe there was something to be touched to that shoulder. Maybe the definition of the fabric detracted too much from the gesture that created it, and there was a rawness in the surface texture lower down, where the turn of her calf and the mould of an Achilles tendon just showed behind a whippy straggle of plants and grasses snagging the cuff of her jeans. These flaws could be dealt with.

No, Julia wasn't the problem. The trouble started again with the man, me, the gamble disrupted at source, if you like, and nothing the least to do with aesthetic scruples or contemporary theory. That frail sketch I'd done of him. Now his dark implied eyes looked accusingly out, until, quite simply, a kind of chaos invaded me—as I'd known it would: this sabotage of a self-portrait becoming routine. Picture me, emboldened by the dawn, beginning in faux innocence to shift preliminary layers into the outline I'd marked out, stealthily keeping going, imagining this time I'd beat it, whatever it was.

No use. Almost as soon as I'd put in the first few strokes, the great lethargy started to take hold and I was thrown off.

Theo, help! I have to crack this. Career, reputation. Painting's my life, for God's sake. Didn't I choose it from my youth? Haven't I always been inspired by the sheer difficulty it always proposed, and by the unearthly pleasure in overcoming it? Am I going to be defeated now by some old, cranky, self-indulgent piece of mental shrapnel? It's not even proper depression; it doesn't obey any known medical rules, and I've come through far worse in the past.

So I mixed another ground and forced myself to apply it. And haven't I kept my guides constantly before me? They never gave up, those saints of the craft, glorious exemplars: Della Francesca, Van Eyck, Van der Weyden, Da Vinci, Rembrandt, my several Spaniards, my beloved Manet.

Okay, internal conflict goes with the territory. But haven't I again and again wrestled with my art, renounced it for significant periods, always re-embraced it, each time like a homecoming. So long an apprenticeship—and don't I live with representation now? Don't I continually thrill myself by the power of image to disrupt every theory and limitation, as though there really did lie in each flat space visual presences magically pre-existing any paltry attempt of mine to bring them out; painting not to cover but *dis*cover. Why, that's the fascination, isn't it?

My eyes closed to a sense of falling, nausea. Even as I gritted my teeth, still vainly willing myself to carry on, some presence had hold of me. Its force seemed to control my limbs. Try as I might, either right or left handed, I just couldn't carry colour up to the surface. Bizarre, that failure of impulse—almost comical, a variant Dorian Gray! I tell you it happened. Surely, someone was present, sneering at me.

I swung round. Mephistopheles? I kept my back to my picture. I let myself peer out over the rims of my glasses through the windowpane. The sea I'd emerged from so recently was beginning to ruffle up. I chewed a brush's end. Then I ripped the spectacles off.

I found my coffee and sipped it, drumming the spare fingers of my left hand on the top of my heavy oak document chest. I told myself this wretched picture marked not just a personal scene with Julia — not just a robbery within a robbery within a robbery — but, if you like, the original theft. I mean the key to it all. By it, *by insisting on representation*, I'd begin to expose the nightmare that lay not only beneath my own work but perhaps even under the original human impulse to create.

So it had to be a *tour de force*, this painting. It had to be done. Through it, I could return *home*, and art — yes, I believed I could even make such a claim — art itself could come home with me. I was almost divinely inspired by all that I'd found myself heir to.

So I'd convinced myself an hour earlier, as I'd struck out towards the rocks at the far side of my bay, the rush and hiss of my own breath in my ears, slick brine dashing my goggles.

Looking back over this correspondence, I seem to have led you in various directions: some sinister island secret, some 'real reason' for my leaving England, a girl in a photograph. These externals now collapse back into the sordid internal. But I can't burden you with it. I *can't*. Don't worry. I'll sort it out. I'll get the thing done.

Subject: War zones

I've thought and thought about your email. Now, it's another afternoon. A hot gust rattles the window catch, the front door bangs, and I agonise. If I ever get my grand design on in London, there'll be repercussions. Or will there? Will it just be ignored?

For I plan a parallel sequence which I haven't told you about, and with which all this is bound up. The idea is for a *double* row of canvases facing each other in one narrow space, the one side to interpret the other.

And I thought of Kell and Ken — all the Frank Street set — with their divine mockery. I thought of Toby Hulme, and Nigel, and then of the critical establishment at large. For them, it's almost a crime for someone to remain upset; or, worse still, to get well. For what's 'well'? Merely a middle class construct, they might say.

They're all so young, so philosophically impudent, and I feel so old. Up there on the castle, Theo, I can hear their voices, too: 'So last century. Stuff happens, Owen. People make it into something. Or they

43

make themselves into something. Or they don't bother, because who gives a shit. Fuck's sake, everyone has a cross to bear; don't you know there's a war on?'

The laughter.

I do still like them all, admire them. By the way, I know Lee Drashkovic from his last show. Tonia Poole by reputation, of course. Her things are so fragile. You'll have real vibrations to worry about, floors, air conditioning and the like, not vibrations in my state of mind!

You got back to me straightaway. I'm touched. I know how very busy you must be. You urge me not to worry—simply to take the bull by the horns and spell out whatever the matter is.

I'm left in two minds, because kindness is a very difficult thing to experience, and I'm certain, one way or another, I shall offend you. My case has no claim on the world. Disclosing it's a little like exhibiting a relic, marketing a disability.

And people can even get nasty; you'd be surprised. It'll mortify my friends. Oh, why should my hands be tied like this by the vile story I'm heir to... or am not.

So I've remained in the house near my computer, near your email, poised between hubris and bathos, mocked by enigma—until just this last minute I saw fins in the water beyond the rocks: dolphins, five, six, more... They were playing. I threw open the window and stared out at them. How they rolled and flashed. How they stitched air to water, all lazy exuberance.

Then the wind gusted hard, but I held the casement by its latch and saw them circle inshore. They were nudging a youngster, shepherding, teaching kindly where the water was milky and beginning to crest. Why, I felt I could almost touch them, gleam-dripping, so it seemed, through the frame and through the spiritous intervening space all the way down to the bay.

And thus I stood, while minutes passed, until, casually, they moved on, tracing the line of the rocks. And eventually, when they were ready, they passed from sight behind the little headland.

And I—eventually—shut the window and bent down to pull out from under my heavy oak document chest the forty or so A3 sheets of cartridge paper I've never dared put my name to.

I mean the images my left hand painted once upon a time in hospital in England. I'd never used my left hand before. Surely these are images I haven't the remotest notion of; they're below-the-surface

44

stuff, nothing to do with me. They concern old family matters—even now I can't bring myself to spit it out—these paintings I've kept hidden, unable to show anyone or to find a home for them. They tell a sad tale: scenes that came out of me. They ended my apprenticeship.

They're strewn about now. I spread some of them across the floor, because here would be the preparatory sketch-work to what I'd conceived of as my parallel row. But they're actually nothing, childish imaginings.

And so I continue my ambivalence towards them, even now, slipping them awkwardly into your field of vision like this after a seascape of cetaceans.

But look more closely. Not so childish after all. Actually, the left hand has an unnerving deftness. How it conjures, with its own absolute confidence, elements of Bosch or Bacon, and also maybe of Blake. See in this one, for instance, the authority of the marks: the curl of an electrical flex, the fold of a dress. I remember I did them in a kind of frenzy, the hand leading, the mind following, only ever half conscious of what might be taking shape.

Here's another, like a team portrait—six characters: a child, a young woman, a man, a fiend, a wolf and an angel. In fact, most of the pictures flaunt a strange little invented family, the angel only occasionally showing up, while the other figures repeat themselves consistently from one painting to the next—like the stolen rushes of a documentary, like random clips abstracted from a concentration camp storyboard. For the setting is nightmarish.

Take this one, here. All five of the basic characters appear, their dramatic tension heightened by strong contrasts between deep lapis blue and a kind of 'keep-off' yellow, their gestures seeking at once to tell and to dissemble exactly what plague overshadows their dark country.

You'll have guessed it, of course. No need for oracles or soothsayers. No gasps of shocked surprise any more these days, but only sighs of weary inevitability. We're all too well aware, today, that children in a police station sometimes have to draw subjects for which they have no words, indeed for which they have no conscious register either. I seem to be one of them, though it was in a clinic that these were done, and I was grown up. Ah, we know for a fact that things do go on in families we could hardly bring ourselves to believe even half a century ago.

Yes, this is all regrettably a commonplace. So much so that a topic once briefly thought scandalously cutting edge and vitally interesting has become all but prohibited in high art. I find cutting edge people today really don't want to hear about it; particularly when the question of memory comes up. No one likes that. And even Scandinavian crime series have exhausted the trope as a plot driver. Sexual abuse scandals do clang on in the news, but the arts have stepped hastily aside. And nobody, but nobody, digs up the recovered memory controversy. That's fallen right off the agenda.

So a culture defends itself, I believe; and who am I to rub anyone's nose in it? That could possibly be the last remaining act of bad taste.

And so I should reassure you after all this, that in these fairly rough left hand sketches I did, the majority are the curious team portraits—of the strange figures in hell that I spoke about earlier—while the abuse itself is *directly* alluded to in only three or four of them, where the full feeling quality of *all* the forgotten assaults is bitterly distilled.

Forgotten. Yes, these images are nothing. They came out of nowhere. They're phantasms, nightmares. No question of *false* memory; I remember nothing. I remain fully amnesiac to everything these paintings contain. If, indeed, they contain anything. Yes, for they were surely just the graphic appendix to a severe mental illness.

Except that at the time my body, under the very mildest of hypnotic prompting, was acting out for my therapist the assaults I'm referring to. And the question 'Was it your father?' always made my head nod, or brought my hands together in a yes. And 'Is it true?' always provoked an agony.

So not quite nothing, then, these paintings. 'Pure machines,' in fact, 'for causing pure emotion,' if poor George Brede could ever have imagined. 1991—I went into the Meredith Clinic a dutiful son; I came out as Hamlet, for my body's story surfaced there suddenly in hypnotic mime and ghostly art. There, by unlooked-for, seemingly supernatural intelligence—albeit I'd had bad panic attacks and incipient suspicions for some months before—I found my dad was instantly doubled with a beast, while I was cast into confusion. Either it was tragedy. Or a freak show.

Well, my dear friend, now I've managed in a roundabout way to set it down here at last: the terrible cliché of the artist's damaged childhood. I wouldn't have told you had I not needed to, artistically. And I know that at the next click of the mouse when I shall have sent this, you'll know these hidden things of me, and I'll be at your mercy.

When I found out myself, of course, in that clinic, I cast about wildly. In one sense, it was the life-long jigsaw piece I'd been waiting for. But, in another, it left me broken. These pictures and their hypnotic enactment came out of me with such attendant punishment it was as though the furies themselves attacked in waves. They did so for months. Between their monstrous visitations, I cudgelled and cudgelled my brains.

What else would you have done? I checked for evidence; I brooded for clues; I ransacked family photo albums, diaries, dreams; I read what scanty medical literature I could find. Because now there was no room for relativism, no closet for philosophy. All at once, truth was critical. The words 'real' or 'imaginary' would determine precisely what I must do.

Yes, there was strong likelihood it had happened. Yes, yes, and yes, what told against Dad made clarity of me—everything I'd painted before, the hopeless marriages, certain childhood enactments, my history of mental illnesses, my dreams, my almost obsessive protectiveness of my own children.

Strong likelihood! For God's sake, it explained exactly why all those years before the discovery I could hardly paint at all—because of a glaring inward world too shocking for any prism that might in those naïve days have transmitted it—even while *all those years* I knew beyond a doubt that I was quintessentially, absolutely and to my fingertips, a painter.

And it illuminated Dad's own weirdness and sudden flight from my life. Yes! But without proof, I say, without proof or memory I had no broker to my revenge.

My mother panicked and clammed up—*Oh! Speak to me no more!* It's almost funny. Clammed up is not quite true. At my first disclosure to her, while I was still a clinic day patient, she was startled and caught off guard. 'Do you mean the same as *my* father did to *me*?' she said. I nodded, not having anything beyond a vague awareness—from a previous admission let slip in a previous conversation—that something inappropriate was supposed to have happened to her. And then she added, 'Oh, *that*'s what your dad always said his own father did to *him*.'

She drove off for a visit to a cousin, but there! There! Categorically and in her words '*that*' was at least *in the family*.

On the other hand '*that*' was an *éminence* still as *grise* and undefined as you like. It could have existed anywhere on a spectrum from trivial to appalling.

Armed with her admission, nevertheless, I had immediate hopes my mother would help me. My heart soared.

Three days later she returned from the cousin and denied everything; upon which I longed to die, as though some eternal grief had suddenly risen from the deep to suck me down.

Bringing my own kids up was what I clung to—kids who needed me alive. One by one, the trails of my enquiry petered out, though, or were fenced off, and I grew more and more mired in an unfathomable country of circumstance, rage and grief—so very like the place shown in the left hand paintings themselves. Because there was no one more sceptical than I! I was scientifically rigorous to the nth degree. Dad had taught me well. I wasn't going to get caught out by any dubious flummery or fashionable prestidigitation. Some part of me—most likely the identical tyrant who is even now policing my self-portrait, Theo, and stopping me from working on it—was always at my shoulder, pouring scorn, demanding detail, chapter and verse, threatening more punishment, humiliation and ruin if ever I took these fragments of evidence seriously.

For, outside the protective fences of the Meredith Clinic, hysteria was already abroad. The early nineties—I wonder if you remember? Psychiatry itself was suddenly a war zone over this very subject: medical shock troops raided and strafed, therapists were sued, some of them pilloried. The press buzzed with diversionary witch hunts. There was a bandwagon, of course, and all kinds of overnight experts sprang up as from sown teeth, pontificating on this side or that.

I couldn't bear it. Infinitely slowly, I got back on my feet. I had a living to earn. I kept *stumm*, slogged the years of depression, shouldered the paranoia, and raised my family.

And I built my career, Theo, because, wherever I hid them, these left hand paintings—now spread out here on my floor—radiated like pitchblende. Of course, I'd seen their significance right from the start. Don't you? If they're true, they become a kind of dynamite, not because of memory, which can be denied—but precisely by memory's absence, by my *a*mnesia.

My total amnesia for Dad's alleged attacks leaves these images as purely physical and artistic testimony, almost unmediated by conscious intention. They remain the missing *marks* in a case that lacks any other overt, corporeal, or historical *scars*; and so become marks in the case of art itself, surely. They make us question all paintings, don't they? They make us question that cosy notion of 'the artistic imagination'.

I think back over the last century and its now famous attempts to access the unconscious. I mean for the sake of art. The Dadaists used automatic writing; the Surrealists tried *grattage* and 'excavation'; Jackson Pollack canonised his own dance, slopping, tipping, dribbling. It was supposed to be *all* about letting the body speak, it was hailed as the body *in excelsis*, digging down under the rational brain. Twentieth century artists so often dreamed of the body, saw themselves as modern romantics, buccaneers.

It was tempting, Theo, such a glamorous letting go. For a hundred Freudian years, the body was said to hold simply the repressed 'drives', the life force: it signified the political elixir, it created the artist as perpetual Oedipal son, as perpetual revolutionary set always to strike the old-guard dead and dine on his forbidden mother fruit, incurring perpetually the father's bourgeois displeasure for the delicious freedom of naughtiness. Of *sin*!

And all that nonsense came to a head in the art games of the seventies and eighties, didn't it? Why, even now, to my amazement, and even after the discrediting of Sigmund Freud, short-circuiting the skull is still held to lead directly to some psychoanalytic treasure chest of folk dreams and transgressive sexual wishes. *Isn't it*?

Nobody bargained for simple replay. Nobody reckoned with a banal document in family atrocity. Still nobody likes to think about it.

But I was cursed to stumble upon the body; and it was my own, Theo. I, that is, and a bunch of other poor unwitting whistle-blowers, weeping children of a new time.

If it's true. If it's true that forgotten narratives of real abuse can show up in the pictures we make... If it's true, no wonder contemporary art has kept its head still firmly in the surrealist clouds. No wonder the medical profession has closed its heart to the implications. Don't I remember all too clearly how my own consultant at the time had wished out loud that I and my accursed condition should simply go away?

But *I* could not, and *it* would not. Because at last my painting began to make sense to me, and I found I knew instinctively and in every detail how to proceed. Artistically, I threw in my lot with what my body had told me. Artistically, if not personally, I backed what was still undecided, and seemingly undecidable. I did it because my gut told me to. My body had to express what the head wouldn't listen to — and that *is* art.

49

I started in a disguised post-modern style—recalling Derrida speaking in Paris when I was there years before in '76. But I made no fashionable jokes, used no ironic pastiche, simply worked up a homage to Artemisia Gentileschi and the forgotten Italians, and smuggled myself in like a child. I did scene upon telling scene, until I struck lucky and you gave me that break against the odds. No one understood—though perhaps they did deep down, and were uneasy. So my name got a little known. And so it went on, Theo. And so we are where we are.

But now from my refuge here I cast about me. For the buried past—or whatever it is—still insists; while Reason, or someone in my head, still denies. And I've exhausted all the possibilities of smuggling and subterfuge. My work is at its crossroads. Art must own its inheritance; it must navigate candidly at last between scepticism and panic. And so it feels that at one stroke my brush could uproot both the modern and post-modern, couldn't it? If only I had the nerve.

Exactly as I decided, splashing down there in the cove, in that joyous pellucid sea: everything, health, life, work, demanded I come clean and tell exactly what it was I'd discovered. The artist must paint the truth. My true self lay fragmented into the six importunate characters of my left hand. It was my allotted task to *recover* from that, and to reassemble myself in a portrait that would emerge only as the whole proposed sequence of canvases took shape.

And surely here at the very start, at least, I could flesh out my own sullied features in the story of that summer back in '76. Surely that was merely a technical matter. I just had to get on and do it.

5

Subject: **Quayside flags**

You're too busy to reply. Of course, I should have thought. Tonia Poole's international now. I imagine you there with a thousand things to attend to. Those strings of feathers, those papers, wires, webs and the scatterings of fibre. I'm a fan of hers—they're thrilling, and what she does is intellectually challenging. No doubt there'll be a good deal of Stateside attention. Probably Far East, too.

Still, I thought I might drop you a line in any case. I'm on my own here for a while and have grown used to a certain pleasing routine in our correspondence—as you know. Just cast an eye over this email if it amuses you, and if you have time. If not, simply delete. No pressure, as they say. Absolutely none.

Eléni has gone to Athens—not business but family. She's discovered new relations there; it was via the internet. And once they heard she was 'in the area', so to speak, they'd brook no refusals. She's sailed off to visit them. I saw her to the port this morning. She was a little flustered with packing and took a while. So I went across to my studio to have another look at those wretched left hand paintings I was telling you about. I'd set some of them up against the walls. Then I took others and grew somewhat absorbed myself, abstracted. It came almost as a surprise to hear her calling, 'Owen! Owen!'

I gathered them all up hurriedly and placed them face down. Not because she hasn't seen them, but because their sheer bleakness upsets her. It upsets me. I showed her them when we first got together; and that, she said, was probably enough.

Alright, the world those characters inhabit is very strange and frightening. And yet I could wish she *would* look at them now and again, because it would indicate a deepening interest in me and my work, which I do rather long for. Perhaps in time.

'Owen, I'm ready,' she called through the door. 'The taxi's here!'

For a moment, it was almost strange seeing her with my 'studio eyes'—framed in the doorway. Eléni is always last minute. She stood with her suitcases, the pretty, dark-haired Greek-American girl I lived with. Almost a surprise; she was suddenly an intruder—so wrapped, trapped and stolen away had I become in my thoughts about the pictures, and in some sense hypnotically regressed once again by them, I suppose. No, of course I hadn't forgotten she was going. Not for a moment. I guess it's just a matter of keeping one world entirely sealed and separate from another — exactly what forgetting is, perhaps.

'Owen!'

'Coming,' I said. I started wiping my brushes, wiping my hands, grabbing the linen jacket that had my wallet in it. 'Just coming,' I put the jacket hastily over my shoulders, 'Darling.'

Dropping her cases at the door, she walked in as if to hurry me up, then glanced at the big Bledlow painting racked up on its stand. It stopped her in her tracks. The likeness of Julia, I suppose. I've got used to it, but after that week's solid work I put in I guess it must have jumped out at her, almost hyper-real. Especially as the most she'd seen before was a mere background mock-up of colour and drawing — you know the kind of reference I'm always seeming to evoke. I mean what we used innocently to call landscape. What I'm trying to do more and more, by the way, is to find how to stitch pure representation into pure painting, though this is nothing to do with the suture problems of reception, which I'm also concerned about... But, heavens, you don't want a digression on theory!

'Who is it?' she asked, staring hard at the picture.

'I knew her thirty years ago. Longer. Just a girl. It's not important.' I grabbed my phone and looked for my keys.

'Knew her?'

'Okay, I was in love with her. She inspired my work. All of it. She was kind.'

'And this?' She jabbed a finger at the photo I'd tacked to the frame.

'That's her, too. Theo sent it on. Or one of his assistants. Someone seems to have mailed it in to them — no name or clues with it. Addressed to me. They forwarded it here. And the really spooky thing is that it arrived *after* I'd begun work on her portrait.'

Eléni flicked at it with her nail. There was an odd venom in the gesture that struck me at the time, though I confess I haven't given it a thought since. I mean until setting it down here.

'Can we go, please, Owen?' She checked her watch. 'Oh, Jesus God! If that boat's on time, I'm swimming to Athens.' She seemed angry.

'It was such a long time ago.'

'I see.' Already leaving the room.

'I thought it would do as a starting point. Portrait of the A as a young M,' I quipped, laughing as I hurried after her.

We stowed her cases quickly in the boot of the taxi and sped off towards the one main road. It took only ten minutes or so to get across the waist of the island. I held her hand in the back seat.

And, of course, we were just in time—Eléni always makes it somehow. The boat was grumbling at the moorings, with a lorry and two vans still loading and the crowd of goers and comers assembled on the quay: three or four taxis, miscellaneous four-by-four pickup waggons, a few families, crates of vegetables and clothing, young men on mopeds, a fat old bloke on a bicycle, a guy with a bouzouki in its case and a couple of farmers with a trussed up sheep. We got out of the car and said our hurried goodbyes. I kissed her. She rubbed her cheek against mine. 'Do you want me to bring you something? Shall I get you some shirts? Nice ones from Athens?'

'No. Not shirts. I can't think of anything, really,' I said. I really couldn't; I felt a bit stupid. '*Típota*, my dearest,' I said. '*Evcharistó. Evcharistó polý*—Nothing at all. Thanks very much.'

'Very funny. Trousers? Shoes? You need some, Owen. I surely do, myself. I'm going to enjoy myself shopping for once.'

'Can we afford it?'

She frowned, 'Oh, you and money!' Then she stamped her foot. 'I'm fed up with not being able to buy this, not that. I'm fed up with your can'ts and mustn'ts. Mustn't I spend my own cash? *Why* can't I, if I like? *Why*?' She shook her head and there was a look in her eye. Then, 'I love you, Owen,' she sighed, and smiled.

'I love you, too, *chrisí mou*. When we get settled, I want to sort out a proper divorce from Lily. She really can't mess us about this time. It'll be fine.' I kissed her again. 'Then we'll have more cash, and we can get married,' I said.

She stared at me, then smiled once more, though there was a certain distance in her look. Our taxi driver had finished unloading her cases. I helped her on board with them, up the rusty ramp and on to the big, shuddering ferry.

Its hooter sounded almost immediately, and the Tannoy chimed for a departure announcement in Greek, and then English. I hurried back ashore. I stood in front of the astonishing Italian constructivist building that runs emptily white all along the quayside at Lakki. Eléni waved down at me from an upper deck. Then she was clinging to a life-boat stanchion while the wind gusted from behind me, and the warm blast came sweeping across a road that was suddenly almost deserted, except for the knot of other well-wishers beside me. The wind caught my hair. It deranged, too, the blue and white Greek flags suspended from a wire between the wharf-side lampposts. It fluttered Eléni's skirt around her legs.

And almost before I could register that the morning had included this strained and rather abrupt parting, the ship was away. Its engines growled, its stern ramp closed, its cables were a-stowing. Its choppy displacement churned up the sunlight on the water as we waved to each other. We waved until she was lost to sight behind the pines and tamarisks of Lakkí bay's northern promontory. Yes, it was unreal, and I felt guilty. I'd freaked her. I shouldn't have mentioned marriage. Not yet. Not till we're better established here and this new paint project looks like a more viable proposition. But our separation is only for a couple of weeks. I took the taxi back, through the strange and melancholy emptiness Mussolini's *Fascisti* created here, the port built almost to designs by De Chirico.

Our door at home keeps banging. As I go to secure the latch again, I half expect to hear Eléni's footfalls on the baked earth outside in this persistent, irritating wind. Just this morning she delayed me in bed, her arms around me playfully as I got up for my swim: '*S'agapó, s'agapó, s'agapó*' — three times, 'I love you'.

I went to my studio. Brushes in hand, I turned to my canvas and to the problematic figure of myself next to Julia that glowed in the light from the window. I sipped my cold coffee, dipped a brush in oil and began working up tone on my enamel plate. But nothing had altered: the minute I started to take paint towards the surface, that same familiar inertia began working up through my guts. My heart thumped, my eyes began to close. It was uncanny. I gave up and thrust myself out, as I've grown so used to doing, into the midday heat.

Subject: **Toned spaces, superposition of themes**

Dear Theo,

I'm wondering, did you receive my last two sendings? I confess I'm alarmed I might have said something out of turn. Or perhaps you're not well—though Jas would surely have let me know if there were problems.

Of course, the Drashkovic event is next and it's still your busiest time of the year. Isn't it. But I do find myself concerned. Neither message has bounced back—I'm worried they might have buried themselves somewhere in what must currently be a very crowded inbox.

Or that my address has somehow got itself listed on your spam filter? Please don't think I'm trying to pester you—the last thing I'd want to do under these circumstances. Just drop me one line if you can, to put me on hold, as it were, and I'll quite understand.

In the meantime, here's a scene for you—on the battlements!

'Just wait a minute for me, Trevor. You didn't tell me there was all these steps. Wait, Trev!'

The husband stops in front of the castle gateway. He looks down over the edge at his wife. She's still twenty stairs beneath the summit of the rock. She's resting one hand against the slope, getting her breath, a plump woman in late middle age, without a hat. She turns her reddened face up at him. 'You'll have to come and help. Please, Trev.'

The man hesitates, then descends. I watch them struggling up together, English holidaymakers, probably staying in one of the converted windmills. Off the main tourist map, as I told you, this island does attract the more determined—Brits, mainly, some Germans and Dutch. 'But it's just walls,' the woman said as she made it to the top. 'There's nowhere to sit down.'

The man nods to me. 'Morning,' he mutters. To his wife, 'There's supposed to be a museum.'

I reply in English and they stare at me. She's mopping her brow. 'Not a breath of that awful wind now,' she says, smiling suddenly as they pass. 'Now we could do with it, of course.'

She's right. Now the fitful gusts of the last week have taken themselves off as queerly as they'd started. The heated air shimmers without movement over the island. How it all warms and distorts, spread out below, a study in inhabited rock. And how the little pastel-coloured boxes of the town simply invite the dab of a brush. Painting, a child could do it! The villas and pines above the road to Áyia Marína, the crinkling olive groves and farmhouses, and Lakkí, the precious deep-water port beyond the donkey-back ridge, its once fought-over sea milky, its air white hot to the horizon, violet-tinged, all of it crying out for some earnest impressionist. Almost there's no horizon, far off Kálymnos and Télenthos jutting out of the southern shimmer where the big boats go through, dolphin flanked.

My heart goes with them. My thought swims under their waterline:

coloured fish flick, stars and shells litter the white sand, raw sponges bulk black on the rocks. Always, the sea-bed shows through, here in the Aegean. So much speaks to us foreigners of another element. I read 'ΜΕΤΑΦΟΡΕΣ — *Metaphors*' stencilled on a rusty pickup van; 'ΕΞΟΔΟΣ — *Exodus*' written over doorways; I offer 'ευχαριστώ — *eucharist*' simply to thank the shopkeeper who sells me my plastic water bottle; his radio blares the rock beat of a τραγούδι — song. Or *tragedy*, give or take the odd stressed syllable. Everything is doubled with an exalted world. I paint what I don't see.

But the devil comes from behind, his company too strong for us. The devil, Theo... Pátmos, Lípsi and the line of the Turkish coast lie just around the corner of the walls, easy sailing. Sun from the white path blinds.

Now the English couple have disappeared. A three-arched church, made of clay, or ancient dough, squats within the castle gateway. Cool as well-water its sudden interior. The miraculous icon of the *Panayía tou Kástrou*, all-holy Virgin of the Castle, gazes candlelit in her golden mount, in the darkness, set in the golden iconostasis that screens the altar.

I love it here. Today, I notice there's a table set out. There are candlesticks, as if inviting to a meal — and a small wooden cross. High up on the wall above it, I read the inscription: 'Εγώ είμι η ανάστασις και η ζωή — *I am the resurrection and the life*'. It's an altered space of kindness, tucked up in a wrecked piece of Byzantine military engineering — as though, suddenly, we're quite *literally* in the presence of saints and sages. Look: each is recognisable by his attributes — no, this isn't western art, because they're also *identifiable* by their faces, the same likenesses transmitted through the millennia. That's the point of icons, I guess, Theo: they're family. They cluster around us like concerned ancestors in a family vault, like distinct shades in a hungry otherworld.

And is it true? Can we trust them, the family of the resurrection and the life? Can we believe something for which we've no conscious personal memory? For here, as everywhere, it's only paintings. And what are paintings?

In a recurrent dream of mine, there is the court of all *my* family, mother, uncles and grandparents, gathered in the cool dark of my aunt's back room in England, and we're assembled to find out what's wrong with me. My Dad is chief interrogator, his voice confusingly, beguilingly kind.

In the same fashion, in this church, all the sainted blood relations of our Saviour appear, only to occlude the meta-mystery of the Father behind the screen. Do you see? The one group maps ironically, in my case, on to the other: the mother, a woman too wrapped up in her own troubled mystery to see what's been going on; the father busy sacrificing the child; the child bearing all the guilt and shame in order to preserve the family. It's a text book structure, intolerably and unavoidably implicit in the *sacred* texts, once we dare read them. How shall *I* ever be saved from the hell behind my back and in my own mind? What resurrection? What life?

And so I'm stumbling out again, almost as soon as I've entered — the external glare immediately sullen, the temperature a fist. This shocking double aspect of the holy family is why I'm imprisoned here on Léros, and why I can't go back or forward, and why the artist who stood with Julia on the Chiltern scarp has no substance in his portrait — nor ever had. Until I know how I stand with my father; whether he really did abuse me — sexually — I can't know who I am.

Julia, then. I met her three years out of art school. It was on a demo, one Sunday, July '73 — a demo against a dictator I hadn't heard of. I'd got some hours a week tutoring at Chiswick Poly. Rosemary Boyle, a woman I worked with, explained to me patiently about Dr Caetano. 'I can't bloody believe you, Owen,' she said, putting down her coffee mug decisively. 'He's only on his way here to London. This living link to the thirties, this bloody dinosaur, this former lackey of Salazar's. He's only coming to visit Ted Heath. It's the slippery slope. Don't you get it? The rise of the right? The Tories showing their true colours at last? This fascist dictator actually coming to visit our prime minister? True colours, Owen!'

'Navy?' I said. 'Prussian blue?

'Oh, for Christ's sake,' she glared at me. 'Sooner or later every one of the post-war gains — health, education, housing — will be down the pan. There'll be beggars on the streets again. You'll bloody see.'

I didn't know why I was flippant with her; I'd read Marx after I'd left Hornsey and been captivated. The tube train filled up with sympathisers at station after station. People held banners and sticks and chattered excitedly. I followed the carnival from Hyde Park Corner, through Trafalgar Square and down Whitehall to Downing Street, where we stopped and chanted. Then we circled back towards Knightsbridge, picking up adherents. Five thousand crammed into Belgravia Square. Above their heads I could just make out the line of mounted police guarding the Portuguese embassy.

There was a stand-off. A hot London breeze sucked around the expensive corners. The sky grew darker. Desultory clashes with the police sent back aftershocks, until, all at once, a far larger tremor swirled through the mass and I found myself separated from Rosemary and the others by a wedge of shouting activists. I struggled crosswise, but the next human vortex swept me hard against ornate black railings at the edge of the square. Crushed next to me was Julia.

Even getting my breath back I was aware of her, her eyes, her short blonde hair, her long limbs. I gave some joking apology as the pressure eased, and she smiled and made room. We began talking.

The demo wasn't her thing. She'd come up on impulse, she said, not for Portugal but for her father. She laughed, because she'd always thought his insufferable bluster, deafness and instability were just a fact of life. Only recently had she connected them, she admitted, with the two years he'd spent grinding his way in a tank across North Africa and up through Italy – in the war against fascism. And then her eyes filled up a little, because here were still Caetano, Franco and some other scaly old autocrats, barricaded in their various corners of modern Europe, for Christ's sake, and still torturing. So had it all been for nothing? She couldn't bear it. She worked in a girls' remand home, she said. For the GLC. For the same borough, it happened, as did I.

Another ripple swept through the crowd. A volley of shouts. Julia tensed, her hand on the strap of her shoulder bag. She said she hoped there wouldn't be a cavalry charge, because people did horrible things, didn't they, like throwing darts or putting ball bearings under the horses' hoofs. She said she liked horses. She drew odd looks. And a sudden flash of light–a man caught us on camera before he vanished into the crowd. Someone shouted, but there were more flashes. A girl was yelling, 'Bastard pigs!' Ten yards away a man was being grappled to the ground. 'Get the film out of it! Kick his fucking head!'

Then lightning, followed by a huge thunderclap. And it began to rain, hot, smoky London drops that beat on our shoulders and splashed down into the basements on the other side of the railings. It grew torrential, and the crowd obligingly dispersed; London trees, parked cars and tarmac came back into soaking view. Julia and I found ourselves scuttling along beside the fancy ironwork. Fat globes drenched our necks, sprang back at us from the pavement to soak our jeans.

We escaped down Halkin Street. We went off and talked for two hours, sitting outside in a café opposite the Park. I remember the striped awning—London just learning in those days to live alfresco. Cloudbursts thudded on the canvas overhead, pedestrians hurried between each deluge, buses emerged from the underpass swishing water from their wheels. Almost oblivious—yet such details remain imprinted on my mind—we chattered and smiled into each other's eyes. But we made no plans to meet again, because each of us was married: Julia to a young corporate lawyer, I to the girlfriend I'd had from even before art college.

Already, though, Julia had left an indelible impression on me. Why? It was the same thing, kindness. Yes, we were physically attracted; but kindness brought us together. She was kind. It set me free to speak, though that seemed just a political thing at first.

Chance sent me on a liaison visit to a Hammersmith secondary school. It was during the three-day-week. Chance brought Julia there, settling one of her charges in the mainstream. Chance contrived a power cut in which we shivered over sandwiches in the corner of a crowded staff room, resuming exactly, so it seemed, where we'd left off. After that we saw each other now and then—for drinks or coffee. She told me of her travels. She'd rejected university: a year on the road with some bloke, taking the hippie trail. India. Everywhere. Afghanistan. She'd spent months there; you could in those days. She'd even seen the Buddhas of Bamiyan. Then she'd come home, to a regular job. And, a while later, marriage.

I met her husband once when he came to collect her: Miles—matey, bullish, on the way up. He seemed okay. What was the harm?

I didn't tell my wife—because I loved her. I gave my feelings for Julia another name: special friendship, a meeting of minds. Platonically, I kept Julia in one box, marriage in another.

But a vision of relationship broke over me whether I liked it or not, and it forced the comparison. Love? I couldn't turn off the blaze in my head; all the more so because my dear first wife wasn't kind, at least not to me. And I'd chosen her and married her in the full knowledge of it.

I left my wife that autumn. It was a technicality, nothing to do with Julia—and I didn't initiate it. Everyone got hitched so young those days, and that was the year marriages first started going down like ninepins—an institution old as the hills suddenly dissolving, as though left out in the rain, the acid rain everyone was talking about;

the economy nearly collapsing, too, because of the oil embargo; inflation spiralling upwards, evoking out of nowhere shades of Weimar... It was bizarre.

Julia left Miles—not because of me. She stayed with a woman friend; we became lovers. It was finances that eventually forced her back to him. And that was why, subsequently, we had always to snatch our hours together. Like that afternoon in bed. Like that moment on the hilltop. Until we could perhaps escape somewhere.

Bledlow:

'We'd better make a move,' she'd said. 'I'm sorry, Owen. Miles will be difficult if I don't...'

Now my eyes are full, even across time and space. Wearily, I make my own move, about to set off home down the rock stairway from the Byzantine Castle. There's a commotion: impossible car horns up here hooting and blaring, cacophony amongst the ruined walls. Impossible! I hurry to the gateway, collide with the bearded priest just emerging from a door by the church. '*Khília signómi!*—So sorry!' We disentangle, we emerge out of the stone arch, we hear shouts, and I look round to the right. Men in sharp suits are coming round the corner of the north rampart. They're heading straight for us.

But the smartest figure carries a bouquet. It's a wedding, of course, not a gang of thugs; not a punishment squad at all. It's the bridegroom's party. And, *of course*, there's a precarious hairpin road at the back of the castle, which I never use and have forgotten about. They must have driven up that way.

No sooner have they rushed up and bundled past me, all smiles and handshakes, than the bride herself appears at the turn, her fussing family doing their best to keep a hoop of flowers over her as she walks. And now my formerly deserted hilltop is all activity.

And *is it true* I have to keep asking myself, even as the guests gather inside the gates. Can I believe my body with its replay of Dad's assaults? Can I have faith? My left hand pictures—they're only the dynamite I think they are if they're true.

Yet if they aren't, why should there be so much mental resistance, so many symptoms—some fiend shutting down my brain, muddling up my thoughts. I can't get a grip on it. I came up here to confront the demons that prevent me from figuring myself—why, I thought for a moment I saw them, in black sharp suits like private security. Instead, they're the heralds of love. Can I ever believe in the meaningfulness of events—as on a stage set between heaven and hell? The groom hands over the bouquet. Everyone crowds into the church.

I need intervention. I need intervention because the evidence I've so long been seeking lies all about us in the fragments of a life, and the left hand paintings *are* the missing memories. For Christ's sake, it's obvious. Memory's shrieking at me! Not so much amnesia as sheer wilful blindness! Then I *defy* punishment. Listen, I'll paint what I'm made of.

I set off down the rock stairway home. I'll do it.

As to Julia and me: I thought our catastrophe was merely the course of true love not running smooth. How was I to know the devil hates most the sight of man and woman embracing?

.

Subject: **Action painting**

Theo?

Alright, then, here's another scene. At least it pleases me to describe them, if not you — so it would seem. I did receive a notification from Jas that one of my Bermondsey monochromes had been sold through your website. I wrote and thanked her; but absolutely nothing from you. Pleases me, I say. Occupies, calms, pacifies, rather. Word-painting.

Julia and me. We crossed the nibbled pasture to where a stile led into the wood…

At least it takes me out of myself, Theo, working out in words what I *still* can't commit to paint.

So I turned on the rickety step, wanting, I suppose, to take a last look over my birthplace. Far off, the little river Thame struggled invisibly south to meet its almost-namesake in the Valley of the White Horse. Shadow swept across, then passed, and brightness rushed on us again, that racing English light. Julia and I ducked under a fringe of almost edible new leaves.

Then the path dropped slantwise. The air was suddenly still. I followed her in a visual pulse of half-illuminated tree trunks as the descent darkened. Our shoes trod an earth rampart, root-fretted; it curved through the wood until, minutes later, we emerged half way down the hill face. A lone cottage marked the prehistoric drove road, the Upper Icknield Way, that bisected the cottage garden and hugged the contour further round. So we retraced our arrival, the tamped earth now bedded white, the track still overarched and dappled. We held hands until another view opened at the bend, directly northeast and looking along the line of the scarp. We stopped. A grass tide far below us flowed into a bay of newly green trees. A solitary church rode at anchor, and, further round, the town of Princes Risborough harboured under the hillside. I pulled Julia to me and kissed her.

'What are you after, now?' she smiled.

I slipped my hand in her coat. I stroked her breasts, her waist, her thighs. I undid her jeans. I remember the touch of her. I smoothed her belly through her clothes.

'Someone might see.'

I was instantly suspicious. I was always just a little unsure of her. Maybe she still clung to Miles. Why else had she gone back to him? But I wanted her again, this time on the earth under the sky — before we had to go back, before I had to surrender her, as always. I pressed my hand further. Now she softened, and I scanned hurriedly around us for where we could go. I noticed the next cloud tear apart and sun strike distant white on an unsuspected reflex of the scarp. It made me start.

'What?' she said. 'What is it?'

It was another chalk sign, maybe five miles away on the hill above the Risborough roofs. It was huge and quite clear. Another cross, its scour shone as bold and emphatic as Bledlow's lay concealed. And from where we stood its lateral was foreshortened, the long and suggestive vertical opening out into the chalk below. I know the name of it now, Theo: it's called Whiteleaf Cross. But from our angle then it was at once so blatantly female, under the mounding top — like some huge public and pubic graffito, that I found myself laughing. It was as though the white cotton cleft against my fingertips had been magically projected on to the landscape itself. Julia laughed, too, until I put all that out of mind and lowered my lips close to hers.

Sudden footfalls on the track ahead; we sprang apart. Two men were approaching — not hikers. The one in front trod carefully in his prim black shoes. He wore a dark overcoat. The other was younger, shaven-headed, burly, in casual jacket and slacks. They hurried towards us.

I shielded Julia instinctively.

'My God, I never thought…' She drew breath, buttoning her jeans. But there was no time to ask what she'd meant, as the man in the overcoat was nearly up with us. It all happened so suddenly.

'Mr Davy?'

'Yes.'

'Mr Owen Davy?'

'Yes, why?'

A paper from his inside pocket. 'It's official business, I'm afraid.'

'Official?' The word disoriented me. 'Who the hell are you?'

No reply.

'Is there something I'm supposed to have done?'

Julia was shouting past us. 'Miles! No! You promised!'

At the bend in the track, Julia's husband was coming towards us, bringing yet another figure with him.

'He told me, Owen,' gripping my arm. 'And I believed him. It was only your address. I thought it was to scare me, Owen. Just to scare me. Honestly, I didn't mean...'

My arms were seized before she could say more. I was wheeled about. Two of them were hustling me back the way they'd come.

I staggered. They quickened pace. For an instant I was aware of Julia half-running alongside me. 'Owen, I'll talk to him. Don't worry — he gets angry. It'll be alright. I'll talk to him.' She was breathless, reaching at my arm. 'Owen, I'm so sorry,' she gasped.

Then she was held, and I was dragged away, too overwhelmed by all that was happening to take in what she'd said. At the turn of the track, I managed to wrench my head around.

I can see it, Theo. Her husband has her pinioned under the high arch of the trees. I hear him shouting at her. She lifts her face to him.

I'd tell my students that paint used to be earth. Perugino learned from Verrocchio how to take clays, stones. Those colourmen ground metals and their oxides, arsenides, chromates; they suspended powders in oil or egg, mixed trance in substance. Love also paints with our flesh.

So pastoral a ground — I was frogmarched to the end of the track and shoved into a car parked right next to my own. A suited, crop-headed youth was already there. Doors slammed. We headed off through the lanes, three strangers and I, unwinding the pilgrimage Julia and I had so recently made.

South we raced on the Wycombe Road, an official-seeming black Rover, bullying aside every other car we met. My hand was damp where I clutched the armrest, my mouth dry. The sky breezed and flickered. The chalk fields folded to right and left, like ridges in a giant molar.

Later, I'd wonder did it happen, or were my kidnappers dark

angels in a dream? I tried to sketch them some years after the event: the three stooges? Musketeers? Men in a car? I drew them standing beside their vehicle on the gravel drive of the house in which I had my studio then—where Julia and I had so often made love. I gave their figures drooping wings. I used coloured inks and the little pen I often carried with me that I'd cut from a clump of bamboo in my landlady's back garden, scraping it down until the nib was fine, flexible as a clarinet reed. It gave a bounding, resilient line: their intricate wings moulted feathers under the plane tree that overhung our Chiswick frontage.

But my illumining hand—no matter for right or left, this time—gave them little detail. They'd become ghosts of their own appearance, perhaps even during the incident itself. And it's only in this effort to keep facing up to my own portrait that the perception of other things comes back, too; nuggets stored just out of reach, so to speak—yes, like ores in the body's earth—so that I'm constantly amazed, Theo, as I write, by this recovery of lost matter, even its most inconsequential moments, in the physical process of transcription. One of the reasons I'm continuing to bother to do it...

The man who'd first accosted me, for example, had silver, neatly combed hair, but I should never have remembered that, had I not typed it here almost before I thought of it. Some black of his lost youth showed through, particularly above the nape. His collar was frayed.

'Where are you taking me?'

'Your place.' He looked round, his face gaunt, his cheeks dry and reddened with minute broken veins, and his eyes blue on either side of a thin, beaked nose.

Then he turned back, leaving his hand resting on the driver's seat. I can see those manicured nails, those peeling finger ends whitened in the grip. And the driver himself: the wiry bristles on the folds of his fat neck...

At the lurch of a sudden corner, we were in a narrow street, the doors of a quaint coaching village accelerating by.

'Left, you daft bastard. You should have gone left.'

The car skidded to a halt. We did a three point turn, the brakes pitching us back and forth, the horn blasting. Antique beams and inn signs gave way to the long, ugly, furniture town of High Wycombe.

'I want to know by what authority...'

'Shut up.'

The mind's eye: now it hovers like a kestrel, a kite, or some Greek mountain bird. I remember the genteel Thames Valley, our miniature rude force barging its way across the narrow suspension bridge at Marlow, slowing only to climb again the wooded zigzag away from the river. I hear in the echo of an abduction—the tyres faintly squealing at every twist and corner, the spongy, stupid, over-engined car thrusting uphill—the patterns of one life overplaying another. And then I'm back down in it, because there's the resonance of a particular feeling, once we'd joined a straight road past Maidenhead Thicket, once we'd lost ourselves in the M4's London-bound traffic.

A feeling. Those things are easier to paint than describe. Or easier to sculpt, maybe. For a tube seemed to stretch out behind us, its membrane more fraught and vulnerable with every mile. It was my connection to the person I held most dear... to Julia and to my beliefs about her... as some multi-dimensional moulding that only the intuition perceives, and which the artist would represent in forms first tenderly elastic, umbilical, musical, now grotesquely blood-ribbed, or with the artificial veins of that other arousal, fear.

I think of *Marsyas* in the Kapoor installation: acrylic sexual gut pulled out in a huge red Ovidian polymer along the top of Tate Modern's Turbine House. I think of passion yanked physically from the red of some idyll, the Titian/Giorgione *Concert Champêtre*, love's conduit suddenly strained to snapping. At its origin, my lover in her violent husband's grasp; at its all-too-generative lip, I.

Bilious afternoon sun. No illusion of speed—my captors relaxing. They chatted amongst themselves. Names emerged: the driver, Benjy; the heavy youth beside me 'the Mole'—nursery creatures grown feral; Benjy and the boss making fun of the Mole as we sliced between Slough and Windsor, over the old marshes, under the bridges and steel gantries. Planes queue in the windscreen, gilded gnats. A jet at take-off rears close enough to touch. A church tower in that wasteland has a fire cresset in its battlements. I keep swallowing a taste of corrosion.

My studio. I'd managed to rent a loft. It was in a house off the back of the Chiswick High Road, and any young painter would have given his eye teeth for it. The space was undivided, the brickwork un-rendered, the floorboards either bare or laid with strips of rush matting. Here, I could live and do as I liked. It was my home. My habitual untidiness made it just the painterly lair you find in every biopic of tortured genius.

A pair of nudes were up on heavy easels I'd borrowed from the poly where I worked—like two-thirds of a Calvary, maybe. Nowhere near finished, they were under the highest part of the rafters, each with Julia's photograph pinned to an upright. All around were canvases half done, canvases stretched and virginal, canvases abandoned. Pieces of artwork on board and metal lined the exposed timbers. Trial prints lay scattered on the floor—where earthen figurines thrust up here and there, as if they were strange hyacinths growing through broken flags.

I had a bookcase, four chairs, a small cooker, some sweet jars full of beans and rice on shelves, vegetables in bags and in boxes. A red Formica table accommodated other random still life. On a windowsill, dead or dying plants; on a desk, picture files and bills, a typewriter, a permanently open toolbox.

A small dormer window blinked over Acton Green and the railway embankment. Another, opposite, stared at a northerly patchwork of back yards. Interior murk swirled inside between them; except at noon, when, if the sun shone—as it had done all the freakishly over-heated year before and was gearing up crazily to do again—then my *camera obscura* endured a blinding girder at an angle through its heart.

And there was a bed, and perhaps some cupboards, and a sack of clay. And a bicycle. I was the naïve curator of myself. Here was my space between two breasts: mortared chimney breasts tapering high at either end, on which depended the roof, the galvanized cold water tank and an identity of sorts. Here I could eat, sleep, paint to my heart's content...

My abductors parked on the gravel. They came up with me. My landlady, who lived on the first floor, smiled and fluttered at them. Her chained spectacles bumped on her bosom. My visitors spoke disarmingly of tea, and we climbed the final narrow stairs, all four of us, into my loft. They occupied my plain chairs, sipped from my ill-assorted cups. There was no phone, of course. They commented on the weather and the drought. The boss leafed through *New Left Review*. Then they got up and smashed everything, systematically.

Benjy started it. I hadn't paid much attention to him; he was about forty, maybe, dog faced, the one who'd helped catch hold of me on the chalk path at Bledlow. He threw his tea grouts over a print, and I saw, helpless, a favourite nocturne suffer a gritty brown rash. 'Sorry,' he said, taking a hammer from my toolbox. 'Official business.' He grinned maliciously at me with his tongue hanging from the corner of his mouth.

I had a photographic enlarger next to the sink. He muffled the hammer with one thickness of towel. Three soft upward blows smashed its lens into the dome. When he removed the cloth, which had become hooked inside, glass pattered softly from the metal shell. 'Oh, dear,' he said.

'Oh dear,' echoed the chap-faced boss, smoothing his coat.

Benjy trod kitchen plates into careful shards.

The Mole picked up a floodlight, found his tongue. 'Sorry.' He unlatched the dormer window and hurled the long stand javelin-like through the gap. It hung on its flex jerking for a few seconds, quietly shattering its bulb against the roof tiles outside.

I backed against the brickwork of the chimney breast and watched muffled explosions, now here, now there: a Venetian bottle against one wall, my slide projector against another. In the lithography press I'd once carefully salvaged from a disused print works, they slowly crushed a small but superb Hendrik Thijssen landscape, which the artist himself had given me. Leonardo's dissections they tore out from my expensive facsimile *Codex*, neatly spitting page after page on forks, kitchen knives, on the handles of my brushes. Purposefully, they ripped the lantern off the remaining lampstand to kebab my own canvases over it. Oh, they were meticulous, inventive. A portfolio of drawings went in the oven; armfuls of books were left floating in the galvanised water tank.

On the end wall I had one large finished work of my own, mounted between reproductions of Manet's *Déjeuner* and *Olympia*. Called *Internment*, it was acrylic on plywood: of Shakespeare characters, Lear, Ros, Doll all wearing rags in an internment camp run by the sadistic, fat and wheelchair-bound 'Staff' — as in a horribly re-engineered Falstaff.

A young man's work, witty in a way and also shocking. It shocked me, my own internal landscape and the repeating, tragic characters even in those days foreshadowing the left hand pictures done in the clinic.

A huge spark fries young Hal on the wire in the night, the way inmates at the Nazi camps used to kill themselves when they couldn't bear any more. His alter ego Mal — a saturnine image from Malvolio — stretches out to him as the arc lights suddenly blaze on. Three violins rescued from a dustbin were nailed along an edge of the piece: I'd found them lying unaccountably one day at a neighbouring college, where they'd lain belly up and stringless, like brown fish in a bucket, with scrolls and fingerboards all awry. A battered, similarly recovered piano keyboard was fixed along the bottom of the picture—as though for an organ, or polyphon, to be played in the form of the picture.

They wrenched it flat, tipped paint from cans, squirted tubes, emptied a pan of leftover food. Pigment pooled, stuff clotted on my figures, ruining weeks of effort. Benjy tussled with the Mole for my bike. He rode it this way and that over my work until colours ridged intriguingly and smeared. The reds slid into outrageous yellows, greens, tomato, pieces of fish.

Then they hoisted the whole plywood panel back upright on the chimney breast. My cast of actors stared out once more, but as if—how shall I describe it—from the flames of some vegetable *auto da fé*. Benjy savaged their eyes with a screwdriver. The Mole took the big pipe wrench I used for my car and twisted each violin to matchwood in his hands. Then he made the subtlest xylophone of the keyboard, quietly shattering the ivories all along.

At last, they turned their attention to the two easels. 'Don't fancy yours,' Benjy whispered to the Mole. 'These photos, though,' said the Boss, inhaling through his teeth.' Soon each portrait of my lover lay ripped and grotesquely ruined in the wreckage of the stands.

They were kinder to me. They only rolled me in the mess of my own paint and gave me a good kicking. My landlady cried up from below, 'Owen? Is everything alright up there? Owen?'

'Alright, Missus. Everything alright,' the boss called back.

Now they were in a hurry. Suddenly, it was all friends, just good-natured horseplay, and we were men of the world together. Which sounds bizarre, yet is consistent, I understand, with a popular hypnotic technique for inducing disorientation or even total forgetfulness of, let's say, a property crime—or sexual assault, perhaps. They behaved *as though nothing had happened*. They each shook my hand in turn; Benjy even winked. 'Better be going,' all smiles. 'Thanks for the tea.' 'Bit like a stag do,' the boss laughed under his breath. He turned back to the chaos next to my desk.

'Sorry, mate. You know how it is. Wife. Nude. Bloke gets upset.' He produced his wallet and extracted a ten pound note, holding it out for me. 'No hard feelings.'

I heard myself pathetically grateful, thanking him as I took it. I shoved it in my back pocket. The Mole was last to leave, just blocking my sink with the sack of clay as he turned on the taps.

I remember wheelspin on the gravel below. Water gurgled and

splashed. Smoke wisped from the oven.

Subject: **The betrayal**

Friendship? Noblest of the Loves? Yet another scene launched blindly into cyberspace with no response. Writing emails, telling stories to myself, it seems.

Theo, I wouldn't have started had you not encouraged me, even insisted.

At least I get something out of it. I get recollection; a satisfaction; a kind of relief from the blockage of my art. For the same West wind I'd faced on Bledlow now fought with the tide, as the ship's safety announcement fought with someone's tranny. A mile out, my ferry ducked its blunt nose, screwed, climbed and dipped awkwardly again as the two most determined gulls dropped astern. I knelt on my rucksack, chary of losing it. I sprawled my arms on the rail.

Glimmering strings peeled off the shearwater with every smack of a wave. I turned to glance at the last of England and saw a clear, miraculous layer of gold above the Channel cliffs. It shaded south into all the Atlantic colours, unachievable in any light except their own.

Day was dimming—the ferry had been delayed. Soon, mine would be a night trip, and there was standing room only here in the bow. Fellow passengers at my back occupied every bollard, plinth and vantage point along the sides of the black-and-white-painted, rust-stained old ship. Suitcases and their owners clogged the decking further aft. We rose and fell, rose and fell. Another mile out, our klaxon blasted an incoming sister vessel. As if at the signal, in the curious, estranged dusk, flasks were uncorked, sandwiches handed out, kids admonished.

I stood up, balancing. A phrase of Da Vinci's came to mind: 'the body of earth has its ocean'. I checked myself over again, one hand on my straps. The cut to my mouth had stopped weeping days ago, though the salt breeze still stung it. Benjy and co had returned to whatever rat hole had brought them forth.

It's the way of such incidents—I mean the trashing of my place and the bruises I received—to remain diffuse in the mind, until we can process them. I'd apologised profoundly to my landlady, as though it were all my fault. Indeed, I half believed it was—that potent word 'official' still oddly resonating.

She'd insisted on the police. But with them, too, I'd felt compromised and responsible; my unconventional life and living quarters on show, my spoilt artwork, my illicit relationship obviously at the root of the trouble.

And, regarding Julia, I felt nothing but bitterness. 'So sorry,' she'd said. Why had she apologised? Whatever it was, she'd *known*. She must have. She was complicit, and, in the process, had smashed not just the physical contents of my studio but the entire construct of my life.

Colleagues rallied round. One offered a bed; I couldn't sleep in my attic any more, that was for sure. The polytechnic's principal insisted I took a break. On a whim the next morning, I'd called George Brede— feeding coins into a public phone box as I explained what had happened. Theo, it was George's idea that I should get right away. Missing the emotional point, as ever, he'd suggested only the grand response. 'England's fucked anyway, old chum. Why don't you go and live in Paris or somewhere? We could all come and visit you.'

I'd had to smile. Yet the idea—and the name of the city—lodged in my mind just as the wider implications of what had happened began to dawn.

Without Julia and my belief in her, I was nothing, had nothing. Why, even my old car was stuck miles away in a wood. I sifted through the mess, salvaged my journals and small portable properties. Just what sort of a life would I be putting back together as I cleared everything up, sorted everything out? Still earning a living at a job I disliked?

Anger welled; a determination took hold. Just go! Now! Maybe this was an opportunity. Seize it! Back yourself as an artist! Aspire! At least check it out. I needed to think.

So I was off on a recce. It shouldn't take long to spy out the land, maybe find somewhere to rent and get myself set up, look at the jobs market. I could discuss it all with parents and friends when I got back. And I'd go to the police again, because, of course, there'd been nothing 'official' at all about the snatch and beating. They were nothing more than the vengeance of a jealous husband, who was warning me off in a traditional—if somewhat excessive—manner and thought he was above the law. I wanted revenge. I'd make damn sure he learned better.

But as day darkened and the cross-Channel tub ploughed further and further out across invisible shipping lanes, I felt cold and more alone. My ribs hurt, my face and stomach still ached. There were kicks to my back and legs I'd failed to register at the height of the attack. The scenes in my flat kept flaring in my head, bruises in their own right: the broken nudes, the screwdrivered *Internment*, the violins' ruptured bellies. And Julia? Now I could only hear the smothered smash of glass, playing and replaying over her last breathless words to me, 'Owen, I'm so sorry.'

I slung my rucksack. I moved back unsteadily between the ship's lifts and dips. A steel door gave on to the boat's saloon. There was a worse crowd there, a fug of tobacco, food odours, a queue to move in meeting another to come out. Strip-lit French families, their kids tetchy from hours of waiting, were crushed at their tables alongside English lorry drivers. Hitch-hikers—students, Americans—crammed any other free space with their bundles. They slumped, sucked cartons of orange. An exhausted young couple lay stretched out along busted Vilene seats.

The ship's motion was blind, our outside blacked by the fluorescents. The floor shuddered to the engines. Eventually, I bought food and a coffee, but was too tired to eat. I sat on my possessions at the one free corner of a table and brushed my hands down my stiffened, paint-soiled jacket.

The woman beside me lit a cigarette, the Frenchman opposite stacked plates into a pile, a child at the next table cried. I stirred sugar from a packet into my paper cup and sipped at it. I made myself bite at my food.

Here, at last, the pieces of what had happened began to assemble. We must have been followed all that day, Julia and I. So it meant that at some stage earlier she must have actually handed her husband my address. Hadn't she said as much?

And who else could it have been, anyway? How else could they have found us at Bledlow? Yes, the thugs had been spying on us. And Miles was waiting there, too. They'd held off until we were right out in the country so as to avoid witnesses, and so that she'd be well out of the way when they came to teach me my lesson. Therefore she must have told them of our planned excursion. Yes; for when we'd got back to my flat, her Mini had gone. Hadn't it? It had certainly been removed when I went downstairs after the attack. I couldn't remember for sure.

But that didn't matter. She'd betrayed me comprehensively. She'd even admitted it.

71

I touched the coffee cup again. 'Owen, I'm so sorry.' And she'd told me she loved me. She... I felt the burn of rage, like an electric arc suddenly jumping across in my head.

Then she still loved Miles. She must do. Or she somehow got a kick out of... rough stuff. The violence. Because some women, sexually, so I'd heard... The womb, the vagina, insatiable... I'd been played for a fool. All along, she'd... And then to apologise!

I stood up and took myself off abruptly, swaying, pushing people out of my way, dragging the heavy rucksack behind me. There was another steel door further aft. A companionway ran beside the car deck where the leeward air sighed, drowsy with diesel as the ship heaved. I gulped it in. I heard the engine's churn, the swish of our wake. Foam lay under the boat's stern, its long streak shimmering opalescent. I looked up. The sky was completely clear and glittered with crystalline points. I looked ahead. The horizon stretched in a long curve dotted with sea lights, reds and greens, the French coast.

Nothing made sense. I leant on that ironwork and watched the wave-tops, the fracture lines, the surface under starlight.

'You have any cigarettes?' The voice was American. A tall, rangy-looking boy with a thin face and blonde, unruly hair.

I shook my head.

'Grass?'

'No.'

'Fuck.' He peered at me. 'What happened to your face?'

'An argument.'

'The other guy?'

'Guys.'

'Oh, right. Steal anything?'

'Pretty much everything.'

'No shit.'

No shit! Oh, why am I bothering to write all this to you, Theo, when you don't bother to reply! Things I've been able to tell no one else. I *have* no one else!

...

I've been out. I've got a grip on my feelings. I've come back to the keyboard. Because the fucking ferryman crosses not only into death, but also back towards life, and I hold something I must set down, whether you read it or not. My visit: the ferry to the neighbouring island of Kálymnos skirts eroded lava, so close. Exactly. I'm in two worlds at once—I told you. Almost, we touch a chine: hardly-

72

inhabited Télenthos, vertiginous island, its sea choppy and dangerous with the *Méltemi*, the Aegean north wind. Engines grind as the captain digs us out. Daylight's astonishing, a glitter of points from wet rock and splintering foam.

This is the safe channel. It's crisscrossed with skiffs and caïques, and we're between volcanic masses, opposing mountains which are brown-white and waterless, this one cracked off from that, so it seems. The wind drops in their shelter. Now the morning's a familiar oven, sun already burning over bald Kalymnian heights. And full ahead from here beckons soft-shaded Mýrties, the village of myrtles.

Land still lifts and falls to the waves imprint. There's a hotel by the quay. Mopeds buzz past. Old Mercedes taxis whisk travellers away. All of them turn south along the coast, past the stalls of groceries and beach toys. It's the way I need to go myself, but the supply of cars is exhausted, and I walk rather than wait. And so I find myself on the road to the Kalymnian hamlet of Kamári, with the tarmac already soft and sticky underfoot.

In fact, the road becomes unbearable; once out of Mýrties it's a mere strip, along which the traffic, though desultory, hurtles. An old bus, with one wheel on the fraying edge, sends up choking clouds of dust in its slipstream. My appointment is not until midday. At Kamári, I take to the hills.

A path of sorts goes up almost vertically beside a roadside shrine. Its saint has only a bottle of Fanta inside the little window. High above are two lonely houses set on their own miniature plateau. I scramble up. A dog barks; its neighbour joins in. I plunge between the buildings and then onward.

This is open mountain, the scrub ever harder and more spiny, the stones progressively looser. My cheap rucksack, far more modern than that thing I carried to Paris, bumps against my shoulders. Stuffed into it is a tube-shaped cargo that weighs next to nothing; yet the pack traps sweat under its straps and becomes a burden. Further still above me, an enclosure marks an olive grove where a single goat stands tethered in a corner of shade.

I stand and look back. So quickly I've come so high above the road. Now the boats in the channel are mere specks, and the bad old tooth of Télenthos shimmers up out of an incredible azure. I told you I needed intervention. I need *some*one…

I pull from my pocket the address I jotted on a single scrap—fruit of a phone call from Marta. It's of a house in the Kálymnos Chóra, or

Chorió; which seems the generic name in Greece for any island's central village. It means 'in the country — *chóra*'. All I have to do to find it is keep the road in view.

My goat path rises. Two basking snakes flash across scree above me, alarmed at my footfall. Instantly, they're lost in a thick undergrowth of thyme, oregano and needle-sharp thorns. I climb past two stunted pine trees. A wall of boulders walls nothing, though beside it the track levels and cuts around a line of the foothills, and all at once I'm so high I can see the other side of the island. Chóra itself lies at the end of a green valley, and beyond it is Kálymnos's port of Póthia and the sea. Behind me, the curve of the mountain is almost sheer lava, crumbling, baking, sometimes overhanging. Then another turn cuts round to a ravine, and the drop to my right is sheer, the way instantly narrow, perilous. It peters out. I put my hand to an edge; I press my finger to the nearest sharp spine. Even pain can deceive, even the rock of dreams can wound. What's real? *Now* is penetrated by *then*; *is* finds itself perpetually interleaved with *was*. Who's in the frame? The encumbrance in my rucksack chafes at my shoulders. I shall have to force a way down. I'm going to Chóra to see Spíros Apostolíthis, the icon painter.

6

Subject: Chiaroscuro, the cave

Dear Theo,

Your long-awaited reply confirms what your silence suggested. I'm very sad to write this. What gives you away is not the things you say — which are unfailingly upbeat and encouraging, of course — but those you leave out. It's as though I never wrote what I did, never put into words the... how shall I put it, *ghostly intelligence* of my father's sexual abuse, this unpleasant little matter that currently so stymies me as an artist.

Well then, I shouldn't have told you, shouldn't have burdened you with it. I should have remained here and kept quiet; dealt with the matter and moved on. Isn't that what people admire? I should have found yet another way to encapsulate the condition — in which I have this accursed misfortune to discover myself. I should have kept on using my trademark artistic subterfuge, symbol, pastiche, displacement, historicity, condensation, witty dissociation or whatever — so that no one ever need be troubled by it. Including you.

Except I can't any longer. I tell you I've run out of artsy tricks to dissemble the entire business as 'fictive imagination'. I mean my concentration on painting the human figure in *narrative*. The human figure *engaged*, Theo: the one subject that can answer the charge that art is 'mere ornament'. Hence, my decision about my new project and my first letter to you. A self-portrait — I was hoping for your continued support and understanding. What I've run into is an uncomfortable silence followed by... equally uncomfortable blandness.

Even as I kept firing off emails to you as though you were simply too busy to reply, I saw precisely what had happened. It's what I always fear. Such *stigma*... There's a Greek word, eh? Such stigma hangs around this subject that hardly any man dares disclose having being on the receiving end, because it makes him, not to put too fine a point on it, a leper.

Listen, two separate nurses from whom I was seeking help... I was in acute distress. They both made the implication, each using almost the identical turn of phrase: 'I have to ask you this, Owen. Have you ever been tempted to abuse?'

Maybe you think it's a reasonable question. I mean on hearing what I've told you. Maybe *I* did at the time. Maybe it was part of some professional routine they'd been instructed to go through in case any children might be at risk in the case. That sounds laudable — even if no other nurses ever asked it. And even if none of them would ever ask it of a woman.

Whatever, I dealt with the question matter-of-factly and honestly both times: no, I had not been tempted to abuse. Yet both times have stuck in my mind, and I still grow hurt and angry in retrospect.

For now I think clearly — aided more and more, so it seems, by this charmed act of writing — I believe I simply saw knee-jerk prejudice in a professional cloak. Actual offenders don't seek treatment; typically, if they receive it at all, they have it thrust upon them. I, on the other hand, was opening up to specialist psychiatric nurses about serious matters. Exactly how serious I was then uncertain. I was feeling suicidal, and in crisis with my marriage and my work. The lightning imputation 'Hmm! Probable paedophile' was at least *medically* uncalled for, don't you think? Surely, there might have been a kinder way of asking it, and they could have let me sit down first. Why, it's the finger of suspicion that makes one think twice about coming forward at all. It stirs up precisely that mixture of guilt and confusion with which the whole thing began.

Forgive me for labouring this point. You can see it touches a nerve. I really do remember feeling inexplicably tainted as a child and strangely cut off from everyone in the world except my father. He and I lived in an arrogant intellectual world of his own construction, but as we kept decamping from one town to another in a seemingly endless chase around the fringes of London, I thought everything was my fault. And I can tell you those nurses took me straight back into all that — cruelly, I believe.

Alright, my mother's fleeting testimony did suggest my father as victim turned perpetrator. But what happened to him isn't *evidence* against him in my case — and the nurses implying that almost inevitably in men it was passed on like vampirism... Do you see? Do you work it out? Theo, such small signs suggest the world regards me askance because of something that, if it was done at all, was done *to* me and not *by* me. Your own palpable disengagement from our correspondence is, to be brutally frank, just another of them.

You write to me first of friendship bound *by a shared concern for something outside and beyond*, and then you shun me. For heaven's sake,

I told you in my last few emails how Julia's jealous husband hired thugs to trash my place in Chiswick. Are you uncomfortable with me as a victim of *that*? Do you find yourself wondering whether I might have been out perpetrating raids on studios or galleries myself? Of course not.

So when one has summoned up the courage—against inexplicable panic and long-embedded threats of the consequences—to spell out to a friend a start in life possibly smashed at the core in the most grotesque way imaginable, how much more painful than any blows and kicks if the friend should turn immediately aside.

You'd never have done so to a woman. I know your generous heart. No, my gender alone opens me to this… this passing by on the other side.

Well, I fought shy of maleness as a child—not surprisingly, perhaps. But nothing could stop me growing into a man. Painting that man, me… painting the portrait of the artist… Can you imagine how fraught it is?

Then, most of all, I'd need a true friend by me. Yet you stand back. Maybe you think I'm a gullible fool who's been tricked by some disreputable therapist into believing outrageous and incredible things. Maybe you simply don't know how to deal with me any more. Then why not tell me so? Why not argue it out with me? I tell you, Theo, the myth of the artist as an entirely self-contained outsider is just that—a myth. It keeps society safe from contact with the uncanny or uncomfortable; but in truth both art and the artist desperately need engagement with other people. As I with you. I *need* it!

There,

> *I was angry with my friend.*
> *I told my wrath…*

I'm unfair. You're just frightened. Everyone is—about this. It's such an incendiary issue, arouses such bitter controversy. 'False memory' and so on.

Theo, I can only trust that you'll take what I've just said in the spirit of… friendship. Yes, I've been furious with you. I've considered breaking off, and to hell with my career. What I'd give sometimes to be at one with the men down there in the boatyard, learning to repair fishing smacks and caïques, working my keep by all kinds of marine *metaphorés*, even by painting the blue and white strakes and the protective eyes upon the bows, longing for a safe port.

But I can't, and the fact that I wouldn't even be able to make myself understood among them is symbolic of the whole predicament. No, there's only one way forward, and I know it. And it has to include you.

I left you in the mountains, I think, on my way to the icon painter. How I wish you'd been walking there with me; for then, perhaps, we shouldn't have got lost—as now it seems we have.

Come, friend. I do need you. And I'm desperate to share with you what happened. Please let's journey on together down to a broad valley on Kálymnos, with the road I'd left running through it and a sprawling village laid out at its heart. Please listen. Don't block me out. Listen to the time that has passed—for it was three o'clock before I was able to gather myself, collect my wits and jam my empty water bottle into the overflowing bin I found beside the only shop there.

Yes, bear with me. I need to tell you. Allow me to continue where I left off. The shop was closed, but I saw reflected in its window the mess I was in from my ragged and unplanned descent. Nevertheless, a little sprucing found only slight cuts to my hands—from where some stones on the slope had given way. The glasses case in my shirt pocket had dug into my chest, but the spectacles themselves were undamaged, and the matrix of scratches on my shins and calves was superficial dried blood, drawn only by the mountainside thorns. A bruise to my hip did bother me—it still does a bit. It came from a harder tumble, and I feel eerily connected by it to my loft studio in Chiswick, having described that to you so recently. Well, it was a foolish venture to leave the road. Had I even come to the right place?

For now it was the deserted Greek afternoon, and Chóra, or Chorió, appeared quite charmless. Above me, on the next mountainside, rose the broken walls of some once high and redoubtable citadel. But here in the valley the prolific houses were mere concrete boxes in a grid. Their gardens sometimes boasted more discarded appliances than shrubs or flowers, and their sky was criss-crossed with power lines. And the abode of Spiríthon Apostolíthis, once I eventually located it, seemed monumentally undistinguished. A rusted moped stood under a sheet of corrugated iron. A child's scooter blocked the tamped path.

But the address tallied with the one on my scrap of paper. And so, flustered and sweaty, I knocked. Sure enough, the door was opened by the same tall, slim young man I'd met not long ago at Marta's house on Léros.

We shook hands. He ushered me in. I wanted to apologise for being so late, but my Greek deserted me, and I was simply awkward. He sat me down at a table as soon as he'd got me through the doorway. Then he disappeared — into what I presumed must be a kitchen.

I looked about me. The room felt cramped and dim. It smelled of a recent meal; there were crumbs on the red vinyl tablecloth under my hand. It smelled, too, of housework, as though someone had not long ago swept the tiled floor and sent all the dust airborne. Everything else betokened a young family and not much cash. The few furnishings were tired and modern; a television squatted on a fruit box between two chairs; a skateboard lay abandoned on the mat in front of it. Next to a shelving unit, a yellow plastic basket was piled with washing, and, amidst a further scatter of toys, a bucket stood where I guessed nappies were soaking. A popular American print on the whitewashed wall opposite me was surrounded by framed portrait photographs, in which one or two of the figures wore traditional Greek costume. I gazed through the half-closed Venetian blind that protected the little window beside me and could just make out, beyond the shaded patio with its plastic chairs and outdoor *foúrnos*, the red and yellow tubes of a brand new climbing frame. But how thick with dancing dust motes were the slatted sunbeams leaking into the room.

Clearly, my host had been expecting me as promised. Clearly, he'd stayed awake, while the rest of the family took their *ypnáko* — their well-earned nap. I fancied I could hear human sounds every so often through the open doorway: the creak of a bed, a faint childish snoring from the back of the house.

What I conspicuously failed to detect were signs that Apostolíthis had anything to do with painting. I could see none of the usual give-aways: no stray jar of brushes, no tube or two of pigment. Nor, most obviously, was there anything remotely worthwhile on the walls. Embarrassed by my late arrival, I began to wonder whether I hadn't got the wrong end of the stick. Greek was so shifting and elusive a language. Perhaps I'd misheard that word *ikónes*. Had our dialogue on art at the party, about which I'd so congratulated myself, actually been on some quite other topic, and was I here making a fool of myself? A drop of sweat fell from my eyebrow to my shirt front. I was dabbing at it when Spíros reappeared.

He brought Greek coffee. He brushed the crumbs from the tablecloth and put down an opened packet of biscuits. He sat opposite me. My dusty rucksack with the tube bundle sticking out of it lay beside me on the floor, and I bent in contrition to produce the baklava I'd packed, unwrapping its paper only to find it crushed and broken from my falls. I set the gift forlornly next to the biscuits.

He made no comment, but the coffee was strong and sweet.

'*Kalós*,' I pointed to the cup. 'Good.'

He nodded. There was a movement of his mouth. I was ready to find him angry; he'd every right to be. Yet the dusty rays between us suggested almost a screen or veil, and his expression remained indeterminate. I found myself wondering, as I looked across at him, whether he didn't remind me of certain painted sarcophagi, the colour still passably fresh, the portrait still almost speaking, even though the identity of the buried young man or woman was shaded over with two-thousand-year-old coats of varnish.

So my thought ran on. Yes, his dark hair just curled at the temples; he was indeed rather neat and 'finished'; yes, disconcertingly like some figure from antiquity, perhaps. Why, he might have worn a linen robe instead of the dark blue jeans and white open-necked shirt in which he'd just greeted me.

I was at once painfully aware of my age, my begrimed clothes, my cut hands with their resinous ingrained pigment. The bruise on my hipbone flared, and the devil in my neck and shoulders tightened into that wretched pain that wasn't pain but rather a darkness — that would accompany me whether I wished it or no. What was the matter with me? In the presence of this Spíros, I'd suddenly become all body and emanation. I'd set out because I couldn't represent myself and had ended up more physical than the man I was asking for help!

It was *help* I wanted?

I'd told myself on the boat that something about him must have made such a deep impression — subliminally — that it would have been only a matter of time before I'd found myself journeying to seek him out. I'd thought of it as a hunch.

The sticky fault lines in my baklava gleamed. He ate some. I bit into one of his biscuits just as he began speaking. I decoded the strong Greek last syllable at the end of a question: '…in a taxi to the Chórá?'

I shook my head. '*Óchi, perpátisa yia meriká khilió metra…* No, I walked for some kilometres…' I couldn't remember any word for 'lost'. I threw up my hands in a kind of desperate pantomime, then stretched out one bare leg to the side of the table and pointed to the scratch marks.

He finished the sentence for me '…*yíro apó to vounó*?'

'Yes,' I said in English, 'I got around the mountain. And bloody hot and thorny it was.' My cheeks were burning.

Now he laughed at me. The delicate mouth showed its fine, slightly irregular teeth with a couple of crumbs of baklava attached to them. My cheeks burned the more—surely in an unmistakable blush—because it occurred to me to wonder what exactly had Spíros assumed when he received a phone call on my behalf? What must he be thinking now? Hadn't I known all along that he understood not a word of English? Had I really kidded myself that my pidgin Greek would allow us to hold a deep and meaningful discussion of West versus East in the crisis of painting, the crisis in my heart and my weird inability to paint my own face?

A species of horror seized me.

Theo, I've never been consciously attracted to males. I told you, I've always fought shy of them.

That said, on just a couple of occasions in my life, abruptly encountering some strikingly handsome young man, I have indeed felt that same blush.

Now I heard myself laugh in turn, a ghostly, rattling laugh. For I was hoist with my own petard. Having staked my career and everything on the authenticity of the body, what had manifested now but the body's reddening—a blush, that sure sexual giveaway—to tell me I'd fixed up an assignation with a young and personable Greek for no other reason than that, unconsciously, I fancied him. Here I was eating cake with him, blithely admiring his smile and imagining him dressed in some sort of fancy linen!

I wanted to leave. I considered pretending to choke and lurching out into the street. Perhaps I could mime needing cigarettes, and then disappear and not come back. I started to get up, but it was too late: Spíros had noticed my alarm and was speaking again. I couldn't meet his eye. Instead, I looked wildly around the room.

That was how I noticed the clue I'd been missing from the start. Positioned behind me, where to someone walking in it would be partially obscured by the door, was a picture, almost certainly an icon. It might mean nothing; most Greek houses had one. Yet to the corner of my eye it looked unlike the usual candlelit Virgin—and it offered at least a pretext for rising to my feet! My heart still distressingly a-thump, I raised my eyebrows to Spíros for permission and stepped over to look more closely.

It was a panel of authentic size, about ten inches by eight, with a carved wooden frame. A spurring knight lanced down hard into the mouth of a dragon. Pain caused the beast to squirm his tail around one of the horse's legs.

I was struck by the composition: the great white horse dominated centre stage while its holy rider was diminutive. I noted, too, the use of text on image: two painted words in the golden glow at the upper level told the saint's name: Yiórgos—George. A pointing hand in a quarter circle, its fullness obscured to human eyes by the frame at the top right corner, suggested heaven's blessing on the struggle.

I thought fleetingly of George Brede, then lost myself again in the painting's disproportion. The saint's foot, encased in armour, was thrust forward and miniaturised still more by its stirrup. The looming crags behind him—eerie reminders of the Kalymnian heights outside, maybe—were scaled down and abstracted almost beyond recognition. The puny dragon... Motion was motionless, presence almost absence. It was an absolute dream of a work.

Theo, we've all had some passing acquaintance with icons; I've looked into them from time to time—I even studied them a little once—but I've always regarded them as a kind of visual dead end. Which makes it all the more strange that I'd come here in the first place, doesn't it, because now I was right up close to one and examining it for dear life. And my college tutor, George, whom I'd once imagined my friend, too, but who'd actually been trying all that time to seduce me... so I eventually realised... You see?

Well, I was riveted to the picture, but at the same time I was thinking maybe I hardly knew myself at all. Maybe I was perpetually giving off signals and the young man in my own current Bledlow painting—whose vacancy it was proving so hard to fill—wasn't a self-portrait at all, but the blatant emblem of repressed desire. Was it just a me I couldn't own up to?

Spíros had moved across from the table to join me. He was looking over my shoulder, so close I could hear him breathe. Sweat trickled in my armpit.

There are moments that have no duration, and we remain forever in a tableau of attitudes: Spíros and I standing there, attracted, perhaps, into the quadrature of this one little artwork.

To paint is, of course, to seek to assemble such moments. For what is this magic we perform but the construction of a space so absolutely and compellingly framed that time finds *itself* confused. A picture forces time's arrow, like a reluctant compass needle, to gyrate now here, now there, until the watcher can only surrender to an altogether transcendent mode. Yes, ours is the anti-Newtonian project, and the viewer is to be drawn by it into the love of eternity, to experience the living world beyond that scientific illusion of its mere dead workings.

Years before—well before the clinic and the foul revelations of Dad—I did a series of small black and sepia ink paintings. You've never seen them, Theo. They were in a gum-thickened medium—after the style of the young Samuel Palmer; reminiscent of Blake's woodcuts, too. They were flawed, but they told a story. A pastoral figure, who is myself, returns home from work late in the evening. It's dark. He parks his bike at the rear entrance to his house only to be assaulted sexually, unaccountably, by an 'angel', who, whispering fiercely, grapples him to the ground. But—equally unaccountably—the protagonist of the scenes, me, rises up out of the body, and, when he looks down, gone is the modern town with its vicious one-way system, where I lived with Lily at the time, to be replaced with rustic monochrome, the moonlit trees stark browns and blacks, the nearby Thames silvering through, and the local hills a web of lines, in whose completion he may summarily lose himself. And does.

All this while, however, the struggle on the ground with the angel persists, and there is something he has to decide, this figure, as he floats high above himself, something he must choose to know, or say. His bound soul, female and hidden separately away, weeps in her rags. His child self, also hidden, separate and elsewhere, cries out in pain.

Yet he can't think of either soul or child, nor of his pinioned body. Instead, while his eye watches the moon tick round—or many moons—he considers philosophically the growth and fall of civilisations far beyond the horizon, beyond homely Bledlow, beyond the just visible Vale of the White Horse. So high up is he; so far out of it.

So I imagined Jacob in the Bible to have been wrestled by the angel at Peniel. Yet was he, too, flooded at morning with angel sperm, enlightenment as rape, grotesque, the rosy pigment on my next transmuted sheet? Indeed, my graphic sequence seemed to end with the 'orgasm' of the attacker.

And therefore far more grotesque, don't you think, that, having completed the series, I gave almost no thought at the time to what I'd painted—to what had come straight out of my 'imagination'. Nor did I pay any attention to its horrific ending. For it seemed as nothing, then, to mix scripture and semen. As nothing, Theo.

Besides, my preoccupation with the work had all been technical—as Gauguin makes Jacob and the Angel flat grey in a field that belts orange back at you over the caps of the women, or Schiele's somewhat similar lovers hunch in their opalescence, or indeed Kandinsky lifts colour generally off into abstraction. So, although one could hardly ask for a more graphic illustration of the abuse that was later to manifest so shockingly out of me, the fact remains that I somehow failed at the time to notice anything significant or bizarre in the narrative I'd just depicted.

Can you believe it? And how many years more must I stay out, floating above my history in this same trance and still failing to own the pictures my body so persistently paints?

My father drew a figure once at my childish request. He sits at our yellow oak Utility table in Aylesbury, wearing his post-war mustard fleck pullover. I'm pestering him. I'm four. His cheek is pinkish blue-white with early morning stubble. From ear to eye runs the tortoiseshell lever of his glasses. Do I love him? He will draw me the figure of a man; I've demanded it. In rapid, reluctant strokes, he dabs a pencil at a lined foolscap pad he has in front of him, and I'm childishly amazed that in his art there are no boundaries, that his entire notion of line is porous, a perpetual nervous hatching, until at last a diffuse male form leaks white.

He'll never draw again. He'll never again make the mistake of giving me a clue or insight into who he really is. Later, he assigns to my mother all artistic faculty beyond the merely diagrammatic. Hyper-intelligent, mathematical, an arch-Newtonian, Dad denies even that he sees pictures in his head. He has neither dreams nor memories, he says. He's wired differently from us all, he says, comes from a different planet—is congenitally *an*iconic.

He's lying. I knew that, even as a child, and challenged him about it. I knew he saw all too well the mental pictures he refuted, had achieved not aniconia but some continual internal icono*clasm* by whose violence he sought to blind himself—presumably to what he'd done. To me.

But he would never, never admit to having a mind's eye. Weird man. And so now I must study endlessly, and without success, yes, like the Prince of Denmark, the gaps in my father's line.

I think suddenly how pure and untainted a form is the icon, and how Spíros Apostolíthis could have been me, the aspiring young artist, the man I'm trying so hard—and failing—to paint. I could have gone to Paris to study, instead of merely to escape. I could have painted beautifully, without this unbearable upsurge of left hand

84

horrors constantly breaking through.

I pointed to the panel, stepping—I hoped not too rudely—back, '*Thikí sás*—yours?'

'*Óchi.*' Spíros tilted his head away in the dismissive Greek negative.

Then he spoke at length, fast. And still I didn't know whether he meant he hadn't *painted* it or that he simply didn't own it and wasn't a painter anyway. So we stood there again, teetering on the brink of what felt to me like a small personal chaos, and saved only by this wooden masterpiece, mysterious in conception, deft in execution and otherworldly in effect. Nothing, it seemed, would resolve into smiles or gestures of informality: another coffee, such tiring heat, these family photographs—soft-furnishings of conversation by which we conspire to cosy out the dragon choice and move, please God, move things on.

No, Spíros and I were a frozen frame, an old Grecian inscription with a missing piece: *please meet our famous local...* Was the word *icon painter*, or not?

Writing to you, Theo, I see so clearly this recurring motif of suspension. And suspension really does appear to be my condition. It continually awaits choice. Choice to descend.

And the choice right here relied not upon some detached academic essay into sexual symbolism—the knight, the lance, the dragon's red mouth, etc, etc—but a right-to-the-moment *reading* upon which my entire future appeared to depend.

I think of it now, the choice, the recurring choice, to drop down into this life, or that... Should I dismiss all the business of Dad's abuse that I'd enacted for Mitchell in the clinic and declare myself here with Spíros in Chóra on Kálymnos simply on account of some repressed Freudian desire for him? Were I to do so, were I to align myself with those voices so sceptical of my 'memories', were indeed I finally to 'discover' myself as some kind of very late-flowering gay, and simply give in to it, cease 'denial' of it, then there beckoned, I suppose, a real niche in the artistic world.

For sure, if I stopped trying to blame my dad for the fact that I kept producing graphically charged material, if I saw the violence of all that as merely stemming from a vast inner resistance to my authentic sexual orientation, then surely I'd have the fellowship I craved; more, the friendship I craved, and that friendship with so many of a similar nature. I'd at last be part of a community, and my praxis would be assured: I'd have my place in, say, the emergent 'post-neo-figurative' movement. Yes, a significant place.

In so many ways, it was precisely the place George marked out for me all those years ago—'You've such a facility for it, Owen. I mean life study, and so on.' (Hardly flattery in those days when drawing was anathema; and there was enough dismissal in his voice to suggest my gifts cut me off from his loftier, brutally intellectual world—as he supposed—and left me merely the unthinking child of fortune. But at least he said it!) 'I suppose you realise you're a *talent*,' he went on. 'I'd have to stay up all day and night for that kind of line.' He was piqued by rejection, of course. He believed that in resisting his advances I was resisting my nature.

So, was I?

Theo, there are some whose sexuality is clear to them; others for whom such things emerge by degrees. We're told. And so, indeed, it seems.

Then was I here on Kálymnos to be enlightened at last by a blush? You see how I do appear to remain hanging.

For some psychiatrists would suggest that the matter my body brought forth in the clinic—and produced elsewhere all these years— might be simply the index of a primarily bisexual nature, the infantile sexual wishes for my father having been repressed in classically Freudian fashion. Yes, suppose Freud's Psychoanalysis was right after all.

But this provokes a still greater matter. For if Dad *is* innocent, and if Freud's seemingly disgusting notion of fantasised sexual wishes *is* to be believed, my *more worrying* left hand images, for example, might also be wishes—that threaten eventually to unearth me as not so much straightforwardly, decently gay, like so many of my acquaintances in the arts, but motivated by completely other, completely horrid and unacceptable predilections. Exactly your concern, as I've suggested, Theo?

Otherwise, what else was my therapist in the clinic asking us to believe but the truly extraordinary proposition that I should have sustained this out-of-the-body *ékstasi*, this perpetual trance of suspended bloody suspension—which is what amnesia implies, doesn't it—for fifty or sixty odd years? Because every incriminating thing about Dad came from my body under that mild hypnosis in the clinic. I repeat that consciously and in any legitimate sense of remembering, I've remembered nothing of any sexual assault by Dad *at all*.

Theo, we've all heard of PTSD. Yes, we now reluctantly

acknowledge that war vets can wall off events that ever afterwards flash and streak, filling their nights with unprocessed screams and their days with suicidal depression. But can we really apply this to childhood? Don't accused parents rightly cry 'false'? For can we honestly imagine a hugely traumatic experience (or more likely traumatic experiences repeated many times over and over again) to have remained so sealed away that not the least tell-tale clue should *ever* leak into the conscious mind? Not the smallest visual flashback? Even under further hypnosis?

Theo, I ask this as one who, years before the first inkling of such things, had already made the most long-term, intense and inward scrutiny of myself. Why, I'd started gleaning childhood memories from the back of my mind soon after my first marriage ended in my mid-twenties; and had kept detailed, candid reminiscences all dated and written down in my notebooks. Not one item there—among, alright, some quite genuinely telling material if you look at it with hindsight—could directly incriminate my father. Which was why that idea had simply never occurred to me at the time.

And hadn't I also in those same youthful years recorded endless data from my dreams—though I admit these did contain a number of explicit references and perhaps many other allusions, which in those days, of course, I would have put down as merely Freudian symbols of perhaps my anally passive *attitude* towards my father—without twigging a thing.

But beyond the personal, Theo. Can we seriously be asked to accept that the whole of culture, the entire body of modern human science and enquiry—I mean, of course, the Newtonian Enlightenment, not forgetting all the romantic, philosophical and theological reactions and revolutions *against* the Enlightenment—has missed, glossed over or somehow been complicit in the historical cover-up of this one class of familial crime? Incest. To the effect that it could be so relatively prevalent and yet so blotted out of the collective mind? For so long?

Well, yes, okay, strangely we can. Strangely, indeed, we've come lately and somewhat reluctantly to acknowledge that incest *does* genuinely take place, and is even quite common, when only thirty years ago it was still denied absolutely, or listed as vanishingly rare.

But this business of post-traumatic amnesia from childhood with *no accompanying visual flashback material whatever*; especially when so many people *do* remember all too clearly the most terrible things done to them…

No, *that's* a step too far. That blows up in everybody's face.

You see? I'm not just a gullible fool. Nor am I trying to escape responsibility for my situation by blaming my parents. I share your reservations; I'm a severe critic. In fact, there's no one more sceptical than I. For surely it's the conspiracy theory to end all conspiracy theories. Surely, the thinking world was right to balk at it—and balk at all the therapists and radical young doctors who began, in the nineties, to propose it.

And the thinking world is surely right nowadays to ignore post-traumatic amnesia as somehow shown up as a species of hoax, or if not quite that then at least under control, sorted, accounted for and no longer the ticking time bomb it had once seemed. For God's sake, my own head always told me it was crazy, untenable. Sigmund Freud, faced with this exact dilemma a century ago, had been right to invent his opposite hypothesis of repressed wishes.

And so surely, now, next to the icon of St George, beside the icon painter on Kálymnos, I should simply face facts, give it all up and bury the idea: the ridiculous idea that I was in any real way the victim of something crucially and woundingly *nasty*.

Even as I stood there, I could feel my hands extending towards him. I looked down. My God: how strange it was, and frightening! My hands were moving of their own accord, just as they'd once done in the clinic. It was a trance phenomenon, and I was permitting it. They were inching towards his waist! The picture—the icon—must somehow have stilled my mind, and now I was on the brink of some appalling indiscretion. And still I let them continue, and continue.

They stopped only a few inches short of his belt buckle. The paint stains on the backs of my fingers were clearly visible. I stared at them aghast. Nothing now could take the gesture back or pretend it hadn't happened. I felt sick.

But then, of their own accord, they turned over. I heard my voice say, '*Íme kallitéchnis egó. K'esís?* — I'm an artist. And you?'

And when I looked up again, his expression was wry, maybe even indulgent. But still he gave nothing away. Slowly, he, too, spread out his hands beside mine, his palms likewise turned up. And maybe his skin showed traces of pigment; or maybe it didn't. The ambiguity, the damned suspension remained. Certainly his hands seemed almost to radiate. And was that from gold leaf—a defining characteristic of the technique I'd come seeking? Or was it rather some besotted glow with which my own perception endowed him? Once again it posed the question: had noble *Philía* brought me, a shared concern for something beyond us? Or was it naked *Éros*?

My embarrassment, so stupid, so long drawn out, so—it felt to me—momentous, appeared never ending.

I was the one who broke it. I let my hands drop. Something between a resigned laugh and a snort came out of my nose, and I turned away, gave up, hoicked my rucksack with its rolled tube of papers on to my shoulder and left the room. I got the front door open and stood just outside in the heat, taking in great gulps of air and looking up at the barren rockscape hanging over us. The blue-white sky seemed to boil wherever it touched the land.

Spíros was beside me.

But then he was ahead, hurrying past the moped in its ugly shelter and stepping over the child's scooter. He turned, beckoning me palm down—Greek fashion—to follow, and marched off. I followed, none the wiser.

He set a keen pace, but I made myself keep up. Then very soon we got out of the village. The glare from its whitewashed walls gave way to the glare from the hillside crag, and the slope was instantly steep, each foothold loose and crumbling to the tread. Up he scrambled. I did the same, hearing as I climbed the clinic matron's ironically accurate words: 'That's a steep and stony road you've chosen, Owen.'

But, ah, how far I was now from that high, oak-beamed room with the little musicians' gallery and the patients taking tea—and that comment from the Matron out of nowhere, after Group... as if she'd known all along what the doctors never suggested: that with many of the psychiatric illnesses there were and always had been options, that the business of healing could be a matter of choice. And that there hung over the whole business the quirky subatomic notion of Uncertainty—the very notion that defined Hamlet and fatally *con*fined him. For only the audience is ever shown categorically that his hunch was right all along.

...

Theo, I've written so much and still have hardly begun to explain what happened. The thing is, I'm still somewhat stunned. I'm urgently trying to digest the experience and its ramifications.

Well, I've swum and been into town: a few hours to think, to think over again what I've already pondered so much during my three days back from the visit.

The truth of the matter—I realised this with something of a

surprise—is that I never actually go very near anyone, least of all men. It's a fact. Other than you, I've virtually no close companions. Nor have ever had. And just look how I manage *our* relationship: with a very great distance in between us! I've never been a proper member of a group or community. And the more I face up to it, the more it's undeniable: I really do seem to avoid contact by every possible means, keep myself apart from almost the whole world, yet contrive to cover this up with my plausible manner and a network of contacts held cleverly at arm's length. So that no one really notices. Not even me.

And so to put myself in close proximity to a complete stranger— with whom, childlike, I had no means of making myself understood— shows up as an enormous gamble and quite uncharacteristic. My God! No wonder I was 'suspended'. I must have been in a state of panic throughout. I can see now that I was perhaps experiencing it just as in my 'angel rape' series; virtually 'out of it' the whole time.

And that's why I haven't been able simply to summarise for you what happened, but must revisit the encounter in narrative form at such length. Because I almost wasn't *there*, but was in some sense gazing down from an intellectual or conceptual zone in which I could hardly feel what was happening.

Perhaps, Theo, that's why the meeting feels so loaded, as I describe it, with a sense of life or death.

I was climbing that goat track up the mountainside. The lava loomed unforgiving a hundred feet above, and I could see no point nor end to our ascent.

Then, all at once, a firmer track snaked sideways, having crossed up unseen from the valley and under the bluff. We followed it, until very soon that same ruined citadel I'd seen from the road came into view and made sense of our direction.

'*Megálo Kástro.*' Spíros stood and pointed, nodding at me before striding on again. Before long, we gained a breach in the walls, only to find a further upward slope, full of broken dwellings.

So we entered the habitation of the past, a refuge from pirates and passing imperialists, and were forced to pick our way gingerly between fallen slabs or whole blocks of masonry. We climbed wrecked streets, negotiated strewn alleys, crossed a ruined *agorá*. A couple of tiny chapels were painted a pristine white as though someone had begun to restore them, and I stopped beside one, turning breathlessly round to stare beyond the walls, right out to the port of Póthia in the east, and the glazing sea.

I stared too long. Spíros was gone when I turned back. I hurried some yards along a vacant façade, but there was no sign of him. So I retraced my steps, peering anxiously this way and that across torn footings, raggedy grasses. Thinking I heard a footfall, I spun round awkwardly. There was nothing. The bruise on my hip ached. Ruefully, I collected myself and wondered what on earth I was doing. Far beyond the walls to this side stood the mountain on which I'd got lost earlier. Its ridges rose hard out of the valley as if to belie the distance. Another sound. Again, I swung round. 'Spíro!' My voice echoed in empty stones, roasted crags. 'Spíro!'

Then I saw him at the top of a narrow set of steps. They led up a small outcrop. A humped portico half concealed by a chine jutted over a fragment of architecture that had long since fallen away, and he was looking down at me from there. The sun blinded and clattered off the rock.

The stairway was hidden in a slot between abandoned houses. I found the place and hurried up. He waited, grinning all the while at my discomfiture. A rust-banded, nail-studded door stood before us at the top. He twisted an iron ring and shoved it open. My gamble had reached its point of decision. I took a deep breath, summoned my resolution and we ducked our heads into darkness as profound as the brilliance we'd left.

A retsina waft struck me. It was mixed with sulphur and earth, perhaps even cloves. All I could see was one barred stripe at my feet. Then my eyes began to adjust. I was in a cave-like space, dimly illumined by narrow slits on either side, and the stripe on the floor was from an arrow loop above and behind us, just now catching the full afternoon sun. This was a little church, its vault hollowed half way into the rock. A large, free-standing wooden structure near the far end gave me momentary pause. I was alarmed by its central position, its heavy bars, clamps and dangling straps. Then I realised I was looking at nothing more sinister than the back of a fantastical old easel. Here at last was the vindication I'd been waiting for. Spíros had turned out exactly who I'd thought he was from the start. Here was his workshop. Something shook in my shoulders as it often does when I'm threatened with strong feelings. Did I sense in this dark interior (if not Plato's cave, then maybe his *chóra*) a cure for my amnesia? That the gamble might have paid off in spades?

I took a step forward and made out several rectangular shapes on the wall to my left—his pictures, of course. And beyond the easel a stone altar, maybe, built into an alcove at the far end. There were homely touches, too: a glimmering white jug on a chest here, a chair and bench there; a small table, some primitive shelves. With a species of joy, my still accommodating vision picked out at last the painter's typical pots and jars, his prepared panels, salvaged frames, upended brushes, his bottles, rags, papers, string, wire and other debris. I felt instantly at home and smiled back at Spíros, who was still in the doorway, silhouetted against the outside glare. I turned and hurried through the glinting light to the first of the paintings.

The image was wholly undistinguished. It was nothing more than one of those Jesus faces common in Orthodox churches — at least so far as I've seen, Theo — churned out by the lorry load in back rooms. They're mostly hand copied, I think, after Theophanes the Greek, but are dross. The light was so dim; I snatched my glasses from their case in my shirt pocket just to make sure, but wasn't mistaken.

I passed further along, so flummoxed I hardly noticed a curious little tempest of eggshells that floated, almost rocked, on the seat of a chair under one of the slots. The next painting was worse. A Turkish delight Mary proffered her saccharine baby from behind a candle extinct in its holder.

I moved on. An idiot with beard and halo held a book. Then four small frames were tacked at random angles on the low tiled arch beside the altar stone. In turn, they showed a schoolgirl with an exposed heart, an anaemic martyr, an empress wearing a dove and a photo-realistic Hollywood angel.

I glanced back over my spectacle rims. My forced smile would be invisible to Spíros; everything else in my demeanour could only broadcast terrible disappointment. As I approached the big easel, I was already figuring how I could extricate myself and get back to Myrtiés in time for the ferry.

The heavy old contraption stood stark against the strange light that speared from the slot above the door. I blinked the afterimage, touched my glasses, geared up for mediocrity and thought I'd found it. Clamped in the black wooden limbs was a regulation-sized panel of Mary as *Theotókos*, or God-bearer. This particular aspect, I recalled from some cobwebby student corner of my past, was called *Eleoúsa*: the saviour and his mother shown cheek to cheek in a pose endlessly imitated and reproduced as the prototype of loving kindness or 'mercy'. It's another regulation tear-jerker in which the child's face is set improbably on a body of little adult proportions, while the Virgin dominates the composition—the great round of her head rounded again with a golden halo that intersects mathematically with the kid's.

I shrugged in scorn and gestured to the arrow slot. 'You paint in the dark?' I said it harshly in English, and it sounded like a judgement. I wanted to get away. I felt as jaded and uneasy as I'd been elated just minutes ago.

He came over, and I tensed almost as if for a fight. But he only unscrewed the panel, painstakingly, in silence, from its clamps. Carefully, he lifted it between his palms, took it a few steps and held it up under the single shaft of sunlight, angling it gently back and forth.

I dumped my rucksack in order to peer over his shoulder. I was still mighty dubious. My glasses lacked the range, and I had to pull them off. Luckily the streak of illumination was so good I could see clearly without them—and was taken aback. All the panel's ground seemed to warm into radiance. The detail awoke, and the entire surface gathered a brushless refulgence in which gold beyond gold pooled beside reds that weren't red and darkness that wasn't dark, until the whole effect was of one shimmer with embedded grains—as though I could suddenly see into the molecular vibrations of each substance. My breath caught in my throat.

He handed the object to me. I jammed the spectacles back on and made the same movement, holding it in front of me under the stream of light. Again the figure came up, almost developed before my eyes— like a photo in the dark room, except here in unstoppable brilliance.

It mattered nothing that the Christ child's expression was half finished. It was of no account that the chalk gesso still showed through, since that was as poignant in its way as the sheer colour everywhere else, colour born out of oxides and earths and such artful matter as spoke after my own heart.

And now the whole function of the design was evident: how child as man and woman as both giver and receiver exchanged unending love; how the female was primary and yet subsequent, how gold exceeded its frame at the top, how the thin red line bounding the Virgin's halo swung high up right on to the edge, so that limitation was deliberately defied—because all creation was suffused now with the same transcendent glow spilling out.

The piece was a delight. I saw its folds and figuring, its stylisation jostling realism, its delicate Greek text-on-image reminding irresistibly of what was always a spoken Genesis—the Word in the beginning, the Logos. I gave myself up to the numinous film of line beside line and tone against tone. Portraiture transcended technique. Mary — untainted yet by any renaissance aesthetic, unreferenced, too, by any standard of modern formulation that I could come up with, neither cubist, fauvist, abstractionist nor naturalist — was intriguingly outbid by her ambience. For the face, in truth, was almost withheld by its ochres, was rendered almost flat against the sculpted pleats in her gold-bordered maphorion of dark red cloth. Yet still she caught to perfection the heavy-faced woman with the broad brow and sad eyes, the elongated nose, the resigned, diminutive mouth, who in every icon gives birth to eternity and hope.

Theo, it was a triumph.

I looked at Spíros in bafflement. He must have guessed my thoughts. He jerked his chin over at the pictures on the wall. *'Kallitechnikí thesaurí,'* he laughed — 'Art treasures.' He said it again, and I got the irony. They were church furnishings, already here when he arrived. He'd found no reason to remove them.

'Ne, Spíro! Katalavéno! — Yes, I understand!'

Then I looked away again and bit my lip.

Theo, you may have clocked my rapid mood swings inside the cave. As I try to document this, I'm increasingly noticing them myself. I was apprehensive when I came in, then relieved that the old easel wasn't some instrument of torture. I was excited and felt justified once I knew Spíros to be an artist, then was extravagantly disappointed at the stuff on his cave walls.

But those swings were as nothing to the one that came over me next. You might say it defied character. It defied, at least, *consistency* in my character, and I can't explain it. Then again I can, but not in a way to suit you, given how manifestly discomfited you've been by the complex clinical information I've already inflicted on you. Anyway, what happened seemed a complete reversal of perception, as though some bitter sceptic in my head suddenly and unaccountably took hold of me. It happened; and that's the truth. Right in the midst of hope and admiration: hope that I might be miraculously released from my amnesia — you remember — and admiration of Spíros's superb achievement, I say, full of generosity and exaltation, I found myself thinking just like my dad. I became contemptuous, suspicious of everything in Spíros's workshop — and of the religious tradition it so patently embodied.

Perhaps it's obvious, though: I was in a dark space with a man, a situation I seem to have gone to extraordinary lengths all my adult life, as I've said, to avoid. Yet that still doesn't account for the sudden switch to scepticism and scorn. Maybe I was jealous. Maybe I begrudged Spíros his achievement. Think of George Brede and his cowboy hatred of all images. Whatever, Theo, the fact remains that all at once, standing there, I had absolutely no time for icons! I was disgracefully ungenerous. My brain simply frothed with derision. Indeed, I reminded myself sneeringly of something I'd looked into once — this long-dormant snippet of information springing remarkably to mind — that just two sources authorised the whole wretched mystique of these so-sacred little pictures: icons credited with amazing cures, icons warding off invasions, icons guarding buried treasure from Moroccan pirates. You know the sort of nonsense.

I don't recall where I read about it: the first was St Luke's alleged painting of Mary and the Child at home — which is a complete fantasy, of course. We know for sure no portraiture accompanied early Christianity; four or five hundred years went by before anyone started making pictures of Christ. Or his entourage.

Secondly the so-called *acheiropoietic* images: St Veronica's Towel and the Turin Shroud, their imprints supposedly 'not made by human hand', their passage through the centuries fraught with trickery and delusion by which they gathered an even creepier sexuality each time their outlines were recycled. Don't you think?

And that's just it: recycled. The truth is that no one has a clue what the original Jesus looked like, or his mother. And so the portrait in my hands became to my eyes in that instant just one more in an immensely long line of copies, each claiming potency out of a plainly spurious likeness.

In fact, I was of the opinion — and this will confirm for you, Theo, what contradictions arise when we launch ourselves into this seemingly limitless Ocean of words — that icon painting was itself the erasure of everything I thought of as art. It was a mere cottage industry, a pre-industrial reprographic system where the painter's own substance and preoccupations — his entire identity — were necessarily set to zero.

I heard my snort and looked hard at Spíros. My visit was a waste. Every icon was a fake. This effort of his, magnificent in its way, was actually no different in artistic implication from the framed rubbish on the walls. It was a joke. It was *the* joke of Warhol's multiple Monroe. At least Marilyn had been real!

He was smiling, but the expression was equivocal — again. And then I hated him, hated everything about him, hated the weird religiosity of his little vault in a cave, in a ruined citadel half way up a mountain. *Megálo Kástro*! Yes, it was all thoroughly *high camp*. Holding his damned icon, I stood my ground.

He blinked first and looked away.

And I'd won, only to find myself wretchedly guilty as I watched him turn and seem to start bustling with his brushes and cloths and pots of substances. Had I hurt him? What was I playing at? I tried to rationalise the feelings he kept stirring up in me. Faces were the very devil. Mary, Jesus, Mao, Madonna. The object in my hands was only a panel of wood daubed with an arrangement of marks. That was the conclusion it had taken the crises of the twentieth century to arrive at. And that was why almost all significant contemporary artists kept rejecting the face. They had to. 'True likeness' was simply part and parcel of that edifice of false consciousness and superstition deployed for millennia to cover up society's vicious abuses—most particularly the familial sexual violence I needed to expose. Now we knew it. Portraiture had come out of the churches, scented charnel houses, and spread abroad in the secular capitalist world only to flatter the fat villains and twisted psychopaths who always ended up running things. Likeness in painting meant joining hands with all I ought to ride out against, not flirt with. Even George had seen that. The face in art was always a retreat. No wonder I couldn't do my own.

I watched Spíros at the bench by the other wall. He was selecting a couple of extra items from one of the shelves. In the shadows, I couldn't be sure what they were.

I took hold of myself. He must just be thinking he'd found a disciple. Naturally, he was getting ready to start work. It was nothing.

He was lighting a brazier beside him. Oh God, like some old Hollywood castle. Now the fire took and flickered, and he held a taper in his hand. Now he was lighting torches on the wall, the kind of outdoor flares you could get in the beach shops. I saw their brackets as the flames licked up. The brazier glowed. The flambeaux burnt. It was nothing. It was theatrical. I stole a glance at the bright doorway. Not just theatrical but practical, too: certain processes required heat, that was all. And light. Gold, eggs for tempera, alcohol base: these were his stock in trade. My shoulders were shaking again. Shadows sprang from the objects in the room and darted eerily.

Once, in England, when I was still quite symptomatic, I was alone with a male photographer. It was a publicity shot for my first exhibition — he was a friend of a friend. He sat me down in his house and gave me a coffee. Then he took me into the garage, where he did his work, and I posed with my coffee cup in the dark space. But his flash failed, and failed again, and he tried changing the bulb units, swapping batteries, checking leads, all to no avail. Theo, his pricy system malfunctioned almost every time he tried to take a shot of me. But whenever he turned away, it fired off perfectly.

I kept apologising. I didn't know why I was shuddering, shuddering uncontrollably. Only afterwards, as I was driving back to my appointment at the clinic, did I remember that along with the coffee before the shoot he'd chatted and shown me some of his own stuff: unpleasantly sexualised work, one or two items involving children, the kind of thing some photographers get up to — unhealthy enough to make some kid-self inside me furious. Furious, I mean, even while I'd consciously blanked out what I'd seen. Furious enough to sabotage his equipment. I *had* sabotaged it; I must have, my inward rage must have stretched a spirit hand into his nasty electrics and disabled them.

But who can switch off fire? Spíros had dropped to his knees. He was gesturing and talking over his shoulder to me. He had his brushes clasped between his hands — like Dürer's hands in prayer, but with protruding spikes. '*Próta próta,*' he was saying. 'First of all.' He was melodramatic, planted in front of the altar. It was mediaeval. It was ridiculous. Now he'd finished his stupid devotions and was standing up, grabbing a torch and coming towards me, coming closer, coming too close. He had a hot flare burning. My shoulders were shaking and he was gabbling at me in his infuriating, kinky language and I could do nothing to save myself. I held up the precious icon in front of me as if to ward him off. It almost hit the flare. I almost set light to it.

It was unforgivable. He stopped dead in his tracks. I was appalled as soon as I'd done it. I swooped the picture down in front of me and pretended to re-examine the brushwork. I even started forward, manoeuvring it back into the light shaft as though it had always demanded a certain extravagance of gesture.

I was unconvincing. He was at my side. I adjusted my glasses, my cheeks burning this time with shame. I looked down at the icon. Once more, the gold gleamed. Here and there were the lines of overlay where he'd applied the leaf, the lines of the swaddling bands more like elaborate robes, the border of her garment, white of the unpainted chalk…

'I'm so sorry,' I murmured. '*Signómi. Lipáme polý…*'

He put his hand on my shoulder. I felt only the portrait's piercing accuracy. Like a wound — it was her, it was simply *her*. Absolutely, the face was nothing like Julia's. Yet I tell you I experienced in that moment the two women as it were superimposed — or was it confused — by an overwhelming likeness beyond likeness.

My eyes filled up with tears.

They fill up now. Theo, I've written all day — all the twists and turns of microcosmic realism. I'm exhausted, drenched with sweat, and hungry. This is the point where I have to break off and send. The rest, though there's not so very much more to tell, follows tomorrow.

Subject: Cyclops

Alright. Here as promised is the remainder of my excursion. It's now the cool of dawn, and I trust you'll still be asleep, and that my last night's email lies as yet unread. The sun's just rising over the Turkish mainland as I write, sun that will take some hours yet to come to you.

Sun overlays the sea like a memory of that gold I wrote of yesterday. Maybe the icon asks which is the representation of which, the heavenly body or the beaten leaf? But this is too much philosophy, and yesterday's frenzy is past. Today I'll be dispassionate, though I confess I'm on tenterhooks to know how you'll respond.

I left you at a critical moment, and you don't yet know how I got out of that cave. It all happened in a flash. Spíros caught my arm and the icon was taken from my hands. In an instant I was twisting free, grabbing my rucksack, stumbling into the blinding daylight.

At once, my exit fell to bathos: one tough English hiking sandal skidded under me at the top of the stone stairs, and I had to throw out an arm. Then I felt the weight of my rucksack slither off. A wild grab for it simply unbalanced me the more, and I ended up on my damn backside. Scrambling to my feet, turning, dashing tears from my eyes, I could only watch the rucksack skidding, bumping down the drop beside the steps to my right. To cap it all, the rolled-up tube of my left hand clinic paintings fell out of it and burst its rubber band. So if I hadn't humiliated myself enough, I had to watch the incestuous sheets separate and flutter over the broken masonry twenty feet below.

I ran down the steps, thinking only to begin collecting them before Spíros should come out.

Too late! His shoes were pattering after me on the stone even as I got to the first image: glaringly face up, of course.

I looked back at him. To my surprise, his face seemed not outraged but concerned. He was even keen, it appeared, to help.

Before too long, we had them all roughly in a pile — it was fortunate there was no wind. But to gather them up he'd had to see them, and now he'd put out several of them on the dust and rubble and was examining them closely.

Theo, I sat down on one of the walls with my head in my hands, resolutely not looking at which ones he had. I didn't even know why I'd brought them — I suppose to show him some of them, if things had worked out differently, and if he'd been someone else. Why, yes, I'd brought my missing memories because I needed to own them. But even then I'd have wanted to show them on my terms, not like this. My concern, of course, was with those two or three in which I'd let the child hand represent diagrammatically — as a child will — the cruellest, most deviant acts Dad had done to me. Allegedly.

These had been painted about nine months after Mitchell, my Clinic therapist, and I had identified them. I mean Dad's acts. This discovery was by hypnotic signalling: a kind of question and answer technique using my hands. I'd never remotely imagined such vile things happening to anyone, and at first I couldn't believe a perpetrator could be that warped. Yet something about them, I can't say quite what, did ring sickeningly true at the back of my mind, and the subsequent act of hinting at them in paint did bring some relief from the pain. I suppose that was what had stopped me dismissing them out of hand. I measured the quantity of pain I experienced in their retrieval and in the many subsequent years' duration of associated illness; and that was only consistent with something very severe. I also think that at that stage I'd wanted Mitchell to see with his *eyes* what we'd only discovered via my hands. So I'd painted for him my left hand paintings. Because then, in a way, I might see them with my eyes, too.

Here, again, this characteristic ambivalence: *I* painted them, yet *I* couldn't own them. They came out of my body, and out of my medically supervised treatment with a recognised practitioner, yet I couldn't comprehend them. Theo, I want to be dispassionate and am not making a bid for your sympathy. Nothing appals me more than the pop-marketing of this sort of suffering, the tear-jerking and packaged annals of monstrous neglect or everyday cruelty. For that

99

very reason, I don't intend to go into any detail here about what those worst allegations against Dad are. Let's just say that my exaggerated response to Spíros's burning torch in the cave may have been related to one of them. Anyway, in the corresponding painting, and around the corresponding diagram, my censorious right hand had drawn a ring of black so thick it suggested some intense gravitational toroid, a circular frame of almost cosmic constriction. Nothing contained within that black ring was ever supposed to leak out. For decades, I guess, it hadn't. But now here was Spíros, a complete stranger and an artist to boot, examining my painted paper sheets at his leisure. What other conclusion could he leap to than that these horrible family secrets were my private tastes, and that I'd brought them here in hopes of finding a like mind?

I stood up, tears streaming freely now as though a dam had burst, and wandered off among the trash and history. The sun was a hammer, the shame unendurable. I stared out at the mountains from a ledge over the slope, seeing nothing. Like Marsyas, flayed, I felt my innards were on display.

And what happened next?

No, Theo. There precisely is the artistic problem. That's why I'm writing to you. Things happening next. Moving on. Moving on is what I need your help with. Release for the victim only happens, they say, with the recall of the abuser *finishing*; because then the worst is over. But I'm nowhere near that in my recovery. I do remain stuck: stuck in the moment of it, stuck in those paintings, I guess, and suspended above them at the same time! That's what I'm trying to tell you. Please, Theo. Ah, what is writing itself but a kind of dissociation.

Something was touching my foot. I paused in my reverie and looked down. A tiny grey-green lizard was on the strap of my sandal. It darted, spangled itself sun-wise on old stones — *moving on* one frame.

The body doesn't lie, Theo. It can't. It only seeks eternally to replay what's been done to it. The body — that despised entity, feminine chóra of 'fantasy' and 'falsehood'... Play tells all to kindness.

I looked back at Spíros. He was still hunched over, still leafing through the sheets. I just let him carry on. My visit to him was a disaster, and I must await the consequences, lamenting, oh God, in the process everything that had happened since that first window of understanding about Dad opened for me. It was a window about post-traumatic amnesia in general, too. It opened very soon after the Berlin wall came down. Through it, clear as a *quattrocento* fresco, we dared to see healing, justice, recovery. But I was lamenting because next came the backlash, both global and quite clearly personal: my consultant slashed my entitlement to care, his voice one evening confusingly, beguilingly kind: 'I don't want you speaking about all this to the nurses. You realise if I had my way, all you *memory* people should be put in one of those bubble things on an island and left to get on with it'.

He smiled, smiled, smiled, damn him, and I smiled with him. 'I don't hold with this abuse business,' he said. 'I've had patients who were sexually abused by their fathers and loved them for it. Alright, Owen?' His actual words, Theo, verbatim.

And his subsequent letter axing my treatment came as punishment for remembering something I'd not even remembered — you couldn't make it up. And he wasn't alone. Pretty soon, everyone in the world seemed up in arms about memory.

A gull swooped out of the birdless void. This is the story of my heart. Not the hero. Not Odysseus after all, but merely Philoctetes — who was dumped on the island of Límnos on the way to Troy because of his stinking wound. So I've done my consultant's work for him: sent myself to an island for the same cause…

Spíros's footfall was soft on baked earth. The faintest skitter of a pebble brought me back. A second gull swung down in an arc, down towards the sparse green vegetation far below, then raced off towards the sea. My eyes had dried. The sun had edged westward. The crests across the valley of 'Chóra' were darkening against it, a fragile blue grey seen only on these islands. Spíros was beside me on the ledge. I could feel his gaze. Down in the village, an engine started. The diesel clatter rose unnaturally clear and distinct in the still air. Shouts too, and a dog barking; siesta was ending.

'*Thikí sas?*' Out of the corner of my eye I was aware of a couple of my sheets being set down upon the rock beside us. 'Yours?'

I turned to face him. '*Málista. Thikí mou.* — Yes. Mine. But they're left-handed. Done with my left…' I tried to assert the case, waving the responsible hand significantly, and separating it from myself. '*Allá aristerochíri. Me ti aristerá mou. Then íne thikí* mou! — They aren't *mine.*'

'*Aristeróchiras.*' Peremptorily, he corrected my stress — and grammar — then shook his head. '*Íne ikónes tis kólasis* — They're icons of hell.'

The two pictures he'd chosen weren't those I'd been dreading. They

101

were, in fact, an untypical pair, whose existence I'd virtually forgotten. Maybe that was why he'd picked them. They made a kind of impromptu diptych, laid out there on the stones: the one a great Satan, or Minos, mounting in judgement over the gates of the underworld, and the other a type of Annunciation, the angel proffering a golden box to the Girl, his wings vibrating. His feather hues were as near iridescent as I could get them with those old clinic materials and in the startle and rapidity of the sketch. I remembered disconsolately how the brush's action and the free flow of images back then had often calmed me. It had stopped me panting like a dog with panic, even allowed some brief flowering at the end of an art therapy session — as in this scene. Or at other times the brush had created countless natural blooms, done wet in wet on bending stems, such joy and beauty apparently only just out of reach beyond the hopelessness.

Indeed, the Girl I'd painted, in her gold dress and blush of illumination, smiles untroubled by the angel. This is not at all an icon of hell. But in the other scene the horned demon towers unstoppably over his country of torment. He holds in one hand his soldering iron with its snaky flex, and in the other a limp figure dangling by the neck like a broken bird. Great heat sparks through his darkened silhouette; the fires of his hellish engines shoot flames high into the night.

I bit my lip and looked at Spíros.

He was speaking. I couldn't understand a word of it. Two women appeared in the gap of the ramparts directly below us, diminutive and still far off, their hiss-clicking, disapproving chatter coming up audibly and mingling with his. Now he was gathering the two pictures and turning away. I followed resignedly, back over the weedy ruins and cobbles to where we'd left the rest of them — from which he quickly made a bundle and handed it over to me before marching abruptly off towards his workshop again. It was obviously a dismissal — I'd spoiled his day with my antics and most of all with my burden of painted evil. 'Thanks,' I called after him. '*Evcharistó. Addío sas* — Goodbye.'

To my surprise, he stopped at the turn to the stone stairs. He was beckoning me again. Nonplussed, I shoved the pictures back in my rucksack and followed him once more up the stairway and in at the open door. The dark space was now flickering with the tapers he'd lit. The brazier glowed. The shaft of light had gone round by the silent traverse of the sun.

Still he beckoned me with that characteristic gesture and I went over to him at the easel where he was fixing his icon back into place. Now he put a brush with a fine tip into my hand — my right. Speaking quietly, he handed me a small plastic pot in which there was already mixed an ochre of sorts. I blinked and stood there, holding the two items, tools of our trade.

'*Prochoríste*! — Go ahead!'

I stared at him, but he was nodding and smiling, clearly indicating the picture he must have worked on so minutely and intimately for many hours.

I hesitated. Then fumbled about with the paint pot — it was one of those small plastic containers that used to house a cartridge of thirty-five mil film — until I got my glasses on. Then I dipped the brush in and looked at him again. He was serious. Mary and Jesus swam in the gloom before me, Julia and a child.

'*Parakaló*,' he said. 'Please.'

I touched the tip of the brush to the blank chalk gesso of the little Christ's unmade face and felt the faintest pressure of the panel coming back in response. It has always electrified me, that first touch.

A brightness flickered at my shoulder. Spíros had fetched one of the beach flares from its bracket and was holding it closer now over the image. Tentatively, hunching a little and resting my forearm on the easel's ledge, which seemed well adapted to the process, I applied the stroke near a red outline he'd sketched. The colour was a similar ground tone to that of the Virgin's face. The pleasure was immediate, the action soothing as ever.

I stood back, heard him murmur encouragement, and returned. Then I let myself paint, gaining confidence and leaving the brush to move as it would over the suggestion of the face. So I carried on for a good five minutes, until I heaved a great sigh and turned to him, smiling, only too sensible of the privilege.

He nodded again. '*Ne*! — Yes!' Then he handed me the flare and took the brush and the little paint pot to work himself on the same features, his touch quicker than mine, the marks a hint more feathered, changing very slightly the direction and — how shall I put this — the *implication* of the surface. I was delighted.

He went to his bench. I held the flare while he opened another of the little photo pots. He poured out some of the contents on to a piece of plate glass. It was a paler shade, and he mixed a tone with the one we'd been using. Now he began raising the Christ's cheek and highlighting the bone of the forehead, the structure of the little nose, bringing up an adult seriousness—which to us in the Italianate tradition always looks out of kilter with our notion of babes, *putti* or cherubs.

From habit, I found myself wondering about 'direction of light', until I re-immersed myself in the picture's own world. Radiance in icons, of course, must emanate *from* the figures of the composition as well as from all around them, and not from any *particular* source. Certainly light must come from the two faces, the one illuminating the other, and I was intrigued to see how he'd handle that, until he lost me in his seemingly effortless working of it. I contented myself with enjoying the delicate strokes and subtle motions by which the divine identity began to take form.

And I was reminded of the clinic once again: that comfort of the materials. Art, I said, is the child at play, and as the day wore on so we played, my pre-verbal teacher and I, in the grinding and mixing of pigments, the stirring of minute quantities of egg yolk and retsina, and the steady furtherance of the image. I saw the raw gold leaf he used and watched the application of the smallest sliver of it to the hem of the child's robe. And while he was absorbed in lining the eye I took my chance to open the chest he kept in the corner and pick up, one after the other, a series of finished icons he kept there ready for despatch. Saints, a Dormition, three holy faces, an Agony in the Garden, Jacob's Ladder, the archangel Gabriel...

And I reflected that even if my whole condition were summed up in that torturer my left hand had painted—the monster looming over his kingdom—nevertheless this interior, here with Spíros, was a darkness redeemed and transformed by the rendering of 'stuff on stuff'—as George Brede had named the process, bless him.

And so, at close of day, I came back here to Léros.

That, Theo, concludes the account of my trip to Kálymnos. What I'm to make of it, I don't yet know. I find myself altered. I see now that suspension out of the body can perhaps equally be expressed as self-imprisonment in the head—as a strategic withdrawal from the violated limbs and trunk into a permanent dreamy intellectuality, even a flippant one. Doesn't our whole cultural tradition since the ancient Greeks support just such a move? And I can also grasp how the sufferer might police—subliminally, but with the utmost rigour—any return to the body, subconsciously peopling the isthmus, the human neck—the choke between mind and body—with mythological curses and villains. That would keep the equally imprisoned memory safely undiscovered below the neck—lest it should burst up and destroy the family, and with it the only survival the child knows.

Spíros saw what my body had given birth to. But then he embraced me as a brother artist. '*Katalavéno*,' he said to me in so many kind gestures, 'I understand.'

Day here is long broken, and soon you'll be waking. And now my hope stands like the morning star on your horizon.

Shall I send this? I'm suddenly frightened again. I've broken an original injunction by telling anything at all; but in telling so much, so very, very much, I fear some very great punishment. And I fear I shall have offended against you, roping you hypnotically into my cursed universe and saddling you unasked with its burden. Is this, too, an abuse, a trespass upon your very good nature? Yet I've sent the greater part already.

Very well, then, so be it. *Katalavénís*? Do *you* understand?

Part II

Family

Subject: **Street scene at night**

Theo, I'm so, so sorry. I jumped to conclusions and blamed you. It's unforgivable. Really, I can't apologise enough. Exactly as you say, a tangle of crossed wires. Do please tell Jas not to worry; there's categorically no need for you or for her to apologise. She simply forgot to pass on that first message — anyone can make a mistake, and the regrets are all mine to express, not yours.

You know, I was so sure you'd look askance at me. So many people recoil. It's somehow easier to focus on monsters 'out there' prowling the streets than to countenance problems inside the home, any home. I just assumed *you*'d recoil, too, and I really shouldn't have. It's insulting to you. And it demonstrates a huge lack of trust on my part. Well, it's actually a lack of friendship, isn't it — that I might for a moment imagine you'd never give me the time of day once you knew. I just couldn't accept you were simply too busy. And so I nursed my anger over several weeks — like a viper to my bosom. As you say, you had consecutive shows to arrange and literally no time for anything else. That's perfectly understandable; I've been there myself often enough.

So I must eat very humble pie indeed. Your reply's full of warmth and understanding, which has quite floored me — to find the relationship still rock solid. As long as you'll accept my apologies, that is! Only now am I getting used to the feeling of relief and happiness.

And not only happiness for that, Theo. My gamble paid off, didn't it! The one I hardly knew I was taking: that my visit to the icon painter should turn out in the end to be a quest for a master, rather than an expression of some previously unannounced sexual desire! Honestly, I'm too old for that sort of discovery. Our meeting *was* about painting, and painting *in excelsis*! The result, now, is a frenzy of work, the flow, the surface, the colour. It's a joy! That sheer technique of his: the ability to put down colour with such incredible depth. Inspirational!

Oil sketches of Paris are consequently flooding out of me. I've put those difficulties of the big Bledlow picture to one side. Let's not worry about all that, now, or mysterious photos turning up. I've gone straight on to map out the next part of the series: the freak summer of

'76. And I'm trying to exploit the iridescent flatness characteristic of the icon at its best. Much smaller canvases.

It's working. I'm right back there in Paris. I can virtually feel the unnatural heat kicking into the brushwork, that year boasting temperatures in northern Europe that were almost Greek. No, they *were* Greek!

My Paris streets are sweaty, tobacco-and-onion spiced. And the light... Ah, the light is glorious! Dave, the Yank on the boat train, and I--we tramp the city in search of food and answers, having slept rough beside the Seine that first foolish night. Christ, we did it for the *adventure* and got rolled by a thief! Head on rucksack, I lost passport, wallet, loose change. I awoke with only that old ten pound note my Bledlow thugs had given me—because that was in my jeans back pocket and trapped under my weight, and even the most silent and accomplished robber couldn't have got it.

Our second night: some student hostel, with iron beds, no sheets, only the blankets of a thousand former dossers. The dormitory hot enough to kill hunger, lull even fleas. Though not the ache of Julia's betrayal.

Rapid oil scenes: what shall I call them, photorealist, labyrinthine, essays in retrospect? Porticos open on to alleys. Alleys link impossibly to courtyards. Here by pissed-on corners, the sun strikes cafés and their awnings. The morning gutters run awash. Dave and I, *apaches* in turn, rinse hands, steal bread, use up the hours.

By floodlit dark once more, we cross a broad road, swerve either side a woman strolling languid. She's petite, high-heeled. She catches us up at the traffic island: '*Vous êtes très beaux jeunes hommes,*' and I turn to her. Through all that shifting metropolis, she looks straight at me in her close fitting dress, her casual elegance, upturned face splashed with moon and streetlight, coiled hair pulled back. I capture her now in paint.

Here's day again, the footsore city parched, ablaze. Here's river and glare, a *bourgeoise* with her dog, smokers in a bar, bikes in the Bois. Here are steps down to the Metro, shop fronts, road signs, the stop-start thrash of traffic. With brush, knife, oil-soaked rag from my wooden box of tricks, I work up the town where art—and Greece—always begins again!

And late, in some stumbled-on *arondissement*, through one more arch to yet another cobbled square, I witness a silent riot. Fifty or so Algerian men; they seem to storm a building, voicelessly, unbelievably — a building not a stone's throw beyond me. It's a fine, sculpted Louis-Napoléon *façade* that makes its own frame, or *parergon*, to the garish windows at street level. Here's night in plenty as a slim arm and even slimmer wrist reaches round to open the shutters. I peer over frenzied heads, catch sight of an unclad white girl posed behind bars. She's just out of reach. There are other near nudes — like Demoiselles — attending. The men merge into one mind, almost one homesick creature, that now whimpers and stretches its foremost hands between the grilles, until the cage door rattles.

Cops come with netted vans. They melt in through masonry: surreal *flics* in full gear — who don't take action, but stand about leisurely, smoking. The night smells of drains and restaurants.

I stack one sketch, begin another.

A big tourist church. La Madeleine? Can't remember. Sightseers divide on the hot steps, or sit, eating snacks, and two men are in debate: Dave and me. He's asking about my passport.

'And?'

'They sent me away.'

'Your British Consulate wouldn't help?'

'Third visit.'

'No kidding!'

'The queues are bloody interminable, and they lost my first application. I filled in another.'

'Yeah?'

'Come back next week.'

'Next week!'

Even before your email, Theo, I'd made one big new stretch of canvas. I'd marked outlines for both brothel and church, its great doors flung as wide as those whorehouse shutters. Because both have thwarted aspirants, and I keep in mind — as ever — Titian's *Sacred and Profane Love*.

In my hurried trance, I paint even the stink of incense. Look here, too, the Virgin and her pierced son. Now I daub at speed Julia's face. Her pose: Manet's *Olympia*. I think of the icon painter. I paint tarts in their electric light, haloed, gaudy clothes dabbed in.

But there's another figure who fleets in the mind's eye. I smile. For see where he comes now, wandering the Left Bank, a guy beyond 'next week', stinking more than a little, bruises still smarting, shoulders almost bleeding from the accursed rucksack.

It's me, poor fool, no food, no cash, no passport. Even my earnest

111

Dave has gone, Dave, my clinging, smoke-wreathed buddy, thoughtless and cheerful as the air.

Rue Cherche-Midi — the strange-sounding name, along with a tease of smells: fresh bread, cooking garlic, like savours behind bars, like sensory butterflies that swarm back across the glade of time.

A troupe of street performers: they push their cart towards me. Intriguingly and by the by, they're a crew the image of my own recently-ruined painting back in England, that one called *Internment*, and its little crew of Shakespeareans.

But it's no hallucination. Two of them have bikes, the kind delivery boys used to ride, their front cradles loaded high with coloured boards and baubles. They stop and set up flares, and at once their made-up faces are weirdly illumined in the flicker.

A crowd gathers. Cars detour to pass, beeping horns battle a miniature barrel organ, while a *grand mousquetaire* swigs down paraffin and holds a brand to his mouth. His jet of fire shoots up into the evening, the flame outrageous against the fading azure overhead. And again it spouts high! A Harlequin juggles clubs. A Columbine strikes attitudes. She changes, twists in the flare-light, soliciting applause.

This happened, Theo; I can see it as though it were yesterday. And then I watched their performance unfold, a *comédie* of love seemingly un-tampered-with since I don't know when.

Until other police came, summer's night fell, and the crowd dispersed in the buzz of engines, the passage of headlamps, late lights in buildings, shop windows. And the players packed up as their torches guttered.

What could I do but lend a hand beside them in the dark. I gathered the mats they'd put down, tied a strap or two, laid one of the Indian clubs tenderly in the panniers of a bike. I held the flag and the *mousquetaire*'s hat under the streetlight while he unlaced the girl's voluminous dress. I helped stow the folding screen they'd used, now for the girl's bedroom, now for the father's study, once for a wall to peer around, once as a window to climb through, lastly as a stretcher for the wounded lover — that was before his miraculous revival by the apothecary's potion! In hope, I rested a hand on the barrel organ between its two large, antique wheels.

The girl, she smiled to thank me, but rolled it free. The *mousquetaire* lifted the handles of the handcart. The cyclists pushed off, unsteadily.

I watched alongside the cops as the bizarre little company passed between cars and melted inexorably into the distance, darkening shapes dwindling towards the river... Fifty yards off, a hundred now, almost lost to sight. I stood, like a blockhead, rooted to the ground.

At once I was running after them, oblivious to the great penance of my rucksack. '*Je voudrais*...!' I was calling. '*Je voudrais*...!' A car swerved and honked.

Painted faces turned as I came up with them. They halted. Breathless, I bowed. I was delirious. I shrugged off the rucksack there and then in the road—in the headlights of another car that screeched to a stop.

I ignored it, gesturing only, speechless, a baby to the 'abstracts'—the players—in front of me. My bruises! Look here! See? I was attacked! My empty pockets—look! My hunger: the mouth, the belly. My hands extended in prayer. Look! Look!

One of the cyclists swung his bike towards me. All the others stood motionless, while the balked car pulled abruptly round.

Surely toxins of exposure had gone to my head, and I was all body, and only body, tongue-tied in the street glow, renewing my claims, miming for dear life (and in these actors' own currency, I must have thought), miming my thwarted calling as a painter, my portraiture of Julia, her traitorous inspiration stretched as though naked in the gutter—a Venus, my head voluptuously on the kerbside—the assault on my work, the beating, my own thugs, the channel crossing, sleeping rough, Julia again and my broken heart.

Passers-by stopped on the pavement.

Theo, I was incompetent. I was everything the little band in front of me was not—for I'd seen their moving tableau with a kind of awe. Yet I know that somehow I even mimed my inadequacy. In my dumb show, I conveyed regret for my shortcomings, and disgust at my sorry state, my hair, my condition—sniffing my armpits and recoiling in dismay.

People on the path laughed. The players smiled and looked at one another. I say, I'd dredged up a certain facility I didn't know I had. Indeed, I don't know what else I could have done, for the plain truth was I'd eaten nothing and drunk less all day in that heat. I had no prospects for the night, no plan, no other resource. I was, as I told you, empty even of desire, adrift on chance.

Finally, I knelt. My little audience applauded; someone threw a coin into the road as though I were actually some coda to the night's enchantment. Still I could hardly resist beginning all over again: in my

113

studio as a painter etc... so possessed had I become by the strange charm of the movements, so desperate to make them understand what had happened to me – and so entirely uncertain whether anyone had.

The *mousquetaire* and the girl came forward. I felt them catch my arms, for I believe, at that point, I must have fainted.

And the next thing I knew I was on the cart looking up, and I could see the deep indigo of the night sky against the passing black outlines of the twin street façades, and could look directly, every now and then, into the streetlamp bulbs. I felt in my back the grumble of the wheels and the jolts of the road; and I heard all around me – it seemed for an eternity – the soft acceleration of cars. Then I slept again.

Briefly.

For I awoke in a courtyard and was brought to my feet. I was taken indoors, via the back entrance to one of those characteristic Parisian vestibules with the lift's iron cagework rising from the centre. The *mousquetaire*, the girl and I went up in the creaking old *ascenseur*. I remember it, Theo; or do I perhaps embroider. For ordinary memory is fallible and as different from traumatic memory as chalk from cheese.

But yes, I *could* smell myself; I still can, almost. '*Je suis désolé...*' I began.

The girl spoke too fast for me, smiled and shook her head. Soon enough we were in an attic flat, unmistakably authentic still, with its strange old furniture, modernist lampshades and unexpected dimensions – exactly as though a play, dream, film, somehow continued of its own accord, with the boundary between life and illusion quite arbitrarily dissolved –

...

Which is quite sufficient on all that for the moment, my friend, for I must finish in just a moment. Eléni needs to be met from the ferry. And I must hurriedly deal with your two questions – that I'm amazed you even picked up on, to be perfectly frank. Let alone that you showed such an interest.

Because you must understand – once again forgive me – I felt in my last two emails as though I were writing almost to myself alone rather than you. I mean as though you were virtually a lost cause, upon whom I was determined to dump my experience with the icon painter before *you* literally dumped *me*!

Firstly, then, I only included that mention of Plato's *chóra* in a spirit of irony; a fleeting anger, if you will. I was confident you wouldn't

114

know the reference, for all your schoolroom Greek. You're a man whose success has come from trusting that brilliant artistic intuition rather than poring over impenetrable Postmodernist textbooks.

I was equally sure you wouldn't *want* to know it. And now I'm hoist with my own bitter little game, of course, for it turns out you genuinely want answers. But naturally I'm delighted into the bargain and will have a brief—I promise you very brief—stab at it here and now, because Eléni... Yeah, if I type flat out, I've probably just got time.

'Chorió', marked on our rudimentary maps. It appears to be the name—together, occasionally, with 'Chóra'—for any central island village. Yes, Chorió just means 'village'. But at the same time, I was familiar with the term *chóra* from critical theory—which I know you absolutely detest. I don't blame you. Not many people can stomach it, even in the business, eh? And a lot of it's so... so up itself!

Oh, Christ, the clock ticking away, Theo...!

Nevertheless there's meat, too, because χώρα (=*chóra*) springs from ancient times and is specially used by Plato; which is how it comes into Post-structuralism etc, etc.

In Plato's *Timaeus*, χώρα is 'a feminine' that suddenly can't be avoided, a receptacle or empty land. Are you with me? It's 'space', smooth wax before the mark, or even—so I happened to read the other day—a mysterious third term briefly invoked for the sake of the argument!

Interesting? Well and good.

So your bugbear Jacques Derrida seizes characteristically on Plato's *quasi* footnote, of course, as one of those wilfully unnoticed dangling ends which are present in even the smartest philosophies or sciences, and which, if deftly pulled, will deliciously unravel the whole project.

Then, in the hands of Kristeva and some other feminist theoreticians, *chóra* becomes a kind of semiotic womb, somehow protected and pre-linguistic—out of which verbal signification subsequently emerges...

Well, you asked, and I'm going for it! But the echoes of this obscurely convoluted stuff only struck me once Spíros and I left his house in the new village and started climbing up to the *old chóra*, where I saw the habitation actually walled in and somewhat womblike for protection.

Bells started ringing at the back of my mind, I tell you, and even as I toddled bemused and rather scared after the icon painter I was intellectually intrigued. How, yes, I was regressed to body language by our mutual incomprehension—and what was that if not pre-linguistic? The walls that weren't walls, the timelessness, the vacancy, you see! And now in front of me was the entrance to his workshop, which was a womb-space if ever there was one! So I hope that makes a little sense and answers your question. But it's a mere coincidence, surely, an amusing footnote and hardly important.

Ten minutes, and then I really must...

Your second point, my clinic. Now that *is* much more of an issue. Just get these few more words down...

I've alluded to the clinic previously often enough, though only glancingly. Which was because I was similarly convinced you'd want no more than the barest bones of my experience there. Again, I can only say I'm intrigued to find myself wrong.

How, then, can I give you some idea of it?

Do you know, the thing that most sticks in my mind is that when I was admitted to the Meredith Clinic—it was just a short drive from where I lived in England with Lily—the old Soviet Union still existed. Yet when I first ventured out into the daylight after a couple of weeks, stunned, still very tearful (and in conflict about Dad, of course), it had disappeared. I mean the Soviet Union. Gone. That's the plain fact of the matter. A great empire far away had simply disappeared.

Curious, isn't it—as if not only I, but everything else about the world, had changed. The familiar universe I'd grown up in had seemingly melted, and its tectonic plates shifted. And what was the knowledge that had spilled out, hot and stinking, from the abruptly revealed substratum? Well, not just the ghost-like intelligence concerning my father, but also a startling truth about the family in general, that incest was, sadly, all around us; that it was, yes, quite common, even: incest—that most sulphurous of crimes.

Theo, forgive me for elaborating. That ferry, Eléni's. It's due very soon. Touch typing, fingers flying, the pianistic joy, the abandon of it! So important...

Because I believe it's now clear that incestuous abuse is an original robbery far nastier than any theft proposed by Milton or Marx, more seismic in its unearthing than uranium. Why, as I've already said, incest's 'discovery' immediately stranded all the Freudians high and dry and threatened to upset a whole century of psychiatric thinking. You're asking for clarification about my 'attack' on Freud. Surely, you're aware of Freud's fall from grace. I thought it was common knowledge. How it was discovered that he had in fact originally proposed sexual trauma as the cause of 'hysteria' in his female patients, only to retract the idea completely when he came under pressure—from himself and from influential others. And how in place of his original theory he shockingly substituted 'Psychoanalysis', which is a wholly invented farrago. Come back to me if you want references, but I assure you Psychoanalysis simply incriminates the victim and exonerates the perpetrator. It blames the victim's alleged sexual wishes, which is disgusting. I have to say it, Theo: Psychoanalysis was to the twentieth century what phrenology, that old nonsense of head bumps, was to the nineteenth.

Well, the fact of the old giant's gruesome fraud was only just leaking out around the time I was first in the Meredith Clinic. It was the pre-Christmas period of '91, and when I learned of it, I heard angels. And my hand painted them.

Because Freud had always been such a vulture of authority to my generation, squatting on the body of Modern Art, his tale always in its mouth. Ach, Freud! Out with him! No, art is instead the child at play—the child so skilled at a perpetual non-occupation of events, shifting out to escape the unspeakable... to escape *real* events. I mean genuine sexual attacks, Theo, not nonsensical made-up Freudian *wishes*. I mean the child so philosophical that the floating mind need never know what the body suffered, must never know...

Listen. I went into the Meredith Clinic in Freud's universe. It was Newton's and Darwin's, too. It was the Cold War era in which I'd grown up, and it was dark even by its own lights, geographically schizoid and locked on a nuclear hair-trigger. And the one thing that universe definitely did *not* contain was incest: so rare and mythical a crime, the textbooks had always said, so deep under oceans or far beyond the stars. Do you remember back then? Exactly! Each one of us was supposed to be subject to Freud's repressed incestuous *desires*; but even to breathe of genuine incest could be diagnostic for madness.

Can you believe that? Why, in my life before the clinic I'd checked real incest's 'non-existence' time and again, because I'd always read and speculated in psychiatry, sociology, anthropology. I guess I'd always been looking for what was wrong with me.

But it's a fact that before the late eighties incest's famous taboo had almost no *referent*—except (let me add for the sake of completeness) via Kinsey's astonishing 'there are no ill effects', or, as I said, Freud's own frankly wicked formulation of the 'Oedipal wishes of infants'.

117

Midwinter 1991 I first saw the Meredith Clinic's oak beams and leaded windows, the ornate brick chimneys, the rippling, uneven roof. Oh, I had no hope, that morning. Work, marriage, memory—every avenue blocked. I simply couldn't go on.

I blamed myself. Dad had been right all along. And I didn't deserve sanctuary. God, I felt such an impostor, turning up—on Lily's company insurance, of all things—to take advantage of this cosy slice of Olde England. The Meredith simply wasn't *for* the likes of me. It was for people with real problems. Or real money. Its bays, its quoins and elaborately carved gables appeared, through the freezing fog, more manorial than medical. Parking was in a neatly screened 'arbour'! Finely raked gravel crackled underfoot, and bare roses wreathed beside an antique entrance whose romantic, iron-studded door stood already open. *Chóra* again?

Yes, the Meredith seemed too good to be true.

Yet the place existed, and exists today, small-scale, quaint, informal, between the motorway and the flight path. It still has its meadow. Sheep still graze the paddock beyond the lawns. There are nanny-goats in the orchard, and blowing poplars screen the river road. And the nurses—most of them—are still kind, I'm sure. In that unlooked-for spiritual oasis, I sheltered from cold and then, as a long-term outpatient, grew acquainted with summers. Seven of them, by the end of it; rose-scented, I feel, not rose-tinted. That's about all there is to it, Theo. That's my clinic.

Christ, the time. Must send! I'll be late. *Very* late!

Subject: **RE Street scene at night**

You misunderstand. I was writing too fast, typing at one hell of a lick. I meant what Dad had always implied—about my character. That I had no backbone, couldn't stick at things.

Rich, wasn't it, coming from him, who could never last in one place more than a year or two!

I did miss her boat. She was waiting on the quayside with her bags, not best pleased.

And now I've just been dispatched to get in some provisions—another oversight. Must see what I can do to make it up to her!

Sent from my iPad

118

Subject: **RE Street scene at night**

No, I've never confronted him. Absolutely not. Confrontation went right out of fashion. The offender's never going to admit what would almost certainly send him to prison. And these days we're hardly ever going to get guilty King Claudius alone on stage confessing his sins!

So I remain in limbo. I don't contact him at all. I daren't. Besides, he's long since remarried and lives abroad.

Sent from my iPad — at the supermarket, in front of the olive oil and tinned tuna!

Subject: **RE Street scene at night**

Theo, I'm not trying to make out all depression is post-traumatic. That was what caused such a rumpus in the first place. Millions of folk get depressed, and I don't want to send whole families running for cover — good, decent ones at that. But my case history is what it is, and I can't pretend I haven't had my share of it. Depression. Must get back. I'll make Eléni a nice meal.

Sent from my iPad — now leaving the supermarket!

Subject: **Theatrical emotion**

Here are Félix and Cécile, my hosts that first theatrical night, in their flat. The *mousquetaire* shrugs off his heavy frock coat; the girl, wearing bra and pants only, smooths cold cream on her face. She shakes loose her beautiful red hair.

'*Je m'appelle* Owen.' I say. '*Je suis… Il y a trois ou quatre jours, j'étais peintre. Maintenant, je suis…*' I spread my hands.

Cécile laughs. Félix scowls.

They live together — Cécile points to the double bed in the corner.

And I remember watching, glazed, almost weeping with exhaustion, as Félix, at a small dressing mirror, tore the false beard and moustache from his face. Then they divided with me what food they had: stale bread and, from their ancient, buzzing fridge, fragments of cheese. How strong it tasted. And I remember being directed, equipped with towel, to the crazy, clanking bathroom they shared with their neighbours. I recall how when I returned half naked, holding my filthy clothes out at arm's length, they sat me in their one armchair and made me hot, sweet coffee. And we talked—to the limit of my French—about who I was and what had happened.

But when Cécile saw my eyelids continually droop and close, she made up an impromptu bed on the floor—from the cushions on which they'd both been sprawling. She bent her lovely face and half-clad bosom over me to drape my body in a thin bedspread.

Have I caught the moment? Ah, I want the narrative mystery about it, almost a mythological study, like that gorgeous Di Cosimo they used to call *The Death of Procris*. But the sketch is also meant to reference, in both style and subject, the endless enigma of Manet. And I have in mind Caravaggio, of course, and Claude Lorraine; and then the endlessly influential pearl backlighting in early Spielberg movies. Yet I do recall the icon painter's shadowless illumination.

No matter. I returned soothed to the dreamless sleep into which I'd fallen on the cart, my vast relief only belied by the tight clutch I tried to keep upon the straps of my rucksack.

I fell at once into a new life, too. Now, Theo, this encounter with moving art, with *Théâtre Inconnu*—for so they called themselves… It stretches coincidence, doesn't it? It out-Nicklebys *Nickleby*. Do you believe me? Do you think I'm making it up? For how strangely fortuitous that someone called Éméric, a member of their troupe, was off in hospital, knifed by a lover. So that the company *just at that moment* found itself in desperate need of a replacement—albeit temporary. And when I begged to be given the chance, how astonishing that Félix, prompted by Cécile, should grudgingly agree to take on *me*.

'Needs must when the devil drives, I guess,' he said, his dark brow furrowed, his full lips pursed. 'Beggars can't be choosers.' (I make a free translation.)

No, the doughty Félix never let me kid myself I'd shown any natural promise or instinctual poise. Quite the contrary: he made it clear that my inhibited, disintegrated effort to communicate—my sheer Englishness, if you like—had grated on him that first night to the point of disgust. Had it not been for my persistence, and for the comic pathos of it all, maybe, and chiefly for Cécile, I believe he'd simply have told them to turn their backs and move on.

She'd pleaded for me. She told me so herself. 'Once we'd picked you up, Owen, and you were jolting along on our cart, spark out to the world, of course we wondered what on earth to do with you. Should we take you to hospital? Should we dump you off with the cops? Félix wanted to compose your foolish limbs in a doorway and leave you for someone to find in the morning. He is difficult sometimes — his lips burn from the petrol and the flames, you understand. His throat hurts him. These are our pains, Owen. And you did seem an encumbrance...'

I looked into her eyes. 'Thank you, anyway, Cécile,' I said.

She smiled, and of course I fell in a sort of love with her as any child falls for sweetness, and we both knew that it was the case, and neither of us minded; although I realise now our instant, innocent and instinctual bond may have been what so tormented Félix about me from the start. For he never had a good word for me. Yet shelter me they did, Theo, and these things happened just as I've described. Just as the muse, the angel... Why, without the miraculous we wouldn't get on at all. The linguistic fabric of the universe — I mean the hyper-rational story we constantly weave for ourselves — really *is* apt to rip apart.

Subject: **Rehearsal**

See the further colour sketches attached. We're at an empty coffee warehouse, near the Quai de la Tournelle, to which the company has negotiated some *entrée*, and I've already been out with them three nights, in the capacity of stagehand only. Now rehearsal has begun.

It's a punishing routine. Ragged and poor my players may be; amateur, they are not. Cécile and Dmitri (one of the bicyclists) have trained together at the Lecoq school — skill and perfect fluidity are second nature to them. The other boy, Zigui, is a dancer, who oozes strength and technique like one of those over-elastic balls that bounce far higher than one expects. The knifed Éméric, bandaged under his shirt, sits intently at the sidelines.

I like this little portrait of him. He's a performer of repute in his own right on the legitimate stage, and I've learnt how he and Félix grew up together in the Midi, misspending all their days in countless daredevil tricks and illusions. Now, in spite of his wound, from which he winces occasionally, Éméric is a lively, ironic onlooker.

But it's Félix, our huge, saturnine leader, who stands stripped

121

before us in singlet and tights, to put us through our paces. Lit only by the high windows of dusty blue that bespeak the glaring day outside, he appears all the shaggier.

I think I've caught him here: muscles rippling, the hair on his arms and chest like some dark, clinging aura. Theo, Félix is unstoppably theatrical, always larger than life, and my picture hardly does him justice. His sheer presence turns the dull wall of empty chests and stacked pallets, from which the ineradicable savour of coffee beans wafts almost palpably, into a backdrop for some menacing dramaturgy.

And we sweating shades face him. Cécile lines up with Dmitri at the front. Today, her pastel green leotard is tucked deliciously about with bits of coloured gauze and wool, which draw attention to the lines of her body. Behind them is Zigui, solo, because two others are late today, and we're all to leave room for them. I, in my shabby jeans and borrowed T-shirt, lurk at the back. I try to keep up with the tortuous exercises, strange routines and subtle moves that form the basis of our craft.

They're an aching encounter. Only five minutes in, I'm grateful for the interruption of the missing pair: the two girls, Minalouche and Marie-José, who scurry in to install themselves. They pick up the class without difficulty under the cloud of Félix's anger, while I can only welter in perspiration and inadequacy until the technique session ends.

An hour and a half's improvisation follows—to which I'm a mere spectator. My new comrades amaze me with their drollery and speed. They love their work, and are dedicated to it. So they have to be, for we subsist on a pittance. But I can't imagine how I'll ever join in, as situation follows situation so rapidly I can scarcely keep track.

Bodies move now here, now there, elasticated by a speech that isn't even standard French but seems drawn up without effort from some formulaic well adapted to every nuance of the action. A flood of story passes before me. Lovers weep, husbands curse, fathers bluster, tricksters thrive, duennas look the other way. Murderers and madmen, jilts and jades, flatterers and *flâneurs* all engage at breakneck speed the mind's eye. Theo, a fool with a spotlight could here generate the whole history of the novel!

Yet all moves on, and if ever I laugh or cry (almost), Félix glares at me fiercely enough to remind me of my status: so out of my depth, in fact, that I continually wonder how I shall possibly match up. Artistically, it's ravishing; technically, it's overwhelming.

Subject: A debut

Here's my fifth day with the company, the day I made up my mind to shed both beard and inhibitions and take the plunge into rehearsal. Candidly, it was either that or go back on the streets.

Shaving was the easier part. There, it was done. I stared into the cracked looking-glass of Cécile-and-Félix's bathroom, to view my suddenly foreshortened face. Surrounded only by the hair I'd let grow long, it looked feminine and naked, the pale jawline untouched by the sun. I hardly recognised myself.

So far so good. But what role could I play in the afternoon? For in that company I remained to all intents and purposes mute.

Yet there was no help for it. And when the time came, and the ribald comments about my appearance had been aired, the technique class had finished and the afternoon's astonishing flow of speaking tableaux had begun, I chose my moment at random, shut my eyes for courage, opened them again wide and simply injected myself into the action.

It was the middle of a parting scene. Cécile and Zigui were locked in some final embrace. For a full ten seconds, I just stood there staring. Then Félix shouted at me. '*Tournez! Tournez! Imbécile!*'

Imagining he was ordering me off, I made to quit the scene as hastily as I'd entered.

'*Non!*' Swearing under his breath, he strode down into the playing space and manhandled me back beside the lovers, at the same time grappling me round so as to open up the action to a putative audience.

In fact there *was* an audience: Éméric, Dmitri and the other two girls were lounging on a couple of boxes in the middle of the warehouse's emptiness. They all looked up at the commotion. The aspect of the viewer—the very notion of perspective, I suppose—was the point at question, and mine was the elementary mistake, one that as a visual artist I should never have made.

Besides, so many *commedia* skills involve precisely this business of constructing and compelling the onlooker by constant visual soliloquy. Novice though I was—*pauvre blanc-bec*—I'd already seen it time and again during these first few afternoon sessions: deliberate and hilarious rifts in even the most forceful action, the performers' abruptly turned faces, the extraordinarily held grimaces. Elaborate excursions from the flow of time, of story.

I apologised.

'Never fucking apologise!' he yelled. (Again, I translate

123

idiomatically.) 'Don't break the spell! Piss artist!'

Cécile and Zigui remained expertly in character, still surprised and in each other's arms. And so, then, I did turn.

I don't know; there must have been something exceptionally slow and stupid about it, because all four spectators suddenly creased up with laughter, and even Félix, whom I saw out of the corner of my eye, strove to hide a smile.

So, in that moment, my question was answered and my role created. Until the wounded Éméric should be restored to health, I was to become the idiot, the stooge or simpleton, a character in many ways vital to the *commedia*, Theo, but hitherto underplayed in this company's repertoire, since our men were all too athletic and too French to want to look that dim, and our girls were all too vain!

So I was told, at least, by Cécile as I massaged her bare shoulders later that night. 'This, Owen, is why we have need of you.' She turned her haunting green eyes up to look at me.

But I'm leaping ahead of myself. The time for the evening performance was fast approaching and the actors needed to explore the new dynamic. I mean, of my inclusion.

It was intensive. They stood me here or there, helped me, railed at me, gave me cues and directions, and coached me in what little I had to say.

I endeavoured to play up. Shedding a few inhibitions, I began almost to enjoy myself – for the scenes became, yes, trancelike; one could be strangely taken over, and lose all sense of time. So that when Félix eventually declared '*Alors, mes enfants, ça suffit!*' and we rested at last, all played out and with the sweat running off us in the heat, I was surprised at how late it was. I felt a sudden rush of adrenalin at the realisation that in a couple of hours I should be doing this in earnest. And for my bread.

Félix never specified the night's action until rehearsal was over. It was to keep everyone on their toes. Tonight's theme, he suddenly announced, was *The Illness of Pantalone*. He'd take the title role himself, and it was to be a traditional performance, in costume. So whatever I'd practised was already redundant – I'd simply have to live on my wits, like the rest of them.

I strained to listen while Félix checked over the skeleton plot, though I managed to grasp very little. Hurriedly, he went on to list a few sequences that had just worked in the session. Then he flipped open a pack of *Camel* cigarettes, moodily lit up and went off somewhere with Éméric. Dmitri also decamped.

I found myself wandering out a few streets away with Zigui and the three girls — and this will explain the smaller attached studies. Theo, I suppose recall has its own still life, for I can see now Cécile folding open a bag of cherries on a bench in the nearby square.

'Take one, Owen. Everyone.'

And how bright those cherries remain, amber and red, in that long departed brilliance; how warm, how very sweet in their criss-cross of thin green stalks — until the sequence runs on again, and I'm following the four back towards our warehouse, back in anticipation along some glowing street of early evening, each of us a touch keyed up and on edge, I note with my painter's eye, chatting of this and that and the sun just dipping behind high roofs. And a slight tidemark of shadow begins.

'*Attention!*' someone says. 'Take care!' Because I'm jumpy, too, impatient of the rush hour traffic, alert to the chatter of sparrows from a little hedge, even disconcerted by the garlic savour from one of this student quarter's early restaurants.

'Owen, it'll be fine. Don't worry,' says the kindly Marie-José.

But I'm only too aware that for the first time I must paint my face like the others, put on the costume I've been allotted and take up the risks and anxieties of my new trade.

For all that, Theo, a glamour clings to these preparations, don't you think? In the glass of time, I see that newly razored face of mine grow less and less familiar, the taut skin daubed preternaturally white, the eyes lined into diamonds and the corners of my mouth over-defined in red and black above my blanched chin and folded white stock. The pulse still quickens, as I realise I've become some never-before-seen creature, about to launch itself upon the world.

It *is* erotic. The girls beside me tend their hair, lift their skirts to adjust a stocking. Minalouche laces Marie-José's dress. 'Pin my strap for me so that it doesn't show, could you?' 'Lend me that rouge you bought. Oh, please.'

The boys return. They fix buttons and belt on their sword sticks. They're tense. 'If you twist round on me again when we're under a window, Zig, I swear you're fucking dead meat.' They pace about in their soft slippers, while I step gingerly in my stiff black shoes, carry myself oddly in the weirdly quartered, musty smelling outfit Félix has found for me in the big laundry basket that serves as one of our wardrobes.

125

And now we must load up our properties and head out into the dusk, Félix stalking in front of us, outrageously transformed by a long-nosed half-mask and fluttering black gown.

At once everything and everyone around me is new born: the hot tarmac, the dry gutters, the doors and apartments, the strolling couples who turn to stare, the passing academics, office workers, tradesmen, that stray dog beside a shutter, a parked car left running, a just-glimmering streetlight, a limp, crepuscular plane tree. Scared and enraptured, I can recall almost too much.

Of the performance, its tale and substance, on the other hand, I remember next to nothing. I spoke of rehearsal as trancelike. Live performance is the quintessence: time is either altered or absent entirely. It leaves merely broken, dreamlike impressions of this hour's passage or that. We occupy, by our intense focus, a universe subject not to human laws but to narrative's, whose dimensions can't be measured, nor its volumes filled. So also in the emotion of painting, my friend, none can tell what was done, nor when, nor how; only that something came forth out of an extreme absorption.

But what's this writing if not a performance? Well, trances within trances defeat me, and of *Pantalone's Illness*, all I can say is that I played my part. I became overwhelmed by it, in fact, that first time. I was pushed here, pummelled there, my new-found comrades now leaping out from behind me, now pulling my mute presence out of the way.

I find myself one moment side-lined in the torchlight, cloaked with intrigue and the night; the next thrust back into an imbroglio of greed, lust, politics and potions. Incomprehension is my role, in my ridiculous stuffed toque. Cécile particularly engages me. Félix and the others hatch their schemes. I stammer, question, halt. The onlookers roar.

Who are they? Where are we? The truth is, Theo, I had just then no sense even of which street or quarter we occupied. Paris became an abstract *of itself*, a vision almost untied from its moorings. Whenever gullibility made me peer skyward, then the stars clustered each time more luminous and densely packed between the tall façades; and, if folly whirled me round, the shop windows and neon signs shone ever brighter and more incongruously than at first. Ever less substantial, in the darkening city, flickered the faces in the torchlight.

So shadows brought us to an end, and illusion dissolved in illusion. The prose world reassembled. First Félix, his long false nose thrown back upon his forehead, stepped forward to receive his applause; then came Cécile and Zigui, with the others flanking them; and I was surprised and not a little gratified to receive my own accolade, along with the smiles and nods of my fellow players.

So the crowd drifted away, and the urban buzz of a summer night resumed — just as it had at our first encounter, when the cops put a stop to things, and I made my spur-of-the-moment decision to follow this retreating emblem of enigma.

So we packed up and got out, with our bicycles and cart, and set off, weaving our way through a maze of side-streets back to base. My head still spinning, I dined on bread and cheap wine with Cécile and Félix up in their flat, and later still — as I told you before — stood, at her laughing request ('Owen, if you wouldn't mind. My Félix is so rough...'), to soothe with my fingers the tired muscles under the skin of her nape — as she sat at her little dressing table removing her make-up. Félix silently removed his own. Then at last, I retired to my improvised bed in the corner of their floor, still sleepless, my mind doubly preoccupied with the sound of their muffled love-making and the far off shunting of trains in the Gare de Lyon. And so began my summer's change.

Now, Theo, you might say that, after so perplexing a fall, I seemed to have landed pretty well on my feet. From nothing, I had at once a kind of plenty: associates, a roof over my head, food to eat, a pretty young woman with whom to flirt, a job — almost a *métier*. And if you detect some genuine rhapsody about the way I've presented my new situation, and about the manner in which I responded to it at the time, you'd not be so very far adrift. Yes, this transient theatre did strike a chord. I worked very hard at my movement skills. I even felt I'd come home to them. Well and good. From whence, then, you could very reasonably ask, come certain left hand colour values of underworld or death-in-life?

Ah but can't death itself put on a seductive mask, first luring us in with relief from pain? The arts, frozen remembrances, places of safety! What was I doing, but cauterising a broken heart and re-establishing my eternal self-sufficiency. Julia? What need had I for her?

8

Subject: **A cuckoo**

You're right. My visit to the icon painter seems to have catalysed the quite joyous interrelation between image and story. Ha! And how relieved that makes me, and doubly excited that you're so on board with it. I wasn't sure how viable. But you're as keen as I am, you say, to hear *what happened next* in this old and long-buried little episode of mine! You even *demand*, Theo. Ha, again! For what is an icon but the quintessential snapshot of a narrative? The icon surely attempts somehow to *embody* story: it should choose just the moment that will echo both backwards and forwards in a persistently textual apprehension. Hence, the text-on-image found in so many of them, don't you think — icons, I mean — something to which I'd never really paid much attention before. And so 'the portrait of the artist as a young man' can be expressed as the sum of such a *sequence*?

Those mornings! There was a café we went to. Just feel with me that sunlight flooding down on us, the red awning a-flutter in the occasional breeze, the blinding reflection from the patch of metal table top next to Félix's folded newspaper. See his tough browned arm across the print, the hairs dark and wiry on his wrist. I have an enduring image of his great hand, its stubby fingers poised over the ashtray to tap the burn off yet another *Camel* cigarette. 'Here, have one, will you?' I remember the taste of them, harsh and unforgiving as the southern sun.

What had I learned of him in my first intensive days? Félix wasn't the most gifted of us. Physically, he was too large to shift into all the shapes that Dmitri, say, could occupy. And he was too much himself to be able to assume Cécile's lightning characterisations. Indisputably, though, he was in charge; his word settled any dispute.

You see my little portrait of Dmitri, too? I hope to have caught his aquiline profile, the early-receding black hair tied back fiercely in a red bandana like a pirate's, the long, elastic limbs and air of petulance. Dmitri could be exasperating and a little lazy. There were girls in his life who worshipped him and who came occasionally to rehearsals in the warehouse. He would play up to them, sometimes in tantrums that subsided as quickly as they arose. But he was talented. He could

Harlequin to perfection, or put on sometimes the braggart Captain.

Zigui was shorter, tousle-haired and gay, most often cast as Cécile's lover, on account of his fine features and stylish movement. He seemed to show a certain gratitude to me personally — a circumstance I couldn't account for, until it occurred to me that our informal alliance with Cécile, Minalouche and Marie-José, which had seemed to coalesce naturally on the afternoon of my first performance, might not always have included him. I guessed my presence altered some pre-existent balance of power; for Zigui and I and the girls continued thereafter to hang together, with our general good humour and the chatter of improving my French. And he seemed happy and relieved at that, while Dmitri and the wounded Éméric took to revolving around us like solitary planets at various levels of pique. Félix, of course, was already quite out of sorts with me, and with Cécile.

I could help none of this; I was the fool. And no one could deny that the newly-risen tensions gave a certain spark to our performances. Beyond that, I believe I brought an extra edge to the company myself, in spite of my technical inadequacies. I say this in all modesty, because Cécile noticed it, too. 'But you've worked so hard, Owen, and have made such progress. And from nothing, it must be said. And now, I don't know, everything is different.'

'Different? In what way different?' I'd just made a sketch of her, and we were sitting together on the lower embankment wall that overlooks the Seine, eating ice cream cones and dangling our legs like children. It was the hour before rehearsal. Ripples from the breeze on the water caught the late sun and burned up at us. Notre-Dame towered not far away to our left.

'Yes, what is it?' she said. 'Two weeks? Three? We've played *The Miser*, *The Baby*, and *Le Malade*; oh, and *La Veuve*. One loses track of them; we know so many themes and variations.' She laughed. 'Well, one loses track of time altogether, do you know? Where are we now: some day in the height of summer, that is all. But you! Already, you, who came to us dumb, Owen, are speaking out to the audience and, in your muddled language, taking them on — which they adore. Already, you bring in here a new element, there an unexpected turn. Do you understand? Your fool is emerging. Soon, maybe, you'll try someone in love. Ah, why not? It's possible. And now in consequence you force us to change.' She turned her delicate face towards me.

'I do my best,' I said. I looked directly into her eyes for a moment and then stared back down at the river. Traffic buzzed behind us on the Quai de la Tournelle.

'Yes, you do,' she said. 'You work like *crazy*! And we...' She put her hand on my arm. 'This Englishwoman. This Julia. She's the fool herself, I think.'

'And I try not to,' I said. 'To think, I mean.'

'Of course. It's painful. The wound is raw. But you'll find someone else, before too long, surely, in your new... incarnation.' She laughed again, suddenly, elfishly, 'Why, I myself, were it not for Félix...' Her hand had strayed up across my shoulders. I felt her fingers touch for a second the back of my neck, the sensuous shiver of fine hairs, the soft, passing imprint of a nail. Then they were gone.

I froze and looked at her sharply, but she'd already raised her legs beside her and was getting up. 'Well, are you coming?' she said. And then, 'You could at least pretend to be interested.'

Astonished, I stood up myself and faced her. She was very beautiful that day, her fine features unpainted, the creamy skin of her cheeks framed by the loosed mass of her red hair. Her slight figure in white top and tight blue jeans was lithe even in its stillness. Our eyes met again, and then she twisted slightly on one flat heel to gaze off upstream.

So direct a challenge; it mortified me. Oh, God! As much as I wanted to possess her, Theo, to devour her lips, sweet flesh of cherries, to stroke her neck, tear free her breasts from the intoxicating cotton gathers of that blouse and then lose myself heedlessly, there and then, in her too sensuous thighs... In spite of all these, Theo, which are the terrible hackneyed clichés of unbridled passion, and yet valid for all that, on account of their perfect accuracy in this occasion, I found myself nonplussed. Improvisation deserted me, though it was the recent staple of my life — and has become the staple of my painting ever after, as it happens. Even though I'd 'loved her at first sight', I just couldn't 'pretend to be interested'.

I tell you, it was as though I had on a lead with me a large sexual wolf who knew exactly what *he* wanted, but whom I held in such complete check that Cécile could see nothing of him at all. Christ, I do believe no sign, gesture, smile or even blush of mine betrayed the slightest flicker of sexual response to the attractive woman offering herself so candidly. And perhaps that was because the lust was not *of* my mind at all, but indeed outside the body, occupying the wolf-shaped space I could never accommodate! It's a surrealist moment, surely, amusing in retrospect, wretched in the occurrence.

What did I do? I turned away, back to the river. A train came past behind us – the Metro there runs in its own concrete gully just before the road.

'I see I've offended you,' she said, when the noise had subsided. She wasn't angry; her voice was simply drained of its animation.

'No! Not at all. I'm very…' I couldn't think of the French word for flattered. I don't think I knew it. 'I'm sorry,' I said. '*Je suis désolé.*'

'Don't be,' she answered, but still in that same flat tone. 'You must think of your Julia. These matters of the heart; of course, you need time. Of course, of course. It's only to be expected.' I heard the soft slap of her sandals on the path and realised she'd already started towards the steps back to street level. After a few paces, she turned and took pity. 'Come on, Owen, or we'll be late.'

I caught up. We climbed to the traffic level and continued towards the warehouse. We walked as closely as ever, but the emotional distance between us, as we chatted blankly of this and that, remained vast. We might as well have been on opposite sides of the road.

That night in performance I was wooden and unconvincing. Cécile hardly ever met my eyes and seemed deliberately to steer any developing action away from me. And after the show there was a new atmosphere in the flat. She was perfunctory in her dealings with me, ladling a portion of sauce on to my plate of spaghetti with a clack of the spoon's edge that bid fair to break the china. Sitting at her mirror, she made no attempt to ask for the, by now routine, shoulder massage.

She took instead every opportunity to become sweetly attentive to Félix, who almost purred in triumph. Once the light was out and a token time had elapsed for me to be presumed asleep in my makeshift bed-corner, their lovemaking – I believed some nights before this in abeyance – was resumed with just enough gusto to make the point that two were the rightful company here, and three was starting to be a crowd.

How could I blame them? I was feeling uncomfortable myself. For a while, it had been a little fairy tale: of a kind and beautiful lady who finds a starveling chick in the forest to bring home and nurture back to health. But I'd turned cuckoo, it seemed, and my fast-growing understanding of *commedia* plots in general and of Félix in particular told me that he, unlike the duped and complaisant songbirds of nature, wouldn't think twice about tipping me out of the nest, were matters between me and Cécile to develop a whit further.

Yet where should I live, if not here? What should I do without these beneficent 'parents', to whom I'd been so recently and so strangely 'born'? I should be dashed.

These thoughts kept me awake, along with the city's night sounds, the old building's inexplicable groans and clanks. What on earth had been Cécile's motives in approaching me? Should I flatter myself she'd actually proposed a liaison—right there under Félix's nose and after so few weeks of our knowing one another? *La belle Cécile*! And what now should I be in the company? What family role could I occupy?

Or should I pre-empt my ejection altogether and quit the group, re-grow my protective beard and try my fortunes yet again with the British Embassy—beg them to contact my parents, for example, or my employers at the Chiswick Poly—and in the meantime hawk myself from café to café in the hope of work as a waiter or suchlike? But I'd still need a roof over my head. And, more seriously, I wondered could such a return to my old life even be accomplished?

For already the daily routines of stretching and flexibility had unstrung some old defences, and my enforced severance from the past felt almost willed. Like it or not, a journey had begun, and I'd begun to embrace it. Cécile was part of it. She'd breached my cover, flushed me out. Sexuality, warmth, other people... I see now with hindsight how the unspeakable past—except for Julia—had always kept me lonely and special; for how does the growing boy contain such stuff? Except to enter, once again, the shifting mummery of his own internal playhouse. Which in that post-Vietnam, still ice-Cold-War universe, I say it again, of Freud, Darwin and Newton, was perhaps the only *authentic* protest he could make.

9

Subject: **Mythical bird**

So glad! Thanks. Interesting. Yes, the brush almost electric, and the paint truly responding. It does have the feel, doesn't it, the 'pace', too, of my Gentileschi sequence. And you've always said the colour and energy all heaping up there was what originally drew you to my work. 'Capaciousness', I think was your word, and I blessed you for it. Theo, I believe we're really getting somewhere at last!

Just in town for a coffee—I have to make myself leave off work for an hour or so each day or I'd run my head completely ragged. Near total recall outpaces siesta, but the crazy thing is I'm scared of losing it, the material. No chance! It's got me in its talons like some great mythical bird!

I suppose at least I'm getting to know some of the café proprietors. And one or two regulars. Trying my Greek. But can scarcely wait to get back to my studio. And the evenings, writing to you, the written text crucially sparking the visual brain and generating tomorrow's work... it's almost hard to waste time sleeping!

Sent from my iPad

Subject: **RE Mythical bird**

Eléni? No, she's fine, I assure you.

Next year? You're sure? Okay. And May sounds fine, thanks so much, Theo. Well, it gives us both something to work towards. And our Americans...!

What should we say: 'Striking a balance between mannerist and anti-mannerist influences'. That sounds plausible, but a little ridiculous. 'A defiant Caravaggist, but also mining Vermeer for a figurative and illustrative *return to painting*'. Ha ha!

But I shall have to spell out again the theoretical justification for such unfashionable techniques, though we need surely have no worries about the subject matter. In terms of contemporary self-portrait, it's a perfectly Modernist, even Post-Modernist gesture.

For, in response to Julia's betrayal, I seemed to make, didn't I, the deliberate move from painting to performance. And what's more twentieth century than that! Behold, the Artist, amid the wreck of images, fire-purging his art of all personal dreaming/memory/reflection! Yes, and of narrative itself. Lo, the Artist in the detonation of 'character' — I mean of course the character of my former English self — taking refuge in these thousand 'imprints of... character': these so flexible stock roles, that constitute a transitory, evanescent and entirely throwaway art!

Was that indeed what I was trying to do in Paris? I do suspect so. To learn the discipline of abandon, to align myself semi-consciously with those movers and shakers of self-dramatization, both then and to come: Beuys, Abramović, Yusama, Gilbert & George, Perry and so on. To purify myself into process, to turn myself into a version of that Modernist and Post-Modernist flowering as 'Anti'-art, the art of the momentary, the lost, the unrecorded, a world of Happenings and Beings? And which now, in paradoxical turn and turn about, I record not with hand held video but in my old-fashioned narrative sequence of oils!

Subject: Monsieur et Madame Godot

But I was right to stay put. Because as time went on, and Cécile cooled, so Félix warmed. In fact, had it not been for that micro-debacle of Cécile's advances, I'd never have gained such theatrical knowledge as now informs my work, and I would have remained perhaps some perpetual fool on the sidelines.

Why? Because Félix was a genius. I think I told you before how he and Éméric came to Paris to set up the company between them. Sure enough, they'd continued to spark off one another for a couple of seasons, and all had gone swimmingly. But in my time there was something in the way Félix spoke to Éméric that suggested differences both of opinion and style, upon which the seemingly unrelated knifing incident had set a kind of seal. Certainly, Éméric contributed little at rehearsals these days. Often, he didn't attend at all. And once, when he stormed out, I could sympathise, for *his* broken heart was plain to see, the bandages all too visible beneath his shirt, the stubborn wound turning his departure into angry slow-motion.

This Éméric. I liked what I knew of him. He had a quirky, peasant face, with floppy, straw-coloured hair. It suited him: a natural prankster. And he could play the guitar and sing. Underneath all that, his wild eyes betokened a sharp wit, though I found his rapid Southern speech hard to follow.

Nevertheless, it was plain to see that Félix was nursing ambitions beyond slapstick and traditional comedy, no matter how brilliantly they were done. He began spending time with me. He cultivated me, indeed, drew me out and enlarged, when we had occasion, on his philosophy of the drama. And I wondered why that was, until I realised one night how strange and possibly even exotic *I* might have seemed to these exotics in turn: an English incompetent claiming to be a bruised and displaced painter. Why, my sudden materialisation might possibly have suggested the very kind of experimental *coup de théâtre* Félix was seeking, coming as it had in that liminal region between performance and the resumption of daily life. I *chimed* with Félix, even as his huge, hairy and agile presence, his panoply of circus skills and rasping, fire-eating speech chimed with something in me — and has continued to resonate ever since.

Theo I attach a pen and ink wash. Ink is good for him, I find, firm of stroke and yet flexible. Yes, a great warmth for Félix began to kindle in me, for how utterly different were our backgrounds: his full of the southern sun, the scents and flavours of the *maqui*, the old, untouched ways of Catholic Provence; mine manufactured out of English austerity, Home Counties perversity and our sad, industrial cuisine. And yet how similar, I soon discovered, were our purposes.

It was stimulating to be taken into his confidence. He told me of the birth of our art. I remember late at night we were in a bar near our apartment at the time — or rather, in that unending heat, at a table outside on the pavement, under the streetlamps and faintly twinkling stars. 'Once upon a time,' he said, 'in the last days of the Sun King, there were troupes of actors in the great Paris fairs. They were like us,' he spread his hands generously, so as to include me. 'Free spirits. But they stole material from the *Comédie Française* and the *Opéra*. And they mocked the licensed players, they insulted the politicians, and they mimicked the well-off, who could afford to attend such places. In fact, they did everything the true theatre should do, but which it did not. So the fucking cowardly legislators banned dialogue from any stage except the official theatres.'

'They were screwed, then.' I laughed, bitterly.

'Not a bit of it.' He broke off while his colossal lungs sucked the burn on his Camel a good half an inch along, and the satisfied smoke wreathed out at last in great, dark billows. 'They used monologue — one figure at a time narrating or soliloquising while the rest had sealed lips. *Mon Dieu, quelle étrangeté*! And how I'd like to have seen it.' He paused. 'So then the authorities, wrestling with the protean nature of art, made it criminal to speak at all.'

'And that did for them?'

'It didn't. They sang. They sang everything.'

'But then fell foul of the *Opéra*,' I said, laughing again.

'Exactly!' Félix laughed, too, his great roaring guffaw. 'So they wrote placards...'

'Like silent movies.'

'...which were instantly prohibited. And so they danced, until dancing itself was forbidden — except upon a tight rope.'

'*Jésus*! What was left?'

'An expressive form so cunningly contrived that it couldn't be outlawed — because it couldn't be defined legally as anything different from everyday gesture: I refer to the art of mime, Owen. And it has survived the two centuries since. Even though,' he brushed off my attempt to interrupt, 'that Corsican short-arse Bonaparte was so frightened of being ridiculed, he passed a decree that no one could even come on stage without turning a somersault or walking on his hands. Unless, of course, he was dancing on a rope!'

'*C'est bizarre, ça.*'

'Owen, it was then under the Empire that for a second time it was ordained no actor could speak, unless he belonged to one of the four classical theatres, I think it was. Who, in a positive orgy of sycophancy, kept presenting Napoleon as some fucking Greek or Roman god-king. So that old art of mime became once again a *necessity*.'

'Ah! So that's why,' I said. 'And why Cécile and Dmitri...'

'Of course. It's obvious. From Duburau at the *Funambules* to Decroux and Barrault — whom you won't know. And now with Lecoq and Marcel Marceau, of whom even you will have heard.'

I nodded.

'Once,' he said, 'the great Duburau, very early in his career, climbed to the top of a human pyramid. Underneath him, down at the ground floor of the edifice, so to speak, sweated a certain Monsieur et Madame Godot, supporting players — literally — who were both drunk.

In brief, they gave way. Duburau fell. He was badly injured. But he got up and continued, and the crowd thought it was part of the show. Owen, salute him. By this symbolic resurrection, Duburau kept alive *le corps expressif*. It's my duty as a Frenchman to do the same.'

Félix, too, was a little drunk—we'd had good takings that night. And yes, I was surprised to hear him utter sentiments so grand, so patriotic, even so philosophical. Yet I've no doubt he spoke from the heart.

Theo, you'll have guessed by now why this matter of silencing so touches me. Together, perhaps, with its solution. But look. In the thirty years or so since the current revival of French classical mime, it's become fashionable to despise the art, hasn't it? Because of the dead end into which it recently shunted itself, of course. But also, I believe, from a more recent cultural hatred of the truly expressive body, and of the child within, and of the miraculous.

In '76, the whole idea of mime seemed new and astonishing, at least to me. Félix enlarged upon it that same evening. He saw mime as a martial art, a perpetual act of resistance to capital or to the oppressive state. Our street theatre was like the *Boxer Rebellion*, he said—using the English words pointedly and unexpectedly and raising a bushy eyebrow at me as he did so. He said the unarmed serfs of China resisted the fucking opium-importing British by honing weapons in the form of their own limbs.

He gave a broad grin. 'Freedom is of the body, Owen. The body cannot lie. The body will rise up in its own cause and find a way. *Vive la Révolution!*' He stood up, and we toasted the sentiment—to the stares of our fellow drinkers, some of whom were American tourists. They jeered: the '68 Paris uprising was still fresh in everyone's mind.

Ah, Félix! His notions. Revolution, Freedom, Marxism: rallying cries then. They touched our intellect, touched our manhood, stirred our hearts. The body; what did we mean by it? It was still partly invisible, hence a metaphor for the poor and downtrodden, and for sexual liberation. Heavens, our naivety! Our idealism!

'Ah, but it's good to speak of these things, *mon ami*.'

I smiled, and sensed that among our company, for all the diverse skills of its members, he'd lacked a foil. That was a part I could play; I knew it.

Another night, his eyes neither smiling nor frowning, he juts one great fleshy hand across the table towards me. Zigui and Dmitri are there and look on. I'm taken aback, momentarily, suddenly lacking the social armour by which one man deals with another. He's in his element; I'm out of mine. What does he want?

No more than my sketchbook: 'Those drawings of yours, Owen. Will you show them to me?' Yes, I remember the scene particularly. My nerves were raw, but all he meant was to be my friend.

Relieved, I took from my coloured jacket pocket my dog-eared sketchbook. Wait, I still have it. It's here somewhere in one of my boxes. I'm sure it is. Why hadn't I thought of it before?

…

Theo, it's taken me half an hour to find, to the sound of these incessant cicadas and one owl crying at the stars. Now the item is right here in front of me: a neat little book once, good paper—maybe I got it in a market. Maybe I stole it. I don't remember doing these figures, life drawing almost a reflex: fast, fast as you can. See, it's full of them all. There's one of Dmitri stretching. Ha, what a coltish fellow! And here's that very sketch I was doing of Cécile, down by the Seine. My God! And Marie-José pointing at Zigui. And Minalouche posing in her flares by the warehouse door. Her real name was Sylvie, you see. She was called Minalouche from the cat-naps she took—she could curl up almost anywhere and fall asleep.

Theo, it's late, and I've painted and written like a madman all day. But I'm very pleased to have remembered this sketchbook—and now to have found it again after all this time. It was with some old desk files of Lily's—I'm an inveterate hoarder.

And so it's true then, what I'm telling you!

And now a dark, hot night lies over us, just like that astonishing summer of years ago. Jesus, I can hardly stop myself typing, tap, tapping with my fingers, my stitch of words pulled again and again across this pale screen. And this, too, is the mime, the mime of the keyboard, the body in motion, speaking, giving its account of itself…

10

Subject: **Rustic dances**

No, nothing more about Spíros.

I did meet Marta today, our doctor friend. The one who gave the party. Theo, I must tell you this. She was driving up from Lakkí and saw me at the bend. The first I knew of it was her big silver Toyota pulling up beside me, the window sliding open: 'Owen. You want a lift to town?'

I didn't recognise her at first, across on the driver's side and in sunglasses. Added to that—ha ha!—I swear I saw spacemen in the back—white body suits, blank faces in silvery helmets! Then it dawned on me who she was, and a closer inspection of the car's rear seats revealed nothing more extra-terrestrial than a couple of guys veiled up in bee-keeping outfits.

I got in.

She introduced me formally. '*Aftós íne o kýrios Cóstas, ke aftós o kýrios Yánnis.*' I shook hands awkwardly through the gap in the seats with the soft, proffered bee gloves. Then she returned to English. 'As you can see, we have work to do. But how was your visit, Owen, my dear? Your trip to Spíros. We haven't seen you. Was it good? Did you talk? You've been hiding away, haven't you.'

'I've been painting, Marta. Unstoppably. And the trip was excellent. Thanks so much for your help, by the way. In fixing it up. The meeting.'

'And?'

'It was inspiring.'

She raised her eyebrows.

'Just... indescribable.' I changed the subject. 'But what about you? Your husband?'

She nodded and braked for a moped swerving up from the beach. '*Polý kalá, evcharistó.*'

'The party,' I said, suddenly. 'We never thanked you properly. It was great. Wonderful. I can only apologise once again for the...'

But she wouldn't hear of it. 'It was nothing,' she said. 'Of course, you must come again. Soon. You and your Eléni. No ill effects?' She turned momentarily from the wheel to flash me a knowing smile.

'None at all. She's not long back from Athens.'

'Ah, Athens!'

We were in the narrow road just above Vromólithos Bay. The flat fronts of old houses lined either side tightly, and there was a shop with boxes of vegetables stacked outside on the kerb. Marta slowed to let a taxi through. 'Well. I want to hear about it. And Spíros. You must tell me everything. But we're almost at the square. Where shall I drop you? You were going for a coffee? Or shopping, perhaps — something for the house?'

I told her it was just a stroll, a well-earned break. So anywhere convenient. More importantly, where was *she* going, because I didn't want to take her out of her way. Which is how, Theo — once she grasped that I was merely relaxing and had no particular destination — I ended up joining her for the bee expedition. She insisted.

So we carried on through town and slightly up country above the bay of Alínda, which is on our eastern coast; and I watched heat mirages on the road while she explained about the bees and the hospital's rehabilitation project.

You remember I spoke of the terrible asylums around, in Lakkí and elsewhere, and of the great scandal when they were exposed? Well, Cóstas and Yánnis, my travelling companions, are actual survivors of that old regime. Former patients. They were in it for years. Decades. Still institutionalised, of course. God knows what they've been through. Marta — psychiatry is actually her specialisation — sees it as part of her medical duty to get involved.

And her moral duty, too. Léros psychiatric hospital, with a dedicated permanent staff and mainland resources, has made good the former disgrace. We're in the forefront of reform here, indeed. And some of those same unfortunate patients now run small agricultural projects: apiary being one of them. They have a unit back at the hospital complex, she says, where they process the honey. And they market it, too, under the label of the goddess Artemis — whose island this once was. I'll leave you to contemplate divine psychiatric honey!

In fact, so significant has the enterprise become that quite a few of the local farmers are starting bees up again in a kind of desperate gamble. In ancient times, she says, Léros was famous for honey, what with all the wild herbs and flowers.

It made me turn and smile at the two figures in the back. Whether or not they smiled back I couldn't tell, because, in that noonday glare from outside, their features were quite hidden by their veils. Why did they wear them? Surely no danger of stings here, in the car—and the day already so warm.

Cóstas was legendary, she said, among the beekeepers of the island. Any problem: they asked for Cóstas. But he only really felt safe when his face was covered; and Yánnis, his devoted friend, kept him company. The two were inseparable; though neither spoke much, she told me, each seeming to know, as though by telepathy, what the other was thinking. She made the point matter-of-factly.

Ten minutes out of Plátanos, we took a dirt track under the hillside. At its end was a one-storey house with a corrugated iron roof.

A young man, in bee smock and jeans, and with a round-brimmed hat, its veil as yet furled, awaited us at the veranda.

Manólis was a prospective honey-farmer: there was some hive disorder, apparently.

Again we made handshakes, Manólis unsmiling. He spoke impatiently, a little in panic, of his investment, before taking us a short trek past his terraced fields. They were just little stone-banked gardens, in which sullen rows of courgettes, peppers and tomato plants wilted and parched.

I walked behind Cóstas, whom I learned to identify as the shorter of the two patients—height being the only key to their ghostly incognitos.

My stay in Paris all those years ago had taught me nothing if not to read movement, and it was as clear to me as daylight that Cóstas was eternally fearful. Though his limbs were almost lost inside his baggy outfit, I could feel how thin they were, how tightly his shoulders hunched, and how his head, even in that strange silvery-white hood, was carried awkwardly, maybe forever expecting or resisting a blow. With his stiff gait, he appeared not so much to walk as—how shall I describe this—*negotiate alien ground*. So my first spaceman impression of him wasn't so wide of the mark: his scuffed trainers lifted and fell as though Earth's touch had always been intolerable, as though he still hoped to string himself up to some more abstract gravity!

Six pastel pale green box hives stood at the far end of a little olive grove. Manólis became animated. He fastened his own veil and began gesticulating at the first hive, all the while turning and talking loudly and expectantly to his guests. (Sometimes, Theo, the local dialect rattles so fast I can't understand a word of it.) Still muttering anxiously, he began knocking his knuckles against the defective colony's walls.

If I, who knew nothing, was alarmed by this stupidity, poor Cóstas was horrified. He hunched ever more defensive, waving his arms protectively as though the swarms of words would sting him—for certainly I saw no more bees at that stage than the ones and twos constantly entering or leaving the slots in the boxes.

Marta rushed to her charge, while Yánnis began his own little yelps of sympathy. Manólis leapt back. He fell silent. It was a moving scene. I thought how trifling had been my own troubles and took myself a few yards apart, where I perched on the flat stones of a tumbledown bank. Cóstas was reassured; Manólis was politely enlightened as to how all diagnosis was to be left to his guest.

And so began an episode that has left its impression on me. For Cóstas was extraordinary, and the source of his reputation quickly became apparent. As soon as he took the smoke can Yánnis had set going, he assumed a demeanour quite at odds with all that had gone before. He even seemed to gain in height, holding the 'coffee pot' smoker with immediate authority.

Soft clouds wreathed him round, and the waft of some piny substance reached me across the grove. When he lifted off the lid of a hive to pull out a frame of honeycomb, I saw how angrily the bees thronged about him, their shape in the air a diagram, full of sharp angles and violent lines, and their sound, yes, with the same note of distress.

But Cóstas lulled them. I could hear, above their noise, faint, dry rasping sounds coming from his throat. He was talking to them, and I swear they were answering. I can't put this any other way: man and invertebrates in duet, for there was also something musical about it. I heard their buzz change, their stridency gradually calm and sweeten into a hum, like honey itself on the air. It was as though they knew he was trying to help them.

And as for the man; I say, that same crippling rigidity—which, in former times and in sad, troubling places, I've seen other institutionalised folk wear pretty much as the badge of their condition—appeared to leave him. He began almost to dance, his simple investigation of each hive perhaps a slow saraband, forward and then back, each gesture flowing flexibly from a centre, the hands touching only subtly this way, now that.

And the bees moved with him, their collective outline, if I looked through half-closed eyes — what Van Gogh calls 'the intense look of a painter' — rounding all the while, at times like a halo, at others like an emanation from his palms.

I made a mental sketch: chalk-white figure amongst pale green boxes in dappled shade. I couldn't but think again of Julia and the hills of my childhood.

Marta came over to sit beside me. 'These moments, they make everything worthwhile.' She gave a little sigh of pleasure. 'So often, with the sick — in the mind or the body, you know… But look. There! He's happy!'

'Yes,' I agreed. 'A transformation.'

'He charms them,' said Marta, abstractedly.

'I guess he does.' I heard myself laugh.

'They cut our funding, of course. These terrible times. It is a race,' she smiled, 'to become… what is your word: self-…'

'Self-sufficient.'

She nodded. 'Before all our work is… trashed. By global economics. You know Soviet Union had bad asylums also. Maybe, they are still there. Places to keep the awkward ones. Maybe, that's one reason I'm pleased not to work in Russia right now. But you shouldn't think too badly of us, Owen. Bad things make some people more determined.'

'Determined?' I said.

'To do what can be done. Even do what *can't* be done. To make the life of a Cóstas here for one day easier, perhaps. And then for another day. And then perhaps one more. One more. Is that really possible?' She turned to me. 'Today I see yes, it is, and I am happy, too.'

'I admire you,' I said. 'Very much. And of course I don't think badly of you.'

Cóstas was working at a frame. He was stripping something away from the honeycomb. Small flakes of it caught in a sunbeam as they drifted down. Yánnis came over to speak to Marta, and she passed on the information to me. 'It's gone a little bad in there,' she said. 'There's some fungus. And besides, the fool Manólis has moved them recently.'

'Can it be cured?'

She spoke again briefly to Yánnis. 'Cóstas can fix it,' she relayed. 'He's going from hive to hive cleaning out. Then it's simply good management. Yánnis will give Manólis lessons. The poor man is so worried he is going to lose his whole venture to these fashionable scares: mites or colony collapse. But it's okay. Like me in my surgery, eh?' she laughed. 'Clean it up and keep it dry. Medicine is so simple!'

But she could tell me no more about Spíros. Does that matter? It's late, Theo. I must break off. What do you think? Two magicians in as many weeks. This island…!

Subject: Nymph under the pines

Ach, you were right about Eléni. I should have listened to you. We had a row, a bad one. Don't worry; it's all over and settled now.

It was my fault, of course. I brought up the subject of drink again. The recriminations lasted all morning. Then, still angry with each other, we siesta-ed separately. The heat hardly slackening, we woke. We went about our business. We circled one another, like wrestlers.

'Did you want to use up some of this bread?'

'Already had some, thanks,' she said. 'I made coffee. There's plenty.'

'Thanks, I've just made tea.'

'Enjoy your swim?'

'Yes. You?'

'Not yet. I'll go down later.'

I retreated to my studio.

Neither did we synchronise at supper.

'I've made leftovers.'

'Do you mind if I eat later?' She wouldn't look at me. 'I'll take a walk, I think.'

I watched her set off under the sporadic light bulbs that decorate the track by the pines. She had on her jeans and a T-shirt, her little back pack hanging from her shoulders. She'd turn left to the port, or right to the town.

I waited. I hardly touched my food. Insects hurled themselves at the fly-screens across the open windows, and my imagination filled up with uncertainty.

It was ten-thirty before she came back.

'Good walk?'

'Yes, thanks.'

'Which way did you go?'

'Up to the castle.'

'That's where I go.'

'I know.'

'Of course.'

144

She spoke no word of the night sky up there, nor of the ships visible in the strait, nor of the glimmering maritime horizon to east or west. No, it continued unresolved, and we slept an uncommunicative night, I on a makeshift arrangement in my studio along with the fume of oils, she in the house.

At dawn, I could bear it no longer. I came in and woke her. 'Eléni.'

'What.' She wasn't asleep—just curled up with a sheet pulled over her.

'We can't go on like this. Just blanking each other.'

She said nothing.

'We should talk, surely.'

She said nothing.

I went to the kitchen. There was yoghurt and some honey. I poured bottled water ready in glasses, filled the kettle from the tap.

Then she appeared, dressed in shorts and a shirt. 'I let myself down.'

'I'm sorry?'

'I let myself down, that's all.'

'It's okay.'

'It's not. It's not you. It just happened, I guess.'

'Well, yes, it does seem to, darling. But, it's okay. We can work it out.'

'Yeah.' She looked abstracted, then found two cups from the shelf. 'You want tea?'

'Sure.'

So she remained silent, attending to her task: the kettle, teabag, spoon, milk from the fridge—whose motor almost never cuts out, these days, so hard it has to work.

The line of her breasts under her shirt, soft flesh...

She took my mug out on to the patio and set it on the table under the umbrella.

I brought my bowl of yoghurt. 'Are you eating anything?'

'No. Thanks. Thanks, Owen.' She turned to me at last, and I began to relax.

We sat, facing the sea. It was slick purple, flat calm, and things were suddenly alright again.

My friend, the sea sends up the faintest beat from the shore. So sensual a calm: I've seen the phenomenon often at the cove. A surface, apparently mirror smooth, is pregnant with rhythm. It frays just at its extremity into wave after miniature wave. Modernist art? Modernism

145

is a retreat. Alright, I do share the Modernist and Postmodernist unease about the figure, about illustration, about the religious — about the risk each poses of a lurch downward into sentimentality. Yet 'figure' is my calling. What can I do? Just keep making sure my work is still justifiably 'contemporary'. It must have an axis of uncompromised pleasure. Christ, I don't want to be taken for some throwback!

Subject: **Two intaglios**

Poor London! The whole of June washed out and now July just as wet, you say. While here the heat just seems to build and build, until even the locals shake their heads. Poor souls, they're full of impotent rage, some turning openly to the far right.

And some just gave up talking about politics when that poor man shot himself in Athens, under the tree in Sýndagma Square. For how can things get any worse?

Instead, 'Εἶναι η υπερθέρμανση του πλανήτη — It's the hyper-thermance of the planet,' they say, mockingly. I love the turn of phrase but feel the despair. I'm almost ashamed to be happy.

It's true enough, though. Here, the air gasps, all movement slows, all stillness turns to agitation. Poor Eléni can model for scarcely an hour before she must shower or swim. (I've managed to borrow her a little from her work, you see, for my purposes.) 'Come on,' she says, and I join her gladly down at the cove, letting the delicious, sparkling sea wash clean away — for half an hour or so — all painterly or compositional questions, all dilemmas as to the management of light in multiple panels, the construction of viewer ditto, and, yet more elusive sometimes, the cultural text or 'myth' that should organise my whole work. Then we sit, side by side on the rocks, drying in the sun. Rain, Theo? We've had none of *that*; scarcely a cloud, dear friend.

And I suppose those Paris nights, a-glitter in the glass of hindsight and my on-going joy in them, must seem yet another affront to you, shivering indoors at your gallery! Time: what is time or time's arrow to the flat expanse of canvas? Look now, I'm fully established as Félix's disciple, and it's the Latin Quarter, the Left Bank, surely the very Paris for which I left England. The mind's eye connives: Picasso, Braque, Joyce, Hemingway — our heroes in their suits, spectacles, cigarette smoke, drinking off their day's struggle with canvas or typewriter. Underworld? Hardly!

Except I'd been transforming myself. Over those Paris weeks I confess I was less and less the youthful modern and more and more Caravaggio's effeminate Bacchus. In looks, that is, not drink! Theo, I was beginning to stand out in company. I was becoming visually anomalous, and consequently *your* glass of hindsight, presuming optic, needs to adjust itself!

So what? It was the seventies, and epicene was par for the course. And what *is* manhood anyway? Must it always show the warrior's strength of arm and voice, his magnanimity in victory, honour in love, his ready, combative temperament, rugged warmth? Why, these were fully on show across the table from me, together with a good measure of body hair. I admired them. Watch: he raises his cognac with one hand—'*À la tienne*, Owen!'—and slaps the table with the other. Félix's maleness fills the space around us. A fire-eater and a *mousquetaire*, he's larger, it seems, than life itself; he almost glows in the dark.

So who cares, if, while imbibing Félix's teachings, I dropped naturally into an appreciative receptivity? Suppose I *was* like the dutiful wife who bolsters her man and, a perfect listener, refrains from contradiction. No wonder he liked talking to me! And what if I *did* dress in a get-up, which, if I painted it for you—maybe I intend to—would raise eyebrows and set you wondering.

The detail? I've appropriated certain items of theatrical costume: provocative, frivolous things. I wear them out on the streets under my ever lengthening hair. I remember a tight cheesecloth blouse I found in the warehouse, with innumerable buttons at the front and puffed romantic sleeves. I remember a belted velvet jacket covered with embroidery and mirrors; a clinging, mohair top. I've taken to heeled clogs. I favour cheap bracelets and dangling necklaces made of apple seeds.

I've said, androgyny was the fashion—along with stars and stripes that year, '76, of the US Bicentennial. Besides, didn't my new trade *demand* a certain 'flamboyance'? I'm among dancers, for heaven's sake, who're given by default to 'female' gestures. You know well enough how we men habitually eschew all but the braced and firm—and the explosive. Imagine instead that your daily bread depended on melting and lyricism. Imagine, too, having constantly to touch your colleagues, physically to catch, hold, flirt, embrace. Why, it's a moving sketch of softness, done in ambivalence. And wouldn't that rub off on anyone?

Yet it hasn't rubbed off on Félix, who habitually wears torn jeans and an old shirt. Nor—now I think of it—on Dmitri, whose casuals, particular as any *Parisien*'s, remain uncompromised. Nor, significantly, has it touched either Éméric or Zigui. Their wardrobes stay male, despite both being unequivocally 'out' as gays.

What, then? By stagy steps and in the shortest time imaginable, I've fabricated a gender almost daringly blurred. I've become a mixed message.

Did anyone in the company comment? No—they were street pirates and couldn't have cared less. Yet I was noticed among crowds. And if I didn't exactly flaunt my new state—I never minced, Theo—then neither did I hide it. So perhaps it wasn't quite nothing, my walk on the wild side.

Freud's technical term, now sprinkled loosely about the language, speaks of 'latent homosexuality'. Or should we call it transvestism and leave it at that? Phenomena of gender no longer threaten us. Do they? We welcome them, don't we? Ah, we celebrate them. Critics write treatises. For artists, they're almost *de rigueur*. So why should my shift seem anything more than a faint wrinkle on culture's brushwork?

And how does it correlate? Sure, following the revelations of the Meredith Clinic, a full decade and half after these, my Paris escapades, I couldn't bear to think of myself as a man. Then, I yearned to be female, so intolerable was the experience of being in my own sexual and sexualised body that I'd have given almost anything to be a woman—or dead.

But just after Bledlow I'd merely had a beating and 'a setback'. So I supposed. And so why should I have chosen so provocative a response?

We must keep objective. Why *was* this tart waiting beneath my skin? She'd been there since I was six, at least, together with the thoughts of death, too. In my teens, I'd covered her up: science and athletics—how Greek! But still hers was a secret, erotic nature. She was in me.

Was that indeed the inner Girl who offered so clear a feminist vision in my Gentileschi paintings, who knew so much more than I did, it seemed, about figures, about their spatial relationships, who noticed the minutiae of dress and décor, could paint so well the folds of fabric? *That* Girl *defied* the erotic. Men were pigs to her mind; the entire machinery of sex she found abhorrent. That was as clear to you as to me at the time and not surprising, given her/my subject matter; for by then I suspected, *as her*, a history of violation that my male self

148

denied — to the point of amnesia.

But the Paris act? Maybe it was something biological, genetic. A 'phase'?

Christ, I had no desires for men. I was in retreat from them. Men, until I met Félix, had been all that was awkward and perverse. Hadn't I just endured men's violent penetration of my place, losing my art, my entire *oeuvre* — such as it was — to Miles's thugs?

Men, those monsters of the outside world, movers and shakers, skirt chasers, hunters, hungry to compete; that inexplicable species, porking and quick to anger.

Male friends? I told myself I had them, but kept them at a distance. I could mix with men, Theo, work with men. But I'd look at their teeth, as of beasts, never the eyes, and find nothing attractive, only horror — which I'd appease. I gave back only the appearance of brotherhood. I mastered by submission, for what we most fear we most seek to engage.

Now you'll look askance at our friendship. I'm ashamed. Should I even click 'Send'? This has already taken me several hours to write, the subject suddenly fraught; and the memories, not to mention the motivations, turned flickering and hard to retrieve. There's some culmination to it, some central warmth of detail that's hovering just out of recall, some significant 'what-happened-next', that for the moment I just can't quite get hold of. Which is why I need to keep unwinding this reel, long sealed and out of mind.

Oh, but show me the man who isn't terrified, at least on some level, of being overwhelmed by his 'female side'. For who can guide us? Achilles, Tiresias? Why, it was only my previous reading of Reich, I believe — he was very much the thing at the time — that gave me the nerve to explore her in Paris. I must have trusted, at least at the back of my mind, that it would be possible to return, not only to England but to my physical gender. By that trust, I was able to venture down the more deeply. Into a kind of underworld. And now your friendship heartens me to go there again. Love, faith and hope — these sureties we must grasp if ever we descend into the flesh. Only by them shall we emerge again.

Φίλε μου! In this email, I've just made for you above two intaglios, miniatures of masculinity — one fine, one swine. You, I hold always as the first. It is I whose inward voices constantly brand me the second — man as monster. Well, you're your *own* man and will take me as you find me!

Subject: **Several masks, certain old characters**

It's alright. Don't worry. Let me reassure you: I'm quite okay with 'disclosing all this'. I'm perfectly *comfortable* with it, as the Americans say. It's not private. Not *classified* or anything like that! It's just the portrait; and a portrait *reveals*. And it's not so much that I can't stop following the thread, unravelling the details, but that I don't want to, artistically. No, I really don't want to get off the ride, not... Not until it reaches its theatrical consummation — which, as I say, I still can't quite...

Because Félix wanted more and better masks, you see — the company used only a few. I designed them, and we made them, mornings together up in the flat. We soaked strips of this or that in paste, moulded them to shapes and peeled off the results over the floor.

Cécile was furious. 'This place is trashed. You two play together like children. If you think I'm wearing one of those nasty little mud pastries...' She glanced at me and swept a hand at our still drying objects. '*Zut!*' She returned to the kitchen, to broadcast her displeasure in crashes and thumps.

Félix winked at me. We continued our work.

We were serious. He'd shown me books of illustrations, and I'd attempted to match them, pushing up the half-mask brows, ridging the foreheads and developing great noses. Raw, they'd looked as bad as Cécile suggested. But by the application of cheap paint and cheaper varnish, certain old characters — Graziano, Coviello, Pulcinella, Arlechino & Co — were beginning almost to cry out with life. Félix watched me bring up the flesh tones: leathery, roguish looks, the yellow of age or pink of simplicity. They were good; he was awed. We tried them on, guying and acting up.

Then I made white, cold beauties for the girls and showed him how to colour them. He grew absorbed, sprawled in the sun-shaft on the rug, lining eyes, reddening lips and, with infinite care, shading bone structures.

At the end of it, to use up materials, I formed certain extra beings: a satyr; a wood nymph with butterfly wing extensions to the face; a birdman with a fantastical beak. As I sat in my fantastical girl's clothes painting my nymph's fantastical shimmer, I observed Félix out of the corner of my eye, following my explicit patterns with his brush, applying the colours I'd indicated on to the birdman's thin *papier maché*. His features were gathered into his own mask of concentration — like a child's, torn between caution and excitement.

I said nothing. We toiled on.

Cécile went to the shops and came home again. At last, Félix got up, holding out his finished object. He moved to the window. There he stood, staring pensively now over the Paris roofs and now down at the birdman face, as though trying to make up his mind about something.

Well, that mask was a triumph, if I say it myself. The poor materials had responded almost like clay: the dramatic cheeks were smoothed round, the elaborate eye sockets had the corners angled up, and the high white forehead was suddenly, in the sunlight, the bone of an ornate skull inset with painted feathers, and with arabesques of blue, red and gold.

'Owen, it's good.' Félix looked at me. 'Magnificent. But it's not comedy.' He laughed, abstractedly.

'I made it as an afterthought.'

'Yes.' He held it once again at arm's length and stared, still seemingly fascinated, into its vacant eyes. On an impulse, he twisted it round and pressed it to his face, pressed it tightly to his features and forced up his thick hair into a black corona.

He held the pose for a second or two, as though to absorb the sensation. Then he turned to me and was suddenly taller, more commanding and yet coldly insubstantial; even his slightest movement — a quizzical jerk of the head, the minute hitch of a shoulder, the quiver of his free arm — suggested some unearthly flying thing that had slid down the glare outside and broken in at the window.

He took a step forward.

I recoiled. Hair pricked on the back of my neck.

He took another step.

Involuntarily, I pressed the wood nymph over my own face.

The sense of danger was fleeting, of course. And my mask felt instantly artificial — so sensitive is the human skin that the first touch of substance dispels any filmic 'transparency'. The birdman was only Félix, and there was nothing remotely supernatural about *him*.

Yet, I was aware I'd reacted. I was aware, too, of my wood nymph's sex. In the spirit of improvisation, I sprang up from the floor and played out, just for a few moments, a maiden surprised by some predatory god.

Was it the mask? Was it the presence of a watcher; or my already ambiguous dress? Theo, you and I were schooled to enter art via the male gaze—we think too often of Leonardo's Vitruvian man in his square and circle.

But every topological point in the male corresponds in the female. I say, the brow softens, the chin narrows, the nose thins and the shoulders contract. The vestigial nipples spread to plump themselves. Elbows, knees: all the joints reflex a little. The pelvis swells into a preserving ark, sucks in the phallic tube and its accoutrements. There's a mathematics to it. And a chemistry: hormones re-equate; some glow of oestrogen fuses through the skin; the rough hair retreats, but doesn't quite disappear. So the genders transform.

Call to mind Daphne fleeing Apollo: Poussin, Pollaiuolo, Tiepolo, Bernini. We occupy first the hand of the painter, then the creamy sensuality of the exposed flesh; and only notice last—if at all—the terror in the girl's eyes, terror overwhelming enough to drive her inside the fibres of the nearest available laurel bush.

I felt it. From island to island, I suffer repetition. I remember not my father, but my mother, chasing me upstairs with the cane—some infringement or other: maybe 'lying' about Dad putting his john-willy in my…? My mouth. I was six. I reached my bedroom and tried to hold the door against her. I can feel the panic of it now, time and space curved into a single heartbeat, within which the free-floating, timeless mind has *time* yet to fashion a shift: I thrust my hand into my toy box for the long-lost cut-out cardboard mask of a grinning constable. I find it in a frenzy and wrench the string over my head just as she bursts in. 'You can't get me,' I yell through my tears. 'I'm a policeman!'

I remember once in a dream I felt such fear of my father that I ran up those same stairs to put on a dress, thinking only to please him, please him, please God. Yes, that was only in a dream, but when I was twelve, in another hemisphere and not dreaming, I changed hurriedly into my mother's clothes for an older boy from our rugby club.

It was nothing: a theatrical illusion. Félix and I broke away from the enactment almost as soon as it had begun. We took off our masks.

'This makes for a different theatre,' he said quietly, tapping the artefact, now merely a domed, decorated surface drained of all power. 'I don't know if we can handle it.'

'You made it,' I said.

He smiled awkwardly. 'I made it to your instruction. And felt it almost like… lightning. It even made its artist jump.'

'Keep it,' I said. 'It's yours. We don't have to use it.'

His nod of agreement made the negative equivocal. 'No, indeed. We don't.'

He stooped, placed the mask back on the floor amongst the others. Then he held out his hand for my wood nymph and called Cécile.

She came in crossly, wiping hands on her apron, and he faced her with it. 'But it's beautiful,' she said with a little gasp, caught unawares.

'Try it,' Félix said.

'I'm cooking.' She was annoyed with herself.

'I want to see you in it.'

She gave her hands a further wipe, rolled up her eyes and put the creation to her face.

She became animated, seemingly against her will. Her glances through the eye slots darted back and forth at us. Then she slipped out of the room, only to reappear, seconds later, holding a spatula. A far cry from my stricken dryad; in the same mask, she was an implacable, beautiful witch.

Félix and I clapped. She played it up, mollified, striding directly into the room, singing incantations to blast now me, now Félix with her wand. We were merry. The little charade charmed a respite in the sulky, offhand mood she'd hung over us all this time. Now we passed different masks between ourselves, fell into attitudes, invented phrases.

And how strangely the sculpted faces shifted figure or feeling: Félix's birdman re-appeared as Cécile's naughty old dame; his strutting, long-nosed Capitano looked foppish on her. My Harlequin was her irony; his Doctor my sorrow.

And the satyr I hadn't even painted made her sink slowly, listlessly to the floor. Before we could applaud, she'd removed it and immediately suffered an unaccountable flood of tears — at finding her naked features suddenly, heartbreakingly, vulnerable. Félix was right: it was no longer quite comedy.

Nevertheless, she smiled at me afterwards for the first time in days.

As for Félix, he began to regard me in a new light. He told me he saw more and more the stimulus I might bring to our direction...

Wait, Theo! I believe the thing I was searching for has just popped into my mind. My God, how the body guides us, speaking of a missing myth, recalling the mask-making, until 'what-happened-next' cannot but spring into consciousness. Keep on! Have faith! Yes, what happened next was the play I designed for him! The play!

I have, of course, always remembered it. Fragments of a script are possibly among my papers; I even know where they might be. Yet in all these recent exchanges—and despite unspooling my Paris to you for days both in paint and in words—I've truly, bizarrely, not thought of it. That hypnotic phenomenon of distraction again. But it'll do. It'll serve. I believe... And I'll tell you the details soon enough.

For we're still with the masks, and I was wondering about my sexuality. A portrait is a portrait, after all.

I *did* consider such a life as Zigui's, or Éméric's; you saw the identical dilemma recur when I was with the icon painter. Was that the real me? Would it account for my difficulties to date? If homosexuality were the answer, shouldn't I face it, like a man!

I watched my two gay colleagues, spent a little time with them, talked to them. Éméric was guarded and suspicious. Zigui, to my surprise, took me for a coffee. He'd discovered in his teens he was attracted to men. Where did he live, I enquired? Clichy-sous-Bois. Alone? No, with his parents, in an apartment block. Was that... inconvenient? They gave him meals and a bicycle. Did that make him happy? Some days, yes. Was he at ease with himself? France was his home. Had he always wanted to act? He had. Did he find it odd playing the romantic male lead opposite Cécile? He didn't. Did he think the old Italian comedy really had a place in contemporary France?

He looked at me as though I were mad.

Ha ha! Our whole rendezvous was a tangle of miscommunication. We left it with no hard feelings and absolutely no intention, on either of our parts, of repeating it.

In terms of my research, however, I learned only that I was closer to a fool than I thought.

Still, at leisure and in my own head, I really did pursue the question of how it would be to dwell forever in the mysterious female that seemed to possess me. Bear with this, Theo. I'm writing too much, here, taxing your patience; but I'm sure it's important.

For one thing, I'd feel safe, you see. I'd be free, free from tragedy, free somehow from guilt and shame and free forever—not least—from that soul-destroying teaching job at the Chiswick Poly, where the demands of other people's painting only highlighted the impossibility of doing my own.

No, as a Girl, I should make my appearance; I should emerge like a butterfly from my chrysalis. It would be as I said before: I'd fly off into the world as naturally as everybody else and find some fulfilling job in the *Arts*. I'd have friends. I'd speak. I'd become 'a character'. If I painted at all, it would be in a lucrative and dependable sub-genre.

Seriously, how tempting it would be to fix as enduring reality something of the witty raillery and light-heartedness I now sipped at each night in our Paris street theatre. So, Theo, I might snap my fingers at the gods and duck out laughing from my fate! Maybe one could even get used to sex with men.

You'll think me so flippant. But I tell you, apart from the fixed point of Julia there really was — there almost is — nothing in my masculine life but recurrent configurations of a sexually confused, metamorphic group: nothing, that is, beside solitary voyaging, days upon days of salt sea, punctuated, yes, by these occasional atolls of other people — which all, I say, turn out to be merely another corner of the identical picture! Why, Lily, and my first wife, and my mother — they're virtually the same woman!

Could you imagine, for example, a more discontinuous or contingent landfall than mine into the lives of Félix and Cécile? Yet what did I find there, reduced as I was to a child by my extreme need and helplessness and almost before I could draw breath? Only a difficult female by whose sexual pique I'm thrown into close involvement with the male! It's like being trapped in a four dimensional crystal; its shape in the continuum allows of no other configuration, because its parts have an eternal molecular binding.

That's destiny, of course. It's uncanny, and nothing I knew in Paris at the time would have explained it. Not science. Not Freud. Nor Jung with his own crystalline structures, the archetypes. The 'anima' — *das ewig Weibliche* — or the sacred marriage, the journey of the hero, the rose, the union of opposites, the wise old man and such-like alchemical confabulations... They're all ultimately too folksy and sanitised to account for the evil that surrounds us.

Nor Reich with his array of character types — *Charakteranalyse* — like the masks I'd just made for Félix and like every other bunch of stereotypes from Theophrastus to the present day. Because Reich, too, couldn't get his head around the consequences of familial sexual abuse, though he'd suffered from it himself.

Oh, God! Just nothing made sense in those days. I might as well have inveighed, along with Homer, against the unwavering wrath of Poseidon. No, Theo, only the extraordinary concept of amnesia, earth-shaking as it was when the tectonic plate of feminism hit that of PTSD, and erupting equally dramatically into my own life as late as 1991, has made any potential meaning out of this rock hard fortune or offered any means at all of dealing with it. Only the possibility that the recurring drama *is* my own supernaturally externalised memory has unlocked my art and given me the will to go on.

So who could blame me all those years earlier in Paris for seeking comfort in being female. And who could blame me for wondering whether I might reify the shift into something more permanent?

What stopped me, when all was said and done, was that the price would have been a lie, an insult into the bargain to Zigui and Éméric — and to all those for whom it was the *genuine* life. Theo, they were right to be suspicious. I had no discernible sexual desire for men; I've told you, I kept them all far off — even my friends. To construct myself otherwise would have been not only inauthentic but another imprisonment.

And anyway, even as I allowed myself to speculate on these things, I was in reality planning this play, this forgotten key, this missing piece, that should display the curiosity of my state for all to see.

And shall again. My play! Yes I'll tell you directly. The play! To be... someone else! Already I could reach out to an audience, once I was in role. And with my broken French and absurd English manner, I was getting laughs. It was noticed. Somehow or other, in a temporary sort of way, I must have had something to offer to *Théâtre Inconnu*.

Divine frenzy: wild and whirling words

I had to break off. A turn in the garden under the stars. A mouthful to eat. The call of nature. The call of Eléni upstairs to come to bed. Am I the drunk one, on words, on memory? I seem in love with writing.

Drunk, yes. Intoxicated. Writing too much. I'm aloft. High! Tell me to stop, Theo. Tell me: 'No more!'

What is it? Memory? Or the exotic? Or the compulsive pleasure of recapturing all that would otherwise be lost?

It's an archaeology, Theo, as though hidden chambers open up, another, and still another beyond, full of the unimagined treasures and grave goods of the past. For they had so much to offer me, my players. I picked up more inklings of their deeper craft. In their shoestring life lay a mystery that couldn't be taught. Félix insisted on it, almost like some Zen master or Dionysiac priest.

There was a night I first experienced it. We'd done some twenty minute piece about circus lovers after the war, I think—a boy, a girl, her fire-eating father. It was a risky theme, with the French Resistance—or the collaboration—still in living memory. You could hear the awkward laughter.

But then we changed abruptly, magically, into something else, and so it was all forgotten. Heavens, my friends could knock up a scene around me in a matter of seconds, so sharp were they, so very full of invention, that all I had to do was move and speak a line in character, and everything would flow accordingly. Self-abandonment was the 'way'; while the moment I grew worried and thought about what I was doing, there was a hiatus.

So I learned to trust them, and it was trance again, it was letting something else take over—like left hand painting.

Often, I couldn't even remember what we'd done, nor how long we'd played. All that remained in my mind were fleeting impressions which were not even part of the action: a face in the crowd, the sounds of cars, the bruised piece of market fruit I picked up from the gutter, the chink of coins into the hat, the smells of coffee, cooking or drains as we wheeled off our gear into the night.

Maybe it was dream. Or was it death? Had they murdered me after all, those thugs in my studio and left me in purgatory? Take care! We meet whom we meet *not* by chance but by the script of divine love encompassed by evil.

No, I won't let you go. My masks turned everything outrageous.

'I said it; you've a gift,' Félix declared. 'This is a wave. We can ride it.' The sun blazed, the moon swam, the lovers swore for eternity and the rest of us excelled ourselves. We became lost in our art.

Emboldened, I made more masks. I set myself free from the formal constraints of the *commedia* and dreamed up images, as with those of the birdman and the dryad, that simply took my fancy. At once, our repertoire gained a dimension. Imagine burning tapers to light us and the sudden appearance of fairies and devils. Yes, first we lulled our audiences with twilight knockabouts. Then, once it was dark, we sprang our new beings at them, the wild torches flickering on our paintwork.

Children cried, and some adults, too.

Once, Minalouche howled piteously in the middle of a scene, so powerful even to their wearers were the creations—terrifying things—not, I hasten to add, through any magic of mine, but by the awful potency of human movement, magnified. *That*'s the effect of these inert identities—the masks. To wear a mask among the masks of others is to enter something of the psychic world of animals. Withdraw the face, and you withdraw linguistic reason: all becomes poetic, sensory, divine, or demonic. I swear I lifted up my own dog-shaped muzzle reverently before putting it on, as if its moulding were otherworldly in hard fact as well as appearance.

Watch through its eye-holes with me. I insist. Marie-José edges towards Félix from the back of our scene, holding against her head the most fearsome design of all.

Pshaw! Of itself, it was no more than a Cubist profile on a stick—another experiment I'd dashed off to use up materials, the afterthought of an afterthought.

But look! So very ghostly do the sideways-painted features render her; and the onlookers, too, seem spellbound. Félix stands in some medical spoof, pronouncing over Dmitri's corpse: 'I am the Doctor and can raise the dead. Take this potion, lad, and lift your head.' He turns, on a sudden, and sees Marie-José, and his own scream goes through him like a knife. Yes, Félix, the consummate professional, the fellow who keeps us on our toes and up to the mark, lets out a yell that makes my hair stand up! Theo, I can almost feel it now; fine sport if it hadn't been so shocking.

All credit to him: he pulled off a *coup de théâtre* by raising up Dmitri, who, equally inspired, pretended to be animated—like a marionette—by that etheric, Egyptian-looking figure standing only half visible behind him. So Marie-José echoed back his every move, and an age-old dualism—of body and spirit—came suddenly up to the minute. If you'd been there, Theo! Sometimes these moments happen, and our understanding of the world is changed. No, really; it was a scene that stays with me, and I doubt there was a soul unmoved at that moving soul.

Other times, alas, the masks were mere entertainment; it's in the nature of a gamble—as was my play. My nonsensical play! The idea for it came to me out of nowhere: from an old tale I'd once read. A hotchpotch of a yarn; I couldn't even remember the whole story. But soon, for some reason, I found myself thinking of nothing else. I pictured its scenes in performance; I began working out effects even before I had the proper text of it: a fortuitous discovery I'll tell you about. It assumed a life in my mind, and I began to consider how on earth I might persuade Félix to take it on.

My play, Theo. I'm thrilled with it, just as I was then. *Jouissance*! My

God, you know how art sometimes feels like jumping off a cliff clutching only the flimsiest of umbrellas. Hold the nerve. Have faith. Keep working at all the sketches and preparatory work. And now the relief! Scenes from the play I made for Félix to organise the narrative of these paintings—what do you think? Describing the masks triggered it; the masks themselves sharpen the imagination. Art is illustration, illustration, illustration. My dear friend, attached you'll find the pictures of all I've done today.

I say, I've tried to tell you too much, far too much, and it's late, far too late. This ecstasy, this floating, soaring delirium of paint and composition is the essence of the creative process. Another face of love? The passion for one's art? Surely!

11

Subject: **Bubbles**

I tried the Bledlow self-portrait again this morning. Hubris. Still can't do it. And so the bubble burst. Now everything feels flat. What's going on?

Subject: **RE Bubbles**

I told you the truth: I *did* conceive a play of my own. *And* I had to start forcing the direction of the company.

Subject: **RE Bubbles**

Because otherwise I should die, of course. Or were we already the dead? Maybe that was part of the *commedia*'s first subliminal lure: a form mummified, preserved in aspic, dissociated from even artistic reality. It was a refuge among refuges. Just another island: the Île-de-fucking-France.

    Sent from my iPad

Subject: **RE Bubbles**

Theo, it was only a poxy little street play. It resolves nothing, I assure you. I've no idea why I was so over the top about it in the first place.

    It *was* nothing. I can *do* nothing; nothing we can *use*.

    My friend, we're back to square one. I'm sorry to have messed you around. I mean with the dates you suggested for the show and so on.

    Sent from my iPad

Subject: **A retreat**

I haven't felt much like writing, the last couple of days. My apologies.

Yes, I do really think Modernism was a retreat rather than an advance. But I'm most likely wrong. By the way, please don't take it in any way as a slight on your gallery. You have a truly fabulous contemporary stable, and I'm so proud to be part of it. I only wish I could live up to your expectations.

Subject: **Golden Dawn**

An interesting idea. Once again, Theo, I'm touched. But the truth is I really can't see the point. The little play spins in its own bobbin of weirdness and obscurity, and I'm seriously doubtful anything much is to be gained from the effort of teasing it out. Forgive me, I feel low and uninspired. Your confidence is inexplicable.

I walked into town. It was late morning; the track overheated. The smell of resin was strong, as always under the pines, some of their bark new-channelled, with a tin-can fixed on for the sap. The taste collects, dark and tarry — to go into retsina, I suppose.

I couldn't resist it. I dipped a finger into the turpentine savour of our painter's trade, while hawk-moths, a couple, flapped in a dance, and cicadas kept rasping — one fat as my thumb on the tree trunk in front of me. Beyond and between these barked uprights, the roasted air set the spread-out land a-shimmer. Then the road, the sea, the town square.

I lacked the impulse to make the customary climb. Instead, I took the street down towards Áyia Marína harbour. When I saw Marta's house, I found myself knocking at her ground floor surgery.

'*Pyos ine*? *Mólis kléno. Éla ávrio.* — Who is it? I'm just closing. Come back tomorrow.'

'I was just wondering... Marta?'

The door sprang open. 'Owen, it's you!' she said in English. 'I'm so sorry. *Yiatí then épate?* — Why didn't you say? Come in at once.'

'Are you sure? I mean... if it's not convenient.'

'*Ne*! *Embrós*! She insisted, flickering between the two languages. '*Pos ise, agapité mou*? — How are you, my dear?'

Theo, I keep trying to capture for you the sound of Greek. Always it ravishes me: the speech of angels? She wanted to make me coffee, but

I declined. So she sat me in the tube-framed clients' chair and took her own place behind her desk.

We chatted of this and that. Of bees. I asked after Cóstas and Yánnis, and she said they were well. 'But still you don't bring with you the pretty Eléni, who sometimes…' She mimed holding a glass in memory of our evening and smiled for a moment. 'Ah, no! *Niet. Óchi!* Eléni has come back to her roots. I'm Russian, but Greece is in my heart. I know it. It is the same for you—for both of you. I could tell as soon as I saw you.' Smiling, she thrust her chair aside and walked to the window. 'This is your home.' A branch hung across outside, heavy with green figs. 'In Greece one is happy.'

'Except that now,' I said, by way of small talk, 'the whole world seems to be trying to make Greece unhappy. And every day the news… The neo-Nazis, what do they call themselves, Golden Dawn? And the homeless and the dispossessed. I hear that in Athens…'

'Athens!' She turned and pouted. 'The islands are the true Greece!' Then she sat down again, this time on her examining couch, and fanned herself with a clipboard. 'I'm sorry, Owen. Perhaps you came here to consult me for some medical purpose, and you find me talking of Greece.'

'Medical? Oh, no. Not at all. I was just passing. I thought maybe to see if you were in. That's all there is to it.' I paused. 'Unless there's a pill to cure the summer of '76!' I laughed.

She stared at me blankly.

'A joke,' I said. 'Just an artistic problem I'm wrestling with. Perhaps a personal one.'

'I see,' she answered. 'Which is to say that I don't. So you are not here as a patient. You're not trying to tell me that your anchorage in the present is fragile?'

'No, no, Marta. Nothing like that at all.' I laughed again, oddly disconcerted by her turn of phrase.

Theo, I left.

This wavy, unreal air, this fount of glossolalia, strange temple of echoes. Greece.

Subject: Clio, the muse of history

She comes down in search of coffee, still blinking night from her eyes.

'Shall I make you a cup?' I say.

'I'll fix it myself. Not going out to your studio?'

'Not painting much, to be honest. Only odd bits and pieces. Last few days I've run aground. Stuck again with that self-portrait.'

'The one with the girlfriend.'

'Ex-girlfriend. Very ex. I'm supposed to be carrying on with France. A play I made. But I can't see the point.' I felt myself sigh. 'I've taken a wrong turn, Eléni, like the whole Paris thing's an irrelevance... Except it still seems to strike a chord with Theo. The colour, the fullness. And he's still on my case to explain.'

'Explain what?'

'Why it seemed important. To my art.'

'Oh, that.'

'He likes the bravura, of course. He says so. Of the figures.'

'And you don't?'

'I'm just really down right now. Whether it's worth wasting the time.'

'I don't know why you spend so much time writing... To him.'

'He's a friend.'

'He's a business associate. This obsessive correspondence...'

'Obsessive? I don't think so. We can stop it whenever we want.'

We stare at each other because of the addict's cliché—the words just came out.

'Oh, sure,' she says. 'My drinking again, is it?' There was a pause. 'And I just had the naïve idea your painting might be about our life here. About now. About *us*.'

'Me,' I said, 'as a young man. Both Greece and France stemming from that first large canvas.'

'From some long gone fuck you once had! That girl. Julia. Pussy *perdue*.'

'From the past and the present,' I said self-righteously and, oh, so pompously. 'It's my work, Eléni. It *is* about us. Paris and Greece. A gamble. Comedy and tragedy.'

She took her coffee upstairs.

Now look what you've done, Theo! Obsessive? *Moi*!? Never mind. It'll blow over.

But I need to collect myself. So the rider collects his horse before a high fence. I confess I *have* been painting again. A little, partly from memory, partly from imagination. I've made a new large canvas, preparing for the play, a drama in masks, preparing for the gamble. I take your point. I have to do something to break the deadlock.

And you of all people will grasp the challenge here for any contemporary painter who risks the human figure. It's how to stay contemporary, how to remain cutting edge—when to many artists and critics 'the figure' is still anathema; the illustrative figure most of all. How to steer between the monsters of regressive art—some mawkish 'pre-Raphaelite' tendency, for example—on the one hand; or pornographic photorealism on the other. How on earth to steer between conceptual and representative.

And don't throw up your hands every time I mention illustration. Is it any more than titling an image? Hmm? Look, I implore the muse: and not just Vermeer's bewitching Clio! Such a painting, that one, Theo, by the way: a painting of painting—Vermeer the artist still ravished by the girl model with her book of Thucydides and her lightest, most heavenly trumpet, the painter as a young man making a complete fool of himself. Over *her*. History of a history, theatre, the death-pale, unsmiling mask, the love letter now un-crumpled she regards on the table: it's the design of designs, all exposed and yet nothing revealed, an illustration of illustration, representation of erotic representation that will not lie still. No, Everything I do must be contemporaneous, unless deliberately done otherwise. Everything must appear the best and most fearless portraiture. At the same time it must be pregnant with story. At the same time, it is itself and nothing other.

For all I've said, I confess… I confess I've seen our letters hitherto as a species of supplement—the little luxury I just came to after the *real* work. And if I did my play at all, I was fully expecting to launch it straight at my canvas—just as I launched it live on to the Parisian streets all those charmed nights ago. You, like anyone else, would surely be interested only in the finished product.

Yet even the little I've done shows me how still inchoate are my memories and how much this correspondence is becoming integral to the whole business: like text on image again; like the cryptic lettering on Spíros's panels. My funny little play marked the end and the beginning of so many things, but it exists in conscious recollection more as a single closed and glittering form rather than spooling narrative. Its actual *mise en scène* is an entirely different trance. Without the teasing of this telling, I'd recapture precious few of its twists. Why, even the lines I spoke have quite deserted me, and I find my image of woman and child—I mean the witch and the boy/girl in the drama—almost a barrier rather than a doorway. And now I've upset Eléni. How did the show open? Who spoke first? Which part was which?

Subject: **Wasted time**

It doesn't matter. It was nothing. I can't fucking do it. We don't have to use it.

12

Subject: Praying hands — the whistle-blower

Okay! If you insist, mate. If you can cope with it. If you think scrutiny might work, then let's put all the tough stuff right under the microscope.

A man goes into a bookshop.

It was me. 1991. Lily and I were having marital counselling sessions, the children just twelve and seven. We were a disaster. I'd grown progressively less able to work, less able to walk in to teach my art classes, more obsessed with the first Gulf War on the TV News: 'Desert Storm' — against the tyrant *djinn*, Saddam, who towered like a plume of evil smoke over poor little Kuwait. I needed more and more time with the doctor, more time off work. I was more prone to say or paint strange things. I was subject to inexplicable panic attacks. Extraordinary, every day, same time, simply panting like a dog.

A man goes into a bookshop.

Of course, I'd read Freud, Jung, any number of others. I'd puzzled over them for years. Nothing ever made sense — of *me*. Nothing!

Until…

Until, ever hopeful, I'd driven one day to Oxford to browse in Blackwell's store: its oh-so-comprehensive Psychology section, which went all the way from whacky Self-Help to the very driest of Academic tomes.

One book almost sprang off the shelf. I can't even remember its name now — I gave it away to somebody. But it was one of the first ever published accounts of childhood traumatic forgetting: by a woman therapist — quite well known in those days — detailing her own sudden and surprised recollection of lost and disturbing events.

A quiet bombshell, Theo. *Never* had I heard that sexual abuse could be forgotten. *Nothing* I'd ever come across suggested it — not even the then new PTSD literature. Why, abuse itself hardly existed in those days. Except I knew it had for Lily, poor thing. But she remembered it, whilst I… I, who'd once actually devoted time and effort to writing a detailed recall of all my past, remembered, as I told you, nothing untoward. Nothing untoward about my father.

But all the way home with this book on the seat beside me, I had the strangest feeling, as though someone inside me was rising up, elated. And when I got out of the car, I went straight up into the loft and dug out my old dream diaries. *There*, yes, and *there*! Heavens, it was almost spelled out. So much, right in front of me all along.

Had I been blind, then? Or stupid?

Or was it just now that I was ripe for it, the lightning-stroke.

For sure, it felt as though I'd been opened with a thunderbolt, god-delivered. Sexual abuse was the one possibility I'd never considered. My lifelong fears and depressions, my sexualised childhood, thwarted adulthood, the poverty, gender confusion, eternal loneliness and the obsessive darkness of it all: everything suddenly clicked into place.

But then it didn't.

For, right at the start of one of our weekly sessions, I mentioned the possibility to my marital counsellor — Don, his name. (They'd decided to take us separately. Lily was with the woman.)

At first, to my surprise, Don thought the idea very likely — in view, he said, of what he already knew of me and our work together.

A fortnight later, though, when I'd failed to provide explicit memories, he wondered didn't I just have an artist's imagination? Was I just perhaps making things up?

I went along with that, Theo. He was the professional, he knew what he was talking about — notwithstanding the fact that this whole matter, pioneered only so very recently by the women's movement, was still clinically unexplored.

So I thrust my suspicions on to the back burner and continued my weekly meetings with him. Don thought I could probably try harder to mobilise my 'network' and use my 'contacts' — effectively, to look on the bright side and pull myself together. It took another few months for the complete breakdown, the clinic and then Mitchell.

You shouldn't have asked me.

Yet you will inquire. You're even forensic. 'What *exactly*?' you say. In what way *precisely* should all this affect the portrait?

You shouldn't come near me.

Tainted.

Protect yourself. For how vague is that phrase itself, 'sexual abuse'. A cliché. A phrase too often deployed, yet so hard to specify. How strange and fearful it feels to write it here, full on. To you. How fraudulent; because, of course, it never happened. Sexual abuse — of me? Don't be ridiculous.

And just see how I wrap it up in email after email, digression after digression, story after story. Like Richardson, maybe, burying Clarissa's rape or Pamela's violent molestation inside a mountain of letters.

But then the 'phrase' encompasses such a multitude of sins and misdemeanours. And who knows for sure what *exactly* might be in the speaker's mind who mentions it, or the hearer's who receives it? Take that comment of my mother's, 'Do you mean the same as my father did to me?'

Well, Theo, I've absolutely no idea what her father did to her. How should I? She never told me. Was there something she once said about him: asking her to sew a button on his flies while he still had his trousers on? Not pleasant for a teenage girl, but hardly an arrestable offence! Was that *it*?

Or was she unable to speak about something else, something more disturbing, because too painful.

And about Dad: '*That*'s what he always said his father did to him,' she's said.

Oh, quite lately, Theo, do you know, just before I left England, I heard from an elderly relative to whom I'd gone out on a limb and confided as I have to you. *She* said my mother had admitted to her—to *her*, note, not to me—that the abuse *had* indeed happened.

Yes; but it was only, she'd claimed—my dear Mother claimed… it was only during the time she'd been away for some weeks in hospital and Dad was looking after me. As if that fucking made it alright!

I think she was optimistic.

Let me tell you, it was in all likelihood a secret part of family life for much longer than that.

If it occurred at all, Theo.

No, it was surely nothing…

But as to what *exactly* she meant by '*That*', or what Dad 'always said', or 'the abuse', we'll never know, because she's never bothered to ask me since or talk about it. And I was too bloody emotionally ill, at the time I first told her, to volunteer details.

Whereas you… Yes, I take it as a professional kindness in you. So few would question further, interrogate, even. Unless their interest were prurient, perhaps. No, they'd be too 'sensitive' about it, not wishing to offend.

But it's the true friend who *must* ask, now that we've come so far; for if these matters impact on one's work—and they do, it seems—and if you're to continue to represent me and show my stuff, then there's that forensic need perhaps for us both... what shall I say: to face facts. A need to classify, yes, *exactly* what strange and ugly creature of the deep now lies dredged up on the table between us. By God, we need its pathology. We need a degree of post mortem analysis. And so on.

The Greeks believe their churches contain a glimpse of heaven. For me, it was the Meredith clinic. Each nurse, in her neat candy-striped shirt and full maroon skirt, appeared — beyond any shade of cliché or irony — to be an angel. Each offered a different face of kindness. I told you how at first I couldn't believe it, nor accept it. Because in that one place there was refuge and warmth, and there was food good enough to gladden the heart — food I didn't have to cook myself and get on the table for the family every night — and there was care and consolation. There was safety. And, as if for the first time, there were other people, with whom to keep company.

Above all, there was help. In the Meredith, shielded around with those gardens that in summer, ah, bore roses, honeysuckle and a host of other blooms, their blues, golds, burnished ochres, scarlets and pinks now wreathed to trellises, now wound on pergolas, now springing in profusion beside the gravelled path, half-hidden beside the brook or fading to green across the paddock, where the two goats grazed beside the one old donkey... Or winter, when I first entered those rooms of old oak and new pine, amongst smells of lavender oil and wood smoke... There and only there, Theo, year round, was the story of my body accepted as true; if not by me, at least by some. And there I was taught to take what the house offered and to try to bring it, little by little, into my own life.

Soon after I arrived, I mentioned my suspicions to Mitchell. He was my appointed therapist there, you remember. I was diffident, but thought I should tell him. You have to be frank about things. Everything.

To this day, I remember his voice, perhaps already lowered and with its own subliminal buzz. 'Maybe you'd like to try a little hypnosis; to see whether there might be something in all of this?'

'Maybe. I'd never thought of it.' I sounded casual, yet was suddenly all ears. 'What does it involve?'

'Nothing really,' he said. 'I'm not naturally a digger into the past, either by training or inclination. But I think it's sometimes helpful if people know their history. Do you want to think about it and tell me next time? Or maybe go ahead now?'

'I don't mind trying now. If you like.'

'Okay.' He smiled and finished his cup of tea. 'So if you just rest your elbows on the arms of the chair. Yes, any way you like. And let the hands come together. That's all.'

'That's all?'

'Sure. That's all it is.'

I couldn't do trance. So much was at stake. I was tense as a fiddle. I was panic-stricken in any case about how I'd ever feed my family again or keep the home together if I couldn't work. So my arms stuck up like quivering aerials and refused to move.

Yet we gave it a shot, and I learned something of his technique. There was no soporific induction, no 'watch the watch and listen to my voice.' Instead, he sought to distract the intellect and focus on some outward part, the hands, as if they didn't belong: classic dissociation. So we were to let the body speak, the arms moving magically inward for 'yes' and outward for 'no'.

I couldn't.

Oh sure, my hands jerked like semaphores and sprang together when he put the all-important question—did your father sexually abuse you—but it felt to me so brazen and mechanical a result that I simply couldn't credit it. Besides, I was already half outside myself—like a scrupulous scientist looking on. Like my dad himself, indeed, perhaps, alert for smoke and mirrors.

In our next session, Mitchell took another tack. He had me place my hands on my knees. Then he invited a finger to lift up: in token, he said, of the Child's willingness to co-operate. I had no time for that. I'd tried all the 'inner child' nonsense years before. I didn't have one!

Still, we began. And no one was more surprised than I when the muscles of my arm suddenly contracted, and a part of myself, in this case the right index finger, sprang up without my say so.

He smiled. We continued. As with the hands, we controlled for a 'yes', and put 'no' on a different finger.

And as before, under the significant question, we turned up the 'yes': the finger raised itself and pointed, rigidly uncomfortable, into mid-air. 'Yes, Dad did it,' said my body. In front of a witness.

I remained sceptical. What, in reality, were we seeing here more than some curious physiological reflex. Like that old experiment medical students used to do with a chicken: you hold the beak to the bench and draw a chalk-mark away from the tip, equidistant from the bird's eyes. The wretched creature stays *in situ* until someone rubs out the line. It's a medics' party trick, and so what.

Never mind that my lifted digits went authentically 'catatonic', and I couldn't bring them down again without Mitchell's gentle permission. Never mind that we repeated the question a few more times with the same result. I was still unimpressed. What phenomenon—other than something akin to the entrancing of hens—did we think we were demonstrating?

Though I *was* persuaded, Theo, or why should I have been there and doing it and letting myself feel so wretchedly, devastatingly ill between sessions as a result—caught between opposing wills.

Oh, how strange to be split in two: the Kid—me—apparently trying to smuggle out messages about some nightmare inside; at the same time another element—still me—confusing the issue, pouring scorn, muddying the waters, beating me up like crazy and doing everything possible to shut up this whistle-blower in front of a concerned professional.

For, just as the story began emerging, I was in the greatest denial. And between sessions—this was still during my first two intensive weeks as an in-patient—I was visited, as I say, with punishment almost physical in its pain and severity. I mean punishment from inside. Like fiends. It was terrible.

Only consider, Theo—setting aside my own case for the moment—the potential impact on art of these details, these quirks of pathology. Consider the implications for portraiture in general. For how on earth are we to represent this splitting? Consider that so-popular Frans Hals: the 'Laughing Cavalier'; more properly, as we all know, 'Portrait of a Young Man'. It's a clear *tour de force*, once you forget the chocolate box connotations. Our Young Man appears unequivocally 'there', doesn't he; and we'd like to meet him.

But what if 'character' is in abeyance in someone? In abeyance in a subject for a portrait. Or if 'character' has never existed. What if other forces seem to battle for the person? How on earth are we to represent that state of affairs upon one flat surface?

I said I couldn't do hypnotism, but something *did* get past my defences. It was a clear December day in the patients' lounge. Cold light struck through the Meredith's leaded bays, while thin cloud drifted across the two little clerestory windows with their quaint, stained glass badges high above the heavy beams and assorted hunting lodge antlers—I was lying on my back in a yoga session. Sure, the place offered such things for us blighted, well-insured patients, stretched out on mats beside the big log fire.

I'd completely forgotten my appointment with Mitchell. When he came to hoick me out, I must have been far calmer and less on guard; because in his little consulting office my arms worked exactly as they were supposed to. More than that: my swaying, praying hands took on a life of their own. They performed that hesitant, almost creaking alternative to normal movement which I later came to recognise as the articulation of trance. Fully conscious while they moved, I went on to experience so striking an enactment there seemed no room left for doubt.

It was a mime. My body portrayed spontaneously a nightmare I'd had some dozen years before—after Paris, but before Lily. I remembered the nightmare vividly, exactly while my limbs were moving: I was shut in a room with some crazy dark 'sister' in rags who was trying to kill me—by forcing her thumb into my mouth. In the dream, a man's head was nailed to the wall above her, framed in oilskin. I'd even done a painting of it all the next day, so very powerful and disturbing had it been.

Nor had I dared go back to sleep that night, I can assure you, but had remained on guard like poor Lockwood in *Wuthering Heights*, counting down the hours and minutes until the first fingers of dawn brought my bedroom back to solidity and the phenomenal world. And now at the clinic, in Mitchell's room, I saw my own dissociated hands dramatize this same theme.

But the hypnotic mime went much further; further than the dream. For the hands descended—I was embarrassed—towards my genitals, and there slowly reversed themselves, scooping, as if symbolically to pick up the organ before returning, pointed together in a telling, rocket-like shape, towards my face. They crammed the fingers so hard into my mouth I eventually had to snap myself out of the trance to put an end to it.

It's not an easy story, Theo. As I said, you're the first to whom I've actually told these details in so many words.

'What do you think that was all about?' Mitchell asked at the end of it, warm but deadpan. I blinked back at him. He was trim and athletic in his blazer and tie, his jaw firm, his full head of dark brown hair neatly combed, more like a sports teacher than a hypnotist—whatever hypnotists are supposed to look like. Or sports teachers.

I still paid remorseless lip-service to Freud, 'A buried conflict over breast-feeding in infancy, maybe?'

Mitchell smiled, wryly, and I had to nod in acknowledgement, because we both knew beyond question that this had nothing to do with breast-feeding. Something like evidence—since we're using that term, Theo—was coming up within only days of our first meeting.

I sat that evening at the big oak dinner table along with the other patients. I made conversation—or didn't: we were a bunch of the usual troubled spirits you find in such places. But I felt secretly transfigured, vindicated. At last, I knew who I was.

And, instantly, I decoded some of the symbolism of the old dream that had so puzzled me when it first occurred: my own body perhaps the enigmatic female figure, the head Dad's, with some, yes, Freudian displacement of 'foreskin' by 'oilskin', maybe, and the thumb an all too obvious reference. Everything made sense, and I'd be whole. I'd be able to paint and could take my place in the world. You see how profoundly the *presence* of the artist to himself must impact on his art? Yes, I was exalted.

Yet, in the morning, a nurse came into my room and found me inconsolable. Tears fell straight on to the tray of scrambled egg she set in place across my bed. 'What's the matter, Owen? Has something upset you?'

'My dad.' I said. 'Because he never loved me, after all.' I wept because the violence of what I'd enacted in front of Mitchell so far exceeded anything I might have let myself anticipate. Prior to that, you understand, I'd imagined my missing 'memories', if they existed at all, would amount merely to Dad's misguided conception of love, στόργη, αγάπη—family love, spiritual love. I'd imagined any conjectured 'abuse' no more than an inappropriate fooling, perhaps, stemming from some naivety engendered by Dad's own brutalised background; really no reason I should be in the clinic in the first place.

It's this question of 'serious' again, isn't it, or 'exactly'. Heavens, I wasn't *in* the clinic as a survivor of incest, but only through my lack of fibre, of *character*, that had meant I could no longer teach at the college, could no longer deal with the behaviour of my wife. So I was in treatment on false pretences, being shown fleeting kindness in temporary respite, before I had to go back and face my responsibilities. Lily was the one with the traumatic background. She was the one needing help. Anything in my own childhood would have been trivial in comparison—I'd believed—and this work with Mitchell was almost entirely an indulgence, a curiosity, you might say, whilst we had the brief opportunity.

Yes, Theo, I'd thought only of some mild impropriety of Dad's, some virtually benign species of his 'overstepping the mark' — for such would accord perfectly with the man I'd known all my life: affable and well meaning, surely, 'so loving to my mother', weak, a degree odd, lumbering awkwardly, perhaps, because of his internal tension, bitter, ill at ease in the world. Dad was someone for whom I'd always felt a little sorry. I'd even looked after him a bit. We got on okay, he and I, now I was long grown up and away from home, now that we met only occasionally, socially. His hadn't been an easy life, by all accounts.

But life-threatening sexual assault...? On me? How old had I been, for Christ's sake? With what frequency had it happened? You remember the pair of little oil paintings you liked at that first exhibition of mine — with the poor abused and debauched Child lying like a foetal ghost in the moonlit landscape beneath the chalk hills? I knew that was why he was hiding there, though it looked to anyone else like some lost kid just curled up. Those hills again, like my sepia sequence. I did it before any of this. I did it without knowing.

But is that where I'm still buried somehow? Under the chalk hills of a Chiltern childhood — Dad taking me up to Ivinghoe Beacon to fly the brown paper kite he'd made for me, and I terrified by the soaring speck in the high wind on the ridge, begging him to wind it in, crying and panicking because it was all suddenly out of control...

So vicious an attack, mimed by my own hands. Do you see how it threw me, how it forced the hard, grainy tears out at last. Why, he'd never loved me at all, must have hated me, rather; I, loving back, had been his dupe.

Theo, the nurse had other breakfasts to deliver. So there was only the winter morning outside and the wintry mood within. How I'd have liked to have discussed the whole episode with my consultant, to have seen similar case histories, or to have known the final validity of 'trance'. None of these was available. The consultant was hostile, as I mentioned, and I, like others at that time, was right at the frontier of treatment. From under the hills of America and UK, countless 'Children', once long ago seemingly Pied Pipered away, were suddenly seeking to return. Therapeutic consulting rooms experienced a flood of refugees, asylum seekers from dramatically remembered incestuous abuse. Society had no idea what to make of them.

And we were our own worst enemies, of course, conflicted, dysfunctional and thrust along Kafkaesque corridors. Once, at a morning 'group', when I tried to suggest to other patients what I was now being treated for, my jaw physically seized up. Truly, my mouth clamped shut; the muscles went rigid. It was astonishing.

The nurse helped me speak; but when I eventually got out my whispered blurt, some woman actually ran from the room. 'There,' I said to the nurse — the same one with the scrambled egg — 'I should never have spoken. I should have kept it all quiet. It can only cause trouble.'

Yes, telling's hard. More than the punishment, there's the belief one carries a fatal cargo — like the Ancient Mariner — and that the mere knowledge will destroy the listener. In this case, you. Then there's the fear of opprobrium. All of these, my friend.

Nevertheless, Mitchell and I went on. Within the blinds-drawn safety of a little glass cabin — it was newly built against a wall in the clinic garden, far from prying eyes — and in the warm security of his presence, my torso began, virtually without prompting, to convulse and to display what appeared to be really quite appalling assaults. And not to the mouth, now. Each time, I feared the episode would go on and on for ever if I didn't wrench myself out of it. Yet, to my surprise, it always ended in a panting pattern of my breathing that sounded uncannily like someone's orgasm — certainly not mine, for I was remote and mortified. I felt not the slightest bit aroused by the whole revolting business.

And so it seemed that the very frequent panting bouts I was by this time experiencing — like a dog — had finally resolved themselves into a 'message' rather than a symptom. I mean that the symptom had first begun to appear about a year previously. But, by this latest stage of my experience, panting would appear as soon as I'd got the children off to school and turned up at the clinic — on whichever of the few days in the week my consultant had left me; out of his own attack on my entitlement.

Clearly, not every doctor at the clinic was comfortable, either, with so noisy a symptom, Theo, nor every nurse; nor indeed every other patient. I'd often find myself panting even in 'Group'; and once a senior staff nurse suggested rather tartly that she was sure I could control it if I wanted to.

But I replied with equal force that the place was a psychiatric clinic, wasn't it, and why should I suppress my symptoms.

They were important to me, which was why I'd never take medication, no matter for the pain or the longing to die. My symptoms were the only thing to suggest to me that what was coming up might be true; I'd spent a lifetime suppressing them, and look where that had landed me!

Nevertheless, I can see in all fairness that my florid panting and dramatic mimes posed a medical problem. Doctors and nurses are sworn to relieve suffering. I was just fortunate—*I* call it fortunate— that Mitchell also agreed to let my symptoms go unsuppressed. And hence gave them the chance to surface. Even if I refused to believe what they appeared to demonstrate.

So it happened that every time I saw Mitchell, and every time we allowed the panting and the muscle contractions to run their course, I was, effectively, raped. And that *did* become too much, turning therapist almost literally into *the-rapist*—you know the old joke (an unfair one, I hasten to add. People are so suspicious of psychotherapy; I assure you Mitchell was just a decent guy trying to help).

And all the while there was something in my head that only inflicted more illness and punishment for allowing such things to be shown. I was a hostage to it, and I still 'remembered' nothing at all.

Mitchell wouldn't be beaten. He returned to the hands and switched to a gentler question and answer technique. 'What percentage of the story have we got so far?' The hands moved on thirty, and we were both surprised. For what more could there be? What worse than we already had?

Suffice it to say that Mitchell's sensitive questioning elicited details of deeds darker and nastier. We turned up modes of Dad's sexual sadism I can't presently bring myself to describe, even to you. In myself, I remained none the wiser, though continuously, as I say, very ill with panic and depression; during which my eternal scepticism would always seal things over once more, like a scab, leaving me unable to put two and two together, convinced I was the vilest of men and making things up. For these new matters strained credibility even further, and I was the more apt to dismiss it all as fantasy, or some brain disorder.

Except that I painted as never before. Indeed, after an interval, while still very ill, and all because of Mitchell, my painting career took off, as you know—and with your invaluable help, of course. It was through the clinic and through you that a door opened miraculously for me into the art world. Because I found ways to get around myself and paint, at last, genuinely from within. And you'll see by now how painting, too, is a trance; how painted *absence* in the self-portrait with which I began this exchange of emails is intimately connected to this same seemingly absent 'Child', who struggled so hard through my physical denial towards a kind of birth.

Last night, I went down to the cove, picking my way in the dark through thorns and wild herbs. The night smells were intense, sage and wild thyme, and the insects at full volume. I clambered over rocks, under stars, stood on the patch of shingle, peering out. No ships, only a few human lights on the leftward promontory, the high castle's silhouette, the warm wind. I stripped off down to my rubber wet-shoes, and waded in, alert to slips and jags.

I gave myself to the element, swam far beyond our little jutting outcrop on the right, then turned around, treading water, to stare at our home, a black landmass. The moon was a thin lunar blade. The sea, my own hands slicing its surface, was silvered. At dead of night, Theo, the element becomes silken, suddenly more opaque below and all the deeper. At night, this benign, tide-less tide fills up like Oceanus with sea snakes, sharks, the trailing stings of jellyfish. Its currents beneath my feet wake malice, luminous-eyed, a cold logic in faint electric voices, limbless clicks.

Night swimmers are buoyed up on death.

But don't worry. No, don't worry, Theo. I was out there no more than ten, twenty minutes and with no other purpose than a dip.

I've simply tried to present the facts. Have I answered you?

Subject: (S)Hades — the play inside

Explosive? Yes, you've hit it! Enact. Mime. Let symptoms play themselves out, rather than suppress, dismiss, or medicate them: that is what's so controversial, isn't it. Very dangerous game, like all such subterranean visits. Oh, we can just about accept post-traumatic stress disorder after combat or disasters. But after childhood? Yes, *exactly*, Theo. Mental illness. Where draw the line? I tell you, people don't like it. The medical profession doesn't like it. Society doesn't like it. Let alone the arts. They *hate* it!

Yet all I've done is to describe the plain facts of what happened to me — *exactly* what happened. I made notes after each session — when I could move, that is — and I promise I haven't embroidered or invented anything. I do still remember, accurately and in detail, what I experienced there with Mitchell; indeed, it was a point of honour to record and remember as much as I could, because I saw just how explosive it was.

You call it a most terrible story. Certainly terrible that anyone should do all that to a child. Or even think of it. Theo, I'm grateful for your condolences and moved by your sympathy; although I still feel a fraud for receiving it. I feel as though it happened, if at all, to someone else.

But you're very sharp on these tell-tale contradictions. Maybe you already guessed at some of these matters in my previous work—you and I have always steered clear of the explicit questions, haven't we, as if by unspoken agreement. Yes, my career began with a gamble. I backed what came out of me. I did it privately; I didn't tell anyone. And it paid off without my having to go into detail. I mean publicly. And then you took *your* gamble on me.

And certainly our western tradition is chock full of agony: all those crucifixions and martyrdoms. So this latest set of disclosures should have done the trick, shouldn't they. Just, as you say, to find ways maybe to heighten the suffering in my face on Bledlow. To acknowledge it, you suggest. The body, too. To 'install' the pain in the portrait—I like your word. It implies something conscious and calculated, and in a way detached, as though I didn't have to believe it in order to do it. Maybe a suggestion of even darker circles around the eyes; or is that too literal. I'm being flippant. I remember as a young man I did wonder why they'd appeared!

Then you point out how I seem to be making sketches of my time in Paris and little portraits of myself without batting an eyelid. But aren't they perhaps quick and small enough to sneak under the radar? They're of being someone else, and I feel I've been far more concerned in them with the application of paint—trying to get that brushless depth Spíros showed me—and not with who's holding the brush itself.

But, dear Theo, I'm afraid that if you really want this Bledlow picture out of me, the full portrait, then there's something more you still need to know about my treatment. It concerns *exactly* that one question: who's holding the brush? It concerns Josh Levinson.

A man rode out of the West. Levinson was my American consultant—consultant in a more benign sense of the word than my unpleasant English one. Josh Levinson was a top U.S. practitioner. He'd really taken up the cause, and he visited England now and then to teach. Mitchell, who knew him, asked me if I'd be a guinea pig. It was about a year into my treatment, and we were still at an impasse. Most of our work was about how to deal with the everyday problems that would continually tip me into panic or desperation. But I can feel even today how, when Mitchell would ask if I could look at something in my head, my eyes would clamp shut so tightly it hurt—as though they were simply refusing to see.

So my guinea pig session with Josh... By very odd coincidence, it was to be held in the same university college—in London—where my father had taught. The other surprise was that it seemed from start to finish nothing more than an ordinary conversation.

It was a Saturday morning.

'Good to meet you, Owen. Let me first assure you I'm not going to touch you.'

'Hi,' I said.

Hand unshaken, I found myself standing on a low dais. All around us was an audience of therapeutic professionals. Yes, I recognised the lecture theatre from days with Dad. It was functional, scientific and 'sixties', all varnished pine and leatherette; quite the antithesis of my gnarled old clinic. And Josh had that Californian candour, a youngish face with warm brown eyes—I recall his high forehead, the hair just receding at the temples, his fine skin declaring the permanent outdoors.

What should I care if he touched me? Anyone could approach me, Theo, and clap me on the shoulder. I wasn't, for heaven's sake, a basket case.

Yet he wondered what would it take for me to feel safe talking to him? And the words 'a barrier, lead-lined' tumbled out of my mouth before I could think.

He nodded, smiled, and I felt such a fraud again: constructed to construct myself into the role of victim. I wondered what details of my case Mitchell had given him. Did Levinson know of my reservations about all this? And what proper detachment, if any, had he enjoined upon those watching?

But I took my chair on the platform, and my smiling inquisitor sat facing me. I just glimpsed Mitchell at the video camera before Josh began: 'How are things going? How are you feeling now?'

I said I wanted to die. I said I saw nothing worth living for. If it hadn't been for my children...

Was I willing to have him help me? Did I want to get free? 'I mean get free of the bastard who did this to you?'

He'd badmouthed my dad. I bridled inwardly. I thought of the only story I knew of Dad's childhood. My cousins had gleaned it from my aunt: of Dad being forced by our seafaring grandfather to eat his own vomit. Christ!

But Dad had told me nothing himself — beyond a kindly one-off in the presence of my mother when I was five: 'Both Mummy and I had unhappy childhoods, and we want things to be different for you.' Surely, he'd done his best.

And both of them, my parents, now, according to my mother, 'sexually abused' — whatever that meant. Dad deserved my sympathy, not these continual vile accusations. What was I doing here?

Yet I nodded and said yes. And Josh and I must have talked a little, establishing the 'rapport' I was fully expecting. But I was... how shall I describe this — I *must* have been almost immediately *entranced* without realising; for time did pass oddly. So skilled a practitioner! I mean before I knew it, he'd pulled a fast one. It came curving out of left field. Had I ever felt there were different people inside me?

Blatant leading of the witness, Theo — I wanted to cry foul! What was he up to, launching straight in about 'the Parts'? Yes, we've all seen films about multiple personality. We know these fables of identity. We knew, even in the early nineties, about fracture by abuse: broken pieces of soul that take on a character within one's 'character', every shard of the holograph retaining a value of the whole. I'd even researched the subject myself in times past.

But here, now, in me? *If* I'd brought it up; *if* a case were ever established against my old man; *if* the matter were indeed so sadistic as my enactments had suggested; *if, if, if... then* such a matter might have been up for discussion! Springing it like this, right here on a Saturday morning... I should have been outraged.

Theo, what rose up instead was a species of joy, because, of course, I did have people inside me. They were the *dramatis personae* of my apprenticeship — witness the group in the *Internment* painting in my Chiswick studio, the one the thugs destroyed. Witness, too, now that *we*'ve brought them to mind, my particular Paris shape-shifts and the whole life of an actor.

But, as I spoke to Josh, the Parisian escapade was all but forgotten, especially the internal dramatization of the *Lion* play — yes, I've just remembered the title. And that old *Internment* painting was certainly the last time I'd deliberately shown them to myself, the People, at least with my right hand.

They'd acquired generic names once. Before all this. It was during the late seventies, I think — again, after Paris and before Lily. No, I'm not sure. It doesn't matter. They were: the Girl, the Headmaster and the Angel — plus the Child himself, now, of course. Of whom I'd had a fleeting glimpse in my work with Mitchell. And the Wolf or Dog, the, hitherto missing, panting one, had also appeared in the Clinic. Perhaps others.

'So you knew all about them before I asked you?' Josh asked.

I told him I had no rapport with them; I found them strange and incomprehensible. But if my painting work felt eternally blocked in my own right, it took off when I was someone else. I said I'd recently portrayed myself as 'the Girl' using the painter's mirror trick, and she'd had the Wolf as companion, her hand resting on his chained collar. Behind her, in many of my 'Gentileschi' paintings — you and I were just then in negotiation for my first show — stood a powerful Biblical figure like the Headmaster.

Theo, I'd *tried* to tell Mitchell about the Girl — perhaps the same crazy figure as in that dream — but he'd been uncomfortable. She was only me 'dressed up', he'd said. So I'd kept quiet, because, to my mind, her existence had always been an artistic rather than a pathological phenomenon, anyway. Every man has a female side; it was Jung, the archetypes, the *anima*. It was Blake, female 'emanations'. It was 'normal'. At least so I'd thought until one of our marital therapists had definitely raised an eyebrow at my secret and constant childhood cross-dressing. That had suddenly made me pay attention to it all.

But certainly not for me those distraught, disintegrated folk in the movies, producing 'personalities' like so many rabbits out of a hat. My inner characters had always been to me more like that feature you find in certain writers: Hardy, say, or Richardson again, or, obviously, Shakespeare — in whom an identifiable group plays out some meta-drama throughout the author's oeuvre.

You see it with artists, too: Picasso — though in the nature of our medium the feature tends to be diffuse. Not that I compare myself to greatness, you understand; but, by my account, my 'Girl' and the others had simply been the figurative foundations of my work, and using them was just what artists did! Which was why I'd never made a song and dance about them, except sometimes flippantly: signing myself off in several names at once in letters to friends, saying to people I could feel another personality waiting to come through... Odd, trivial things like that, years before.

Josh's question, nevertheless, speared like the sun. I listed their characteristics, and it was suddenly as though I'd kept vividly in touch with them. Which I definitely hadn't, Theo, because marriage to Lily had meant I'd buried most of them for years. Well, my role in that marriage was effectively female and housewife-ish, but I'd never made any sense of it; or really established the connection. No, Josh genuinely unearthed the Parts, and did it without my even realising.

And this is surely the way of memory, that when it *is* recovered, it's as though it's never been gone.

Maybe no smile reached my face, but deep inside I could feel my heart lift and sing. No one had ever asked about the inner people, the 'Parts', nor offered to take them seriously. It opened their prison gates. The Child was happy.

'I wonder, could you try something for me?' said Josh, smiling himself.

I nodded.

'Would you be able to gather all the parts together, the Wolf, the Girl, the Headmaster and the Child, and bring them towards the Angel?'

'In my mind?'

'In your mind.'

Theo, it was like herding ghosts. There stood the Angel, his glow fading, his wings suddenly faltering; here was my little party of masqueraders stumbling about in the shadows. They wouldn't budge. Besides, I felt at once that the whole nature of the Angel was terribly compromised — by that angel-rape sequence I'd done. Was the angel really 'good'? I couldn't be sure. Nobody could trust anybody.

'I can't. I'm sorry.'

Josh was ahead of me. 'That's okay. I wonder could you maybe think of an occasion when someone, or something, stopped you from being with other people.'

With Mitchell, my disbelief often out-guessed the therapist. The more I *tried* to see, the more I'd shake my head, and dismiss as of no consequence whatever grotesque flitting things might squeak into my head.

But Josh must have well and truly hooked me, because an image came promptly on cue, a scene I'd honestly never accessed since the event. I was seventeen or so, and a concerned schoolteacher of mine, whom I'd liked very much, had phoned to invite me for tea that coming Sunday, at a country vicarage with his wife and father-in-law. My father was holding the receiver, giving him a hard time. 'Why?' he was saying. 'Why do you want him?'

'Let me, Dad,' I'd interrupted. I'd taken hold of the phone and got the directions. 'Yes, yes, I'd be pleased to come. Thanks very much. I'd love to.'

The memory, then, is of Dad standing there with the phone still in his hand, his face severe, his words aggressively protective because he thinks someone's trying to convert me to Christianity and he wants to put a stop to it.

Josh began to bring me out. Of what? I felt tricked. Was that *it*, a flash of Dad being curmudgeonly? How could that possibly help?

But then we came to his exegesis, and he began to include the audience. The scene with the phone, he acknowledged, contained absolutely no evidence of abuse. Of course not. It was indeed just a trivial moment from a far later period in my relationship with my father than any of the matters under question.

That was true: I hadn't been the least intimidated by Dad's behaviour with the phone, merely embarrassed at his rudeness, and then I'd done just what I wanted to — brushed his objections aside, and driven calmly to the vicarage on the Sunday, where religion, that bugbear of his, was never once mentioned.

Yet even *I* couldn't dispute the fact that the long buried incident had given us exactly what Josh asked for. Here was an image, promptly to order, of someone or something that had tried to prevent me from being with other people, people I liked, who cared about me. It was Dad himself.

Josh spread his hands. 'We have a collection of *known* parts, internal characters that Owen can't seem to move on. What if they're thwarted by another, far stronger entity, who has always, so far, lain *hidden*?'

I remember his warm West Coast tones, and there was the very faintest hint of triumph at what had happened. 'Let's call him the Father,' he said, 'because Dad was the guy who showed up today. And let's say that he, too, is a genuine part, a truly *missing* part, one we've discovered only here, today. But let's also say that this is a fairly typical finding in my experience of working with sexual abuse victims, and that his function is literally — as in our example — to keep Owen from getting close to anyone.'

I heard sounds from the audience.

Josh sat back in his chair and looked out. 'You may be asking what is this business of multiplicity, anyway?' He shook his head.

183

'Remember, a child experiencing incestuous abuse is still a child, and children are naturally problem solvers, thinkers. Children are dramatists, too: they make up characters all the time. What better way to deal with the shocking abuse of trust, what better way simply to survive, than by making up, creating, surrogate selves to go down and take your part on that stage, as it were, to suffer the crime being enacted, and to experience and contain the horror of it?

'And what more imperative, afterwards, than to *leave those selves behind*?

'Just as, after a tragedy, the actor hangs up his mask, or removes his costume and make-up and returns to everyday society. Remember, the incestuously abused kid has always to "act normal" in everyday situations, so as not to give the game away.

'As practitioners, you'll recognise, all of you, I'm sure, the phenomenon of dissociation, itself a hypnotic, or self-hypnotic, function. By dissociation, by leaving the trauma behind, the elements of the abuse become distributed, compartmentalised, psychologically sealed off. That way,' Josh gestured towards me, 'we can perhaps understand Owen's Girl and his Wolf. They're coping identities. But what interests us here today is why he should ever have made such a secret creation as the fellow we've just identified, whom we called "the Father".' He turned to me, 'Why would you do that, if your dad was *in reality* the very person who'd raided and terrified you?'

'Quite,' I said.

He shook his head again. 'Why should any child choose, by making a policing figure in exactly the image of the abuser, to live in spiritual loneliness and isolation, keeping himself—or more often than not *her*self—cut off from the warmth of other people? For life. Aren't we here to tackle these... bastards? Don't we all feel an extreme repugnance at any idea of the abuser himself being internalised?'

There were nods and coughs.

'Quite,' I said again, softly.

Here came the hypothesis. Josh predicated the formation of *all* the parts on the need to survive the abuse. But the most crying need was for the secret to be kept. The secret of the abuse threatened, if it ever came out, to destroy the victim's life support. It threatened the child's only possible source of love, the family.

Logically, then, and despite appearances, he said, *all* the parts, including the tyrant—the internal denier—could have only a benign function for the child who'd conjured them up. 'We have to remember,' he explained, 'that the child to whom incestuous abuse is happening has just the world supplied by the abuser and his family to build from. Nothing else. So we mustn't judge him, or her, if the image of his ultimate defender is modelled on the violence he's been shown—by the abuser himself. Or herself,' he added. 'Because women also abuse, sometimes.'

He looked around him, holding everyone rapt, including me. The main road outside hummed with traffic, but we heard little of it. 'Everybody,' he said, 'we must all of us keep in the forefront of our minds the point I've already made: that this 'Father' part is *not* the abuser—one can't internalise a real person. Owen, here, hasn't got the perpetrator living inside him. And we're not talking evil spirits—or vampires! It's merely a self-protective image, an icon, if you will, fashioned out of the most frightening person the victim has to hand. As we've said, the only function of such a creation *must* be positive and not the negative it appears. It *must* be simply to ward off further danger—either from attack by others, or from decent people finding out what's been going on.' He paused. 'What does this mean for us, who're trying to help?'

Silence.

'It means that a very powerful force, left over from childhood but still active, will do all he can to keep Owen away from us. He sees us as dangerous—to Owen, to Owen's family, to Owen's survival. That creates great difficulties for any therapeutic intervention, of course. But it also means that he—it's mostly a he—can be reasoned with.

'Do you see the difference? Real-life perpetrators, the bad guys, abusers, bullies, torturers and dictators know that if they ever let go of power, if ever they come out of their family fortresses, their political gangs, their crooked empires and failing states, then the exposure of their crimes will instantly convict them.

'The interior figures, by contrast, no matter how monstrous they *seem*, are children themselves. We must treat them as such, as determined, needy children. We mustn't seek to punish them. We mustn't hold up our hands in horror when we find them. We mustn't hate them. Despite their often fearsome appearances, they're only trying to keep safe the traumatised self, in the only way they know. By a kind of internal violence, they're trying to keep the real self away from other people.

'And so, you see, the therapist *can* succeed with them. We *can* try to reassure them and draw them into dialogue. We *can* try to prove to them that their draconian inner regime is no longer necessary, that things have changed, that little Owen has grown up, that it really is safe now to let go and to let the Self, the truth, come out of hiding. Our task as helping professionals—as always, ladies and gentlemen—is one of creative negotiation.'

13

Subject: **Dawn of Gold**

I made a mask and hid it in a bag.

The play, Theo. It'll take me a page or two, no more; and then the players vanish, I promise. Into air. It is indeed a kind of empty heaven, yes, to parade the old, primitive icons of the people, wisecracking and dressing them up. Empty, insubstantial. A page or two, no more...

And yet this play is itself a kind of cardinal painting, a *Primavera* — a rite of Spring — whose powerful forces gather in a circle. But not around the maypole or phallic totem. Rather they dance around a central nothing: or at least a character so vague and ambivalent as to amount to nothing — myself. Played by Cécile, in this mask.

One morning, when Félix and I were at the café with the striped awning, I had the mask in a bag. I placed the bag on the table. 'It's a kind of fairy tale,' I told him casually. 'Symbols and nonsense. Not to your taste at all.'

'Eh?' He looked up from his pencil and paper. He was adding up our takings. 'What do you know about my taste?'

'Nothing, *patron*, believe me.'

'I believe only that you're mad, and an idiot.' He ignored the bag and offered me a cigarette. I took it, lit up, coughed and laughed. But then, almost as though on cue, he gave away the very thoughts I'd been formulating myself, though he spoke cloudily, as one simply musing aloud. 'Owen, *mon ami*,' he said, 'we balance on a knife edge.'

'We?'

'The company.'

'Ah. Money?'

'No.' He blew out his smoke and tapped the accounts in front of him. 'The money's good — for a change. Everything's good, in fact. Too good. Can it be too good in our business, Mr Englishman?' He pointed to the sun. 'Only half the season gone, and this unremitting... Such hot weather is a little crazy, don't you think? It forces the pace. There's an "air". I have a feeling.' He tapped his forehead significantly. 'The stabbing with Éméric was bad enough. Soon, something else will happen; someone else will burn out.'

'I'm sorry?' I hadn't understood the French.

187

He explained, and I saw my chance. Indeed, in an odd way, he'd fallen right into my design. I took the mask out of its bag. It showed a poignant face, Theo, quite small, divided half male, half female. 'It's from my roots,' I said. 'From Wales, *du Pays de Galles*. From your roots, too, for *Pays de Galles* is equally France, and we're brothers under the skin.' I smiled.

'*Merde, alors*!' He threw up his hands.

'A kind of fairy story. A myth—as I said.'

'What is?'

'My plan.'

'You propose…?

'A new direction, Félix. *Avant garde*. Political. And at the same time mysterious, absurd.'

'What, Ionesco? Beckett? It's been done. Almost old hat.'

'*Mais non*. It's an idea.' Now I tapped my own forehead. 'An idea almost fully formed.'

A laugh burst out of him. 'Fully formed, is it?' he said, sitting back in his chair to stare at me, then at the mask, and then back at me. Thick smoke curled from his nostrils. 'You're a dark horse, Owen. Am I to understand you of all people have a play for us?'

'It's nothing. A folly. Like I said, not to your taste at all.'

Now he leaned forward. 'Shouldn't I be the judge of that?'

'*Un petit geste*.'

'Tell me!'

'*Patron*, I hesitate even to trouble you with its name.'

'It has a name? Fuck you, tell me! The piece!'

Already he was soliciting the title and calling it a 'piece'. I drew smoke from my own cigarette until it glowed even in that sunlight. 'It's *about* naming.'

'And?'

I jerked the line. 'The name of the naming is *The Lion with the Steady Hand*.'

Too strongly. All the interest went out of his eyes. He snorted; for, Theo, the title sounds ridiculous enough in English, and you may imagine the hash I made of it in French. I remind you that when I report these conversations, my dalliance with them tends to smooth out the halts and limitations of my tongue.

'You're taking the piss.' He shifted in his metal chair and glanced back down at his calculations.

'But here, look.' I put the mask up to my face. 'It's a child—see!—

who can't decide whether he's a boy or a girl. And a witch' — now it was my turn to point up at the sun and then far away to a hypothetical moon — 'called Silver Wheel!'

He sat up again. Faces turned in our direction. I brought the mask down and handed it to him.

He turned it over in his hands. 'A fine thought.' He stared at me. 'And *Roue Argentée*, is it? Well, I don't know what you're talking about.' He stood up to go, reaching into his pocket. 'There.' He flipped out coins on to the table to pay for our coffee. '*Roues d'argent.*'

I stayed him and made him sit back down. 'Some nights ago, I woke from a dream. No matter for what; it was a bad one — I'm prone to them — heart thumping, cold sweat, compression of the chest. To avoid falling back into this dream, I kept my eyes open by staring upwards. It must have been, what, half past four — I don't know. Dawn was breaking, and there was a hint of light from the curtain edges. I could just trace a crack in the ceiling plaster, just catch the agitations of a spider mending her web in the corner. I listened to your deep slow breaths and that soft sound Cécile always makes in her throat when she's asleep.'

He smiled, despite himself.

'Suddenly, Félix, don't ask me how, this drollery, this old abandoned folk tale came into my mind, so vividly, do you know, that I saw its episodes almost projected above me. At first, I dismissed them. But they returned. I thought of other things. They persisted. Then I started enjoying them. At length, I began to wonder: could this be something for us, a drama, a *comédie*, yet all the while a romance, and with that again a political satire. My mind, you see, *patron* — Félix — was racing, and there came no more sleep for me that night. But, as you say, I am an idiot, and it's probably nothing, so far away from our usual stuff. I suppose our masks must have set something in train...'

And *you* will see, Theo, how intently I was selling it to him; just as I appear now to be selling it to you.

Or was it my body trying to sell it to *me*? For I say it yet again: all art comes from the body, and the play *is* the portrait, the portrait of *absence*, shall we call it — since we're searching for what is exact, with your demands, your detective insistence, your strange curiosity? I'm not used to it.

But indeed I was in earnest, hoping to reel him in just when I seemed most casual and offhand. If I wasn't careful, he might refuse

189

point blank, and this mounting urge to see my story brought to life by our mountebanks and ragamuffins—who subsisted, barely, in the twilight of Paris and on the very fringes of society, playing over again (albeit with the addition of a few of my fairy masks) only what they were accustomed to: the old man, his daughter and her lover, the rivals, the doctor, the smart employee, his girl and his boss—would be lost. And I with it.

'Well?' he spread his hands.

'It is something of the north,' I said, 'of the forgotten. Something beyond the edge. Magical. And you see, Boss, as I lay in my bed looking up, so Cécile curled herself against you, and her breathing grew gradually calm and deep; and I saw on the ceiling the pair of you and all our... family in "The Lion with the Steady Hand". And I was the missing part. Then, just as I tried to catch hold of what that might be, and how my small role sharpened the thing to a point, the sun rose and a burst of light from the window put an end to my scheming. And the vision was gone. Maybe. Yet I shall work it out. You see if I don't!'

He stood up a second time, and that was that. We left; and there was no more talk of this '*piéce*' in the days that followed. Normal rehearsals continued in the warehouse every afternoon—as I imagined they always had—and necessity drove us to perform each night, except for our languid Sundays.

But the bait had been taken. Félix was intrigued despite himself, and I knew he'd come back to me.

Alors, everyone was already pleased at our slight shift in repertoire, and takings stayed up. And all was absorbing; and exhausting enough to keep at arm's length, still, the chagrin that had brought me here— Julia's betrayal. Biding my time, I told myself how lucky I was both to find my feet and lose my cares in these quick-fire stories we made. That in itself was a fairy tale.

So we went on, Theo, for at least another couple of weeks.

Then, at last, and to my gratified surprise, Felix returned to my play. He said he'd been thinking about it. 'The *Lion*, Owen. Well?'

So let's approach. What exactly was this 'Lion with the Steady Hand'—or *Lion, Tireur d'Élite*, as the title became in our version. Google it, Theo. It has echoes of Robin Hood, or the Biblical David, and I'd found it first as a student. It's in Robert Graves's book *The White Goddess*, that breathless monument to idiosyncrasy. Google that, too. An argument of obscure myths, the 'Lion' story being one fragment among many.

It's an argument of barking nonsense, of course. Poor Graves. Poor all of them, his whole brutalised, Spartanised generation. Graves postulates a religion of infatuation and betrayal that seems merely to enshrine his experience of sex after the trenches; and the flatness of his subsequent poetry reveals the thesis of *The White Goddess* as a supreme intellectual folly. It simply allows him to mythologize away the cruelty of Laura Riding, his self-obsessed lover. No matter what you tell yourself, you can't write good love poetry about someone your body must, of necessity, detest.

Theo, I think of those other artists and poets who survived Armageddon: the Nash brothers, William Roberts, Gertler, Sassoon, Blunden *et al*. Graves knows them all, mentors some; he marries Ben Nicholson's sister, for heaven's sake. His influence is colossal. His readings of modernist poetry inspire Empson's. By the fifties, Hughes and Plath owe a debt to him. When I was an art student, folk still took him seriously as a critical tool. I remember his ruggedly smiling features, his assured, outrageous classicism. I tell you, Graves gave the impression of having got over his shellshock. *Goodbye to All That* seemed, as the title suggests, to put a line under nightmares, flashbacks and panic fugues. Yet maybe his PTSD remained the most florid of them all. Maybe poor RG stayed mad as a hatter—taking himself off to a Mediterranean island and living in a perpetual dream of the past where reality could never again impinge upon him.

But for 'all that', why, as I languished in Paris, did *The Lion* so captivate me? I could say nothing to Félix, when I'd explained the story of it.

'What is this stuff, Owen? My God, it's impossible. Absurdity upon absurdity. I was crazy to listen to you. No theatre in the world could ever contain such a farrago. And no one would understand it if it did.

I begged him to suspend disbelief. 'Let me have only one afternoon with the company. If I don't convince them—and you—I'll let it drop. I promise you.

He stamped under the table and twitched a little more. Then he turned back. 'Bastard! Oh, very well. In four days' time. That's next Tuesday, isn't it? You can have all afternoon. But if it's a fiasco, Owen...'

I took note of the threat left hanging in the air. The fact was I had no idea exactly how I was going to turn the love story that was haunting me, full of strangenesses, of shape-shifting, ambiguity and rebirth, into the viable political drama I'd pitched to him.

At last, I took a risk and spoke to Marie-José. 'Listen, I've got three more days to make a whole show, or I'm out on my ear.'

She stared at me, her grey-olive eyes wide in her fine, slim face. I remember the noonday traffic beside us and the light flooding down on the wide pavement, the railings, the dusty Metro sign for the Gare d'Austerlitz.

'I don't know what to do,' I said. 'It's here in my head, but I can't get a grip on it.'

'What are you talking about?'

'I can't tell you. Help me. I want you to help me.'

'You're hopeless, Owen.' She put her arm on my shoulder.

I dashed my hand at my eyes, laughing. 'You'll see, Marie-José. If I can just...'

She silenced me, laughing too. We embraced—as we often did, working so closely together.

Then we walked into the Jardin des Plantes. Theo, I recall noticing how, in the beautiful avenue, the leaves above were still and lifeless from the drought. 'Félix will fire me if I don't pull some rabbit out of the hat. Then where will I be? In the gutter? In England?'

She touched my shoulder again; her long, delicate fingers, her expressive hands. 'What's the matter with you? Félix won't fire you. You two are thick as thieves. And you work so well together. You must know he relies on you.'

'Relies on me?'

'Everyone sees.'

I relaxed just a little. We sat down on a bench, the tall, dark-haired girl and I in my clinging, misleading clothes. There were ducks on the shrunken water. Animals honked and screeched in the zoo not far away. I tried to tell her my plot; it defeated both of us. Nevertheless, her words had struck a chord, and suddenly a character I'd improvised one rehearsal with Félix popped inspirationally into my mind. I'd played a petty tyrant who'd both surprised and horrified me with his force. I hadn't known he was in me—a direct antithesis to my soft exterior.

With that tyrant, in a flash, was born the play's *raison d'être*. I saw a Parisian dreamscape with echoes of '68. There'd be a whip-handed capitalist bossing a stable of actors—just as Sun King Louis's chief of police once 'owned' the *Comédie Francaise*. I'd play him myself as a kind of arch-Félix: a little satire on our leader. The company would appreciate that, and it would sell my play to them! Almost instantly, I had the character's name: Flea — *Puce* — a diminutive title that belied his great bloodsucking power. But, to bring our enterprise to life, I'd cast Félix himself as the actors' champion who, in the spirit of those players of the old *foires* he so admired, would lead his fellows against my dull, artistic tyranny and propose a radical new direction in the shape of *The Lion with the Steady Hand*.

I hugged Marie-José in relief and kissed her cheek. She kissed me back — on the lips. We smiled, surprised, and I laughed. Then we got up and looked about us at the lawns and trees, and hurried back for rehearsal. But I left her at the door to our warehouse and took myself off to the river with pencil and paper. There was no time to lose.

I worked all over the weekend, beside the river, in odd corners, in the bar and late into the nights at the table in Cécile's kitchen. By noon on the fourth day, I had the bare bones of a script. Scripts are anathema to an extempore company; but Félix got me copies made somewhere, though he'd had no time to read it himself.

I remember that still-sweltering afternoon. The warehouse walls oozed their stale storage smells, and my colleagues gathered in knots, talking, smoking, stretching. There were no absentees; even bandaged Éméric showed up, now thin and melancholic. Then Félix sat us round in a ring, and people looked at each other with puzzled faces. How nervous I was when he handed the floor to me.

But I'd planned the moment. We had amongst our properties an old tail coat and a black opera hat. I put these items on and launched into my character. 'Up, you dogs!' I cried. I took a belt for a whip and cracked it at them against the floor. 'Up now! *Levez-vous, connards*!'

To say they were astonished is to understate the case. Here was their Owen, the tentative parvenu, the quasi-transvestite idiot who'd been for so long scarcely more than a passenger, now suddenly turned fire-eater. I confess, Theo, I had some flavour in my mind of that domineering Lautrec ringmaster — and of Beckett's Lucky and Pozzo, of course. All to the good; my friends shambled to their feet, half accepting, half resenting the illusion.

I told them, as I would in the play itself, they were all shirkers and lazy slackers. They looked blankly. I chided them, cracked my whip again. One or two began to catch on. There were grumbles, audible curses. 'You!' I said. 'I rescued you from the gutter. I did! I saved you from starvation and the streets. Now you know where you stand, you know your roles and you'd better perform them well if you want to eat. For I'll brook no idlers nor freeloaders, tolerate no complaints! Just

remember how it was before. Eh? Do you want to go back to all that?'
I slashed my belt across Dmitri's back.

But then, as I stalked to one side, Felix leapt in. And he began
immediately whispering of *Lion, Tireur d'Élite*, as though it were a
talisman, a code name or password. He gathered them all around him
in a conspiratorial huddle. Then he handed out the copies.

And yes, Theo, the charm works: the action does come back, the
immersion of writing begins to project those images again upon the
walls of my mind exactly as I'd hoped. The players do rebel. They do
put on the new and challenging play—as an act of defiance. And
Cécile is once again the sacred child Llew—i.e. Leo—the 'Lion' child
who springs large as life from a casket of imprisonment. Cécile it was
who wore the mask of half boy and half girl, her sudden red leotard
and Lincoln green jerkin a sexy draw to the crowd. I can see her now,
so swift and mischievous, her movement almost shape-shifting, her
tours de scène seemingly without locomotion.

'I am the Lion, the sharpshooter,' she would declare. 'My perfect
aim can split the leg of a wren. I am a story of birds and animals. But,
oh, you are the witch Silver Wheel—*la sorcière, La Roue Argentée*.' And
that was Marie-José, who with her height and presence and her moon
mask against that curling, spilling raven hair, would hold Cécile and
Félix, the poet-wizard, trembling in her gaze, transfix the audience,
too. 'The child is not mine. I will never accept him, never name him.'
An *impasse*, until a shimmer of Félix's counter magic makes Cécile,
masked, fleeting, ambiguous, reappear from another quarter to taunt
the witch. Who retires, for the moment, vanquished.

Then I'd jump up from behind the cart, lift my top hat and prowl
the arena as though I still owned the city. I'd crack my whip with a
scowl and intone in my sinister foreign accent: 'Back to your work you
rogues and dogs, you sly creatures. I took you from nothing. And
without me you'd *be* nothing. Nothing, I say! Bah! You're not worth
your keep.'

And Cécile would explain in an aside to the onlookers, 'Look. Don't
you see? He's the brute who enslaves us, who keeps us all in poverty
and servitude. We mock him, call him Flea, the bloodsucking
parasite.' And so I snarled at them in my sombre tail coat, hunched
my cruel shoulders, ground my teeth behind my fat, plutocrat face
with its wicked moustache, and fired off a burst from my plastic
machine gun.

The crowd hissed and booed. And when, in the mid-point of the action, I managed to force my characters to labour at a mill (using one of the bicycles on its side and a couple of sticks), I'd flick a switch on the battery in my pocket at the exact moment the poor slaves ground their capstan — which they did with wonderful contortions of strain — and a ring of torch bulbs concealed in plastic ivy would light up around my hat brim, showing my credit from the toil of others. The audience roared.

Zig was the rival lover; Dmitri a kind of brilliant universal for stone or tree, courtier or executioner. And surely it was Minalouche whom we pretended to puff up with a foot pump like a sex doll as the Bride of Flowers — Blodeuwedd — how well that went down. And it was Félix who both enacted the revolution, turning my own weapons against me, and who also played so cunningly Gwydion/Woden, the philosopher, intellectual, poet and original magician:

> *Pendant les nuits, j'ai étudié –*
> *Pour gagner mes puissances –*
> *Et maintenant vous me volez*
> *Toutes mes jouissances...*

And so it was that we were going out in public with the show, and were a triumph for at least a month, pulling a pretty girl out of the crowd each night and making a happy ending via a little impromptu marriage. And after that the thing was gone, finished, *kaput*, for its final form was never written down but stored only in our body memories — just as the old ballets and interludes of the past live on only so long as there are new generations to learn them — by sheer bodily imitation.

So my play just flew off, like a dream, into the ether, never to be heard of again. And where are we all now? And however did so chaotic a plot so work upon its hearers?

I can't tell you, for I was only part of it, and the part cannot comprehend the whole.

Subject: **Implacable kingdom**

Mitchell saw me to the door. The warmth and, indeed, the unaccustomed interest that I'd just been shown ended abruptly. I was out in the cold. But I understood at once, Theo, the enormous significance of what I'd just experienced. Josh had fished out a key figure, the 'Father', the 'Tyrant'. It *was* the key figure, the one that was holding me back—then and presumably still now—an idea I'd never heard tell of in any other psychiatric source, neither from Mitchell nor in my own reading. And I've never heard it since.

But he was surely right; the role of such an internalised 'Father' would indeed be crucial. What would have happened to my family if, as a young child, I'd let anyone else see 'the Others'? I mean the Parts, of course: maybe in the pictures I might have drawn as a child, or in my too-precocious sexuality, my regular dressing in my mother's clothes or exposing myself to other six-year-olds—or both. What would have arisen from a revelation of such secrets to the social milieu, or to school?

I remember there was occasionally such leakage; maybe 'the Father' was never in full control. And maybe that was why Dad kept us moving from place to place, job to job. Awkward questions could have brought about the devastation of my mother and the removal of the man who was the only love I knew, my mainstay, my ironic help and protector in the dark terrors that racked my nights. Gaol for us both, I might have believed—he might have told me. Death for my mother, it may be that he threatened me—for that's how it came out with Mitchell, once. Better far to shoulder the guilt myself in an iron regime. So 'the Father' should keep me isolated. On my own island, if you will.

Did I see Mitchell's video of it afterwards? I couldn't face it. Or wouldn't. I knew he was disappointed about that, though he tried not to show it.

But let me spell this out, Theo: a lot of nonsense has been talked about multiplicity. It's plain as daylight that all models of mind propose some primary splitting: soul, will, head, heart, conscience and what have you. Freud and Jung hived off 'the unconscious' and then filled it with id, superego, shadow, persona and the rest. We all have sub-personalities; we all have conversations with ourselves. It's impossible not to think of the mind as a theatre! Even our clothes change our behaviour. We each fashion ourselves on our close family, like every other creature. We imitate bodily those we admire, both consciously and unawares. We adore acting. And that's why florid cases of multiple personality often lead us nowhere, except into a morass of uncertainty about who's kidding whom! In art criticism, too, Freudian theorists adopting the idea have particularly muddied the waters, starting as Freudians always do from false premises and blurring the difference between traumatic and non-traumatic effects.

No, Josh Levinson's demonstration on me that Saturday morning wasn't *about* the many facets of 'regular' human personality.

It *was* about their post-traumatic manifestations, however. I see that now. I've spent years thinking about it and trying to find the few bits of proper writing and research that are out there. Josh's lesson was startling. Through childhood abuse, the true Self retreats into hiding, and overall control is seized by a shadowy authoritarian part, modelled on the abuser.

This figure tries to shut up shop and stifle dissent, and that's what promotes the strange so-called 'multiple' dissociative effects, as the child grows into a teenager without a proper Self to take charge. Then other, split-off elements launch bids for power. It's like a failed state run by kids, who can neither cooperate nor trust each other. It's like *Lord of the Flies*, Theo. This distinction between healthy and post-traumatic; it's absolutely pivotal. Healthy folk have a central Self in touch with all the various faces of their personality, their 'parts'; but people from traumatic childhoods mostly have an absent Self and sometimes wholly dissociated 'characters'. They're the ones who become autonomous or semi-autonomous.

But I couldn't see that at the time. My friend, I was deeply conflicted about Josh's session with me. Nevertheless, I hope you'll grasp how pertinent it is to my Bledlow crisis and the subsequent visit to the icon painter. In Bledlow, I'm trying to paint someone that almost literally isn't there. Who's holding the brush? The true Self is still in hiding, his kingdom is still being run by the powerful others, his operations and employments in the world are still being managed under the masks of childhood 'coping people'. There we have it. No wonder the paint won't colour me!

Subject: Janus

What happened after Josh? I went down, far down, in fact. My mind went dark. I lost touch with all the Parts. Worse, I completely forgot the Angel. For years.

On Josh's instructions, Mitchell and I were to try to bring 'the Father' to the negotiating table—to reason with him and persuade him his harsh regime was no longer appropriate.

We did try. We tried for some months, but he was too strong for us; which is to say that my real self was so weak, so absent, that I failed utterly to marshal Josh's powerful insights against the Father's punitive scorn and scepticism: mine. In fact, even as that amazing session ended, and I wandered out from the building into the February streets of West London, I began to feel colder and more desperate than before. I remember sitting in a café over a tiny espresso cup, sensing all hope and excitement drain away with each bitter sip.

All this might have made me curse Josh for a fraud—the Father's idea exactly. Except that I clutched at one straw of faith. For he'd spoken of love, and—intellectually—I could see the problem: it was that I still didn't feel safe in my outward life. I still didn't know love, the subject of these letters. My life remained ruined, and nothing in it existed to disprove the childhood thesis that life without Dad—the one person whom I believed had loved me—was untenable. Dad's double face: both original protector and original violator, the angel dissociated utterly from the devil... Dad had been my refuge as a kid, far more than my mother, with whom I don't seem to have had much of a bond at all. I seemed to know no other love than Dad's. I would find no other love than Dad's.

And adult experience has proved that true, I suppose. Until Eléni, of course. No, it was always like one of those fairy tales—*Beauty and the Beast*. For only if I could find someone who would love me, do you see, could I prove the Father wrong: that there was in fact love in the world outside of Dad.

Ah, but the Catch-22 was always that the Father's whole rigid judicial function, according to Josh, was to keep me *away* from closeness of all kinds. So I'd always be steered clear of real love; while at the same time left, I have to add, ironically vulnerable to unforeseen predators because of the intolerable loneliness of a life without associates. What a bind!

And I've said not long ago, haven't I, that it's true: how the fact of the matter is that I really don't let myself get close to people. Though I hide this truth from myself and others by appearing almost perfectly functional socially. Which I'm not. So for all the revelation of my encounter with Josh, Dad still remained demonstrably right, his perverse scientific view of the world as a wretched, meaningless place all the more vindicated. Why should I place any trust in Mitchell or Josh, or therapy in general? Oh yes, 'the Father' went to work with a vengeance.

Subject: The deepest circle

You genuinely want to know? I got three years. Three more years, that is. I mean of severe depression, and God knows it felt like prison. Worst were the mornings, the hammer of despair coming down a second or so after waking, the empty bedroom stuffed with some poisoned psychic cloak I had each day to put on, just to get the kids to school, just to cook food for them in the evening. All movement slowed. My stomach churned; my blood ached. But it was nothing, and I was a fraud. At any time, I told myself, I could have got up, run and shouted with the next man.

I longed to die, but would still take no medication. Because I had to know the pain's fullness — like Odysseus strapped to the mast. Death sang. I conjured extinction every hour as the starving conjure meals, longed-for oblivion.

And thus, by indulging Death, I contrived to live; for I knew, as did Mitchell, and Josh, too, that survival was the only revenge. To endure, to survive with honour, to do what was right, decent and honest in the face of evil — that was the one remedy. Why, it was Christian, too, never mind Josh was Jewish and I was something uncommitted. Survival was a duty to everything, to my kids, to their absent, troubled mother and to my art. It was demanded. That knowledge makes you bear pain you couldn't deal with otherwise.

Nevertheless, Theo, for those years I saw only the ape in man — or woman. This was when the left hand paintings reached their apogee. Why not? I could do nothing with my right. This was when I ground out those 'team portraits', setting myself in faith one single constraint: that though I myself could neither work with them nor make sense of them, every picture should include them all: the benighted, Angel-less Parts.

Yes, their left hand world is almost entirely unlit. Their blacks, their deepest purples and ultramarines are ripped apart, and the torment of my people occupies only the rifts in colour. Where do they live? Where is this Cimmerian place? I've asked that question since my student days, when I first noticed the Parts in my work. And I've asked it all the more pointedly of late. Just what pocket of space/time, what hell, what unmapped region of the body or mind, do such dissociated shades occupy? I mean when they aren't out. I mean when they aren't seizing the executive function and running/ruining our lives.

At my lowest point, Theo, I painted that diagrammatic scene — the one I thought would prove my ruin on Kálymnos—and then drew the blackest, thickest ring around it. With that, I hid all the left hand paintings away: gave them to Mitchell to keep in his loft, miles away, in case 'the Father' sent, yes, the Thought Police to find them. Those were the precise terms I used.

The depression began to lift. My bloodstream felt a little cleaner. By '96, I'd had another spell in the clinic as an in-patient, but I'd responded more quickly. Josh reappeared in England; Mitchell videoed me at another session.

No college lecture theatre this time but a grubby community centre in East London, with an audience far smaller. For 'recovered memory' had become decidedly 'dodgy'. Do you remember? Officialdom and the press had joined forces; all therapists and 'survivor' groups were suspect. The arts establishment, if you recall, was particularly hostile, and government bigwigs had been appointed to report on the whole 'explosive' issue.

Nevertheless, Josh and I faced each other across the platform. We chatted as before, and the camera whirred. I told him ruefully how the fallout from our first meeting had given me such a hard time. 'Sorry to hear it,' he smiled. But I didn't question the validity of what we'd done, because I knew—I did know in my deepest core—that it made complete sense. Even if consciously I didn't believe it.

We returned academically to the Parts we'd elicited, Josh and I. We considered their possible functions: the Girl maybe to handle interactions with the male world; the Wolf to locate rage and the sadly inevitable sexual arousal; the Child, pallid, shimmering and always cruciform, his arms as though drawn out with ropes, a centre for the original pain; the Headmaster trying to keep the body from acting out, and the tyrannical Father guarding the secret. Still I had almost no idea of them, shades lurking for blood. They wouldn't speak to me, and we were getting nowhere.

So I mentioned the left hand paintings, including that most fearful one.

Josh's gaze sharpened. 'Who painted the black ring?'

'The Headmaster?' I muttered. 'Or maybe the Father?' I wasn't in a trance. Or was I?

'I'm going to set you two tasks, Owen. One is to find an alternative occupation for whoever drew that circle. The other is to have a celebration.'

Again, it was only afterwards I grasped what he was driving at.

That circle in the painting *was* the amnesia. How did I describe it to you—ah: *a ring of black so thick it suggested some intense gravitational toroid, a circular frame of almost cosmic constriction. Nothing contained within was ever supposed to leak out.* That painted black ring fought to suppress what the image exposed. Do you see, Theo? As I told you, nothing would persuade my internal tyrant to release his grip until he saw evidence of a love greater than Dad's, and I hadn't had much luck with relationships—to put it mildly. To be able to celebrate, to love, to trust the world; that's what it would take. It was the same philosophy as the clinic's: to take a glimpse of Eden and bring it into your life. To make it spread.

At the same time, the brutal Father needed an alternative occupation, so that he didn't, in the pique of rejection, pull down the whole show on top of everyone. Naturally, I mean suicide.

But now, here, the internet... Evil deeds can no longer stay hidden. I feel the change, all kinds of crimes brought out of concealment. Matters shifted once before for me when the Berlin wall came down, when the Iron Curtain collapsed. And then there was the backlash. But now I feel hope again. Eléni and I, we'll work things out. We shall. The old regime will crumble in the new world's openness. The little Child will step forward from the grave he shuddered in, Theo, leading the other parts up into the light.

Subject: Champs Élysées

So long I've made you linger with me in this underworld. You and I, interrogating shades and ghosts together in this quest for *exactly*. We've seen heroes at their exercise and glimpsed, too, the pits of torment.

And now? I suppose I stand before you quite naked.

Don't laugh! You know those eighteenth century anatomy engravings where the subject peels back his own skin. Even so have I revealed my innards, my most private nerves and sinews.

Ha! You wanted the truth? I needed you to understand. I *needed* you to see *exactly* how it all works. I could only do so by telling the stories no one else wanted to hear.

People imagine desire is free. They can't conceive how some, given all the choice in the world, keep falling for the same misfortune. I point to that black sphincter in my left hand painting, a ring so intense it bars love out and traps only torture within. That gravitational ring shapes the world, shapes my life.

Even now, inside that ring, live the creatures of my underworld. Imagine it will you, once more. Now. Imagine a child faced in truth with outrageous assaults by the love giver. The child's only medium is the stuff of mind; his or her only tool the will to live. Maybe not the first time, nor even the second, but soon enough he learns the habit to take the medium of his own being and fashion from the abuse itself two separate worlds of good and evil—or die in that intolerable regime.

I tell you, the harsher the censorship, the more divinely inventive the child. At least Freud was right about that trade off! The child pastes cold, good, sainted icons of an ideal family in front of his eyes, and these exact his waking tribute. Behind them, in the underworld crypt of the body, of the muscles indeed, are pent the nightmare selves trying to play out the real time abuse and its aspects. Their terrified souls still wander the chalk hills of home, or drift far out into the remotest galaxies. Their existence, for the sake of the family, must never come to light. And who else can hoard them from view but their dark constrictor, fashioned in no other likeness than that of the abuser?

Voilà! Flea, in my Paris play! Flea, the parasite, whom I played myself, who sought tyrannically to control his company—of actors, Theo. Of Parts! You see! Played out all along as soon as I got to Paris. And in the midst of it I played the tyrant trying to stop them playing out a give-away story. For in Paris, stripped of girlfriend, family and employer—those ornaments of reason—I first learned, as we've now teased out, the body as medium. In Paris, before I knew or suspected a thing about Dad, I let the story smuggle itself through. The play: the loveless child, the gender confusion, the problematic mother, the sexual curse, the contrived marriage, the betrayal, the suggestion of dark, life-threatening deeds in an altered state, and the mind leaving the violently penetrated body in the form of a bird, who then remains in a permanently dissociated condition high in a tree, his wings flightless and his entrails gobbled at by a rooting sow?

Oh, to what lengths, Theo, must art venture to smuggle its image! For as much as the *Lion* answered the needs of my left hand, so Flea's canny political meta-structure masked or, with a figurative right, drew a ring of censorship around everything the play might reveal. Self-mockery and youthful radicalism washed it of all portraiture. For sure, no implication of my real father should ever leak out, even to me. Of my mother, perhaps yes, in the person of Arianhrod—Silver Wheel. But of 'that incestuous, that adulterate beast'—assuming such to be the case, Theo—no, not a whisper. I tell you, the drama, by now so deeply disguised and intricately convoluted, would show up as nothing more than a riotous, if perhaps thought-provoking, piece of carnival! And so it did.

But is that play, then, the very distillation we're seeking? The emblem of everything? The crystal at the centre? The supreme organising element around which this whole project of portraiture should coalesce? Can't we now simply assemble the failing Bledlow portrait out of its 'parts'?

Alas no. Alas, it's insufficient. Theo, my oeuvre-to-date is already a colourful and engaging drama of the Parts, which you've championed with your heart, perhaps without your head knowing quite why. And I, the perpetual fool of it, have continued to hide even as much as I've disclosed, dissembling, yes, smuggling in the horrible legend of my family often enough, but as though it were some distant folk tale, some 'fiction' that hardly touches me, almost an entertainment. And so it never gets to the heart of things. And people can still say it's merely imagination, isn't it, art, a pleasing adornment, a sensuous *divertissement*, a healthy relaxation, a vitamin supplement, an inessential *parergon* to the hard and scientific facts of life that really matter.

Which I don't believe. Because art—art in its proper sense, Theo—is the real thing. Art should be truth and not fiction. And that is dynamite. And you, by your belief and mounting enthusiasm would seem to agree, would seem to be intrigued and wish, as a true friend, but also a true patron of the arts, to drag the real thing out of me. But even now, I tell you, having stripped myself virtually to the bone in front of you, I still can't do it. Because telling isn't enough, and my Self, my true face, still seems to be a prisoner of some dark, Goddess-worshipping, pre-linguistic cave. And that's why these Paris paintings still encapsulate only my absence, the underworld summer of the Parts, my sterile multiplicity without centre.

Subject: **A sacred grove**

Yes, I do realise you're concerned. Alright, then, alarmed! 'The convoluted intensity of this writing,' you say. 'This persistent, chaotic

203

energy,' you call it. You suspect I'm mad. There's no need to. It's okay. I'm okay. I assure you I do take it all as seriously as I can; I've lived with it long enough. But I can deal with it. And Eléni's here to keep me on the straight and narrow. Bad the past may have been; we don't know. Yes, if you like, devastating, even. But I seem to have survived it, and now it's all very, very far away. Rest assured, I'm doing fine.

Listen, something just happened. As if the bees… I have to tell you.

The day began uneventfully enough. I designed the empty circle idea of the play; the dance of Spring. Then Marta picked me up at the corner again. 'You're a bad man, Owen. You should bring her. Look!' She indicated a bunch of roses on the passenger seat.

'Marta, Eléni has to work. She sends her apologies. But flowers! It's too kind of you.'

'It's nothing. My courtyard is full of roses.'

'Eléni's the one bringing in the money, I'm afraid, at the moment. UK office hours. You know how it is.' I got into the car, cradling the roses in my lap. I glanced at the back seat. No spacemen today, but a tiny old lady, her cheek browned and lined from the sun, staring away from me out of the rear window. She sat so prim and self-effacing she was almost lost in the car's upholstery.

'*Yeia sas, Kyría.*'

No reply.

I raised my eyebrows to Marta as she let in the clutch.

'Her name is Elpítha. It means Hope. She lives in her own world, but enjoys a change of scenery. In ours. So today we visit *my* bees.'

'Yours?'

She nodded. 'You can both of you help me.'

The car swung once more through the narrows. But this time we turned up a steep track immediately before the town; then a winding trail amongst dried and craggy slopes. Marta stopped at a rough pull-off. Ahead, were glimpses of the sea towards Kálymnos and Kos; behind, a wonderful view of the castle. We were near the top of the ridge. The ground at our left fell away sharply to a valley. Marta opened the car boot. It contained a tool bag and four bee suits—of course, one had been for Eléni. She took out three.

Elpítha was first ready. She turned about and about on the track, poised and veiled, as though momentarily occupying some 1950s catwalk. Then she led us beyond the car and into a narrow chine. I followed Marta with the tool bag.

A gnarled holm oak kept the chine's far corner. Behind it, at an angle invisible from the track, there opened a lovely secluded terrace couched among rock faces and carpeted with small white boulders, through which grew our ubiquitous dwarf sages, purple-flowered thyme clumps and thorn bushes, together with miscellaneous spearing yellows and other miniature vegetation. Upon all this were six hives.

I stopped, delighted. I heard only the wind and Marta's bees about their business. Theo, it was—how shall I describe this—an authentically idyllic spot. It seemed for a moment to reach back to the roots of poetry: to some hypothetical Ur-Greece, where it had all first happened. I mean divinity impassioned for human features, the god overjoyed by physicality. I mean that legendary epoch before the classical, perhaps before Zeus, certainly before Christianity, before rationalism and macroeconomics; and before matter was declared inert and production turned over to replication—our never-decaying detritus of plastic bottles, say, and plastic bags, and shattered, indestructible junk that, even on Léros, still shows starkly and too often. I mean a time before art was made trite or clever; the time of Theocritus, Pheidias, Sappho, Erinna, Apollodorus, Praxiteles, Apelles...

Forgive me, I'm doing it again, aren't I. Going frenziedly off on one. Is it madness? Feigned madness? But I really do have to pinch myself here sometimes; that *they* actually voyaged this cross-ferried archipelago. For I see now that Greece isn't so much a country but a mysteriously circumscribed expanse of water, upon which everyone must travel and through which the numinous sea bed continually breaks. But those great ones, and the rest... Ah, they could pass any day such a beautiful *témenos* as the nook I now saw before me.

'Light this.'

'What?'

'Light the smoker.' Marta opened the lid of the contraption and handed it to me. Inside was a heap of pine needles and wood shavings, together with a torn strip of newspaper. I was able to read it through my bee-veil, so bright the sun: Γνήσια Ανταλλακτικά και Αξεσουάρ—only Genuine Parts and Accessories. Even a car franchise ad seemed momentarily transcendent.

She rummaged in her jeans for a book of matches. 'Here. And puff it.' She mimed.

I worked the bellows. Wood sparks flew, and the air filled with that spirity waft I remembered from the previous occasion. We put on our gloves.

'Come here. No! Here beside the hive! Or they'll think you're a bear. Smoke at the entrance. That's right. And the gaps. There, and there.'

With a blunt blade from the tool bag, she levered the hive open. A circular shape of insects appeared across the sticky tops of the frames inside. Each bee, disdainful of our smoke, seemed still to push or pull at their oozing collective substance. Marta took out a frame to inspect it. I saw the hexagonal cells and their tireless creatures. I could see, too, Marta's veiled features bobbing close to them as she worked.

Faiyum portraits. Spíros himself, the icon painter. Theo, beeswax is the quintessence of medium, a sweet, pliable, imprint-bearing 'stuff' that takes us always outward to relationship and never to the conceptual. This, too, shifts back in time. Homeric bee maidens spoke honey-drunk truth, or, deprived of their honey, swarmed like Furies. So Di Cosimo painted a honey carnival where art still undid philosophy, and the quest for likeness used both 'wax encaustic', or 'wax direct' upon the cheekbones of the dead. Besides, my Greek word 'therapy', which the arts world hates and mocks, has its origins in the honeyed cataplasm for a wound...

Yet again, I brought myself back. Marta handed each frame to Elpítha, who carefully replaced them. Herself occasionally enwreathed by my smoke, she checked all the hives. And so before long we were done and the little ministration was over.

Once she'd made sure there was water in the plastic drum, we took off our white overalls and got back in the car. I suggested coffee, because I was unwilling to relinquish the company.

So Marta drove us down to the quay at Pandéli, and the three of us sat at a taverna by the sea, the tables set on a shingly strip of beach. Our neighbours were tourists: British, German, a Swedish couple, an Italian family. Marta and I devoured toasted sandwiches, while Elpítha merely held her coffee cup with extreme daintiness and looked out over the unruffled Aegean.

'She's fond of the sea. What do you say in English... in tune with it. *I thálassa íne o erastís sou. Étsi then íne, agapití mou* — The sea's your lover. Isn't it, my dear?'

Elpítha appeared for the first time to take notice of our words. She turned suddenly to look directly at Marta, and then at me. '*Málista* — indeed.' She smiled for a moment, and her normally abstracted face revealed the faintest blush under the lined tan of her cheeks. '*Málista*,' she repeated, before turning back.

I wanted to say something to her, to thank her perhaps, or at least acknowledge her; but a sudden movement at the edge of my vision attracted my attention and made me glance to my left. A couple were about to settle at the next table but one. I don't know why I should have noticed them. Obvious enough tourists. Neither was young. The woman, blonde, had her back to me. The man was just removing his hat and sunglasses to mop his brow. He was bald and craggy-seeming, and as he lowered himself under the protection of the table parasol, his face was lit by the full afternoon glare. For a second I found myself unable to look away. We caught each other's eye.

Then he settled into his place and said something to his wife, and they began discussing a menu.

I turned back to Marta. 'Your bees are completely fascinating. What an experience! I'm so grateful.' I said how privileged I felt, and asked her about the thyme flowers and where they grew most.

We chatted a little more before I found myself snatching another look at the newcomers. The waiter was just at their table, and the woman angled her head up towards him so that her profile, along with the husband's full face...

Theo, they were suddenly caught together — in the same frame, so to speak. I heard myself gasp as I stared, unable to believe the astonishing conjunction I had before my eyes.

'What's the matter, Owen? Owen? Is there some problem?'

'Those people.'

'Yes?'

'I know them. It was... I was once...' I felt I was falling.

Christ, the years change us inexorably. Dear God, without a constant visual update of family, colleagues, friends; well, which of them would we ever recognise after a few decades! Think how it is with school reunions and such like. I tell you, had it just been him, sitting there, or just her... If they'd come to a different table... Or if I'd passed them in the street, for example, or maybe even shared some boat crossing or bus ride where one is well accustomed to seeing — and ignoring — holidaymakers of a certain age and in all degrees of sartorial informality...

If it had been any of these occasions, I do seriously doubt whether I'd have registered the couple now sitting only yards away from me. I say again, they might have come and gone without my being one whit the wiser — but for that momentary quirk of alignment by which this face suddenly appeared in narrow visual context with that.

Theo, I can still hardly credit it as I write; for you'll have surely guessed by now, my friend, to whose likenesses I'm referring. Slowly but unmistakably, my legs began to shake and my stomach feel as though it might dissolve its lining.

'Do you know them? Do you want to go and speak with them?'

'It can't be true. What on earth…?'

'Have they upset you? Do you want to leave?'

'No!' I recollected myself. 'I'm sorry, Marta. Rude of me.'

'Not at all.'

I jerked my head once more at the pair. 'That woman. I've just spent several weeks painting her. I haven't seen her for… it must be over thirty years.'

'Painting her? How painting her, Owen, if you haven't seen her?' Marta's voice was soft.

'I know her face. By heart. And… from a photograph. And now she's here.'

'Are you sure? Are you sure it's the same person, I mean? That you're not…'

Her face was invisible again; and *he* had replaced his sunglasses. They were both looking in different directions.

'Mistaken.' The word on my lips sobered me. 'Yes, of course,' I breathed out. 'Perhaps I was.' For almost certainly Marta was right; I'd leapt to a startling conclusion on only the merest flash of evidence.

I struck my head several times with the heel of my palm.

'You're overworking, maybe,' she said, gently. 'You English. Overworking. Eléni, too.'

You see, Theo? Like you, Marta was growing concerned. Even Elpítha, formerly so abstracted, gazing out over the waters or picking up the pebbles at her feet and casting them down again, was now peering at me intently. Madness?

'Eléni's American,' I sighed. 'But, yes, maybe I am. Overworking. It's just that the man, her husband, if that's who he is… It looks so like… like the husband of someone I once used to know.'

Smiling, Marta stood up. She looked at her watch. 'Forgive me, Owen. It's a little later than I thought. I have a patient to see. My apologies. We must go back to the unit, Elpítha and I. Shall I drive you home?'

'Home? Oh, yes. I'm sorry.' I got up, too.

But it struck me at once, Theo, that if I left now, abruptly, I'd never know. I might never see them again. 'No. Actually, Marta,' I took out my wallet. 'I think I'll stay after all. D'you mind? I think I'll maybe wait and watch where they... I'll see to the bill. You go. Drive Elpítha back; I've kept you both far too long anyway.'

She put a hand on my shoulder. 'If you're sure, Owen. Thank you.' She looked at her watch again and took Elpítha's arm. 'I didn't realise the time.'

But Elpítha stopped for a second as she passed me and handed me four of her stones, all of subtly different colours. With a sudden girlish embarrassment, she embraced Marta, and reached to embrace me, too, a kiss on each cheek. (Theo, I have the stones here in front of me now: one reddish in character, one almost jade green, one black and another of a beautiful grey smoothness.)

Touched, I watched the two women go. Then I returned, my hand still shaking slightly, to my cup, my plate and my amazement.

Part III

Eros

14

Subject: **Roses**

What shall I say, Theo. Apart from the palpitations, naturally, I did all the right things: avoided any further eye contact, waited patiently and kept the couple under discreet observation, while I pretended — for a long time — to consider the coloured dessert items on the plasticised menu fixed to our table.

At last, my strangers finished their drinks; the man was looking at the bill. I snatched my own bill and hurried inside to pay it directly at the counter. But then I remembered I'd left Eleni's roses on the chair beside me. As unobtrusively as I could, I darted back to retrieve them and then sped out again on to the pathway — in time to stroll casually past my subjects as they emerged.

To no avail. I got a close view of them, but they were in their sunglasses and hats. Julia and Miles — or merely some harmless middle aged couple who, by their vague similarity to folk long lost, had the misfortune to trigger off that sudden physical reaction?

I followed them to their hotel. At least I know where they're staying, Theo.

That photograph, pinned to my easel. Someone at your gallery *must* have forwarded it. Who but Julia could have possessed such an image? Who but Julia could have sent it?

Subject: **The Ambassadors**

I left the house early this morning. I took a pair of binoculars. Their leather case bumped against my hip as I walked, and I got only a few paces down the pine track before I decided against them.

So I began again, with just a cloth bag for some groceries. The couple's hotel is on the Pandéli Beach Road, which runs parallel to the main route to town but drops down somewhat lower and nearer the sea. A small convenience store huddles on the opposite side. I bought a few odds and ends and continued on past the hotel front.

It has a wide and imposing terrace, raised up to take advantage of the sea view. Tables with parasols are permanently set out. A waitress with plates of food and jugs of coffee was flitting between breakfasting guests.

But I failed to spot my quarry. Theo, what am I doing?

The road beyond climbs back to the edge of town. So I waited up there a little, watched the traffic, such as it was, and bought *Ta Néa* — "The News", from a *perípteron* — one of those little winged kiosks the Greeks favour. Then, as slowly as I could, I returned by the same route. I stopped alongside the hotel terrace and opened my paper.

No reason to stand and nowhere to sit — the beach was just too far off to offer any pretext. I mean, for loitering. And, of course, there were no English shop windows to stare into — the kind always at hand for the English TV sleuth. So I had to remain in the middle of the path, pretending to be absorbed in words I mostly didn't know and surely making myself more conspicuous every time I glanced up to check on the breakfasters.

I moved on a few paces. I still had that slight instability in knees, those incipient butterflies in the stomach. Turning the *Ta Néa* pages, I shifted my sunhat and mopped sweat from my brow. And with all this, I kept looking up at the hotel terrace and then back to more fragments of Greek news: high temperatures for Thessaloníki and Athens; football — Olymbiakós losing to AEK; the debt crisis, the debt crisis and the debt crisis again. I swung away. The sea sparkled in the distance. I swung further, allowing my leisurely pirouette to continue right around until I saw the terrace once more. No change.

I checked my shopping, took a few more steps and returned to spell out the baffling words of the Greek stock market analysis, until I judged it reasonable to look up again. Still no change.

Devoid of other ideas, I scuttled back across the road to the shop, emerged with a small bottle of water and crossed again to drink — sip by patient sip — seeing only a family with two children finish their breakfast and re-enter the hotel. The waitress bustled out to tidy. Breaths of wind ruffled the parasol fringes.

Theo, I hung on there as long as I dared, eventually conceiving the plan — faintly comical, at least in retrospect — of staring up and down the road and tapping one foot as though expecting a taxi. After which I saw nothing for it but to give up and wander home. *Flâneur* did I think myself? Secret agent? Fool, more likely. It was to a degree preposterous. What on earth was I hoping to gain from such a pantomime?

Ah, but doesn't Fortune always demand we nearly fail before she deigns to lift a finger? I reached the turn at our end, where the beach road climbs steeply to firmer ground, and there allowed myself just one more backward and farewell glance—only to find that several new guests were emerging from the hotel on to the terrace; indeed, a promising-looking couple was even now hovering beside one of the tables nearest the path.

I gave them time, then strode back. It *was* the same two people. Now I was no more than five or six yards away from them, though standing slightly lower because of the sloping ground. I resumed my taxi-waiting—heart almost painfully thumping; opened my paper; peered over it.

The man was bald at the crown, as I said. The rest of his hair was clipped short in the pepper-and-salt texture that comes with age. Now, finally, I could study the craggy visage, the skin somewhat ridged and tired-looking, the jowl just sagging away from the jawline. He was pale, even a little mottled—by which I assumed the couple were at the start of their holiday, rather than at the end. Heavily built, he wore an open-necked, short-sleeved shirt in a style—or lack of it— that could only be English.

Over the edge of the *Gnómes*, the 'Opinion' page, I mapped my memory of Miles on to his features. I tried to compensate for dramatic hair loss, thickening of the flesh, failure of tone, excess weight...

But this is to prevaricate, Theo, and spin out the details, for it didn't matter a damn whether Miles was Miles unless Julia was Julia.

The woman, then. She was blonde, I said. So are many, who'd be grey but for a bottle. Yet there was no getting away from it, the cut of her hair was very much as Julia's always used to be, with the short, flyaway wisps made to frame the head *comme une gamine*. And the root colour was dark, intriguingly—not silver. Her flesh, too, remained almost un-weathered—unlike Miles's. Curious.

Alright, Theo, not just curious: I was riveted.

But what of her *features*, those ratios everyone decodes—but which only the artist understands... I mean as to how the eye seats itself between cheekbone and brow, the exact flare of the nostrils, the crucial relation of top lip to septum, the whole notion of mandible with its attendant musculature?

Well, indeed, they scored pretty highly. I knew them, as I told you once before, almost by instinct.

Then why was I still unsure?

215

Beauty springs out of regularity, not from distinctiveness. Take the extreme case: had Julia been marked or disfigured at birth, identification would have been simple. But she was not. She was far too near the 'fortunate' end of the spectrum of looks. And the closer we steer to that troublesome Greek concept of ideal form, truly, the less we can tell one face from another.

Ha! I once knew a top fashion model whom I couldn't even pick out in a photo she showed me, so similarly perfect were all the other girls—and so similarly made-up. But that's the other extreme. No, recognition is negative; as with sounds and signs, we distinguish by what is not... Besides, my attractive holiday subject had grown a little fuller in the figure than the Julia I remembered. The Julia I remembered...

I should describe what she was wearing.

But to be honest I didn't notice, so intent was I on whether or not this was the lover and betrayer, whose portrait—along with the snap—was up even now on the stand in my studio.

Intent, Theo. And breathless. I made myself walk on a little. Then I hung about until they'd finished and gone back inside.

My next idea was to appear on the upper road and catch them leaving the hotel's front entrance. That failed: I missed them.

But I did return to town about seven-thirty this evening. Why? Because, as everyone knows, the English tend to dine early. And we have a finite number of restaurants, all outdoors. Sure enough, I found my couple—they were upstairs at Yiorgákis's, close to where I'd bought my paper. They were eating together without animation, she in a sage green dress, he in shorts and a pale blue shirt.

I greeted Yiorgákis and found a table. What will you think of me? I ordered a beer and a dish of fried courgettes. Yet almost at once I began to realise... Now you'll smile, perhaps: I began to formulate the difficulty that, absorbed in my surveillance, I'd failed to think through—because, once again, of course, my stakeout was immediately, tantalisingly, indecisive... Yes, I began to realise the problem I hadn't foreseen: that I might *never* succeed; that the indeterminacy was perhaps absolute.

Do you see it? You'll accuse me of intellectualising again. But surely, it's crucial. Why, I could be sitting right next to them for hours—for eternity—and still be unable to make up my mind. Only with hindsight does that fact become obvious. Identification here wasn't intrinsically visual at all; it could only be established via some other intervention than the gaze: by speech—names, history and so on, matters categorically removed from the ocular involvement, from the compositional trance of the artist, that eerie place where art intersects with life.

No, we were rather in the territory of *authentication*, better resolved by title, provenance, what's on the frame, or through jottings made in some label, perhaps, on the back of the panel...

I went home and paced about my studio, beginning to be alarmed by the voyeurism I was adopting. Beginning, too, to remind myself of your anxiety, and Marta's, about my mental state. *Had* I simply been overworking? *Was* I actually going crazy?

And why, for God's sake, was I *eschewing* speech. Why didn't I simply go up to them and ask them who they were?

Because...

Because there was some burst of feeling which Julia still had the capacity to inject into my bloodstream? Sending me that photograph...

If I could just come across her on her own...

But she wasn't going to be on her own. Holiday couples remain almost superglued together.

Much later, Theo, and still perplexed by my emotions, excited, guilty, ashamed...? I sat down to write this email to you. And found in the process the intuition stealing over me... almost the profound conviction—these also sound like elements of madness... I tell you the sense grew inside me that in this case the establishment of reality, one way or the other, wasn't even the straightforward matter of identification that it had so far seemed.

No, an insistent little chime in my head held out that maybe, here and now, all this wasn't purely *about* external phenomena. You understand?

You couldn't be expected to. This is so interior, it's so... I don't know how to put it. I'm saying that this decision concerned *me*; that, having painted the Bledlow picture in the first place, I was still a player. I could make the difference.

And that calmed me. I don't know. Can you possibly accept anything so off the wall? Ah, we have these compelling feelings; they're nonsense, superstitious, magical thinking. Yet I have known occasions, Theo... *a toroid, a circular frame of almost cosmic constriction...* in which the normal presentments of time and space were possibly— impossibly—gravitationally, even—*curved* around. You've only to look at the chain of events: the painting, the photograph, the bizarre happenings in the icon painter's workshop and the appearance now of this tantalising woman. Not isolated contingencies at all, but *linked...* perhaps. Do you see? Linked, even, as Jung suggests, by *meaning*. It was another of those moments when choice really is more than election.

My friend, this is how I explained it to myself. For I reasoned that if I risked nothing more in this flow of events, if I allowed myself to rest enmeshed in the symptoms of mental illness that had surrounded me for so long...

In other words, I told myself that if I failed to act further, then most likely this woman wouldn't be Julia at all, and the world into the bargain would remain stale, flat and subject only to the tedious march of evolution and the tiresome number crunching of probability.

Indeed, the pair of holidaymakers in question would simply shake their heads: 'Sorry mate. We're Paul and Jenny from Leeds. Or Roy and Sheila from Worcester. Or Ted and Mary from Barrow-in-Furness. Always come to Léros this time of year. Nice enough little place, isn't it. Off the beaten track. You here for long, yourself?'

But if I *committed* myself, Theo... If I made... what? Some *significant* choice... Exactly, it was a kind of quantum reasoning.

Is it a sign of madness? My hunch was telling me I had a role in this, and that what I did next would potentially turn the stream of events; turn not just events waiting to occur, but — it sounds incredible — turn even their history with them. That Ted and Mary wouldn't have come to Léros this year, that Roy and Sheila were in some other, irrelevant street, and so on... and that this *would* be Julia.

Yes, I told myself that the situation really did solicit some key *move* on my behalf, *phíle mou*, by which I might gain some control and might even ward off, perhaps, some looming embedded tragedy — *the* tragedy, the inevitable old Greek tragedy of incest, with its recurrent bad outcomes and devastations of mind and fortune, to which I seemed unwittingly to have become the permanent heir.

Eléni was asleep. No noise or glimmer from upstairs. I went outside and had only to walk to the wire gate to find myself surrounded by that sound from the coastal scrub, as though every insect belonging there rasped in frenzied chorus. And the creatures in the pines, too: a joint ecstatic *chirr* which, combined, rose up faultless to the heavens and made, it could be, whole galaxies vibrate and the prime stars throb with unusual light.

I was transfixed. To dare. To practise darkly upon the universe. The sea glittered; the outline of the bluff almost glowed. I caught the air's resinous tang and allowed my thought to stray down along the beach road—to that hotel only half a mile away, between me and the dark mass of the castle.

I hurried immediately to my studio, flicked on the bright lamps. Blinking, I crossed to my stand. Bledlow and its two figures stared back at me, the one Julia, the other mostly a blank, me. Julia was perhaps even now on the island...

I picked a brush from one of the jars and began wiping it on a cloth. I put on my work glasses. I looked at the photograph pinned to the woodwork. Control? Everyone knows the worst feature of abuse is the loss of control: over one's own body, over one's destiny.

So why wasn't I boiling with rage against Julia right now?

Perhaps I was. Anger surged up for what she'd done, from my stomach, my diaphragm. *My art* had brought her here. I had her in my power. I had occasion for revenge.

I looked around me. For the flicker of a god? None spoke.

Should I pray on my knees like the icon painter? The ancients reached for sacrifice: goat, bull, horse, wife, even a child. Should I cut myself? Was I supposed to burn a favourite painting? This one? Give it up?

I remembered Agamemnon, knifing his daughter for a war; Idomeneus, slaughtering his son on his return from it; Abraham nearly slitting Isaac's throat. They made deals with deity. They gambled with violence. Julia could be at my disposal, and I'd have the upper hand. At last.

Theo, just as we must reject an abusive universe, we must also reject those antique power bargains with some blood-soaked spirit concept or other.

In the same breath, then, we must reject all modern dog eat dog world-views: power over others, sex and death, survival of the fittest. These are in no way authorised by nature, despite Darwin.

Control over my own body, that's all I have a right to demand. For we still espouse, don't we—if not on our knees—the new dispensation under which love becomes love, rather than mere passion, and in forgiveness all are set free, even our enemies. My painting was itself; it told its own truth. It should remain unharmed.

I turned away, momentarily nonplussed. What, then? For the ball was in my court. What hadn't I already tried?

I saw myself having wept outside the icon painter's cave. I saw myself in panicky frustration trying to gather up my scattered left hand paintings—up there on the scorched volcanic crag, exposed to the pitiless sky.

An idea formed.

I positioned myself fully round to the right of the easel, my cheek not so far from the extreme edge of the canvas. From here, I could see nothing of the Bledlow scene itself—only blurred gradations of tone, with all the picture's content now condensed by extreme perspective to a narrow band or strip.

Well and good. I picked up this morning's palette in my unaccustomed right hand and peeled off the cling film. I grasped a fine brush in my neglected left. The left hand, Theo. I took some colour with it and touched it to the work. The shank felt instantly alive, the fibres responded to the surface; for the Child was still there in my muscles, eternally present.

How shall I convey the experience? The painting left hand at once moved with a will and certainty of its own, leaving me almost literally the bystander. It worked fast, too, on the intensely angled canvas, choosing unexpected tones and mixing them directly on the cloth, in line with my squint-eyed view. Proportions appeared, outlines moulded now here, now there, in tints and half-shades—that weird assurance of the left, which I, even with my adult training, did not possess and never could: the application of flesh, the construction of presence.

I let it continue. It worked, and I watched, fascinated, a little aghast, for upwards of half an hour. More, maybe. I can't tell. Only when the images were secure to that extraordinary take did I switch back to my right hand and, still in position, still at that almost blinded angle, awkwardly touch in the details, conspiratorially, excitedly, with even finer brushes: the whites of eyes, or points of light in the lips or teeth. All the rest I left to trust.

At last, I stepped away and round and confronted the picture face on. What would be the result? Would I have ruined it? Theo, what had I *done*?

Face on, it turns out I've made only the most subtle alterations to my Bledlow: certain patches of dark or light appear upon the hillside, or in the shadows, even intersecting the figures. Face on, my night's work looks virtually nothing, strange anomalies to the attentive viewer. The painting, I think intriguingly, actually benefits.

But if you stand to the side—you know Holbein's great device... if you view the piece from far round to the right hand side—then, once your eyes have accommodated, you'll make out the cruciform shape of the Child, shuddering under the very substance of the chalk. And now, too, amongst the trees, lurk, like mythical creatures, the just discernible living forms of the Girl, the Father, The Headmaster and the Wolf.

15

Subject: From the sea

Two soldiers were at the door this morning, a man and a woman. They had rifles at the ready. The man barked something in Greek. I couldn't reply. The woman took over, with that same pedantic exasperation we English use on foreigners: '*Chartiá! Tavtótita!*' Her gun barrel stabbed at my chest.

How vulnerable the nippled skin — I was wearing only my shorts. Horribly useless my bare feet to get me out of there. Last ditch etymology saved me, Theo: 'charts' are made of paper, a 'tautology' is an identity. Identity papers: they wanted our passports.

They pushed inside. They poked around the ground floor rooms while I rummaged in files and boxes. Eléni came down. They shouted at her.

Once I'd found those precious red booklets, the mood changed. Our guests apologised for any disturbance. They bid us '*Yeia sas*' and left with half smiles. Eléni's phone was on the kitchen table. I snatched it up in the elation of relief, and, hastily sandaled, rushed outside.

The two *hoplites* — they actually still call them that — were sauntering via the wire gate down the goat path towards the cove. I followed to the edge of the dip, only to see another eight of them waiting at the beach. All bristled with weapons. Drawn up on the shingle was a substantial rubber inflatable with a machine gun mounted at either end. Our visitors re-joined their comrades and conferred briefly with an officer. Then two other soldiers appeared from the far track — coming down, I guess, from our neighbours. The whole squad re-embarked. Theo, I was just about to raise the phone camera for a shot of them, when one turned in my direction. We shared a moment of understanding; the Greek military's extreme touchiness over being photographed. So, regrettably, you have no picture of this drama, and I've just escaped gaol for real spying — as opposed to my recent private eye snooping.

As to that, by the way, I managed to stop myself charging off today on another wild goose chase. In every reasonable probability, it's not Julia at all. Safely back at my easel, I'm pondering the fine line between 'visionary' and 'seeing things'. If not quite overworking —

Marta's word — then maybe I've been overexcited. I feel some measure of *chagrin* in relation to last night's episode.

Back to our soldiers: seconds after my attempt at a photograph, they were off at high speed around the bluff to the south, and the incident was no more than a wide foaming wake left behind them.

'What did they want?' Eléni stood, white and shaking.

I shook my head. 'Looking for illegals?'

'Oh, right. I guess. Yeah.'

Theo, they flood over from Turkey. In boats. It's a route into the EU; Greece's big headache. Well, Greece's other big headache. And now the Golden Dawn, the neo-Nazis: immigrants are even more in the firing line. They beat them up.'

'Can I have my phone back?' Her hand still trembled a little. 'I'm expecting a call.'

'Who's that? It's a Saturday. You okay, darling?'

'Just someone I met in Athens. I'll take it upstairs.'

Mentioning Marta: she drove me up to her hives once again. This time she didn't bother with bee suits. We sat on rocks in the shade and just listened to the humming sound and watched the indefatigable creatures coming and going. So I began sketching her — in her wide-brimmed straw hat. She wore a white short-sleeved blouse and a calf-length denim skirt. I dashed down the outline of the folds and the angle of her feet: she had on neat tan sandals. Then a couple of lines for her brown hair tied loosely back under the straw brim. I caught the regular features, the intelligent eyes, the generous mouth. I hinted the silver earrings, marked the creases in the loose cotton below: collar, sleeve, curve of breasts. She was flattered, but held herself tense.

'You don't need to keep still.'

'Really?'

'No, really.'

So she let herself breathe, and then sunlight seemed suddenly to flood around us, a bright, peripheral curtain.

'And now this... person has shown up,' she said. 'This woman.'

I looked up sharply, but Marta held my gaze, until I flicked down again, hurrying to detail the eyes. 'What do you mean?'

'At the taverna,' she laboured the word with her accent. 'On the beach. That couple. Did you find out who they were?' She got up to walk close to one of the hives. I watched her incline forward. On a new sheet, I caught the flexion of her spine beneath her clothes.

'I couldn't be sure,' I said. I went and stood behind the hives altogether, capturing impressions as she moved among them, trying not to think but to leave all to the hands. And the charcoal stick between my fingers scratched away of its own accord, a pointed black sharp, a broader flat, a curved edge.

She turned, now here, now there, and spoke about her family. Two boys: 'Istvan is seventeen, Pávlos fifteen. They are at school in Athens. And here I'm only a family doctor. Part-time. And wife. And I work at the psychiatric hospital when I can.'

She told me how she'd studied medicine in Soviet Russia and then come to Greece with her husband. She told me about her father, a family doctor himself, and how she'd felt, as a girl, that she might have inherited a certain gift for illness — for perceiving and diagnosing it, that is. *Talant* was the Russian word with which she tried to explain it.

Intrigued, Theo, I conjured up on a separate page some winter forest — my hurried trees like the blobs and dots of early Kandinsky — and a wooden house, where the aspiring girl, in the embroidered boots of Russian fairy tale, argues the spirit with her sceptical, white-bearded father.

'But now I don't have it. My gift.' She was matter of fact. 'Not any more.'

'Why not? What happened?'

'Nothing happened. I just don't have it. I don't know. I'm still a good doctor. I'd forgotten all about it until today.' A bee detached itself to settle on her hand. It traversed the ridges of her knuckles. She looked down at it, and I couldn't but begin sketching again: the angle, the shaft of sunlight now catching her facial bones, the illuminated arm and the insect briefly incandescent before it sped away. She followed it with affectionate eyes. 'What is *your* father like, Owen? Is *he* alive?'

'He lives in Berlin. Been there fifteen years. I've chosen not to be in touch.'

'Not to be in touch? Chosen?'

'Yes.'

She paused. 'May we know why?'

'Do you mind if… if I don't say? For now?'

'Of course. I'm sorry.' She paused again. 'Does *he* know why?'

'He hasn't complained. Maybe I've always rattled him.'

'Rattled? What is rattled?'

'Frightened. Things I might have said or done.'

'Frightened? Frightened of his son?'

Theo, I've always thought I had a very clear perception of my dad. And just for a moment, then, I thought I heard his voice. And his face came so suddenly to mind, complete with horn-rimmed glasses and bitter grin, that it made me jump. *Hello, Owey.*

But then I fished for other recollections and found them absent. Who was he? Where was he? In the splash of thoughts triggered by Marta's question, I got another glimpse of him: eating—coarse, unmannerly—at the table with my mother. Then I saw him mixing cement when I was three, adding water to a hollow in the grey heap, churning it in with a spade until the sheen of the mess was Louvre-patterned by his jabs. I saw him cursing to dig out the roots of a tree stump, his trousers tucked into his socks. Then he was emerging from under some old Morris car we had, his face smudged filthy with grease...

Yes, those apperceptions were laced with disgust. But, scrambling up cliffs with him, again when I was three, maybe four, I felt fearless and happy. Once, I saw my mother weeping in his arms—some private grief: the death of my brother just after his birth; my sister, later stillborn. Did Dad ever weep for his lost children? Did I?

I recalled photos of him: in sports jacket and tie, sitting, pen in hand, at our table. In my aunt's garden, he was pulling a mad face—a man in his forties—when everyone else was just smiling for the camera. In his swimming team at school, he sat bolt upright with six or seven other young men, all in those dated one-piece costumes, behind a shield trophy. He held his knees together in a strangely forced, and, now that I come to write it, slightly effeminate manner.

What was he like?

Like nothing. I smelt the sour tang of his breath, heard his grudging laugh—sensations at once eerily, uncannily present.

'Yes,' I said, at last. 'He wants grace.'

'He is... what is your word... clumsy?'

'Graceless. I can't put it any other way. He aspired to... grace. When he was a schoolboy, a scholarship boy from an uneducated home, he did sports—gymnastics, diving—that courted such a quality. Grace, he admired young men who had it, men whose bodies moved properly and easily, who could make things with their hands. He liked working men, craftsmen, mechanics.'

'He liked men?'

'He knew nothing of girls. He was working class himself—always spoke with a London accent. But he never went to pubs, never drank, never flirted—the idea! At least not with women. Had no interest in racing or football. Maybe he did once have comrades; I've a notion he was once a communist. At university, maybe. But I'm not sure.' I shrugged. 'I know so little about him, because he gave nothing away. He should never have married.' My charcoal stick halted. 'For when I pressed him once, Marta, he said he'd tried to break it off with my mother, while they were engaged. He knew it wasn't right, he said. But she'd threatened to kill herself, and so he'd felt trapped. And so he exhibited more and more, as the years went on, that lumbering, self-mocking, entirely negative... gracelessness. He came to disgust me, the man whom, as a child, I'd seen as loving my mother with such purity—a purity I could never reach, because I felt...' I paused with an apologetic smile, 'because I felt strangely evil and contaminated. That's how I remember him: as a bitter intelligence, working in electronic control systems, you know, government contracts, intercontinental ballistic missiles—maybe aimed at you, Marta. This man who'd once been a Conscientious Objector! Objector to the war, that means. Jobs here. Jobs there. Then university tenure...' I spread my hands '...stuck in a godless body...'

She was listening very closely. Then she said, 'He sounds a robot. Or a golem.'

'I believe inside his head there was a safe place he'd made. It was purged of all images, of all memory or emotion. It was a place governed only by voltages.' I laughed. 'By electrical currents and the soldered resistances of his own designs. There, in his head, he was God. No women, nothing emotional. There he'd feel neither pain nor guilt, love nor remorse nor... nor anything. It was a sanctum he'd defend to the death. He'd dig in and fight, if I ever questioned it.'

'It is from some Soviet *gulag*, perhaps, this sanctum place?'

'Science, I mean.' I swept on, my charcoal sketches momentarily forgotten. 'I think of science as a closed philosophical vessel emptied, by definition, of the observer. A place of soulless experiment; he *had* no pleasures... no public ones. He'd no time for art, music, theatre. Why? Because with them came feeling, the body; and he was scared. He read nothing. Except science fiction.' I made another laugh. 'Science fiction! Monsters, mechanical androids, witch temptresses— all the clichés of sexual disturbance! Only, played out by spacemen with Greek sounding names!' There. My extraordinary confessional speech ended.

'My father was a scientist.' Marta said. 'Doctors. Without science, my patients die. Without it, my bees die. I am a scientist. You're a scientist, too, Owen. So are we all—or we're crazy. We can't give up reason. That would be madness!'

We both laughed. 'Of course.'

'So science is what works. Everything tested, nothing taken on just say so.'

'No,' I cut in. 'That's what *he* used to say. But science only 'works' by disallowing the body of the observer.'

Marta sat silent. I was acutely conscious of the sound from the hives, like some low mains hum in my childhood, as though Dad were here, even now, trying to fix a piece of circuitry behind the holm oak tree at the entrance to the dell. There was almost the flux smell of solder on a hot breath of wind.

I heard myself laugh once again. 'He used to claim he was a Martian—it was his joke. Not funny. Science was his religion. This man who loathed belief believed fanatically in the cult of intelligence. A monstrous baby so split off and cast out, an entity so withdrawn from his own flesh that he saw nothing wrong in subjecting all Nature to torture, to experiment: as though she, too—Nature—felt nothing.' My wave crested in scorn. 'Science! A great brain given licence to pull the wings off flies. Off bees. Off boys. "Never trust anyone, not even your own father"—that was his teaching to me. He taught it by constant word and—presumably—by deed. Had he ever acquired the humility to study anything human, Marta, he could perhaps have gleaned that the ancient Greeks abstained from experiment not because they were stupid, or superstitious, or just plain idle, but because they lacked that terrible, psychopathic permission to do whatever they damned well liked, because maybe they still had a sense of something prior to pure cleverness, a sense of that holy Receptacle from which the Demiurge brings order. They still had a sense of *chóra.'*

I looked straight at her, finally lost for words and feeling instantly ashamed for lecturing again and in such a renewed flood, for cleverly quoting Plato and showing off my eloquence by dragging in that word not even from her own near perfect understanding of Greek. A squadron of bees formed a sudden cloud around her hair, then dispersed. A small, mottled lizard flicked its tail on the sun-bleached stones beneath her feet.

She shook her head.

I turned away to the entrance to the dell. A stretch of sea was just visible between the hills. Theo, my eyes filled with tears, as they do now, because I remembered the only time Dad had seen his grandson, Arun. He and his German wife were visiting. My boy was three. They'd called in just at the last minute, almost as an afterthought, having already been in England a full fortnight—he'd admitted on the phone—staying with friends. They'd bought presents for our kids, of course, and wanted to drop them off.

So I'd watched Arun do all he could to engage this new-found grandfather, monopolising him in the way children do, showing him toys and games, talking incessantly, expecting all the joy and warmth that youth arouses in age. And I'd seen my dad flounder. No touch, no embrace, only a near perpetual glaze, with lifted brows, a forced smile, as he tried to manage the stream of child-hearted chatter. Why, he was so agitated and embarrassed he could hardly wait to get off—off to catch their Channel ferry, he said. Can't stop! I'd never known him so ill at ease. No, they really couldn't eat the meal Lily and I had prepared. Sorry, there just wasn't time.

And there he is at last, Theo, pincered by events. Maybe a whole day with us would have exposed him one way, while his failing to call in at all would have scuppered him another. So his tale of a ferry deadline was aiming—pathetically—to appease both counts. Because he must have known that no amount of presents could have made it acceptable simply to dump them at the doorstep with the engine running. And so, for some hours, he had to endure the child of his genes, Arun, during which no self-abstraction, effacement of image, repudiation of story, denial of drama, no lofty denunciation of human kind, no hyper-intelligent philosophising, no pulling up the ladder into a zone purged by strict mathematics of all metaphor, play or ambiguity… not one of these, his lifelong Modernist or Scientific strategies, could shield him.

Oh, my friend, what recollections did my son stir up for him? Was it just the memory of his own child self? Or was it perhaps the recollection of me…?

As to Josh Levinson, you ask, I'm afraid I've no idea. Yes, I did hear from him again. It was some years later—there has to be a time lapse, for professional reasons. Things weren't good for him. He was being targeted. Persecuted, if you will, like a lot of other therapists in the States at that time: death threats and so on. For what? For listening to people and trying to help. For taking abuse seriously and seeking to understand it.

Theo, I'm glad I told you about Josh and about the Parts; frankly, I've no idea where Josh is at the moment, or what he's doing. And despite my personal failure, my failure to take seriously the tools he offered, I feel I did have a duty to record for you in that email what I witnessed of him: just in case the information might be in danger of being lost forever. The whole question of traumatic memory and its treatments seems these days to have been kicked into the long grass. I mean, you never hear of it, do you.

Finally, my 'gesture' — and all that about a sacrifice. You're perturbed again, I can tell. My talk of resolving an indeterminacy by choice and 'participation', by doing a funny bit of painting sideways with my left hand; I know it exasperates you. Shocks you? Not the painting, of course, but the fact that I take it seriously; that suggestion of mine that it might somehow alter the course of events. Alter even history, didn't I say? Oh, Theo, you always tread so carefully, but I know you worry.

I *have* been there, of course. Times I thought I was getting messages from the TV, when I believed the outcome of the first Gulf War depended on me and what I had to say to Lily…

And so when you find me linking a decisive moment in my own treatment to the end of the Cold War and such like — I did, didn't I. Well, it can only unsettle you. Of course. It unsettles Marta, too, doesn't it! My anger at 'total science', Science with a capital 'S'; it seems to speak against the modern God. Against reason. Which I do not, Theo.

But I can almost hear your alarm at an apparently recurring psychosis. And that will make you question everything I told you of the enactments in the clinic, the body's demonstrations, the mysteriously gathered information — as the products of severe derangement. Oh Jesus, now even as I write about hearing your alarm and knowing your thoughts, it must sound exactly like a delusion of telepathy, like the 'voices' of a madman. Worse and worse!

Subject: At the court of Alcinous

It's late. Come, let's deal with it all and put it to rest. I try to be rigorous, scrupulous. I seek to observe and record only what I've noticed — or experienced. That's all, honestly. But if an event exceeds coincidence, if it flies in the face of everything we think ought to be the case… Julia? Of course it isn't Julia. I realise that, Theo. But I've got to be rigorous and scrupulous about my own perceptions. I need honesty in my art. And perhaps the world really isn't as we've been told! More things in heaven and earth, you know…!

I'll make that comparison again, which I hope you won't take amiss. Your fine intellect is civilian. Yours are the graces of humanism and peace. Great learning, long years of experience, a wonderful instinct, warm emotion; these are the tools of your trade. Your success and the esteem with which you're regarded in the art world bear witness to them all. I admire you unreservedly.

My stance, by contrast, rests obscure; I claim it's almost military. My artistic battle is nowhere if not in *that chóra business*, as you call it. But don't just dismiss it. Odd things do happen—even to sane people. You see, my cranky 'soldiering' has witnessed many strange sights, and I've had to campaign in foreign parts. I've seen the sack of philosophy, the rout of Modernism. I mean Deconstruction, of course, and I'm speaking figuratively. It's just in fun. That great siege is far off, now, from the everyday, though all the world knows the rumour of it. Deconstruction—almost a household term in its misuse. The struggle itself has fallen into a kind of myth, hasn't it? Academia preserves it after a fashion; but in no place else, nowadays, does 'theory' count for a button. Why, in our current great populist reaction against the intellect, it's only the market that calls the shots. Critically speaking, we're back in the eighteenth century. *Taste* rules, don't you think? And, of course, money!

Yet the 'heroes' were legendary. Derrida, the Algerian Jew, our Agamemnon; Barthes, the Achilles who dragged the Author's body behind his chariot; fierce Foucault; Kristeva the doomed prophetess; Bakhtin and rash Baudrillard; frenzied Althusser; old Saussure himself! Paris—I mean the city—was the start of it.

But if I do make a burlesque of this, Theo, my purpose is serious. My duty: it's in the matter of what we bring back, isn't it? How we tell it. An artist is nothing who has nothing to say about the wider world, focusing only on his inner condition. And so maybe there *is* some salvage from that foolish 'war'; such a byword for folly, wasn't it, a critical prestidigitation that promised wonders, yet fell to nothing. Nothing, yes. For Derrida is dead, our heroes are dust, our troops scattered. What's left but a scrabble for profit in the ruins of a once great discipline: where postmodern irony licenses—ironically—the

230

very market that so routinely scorns 'theory'. And this is the travesty.

Yet *I* say it mattered, that fight. I tell you, art itself is amnesiac. Art forgets its own history. Contemporary art floats high on its own trite 'intellectualism', far out of touch with everything! Listen, Manet painted sexy *Olympia*. Revolt, shock and desire went on to fuel Modernism: the psychoanalytic son against the repressive father. That's what we're told; the legend of the new.

It's nonsense. It's the fruit of Sigmund Freud's disgusting and wicked self-persuasion that incest wasn't a real danger at all, but was *every* child's fantasy.

I'll tell you the truth. Manet painted the family. At its heart was Olympia, the whore, who *might* let her black cat out of the bag. She's not intimidated: and *that's* the scandal. But here was no young painter's rebellious sexuality. For whom could such a cliché offend? Paris had whores, nudes and titillation for every youth and made no secret of it.

No. Manet's so richly allusive style brings all art history back home to a *family*, crippled—as it happens—by incest. Olympia is shown lying in his parents' house. You think I'm making it up? Did you know Manet had to marry his father's mistress? His disowned half-brother became his stepson. Call it Oedipal if you like: Edouard Manet's stepmother was his own wife. Something else was rotten: both *père & fils* were to die of syphilis. Poor Victorine Meurent...

A painting of horror, not arousal, that was the outrage. It touched everyone's guilty secrets. And after that do you think seeing was easy? The plain fact of the matter is that no one post-Olympia *dared* paint the image, the icon; not because it was sexy, but because it threatened our most sensitive of inscapes, the family. What was Impressionism but a loss of focus? Never mind 'light' and *plein-air*; Impressionism is a *retreat*. You asked what I meant about this once, and I never really answered. It's surely a retreat from woman, from sharp-eyed sexuality. And then Picasso himself recoils from the *Demoiselles*. What's Modernism? It's the abandonment of *desire*. Modernism *averts* the gaze from sex—as children do when the reality is too terrible. Ah, they fix their eyes on some irrelevant object. They distract themselves. They intellectualise, dissociate, become *metaphysical*, mechanical—see anything but what is central to be seen. I should know. So the truth about Modernism is that it looked away, and art became more and more the *avoidance* of illustration.

Hence, the triumph of *parergon*: frame, decoration, background. So

231

indeed Kandinsky banishes both St George *and* the dragon to the extreme corners, beyond the frame, even, and concentrates only on the space opened up by the lance. Pattern, shape, colour; now a whole consciousness of aesthetics beautifully abducts the canvas. And narrative evaporates in the devastation of faith, where no version is authorised save Science's chronicle of random catastrophe. That's a tale, Theo, whose god is a psychopath, as my dad told it to me, and this, too, fits the historical facts. Surely, our adherence to the dark myths of Science is a post-traumatic phenomenon — the consequence of two world wars. Surely, now, we need far more to *remember*: to *illuminate*.

You'll say nothing is more despised in art now than illustration. Yet what else did the masters do? They located us in story, not philosophy. We must return to Manet. We must help stitch the wound he left open, his nerve and body broken. And *that*'s where Derrida comes in. But do you see, my dear friend, how this touches me, who have searched for my own account, only to find it the tale of art itself? I've lacked precisely what my body, my left hand, knows, and what I couldn't bring myself to see. At risk — if I went under — was that scene, that illustration, foreclosed by a frame, *a ring of black so thick it suggests some intense gravitational toroid, a circular frame of almost cosmic constriction. Nothing contained within is ever supposed to leak out.*

Theo, I'm not mad. I beg you not to be distressed by my little left hand 'gesture' of those figures, or by my rhetoric. Look at it this way: at least it helped me make some progress with the Bledlow painting, and that's to the good, isn't it? Ach, we artists all have our weird ways of getting on, and it's only a kind of dialogue with myself. Nothing more, I assure you. Such moments attend, it seems, the arduous march, the still more arduous homecoming!

And no, of course nothing's happened about the woman since I painted my 'ambassadors trick'. Nothing will, now, we can be sure of that. Wild goose chase — I told you! So don't worry. Everything's fine. I'm getting on with Paris. By the way, I went on to tell Marta about the Clinic. Well, I alluded to it. And about Josh. And Dad. The abuse. Sort of. The Parts. In a manner of speaking. She seemed interested — unless she, too, thinks I'm off my bloody head!

16

Subject: **On a plate**

There's a coast path. It's almost invisible; no one uses it. It meanders across the rise that separates us from Pandéli Beach and then joins our goat track beyond the end of the garden. I saw someone walking there as I returned from my swim. She was maybe a hundred yards away in the open scrub: a woman in a pink dress. I just made out a straw sunhat. And she was carrying a few long objects and awkward bits and pieces. I guessed she might be looking to set up a picnic table somewhere further round and I confidently predicted the imminent appearance of a couple of kids and a husband.

It was a little unusual, though. The coast path is mostly un-trodden, as I just said; I've hardly walked it myself. Far easier to get to town via the pines and the main road. And besides, holiday makers tend to stay close to the principal beaches, where they can spit-roast themselves on sunbeds; or splash about; or go to the little shops and tavernas.

So I climbed on up to the house, where I began work as usual. Nothing else disturbed my concentration until I stopped at about eleven to make coffee.

In hat and sunglasses, taking my cup out on to the patio, I had my first surprise. Call it that, Theo, although the word 'surprise' now seems barely adequate to keep pace with what I'm about to tell you. The walker in pink hadn't passed by at all but was seated not far off with her back to me—in the patch of scrub beyond our wire gate. She'd been there all that time, Theo: on a camp stool under a folding parasol. She had a portable easel set up in front of her. She was painting a view of the cove and the bluff.

Even so, for the moment I merely lifted an eyebrow; and that's the truth. There are worse things for tourists to get up to on holiday, and my mind really did remain preoccupied with some new Left Bank oil studies I'd just got down. So I simply looked on abstractedly from my chair.

But something about her struck me as familiar—despite the fact, you understand, that her straw hat almost completely obscured her head, and the loose linen dress did little to reveal her outline. Sure enough—here came my second surprise—the more I began to take notice and to 'wise up', the more certain I became it was the woman herself, the one I'd been agonising about.

My mouth went dry. Of course it did. Jesus! I put down my cup and stole to the fence. No question: as she turned to adjust the angle of her parasol, I recognised those features I'd been observing on my missions of a few days ago.

God in heaven, how could this have happened! What do you make of it, Theo? Cancel all I said. Here *on a plate* was the opportunity I'd thought so unlikely, the chance to approach her on her own. On a plate, I say: ha! Christ! What do you think? Like the fairies in the song: right at the bottom of my garden!

Heart pounding again, I checked to both sides. Even now, Miles might be on his way. But surely, Theo, it *wasn't* Miles. And this *wasn't* Julia. It stretched coincidence too far. Still, the coast (literally!) was clear. I bit my lip. I couldn't turn my back on it. The chance. Could I. Not now.

Easing open the wire gate, I crept towards her, the solitary painter, picking my way in a small circle around to the right through low thorn bushes and tufts of browned sage. Until I could approach her almost from the direction of her own picture.

I was a few steps away. She gave a little jump of surprise. 'Oh, I didn't see you!'

'*Kaliméra,*' I said, my sunglasses and hat offering perfect protection.

'Kaliméra.' She looked anxious, the word hesitant and unpractised on her lips. 'I'm sorry,' she said. 'Am I allowed to paint here? It's not private property, is it? I'll go if it is.' Putting down her paint and brushes, she began as if to pack up her materials.

The voice: familiar? I couldn't tell. The intonation? I didn't know. Caution threw a cloak about me. A sudden cloak. I continued in Greek.

'*Óla kalá. Íne endáxi, kyría. Prochoríste*—It's fine. No problem, ma'am. Go ahead.' I found myself nodding energetically and gesturing for her to continue. A cloak of invisibility, Theo.

We were silent a moment, she seemingly reluctant to continue painting, and I at once unsure what my assumed character might say next.

Then I remembered my abandoned coffee cup. '*Tha thélate na píite káti*—would you like something to drink?' I mimed the action. '*Kaffé? Chymós?*' I squeezed imaginary fruits between my palms like some holiday waiter. '*Neró?*' I pointed to the sea.

234

She cottoned on. 'Well, yes, actually a glass of water—neró—would be marvellous. I've already finished what I brought, and it's so hot.' Laughing, she repeated the pointing gesture and held up the empty bottle as evidence. 'If you're sure. That's very kind. I don't want to put you out.'

The voice; it pierced my charade. I racked my brains again, all the way back to the house. Did I recognise her? Or was I being a hopeless fool? My heart! I fixed a glass of water with some ice and carried it back out to where she'd resumed her work.

'Thank you so much,' she said.

'*Parakaló.*'

She drank. Slipping up my sunglasses for a moment, I took the opportunity to look at the picture she was doing. It wasn't bad. I clapped my hands and nodded in approval. '*Brávo!*' She'd used an obvious Impressionist technique, striking colours on in dabs—as outdoor amateurs do all over the world. Yet the marks had assurance to them, and the canvas already revealed a strong and strikingly individual sense of design. Julia had never painted.

'Well, I don't know.' She smiled self-deprecatingly. 'It's a start, I suppose. I've only recently taken it up. Something I've always wanted to do but never got around to.' She made explanatory movements with her hands, which I pretended not to understand, smiling back.

What a situation! And yet here we were, suddenly interacting in a way… yes, in a canvassy, oil-based, substantial way that could never have come about, I guess, had I launched in straightaway with English.

I looked at her painting once more. '*Íne kalí*—It's good.' I clapped again. Did I remember Julia once saying she'd wanted to take Art at school?

But she was getting up. 'Actually, I do think I have to go after all.' She showed me her watch and tapped it, lifting her eyebrows and jerking her head back in the direction of the town. 'My husband… I didn't notice. It's getting on. I think I've made some progress, though.' She began packing up her things, tubes of paint, clunky old mobile phone, box of tissues, bottle of sunblock, the pouch of her sunglasses. I watched her tear a length of cling film off a roll, hastily wrap her brushes and then flatten some more over her tin plate palette—a tin plate strangely similar to my own.

I collapsed her parasol and laid it ready for her.

'Thank you,' she said. 'Thank you.' She was hurrying a little. My presence unsettled her: an unsolicited male, standing attentive in a secluded space, a foreign country. She laid her canvas carefully face up across some thorn bushes and folded her portable easel. She looked once more at her phone, checked it rather earnestly, then fiddled to extract her sunglasses from their pouch, pressed them to her face and began gathering everything for her trek back.

Except the painting itself. With her hands now full, there seemed no way she could pick it up. And so I came to the rescue, lifting it respectfully and holding the painted surface towards me so that she could just grip the wooden centre strut between a spare thumb and finger. That way it would hang without smudging.

'I should have thought about this, shouldn't I! Before I started out. That it would still be wet, I mean. This is the first time I've... So stupid of me!' She enacted the difficulty with her eyes and expression, smiling now in resignation at her awkward burden.

I smiled back and made a face in sympathy. I could have offered to carry it for her; or the parasol; or the easel. But she'd surely have suspected my designs. I wanted her to come back. She hadn't finished. I was desperate for her to come back. '*Ávrió?*' I said.

She inclined her head in puzzlement. '*Ávrio?*'

'*Ávrio,*' I repeated. I pointed to an imaginary watch on my own wrist, circling the hour round many times with my finger. I pointed to her and then to the place she'd been sitting and swept my hand open in a gesture of welcome. I pointed to the sun and indicated that it would set and rise again over the sea. '*Ávrio.*'

'Oh, *tomorrow*. Yes, I shall have to come again, shan't I. It's such a pretty scene and there's still a lot to do. If that's alright, of course.'

Theo, I nodded as though I understood every word—which, of course, I did. She looked at me suddenly, but now we were both masked—by our sunglasses, of course—but also, I hasten to add, by the extreme unlikeliness of what was occurring.

'Yes, tomorrow, then. *Ávrio,*' she said, suddenly a touch embarrassed again, though with her accent noticeably improved, as though she'd listened to me and tuned in. I was impressed. 'And thank you once again,' she said. 'For the *neró. Evcharistó,* I mean.'

'*Parakaló,*' I said again, and inclined my head in the suggestion of a bow.

So she walked off, picking that barely visible path between the stones and dry vegetation and managing her various burdens. And I went back to the gate and watched her. After about thirty paces, she turned and smiled. So I waved; and she made a kind of acknowledgement with her head and body and continued on her way.

That was actually yesterday, Theo. And I got through the rest of the day. Somehow. Without writing to you. Then, this morning, '*ávrio*' didn't happen. She didn't show up. I checked in case you'd had a chance to reply to my last. I could have done with just 'hearing your voice'.

But now… Oh God, oh God! Theo, I don't know which way to turn. What was it? What's going on? I spent a while trying to work, but I was all over the place. Siesta time, and I keep thinking and thinking about what's happened.

Subject: A storm

And now another twelve hours have passed, and daylight has long switched out. The night, for once, is overcast. Maybe a storm brews. Gusts of hot air rustle the vines. I don't know.

It's later still. The sticky, heated oil paint on my clothes fumes in my nostrils. Eléni already asleep; I, awake. I hear—as always—calls from strident insects. They, too, await the rain. Yes, there was lightning, far off over the Turkish coast; no thunder yet.

And I remain completely 'wired', do you see, Theo, by this bizarre circumstance. Not only was the woman *detached* from her husband… That would be significant enough, though not past credibility, not past coincidence, chance, luck, what have you. But she *also came to sit for a number of hours precisely outside my back gate*—which surely appears to strain even the driest statistical apologetics. Doesn't it?

Or am I making something out of nothing?

Yet look at it. Just a day or so after I assured you the little thing I did to my painting, the sideways Holbein 'gesture' I made, was *simply* a gesture, Jesus Christ, it's risen up to confound both of us. It confounds you because my madness has come true; and it confounds me… because my madness has come true! I'm assailed by… by horror and confusion, Theo, if I'm honest. I'm asking myself yet once again that question no true madman ever asks: am I mad?

Well, either I am; or the simple act of putting brush to canvas has endowed me with a brand of supernatural power that actually forges events. Which is very frightening. Not to say grotesque.

For where will it end? And where did art begin? Altamira,

Lascaux—the shaman going down under the skin of language, going deep into some sacred cave basically to decorate the walls. Except this 'decoration' was supposed to tickle Mother Nature's womb, I guess; to bring forth deer, antelope, bison—or maybe even some lost lover held captive in the house of darkness. Just imagine that proto-artist, proto-sorcerer with his guttering wax-light and clay pot, spitting and blowing his astonishing ochres on to the rock. Is that suddenly me, and am I poking about now in the goddess's secret parts, her privates, kissing again the lip of the underworld, *that chòra business*? Memory, dream, criss-crossing desires—does writing, too, conjure up lost souls?

I *am* scared, Theo. And at the same time buoyed up. The missing? The dead? Dare I put brush to canvas now—or finger to keyboard? Oh, the beating of wings, the potential, benign or Faustian. Let the philosopher examine his soul.

I'll do it. Because if I'm not mad, then it's my wound. Yes, I've heard it's often the vilely abused have this psychic traction on space-time, able to call spirits out of hiding. Theo, it's Dad's legacy. Dad forced me out of my body, forced me out of language, too, that social medium, and left me floating. Floating above it all, that's what offers this so dangerous capacity to meddle.

But I'll do it. I'll go on. Because contact is the only answer. The risk of another person is the only way back into the flesh. I spoke of sacrifice a while ago. Then let me sacrifice my scepticism, my denial.

Ah, where are we, all of a sudden? So soon! Lost voices surround us. Shapes beckon, now this, now that. Here's one, a figure from my youth. Who?! In this dark and midnight place! Who makes his way, there, through the shadows? Be still. No reason for alarm. Why, it's only Piotr Benkowski, little visionary, counsellor, adviser. And the hairs on the back of my neck lie smooth again.

Theo, did I tell you of him? Maybe not, after all. He was at Hornsey, a tutor of some kind—my art school wasn't all George. I shadowed Benkowski in my second year for his woodcuts. His was a gothic chiselling, a kind of graven image quite out of fashion then, and perhaps now. He hid himself almost unobserved in a prefab the college owned, and was chiselled himself—he'd been in a concentration camp. Perhaps he felt at home in that functional concrete hut by the Hornsey boiler house, where no one else would bother him. Benkowski told me first of Jung's concept of Meaning.

Have I *never* spoken of him, Theo? Did I perhaps 'forget' him, too, leaving this second mentor so long in his ugly, unexamined space?

238

Piotr was a hardliner in the way of Dürer. He was nothing but line, in fact: a Polish half-Jew who made prints by the wrong method, out of the wrong, outmoded subjects.

Piotr Benkowski grew more English than the English. He poured tea and scorn on the psychoanalytic obsessions of the faculty, forked slices of toast against his small gas fire and the faddist *avant garde*. He showed me the tattooed number on his arm, from the concentration camp. Behind us, disorderly on a bench, lay his woodblocks for *Sir Gawayne and the Green Knight*. Piotr laid a finger to his nose and laughed grimly. 'An ink for an ink, an antidote for a bite. It lies here,' he tapped the book he was illustrating, 'this is native comedy, this map of archetypes; and you English don't regard it.'

I used his pass to the British Museum—to read not Gawayne but the Carl Jung he insisted upon—turning page after page, day after day, in volume after labyrinthine volume. Each time, I was afraid he'd be dead before I got back, self-stabbed with his own gouge. It was a relief to find him still at work. 'So now you have voice in either ear, boy. Me and George. Which will you listen to?' His laugh was a rattle. His microscopic blade cut fine spirals from flat white holly. I watched a negative wood block take shape: the plaited mane of the charger, Gringolet, then Gawayne's breastplate, his gorget, his questing face part-hidden by the cheek guard—like Dürer's *Knight*, indeed.

'What spurs him on?' I asked, naïvely.

He looked up at me, his small eyes suddenly alight. 'Gawayne is almost afraid to die, almost not. When I come first to England, I say to myself, here is magic island.' Then he pointed to the figure. 'Gawayne is young man, tries only to do his duty. He goes out into the bewildering world, but nothing is what he thinks, nothing what he is told. This is true, eh? The more they say one thing, the more it is another. George Brede!' He laughed and spat at the fire. One column of it puttered and went out, and there was a smell of gas before it caught again—exploding casually from the latticed fireclay. 'George is flat surface.'

He mimicked George at work, then paused to sip his tea, from an elegant china cup amidst the coarse debris on his workbench, under the coarse angle-iron of the corrugated asbestos roof. 'Sex and absurdity, says Existential George!' He spat again. 'Bang, splash makes you artist! But Gawayne finds the game of not quite sex and not sure death. It is so strange. Not game, but it is. For real. So Gawayne must make choices, and right choices. Artist is bewildered warrior, Owen.' He laughed again. I ate my toast, intrigued.

239

I thought him embittered, yet I'd take off dutifully to my place in the Reading Room. Indeed, I swayed by tube to Holborn so often when I should have been in a studio or at some lecture. There, I immersed myself in Jung's crazy fountain of words—where logic is itself dissolved. Yes, I swam at the desk beside madmen and mermen. With misshapen creatures, I schooled, little knowing I was one of them.

I think now, Theo, of Benkowski's woodcuts, his *Gawayne* cycle imbued with the camps and torture, rootless humour and survival. I see his face, lined like his art. I hear his voice speaking of his 'long journey on the arm of death'. If George was public show; Piotr fought the private dragon. I learned soldiering in solitude.

Frames and containers preoccupy me suddenly, La Madeleine's stonework, the brothel's stucco; within delimiting structures we try to lead our lives. At night, though—here, now, in this sweaty dark—implacable weight and substance become permeable. Paint itself tells the tale: there's pallor under it in the scraping off. Darkness turns transparent.

So when we're locked asleep, veiled whispering dreams steal in through concrete walls. Sure enough, Theo, since Eléni and I came here to this white-washed box-for-strangers, rendered and plastered a good inch thick—well sealed, you'd have thought—my dreams have followed me and found me out, still keeping up their unfailing attack. Hardly a night I don't wake in a sweat from this strange beast or that abhorrence. I dream despair, too, hopelessness, anxiety—states of profound illness, which upon waking are cured. Almost.

Spíros Apostolíthis, the icon painter, took my nightmares away. That first night back from Kálymnos, it was no coincidence: having touched the icon, or been touched by it, I was drowsy beyond belief. I passed into so dreamless a rest I've never had. And woke relieved. For two days, maybe three, I felt that same pleasing stupor. And there was serenity, Theo, as at the gates of vision cleansed. Why, it was suddenly pure artistic indulgence to drowse, a pleasure unalloyed, in fact.

And then, all at once, I was full of dauntless energy, feeling my spectral limbs fill up with... what shall I call it? Presence? God? I sprang to my canvas, as you know, painting so many images of Paris. Theo, I swear it must have been the icon—or the man. No, I assure you. Before Eleni came back there was a clear interval when the icon painter and the astonishing holy face he showed me took my bad dreams away.

240

Subject: **A storm** *contd.*

Sleepless, Theo. I'm sorry. I sent the last but have come downstairs again almost at once. Typing's an opiate; forgive me clogging your inbox. Delete this unread, if you like. My dad took my dreams away when I was six — to hide the crimes? For what if I talked? They were nightmares so bad I dared not sleep, and Dad, a mystagogue that year, taught me a mantra: 'I must not dream, I must not dream.' I repeated it for ever, and it worked! It gave me mind control! Ha! Ironic Dad, who first told me of 'bad dreams', standing beside my cot some earlier year, to explain away — as I've heard perpetrators often do — my loud *undreamt* distress. So Dad played my cause and cure, devil and doctor, rapist and therapist. His cursed hypnosis proved the best of all.

Only years later, in my twenties, did I feel robbed. I started to regret having stifled those terrors and buried them so deep. What had they been? So I began a hunt for dreams, recorded a thousand and one dormitions in my Chiswick studio — that is, before it was trashed. For from dreams would come the answer, I was sure of it, to the enigma of myself.

Theo, I believed in Jungian 'meaning', but the hunt grew into an obsession, and I withdrew into myself. Sometimes, I could hardly wait for dark: to see what horrors would transpire — or visions, bright coral-encrusted. No LSD, I swear, yet unbelievable what seas oftentimes I floated, or stars under whose radiance I flew.

By day, I kept peeled that inward eye. A good field worker, I'd sit and analyse. I wrote before I painted. Cross-correlating, I indexed my own archive; but the dream-themes out-multiplied all system or catalogue. Often as not, I caught three or four detailed sequences per night.

But I didn't care. My waking purpose? To undo Dad's spell; to dig up what grave goods — or bads — we'd hidden together.

Particularly, I'd transcribe the symbols. Embedded deep either in Freud's *Traumdeutung* or Jung's *Aion* lies the lure of truth. You'll know this. Truth is dream's unicorn far from home. And I'd catch glimpses of the creature, too, in some morning thicket. Why, perhaps then I was indeed artist as shaman, now voyaging at large upon the globe, now seated at study with the ghosts of ancestors in some cave.

Or, I was lone prospector, even alchemist, sifting, refining. For every nugget wears a ton of dross, and not every dream is 'great'. I use Jung's term — *der große Traum*. I mean the kind of dream far beyond the common run, the rare sort we might act upon: Jacob's vision of the ladder, say, or Joseph's of the fat and lean kine, or Aeneas's of Anchises—or, dare I say, mine of the crazy sister Girl, the one I told you of, with that 'finger' in my mouth. Ah, but I've dreamed all kinds: Freudian dreams, where the sexual symbols are so perfect as to bear Freud out to the letter; Jungian dreams, in which some archetype repeatedly suggests itself; dreams of pasts and of futures foretold, sometimes genuinely; dreams with poignant plots complex as movies, and dreams as random and empty as those science's dreary sleep labs uncover. I've had the gamut of them. Dreams are like children; they appease or mock.

But, in sad truth, truth always escaped me; until I was, yes, mad or close to madness, sitting in my brick-raw studio, ravelling Meaning. *Melencolia 1*—I said I think I have been mad, Theo, except when I was with Julia. Madness is so sure of itself, madness is always pursuant: of just one more twist, another turning, following that clew—or clue—until truth should, would, must, surely, stand revealed.

In truth, too, it did. But that was when the dreams most blinded me.

There, far off, first thunder! Lightning over Lésbos. Lésvos, I should say.

And they must live over their past lives again—by drawing or enactment, by dolls or toys or airy shapes, by dreams, by left hand paintings—as if those lives were indeed ever present.

Thunder again. *Intonuit laevum!* My screen crackles. Louder! My God, Theo, all that time ago in that cursed studio and I was actually being given the truth—I mean, certain graphic sexual dreams about Dad. Was that the truth? I told you I went back to the flat and retrieved my journals. I have them now always in front of me. Look, here! And here! But ah, my thought, like that of the whole century, was clouded by both Freud and by Jung, George and Piotr, in either ear. I'd tell myself, 'No, anything literal must be discounted: only in some symbolic, cloudy, 'psychoanalytic' or even Jungian way must I be—that phrase—'anally passive' to my father!

X marks the spot. That unmentionable spot: anus, rectum, sphincter or even 'toroid'—ridiculous Latin and Greek names for an arsehole, the location and origin of it all. Perhaps I can't feel it, can't feel my own body. How would I know? That's the sadness of it. I think of the poor Kid—me—trying by hook or by crook to get through to… me. And the Censor—myself—the stiff-necked artist, wilfully, flippantly explaining away all his bad and peculiar sufferings as mere metaphor.

My heart breaks. We were so deadlocked in madness, again and again. England? Better to trash the place and leave.

The full storm comes on cue, the first big-bellied drops of rain, dark sounds. I've opened the window, Theo. The annunciant gusts have stilled; now I hear just heavy globes tap, splash, dash on the patio stones. The sudden lightning flares, even though the streak itself is out of sight—somewhere over the northern hills; most likely Parthéni, Kastéli. Yes, there's the thunder, loud, five miles and counting.

Footsteps above me: Eléni wakened by it. We're here in the same house, under the same storm, sheltering. And now again and again the stone-flat sea's lit up; the night cracks and roars. Now we're a-drench, and the damp air pants in at the window, smelling of dust. I defy the psychoanalytic remnant of the age, Theo. We're not *neurotics*; we who cannot choose but be artists are not *narcissists*. I spit on Freud, like Piotr spat on George. We're not indulging. We're not 'expressing ourselves', our creativity or our sexuality. Simply, we're asked to mediate. For the material comes from the holy Child, from the body—and the Child is in hell.

Subject: A storm *further contd.*

Ach God. No rest. No damned rest. Footsteps again, in between thunderclaps, and dreams won't lie still, but, muttering in the voices of Hermes, they escape all definition and interpretation. I've had help for paintings from dreams. I've had inspiration and warnings. I've had maps and diagrams, detailed precognition of events I could never have anticipated. I've had dream meetings with some former lover, followed by the unexpected letter from her next morning, quite out of the blue.

And one night during my treatment, Theo, after a day in which Mitchell and I had sought vainly for the key to an intuition of torture I'd mentioned to him—so often my childhood thoughts were filled with just such a terrible apprehension—I dreamt my father as an unwelcome young man.

Heavens, how Zeus shakes us all, and rain sluices down.

Fresh-faced, he was, and slim, his features handsome, though never classical, Dad, but pale, Nordic, not those you think of for a fool. He came to meet me from a shop door—it was in the precinct near my home—I was married to Lily, then, while Mitchell was treating me.

From a shop door, I said, an electrical shop. Dad carried a paper bag, large, containing one item. I spoke to him, in dreaming surprise, 'You look smart. What are you doing here?' The young man in his prime — Dad — a portrait as I'd forgotten him, child-eyed. Dad held out his hand. I refused to shake it. He passed me the bag.

Theo, inside was something heavy, dream-coiled with flex. I thanked him. He was gone. Then, at a stall — now we were in Mitchell's town, the covered market — and I carried for sale a heavy item of electrical equipment. I was beginning, still in the dream, to get on the trail of how there might be torture without leaving marks. My apparatus was a grey metal box that seemed — still in the dream, I say — almost to leak sadness. Indeed, the stallholder, a small and chiselled man, called it a 'concentration camp drill'; and now the box on his table was intense pain and grief compressed. His? Mine? I could almost say Léros's.

For as I approached this metal box, I could feel the pull of it, an intense gravitational tug of sorrow that bid to lay me low. Theo, I couldn't bear it. I became agitated that, in the words I wrote down immediately upon waking, 'I might have been electrically tortured and had soldered the leads myself — to my father's appliance'.

I made nothing of that. Nothing at all — it was incomprehensible, even though we were 'on the case' of the darker abuse and this was long after the era of the dream diaries. But the dream was for Mitchell, not for me. And Mitchell duly opened the bag, so to speak, and the metal box, too, at my appointment that very next day.

That box had really existed. A six year old, I *had* helped Dad solder its electrical innards: an invention he was working on at home. He called it a 'lid-lock'. Holding the little iron, because my eyes were young and good and 'so much better than his', I *did* make the minute soldered joint he'd wanted.

But the paper bag! Ah, that contained his other iron, a larger one, solid, pre-war, bulb-nosed, slow-heating. Only by Mitchell's art, I mean by his interpretative skills, asking the hands: is it such and such? Yes? No? Is it such and such? Only so did we find an answer — connecting solder with the thing in the bag, and with the business of locking up the memory. Yes, hypnosis revealed the particular disgusting use Dad found for this his large electrician's tool, though I didn't believe it then, and struggle to now. And so it was this 'Child' I speak about, my body's non-Newtonian sprite, who first brought up the vile subject, who produced the dream, who smuggled his

244

'torture'—for Dad would always turn it off in time; he wasn't a bloody psychopath for Christ's sake!—through to Mitchell. It was his 'warm-up' device. And the sadness was the Child's, mine indeed, lid-locked and sealed by my father's original spells.

Theo, I weave you a midnight web, out of these shadowy figures, out of Julia, Piotr, George, Dad. Out of the icon painter in this storm. Marta, too. These strands make up a membrane—as perhaps in Pinturicchio's Penelope with the Suitors—between my heart and the dark overwhelm of remembered rapes, cunning torments. I say, we're close to the brink of *chóra*, where truth waits and male endeavour dissolves; but it isn't Kristeva's formulation of *chóra*. It's the female space of my own body, and Paris will be my sign for it. We enter symbolically via that chalk cleft Julia and I saw on the hillside the second before we were snatched apart. Whether I like it or not, I've become that primitive philosopher-artist. I've summoned this woman to my island. What, then? What next?

17

Subject: **RE A storm**

You're awake? At this hour? When I clicked 'Send', the last thing I imagined... Theo, it was almost a rhetorical gesture: I said you were hardly supposed even to read it. I didn't expect you... At this time of night!

I forget you're a couple of hours behind. But still... Look, don't trouble yourself. Please don't stay up on my account. It's okay. It's fine. You need your sleep. Take no notice of my ramblings!

Subject: **RE A storm**

I'm not used to this. You're concerned, you say. Still fucking concerned about me! I'm touched. Honestly, it's nothing. The soldering iron. Really, I didn't mean to tell you. It worked its way into what I've just sent you, wouldn't leave me alone. But really, it probably never happened. Most likely, I made it up. Except I didn't even do that! For the whole episode came out between Mitchell and my hands. Honestly, though, it doesn't affect me. Revisiting it. Not after all this time. For Christ's sake, you didn't think... did you? Theo, I keep telling you, I plan nothing stupid. Don't worry. You *must* sleep now. Your work!

Subject: **RE A storm**

Still raining? Yes, it is. Almost beyond rain! Lightning still flares; thunder still wheels and cracks overhead. Now *you* can't sleep? Pull the other one. I'm on to you, my friend. It's just some ruse on your part, a ruse of kindness. You *are* just trying to take my mind off... off everything. And, I do confess, some vague emotion I can't give voice to now constantly rises at my throat and eyes, tonight, while the rain outside unloads in torrents. So yes, I really do appreciate it—that anyone would be generous enough. To offer to stay with me, I mean. I can't get over it, and maybe that's half the emotion...

Subject: **RE A storm**

Alright, if you insist. If you really want to take my mind off 'that soldering iron business', I'll tell you about him. Although nothing in the world will persuade me that you of all people are the least bit interested in Derrida. I'll humour you, Theo. It's a diversion, since now we're both stuck here wide awake. And no I'm not drunk; just a glass or so. And, yes, I did see him once, heard him lecture. Went with French friends to the École in that same summer's heat. '76. None of us understood a word, if you want to know. And I was inclined to think no more of him. So recondite and difficult a *poseur*; what did he think he was stirring up? I quite scorned the whole roller coaster of a 'campaign', in fact, tried not to get caught up in it. I played, if you like, the reactionary, imagining to dismiss Derrida as just another passing fashion—as do all Englishmen, of course, who prate 'mumbo jumbo' to whatever challenges their cosy *Lógos*.

It was only much later, Theo, in the wake of the Post-structuralism conflict, that I saw the force of it. Well, it was unarguable. It laid siege to serious philosophy; I mean rigid, pompous, academic philosophy. Derrida—not just another muscle-bound superhero, but mercurial, witty and mining at the whole grim citadel. It took me another decade, and I shan't go into that. But I pricked up my ears at last, and scurried to read and reread works more mazy of access than any yet, even Jung's, because I, too, had spent years seeking—and failing—to undo the trick of it all.

Now consider this: Derrida exposed a universal sleight of hand—showed how every philosopher must always slyly suppress the reverse proposition of his own text. And he taught that language won't be constricted, and that all who seek to nail one intention to this or that written construction are deluded. But Dad was my first academic. Dad made a nutshell of the universe. Dad constricted the play of my language, so I could never give tongue to that torment, and I was locked in tight to that cold scientific perspective—lid-locked! I was neatly soldered up with logic and his sadistic experiments, where all my fears—and his deeds—were just 'bad dreams'.

Subject: **RE A storm**

Are you sure? You're a glutton for punishment. Very well, I made a joke of the battle, didn't I, some nights ago. It happened. '82, this time.

Don't you recall? That huge Post-structuralism controversy? It even leaked out into the broadsheet press. And the news programmes. Imagine, critical theory on the news, and all kinds of profs and so on drafted in to try to explain it! They failed, of course. You *must* remember, Theo.

But Derrida triumphed. He *did* topple philosophy — with its topless detachment! He overturned its sceptic self-hire to what Barthes called *the fascism of language*. Derrida went for Plato and demolished the root of it. He took apart Plato's puppet play; how Plato's illusion of Socrates was our universal delusion — a delusion that made speech the vehicle of pure thought, and writing merely its poor record. He did it!

Subject: RE A storm

No! You don't understand. Derrida read Plato's reverse: that writing *precedes* speech. Theo, because of Derrida, *nothing* is as we believed it was, as we've imagined all these years. Philosophy has *all* been an illusion, a version of hypnotism. You can't just wave this away.

Subject: RE A storm

For God's sake, you're not getting this. Listen. Pure thought doesn't even exist. And language *isn't* a thing we've made, like some stone tool. We don't think language; language thinks *us*. It *makes* us. And language, with its structures and pathways, may never have begun nor will ever end; language may never have 'evolved', certainly not from animal grunts or primitive squeaks. Language has always been quite separate and of itself; it has *no necessary relation* to reality, to physical experience. Language may be genuinely *meta*-physical!

Do you sync with any of this at all? It's not 'body and mind', but 'body and language'. Theo, you're such an innocent. Where've you been? We *live* in language. We can't even *see* — except through language. Let alone paint. Yes, I mean it. Painting depends on language. There's no innate intelligence but the intelligence of language, and it's not the capacity of our brains at all that distinguishes us from beasts, but merely our involvement with language. Animals: they experience things directly; we don't — because we're trapped in language.

And when we seem to find order, that's the order in language and not nature. I say it again: thought conforms to language, not the other way round. Intelligence, consciousness, these are linguistic phenomena; we don't possess them, we *join* them. Which gives us society, makes the violent immediacy of the world bearable. Ha! Language is the ultimate social networking site. It frees us from rash thoughts, keeps us out of trouble. Hence, the effectiveness of talking therapies, by the way. But once we're 'in' language, we can't get out— except through poetry, or art. That's Barthes. I tell you, for Hamlet's need, Horatio's academic philosophy must *always* be bankrupt. The minute, as children, we first cling to our pronoun 'I' in the sea of language we give up truth, reality, body, mother, world. Reality, as it beats in upon the animal kingdom, becomes something we can never, ever, know again.

Subject: RE A storm

For fuck's sake, old friend! I'm not saying reality doesn't exist. That's just something you've heard. Me, I'm saying the opposite. It does exist. Reality is still 'there', and Derrida might have bid fair to restore Blake's divine universe. But that he and his captains, carousing and tempted by Freud, made the cardinal error. It was *they* who preached that if reality was unknowable, it didn't *matter*.

Subject: RE A storm

It matters crucially: the truth about events. Take my personal history, as to whether Dad was guilty or not; it matters, legally, criminologically, medically. It's the basis upon which I must act. But drunken Baudrillard shouted his latter follies. They all did, and there's your nonsense. *There*'s mumbo jumbo. Ah, but the whole damn victory collapsed into relativism.

Subject: RE A storm

See what you've done! You've pressed me into setting out my artistic manifesto. I might as well. I've never shouted about it. Least of all to you. My artistic manifesto is based on what happened when I surrendered my muscles to the Child. It's based on the skills I learnt in Paris: mime, *the only art* that has that 'pre-linguistic' capacity to offer direct and *real time* replay, that can, perhaps, take us closest to the direct experience of animals, that might steal under language and find, in the living body, the *reality*.

What's my 'purpose', then, as you say? Explicitly to reach back to Manet and stitch up that huge fucking wound.

Subject: RE A storm

Theo, it's glaringly obvious. Modernism *is* a wound, and Postmodernism's no healing. Don't you see? From Manet onwards, the sexes become increasingly estranged. Look! Read! It happens in art, in music, in literature. The retreat from Olympia, say, the retreat from Estella in *Great Expectations*, Zola's *La Bête Humaine*. Take Wilde's *Salomé*, Beardsley, Klimt, then Picasso's shocking *Demoiselles*, the Yeats plays of beheading — and so on.

Subject: RE A storm

That's right. It's everywhere. After Manet, high art's images of woman grow more and more frightening, more sadomasochistic, more abstracted, until, soon after the turn of the century, the nineteenth/twentieth, I mean the female figure disappears almost completely. Alright, I know, with a number of honourable exceptions, late Picasso, Matisse, Moore and so on. But, why?

Subject: RE A storm

Agreed. Science. And the decline of religion. Or Science *is* the new religion. But surely, Theo, it's chiefly because women rose up vocally at last to claim their revenge. For millennia of violation, I mean. Isn't that the case? And no man could answer them. Not with integrity. Not without owning up to a whole catalogue of abuses.

Subject: **RE A storm**

Of course. You're right. Commercial art and the new popular cinema have been full ahead at the same time continuing to exploit sexy images of women. But I'm talking about serious art, honest art, the art that always looked most penetratingly at relationship and the human condition. Art that shouldn't be expected to appear 'transparent' and 'accessible' to everyone and his brother without any effort. Art that has the right to be difficult and to explore—as neither high nor low art currently does—into the interior of real pleasure and real pain. There, we lost the female figure almost entirely.

Subject: **RE A storm**

Alright, but you must see that anyone with half a brain or any artistic soul at all in those days simply *couldn't* go back to painting the figure, or composing harmonic music, or writing happy-ending love stories. It would just have been reactionary. Head-in-the-sand stuff. Like people still bloody tut-tutting and shaking their heads in front of Picassos and Braques. That's low grade anti-intellectual fogeyism! Picasso took art in the only direction it could go, and to deny that would have been to blinker oneself to the philosophical force that drove Modernism in the first place.

Subject: **RE A storm**

Theo, I'm *not* going back on myself. I *am* a figurative painter, but what I'm saying is that if anyone really does want to heal this 'wound of Modernism', as I choose to call it, it has to be done properly, philosophically, on art's own ground. Because all those great modernists weren't fools. They were superb. They truly grasped the implication of their times. To think blindly, as some conservatives actually do, that you can just wind back art's clock, like Hitler, or Stalin, or even the more pettily outraged campaigners with their 'family values' and so on, is just stupid, totalitarian and ignorant.

So no, what I'm attempting is nothing like that. Look, I make no apology. This stuff is hard, and I'm fed up with artists having to keep quiet and make things easy for people. I'm fed up with leaving the interpretation to ill-informed critics. Ha! At least we can say things like that here in private between us!

But no, the job has to be done with the utmost intellectual rigour, caution and self-examination. Theo, it's not enough simply noticing that the conclusions of late nineteenth and mid-twentieth century philosophy—I'm thinking Schopenhauer, of course, and Nietzsche, through to Heidegger and Sartre, and Comte, too, in his own way— are fundamentally depressive. It's not sufficient to recognise that the habitual ascetic and profound withdrawal of the 'great philosophical mind' from communion with others in order to 'think' and 'philosophise' would be a huge bloody psychiatric danger signal in anybody else. It doesn't solve the problem just to realise that their eternal scepticism annihilates faith and hope—and consequently the prospect of fulfilling relationship. It's no good just smartly observing that the very similar depressive and existential conclusions drawn by so many abused in childhood are labelled medically as mental illness rather than philosophy! We may wring our hands over the loss of God and the desperate *huis clos* it left us in. So many Modernist artists did that, too. But the devastating logic of that whole philosophical drive remained unassailable. Two horrific wars—such a wound—and then the on-going threat of nuclear annihilation all bore it out to the letter. God *was* dead. The world we occupied was *indeed* a mere speck of irrelevant dust at the edge of a violent, abandoned and hate-filled universe.

Until Derrida, Theo! I'm serious. Until Derrida: who showed that there are *no* answers in philosophy. There can *never* be answers. Reasoning can deliver *nothing*, because reason is trapped in language. He showed that philosophy itself was trapped in the delusion of the philosopher's hearing himself speak. I shan't go into that, but do you see? Derrida freed us from those mortifying philosophers who underwrote our despair. He even frees us from Science. Derrida suddenly gave us licence legitimately to imagine a different world. If the new vision didn't in his hands turn out to be the divine one I suggested, that seems to me entirely because his conclusions were

252

instantly contaminated with Freudian psychoanalysis—which is demonstrably fraudulent. But he wasn't to know that at the time.

Nevertheless, *with* those psychoanalytic rogues, Freud and Lacan, Derrida offers only a blind alley to those seeking recovery.

But *without* them, the world suddenly opens up…

You see now how crucial is our man, this Derrida. That it's Art, not Science; fiction not 'fact', that can give us the truth about reality. That's a revolutionary statement, Theo!

Imagine a time when people actually *believed* in the divine universe. Imagine how it would have felt when the sacred texts, Christian, Neoplatonic, Islamic, Hermetic, offered *genuine* maps of the world. So Botticelli, Michelangelo & Co weren't just playing at *decoration* when they painted the human figure. They could see their work as genuinely magical, genuinely sacred—in a way that has been denied to art since Newton (and latterly since George Brede!) chased all the gods and spirits out of the landscape. Every subsequent painter of classical scenes is, yes, a mere fanciful illustrator of Ovid, or the *Aeneid*, or whatever, no matter how fine a technician.

And so we had those stagnant forms and stuffy academicians—that brought about the Salon de Refusés and the birth of Modernism. Modernism was Modernism because no one could believe in the image any more.

But now, Theo. Now, post-Derrida, we have the chance again to make art, if not exactly out of 'faith'—that's a silly, Victorian, PRB sort of aim—but out of love. Love as the organising principle, love as represented by the human form in movement: *La Primavera* again as a statement of… Of reality, Theo. That's why I'm a painter of the figure. Not for decoration, not for commemoration, not to please the multitude, but to make a representation of the truth. That's what I'm trying to do, Theo. It's a duty. Not fashionable, not easy, not authorised, but *accurate*. It's the dance, the cosmic dance that some of those quantum physicists used to speak of. It's the play: the bride of flowers, Blodeuwedd, the dying and resurrected hero, Llew, the magus, Gwydion, the angel, the betrayal.

Every few centuries comes someone who flings open this philosophical window. Artists see the vision of it, and Art bursts into flower. Briefly, the world fills up with the possibilities of love—before some monstrous regime and its 'philosophy' shuts it all down again.

So I say once more: *with* those psychoanalytic rogues Freud and Lacan, Derrida is just a quirky irrelevance. *Without* Freud, Derrida makes everything at once pregnant with a kind of joy, like the Spring. The human figure, Theo! The human figure, trailing flowers... Hence my artistic purpose: it's to un-seam Derrida from Freud. That's what I've been trying to do all along.

Subject: **RE A storm**

Go to bed! You take me to task for intellectualising, for philosophising myself. Alright. Consider it might be no more than a symptom of abuse: floating above reality and relationship...

Bah! Isn't that exactly what art itself has done for the last hundred and fifty years? And contemporary art still hangs over the body of tradition, doesn't it, quite absorbed in its own theoretics. It looks down ironically, if you will, from the philosophical cross to which it remains nailed. Contemporary, post-modern art is still desolate, intellectual, flippant. Just look at all the big galleries — and your own stable, Theo.

For me, healing must come with the ability to bring the sexes together artistically. It's *pleasure*. Pleasure in a sacred marriage, if you like, the alchemical ιερός γάμος at the traditional end of a comedy. And that's almost a forbidden subject, isn't it. In high art. It flies in the face of everything 'contemporary' and currently 'orthodox'. It's a heresy, and I shall no doubt be hauled over the coals for it.

But you'll see now what I was attempting to do in my Bledlow picture, and why its failure led to all that has since passed between you and me. I was anticipating that the piece would exhibit an original *wound to relationship* — showing Julia and me in a paradise immediately to be disrupted. A 'Fall' if you will — the exact emblem of this Modernist jinx. This Fall then initiates my 'portrait of the artist as a young man'. After which sequence I planned gradually to catch up with myself and to move on to the respective efforts that both Eléni and I are making to build a new relationship out of the pieces. As a defiant act of recovery, Theo! Of *resistance*. You see? A long term artistic plan! And a personal one!

Yes, Bledlow was to be a perfect statement of the *problem*, Theo. But not of the *solution*! That's why I'm so *bewildered* by the appearance of this painting woman. Surely, she throws a huge spanner in the works. Eléni and I were putting our money where our mouth was. You see? Hard; but then relationship *is* hard. Eléni's the gift I've been given. But now this... this Julia-*ísos* — Julia-perhaps.

254

Well, at least I've engaged you. I've caught your interest. Have I even challenged your gallery! Ah, when it comes down to it, maybe I'm just a crazy in the night. Who can tell! A sleepless old soldier; or is it sailor I am. What do I know of these rarefied matters? But do you see at last? Do you see how Derrida's jemmy might lever art off its cross.

Derrida might have let the body's history underwrite expression, finding a resurrection in the derided voice, saying 'Yes! This happened; here are the scars to prove it!' From Derrida might have sprung faith. Hope, too. Even love. Other stories – decried as fictions – might have combated Science's story – authorised as fact. Art might have mutinied against the accepted hierarchy. Do you see how Derrida's tragedy wasn't that he was wrong. His tragedy, like Agamemnon's, was in sacrificing his virgin thought almost blindly to Freud, whose falsified tracts, whose denial of the body's heartfelt cries, could not but turn him, and his followers, to morally offensive...

Ah, stop my brain, my fingers! For, as I write these words, the whole sky lights. The headland leaps clear as day, and it fades again in what I've just done. Theo, I disclosed to you the very worst of Dad's abuse and then covered it over again. Disclosed my manifesto with screeds and screeds – pages – of philosophy. Even as I debunk it! Jesus! Soliloquising on the edge of the grave! Intellectualising, I spur my furious hobby horse! And all to put an intense black ring around the hideous revelation of Dad and his iron...

Dripping foliage outside; the deluge slackens. The storm moves south toward Crete. Now the black air steams at my window with wetted rock and goatish herbs. That photograph, Julia and me, looking so happy.

Only, I see at last, these acts of writing to you about the accident of my condition – a literature I'd normally keep to myself – our whole string of emails of my treatment in the clinic and how I came here... *This* is what might threaten the whole critical juggernaut... Heaven's noises; one late forked flash! ...because *you*, Theo, my singular reader, might see the damn'd incestuous villain's guilt, might judge from all this body of evidence – even if I still struggle with it – that the need to paint, sculpt, or write really might not proceed from the human creativity we so pride ourselves on, nor from 'genius', nor 'imagination', nor 'self-expression', nor heedless play, nor, most of all, from some stupid idea of the repression of allegedly paradisal pre-linguistic and incestuous Freudian *wishes*! No, but from the *real* murder of feeling, from the sexual and political violence implicit in our vaunted *philosophy*, and enacted in genuine abuse.

Art as the evidence of our penetration by evil. Art as the political struggle not against God the Father but against the Devil Father of Lies! Wouldn't that, Theo, rewrite our modern assumptions? Wouldn't that upset the prevailing cosy deal between academia and the arts market?

So the arts might take themselves seriously again: science's antidote rather than its fucking placebo, its foreground rather than its frame, its muse rather than its whore. The arts might become once more what they always were — a constant reminder of evil's attack. Upon love.

It's dawn. I've slept a little, curled in one of our armchairs here — thanks to you, my dear friend. You talked me down, as though I were some sky pilot unable to land. Or you let me talk my*self* down, should I say. *Your* faith: you gave me licence to rave, no matter what babble it was! *Your* hope. *Your* love. Oh, you took the risk of me, and I'm inexpressibly moved by it.

Have you slept, too? I trust so.

Outside, the drench evaporates. The Aegean lies blue under rinsed skies. From this self-same sea, love rose foam-born, so myth has it: Aphrodite, shell-borne intercessor between God and man. Love is the divine link the icon painter showed me in a vision in a cave. I think of those four Greek labels: *Philía, Éros, Stórge, Agápe*.

And of a woman who came to paint outside my back garden. My true friend, I review, in love, all I've written to you this long night. Meaning? Choice? My rage at Freud — and Jung, too, that dreamy obscurantist? I've spoken of Derrida. Theo, surviving them all imposes a burden on me, whose destiny it has been to sail strange seas and make landfall on islands none has recalled. All art is religious, all art illustration. The story we must show is one of love, and I must survive again and tell the tale of it. A warrior, I must take the risk, the spiritual gamble of my own recovery — to become a man. And even so shall I draw, by this pre-potent play of energy, the woman in the straw hat, whoever she is, to visit me again!

18

Subject: Lemons

Her easel in the exact same spot, her sunshade fluttering at an angle in the breeze.

I'd been in my studio, of course. Eléni has had to jet to Athens for another couple of days. Because of the riots, she says; this continuing Euro crisis… and I'm my own boss again. Once more, it was about eleven when I saw the woman, just as I crossed to the house for my break.

In England, after such a deluge, we should expect evidence: puddles on paths, gutters awash, lawns a-glisten. I think of stark birdsong in lush growths bowed down, from whose leaves the wet still drips. Not a bit of it here. The storm might never have happened. Our ground becomes almost instantly dry, our vegetation once again parched.

And there she was.

I found a juice carton in the fridge. Like some elixir, it claimed nine different fruits. I poured two glasses, rammed on my sunglasses and hat and took out the offering on a little tray—making my way carefully down to the wire gate and round again through the scrub until she saw me.

'Oh, it's you,' she said, her face brightening.

'*Yeia sas, kyría,*' I said, and held out the tray. '*Akóma káti na piíte.*'

'Is that for me? How kind. Thank you so much. *Evcharistó.*' She put down her brush on the ledge of the easel, took one of my tumblers and sipped. I sipped at mine.

'This is delicious.' She raised her eyebrows.

I listed random words for fruit from my CDs: '*Portokália, rothákina, pepónia, míla, achláthia, lemónia…*'

'I know that one,' she laughed. 'Lemons!'

'*Ne,*' I said. 'Lemons!'

'That's it! Lemons!'

We laughed together.

I looked at her painting as I'd done before. The top of our bluff was now strongly dashed in over quite a subtle delineation of the horizon. She'd even made a suggestion of the Turkish coast—today very faintly visible. The body of the sea, however, and the contrasting upthrust of bare rocks were hardly begun. Not to mention the sky. It all felt as though she were hesitant, unsure how to proceed. And I believed I knew the reason: the daylight was so brilliant that every colour seemed slightly to oscillate; nature was blinded by her own creation. That was it. Homer's bronze reflective sky shone unpaintable, while the sea flounced and sported to every motion of the breeze.

If I could establish myself before she left. As a fellow painter...

'*Egó*,' I said, pointing with both hands at my chest. '*Íme kallitéchnis k'egó.*' They were the same words I'd used to Spíros. 'I'm an artist, *too*.'

She looked blank, and I willed her to understand, nodding at her painting. 'You like it?' she said, juice drink in hand. She stared at me. 'You want it? I'm afraid it isn't for sale. It's not even half-finished, anyway.' She was shaking her head.

'*Óchi, óchi!*' I shook mine. '*Then katalavénete*—You don't understand!' I tried again, building up from first elements, as it were. '*Egó*,' pointing at my chest.

'Okay,' she said. 'I've got it. "I" It's like Latin, isn't it. *Ego*. We learnt it at school. How strange.'

I nodded vigorously and pointed again to myself, imitating her English: 'I'. But before I could ham it further, there was a stream of music from her bag.

She dashed down her glass and rummaged for the noise, flinging me a hurried 'Excuse me'. She peered once at her screen, jabbed the button and snatched the phone to her ear.

It wasn't the husband. She seemed relieved at the call, but agitated, too. Strain my ears as I might, I could hear nothing of the other party above the sough of the breeze, the insects' murmur and the waves' low, insistent crash, crash on to the beach below—sounds a moment ago all but inaudible.

But her tone suggested a male. A son, then? Yes, some grown up son about whom she was anxious, and whom she could still address with some impatience. Why hadn't he returned her calls? Where had he been? Indeed, I'd almost plumped for the son, when 'Your wife!' she cried. 'Why? When did she decide to do that? Can't you get out of it?' A pause. 'So where are you now? In Rome?! Why?!' He had an explanation, but there was anger in her voice, mixed with disappointment. 'So you don't think you can get here at all? Oh, Stefan!'

Theo, I shall eavesdrop no longer on this conversation—at least not here in my email. It ended shortly afterwards, with certain breathy endearments and an agreement, I gleaned, that he'd call the following morning at the same time—which would be safe, she told him, 'because I'll be out here on my own again, painting. This place I've found, where no one comes, except... Oh, just a bay and some rocks. Well, I've got to have something to show for it, haven't I.'

So she had a lover. Whose name was Stefan. And I'd been quite wrong about the intensity of the light and all that business—her picture was merely a pretext. Stefan had a wife, who was being difficult. He'd made it to Rome—from wherever—but their Greek island tryst was now off. I'd learned these things; I must immediately appear not to know them at all.

She remained crestfallen. She put the mobile in her bag and gazed bleakly out past her canvas, seemingly oblivious not just of my existence but of the world at large. I was about to steal away when she turned her head. 'I'm sorry,' she said. 'Don't go.' She motioned with her arm. 'Sorry about that.' She picked up her drink.

I nodded, pretending to respond only to her gesture. '*Then pirázi kathólou*—It doesn't matter at all.'

What had I expected? Julia and Miles the devoted couple?

...If Julia it is.

Again I cudgelled my brain for that exact voice. But it was so long ago, and everything changes. Nor did she give any sign that she recognised mine, nor the contours of my face behind my dark glasses, nor the way I moved, nor any element of me. Everything changes, my friend. Everything is covered over and buried.

Subject: Point of Entry

Today she came much earlier. I didn't delay. I found a small folding easel of my own and carried it boldly out—wearing my usual sunglasses and hat. I planted the easel in a space just to her left and paid no heed at all to her surprised expression. Then I went back for my things: a workbox of paints, brushes, knives, the oil pot and so on, and several smallish canvases, of which I made play in front of her, so that she'd have no doubt they were empty from the start. I clamped one of them up on the stand, but angled it just out of her sight line. Then I brought myself a dark green plastic chair, together with the cheap garden parasol that Eléni and I had brought from England.

'*Kaliméra*!' I hammered the parasol's lower section into the ground. I erected the shade, swung my sunglasses up on to my hair like an open visor and sat purposefully, giving her only the merest sideways glance before settling to my trade, choosing colours and beginning to squeeze out paint on my own tin plate.

'*Kaliméra*,' she said, with perhaps the hint of a smile. Though I did notice, too, a certain puffiness about her eyes.

I worked fast, Theo. So much light—no need for spectacles. You'll like this sketch; it's of Cécile and Félix as Llew the 'Lion' and Gwydion the magician, with Minalouche as the inconstant flower bride. And there's the suggestion of myself lurking in the role of Flea at the edge of the canvas. Here are the shadowy faces of the audience, here the shop fronts in the streetlight. And just imagine for a moment how it might have been if, by some quirk of history, the Renaissance had endorsed Hesperian myths instead of classical ones: we might now have a Botticelli of Blodeuwedd; a Di Cosimo of death by riddle; a Leonardo anatomical of a wren's leg!

Yet all such froth and speculation felt this morning, even as I worked them up in paint... they felt again as merely a kind of golden captivity, or persistent state of chrysalis: the Parts—certainly the Girl, certainly the Child, say, cooped in that Paris room with those surrogate parents... the Parts strutting their stuff as, to be sure, they seemed immediately to do after Bledlow without so much as being asked or called upon; the Parts I hardly knew suddenly let loose and rushing out upon the world, Paris after Julia: melting down love for art...

My painting companion stole glances. Of course she did, though she could see nothing of my work. But she refused absolutely to give in and ask questions. No, she played her 'part' and carried on at her own scene—in which, via my own stolen glances—I saw her sea begin to foam at the base of the bluff, and some of her sky achieve its heated, almost colourless, colour. For she, too, seemed energised. Today, she painted properly, if not quite in my own buzz of composition, then with conviction. And so was it no longer such a cover for something else...?

While she was absorbed, I dropped my sunglass visor back down over my eyes and hurried indoors for the nine-fruit juice.

I handed her the drink again, waiter-like from my tray.

'Thank you so much.' She sipped at the tumbler. '*Evcharistó polý*,' her accent and stress more confident.

260

Her picture: I clapped again. '*Brávo!*'

'I'm not sure,' she clicked her tongue. 'It's coming, I suppose.'

She looked pointedly towards my easel. 'Well, I don't see why I shouldn't.' Her lips compressed and, holding her glass, she stood up and stepped round to get a full view at last.

Her jaw dropped. Her face screwed up in puzzlement. Then she peered at me. 'But I don't understand,' she said. She raised her eyebrows and made an elaborate mime, pointing out to sea and then to my animated characters, shaking her head and shrugging her shoulders. 'It's not from life at all. You're... it's something else!' Her tone — indignant, bewildered, amused?

'*Apó to Parísi.*' I said.

'Parisi?'

'*Parísi. Ne. Bonjour. Comment ça va?*' I gave it some Gallic shrugs.

'Ah! Paris!'

'*Ne,*' I nodded vigorously. 'Paris.'

'*Mais vous parlez français?*'

Julia spoke excellent French. '*Óchi, óchi,*' I said, quickly jutting my chin up. '*Óchi français.*'

'Then why?' she spread her hands and glanced about her in frustration. 'What...? Why Paris?'

'Paris.' I continued to smile and nod.

She eyed me very closely, as though seeking to pierce the disguise of my shades. Then she turned back to my canvas, making the clapping gesture in turn. 'It's really good.'

'*Íme kallitéchnis ki egó.*'I gave a slight bow.

Now she twigged the phrase. 'Yes of course. An artist. And a good one. I'm so sorry. Sorry I misunderstood. Rude of me, assuming you wanted to buy.' She laughed and paused, as if in a private reverie. 'I was once...'

But the phone went off again in her bag, and she squatted to retrieve it.

'Yes, Stefan. Painting, of course. The bay. No. Yes. Yes, I realise. Look, there's somebody here. A Greek, an artist. For heaven's sake, it's no one. It's no one! I know I did. Sorry, it's awkward. I can't talk now. Yes, of course I do. It's just that it isn't quite... Look, I'll call you back. Stefan? Okay. Yes. You, too. I'll call you.' She killed the conversation with an apologetic glance to me and slipped the phone into her bag.

So we remained, examining our drinks and smiling at one another.

Oh, theatre! Transformative, shape-shifting comedy! Am I the puppeteer, holding the strings?

So much of our great painting tradition originates from staged life: the contrived perspective of the old religious pageants, with their elaborate three-sided nativities, their symbolic mountains or engineered gardens, both of Eden and Gethsemane. Don't you agree; theatre is midwife to our whole endeavour.

Your latest has just arrived, and I've read it. Quite! Yes, I could quote you Picasso's Blue Period, and his Rose, too. You're still so scathing about illustration, Theo, and I'd reply that we see Picasso's theatrical figures, don't we, through the lens of a hundred years. Our hindsight is tutored in mistrust, some of it Picasso's own. I mean mistrust of the figure. We know his inscrutable faces and morose bodies stand exactly at the point — under the artist's apprehension — of giving way altogether. Before long, they'll fracture and flatten to Cubism, and then the human form will vanish entirely, like the soon-to-be-displaced of Europe, into a taste for abstraction. Outline will fail and colour drain through it, unbounded, as though no skin could hold what blood is to be shed. Two world wars.

Sending now in hope to catch you before you log off.

Subject: The treachery of images

I agree. Such was our birth century, yours and mine. We must seek to understand, but perhaps not so blindly celebrate its iconoclasm. It seems such a perfect progression, now, indeed, from Pablo's mournful jugglers and *saltimbancos* to the alleged freedom of the Modern: Cubism, Expressionism, Fauvism, all the way to the fifties' *Avant Garde* and the rest. But listen, Picasso's player folk are parts without plot. Torn from their comedy, they stand or sit, as immobilised as Joyce's *Dubliners*, because their *theatre*, that always religious structure through which art once imagined the cosmology of hope, is already blown away. So here, too, we discern icons of hell: Picasso, the master, dreams wars to come. His work *is* prophecy — reflective, melancholic in the true sense — and that's a sadness. Truly we shouldn't mistake crisis, as Freud does, for normality.

Ah, you know too well how Paris was an epoch to which I pinned my hopes in glowing imaginative colours right up to a couple of weeks ago... Indeed, that heated sexual ambiguity really was the spur to my later 'Gentileschi' paintings. Yet in comparison to working here beside my tantalising companion…

For surely this vital contrast, her flesh-and-blood against my frigid Paris masquerade — of blown identity, *appearing* gay not *being* gay — brings everything into sharp focus. Paris, the summer of my former days, compared to the winter years of marriage to Lily, the breakdown, the illness…

I called Modernism a retreat. Theo, this woman's presence here next to me shouts suddenly that my venture to Paris was a retreat if ever there were one. For there I didn't so much lose myself in art as *become* art, in my make-up and post-traumatic overwhelm. I allowed myself to die and to fragment. The symbolic hermaphrodite, said the old alchemists, 'needs fire'. I was, yes, a hermaphroditic *confusion*: of performance, intellect, the Parts, brief chronicles. I repeated abstracts in a kaleidoscope of recycled stories. I perched above reality, like Yeats's golden bird, like the mortifying eagle in *The Lion with the Steady Hand*. And maybe I've stayed that way. Even with Eléni, maybe I'm still a husk, incapable of emotion, failing genuinely to paint this story of mine which has the power…

I'd done three adequate sketches this morning before the oil became loose and the colour sticky. My companion was also feeling the heat, constantly mopping her face with a tissue. Soon, the day was too fierce to continue. She tapped her watch and began to pack her things.

I intercepted her work and held it up as a surreal backdrop to my figures. Her paint application was skilful. She was talented, her seascape well on its way.

But that was when its emptiness struck me. She'd edited out all the yachts and freighters of our waterway, leaving only the distance. Why, it seemed she was trying to do Greece without the Greeks! I felt her watching me and grew angry: that we were *both* somehow in retreat from the world.

'*Yia póso keró tha mínete stin Ellátha?* — How long are you staying in Greece?' I slammed down my dark glasses over my eyes and turned to her. I had to know. It was imperative. I did everything, indicated the island, pointed to the sun and so on. I mimed sleeping and waking and then sleeping again. I rested her canvas on the ground and made flapping gestures with my arms to show her leaving by plane. '*Póte févyete?*' I said, insistently. 'When do you leave?'

Previously so acute, she now misunderstood — perversely. 'I'm Julia,' she said. She pointed both hands to her heart and said it again.

'My name, if that's what you want to know. It's Julia.'

'*Dzoúlia*,' I repeated, stupidly. '*Dzoúlia*.'

'That's it. Nearly,' she laughed. 'Julia. And you?'

I was in role, two places at once. I had no clever answer like returning Odysseus, who in disguise spun yarn after yarn to melt Penelope's heart. I opened my mouth.

'*Me léne Spíro. To ónoma mou íne Spíros. Spíros Apostolíthis.*'

'Spiros?'

'*Ne.*'

Subject: The persistence of mime

Her foreground: bright, bleached stalks, scrub, low sages, thyme in flower. With their goat-resistant spines and bitter leaves, they baffle her. The morning sun lurks over the horizon, and I watch her try now this, now that. She scrapes off, starts over. Still the effect eludes her.

And you and I, Theo; your email! Why, you're as excited as I am, old friend. We're both of us quite beside ourselves. Because we've done it, haven't we! It's her. It's actually Julia! Do you know, I can't help thinking of that scene in *Pygmalion* when Higgins and Pickering bring Eliza back from the ball, and she's turned up trumps. But all they can do in their self-congratulation is ignore her. Which is simply to say that Shaw finally 'discovers' his male and female leads centre stage together, and then can't bring himself to marry them off!

What am I saying! She ruined my life! Now I've got her at my mercy… in a manner of speaking.

She looks up at last, and this time I leave my visor raised — deliberately. I point to her workbox. I lift my brows. She nods.

Still in my outrageous alias, though, still Spíros, still somehow mumming it on the very brink of her credulity, I pick out a paint-stiffened, neglected old brush with fibres missing. I work it against a rock. I take colour from her tin palette.

'Go ahead, if you can help,' she shrugs. 'I don't mind.'

I lean over her shoulder, close, my cheek almost against her hair. I spike the brush to her canvas.

A gasp, 'Oh, yes.' She clicks her tongue. 'Of course. Why didn't I…?'

I work a moment more. Her hand, her voice. 'May I?' she says.

'*Vevéos.*' I pass the brush.

She tries. Again. She breathes out crossly through her nose. Very gently, I put my hand over hers. I hold it just firmly enough to sense the response of the brush. I feel her fingers relax into mine. We work, making the colour talk in fine dry points, for probably no more than a minute, teasing out thorns, suggesting leaves.

I let go. A stillness.

'Thank you,' she says at last. She turns her face up to mine. '*Evcharistó.*'

Eyes unprotected. She must see me, know me.

But she gives no sign.

'*Parakaló, kyría.*'

I step back, Theo. How long do I have? '*Yia póso keró tha mínete stin Ellátha.*'

She shakes her head.

I point out to sea. '*Póte févyete?*' Then to her, to indicate going.

This time, at last, she understands. 'We've got another three weeks here.' She holds up three fingers. 'At our age, time is…' She shrugs, smiles.

'*Tris méres mónó?*—Only three days?' Pointing to three traversing suns, I show helplessness, deliberately obtuse. I raise eyebrows at her painting.

'No,' shaking her head and laughing. 'Three weeks. Three *weeks!*' Her hands twice showing the full ten fingers. And then one.

'*Ah!* *Yia tris evthomáthes!*' Every sign of relief.

And when she packs up, I take hold of her painting again. She speaks in Greek—my Greek, bits she's cottoned on to. '*Óchi ávrio,*' she says, shaking her head. 'I'm afraid I can't come tomorrow.' She points to her watch. Now she makes four days go past by circling with her finger and then holds up the sign for four. '*Óchi ávrio.* Four days,' she says. 'We go to Sými.' She mimes painting and shakes her head again, gesturing seaward. 'Sými. For four days. Four days. Or five. Yes? *Ne?* For a trip. But I'll be back.' She smiles.

What then, Theo? What do I want? Let her have Stefan. Let her have Miles, even. I am, in a sense, by this, enough on fire.

19

Subject: Shipwreck

I see what you mean. Yes, I did have a 'steady hand', didn't I.

But not any more, alas.

Theo, I'm writing this in a state of shock. Eléni's leaving. I mean quitting for good. She landed from Athens at eleven last night, and I could tell she was different: something stagey and irritable about her, a certain little *business* with the suitcases as she came out of Arrivals. I felt, even in the dark outside, that she made merely the simulacrum of a homecoming. And the kiss—what are these nuances of touch and gesture? We pick up flavours directly from the ones we know best, or thought we knew. I asked her there and then what was the matter.

'Matter? I don't know. What do you mean? I'm tired from the trip. Haven't I a right to be?'

At least I'd flushed out a reaction. I stowed her luggage in the boot of the taxi and sat beside her. It was a strained atmosphere. Our tiny airport is in the north, the military area of the island. We said little, the long road home. Once here, I made her tea. We drank it in the kitchen, the naked bulb on the ceiling staring and unpropitious.

'Do you want to tell me why you're different? Darling?'

'People do change,' she said. 'I suppose it'll take me a while to come back. Owen, it was such a good break, so refreshing to have time to myself. I mean really to myself. Athens is spoiled, of course, and there's no money. But then I didn't spend all my time in the city.'

I asked where she *had* spent time. It emerged, of course, that there was some man. She'd met him the visit before. Purely platonic, she insisted: just 'bumped into him' again, and they'd simply got on well. A young architect, friend of the family; and yes, they'd had such a great time together, so refreshing—that word again. Everything had made her think. So not surprising, she said, if I found her different.

In bed, I challenged her further. Perhaps I shouldn't have. Perhaps, if I hadn't, she would indeed have come back in her own time.

Oh Jesus, Theo, I feel terrible. Sure, sure, if I'd left it alone, she might, yes, have come back. Yes, maybe she would, once she'd 'sobered up', as always—is that too cruel or inappropriate a metaphor?

266

But is getting her back what I really want?

I haven't told you this—of course, I haven't—but she's been prone to one or two of these 'excursions' in the past. Someone called Kieran at least I knew about. Prone to excursions—another little foible, you might say, along with the booze. But do *I* want to be prone to them, too? For the rest of my life?

God, I look at the whole set up and I want to kick myself. What a fool I was to believe she'd genuinely made the commitment this time. Fool! Fool! Fool!

But I'd reason to, for heaven's sake! Hadn't I? Given this whole joint venture and all we've been through with it. Given that we've just tied ourselves tightly and financially together into this house in Léros!

Anyway, I kept on and pressed her about Athens, and that's when it all blew up. That's when she exploded into a decision. The rest of the night was naturally horrible—and final, as it's turned out. I still don't know what really went on with the young architect, and I don't want to. What matters is that in the depths of our confrontation, she called the whole thing right off. I mean our thing.

My dear friend, there's such a wreckage in my heart—I'm all washed up, and I guess it'll be a while before I'm used to it. Right now, I don't know what I'll do to keep going. I mean money-wise. Gone is the privilege of my days: artistic licence—now there's a laugh! Why, these last few days we've been celebrating, haven't we, you and I. We've been speculating wildly about magic, Julia and alchemy and how to play it next. And my Artistic Manifesto! As though it were some late night game of men we'd stumbled upon. What does any of that matter now? No, all at once I'm strewn about in pieces and the only question is one of survival.

I'm done for, Theo. I have no income. Suddenly! Suddenly, I have no income at all We were living on hers. My only chance is to sell a painting or two.

Any painting, Theo. And sell it at once. I'm trying to put a brave face on it, but now I find I depend upon you absolutely. I'm so sorry. Tell me, while I think of it, is there any news from our American friends? Could they offer a spar to cling to?

And do say how are things with you? How is Fran? I send you my best.

Subject: Rejection

Oh, infuriating, the States! This 'thanks, but no thanks'! What's fucking wrong with them? I thought the deal was virtually a formality, after last time. Another body blow.

Thank you, anyway, for forwarding it; and for your commiserations. So glad you're both well.

Subject: Dissociative bodily symmetry

No, everything is just as it was. Eléni and I exist in an undeclared truce. At breakfast, she holds only icy converse, while I reply in kind. I glimpse no reconciliation. Neither of us wants one. It's unlike any of our other rows; we've made ourselves stonily separate. We know each in our heart of hearts that there's no going back. You query the finality. You don't know *us*. You don't know *her*. She's an odd girl, she really is. I don't know what I was doing with her in the first place. She kept protesting love and permanence, and I guess I... Older man with a young woman. Shocking! Disgusting! I guess I'm just getting what I deserve.

Theo, my impulse collapses. The upper lip unstiffens, and panic, that old companion, rises. Ah, nauseous.

Faint; I thought I'd got free of it. How wrong! Forgive me. I sound hysterical. Christ knows this happens all the time: man meets woman; they get together; they split up.

Well and good, they're adults. Arrangements are made, property divided.

Well and good... The pain, I can bear. I've been through these acrimonious splits before.

But the panic...

Why did I allow myself to become so totally *dependent* on this woman? My God, it was set up like this precisely so that I *could* paint!

I can't blame her. Surely, she was generous. But, as I said to you once, until very recently I was bringing in as much income as her, and now, with the failure of this American deal, she's suddenly the only earner. At a stroke, I've no income at all, Theo, and my self-indulgent struggle to see my way through this current work... It all takes such time. And she wants to leave *now*. Leave — just like that. She'd go this minute if she could.

She promises not to touch our joint bank account — out of good will. 'You'll get a job,' she says. 'You'll find something.' She patronises. She almost pats me on the head.

There are no fucking jobs, Theo! Not for the Greeks; certainly not for me. There are only our loans to service, bills to pay. Not to mention what it costs simply to live, even here. And if I have to give all my waking hours to survival, then art, the Child, is lost. That's the nub of it. Art is the Child's only voice, high art, difficult art, the only way I can tell his story. That's why I'm panicking, surely. It's a Part, an overwhelm.

No, the house will have to be sold. But even that will take money, money I don't have...

Still too raw to paint — indulge me in this. I try to reply to you, seeking in vain the dance of the fingers that I enjoyed so very recently, that sweet interplay of hands, as though continually improvising, perhaps, at the piano, each word next its fellow, whole sentences plaited out of some strange dissociative bodily symmetry. Bunkum!

Write of what? Hypnosis? All trash and trickery. Mitchell Stevens at the Meredith Clinic with his attitudes of prayer! I couldn't do it, anyway, just as I can't write now. The icon painter? Can't focus. Hands shaking — it's hopeless.

Subject: **A box for strangers**

Eléni's somewhere about the house. Outside is the heat and atmosphere of another day. How on earth am I going to deal with this, Theo? How?

Subject: **Ocean, with dark sky**

You don't understand. After the clinic, a door miraculously opened. I found a way into the art world, and I tried to take advantage of it. Then, infinitely slowly, I got human again. Eléni came, and I tried to belong to her. But times have grown hostile. I took a false turn. I'm like the poor Abbé Faria, using all his strength and wit to tunnel for years through rock — only to find himself in another prisoner's cell!

The devil smiles. The Child's angry. God's angry. The Son and the Father; I can contact neither. I'm dead, Theo. Ditch me. I tell you, rationally, objectively, I have no future.

Subject: Woman laughing

Contacts? I *have* none. Enter *my* universe, for Christ's sake. It's light years from yours! My family are all estranged from me—because I raised the spectre of incest. You don't know what it's like! Friends, I've left them behind. My *only* 'network' is interior: the post-traumatic Parts. And a useless bunch they are!

As for employment, even in England, no skill or cunning of mine, other than in painting, carries the slightest weight in the commercial world. I'm not young. I'm long out of touch. Any work I got would be minimum wage and all hours. Those are the facts, Theo. The dream's gone. This vortex won't spew me up again.

As for the survivor support groups you talk of, there *are* none. They've all been long killed off, and I haven't the nerve or the energy to keep going it alone. Besides, I don't even believe I am one: 'survivor'.

No it'll all come down to medication, I know it, just to keep a little dead-end job and a bedsit somewhere. I'll be rendered 'normal'.

For who'll believe what I can't back up myself? And Dad will have been just a guy. My symptoms? Mere chemical aberrations in the brain. Or something in the genes. Ah, Science! Sure as lobotomy, everything will go. Most went by the end of the nineties; and then came along all these famous 'international security threats' we live with. No patience with the likes of me. Or time. Goodbye, then, to both body and art.

Glad at least that I've passed on Josh's work. He was targeted, I told you, back in the States. Persecuted, actually. I feel like the last person in the world.

Eléni's phoning the architect. All hours of the day she does it, now that her mobile phone bill's 'her own'. I've made up a bed by my computer downstairs. But always I hear her, above me, in *our* room, gossiping on and laughing with him sometimes for an hour or more at a stretch. I don't hear the actual words, but just the happy chirrup of people who're so pleased with themselves. *He*'s besotted, she says, smiling. *She* simply has 'no one else to talk to'. *I* keep asking myself why I should care so much, because I don't believe I'd want her back even if it were on the cards. Truly, it's over. Then why is it so hurtful that she laughs and chatters all hours with my replacement?

Because it's cruel! She flaunts her power over me, and her love turns to indifference; what was once all is suddenly nothing. She thrusts this discontinuity in my face because I won't let her simply disappear over the horizon. Just as she scarpered from my predecessor, now I think of it. She seeks to hurt me because I've insisted, Theo, that the length of our relationship—mark you, a full seven years in UK prior to this venture to Greece—entitles me to some consideration. Doesn't it? Or is it acceptable for a person just to vanish? On a whim? Someone who was insisting she loved me the very morning she first went off to Athens? I told you she was something of a one off.

She disavows any claim to the house—presumably the architect...

Our balance in the bank will last about two months. By which time, she blithely suggests, I should have been able to get a job. Portering down at the fruit warehouse, filling shelves at the big Lakkí supermarket? Ha ha! Greece is in financial meltdown, and I can't even really speak the language.

This is another punishment. I shouldn't have gone to the icon painter, should never have shown him my paintings—never let the secret out of the bag. I should never have told you about the abuse. All hell has blown loose.

The Child, he kicks and screams. I don't know how to comfort him. Painting is the accommodation with him that lets me function at all. Now my body's awash with fear. His fear. The Child's alive inside me, unprocessed, in real-time. It's like some horror film, Theo. Like Llew, even, in the play, who can only be killed in a riddle: neither on land nor in water, clothed nor unclothed, neither in darkness nor in light, indoors nor outdoors, riding nor walking. Ludicrous! And the bastards build him a thatched roof without walls, with a bathtub lodged over a river bank, and Llew anoints himself at twilight and poises half in and half out of the tub. Strangely complaisant, he stands naked but for a net, and rests his free foot on a tethered buck! Thus stably unstable, he receives the appointed spear through his side. Strangely complaisant, Theo. That's me, eh? Ha! That ridiculous play... of the Child! Of my body! Of the saviour. He's so foreign, so 'other'. His alien story insists, and that's my art. But if I can't paint, the illness that isn't an illness rears up again, and I can't act. I'm back in my bedroom in Aylesbury with Dad.

Subject: **Woman with a comb**

Your news comes as a ray through clouds. This commission you speak of. It changes everything—if I can get it! Theo, you're a genius. How on earth did you fix it? And are they really interested? I can hardly believe what you're telling me.

I got straight on the case, of course. Eléni was the first port of call.

She agreed to talk. 'Well?' she said, 'Go on.'

I explained what you'd written.

'Wow! Good for you, Owen. So things aren't so terrible after all, are they.'

'It seems not. Suddenly.'

'Is that it? Can I go upstairs now?'

Theo, I can hardly believe her myself. So abrupt! No regrets or tenderness; on her return from Athens, she swung our relationship through 180 degrees in as many minutes. Was she always so hard? Or am I just a hopeless judge of character?

'Not quite,' I said. 'I need your help, Eléni.'

'Oh-oh!'

'You pulling out...'

She sighed impatiently. 'Owen, I've given everything. I've tried my hardest. And still you make it my fault.'

'I'm not making it your fault. It's just how it is. You said you were totally committed; now you're not. That leaves me unviable.'

'But now you have this opportunity, don't you? From Theo. The wonderful Theo. That's what you wanted to tell me, wasn't it? Owen, give me a break. I can't take any more criticism. Everything gets thrown in my face. I can never win with you.'

'What's winning got to do with it? And what option did I ever have?' My feelings got the better of me. 'It's not a game, Eléni! Nothing of mine gets resolved while we're always so busy dealing with your *stuff*. And now we're dealing with you all the more!'

'Dealing with *me*?' She glared. There were sudden tears of anger in her eyes. 'For Pete's sake, it's always you and your goddamn paintings we're dealing with. You want my view on this, you want an opinion on that. You're stuck, you're unsure: your lines and designs; your little moments of colour; where should this motif lead; what point should I be making here? It's exhausting, Owen! I'm tired of helping you out. I hate your fucking art and all it stands for, and I don't see why you can't just get on with your life. Now you've gotten this commission...'

272

'I haven't… gotten it.'

'You'll get it. You're good. Very good. So why can't you just move on and let go. And let go of me.'

'Because I don't have the money!'

'But I've seen to it that you *do*, so don't pull that on me! I've told you I'm leaving you the bank account and everything we have, and still you agonise and make demands. Dear Lord, I just want to be normal. Normal people relax and enjoy themselves once in a while. Life doesn't have to be such a fucking journey. And it doesn't have to be so penny-pinching and cautious. That's no fun for a woman. Well, is it?'

She was persuasive. I saw myself through her eyes.

But I'd spoken the truth, Theo: she *had* needed enormous emotional maintenance all along, for her career, her fears, her dealings with her family, her own significant post-traumatic depressions, her… her incipient alcoholism—for now at last I must come out of denial and put a name to it. And she really hadn't ever *volunteered* much interest in anything I was doing. Certainly not lately. And if ever I showed my own symptoms there'd be a punitive silence, and she'd make a calculated move away. That's the fact of the matter. My friend, if there'd been much emotional nourishment for me in the whole shooting match, would I need to have been pouring out my heart to you?

'During our relationship, Eléni,' I said, 'it wasn't in the least unreasonable of me to ask you to be involved with my work. It would never cost you more than a conversation or two—at the most.'

'A conversation or two! Fuck, Owen, I've given it my all. And gone without myself!'

She was building up.

'People like you and me…' I said , as delicately as I could. 'People with emotional baggage, Eléni. People with… stuff… Look, there's no avoiding it. With us, it was never going to be perfectly-settled-boy meets emotionally-secure-girl. The challenge would always be how to deal honestly with what comes up.'

'Oh, you and your "challenges" and "what comes up". Fucking therapy-speak. You so love it, don't you? You're always wrestling with your screwy demons, your ridiculous "parts". But what real courage do you show, Owen?' She made a gesture with her arm. 'So your dad used to stick his soldering iron up your ass. Or not. Get over it. Have the guts to go out there and face real life for once. I've taken

273

enough. You and your memories you can't remember. For me, and for plenty of women like me, I can tell you, forgetting would be a luxury. Plenty of women, Owen. So many. We try to get on with our lives. We try to put what happened to *us*... we try to put it behind us. But not you, of course. You're a *man*. And you have to know different, don't you. Well, fuck you. I'm fed up with being in the wrong. Do you think I haven't done my best? Well, do you? I really can't bear it any more.'

Her eyes were bright with hurt, her cheeks blotched with genuine emotion. I was moved and on the point of believing her, that it was I who was being cruel and unreasonable — for surely one of us was.

We were in the kitchen. I glanced through the window. No sign of Julia. Had she ever been out there, just beyond the fence? Truly? To all my perspectives, it seems, clings a dilemma about reality. Eléni, sadist or victim?

No, I mean it, Theo. What's sadism but a game enforced — by the one with no risk of losing. I have to admit this: sexual sadism genuinely seems to interest Eléni. It disgusts me. Clearly, I've been in denial about everything and knew zero about the true nature of our relationship!

I turned back, summoning up the courage she said I lacked. I launched my one shot.

'I don't think you *have* done your best,' I said. 'The first step was always yours. You never made it.'

'What in the name of shit do you mean by that?'

'The alcohol, of course. And the drugs.'

She looked shocked. 'I haven't taken any drugs since I met you. All that was just recreational.'

'Was it?'

'Sure.'

'And the booze?'

'I like a drink now and then. So that's a crime, now?'

I looked down. 'We both know it's more than a drink now and then.'

'You're so fucking puritan.' She turned on her heel.

'What else can I be?' I said. '*I* can't *afford* to put a foot wrong. Listen. Back in England, while the pressure was on with Lily and we had all that trouble with Arun, you were up for the struggle, and I really admired you for it. Now there's no pressure on you, and you're claiming there is. What's really happened is that you didn't want our relationship in the first place and Léros has exposed the fact. I just wish you'd said so years ago when I kept giving you the chance.'

That brought nothing but swearing and slamming of doors.

I followed her up to the bedroom. 'Well and good,' I said. 'People make wrong choices. Things don't always work out. I'm sorry for that, and we have to part. You'd like to get out quickly; I accept that. But what I don't understand is why you can't, just for one minute, Eléni, see where it leaves me. Unless you cut me some slack, I'm finished. Don't you get it?'

'Don't be ridiculous. People break up all the time.'

'Yes, they do. But if they're adult about it they at least talk terms.'

'So now you're pleading with me.'

'I'm not pleading.'

'It sounds like it. Is that the act of a gentleman?'

Now it was my turn to be shocked. *The act of a gentleman* — the weird phrase sounded so odd on her lips. Victorian, or deep South, a little askew, just out of context; almost as though for a moment she weren't quite present but overlapping with some other event.

Theo, I learnt from Mitchell to pay attention to such things. They're giveaways, he said. And it's Josh's notion of trance, too, not as a separate, sleepy state, but as a constant, almost natural occurrence. Not Eléni's fault, poor thing. It had happened in the States: an older man, she'd been only thirteen. Why, I seem to be giving you the impression this rape business is so everyday. Sadly, it is. And it had left her damaged and furious, of course.

The parents never knew, and the matter lay unhealed. Along come I, many years later, an older man among many older men, half in my own trance, perhaps, and ready to accept her local revenge drama because of my inherent guilt — for *being* an older man. Though I have to say I did keep trying to stand up for myself. But maybe that was all part of it. I tell you, I see now that a subliminal sadomasochism was perhaps actually the glue that held us together.

Whatever, in the present situation it wasn't that she *couldn't* see where her move had left me; it was that she *wouldn't*.

Oh, Theo. I glance over what I've written and see only the creepy self-justification of... indeed, a disgusting, predatory old man — the pretty young girl, the waspish nymph, simply trying to escape from him. To get away. Daphne, the nymph, desperate to get away. How sick and deluded I was to think she loved *me*, and that we were linked despite the age gap. Linked through a meeting of minds, through art... I was tempted to crawl away in self-loathing.

275

But did not. I stood my ground. I saw my one chance... which was to stay cool, insist on the facts and just hope her better nature might break through.

I spelled out your news again: the Far Eastern corporate buyer, the new European head office. I told her this daring plan to use the whole arch inside the foyer as a major artistic statement. 'Theo says they'd already mentioned my name when they approached him. It's a genuine opportunity, Eléni.'

She stood at the bedroom window looking landward, her black hair a wild mass against the evening sun. I watched her twist in her hands one of the tortoiseshell combs she wore. The plastic snapped. The piece fell to the floor. She twisted the remainder until that, too, broke in half.

'You hold all the cards,' I said. 'If that was what you've been wanting, then you've got it. But the fact is I'm not crawling or grovelling, and I don't deserve punishment just because I'm a man. I'm not *that* man. I've never done anything cruel or illegal or degrading to you. You have a claim on revenge, but not over me. All I can do is appeal to the humanity I know you possess. And if you turn me down, so be it.'

She looked at me. Her lip curled. Then she stared back out of the window. After a seemingly interminable pause, she let go her breath and turned around again. 'Alright, what do you want?'

I felt a surge of relief. 'Time,' I said.

'How much?'

'Time for two finished pictures and an overview for the client of the whole project—fully worked out with detailed, painted sketches.'

She gave another snort.

'And a little critical help,' I said.

'You're joking.'

'Your eye's so good. My objectivity's all to pot at the moment.'

'Oh yeah?'

'Because of the panic.'

'Panic!' Again her lip curled.

'It's the Child,' I said. 'I'm not apologising. It's just a fact. It goes with my territory.'

'The Child!'

'Yes, the Child.'

There was a pause. She wrestled with herself. 'How long, then?' she said at length.

'Two months.'

'Two months!'

'Theo's offered to help in any way he can. He thinks I should work on Paris.'

She looked up, sharply.

'Not travel there. Hardly in a position to do that, am I?' I gave her a grim smile. 'And that's not where this head office is, either. It's just that he's taken a cool look at my options and reckons we can map my Bledlow Paris sequence pretty much on to the client's aspirations. And with my previous track record, he honestly believes he can get me something substantial up front. Then at least I'll have options. Eléni, it feels like a miracle; I can hardly believe it. So all I'm asking is for your continued financial support. Just until shipment. In the circumstances, I believe that's a reasonable request. If you agree, I'll call Theo back first thing. Because, other than that, right now I simply can't think of a way out.'

'Two *months*!' She spat the words out.

'Out of seven years,' I said.

Still she hesitated, seemingly wrestling with herself. Eventually, 'No, Owen. I'm sorry but I won't. I won't do it. Fuck you. You've no right to ask me to put my life on hold like this.'

She walked out of the room, and I would not follow her again.

Subject: Charity

It was so good to hear your voice. Touch base. Theo, I'm profoundly indebted to you. I said you were a genius. Look, I'll fulfil the deal. Don't worry, I'll deliver. Eléni or no Eléni, I'll find a way. This corporate buyer of yours wants bold colours, figurative style. I'm up for it. If need be, I'll go to Marta and get some medication.

Subject: A jar of pills

'She's confused. She's young. She'll change her mind.' Marta was exasperated.

'I've been a fool. Her longest affair before was with a woman, so maybe she... maybe she was never... But she always said she *was*, and

277

what was I to do? By then I was trapped—financially, I mean.' I felt unexpected tears behind my eyes. 'I'm very lucky. I have a commission—I hope. I have two months to paint something saleable. I mean good money. I can't... You see, I've always refused medication. I've always tried to bear whatever came along, because...' I stood up. 'Right now, I just need to work.'

It was a low blow, Theo; I shouldn't have betrayed Eléni's lesbian history like that. To Marta, or to you.

Marta gave me tranquillisers. They're little blue tablets in a jar. She furnished me with antidepressants, too, though those won't kick in for a fortnight or so. I took a couple of each straightaway, Theo. The blue ones work, I think. They're even good: not so drastic I can't keep awake, nor so weak I can't paint.

But Marta? Why did she care so much what happened to our relationship? I mean Eléni and me. She was almost cross *herself*. I can tell you, I've racked my brains for her motive. I like her enormously; but, in all honesty, I hardly know her. Still, she seems to have taken me somewhat under her wing.

20

Subject: Flotsam

Something else has suddenly happened.

It was late. I'd switched off my computer and was about to get into my makeshift bed when Eléni's phone went upstairs. I heard her answer it, of course; no prizes for guessing who. She feels no compunction about being as loud as she likes up there—at whatever hour.

I decided to decamp to my studio, and I don't know why I hadn't thought of this before. Maybe ceding territory marks a certain defeat; maybe I'd felt constrained by the downstairs bed I'd already made up. My rage this time was intense, however, and it drove me to gather up the sofa cushions and get right out of the house. The night being so hot, I needed no covers. Amongst the comforting smells of my day's work, I got a few hours' sleep and awoke just before dawn.

I thought to catch the sunrise. With my bathing shorts, towel and beach shoes from the porch, I crept down to the cove. I have to tell you what I found there.

There was enough light to pick my way. Petulant waves, a hot wind blowing all night. A rare lens of cloud took on the merest touch of pink over the Turkish mainland, cloud that wouldn't last five minutes once the sun was up.

The beach is only a yard or two of shingle. I threw down my towel and paused briefly on the stones before wading in. To my left was the jut of hard land where the island shapes itself to the sea; to my right, familiar boulders against the bluff. No clue in that dim grey alerted me to anything else.

I only saw it as I swam back. An extra form, like a rock. Half in, half out of the water, it lay disturbingly un-rock-like once the first rays surfed the low crests, and the wind flicked droplets off in bright, momentary skeins. A flap of shirt lifted from its bulk. And there was a hand—pale brown—stretched out as though to cling to pebbles; a hand I might almost have trodden on just minutes before. I shivered as I stood up.

A gull swooped. I looked towards our house, then back at the already huge sunrise. I clambered from the shallows, towelled my chest and arms and trod cautiously around the object.

The hips, beached, were awash. The legs, in jeans, lay eerily foreshortened. The thing appeared to kneel below the rock shelf. One foot moved in the slight backflow—as though still trying hopelessly to swim. The torso remained inert, the flap of shirt revealing, every so often, a line of mottling flesh above the belt. The head… I made myself snatch aside a hank of wet, dark hair. It was a dead youth.

I retched. The gull swooped again, closer. What was the Greek emergency number? Which words would I need? Should I even leave the body?

I stared around me: the headland, the bluff, the perfect sea.

The corpse made a noise. I swung back. It was moving. My God, Theo. Again, I nearly vomited.

Then fellow feeling arose, and I made myself confront the thing. 'Wait! Listen! I'll help!' I said, automatically, feebly, bending closer.

The face lifted from the gravel. I peered at it: Greek-seeming, Turkish, Italian? It was bruised.

The mouth opened: a word, more like a gasp. Some language I didn't understand.

I reached down, repulsed. I got hold under the arm. 'Careful. Take it slowly,' my voice still strangulated.

The figure crawled. It was disgusting. I gripped the other shoulder. Straining, I managed to pull him out of the water. 'My house. It's just up here.'

I don't know how I got him to his feet. Should I have? He tottered. I wished he hadn't landed himself on me. I put my towel around him and pushed and propped him up. 'Come on. You can do it. Here, this way. Up here.' He took another step. He was shivering. I got his arm around my shoulders. 'Come on, then. Come on. Quick.'

Yes, some intuition told me not only that he was at risk of exposure, but that neither of us should be visible down there on the beach any longer than necessary. We all know the Greeks are angry. Gone, under the great economic betrayal and a deluge of illegal immigrants, is a large part of that legendary hospitality.

But his exhaustion was like a sea anchor, seeming to pull him down, bidding to wind him back to the element, his blanched face next to mine, the large brown eyes, the slightly pimpled skin, the wet, black hair, the smell in his laboured breath of both garlic and seawater.

We reached the footholds to the goat track, nevertheless. 'That's

280

right,' I said. 'And now there.' I tried to hurry him. I willed him upward.

We got to the top. I was bent over with him, spotting each footprint between stones and scrub. 'Not far now, mate. Come on.' Damn him, the dawn already brilliant: 'Only a little further. Only a few steps more and there'll be help.' I saw his eyes flick towards the house, but I kept my attention on his feet, steering them while planning in my mind what we'd have to do with him. 'Eléni will make you comfortable. At least she'll do that. And I'll get on the phone to someone. Maybe Níkos at the post office. Someone who might know what the fuck to do.'

'Can I help at all?'

The sudden English voice out of nowhere! It made me start.

'Please, yes,' I answered without thinking.

It was then I looked up from my burden. I found myself directly eye to eye with Julia.

Which was it: my voice, my towelled hair, the un-looked for intensity of our mutual gaze?

For *directly* the spark of recognition jumped.

'Owen!' She stumbled and almost lost her footing in the scrub bushes, her hand over her heart as she tried to get her breath. Her painting equipment clattered to the ground.

I hunched, stock still, the half-drowned teenager hanging from my shoulders: 'Julia. I'm sorry, Julia. Look, I'm really sorry.' It was a sorry speech indeed. Pathetic.

She recovered. Suddenly, she couldn't resist stretching out a hand to touch my cheek, extending the tips of her fingers like a child. I felt it, almost electric.

Then she drew back. She was furious. 'What...? What have you been...? Owen! Owen, I don't understand. All this time it was you, and you didn't tell me? You let me...' She stared, searching my features—as if now to pierce the disguise I'd already removed.

'You're right,' I said. 'I'm sorry. I...' The weight of the boy.

'Why? For heaven's sake, why, Owen? You! Here! Oh God, how strange it sounds to say your name, right out like that, after all these years. I don't know.' She turned away and put her hand to her head. 'I need to get my brain together.'

Immediately, she swung back. 'No. I shan't give you the advantage. It's... It's...' And again she stared, lost for her words, scanning my face in disbelief.

The boy coughed and groaned. It made the point. She got straight under his other arm, and we helped him inside.

Subject: **Lawless waters**

That was this morning, Theo. Eléni and I have spent time with him. He's well. And now he's asleep. The event has borne out my hunch for discretion, and you'll have guessed it at once: we have an illegal on our hands. I've heard that the people-smugglers throw them overboard without the slightest hesitation if the coast guard show up. Or the boats are so overcrowded they sink anyway. Or sometimes the Greeks see to it on the quiet—these waters are lawless.

Julia stayed briefly. In fact it was her rudimentary tags of Indic or Farsi from her travels all those years ago that eventually elicited a fact or two about him. Her year on the road; I think I might have told you. India. Afghanistan. Iran. More than a year.

Subject: **The sea's egg**

He is Afghan, as you suspected. He's called Nasir. He in turn has a few English words—in this polyglot world! Julia told us how they'd run after anyone when she was there: 'Lady! Lady! You want?' Most likely he's learned something from the Nato troops. But what precise circumstances forced him to try his luck overland from Afghanistan to the Turkish coast—and onward by sea to here—is beyond our communication.

So there we were, Eléni and I, in our downstairs room, Theo, an awkward duo gazing at this 'other', whom the sea has laid at our door like an egg.

The situation is no joke, though. God knows how many hours he spent in the water. Where he'd learned to swim, even—the Kabul River? It's a miracle he's alive!

Of course, he's very withdrawn; and completely exhausted. He's in the bed down here—'my' bed, until lately. And neither Eléni nor I has the heart to turn him over to the authorities. Not yet. Not now. So we've pretty much compromised ourselves, haven't we?

Ought we call a doctor, no matter what?

Marta?

We hesitate.

Theo, what *should* we do? *And who is my neighbour*? I don't trust the soldiery with him. I told you, times have changed. It wasn't so long ago that even *shipwrecked* illegals were treated with generosity, or at least according to the law. Not now. And I've no idea of the penalty for harbouring aliens. On the other hand, I doubt the army will be back just yet, unless other survivors show up on the beach.

All my instincts, though, are that Nasir is probably singular. And rather remarkable. I guess, once he's recovered, he'll have to take his chances. On the island, perhaps. Or we'll find him some money for the ferry.

Of all the things to happen, Theo! And now!

But how paltry appear my worries next to his. What matter the 'Parts' now, or the niceties of memory? And who's Derrida but a theoretician so rarefied that not one in a thousand has heard of him, still less gives a damn?

Yet the odd thing is that Nasir delays Eléni's threatened departure. He buys me at least a little time. If I can use it. I'm ashamed at so mercenary a take, yet it would be false to deny my temporary sigh of relief.

And Julia? She left us once he was settled. She left with a great deal unsaid and a look of fierce enquiry in her eye. But again it was impossible to talk, there, at the garden gate, with Eléni watching hawk-eyed from the patio.

So now I sit at my keyboard, and Nasir lies only a yard or so away. I can hear him breathe.

Subject: Empty egg

He sleeps most of the time. On that bed next to my computer. Eléni and I remain at chaotic odds with each other, yet strangely focused on the needs of this our adopted… our adopted what, Theo?

No. No sign of Julia.

Subject: **Malingering**

Questions, questions! I'll get to them. I suddenly had a bad day, that's all. Out of the blue. Call it depression; though I don't know what kind of depression comes and goes just like that? It couldn't have been Eléni; that situation stays the same. Is it Nasir, our cast up mer-boy? Has the concealment somehow ensnared me? Has the deception we must now keep up perhaps cut me off in my own mind from Marta's good offices? Stress and tiredness?

Oh, but it's Julia, isn't it! And Miles. And Stefan! Or must we simply imagine some inscrutable interior force, like the vulcanism constantly at work under the Earth's crust, which erupts entirely according to its own schemes?

Unless it was something I painted...

First there was sadness behind the eyes — undischarged. Then that old familiar paralysis: nothing to be done. I call it old. I call it familiar, remembering the years of the clinic; but it won't, of course, be familiar to you. I've told you about struggling to paint, but not about being unable to move at all.

The only phrase I can find is 'nauseous gravity', for the downward pull is so strong the muscles can't operate, while the vile sensation seems to emanate from the stomach. At least I didn't duck the light, as I used to. I sat in the sun — I even got a little burnt. One's never really paralysed, of course. Had some emergency arisen — Nasir in crisis, for example — I know I could have leapt up and dashed about with almost no problem. As I said once before, I think, there's nothing the matter with my function. In all departments.

So it's only a kind of malingering.

Isn't it? Just when I'm needed?

Luckily poor Nasir mostly slept, helpfully postponing the awkward question of what on earth we're going to do with him.

Of his native griefs we can know nothing. But they must be significant.

So my strange, one-day depression seems merely to be a disorder of the will, as though — in the glaring absence here of Taleban, air strikes, civil war or absolute poverty — some self-indulgent sign from another dimension was posted. And I, as self-indulgently, answered it. The result: immobility. I kept my head above it just enough to let my eyes dwell on the little rose bush Eléni planted no more than a month ago. It's come into bloom with a delicious deep red, but I've never really looked at it; what with all our difficulties. Those lines of Keats:

> *Then glut thy sorrow on a morning rose*
>
> ....
>
> *And, if thy mistress some rich anger shows,*
> *Imprison her soft hand, and let her rave*
> *And feed deep, deep upon her peerless eyes.*

Rose, mistress and anger were all pre-installed (through the open upstairs window I could hear Eléni's repeated business calls, brusque and unsentimental to the point of rudeness, punctuated by the hard rattle of her keyboard). But I could sate myself as instructed on none of this, because emotion still failed me, and the dry experience of the rose bush, its buds and leaves, was far closer to Coleridge's *Dejection*:

> *I see them all so excellently fair;*
> *I see, not feel, how beautiful they are!*

My friend, I labour this point grotesquely, and complete with literary allusions, because I believe that during my bad day I achieved a minor triumph, even taking into account the worrying dilemma of Nasir and the loss of yet another day's painting. You see, these bouts usually preclude any reflection at all, and so the absorption with the rose represented real progress.

Still more significant was the strong hunch that the feelings I was experiencing weren't 'mine' at all. I had the intuition that, instead of just suffering pointlessly, I was performing a kindly act: almost as though I was sitting by my poor Child's bedside and sharing, at least in some degree, his state. As if Nasir has brought more than just himself out of the deep. And, if Eléni at least ministers to *his* clear needs, I can now deal with *my* cloudy ones. Can you believe that?

Nevertheless, I wished with all my heart for the affliction to stop.

It did, in the early evening. I made food for the three of us. Eléni and I were cold in our usual non-intercourse across the supper table. Then she went to Nasir to help him eat and remained with him, trying, I think, to equip him with a few sentences of English. I drifted out to look at the stars, and then sat reading and listening to some Greek music station in my studio. In due course I went to bed in there and lay awake on those sofa cushions.

Nasir: so curious an event, so hard to decode. As much as he delays Eléni and buys me a few days, his constant maintenance — water, the right kind of food, reassurance, entertainment — prevent me making use of them. Of the extra days, that is. Zero sum.

A purely random wash-up, then? Meaningless as driftwood? Existentialism fighting back? For God's sake, his mere presence puts us in jeopardy. Surely we'll have done enough by just getting him back on his feet.

Yet maybe I've never properly credited the generosity with which I myself was taken in. Did Félix and Cécile run risks, I wonder? And was I too bound up with my own troubles to care? A story can be a mirror, and not always a flattering one.

I *have* also spent time myself with Nasir. I like what I can know of him, and the rest we have to take on trust; trust that he's a 'civilian' and not about to kill us for being Western!

Besides, would it *really* make any difference to find out he was one of 'theirs' and on the run, possibly running from our own side? To find he was not only an illegal alien but also an enemy? Surely it shouldn't. He stirs about a little lately, and the bruises to his face begin to subside. I'm not so sure they all came from the stones on the beach.

I've just thought of my son. Ah, Theo, that was it. That was it! Surely my bad day was *Arun's* despair. Of course. My *son*. *My* son. Things must be rough with him. Laid low. That's what I was feeling. Where is he now? How is he? My son! Oh, God!

Nasir has been with us three days. Just now, Eléni's watching English TV with him. We can't go out. I suspect it's because neither of us quite believes the other won't shop him or throw him out. I mean in the great pressure we both have at the moment to get on with our lives. And what if someone called and saw him—Marta, the neighbours, the police? Something will have to be done. And soon.

Meanwhile, Theo, tonight is stifling; the fly-screens are up and the windows wide open to try to get any draught at all.

Subject: **Light**

No she didn't mention her name, I think. So Eléni didn't realise that Julia was Julia. And still doesn't, I believe. Julia just helped me indoors with Nasir and got him sat down and so on. As far as I can be sure, Eléni assumes she was only someone passing. Going painting, she said—which was true. Julia, I mean. Catching the dawn light, etc.

So you're absolutely right. In the kerfuffle of his being here and what we're going to do about it, and feeling so bloody ill yesterday, I'd overlooked the blindingly obvious. Random, was I saying? Zero sum? Meaningless? Nasir effectively knocked our heads together, didn't he. Almost literally, Julia and me! Had it not been for his misfortune, I'd still be pretending to be Greek, and she and I…

Subject: The artist in his studio

'I couldn't get away,' she said. 'Till today.'

It was on the path at the back. I saw her from the window. I went out and spoke to her.

She was still fuming. Understandably, Theo. 'Sure?' she said. 'What do you mean, sure!'

'To be sure it was you.'

'You couldn't tell, Owen? You didn't recognise me?'

'You didn't recognise *me*!'

It was a poor riposte, and she took me to task for it.

'You were hiding behind your sunglasses. You were speaking Greek! And you had that… stupid hat on.' No laughter. Her feeling overcame her. A hint of tears. The wind gusted in the pines, and the sea slapped at the cove in little waves.

Then she collected herself. 'But you're seriously telling me you saw me for days and still didn't know me? Am I so very old and ugly?'

'No, of course not. Quite the contrary,' I said. My gallantry jarred the moment it left my mouth. 'But I just couldn't be certain.' That was the plain truth, at least. I made her face me. 'Come on, Julia. Would you have ever known *me*? In another country? If you'd happened to pass me in the street?'

'Hard to say. Now I know it *is* you.' She stepped back to squint at me, any latent comedy still eclipsed by her real anger. 'Alright, maybe I wouldn't, Owen. It's possible.'

'You see?'

'Oh, no! That doesn't get you get out of it. Why didn't you speak? Why didn't you just come up and ask me?'

I hesitated. Because I couldn't believe it? Because I couldn't bear the thought of losing her — again? Because I was angry? 'Because you were with Miles,' I said.

'Ah.'

'Yes.'

'It's because of Miles, is it.'

That gave me my chance. I glanced back up to where Eléni would be at work at her computer. 'Look, Julia, come with me.' I held out my hand.

'Where?' She took it, and I remembered at once how it felt to be linked to her, the warm, intimate contact of her grip.

'To my studio.' So I led her in again through the wired back gate of our garden; the gate through which, just a couple of days before, we'd brought the sea boy. 'We have to keep quiet.'

'Why?'

'Because Eléni...' I kept my voice low. 'You saw her.'

'That girl, yes. Because she what? Aren't you allowed visitors, Owen?'

'It's just... Oh, forget it.'

'I will. But the Afghan lad, Nasir. Is he alright?'

'Yes.'

'Is he still here?'

'Yes. And I heard what happened. What brought him. They were talking about it earlier, down in the shop. There *were* illegals out there that night. They were chased by a Greek patrol. But he's safe. For now. He's watching TV. So come on.' I put my finger to my lips and led her across the parched ground until we slipped unseen into the security of my studio.

She noticed the improvised bed. 'You're sleeping here?'

'Yeah. That's why... We're...' The drift of my relationship with Eléni hung in the air.

Julia looked around at my work. 'I still recognise your style,' she said. 'I have to confess, I've followed your work. A little,' she added.

'You didn't recognise it when I was painting next to you.'

'That's not fair.' She moved among the canvases, lifting now this one, now that. 'They're good. I like them. Damn you.'

'They're mostly sketches. Just ideas. A commission I've suddenly got to...'

But her eye had lighted on the Bledlow canvas in the far corner. She went over to it. 'That's me. Owen? It's me, isn't it? Christ! You've been painting *me*.'

'Yes.'

She rounded, so angry again. 'You've been painting out there alongside me and... looking at me... and then coming back to do this?'

'No.'

'What d'you mean, no!'

'I didn't. I haven't. It was before. That's what I wanted to show you. I did this picture ages ago. I did it weeks before you even came.'

Her jaw visibly dropped. She swung back again to the scene. 'That's my old Afghan coat I'm wearing. They were all the rage, weren't they, but mine was the genuine... Oh God, it's us. It's us when...'

I saw her staring at the sketchy, ghost-looking figure who was, and was not, me. Then she swept her astonished gaze slowly back across the rest of the paintwork, raising her hand unconsciously as if she might need to touch the dried pigment to believe in it.

'I began it soon after we moved here,' I said. 'Back in May.'

But then she saw the photograph pinned to the leg of the stand. 'Oh, so you got that!' She turned once more to face me. 'It arrived. Here. That explains it.'

'It was forwarded here by my gallery.'

'It *was* a long shot. I don't even know quite why... I never really imagined...' She was staring abstractedly around the room, and, for a split second, an angle revealed her face almost doubled by the younger features in the painting behind her. How could I ever have doubted? 'Right, Owen. Okay,' she was saying. 'So you just did all this from the photograph.' She gestured at it.

'No, Julia, that's the point.' I admit I savoured the moment, Theo. 'That's what I'm trying to tell you. I was already working on the picture. The portrait of you was virtually complete before the snapshot even reached me.'

Poor thing, each new piece of information gusted her back and forth like a weathervane between painter and painting. She shook her head. 'You're joking. You're making a fool of me.'

'I'm not, though. I was as blown away as you are now when that photo turned up. And I am still, except this sort of thing does seem to keep happening. But I didn't know what to think. I swear to you: your portrait was already finished. Then I ran into problems. I couldn't do mine.' I paused, because a sudden thought had crossed my mind. 'D'you know, I've just remembered. There was a morning Eléni came in and...'

Julia interrupted. 'Is she Greek, or something, the frosty one?' She raised her eyebrows. 'Your girlfriend. Your wife...?'

'Ex-girlfriend, Julia. Very recently ex. We've... This is our house. But back then she came in one morning and saw the whole thing, the photo, the painting. Maybe she drew some conclusion... I don't know.'

'Owen...'

At that moment I noticed Nasir slipping stealthily down the garden towards the coast path. He just happened to turn at the wire gate and look back towards the house. Catching sight of me at the window, he hurriedly switched both demeanour and direction and started back towards the studio door. Julia and I both dashed out to him. He looked distressed.

We shepherded him back to the house as quickly as we could. I turned off the TV and sat him down. Only by the aid of Julia's few odd words and phrases did we eventually establish quite how upset he'd become, stuck here in a strange house and among strangers, not knowing our intentions. He was scared. Of course he was. Scared that whatever happened he'd be caught, imprisoned, beaten up, sent back — whatever. Theo, we might have foreseen this; but he'd seemed quite content until now. The good news is that he *is* much recovered; the bad is that this makes him strong enough to do something stupid if we don't get our act together.

What might that act be? Just how can we do anything that doesn't plunge him — and us — into a worse mess than he's in already. No doubt he's come to the same conclusion, and that was why he was thinking of chancing it alone out there.

He wouldn't last a minute. Not in his present state. I think we did right. To get him back in and try to calm him down. But something has to be done, Theo.

Eléni appeared. She grasped the problem, but was cool with Julia. 'Just passing again, were you?' and Julia could only bluff out that she'd also been concerned and intrigued. Clearly, Eléni suspects. But Julia's been in on this from the start. If we can come up with a solution, Julia will have to be part of it. Besides, Nasir likes her; there's a bond between them. She seems to soothe him, and we'll need that if we're to get him to cooperate. If he decides to cut his losses again, it could spell disaster for us all.

But no more bad days, Theo! Quite the opposite. With all the very real dangers looming, I find myself excited, oddly 'high' again. Not so oddly! But a strange, surging, elated mood. I made no bones about asking for Julia's mobile number in front of Eléni. Well, we have to be able to contact her!

21

Subject: Laestrygonian

Now it's over with, I can tell you our outrageous plan. For we did hatch one. Risky and ridiculous it will almost certainly sound, but we could think of nothing better.

It began early yesterday evening, just before dusk. It was lunatic. Nasir and I set out across country. He was dressed as Eléni—they're both much of a height. I should add that he'd already been wearing an old pair of her jeans, because they fit him, and a T-shirt is a T-shirt is a T-shirt.

But to help the disguise we paid particular attention to his walking sandals, trekking stick, and sunglasses. And, despite the heat, we put a loose denim waistcoat of hers on him to hint at a small bosom.

We each carried rucksacks containing a change of clothes: for him. And some food for the night. And, crucially, a large empty holdall with airport labels, concealed as flatly as it would go. The aim, as you'll have realised, was to simulate one of our hikes.

Theo, I'd considered waiting for the full cover of darkness. But surely we'd have looked more suspicious when walkers aren't so generally out and about. Paradoxically, it was less risky to be brazen. We'd pass ourselves off as a known phenomenon—Eléni and me out walking—and trust to luck.

How very scary! My heart pounded as we got ready. In fact, we were all a little lightheaded; Eléni giggled once, but it was sheer nervousness.

So we set off. I should also say at this point that I'd laid out the whole plan before Nasir in the form of a storyboard—a little graphic novel, if you will. That was Eléni's idea. I won't relay her joke about my art being good for something at last. But it does feel strange to be putting aside our differences and working together; a relief from the outright hostility. We'd offered Nasir the paper and pencil, too, forgetting where he'd been brought up. Making images wasn't a priority in his education, though he has a fine calligraphic line. Hardly any sense of representation. So we still know almost nothing about him, and it isn't our brief to extract more.

I should also add the detail that we'd contemplated buying a female wig somewhere in town, to match Eléni's dark locks. But the over-theatricality made us think twice, never mind the trouble of finding one. We settled for a headscarf under Eléni's khaki hat—the very unglamorous thing you've seen in the photos—and we let the folds hang down at Nasir's back as though after a hard day's walk in the sun. Despite this torrid weather, we had to stick with the jeans to spare him shaving his legs. We did put a little make-up on his face. He ran to look in the bathroom mirror—and came back shocked and grinning. And we laughed, too. It relieved the tension.

So we took the beach road, exactly as if Eléni and I might have been heading for one of the tavernas. We passed Julia's hotel; I kept an eye out for Miles. Then we climbed back to the main road just as the sun set and headed daringly into Plátanos itself. The streetlights and shops in the town square seemed at once too bright. A potent half-moon glared down already. But there were a number of tourists and holidaymakers about, some dressed, as I'd hoped, in quite similar fashion. 'How're you feeling?' I asked Nasir, purely to ease my own nerves, and he nodded at me, forcing a smile of incomprehension through a mask of fear—a grotesquely girlish mask.

He was game, and I admired him. My nerves were just getting to me. I was like the kid who's found some stricken bird quivering on the woodland floor; the urge to help is overwhelming, yet the creature mostly dies.

But it was either this or nothing, and we kept up a confident pace past the castle steps and on down the slope: I averted my head from Marta's. After all her kindnesses, I hated the thought of deceiving her. Or, worse, implicating her in our plot.

We passed safely, however, and down through Áyia Marína. There was Julia, waiting at the last taverna, where the tables spill out under bright electric lanterns towards the harbour front.

She got up, and we made the show of English people meeting one another by chance. I stood with my arm on Nasir's shoulder for a moment, and we all three moved on a little way—along the sparsely lit coast road.

At last we could talk. Nasir was pleased to see her. She took pity and embraced him, and they shared a moment or two in pidgin fragments before she turned to me. 'Owen, look at him! What are we doing?!'

'I know. But we've made it this far.'

'And no one noticed?'

I shook my head.

'Christ Jesus!' she said.

'What about Miles?' I was concerned. 'You managed to get away?'

'Miles is on a boat. He's out on a trip, Owen. A little tuna fishing. It's one of the reasons we came here.'

'And he gets back?'

'Tomorrow morning. It's overnight. So...' She hesitated. 'So, if you like, Owen, I could come a bit of the way.'

I looked at her, on the point of refusing. It was too dangerous. But the look in her eyes changed my mind. I took her hand and squeezed it. It was only the second time I'd touched her, since... since Bledlow, if you think about it. It brought back a world more feelings. And memories, Theo. Of course it did. It brought back a great deal. She slung her shoulder bag, and we placed ourselves on either side of Nasir.

Now Nasir and I could come into our second characters: anonymous male hikers perhaps returning to their hillside apartment by moonlight after a daylong jaunt. And now Julia made a companion, which was perfect.

Soon the town lay far behind us. We strode out. Nasir proved a gritty walker, despite what he must have been through—or perhaps because of it. We spiked the roadside verge with our English trekking poles, and the tense mood lifted. Julia and I chatted across him of this and that. Cicadas sawed in the vegetation. Occasional night creatures scuttled from our footfalls. Once, the quiver of wings suggested a small owl flapping close. Moonbeams, challenged only by the headlamps of an occasional taxi, fell slanting over the island's warm dream.

We took a break. We drank a little from the bottles we'd brought. Julia wetted a tissue and scrubbed away at Nasir's make-up. I took stock of our situation. It was another six miles to the airport, in territory I'd never explored. The later it got, the more odd we'd look, pushing on in the dark. Someone might offer us a lift—one car had slowed ominously. So now we took to hiding at the first sign of headlights, which was easier said than done in that low scrub. Once, with a stifled scream, Julia lost her footing and fell.

Nasir was with her instantly. He was kneeling beside her, speaking, his voice concerned. I bent down to her. 'Alright?'

'I suppose. Just my hand.' She held on to Nasir and got awkwardly to her feet, peering in the moonlight at her right palm. 'Thorns. Ah,

293

God, they hurt.' She sucked the wound. 'Owen, is this the only way? Aren't there footpaths, side roads?'

'Eléni and I scoured the map. We looked on Google.' I rummaged in my rucksack. 'Damn! Forgot the iPad.' I stood up. 'Oh, well, there's hardly 'street view', is there. But even the best satellite pictures show only this one fold through the northern *massif*.'

'I know,' she sighed. 'I looked, too. It's just… I'm sorry.'

'Don't be,' I leaned out and touched her shoulder. 'Won't Miles…?'

'I said, he's out overnight.' She looked off into the darkness. 'You think I should go back?'

'I don't want… I don't want to put you…'

She smiled. 'Miles won't know. I shan't tell him. Will you?' Now she laughed and took a swig from her water bottle.

I smiled back. 'You're sure?'

'In for a penny, Owen? This is too good to miss!' She put her arm around Nasir.

I shook his hand. He spoke. I could see the whites of his eyes, but not his expression.

We got a glimpse of the airport runway about nine. But it was far in the distance, its lights shooting out to sea through a notch in the black, encircling hills. From here on, foot-weary as we were, and with our shoulders beginning to ache, we could anticipate just a very gradual descent to the small plain of Parthéni, the vale of the Virgin. Not Mary, but someone far older: Artemis the huntress.

We fell silent. Each of us was locked for a while in the abstraction of hard walking. It occurs to me now that if I'd allowed myself to mull over how stupid and potentially dangerous was the little enterprise we'd embarked upon, I'd never have gone a step further.

But I did not. What I found myself thinking pretty intensely about, of course, was Julia. Here I was with her, the last person I'd ever have expected to be my companion.

And I was held apart from her, so it seemed, only by the presence of this Afghan boy, plucked from a sea of refugees: Nasir, whom we were both seeking to help — almost as though we had a child together, Julia and I; almost as though we were nursing our kid through some local problem or teenage difficulty.

Towards freedom, I supposed; that he should soon translocate illegally again and disappear into a different sea.

It was true, only Nasir's shoulder-width made the distance between us. But, do you see, he was also the mysterious glue that held us fast together. For now.

What, then? If Nasir was an enigma, how much more was Julia herself, whom I'd spent such a good part of my younger days regretting—and eventually filing under that label 'betrayal'. Again, Theo, we interrogate this bewildering reality. How was it my hand had re-visited her in paint, unearthed her, almost, just as soon as I'd made landfall on this isle?

I tried to hold the notion of betrayal still enough to be examined, but it kept eluding me. She'd cheated, hadn't she? She'd handed me over. And yet here she was *again*, apparently in harness with Miles *again*, and I was allowing myself *again* to be lulled into a fascination with her.

There, I *was* enraptured. I confess it, and that rapture was quite likely the reason for the absurd burst of creativity and enthusiasm that even seemed to include the performance art of walking slap bang into the vale of Artemis with her and an illegal alien. Indeed, here was true *chóra*—'country, open space' of a threatening and dangerous kind. It was, in a final sense, re-entering the chalk sign of home.

And yes, Theo, I knew my gods and goddesses. I knew them from childhood, as I've said; I knew them from art history; I knew them from research, and from the thousand and one ways the classical deities still pop up all about us. And I conjured this one in her lunar disc and castled headdress—a weird construction: Artemis. She's Graves's 'triple goddess', of course—that shell-shocked masochism of his. Shakespeare's Hecate, too. I thought of her restless hounds, her male-hating arrows, her subterranean caverns. Bloody, bloodthirsty idol to whom Spartan schoolboys were flogged to shreds. Ha! Feminism enlightened us, Theo, but *woman*...

For a moment or two, I let her damned betrayals well up, and they bathed me red. I was angry. At Julia, of course. And I conceived the entry of evil into the world, somewhere between language and love. Evil spied a chink, and *she* did nothing. Ah, my friend, there in my mind stood, as ever, our dark primordial parents, mine: that graceless, clever man and that wretched, implacable woman, who let it happen.

But then I thought not of Artemis, but of Artemisia, the lovely, wounded painter on whom I'd based my technique, and how painting as a 'Caravaggista' had been just enough of a conceptual statement to get me recognised. As *you* remember, of course. And as poor Artemis was spied upon by Actaeon, so Artemisia Gentileschi painted the naked Susannah being gawped at by the Elders. In the artistic disguise of Judith and her maid, she took her revenge in oils on the drunken Holofernes, hammered her tent peg into sleeping Sisera's skull. I thought how brave she'd been, meeting her violator and tormentor head on with such calm fullness of colour, such triumph of texture. Artemisia! The herbal name medicinal as its own cloud of wispy leaves.

And Julia?

But the moon was sinking in the west, the darkness proving ever harder to negotiate. Much of the region, according to that useless map I'd deliberately left back at the house, was military. Beyond and to the west of the airstrip, it was marked 'restricted'. Hadn't I read, somewhere on the internet, that the Italian barracks—in which the Greek Colonels had a notorious torture centre—still stood? Was it my imagination, or did a disquiet settle over us all when, at long last, we neared the airport buildings and took our turn off to the left?

Engines growled behind us. A fast approaching convoy of lights sent us scuttling deep into the vegetation. We crouched and hid our pale faces—not a moment too soon—as a jeep and two heavy lorries made the same turn and sped past us. Their painted camouflage was clear in the headlamps, to our furtively uplifted eyes.

I'd failed to anticipate armed transport. How suspicious we'd look out here, with no passenger flights this time of night, no tourist nightlife for miles. I reached out and felt for Nasir as we stood up. He was shaking. 'It's alright,' I said. 'They can't have seen us.'

Julia made signs and touched him. He seemed to calm down.

Then, my own heart thumping, I took *her* hand again. And she returned the grip; until we carried on with him as before, only to see the last sector of moon vanish behind the westward hill. It left us scouting cautiously along the tarmac's margin. There, according to Google Maps, we should soon find a certain track.

There was no sign of it. Only scrubby trees in faint silhouette that seemed to make one continuous, impenetrable edge. Minutes passed. 'We've gone too far,' I whispered. 'We must have missed it. God knows where we are. If we're not careful, we'll bump into some guard post or checkpoint.'

Julia hummed—literally, but in a way detached, as though she were briefly elsewhere. 'Perhaps just a little further,' she said. She hummed a measure more, louder this time. The sound carried dangerously on the still air, an unearthly cadence.

'For God's sake!'

Some Afghan song, I supposed, though a listener might imagine it Greek. And Nasir responded, looking at her, smiling, nodding. How odd a thing! Clearly, they'd both got over their fright.

'The track was in half a mile,' I said, still agitated. 'We've done more. A lot more.'

'Another few minutes. Owen?'

Her eyes held just a glint of starlight, and I felt she was smiling. It suddenly struck me that her voice's timbre had been like that of the bees coming and going through their warm glades.

I brushed the thought away and set off again, moody and doubting.

Sure enough, we came before long to a gap. There was a sign stuck up stark on a pole against the glittering midnight sky, and I reached up like a blind man to feel for impressions.

'You were right.' I had to admit it. 'There's a clear capital "A" right at the beginning of a word. A for Artemis. It has to be.'

Now she laughed out loud.

'Shhh!' I hissed.

'Sorry!'

'The dark,' I whispered. 'It disorientates, I guess.'

'I guess.'

'Sorry.'

'It's fine.'

I took her hand once more, and we followed the track. But now she sang out loud the words of the song, the foreign sounds colouring the unrelieved dark.

I listened, flummoxed: some fêted *ghazal*, perhaps, coming back to her across all those years, from Afghanistan, when she was there before the Russians and the Taleban. Before the Americans and us. As for the path, maybe she'd simply remembered the Google map better. Maybe she was just a superior navigator. It was nothing, and I gave up trying to keep her quiet.

Past the shapes of taller trees, we found another gap. With another illegible sign. But there could be no doubt we'd reached our goal. Here, by the just discernible outlines of its perimeter, was the wide enclosure we'd seen on screen at home, and within it should lie the flat stones and ruined fragments of the island's only antiquity. We ventured in.

Theo, not for Léros any famous philosophers, healers; nor any saints. Nor inspirational Lesbians. No bellowing Minotaur favoured us. No oracular Sybil. Absolutely nothing heroic, barring the couple of ships we sent to Troy—so claimed the *Iliad*. Just this sole patch of archaeology.

It's the corner of a mainland tale. Did you hear of the Calydonian Boar? Meleager killed it, but died himself in some characteristic family horror. The goddess took pity on his weeping sisters and brought them to Léros, where they lived in her temple precinct as chickens, guinea-fowl—the Meleagrids. Yes, peel off the Homeric glamour and you get these farmyard moments. Here once stood a temple to angry Artemis. With hens! And here, according to our plan, Nasir would spend the night.

Our knapsacks contained his clothes, you remember. And then extra clothes for stuffing. Plus a little food and water. Together, more by feel than sight, we packed up the holdall to make it look like a large item of flight luggage. 'Feel alright?' I said, nodding and raising my eyebrows at Nasir.

He nodded back, but starlight revealed his wide, fearful eyes.

Julia put her arm around him again. 'Well,' she said in a low voice. 'It's only a few hours, after all. And it's hardly cold, is it. He'll be alright. And I suppose I've had my escapade. And Miles... It's really late, isn't it.'

She didn't move, though, and I couldn't make out what she was thinking. I told her about the sacred chickens. 'Right here, maybe.' I tapped the ground with my sandal.

She laughed, and we were still for a moment or two more. 'Owen, I can't actually do it. I can't just leave him here. All on his own. Who knows what might happen?' She gestured into the surrounding darkness. 'Think about it. This is the really weak part of the whole scheme. What if he panics, does something stupid. Who knows what they've got switched on out here. Radar? Night vision? Suppose he broke for cover; they might even shoot him.' Her eyes met mine. 'So why don't I stay?'

'Julia, I've got to be back at the house.'

'I know you have—for tomorrow to work. But I'll just stay here with him, shall I? There's no reason I shouldn't. And then I'll get myself taxied home somehow in the morning.'

I was completely taken aback. 'Suppose Miles gets home before you?'

'Shh! Now *you* need to keep your voice down. Don't worry about Miles. He'll assume I've gone for a swim. Or something.' She smiled in the moonlight. 'Anyway, Miles can manage for one night. Don't you

298

think? Without me.'

'I've lasted for thousands.' It just came out like that.

There was a pregnant silence, there in the night.

I broke it. 'You really mean…? Christ, it's crazy. You're really sure?'

'I think I am. Yes, quite sure. I've made up my mind.'

'Text him then. In the morning. To cover yourself. Won't he…?'

'Text him that I've decided to spend the night with an Afghan boy at the temple of Artemis?' Her eyes glittering. 'Not totally convincing, Owen, I'd have thought.' Smiling again. 'When it comes down to it, there's really no lie that wouldn't sound more suspicious than the truth, is there? No, I'll leave any explanations till tomorrow.'

'Julia…'

'It'll be fine, Owen. Besides, they might pick up the signal or something—the phone signal, if I… Who knows what they can do.' She spread her hands.

I could see the logic. Her staying would indeed secure this weakest link. I was astonished; and filled with admiration. At her courage. Truly, it would turn a very flaky and hare-brained scheme into real plan of action. 'Very well,' I said. 'Thanks. Thanks very much. It's a wonderful gesture.' I hesitated. 'So yes, I'll get straight off, then. I might as well, I suppose.'

'Owen… I'm really glad. I mean, for the opportunity. Because, yes, we couldn't have just handed him over, could we. We couldn't.'

On an impulse, I embraced her. Theo, we clung together for maybe a few seconds too long. Too long for the indeterminacy of the situation. But how good it can feel, the softness of body against body, and… Oh God, what can I say? The memories, the thoughts and feelings, the fragile glimpse… Of what? Of what shall I call it? A homecoming?

'Till morning, then,' I said, disengaging. 'Julia.'

'Till morning. No. I probably shan't see you in the morning. Till soon.'

I turned abruptly—far too abruptly. I set off towards the entrance to the enclosure. Once on the track, I looked back, but could see nothing of her, or of Nasir. I listened, but could hear nothing either.

So I began my journey homeward, still amazed at where I was and what I was doing, and full, too full, of those confused emotions.

For sure I had time enough to think, retracing that long road under the wheeling summer constellations, feeling at my back the first strong gusts of the north wind, the summer Méltemi, as it picked up again from the blow earlier in the week.

We'd still had no opportunity to talk, Julia and I. Not about the past. All our time had been taken up with Nasir.

Nevertheless, I was so glad she was with him. He'd even be able to sleep, maybe, having come so far and by so many roads. And she'd remain on guard, through the night hours. I imagined her there at the temple ruins, sitting on one of the slabs of excavated stone, maybe singing that unwise song to him. More likely, she'd busy herself with something practical: taking out the food, getting him to sip at the water bottle, putting on mosquito repellent. I imagined her prospecting cautiously in the dark for a shelf or nook, out of the way of snakes or scorpions. It even crossed my mind, Theo, that she might be thinking of me.

There was no traffic on the road. The hour? One in the morning, at least. Hardly a light on the looming hillsides. My sandals echoed strangely, and I thought of Julia all the more, saw her walking quietly among those stones, like Artemis herself, perhaps, abstracted, meditating, as I, upon the past.

What was I to make of it? Of her? And when I say thinking, perhaps that wasn't the right word. For it wasn't quite 'thought', in which meaning is pulled along in sentences from one construction to the next. No, Julia was just *there*; she was all around me. She was in the faint dark shapes of the landscape, in the night scents from the herbs and the unceasing sounds from the undergrowth. She was in the breath of the wind and the spill of light from the pulsating stars overhead. No matter what I saw or felt or heard, they were all somehow Julia.

And that was a kind of ecstasy, so that I hardly noticed that footslogging route back to Áyia Marína and Plátanos. Then, oh, how eerie the town felt without its lights, the castle a black bulk, the sea a black line, under which some far off voyaging vessel showed just one spot of red. How the crickets by the shore grated their mad bodies, and the ghostly pines creaked and sweltered in the wind.

It was then that I remembered your latest. Only then, and all of a sudden. That link you sent. I said my emotions were confused. But this quite topped it. That article in *The Guardian* — a journal one would have hoped knew better. Theo, I'd only had time to glance through it before getting ready yesterday, and had wondered from the start what you could have meant. I confess it had rocked me, coming embedded there just after the great news of your Katya Schelling success. And

300

your bald commentary: *I thought this might interest you.*

These things… They come always like a blow. On reading it, I'd felt quite sick for a minute or two. Felt destroyed almost. Did *you* think I was a fraud? That my whole being, my purpose, my existence, my art, was nothing, except—to paraphrase the wretched article—'an attempt to blame others for my own problems'?

Underneath all that, I'd felt scared. But, by then, we were in the midst of all the preparations for this mad plot of Nasir, and I had to get on with them.

Now, though, it sprang up at me and caught me off guard. *Why* had you sent it? Did you believe it? Did I? Why *now*?

These people, Theo, I remember when they first showed up. About '93, wasn't it? I'd been working with Mitchell maybe a couple of years. Yes, I'm pretty sure I'd had that first session with Josh. Then the media—the quality media, mind you, the broadsheets and BBC and so on—they began running this stuff. My God, it sounded 'Official'. It sounded 'Scientific'. It sounded for all the world as though there was some medically attested cloud of behaviours that had recently been identified. Oh, yes, it was a master stroke, and the press swallowed it whole.

A classic backlash! I can see that now; Mitchell was abreast of it, which was a help. Josh, in the States, was actively taking them on. But a mob it was, the same sort of mob that always springs up to defend vested interests. Theo, I won't go into the details: the fact that, clinically, there *is* no such 'syndrome'; that the claims they made were mostly misrepresentations and the experimental data they used hijacked from tin-pot experiments.

But can you imagine how it felt back then, after all the pain? And, more to the point, after the incredible sense of liberation we'd got from our therapists: that the pain was suddenly worth bearing, and that things had at last started lining up, with life, with ourselves, with the kindly God of whom we'd been deprived? That recovery was at last possible? To have it all trashed! To be set down as shifty inadequates manipulated by an equally shifty, unregulated bunch of charlatans. Theo, it was horrific.

So I got home in some turmoil, with my head full of Julia, and relieved, yes, that the first half of the Nasir plot had gone well, but also troubled by this damned link of yours. Troubled, did I say? I was furious. That old wolfish anger; I could almost feel my lips draw back, my teeth exposed—a racing, calculating anger. I realised quite how much I've lived under the shadow of these folk, even down to the present, and quite how shaken I've been by their hostility. God, they'd made me feel insane, out of step with everyone normal, hated, guilt-ridden. By the mid-nineties, they'd already sabotaged my healing and maybe that of countless others. They successfully killed off any support systems. With their threatening, mocking charges, they started a re-traumatisation, and the attempt at recovery itself became unsafe: both clients and professionals keeping their heads down.

My small hours ticked away. I couldn't sleep, pumped up with this sudden, all-consuming anger: against you, against everyone I'd ever trusted. I sat at the computer, speechless, alternately typing and clawing my coffee cup, hardly conscious of Nasir's empty bed, or of beloved Julia, likewise awake, on guard in that temple.

Beloved! The word was a sudden typo, Theo, an involuntary mistake. But it was not. For how could Julia's staying out all night with Nasir be the act of a betrayer, when I knew, I *knew*, deep down in every bone of my body, that she simply wasn't the kind of person who'd hand him over to the authorities the moment my back was turned. Of course she wasn't. Then what on earth had I been thinking all these years...?

Beloved Julia; it cleared my eyes. It sent down the furious Wolf, always so quick to leap up. Beloved Julia: out there, in the field of so much peril, the 'restricted' landscape almost electric with echoes of punishment and cruelty. I'd trusted her, implicitly, like a Child... Why, betrayal hadn't even occurred to me.

And you, Theo—did I seriously want to imagine after all this time, after everything you've been to me in this so lengthy exchange, that you'd suddenly turned on me?

Trust; it is that most difficult quality. Faith; that anything good might persist for longer than a moment or two. Be still and think, I told myself. Dare for once to believe that love endures, that love might not always be blown to pieces by the passage of a day or the ticking of an hour. So I re-read the pathetic little *Guardian* piece again—fetched in on a slow day, no doubt, to fill space.

And suddenly it couldn't hurt me. Its points were merely 'old hat' recycled, and I saw that when you'd sent it you really had meant no more nor less than your statement 'this might interest you', and it was not sent through any calculated hatred or intrinsic loathing you had for me.

More than that, it actually became a gift, my friend—the cause, as I felt, for rejoicing and celebration. Because I realised something in a flash, almost in the same breath as *beloved*… I realised something I'd never for a moment suspected before – that the cries of this angry mob were the perfect mirror of my own scepticism!

For what else have I been doing all along *myself* but setting the standard of proof cruelly, forensically, out of reach? My poor body, producing for years these heartrending messages, paintings by both hands, enactments… And what have I demanded of it every time? Exactly what this backlash always demands: more proof! More proof! Proof in perspective. Proof in 3D. In Technicolor. Whatever I have, it's never enough. I routinely call my Child self a liar because it can't come up with scientifically watertight evidence that will *always* be far too absolute for someone so young. You've heard me do it. God! I finally began to understand!

I remember Mitchell saying once in face of my tedious and seemingly indestructible denial: 'Well, *something*'s making you like this.' Theo, I made no reply, because I couldn't get a grip on what he meant. Even at the height of my illness, when we were actually uncovering the details and I could barely move for days for fear and desperation, and my dog-like panting attacks came in almost continuous waves, I kept insisting to myself that I had no symptoms at all, that my claim to care and treatment was pretty much of a fraud. And that's just what *they* say, these people!

And I've been so muddled ever since, so *discontinuous* – not knowing whether I was good or unforgivably bad – simply because someone in my head would never let me put two and two together. Theo, I embrace you, whatever your motives, and I'm so thrilled you sent me the link. Yes, they're savage, these folk. They feel attacked and have no kindly eye or ear for us, who, to be frank, seek mostly only authentication and an apology – with maybe a little financial help with our treatment. No, they'd rather get vicious. My own mother's done as much, in a manner of speaking.

But context is all. We know from children themselves the prevalence of intra-familial abuse today. So where's the surprise if it was just as prevalent fifty, a hundred, a thousand years ago? Didn't the ancient world run on it? Here, in Greece, wasn't pederasty a way of life, a production line for soldiers?

Theo, it's Dad in me! It's him! The Father! Flea! Why, even as I idealise my conscious memory of Dad, so my scepticism has all his trademarks. I mean the side of him I keep contriving not to recall: the iconophobia, the wilful category errors, the closed thinking, the ruthless, quasi-Jesuitical persecution of anything he perceives as heretical to Science—together with that tireless, fundamentalist atheism. The mob is in me, and its clever face is Dad, whose hyper-intelligence shuts light out, shuts Julia out. Dad hides the quivering whistle-blower Child in a black hole and punishes him continually. I think, dear Theo, my very dear friend, you might finally and unwittingly have flushed the Father out. And could that mean that Julia…? I don't know.

The rest of the plan? Oh, it was simple: to pick up Nasir at the airport in the morning as though he'd just arrived. The clothes and pieces of western kit we'd carried were all bought for him by Eléni. She'd even got smart shoes, along with some strong hair colouring from the *pharmakío*. She'd spent hours streak-bleaching Nasir's black hair, and so all he had to do this morning was get himself round to the airport in time for daybreak. Quite a lively scheme, don't you think? If it hadn't all been so insanely stupid, if Nasir hadn't been in fear of his life, if Eléni and I hadn't been in the midst of our acrimonious break-up, and if I hadn't been struggling with my perennially active demons, it might have been fun.

I ordered the taxi. Eléni and I drove in it to the airport. And there he was. It needed a double take to recognise him, because Julia had left him entirely convincing, in sunglasses and smart outfit, the hair swept back like some trendy guy. We greeted him and made sure the driver got a good look. Then we boldly hung around.

We got another driver to take us to Plátanos and had as public a coffee as possible, with the labelled holdall prominently on display on the pavement and Eléni embracing Nasir now and then.

We took lunch down at the harbour before walking back through town to the jetty for a leisurely drink.

Finally, we commandeered the one remaining taxi on the island to bring him home.

Theo, in so far as we're all still out of jail, it was a small triumph, and, in the island's subliminal perception, Eléni has a visiting brother, or friend, or whatever. And so we've bought ourselves a little time and space, I believe. Nasir will pass among Greeks as American or European, and his style will pass among everyone as entirely legal. At least in the very short term while he recovers. As for the future, we'll have to think again. He can't stay here forever. Tell me, my dear friend, do all your artists lead such lives?

304

22

Subject: **RE Internment**

What on earth do you mean?

Subject: **RE Internment**

My painting, yes. Called *Internment*. Yes, I know exactly the one; it was destroyed. I told you. Along with all the other stuff in my studio. 1976. So what about it?

Subject: **RE Internment**

Theo, I'm supposed to be the Socratic one — the one who's always up in the theoretical clouds, 'intellectualising' — not you. I still haven't the faintest clue what you're driving at.

Subject: **RE Internment**

Re-assembling?

Subject: **RE Internment**

Oh, Lord! I see it now. I have to confess it once more, that you're a genius, a masterly eye, a fine iconologist. Just let me set this down. I need to get it straight: the military landscape, the dark, the sense of imprisonment and danger — yes, electrical danger. You're saying the figures in that painting, *Internment* — the Parts, of course, in a way scattered by Julia's 'betrayal' and the assault of the thugs — are now re-assembling. How curious! And yet it stands up. After a fashion.

So the figures in that painting my thugs destroyed — the Parts. Yes, this we already incline to…

I have to say, I'm astonished by your analysis: Julia: the Girl. Nasir: the Child. Of course, pre-figured all those years ago as poor Hal, arms heroically outstretched on the wire as he fried. Outstretched, indeed, exactly as in the later left hand paintings. Ah, Nasir, his arms flung out over our shoulders when Julia and I pulled him up from the beach! Held so between us ever since, it seems. Not fully reflected in the *Lion* play, though, Cécile and so on. Of course, I didn't even understand at the time why I'd painted *Internment*. I was appalled that my imagination was so unremittingly dark. But then I was just scratching the surface, quite horrified at what violence and terror lay close underneath the mask of good fortune I presented to the world.

And the Father, of course, Staff, the wheelchair-bound 'camp commandant', from under whose radar *we've* now just escaped—as if by the skin of our teeth. Yet it wasn't until my rant, you say—about the article in *The Guardian*—that you slotted it all home. I salute you.

But what are we to make of it?

By the way, I suppose you're right about committing our Nasir plan to writing. I must be more circumspect in future. At least it was only to you and not broadcast on Facebook!

Subject: Courage

The Girl, somehow made flesh! You spur me to action, like some wing-footed messenger in a dream. Ha ha! Yes, but the risk…

Subject: RE Courage

But she herself is a field of danger, Theo. I tell you, her allegiances, alliances—Miles, Stefan, for a start. What if… What if it's all a trap? I mean a spiritual trap. An emotional one. I've known such happenings. I have! Things aren't what they seem. Theo…

Subject: RE Courage

You're right. Faint heart, etc. And all very well to style myself a warrior. But to be a man, yes, to be a man is always to make this

306

ordinary gamble, accept this simple risk. Why, it's nothing in truth, is it, the risk of making the sexual approach. Yet I have to admit, now you pin me down, that I've always slyly avoided it, having taken up in the past with women who pursued *me*, rather than those I might have pursued myself. Julia was the exception. But at all other times I avoided the risk of rejection. No, it's true. It's the risk every man is supposed to be man enough to accept. You see how I've hidden, so covertly, so secretly all along, in the female role.

Money where my mouth is? For sure.

23

Subject: **A serpent, coiled**

'But you didn't ever write. Or ring. Or try to make contact in… I don't know, in *any* kind of way. You could have reached me. You could. You could have come to the house and waited till the coast was clear.' She looked about to cry. 'Instead, you just disappeared. You *disappeared*, Owen. I went to the flat. I went, once Miles had calmed down. But you'd gone. You'd *vanished*. No car, no nothing. Your landlady couldn't tell me anything, either. It was horrible. I even wondered… I thought they might have killed you.'

I stared at her, dumbfounded. We were up at the castle, on the road overlooking the sea. It was late afternoon, and the long shadows of the huge walls cast a relief from the day's swelter. But her words rewrote everything I'd believed. 'You came to my flat?'

'Of course I did.'

'When?'

'I told you. When Miles had calmed down. He was angry.' She lowered her eyes. 'Very angry. I'd hurt him a lot.'

'Oh, right.'

'Yes. Well.'

I bit my tongue. 'Julia, I'm so sorry. So sorry.' I looked away from her. Two or three yachts were scurrying across the seaway, aiming to make Áyia Marína before dusk. 'It was bad?'

'I suppose.'

'Wait, though. I'm not getting it. I've thought, all this time… I have to say this, Julia. They knew where we were that day, Miles and his boys. They knew *exactly*. There's no way around this. They *intercepted* us at a place we'd planned to go, way out in the country: a place no one else could ever have guessed. *I* didn't tell anyone. I know that for a fact. And all I could remember were your last four words to me: *Owen, I'm so sorry.*'

She jerked herself away from me. 'You thought *I'd* done it!? You actually thought *I'd* set it all up? Genuinely?'

'How else could they have known?' I spread my palms. 'Julia, you were even apologising for it as it happened. You were saying sorry!'

'You think *I'd* get you hi-jacked and beaten up? You really

308

believed...!'

'I didn't want to! Of course I didn't. It was terrible.' At last I saw the full flimsiness of my position. 'But how *could* it have been anything else? Right as they were dragging me off, you said *Owen, I'm so sorry.* What other possible interpretation could I have come to?'

'The real one, for God's sake, Owen! Didn't you have any *faith* in me? What *idea*...? Owen, what awful *conception* of me must you have had? Couldn't you believe in... our love?' Her eyes were brimming again. 'Love, Owen.'

I put my hand up to her face and with the back of my fingers touched her cheek as gently as I could. I felt her tear run down. 'Tell me, then. Please.'

'There's nothing to tell.' She sniffed and dashed her eyes with the back of her hand. She rummaged in her handbag for a tissue and blew her nose. 'I didn't know anything about it. You remember Miles was always suspicious. He still is. He always used to think I was seeing someone, even when I wasn't. He'd make me account for all my actions, everywhere I went, who I was with. So then when I *was* seeing someone—you—we had to be really careful, didn't we. We had to work around it. I suppose I *was* sort of resigned to him finding out eventually, but I kept just putting it to the back of my mind. I suppose I was just frightened, Owen. Well, obviously. What else do you do?

'And then,' she said, 'when it happened, when he did find out, it caught me by surprise. It was immediately before... that afternoon. He'd somehow guessed it was you. He said your name one day, out of the blue—you remember you'd met him that time. It came up in some conversation we were having—don't ask me how. Maybe he was fishing. Oh, yes—fishing, Owen. Fishing for clues; about my work, probably, wanting to know what had kept me late. I denied everything; of course I did. As convincingly as I could. I tried to sound casual. But I can only think there must have been some look in my eye or some expression on my face that gave me away.'

I wanted to interrupt but let her speak.

'There must have been, Owen, because he latched on to the notion there and then. And then he wouldn't let it go. He just wouldn't. He asked me the next day where you worked. Straight out. Well, I couldn't refuse to tell him, could I—how suspicious would that have seemed? So there it was. And that was all it took to set him on the track; because of course he knew someone. Someone in Hammersmith Council. Some mate, some buddy who'd readily do him a favour, and who had access to the payroll. He always did. He always knew someone, Owen. Mates. Blokes he'd met. Buddies who owed him one. Miles gave this buddy a story and the rat simply handed over your address. Easy as that. Miles even showed it to me written down on a piece of paper. He was laughing.'

'Bastards! Both of them!'

She sighed.

'So he *did* watch us at the house?' I said.

'I don't know. He must have done. Or set those people to do it.'

'The Boss, the Mole; I made names for them. Who were they?'

'I've honestly no idea. I'd never seen them before. Owen, that time he went further than I'd ever have imagined. I knew he'd do something; but *that*! I never dreamed... I thought it would be just me. I felt horrible.' She touched my arm again. 'What happened?'

'Not so much. They roughed me up. Ruined my studio.'

'What, your paintings?'

'More or less.'

'Poor you. What can I say?'

We looked at one another, then away.

'But at Bledlow ridge,' I said. 'When you said you were sorry...'

'Sorry. Yes, I was. I was sorry because I'd told him where you worked. That's all, honestly. I hated myself for it.' She dabbed at her eyes again. 'Owen, you do believe me, don't you?'

I could feel my brow furrowed, the muscles of my forehead contracted as I worked at the difference between perceiving and believing, the sudden sweeping away of a half-baked, paranoid, yet so very powerful construct. 'Of course. Of course I believe you. And *of course* I'm cursing myself for being so blind, so crazy. These things, you know...'

But she couldn't *know*, Theo. She couldn't know, or imagine, the particular personal madness and descent that had been triggered in me by the events of that day on Bledlow; because it was only just now that I was seeing them for myself.

When I'd last known Julia, I'd imagined I was the most sane and normal person in the world. That huge lack of faith I spoke about, the deluded thinking—which had masqueraded so convincingly at the time as rational decision making...

And the only conclusion I can draw, my friend, is that it must have suited me in some way to think of her as a betrayer. It must have suited some 'part' of me to turn the person who loved me, and whom

I loved in return, into an object of anger. And my insatiable anger, my blind, concealed, insensate and indiscriminate rage, has fed upon that thought, quietly, serpent-like and coiled almost unshakably at the back of my mind all these years. Right down to Eléni, whom I so stupidly trusted even as I kept scribbling to you about Julia's inconstancy—even as she was off screwing her wretched Athenian. Now there's the full hundred and eighty degrees of misperception, Theo. Ah, monstrous anger has constructed all my attitudes and opinions, the furniture of delusion!

The worst thing about it was that I might somehow have intervened to save Julia from *Miles*'s anger, had I not jumped to conclusions immediately after the thugs wrecked my studio.

Or, if I hadn't been able to prevent that, at least the incident might have precipitated some resolution for her. *If* I'd played my part, Theo. And she could have escaped from a bad situation. With me.

'It wasn't that bad, Owen. Miles was...'

'Tell me.'

Theo, she talked for a time about her life, her family; and, believe it or not, seemed able to explain Miles away. There was even a strange fondness for him, I thought, in her tone. I told her something of Lily, and my children.

I guess it's easy for me, now, and with the perspective of hindsight, to characterise Miles—that controlling, obsessive scrutiny of her activities, the overmastering suspicion, the rapid resort to aggression, and so on. Tolstoy was hopelessly wrong about unhappy families. The sad truth is that they're unhappy in only a very few routine and predictable ways, as that glorious novel of his itself proved, indeed: controlling husband, desperate wife, judgmental society. Only the details, times and landscapes of unhappiness tend to vary.

God, I'd really like to think we're clear now about violence against women: physical, sexual, emotional, financial, whatever. It lurks so often unseen, and so much in mental health is about the bullying still going on... So I believe, at least. Flawed childhoods set us up for adult relationships in which we misperceive the present, explain it away, compartmentalise it, or even blame ourselves. And that's another reason why Psychoanalysis was always such a pernicious red herring, with its flimflam about sexual fantasies, compounding both society's and the victim's own denial. Pernicious that it once led us to imagine some women actually got off on being knocked about. I confess, Theo, I resorted to that thought myself in the aftermath of Bledlow—just to

311

try to make sense of Julia's behaviour. It's shameful, and I'm sorry for it. And I note here, with as much humility as I can muster, that for all the vaunted feminism of my painting stance with you, my bitter ego has clung to the Julia myth right to the last, only admitting to the streaks in it over the past few months — indeed, only during the composition of this strange Bledlow painting and all that has since flowed from it.

'Owen…'

'I'm so, so sorry.'

'It wasn't your fault. It was just…'

But I couldn't let the halting explanations go on. My feelings overcame me. I turned to her and took her in my arms and felt again the body I'd known so well. She resisted at first. She pulled away — yet only half, for her hands were on my shoulders, and she made no attempt to remove them. She gave herself gradually to the embrace, holding me tightly, as I held her. So our bodies closed together, and our cheeks rested the one beside the other.

Theo, I don't know how long we remained there. Touch removed us from the world, and it was a timeless time, more than just minutes, more than any normal segments of the clock. No one passed. The sun went down. Maybe we clung there an hour, maybe longer. I can't say. It was as though, having found the moment, neither of us could bear to release it and so return us to speech and all the fragile details that had led us to this point. It was as though we must somehow make up for all the years that had kept us apart, in case they did so again. Far better, we thought, to stay locked and let our souls converse — if anyone still dare speak of soul, Theo, and in that word emulate a subtler, richer, more accurate age of love. Yes, I mean that, my dear friend. *More accurate*, like Donne's *Exstasie*.

The bright moon flooded its light over us, and I leave you for the moment with this seemingly endless embrace, made temporal only by each slightest shift of hold, each smallest adjustment of stance, each gentle pressure of head beside head, mine lifted only to print kisses on her hair, her ear, her soft neck, her beloved cheek. Oh, that I could paint all this!

24

Subject: **RE Resolution**

But he bites my back, almost at my ear; almost as an audible voice.

Anyway, I've nothing to offer her, no matter what you say. I'm a husk. Clapped out! The Parts? They're all agitated, I guess — if they exist at all, Theo.

Because this... this is really rocking the boat, putting a cat among their pigeons, upsetting the apple cart.

Isn't it, Theo?

No. How can I trust her, when she has Miles and Stefan, and God knows who else already on a string?

Subject: **The kiss**

We contrived to meet on the other side of the bluff. We chose the dry valley of a stream, where it ran into the sea.

Privacy is rare on an isle like this; the low vegetation offers neither cover nor comfort! Even out of town, in these wilder regions, where the occasional stunted holm oak or wild olive shimmers in a waste of grits and ochres, and the scorched rock drops abruptly to the Aegean, one can still remain in view, say, of the lone rambler up on a path of tamped stones, or the fishing boat suddenly rounding the headland, to ply its nets back and forth in the bay.

Nevertheless, we put down a blanket. We tucked ourselves into the chine. We could hear the waves lap on the shingle and the warm wind bristle in the vegetation. The night, keeping us apart, had been divine torment. Now, by day, we lay close together in the blaze of morning. And I couldn't but stroke her thigh through her dress, or touch, continually, the fine brown skin of her arm, until our hands linked and she nursed my fingers in her own.

They tell you the kiss is modern. Search your old Greeks, Theo, and you won't find much of it — except between men, and mostly for greeting. Oh yes, authorities suggest their kiss was for affection, not arousal. Mothers kissed children; shepherds lambs! It's borne out

313

today. *Philí*, the word, owes more to friendship—*philía*. Don't worry, I shan't be kissing you!

Was it the Romans, then, who first romanticised it? Did Catullus crave his thousand kisses from Clodia Metelli even as all other cultures thrust and lusted in complete ignorance of this one tender supplement?

No, Theo! For sure, the *Song of Songs* sucks erotic kissing far back into the Semitic Bronze Age. And what other giveaways may lie yet undiscovered in fired tablets?

And besides, a canny glance or two at Theocritus shows how the erotic kiss was actually very well-established, whatever historians may suppose. And what about Indian sexual culture? For how, Theo, can such pleasure to human kind have remained simply unexplored during all the millennia of our evolution. It's a nonsense. Someone— some two—*must* have discovered it, and that well early in the dawn of time.

And they'd have spread the word, wouldn't they? For the lips are marked out in humans as in no other creature; flushed and fleshed with the same tinge as every other erogenous zone. It doesn't take an artist to see that. To see how, in our species—the erotic ape—the dark of the lips complements exquisitely the skin, itself an organ so nakedly, exquisitely different, and in itself so incredibly, availably sensuous. The lips above all clamour for touch of lips, because we are designed for love!

Ah, but the kiss is more political than sex, and Julia and I were at once its radicals. The kiss is the true forbidden fruit; it undoes the Fall. It threatens the tyrant far more than sex. Where the kiss lacks, it must have been suppressed. For sure, our kisses challenged not just Miles, but all structural hatred and envy. Paolo and Francesca were forever denied it; and that's the hell from which Rodin tries to spring them. The hope—to borrow Yeats, too—that lip would be pressed on lip! Ah, Rodin's sculptural gestures are a response to Manet. Rodin bids, suddenly, and almost from nowhere, to restore Eros. Alas, that our own century's art is otherwise devoid of it. Of kisses.

Julia and I shared our breath, our mouths, our selves, while the sun moved overhead. We were in paradise with lizards and butterflies. Birds forgot to be wary. Lesser winged creatures zoomed or hovered over us. Bees hummed at the thick-flowered oleander that had seeded and sprung up not far away. We hardly spoke.

'But what happened then? I want to know, Owen. I need to understand.'

We were at the castle again, and she'd told Miles she was shopping for gifts. I'd told Eléni I was walking into town in search of ideas; though God knows Eléni doesn't care these days what I do one way or the other. We were outside the high Byzantine walls, looking west this time over Léros ridge to the port of Lakkí, and to the other islands beyond. I was content to talk. But things were growing urgent. Theo — her looming departure.

I outlined my disappearance, my sojourn in Paris. I sketched my dissolution into a fragmentary, speechless body. I was trying, of course, to lead round to a certain subject. For wasn't my Paris experience the reason I could subsequently make mimes for Mitchell? Dad forbade me speech — or my mother would die, he said. And you remember the French authorities once banned speech and so brought forth that wondrous art of mime, so despised today. Yes, I desperately wanted to tell Julia about Dad, but loquacious as I was — as I am, my friend, as you know so well — on this matter again I couldn't make my lips move; they felt almost physically stitched up.

I did explain my feminisation: the long hair and newly-shaven cheeks, the sparkling clothes, necklaces, bangles, the tripping clogs.

'But that was just the fashion,' she said.

'I went beyond fashion.'

There was a pause. 'What are you trying to tell me, Owen?

I'm trying to tell you I'd no desire for men. And yet this female Part... I did use the word to Julia, Theo, '...was somehow waiting, dormant inside me,' I said, 'like the sleeping beauty. I... When I lost you, Julia. When I went to Paris... she — the Girl — just came out. *She* was sociable, confident, witty. *I* was not. That's what happened.'

She looked at me steadily, until I grew embarrassed. I rattled on stupidly about Félix.

'You were in love with Félix?' she said gently.

'You misunderstand,' I came back with sudden sharpness. 'He was my friend. Maybe the first man I ever trusted or warmed to. After Dad.' *For thou hast been as one in suffering all...* Oh, my friend.

And now, writing to you, Theo, I see myself sitting there at that Paris café, dressed to kill.

Was Julia right? Is she right to be suspicious in her turn? Was that the purpose of my rig, after all, not to ensnare Zigui, or the others, but

315

Félix? No, I swear not. The opposite — if anything, of such a Freudian reading: it was actually to get clean out of my sullied skin into a land where I should have fellowship, and into a gender where sex would only be play-acting.

But now she redeems that.

Subject: Julia naked

It's the makeshift bed in my studio. She brought yoghurt and honey. The sheet we've occupied, Julia and I, remains rucked and scrunched into ridges, as in the Titian *Urbino* — which I now joyfully have in mind. Ah, but it's an excitement to tease all those heaped folds and bluish yellow shadows out of the creamy white. Painting this makes me rearrange my thoughts. Now all the Paris scenes will in some way add up to this central nude. So I've decided.

And the delight of flesh! So long, I confess, since the brush tasted this full candour or could luxuriate in complex skin tones: the palette taxed to its limits with titanium, barium, carmine, sienna... Flesh tones: I'd gladly list every name, as of earthen muses constantly before my eyes. This subtlety, if anything, is a homecoming.

I'm sorry for my silence. You'll understand.

Nevertheless, the work proceeds, and if this piece — the nude — will go centrally over the arch, that opens a space far left for the Bledlow scene, using the others between them as the top line of a double row, their intention mysterious, their colours tending always to the scheme that relates the start to the centre. For their shapes are thrown curiously into context — as though they knew all along that Julia would return; it's uncanny.

But then so much in painting is less about invention than discovering what's underneath. As with the chalk hill, we scrape off to disclose. Which would imply a future already figured — an absurd proposition, Theo, yet perpetually demonstrable by this act of setting medium to surface. No, I can't ignore the fact that the finish really does seem to lie like the image of a crystal, fully formed and timeless, under all aspects of the work.

I come back, too, to the warrior: if it's to be worth anything, art is a violent encounter with extreme forces. On land, one can seek only to hold steadfast and ride ahead; at sea, to steer a true course no matter what wind buffets.

Subject: Assembling

Glad you like it. Double row means that the lower, or under-text of the concept can now accommodate certain more *left hand* images—as if in a miniature *Theatre of Cruelty*, a kind of lens by which to scrutinise the larger.

Sent from my iPad

Subject: RE Assembling

No, she's absent, now. She's at her hotel, with Miles.

It *is* from life; she *was* here with me, in truth, in the flesh.

And now the paint traces I make serve to re-suggest, to re-present each lovely moment of her presence—that slightest darkening of tone beside the throat, the sun-damaged skin beneath the collar bone, the crease under the left breast with its hint of purple shadow. And here the movement of belly into hip, the little moles there, and just there, the caesarean scar with its protective sag of flesh, the tan lines and weight of the thighs, their slight compression one against the other, an articulation of the small bones in the hand against the wreathing pubic curl... Oh, my description of her here on the screen makes her now twice removed. For all is a species of memory; with intimacy perhaps deferred even as it takes place. Surely this is the artist's ultimate challenge: the perpetual offstage-ness of the beloved. If he can bear it.

Subject: RE Assembling

Only because we were talking, after we'd made love; Eléni had gone off to see about her flights.

'They gave me ECT,' Julia said.

'When?'

'About seven years ago. "Severe agitated depression" was the diagnosis. I was glad, Owen, at the time. Under anaesthetic, naturally. Shocks did what nothing else would. And now I don't ever want to go back into that pit... that pit of absolute darkness.'

'Nothing else was on offer?'

'Pills. Anti-depressants. My doctors boosted up the dose. For weeks, nothing would touch it. I was desperate.'

'Didn't you have counselling? Therapy?'

'On the NHS? They never mentioned it.'

She showed me photos of her children on her camera; then some of her own paintings.

'Do you *never* paint people in them? Not your kids, even?'

'Here,' she said. 'This one, and this.'

She said she'd remembered, but only in her forties, being molested as a child quite often by an older cousin—at age nine. She hadn't forgotten it before that, just never thought of it, much less given it a name.

'Maybe that's what forgetting is,' I said, quietly.

'I wanted you to know about it. All those years ago, when we were young together, I didn't connect it with anything. I didn't think... We were... Things were different.'

Theo, there's no Eros without the figure. When art shuns the face, the nippled breasts, the spine's sensuous path—I travel it with the brush—the narrows of the waist, the genitals' occlusion, the leg's soft curve, the foot's heavenly arch... When every explicitness in these is routinely eschewed by the artist and left merely to the pornographer, then art has voided desire, shirked responsibility. For unless art owns the arousing figure, only the intellect is ever engaged. And that any child can do; for children's art is all intellectual, spiritual, conceptual. And we're not children. Contrary to Freud, only the adult is the sexual being, having suffered pupation and emerged, winged, to the delight of day.

Subject: RE Assembling

How on earth am I going to get them to do that? Yes, always they're there, waiting, and if ever I let my guard down, I can feel them. For they long to surface—just as the sweats and tremors of the shell-shocked soldier besiege his fortified mind and seek to visit the battlefield once again upon his nights. You understand me?

Because the essence of post-traumatic stress is muscle pitted against muscle, with the urge to relive fiercely resisted by its own refusal. That's why it's *stress*, Theo.

Co-operate, though...?

Yes, I know it's what Josh suggested. I just don't know how. I don't know where to start with them.

But at least the Father is silenced. I haven't heard his 'voice' at all. And so am well, and it's a joy.

And I love your notion: 'to make space for the artist'. Of course! You mean full Renaissance perspective? Brilliant! To create space for the missing self-portrait, myself. Indeed, she needs him, the nude. See how she staled over the centuries, exposed in her private room to public show. Right down to Manet: Olympia's hard whore stare, a complete loss of trust in love, daring the family, daring the man to come forward, come into the frame, Monsieur.

Oh, that prettified shape—*Olympia*. See her servant offer it, the vulva of infected flowers funnelling down only to her speechless revenge. Then a century and half's blood chaos on the canvas—the art we grew up with. No, I don't blame anyone for the retreat from perspective.

But you're right, I must make *chóra* relocate itself. Perspective: which is *making perspectival room* for cavity as space-time, the wordless country between Julia's thighs.

So I make hints of her openness; they stiffen me again as I paint. Here's the female cleft upon my chalk-white canvas. Only a precise conformity to the erotic *shape*, passionately, painstakingly delivered, makes the cock stand—as the Greeks knew. I love her attributes. My lust for her objectifies them; it's love in action. Only an accurate portrayal identifies *her* nakedness from any other's! Ha! The eyeball's a camera, whether we like it or not. And all our known personal scenes and memories do principally come to mind as through an optic *lens*.

Theo, not only has the beloved been offstage, but I, too. My True Self must enter to Julia, stage right, or left. He's coming, I can feel it. But can I bear it?

Subject: RE Assembling

Thanks for yours. I'm just making a vacant landscape visible through the window. Clearly, the emptiness in her own paintings is her desire for cleanliness. After her cousin's interference, I mean. So this whole piece will be an image of her. See her mouth just open, too, the lids lowered? See the slight charge at her ribcage, as though the chest still heaves and she's just breathed hard. Julia is neither Titian's diva, nor

Olympia; for this breath animates her. Whether orgasm or ECT, I'm content, Theo, for both *are* her; both are her history. How in truth do we paint what's written on the body?

25

Subject: **Life class**

Marta called. It was this morning. Eléni showed her into my studio —
Nasir was with her.

I took off my glasses and looked, blinking, sweating and holding
my brushes, from one to another. Then Eléni swept Nasir back to the
house.

'So,' said Marta, smiling. 'You have a guest. A relative, I
understand. I heard something of it.'

Aha! So the plan had worked! But now I had to deceive the one
person I didn't want to.

We'd been expecting such a moment, of course. Even so, I stood
both awkward and embarrassed to trot out our pathetic story —
pathetic in all senses of the word. 'A distant cousin, actually, Marta.
We don't know him so well. Eleni's family in New York. He's visiting
for a week or two. Hasn't been well. A tumour on the throat.' I looked
down, ashamed at the blatant absurdity. 'Benign. As it turned out. The
tumour.' I cleared my own throat. 'And the operation was successful.
Thankfully. He's come out here to convalesce. To us. To Eléni.
Cousin.'

'Convalesce?' The word was unfamiliar to her.

'To recover. Restore one's health.'

'I see.'

'To get away from it all.' I heard a shrill note in my laugh.

I tell you, Theo, we'd agonised over the language question for
nights. We simply couldn't come up with a convincing nationality or
ethnicity that might stop people — say, someone as polyglot as Marta —
from trying to speak to him.

'He has to spend a lot of time lying down. Fresh air, complete rest.
You'd know, of course, as a doctor... The family thought of us, Marta,
and here he is.' Lame, desperate stuff — absurdity upon absurdity! In
the flustered dialogue of farce, I almost heard an audience again.

My guest too, perhaps. She made a sound in her nose, and I knew
she wasn't convinced.

Yet doctors don't meddle with the patients of others, and she
seemed willing enough to play her part. 'Very nice I think for you.

321

Fortunate. Considering your sad... Owen, when you told me of you and Eléni... Bah! But it will help, I think, to have someone... what do you say? I have read this expression, *to oil the wheels.*'

'I suppose it will.' My laugh again. 'Buys me time. A bit. For my commission.'

She looked away a little, then back. 'Owen, I heard also another thing. A lady. An English lady.' Her eyebrows lifted interrogatively. 'Who visits, too, sometimes?'

My heart was in my mouth, but I gazed at her as blankly as I could. And why, Theo, did I hesitate to tell her about Julia? I don't know. A medical practitioner, an authority figure, who seemed to have some investment in my happiness with Eléni; it felt a little like my mother, I guess. And, with such an important issue, perhaps I couldn't be sure whose side she might be on.

She shrugged and looked away. 'Ah, well, these rumours...' She touched at her hair and shifted the perched sunglasses. 'And what's his name, the cousin?'

'Na...' Oh, God! She'd caught me off guard, hinting at Julia and then suddenly returning to the boy. And just when I thought I'd got away with it! The name, of all things! In our desperate, ludicrous concoction of the speechless cousin, we'd forgotten to think of a name.

'Paraskeví.' It jumped into my mind. I'd heard it before, Paraskeví. Seen it? On a poster? On the old church on the way up to the castle? Some saint? Something religious? The word, too, for a day of the week — Friday, weirdly. Too late I realised I'd got the gender wrong.

'He has a girl's name?' Marta stared hard at me.

'Sorry. Paraskevós? Paraskevás, is it?' I bluffed the masculine. Then adrenalin spoke for me: 'The family calls him Paddy, anyway. He has no Greek at all. Completely Americanised.'

I stared back at her, until our gazes seemed to twine into a kind of understanding.

She turned at last to glance around, taking in the trials and sketches and half-done canvases stacked about drying.

I wiped a sleeve across my brow.

'So I track you to your den at last.' She was lifting a painting by its edges. 'But this one is striking. And this. Strange scenes, strange moments of detail, Owen.'

'They're not finished.' I explained, relieved. 'They're all to hang together. Close in tightly, next to one another. In frames.' I spread out my hands. 'Frames within a frame. Like your Orthodox iconostasis

322

...stases? In your churches. With the central doorway, screening a mystery. There's a large doorway leading from the main space of our building... The commission.'

'May I?' She rummaged through the Paris courtyards, interiors and *genre* moments with their cast of players. 'And this is the project that will save your...' she hunted for the word.

'Bacon?'

She was blank.

'It's another expression. Yes. I'm hoping so.'

'Then no change? You and Eléni?'

'No,' I said. 'Nor will there be.'

She frowned.

'Everything between us is over. It's finished, Marta, I'm afraid. Despite... Paddy. She's only left me time enough to put this commission together in outline. I have to finish some key elements to show the client. Theo, at my gallery, my friend, my... life-support actually. He's still confident. He likes what I've sent him. He likes the overall conception. If all goes well...'

'Then?'

I shrugged. 'England, I suppose. Put this house on the market—if you can sell houses any more. My son...'

We stood in awkward silence, our earlier confusion symbolic of this unforeseen gap between us. This gap created, I mean, by the existence of Nasir. And of Julia.

'Can I get you coffee?'

'Thank you, no. I regret I can't stay. I only came to tell you some news. Spíros is coming. Here, to Léros.'

'When?'

'Soon. He, too, has a commission—an archangel. *Áyios Michaél Taxiárchis*. For the harbour church. Yes, just down the street from me. Now that I've seen your work, I'll be able to tell him. He spoke of you. He would like to view, I know.'

'He'd be welcome. So much has happened since... since I went to visit him.' I stuck my brushes in a jar of oil. 'Inspiration. Another thing I have to thank you for.'

'Owen, no one is ill on Léros. My surgery is finished. Will you come to my hives?' She said it all abruptly, her Russian intonation at once thick and enigmatic, as though she were consciously staking out a position.

'I'd love to, Marta.' I looked down. 'But I really must get on with...

with this, my work. The pressure of time. Forgive me.'

Yet we remained standing there, in a rather English way, as though politeness demanded a little more before we parted.

'The anxiolytics? They're working?'

'I don't need them so much.' I smiled.

'And the Paroxetine?'

'Actually, I've left off with them all.'

'Left off?'

'Discontinued.' I let the breath out through my nose. 'Alright, I'll tell you the truth. A few days ago I threw the whole lot away. I'm sorry. They helped initially, but I needed…' Again I was deceiving her. The reason, of course, was that psychiatric drugs are no friend to erection, even less to ejaculation! 'I needed to be in touch,' I lied, 'with the paint.'

'Ah.' Again, that searching look. 'I see. Very well. If you feel you don't need them, yes, then that is good.' Her eye strayed over my pictures again, and I realised with a start that a section of nude Julia was quite visible over by the window. 'Yes, if you feel, Owen, that circumstances really have changed.'

'Please don't think I'm ungrateful. The pills did help. Genuinely. I can only thank you very much for helping me.'

'It is my job. But I have been thinking,' she said at last, looking directly at me and then away again. 'About what you told me. What I think you told me. Your treatment. The American man, Josh. These "Parts" you appeared to suggest…'

Theo, you remember I said I'd told her about them. A little. With the change of subject, some of the awkwardness between us seemed to melt, and I spoke a little excitedly perhaps, almost jumping at the chance and opening up the conversation again. I said that after some recent things I'd tried talking to the Father in my mind, trying to get him 'off my back'. Thanking him, Theo, but asking him once and for all to stop making life so bloody difficult. Then I felt I was saying too much, presuming, foolish.

But she was alert. She sat down on my makeshift bed, curious. 'Did this… talking work?'

I made light of it. 'He wouldn't cooperate, no matter how I tried. He refused to talk back. Kept disappearing—it was bizarre. In the end I had an idea and put him in the Angel's downdraught. Interesting, about Spiros's commission, by the way.'

'Downdraught? Angel?' She wouldn't be put off.

324

And I was glad, despite my reservations—joyous, as with Josh—suddenly to find myself talking about the Parts. 'It really annoyed him. A great golden force flooding down from the outstretched wings—Dad always hated religion. I didn't want to hurt him, but he was pinioned there. Pinioned by Good, so to speak. And there he's had to stay.' I grinned at her, again a little crazily, and yet—I say it again—it was a profound relief to speak like this, to someone who was actually interested. 'That was some days ago. I've checked on him a couple of times, and he's still furious.'

'And now the Girl has shown up.'

Now I looked at her very sharply, and she held my gaze, until some inclination of her head seemed to indicate the nude of Julia.

But then she abruptly changed the subject. 'So you understand them better, perhaps, these... Parts? Now that you've left the Father to... to fry?'

I fiddled awkwardly with my jar of brushes, dabbing them about in the oil. But I was also fired up, Theo. 'I know them only through my painting. Marta, truly, I've no sense of them. This whole business, everything; it's boloney. It's just a leap in the dark, an act of faith. Faith in what, I ask myself. In me? Josh? God? I try to see the Parts in my mind, Marta. It's ridiculous. I can't. Not convincingly. I'm trying to suggest them in these Paris scenes,' I gestured at the nearest oil sketches. 'But it still feels mad. There's absolutely no feedback from them. As soon as I wake, they go silent. It's nonsensical.' Her face was, for a moment, I noticed, full and ideal. 'So there really is nothing to suggest any validity to them.'

'Except this... woman.'

'Very well. Her name,' I said at last, 'is Julia.'

'Ah, Julia.' A hint of smile on her lips. 'Another name to... to conjure with, you say, don't you.'

'Yeah. You have very good English.'

'Thank you. I learned in Russia, and then from reading and movies... So you put Father on hold. And straightaway this... Julia. She shows up.'

She was reluctant to go. What did she want, Theo? Was she jealous? Was she trying to have an affair?

It wasn't that. She was somehow serene. But she spoke about herself, about when she qualified in Russia, soon after the fall of the Soviet Union. She took psychiatry, just as they realised how hurt they'd been, and how the Americans just left them to rot. Stalin, the war, the KGB, corruption, vodka, gangsters, Afghanistan—all that backlog, and the Russian people were crying out for healing. And she'd heard of all these controversial new ideas suddenly coming out of the West: PTSD, amnesia, dissociation—psychiatry in uproar.

But then she fell in love with a Greek man and left the country, as I told you; married, came here, had kids. And when she turned around—a family doctor helping out at the hospital, yes, and happy, of course, very happy... When she turned around, all that had gone. Vanished. The post-traumatic genie back in the bottle, so to speak. Exactly.

'Except for maybe here on Léros,' she said. 'Because here trauma lies all around us, Owen. Psychiatric trauma, exposed, on the surface. Cóstas, Yánnis, at the unit. Everyone. It's documented, very severe, and plain to see. Yet one treats still almost in the dark, only with kindness, endless kindness. Hardly with drugs at all, you know. Yet always a little in the dark, feeling our way...'

And so, Theo, when I show up on the island with my passing neediness and blather about the Parts, well, she's intrigued, curious.

But it's almost as though she seems to know already, and that I'd just 'woken her up' as she calls it. Her lost gift—'talant'—you recall? Maybe. Anyway, she tackled me head on about my attitude to the Parts. I'd tried to change the subject: back to Russia and her upbringing. And she did speak touchingly again about her father, Theo, also a doctor, you remember. In Russia. Dead, now. How she'd loved him. Yet she wouldn't be diverted. 'Russia is...' she made a wide, sweeping gesture '...impossible. While you, Owen. Still avoiding the issue, eh? These Parts. They're you.'

She leaned forward to touch my arm, my face, in that diagnostic way doctors have. Yes, moved the focus firmly and conclusively back on to me, as though she'd revealed quite enough of herself for one day, thank you very much. 'You'd better believe it. There's no doubt of you, Owen. No need to cling to...'

'They're real,' I said, almost picking a fight, almost contradicting myself.

'Of course.'

'No, but real. Too real to "own". They're not just imagination. Not just the dreamy productions of some artist. They're real! But I have no knowledge of them. And they despise me.'

'What?'

'They despise me.'

326

'Why?'

'Because they see me as weak, while they're left in charge. To do all the work.'

'You speak of them as an ancient might speak of the gods,' she said.

Abruptly, she made her farewells and left. Ashamed of my deceit over Nasir, I felt a hypocrite kissing her cheeks. And so odd a conversation. Her own kindness. Her frank attempt to help. I didn't let her—even though, by some starry insight of her own, she was saying nothing more than the same conclusion I'd come to myself over the Laestrygonians: that the Parts were just me.

I can't handle it. I push people away. The Father must still be very active, very persuasive.

I don't understand why she seems to care so much. About me, Theo.

Subject: **RE Life class**

How can I? Julia's at her hotel. I haven't heard from her. I can't get to see her, and time's running out.

Subject: **RE Life class**

No, she's not answering her phone. Don't you think I've tried! Or texts. It's a trick. She's been leading me on. She's set me up again.

Subject: **Actaeon—after Titian again**

Maybe she's… She had ECT—Julia. ECT broke Artaud's spine. I read it. Fifty-one shocks to the head they gave him, June 1943 to December 1944. The dates are chilling, Theo, as if Vichy's asylum bids to rejoin the war outside. I have a drawing of Artaud's—a copy—the rays of electricity apparently streaming into his own naked form… although such images are common enough in the distressed, with or without ECT. But if he'd been anaesthetised, would it still have been torture? Torture that doesn't leave a mark—except upon the soul.

Maybe she's been lying to me all along, Theo.

Subject: **RE Actaeon — after Titian again**

Intellectualising? Floating off? Artaud *is* relevant. Artaud would have brought all violence centre stage. Anti-writing — his Roman theatre of blood and spectacle. Howls, huge disquieting movements… Derrida & Co, those connoisseurs of screams, made Artaud their Christ on a stick, their tortured genius. I despise them by turns. Agamemnon! Always, always, Theo, Psychoanalysis turns a blind eye to suffering, patronises pathology, wanks off on it. When pain becomes fashionable, Eros is trashed. Look, look! Artaud himself said his epiphany came in the Louvre, at Van Leyden's *Lot and his Daughters*: incest foregrounded against fire and destruction.

Maybe it's me. Yes, of course there'll be an explanation. The Headmaster, you think. Yes, alright. Maybe trust…

26

Panic, Theo. Yes, she's replied; everything's fine as far as that's concerned. Yes, it was Miles, nothing to do with me, and we're due to meet tomorrow. All that is as it was. Except for me: breathless, my fingers skidding on the keys, the instant sweat cold even in this heat. My friend, the commission you so kindly secured me...

Ah, it was well on its way, perhaps, and I could have fudged it; until comes she, my lover, whose return, yes, it justifies my entire design, from Bledlow on—but for her one sweet, reasonable, soon-to-be-posed question, *what happened next*?

For she's bound to ask again. She must. And I'm caught there, Theo, I'm hoist!

You two! You gang up on me! You make me colour myself in, so that at last we shall see him, me, 3D, come to answer charges, even in the perspective court I so recently seem to have made for myself, setting Julia naked in my studio. The court of all my family.

Theo, there's nothing for it but to ditch this whole project. Forget me. I can't do it. Give up on me. Dear friend, your efforts have been magnificent, your generosity boundless, your patience unflagging—but I'm not worth the candle. It's off. Don't protest. You don't know what I did. *What happened next* when I came back from Paris so torments me.

I want to hide. Earth, open and swallow me deeper than the grave.

I've *been* hiding, you see, here, on this island. It suited me. Theo, she'll want the whole story, and I'm speared on my own gender. Admit it, men are to blame for the whole gamut of it: paedophilia, rape, molestation, procurement, trafficking, harassment. Women are innocent, almost always. For God's sake, that's why we hand them our kids. Women are genetically, hormonally 'good'. I mean this. Hard line feminism has it: and that's why I was happy as a girl, in Paris—if only in make-believe. My Girl, a hard-line feminist if ever there was one. By being a girl I ducked my male shame!

Ah, hard to catch *this* feeling, my friend, hard to name it in time; because it always pulls me down, this sudden dull vacuum in the chest, this breathless retreat of the world. Panic, yes. Panic, of course;

because feminism made the breakthrough, and but for the women's movement, incest would never have been so much as whispered. And all those sociological textbooks would have stayed as authoritatively *stumm* as they were in the sixties and seventies. No, it's those rigorous, brilliant women who brought it all to light; women who suffered the abuse and violence in the first place—and then suffered the backlash for speaking out. Women *should* be hard line. Feminist theoretics *stick*; it's only guilty men's squirming that seeks to sweep them aside. Theo, I am one such, a guilty man.

And there we have it—after all my intellectualising and periphrasis. There we come at last to the *what happened next* when my Paris summer ended and I returned home. For which guilt, now let me admit—let me at last *confess* to you, Theo—I find it hard even to show my face in the wider world; and for which, yes, in the constant concept of my mind's eye, I repeatedly send myself to prison.

Or to exile, away from people, away from love—*vide*, here. Yes, Léros is a prison, far from the warmth and comfort of society, of friends or family—where I admit I expect only hate mail, or to be spat at in the street; or the brick through the window, the mob, the dawn arrest, ostracism, beatings, torture: *if* ever it came out—as surely it will the moment I lift my head an inch 'above the parapet', the moment I supply, in public, the lineaments of my fleshly truth. Ah, the closer we come, Julia and I, and the more divinely intimate we are, the more my guilty heart knocks at my ribs. Oh, it does, Theo. Yes, if closeness brings up poor Julia's ghosts, it brings up mine, too.

Subject: RE Courtroom—the summons

Society portraits, then. Anodyne abstracts, polite landscapes. You say it just sounds like the Father. You say it's lies he pours into my ear— the devil on my shoulder, just out of vision—that I'm so bad, so unutterably bad. I wish I could believe you.

Sent from my iPad

Subject: **RE Courtroom — the summons**

Panic is the Wolf boy on all fours I drew once for Mitchell and never drew it again, never again because it made me so ill, his body marked, hind parts misshapen, still in that bedroom in Aylesbury: lino floor, galleons on the wallpaper, dull window, empty fireplace, my Nan's dressmaker's dummy headless, heedless on a stand, the tall painted cupboard, the Wolf boy still held, yes, shafted in a gravity so intense, space-time so warped and so curved that just to approach him, even in thought, made me suicidal for days... the boy who brings back not only what was done *to* him, but the guilt of what he, in turn, will have done, *has* done, because he grew into me and wore, in my amnesia, man's apparel.

Sent from my iPad

Subject: **RE Courtroom — the summons**

Time ticks past. The bay outside stills, the castle promontory steadies. By degrees, air's rational once more, and the panic attack, a mild one, subsides. I'm myself again. Just give me a minute or two more.

Subject: **RE Courtroom — the summons**

My friend, there's the faintest light, the narrowest chink, as if to squeeze between two almost touching stones back into the world. I've never discussed my transgression, so ashamed of what it might label me. Not that it's hidden, indeed. How could a matter of record be secret? But I never speak of it. And I wouldn't speak now — had it not just occurred to me again, yes, increasingly in flashes these last few months — you remember that morning Eléni and I were so new to the island, and the invitation slipped under the door... Didn't I lose my nerve then, in these same terms? Until Eléni made me go to the party? Oh, Jesus, didn't I think I was depraved, already hated, for having a partner so much younger?

But didn't the event itself put my fears to rout, making way for Marta, Spíros — for Julia...

Then maybe there's the slimmest chance... Let me explain: that

331

when I so slander my maleness there's just the possibility that self-hatred, too, springs from distorted perception...

But then the hard line feminist canon I've always espoused would have to be skewed too? Is that possible?

Well, perhaps. Theoretically. Then could my self-loathing perhaps be merely symptomatic? That this crush of guilt I've borne so many, many years, ever since I returned home from Paris, in fact—why, no, for I felt it even as a child, crippling... That this guilt could in some way turn out... in some way, Theo... some way that even now seems far-fetched enough to be miraculous, like the touch of a true icon, maybe, or the presence, even, of an Angel... that my crippling, imprisoning guilt might turn out... were I to speak to Julia, I mean, to confess, as it were... not just my self-loathing but the actual *what-happened-next*... that my criminalisation might turn out to be, dare I say it... at least to some extent... illusory?

Oh, God, there I shall be, watching for the corners of her guiltless mouth to show the first flicker of disgust—that she'll try so hard to conceal, but which *will* break through. The corners of her mouth... If she were to be appalled, as I am, then this one person, Julia, would be jury enough to condemn me for ever.

You see, my dear, dear friend, how I try to work all this out. For if I didn't sit here and write it down, I might truly go mad!

Subject: **The Arrest**

I've heard from Lily. Arun's in trouble with the police.

27

Subject: **A Constructivist café**

We meet in Lakkí, the deep water port. It's out of the way and has an emptiness, even at the height of season: *Il Duce*'s wrong townscape, wrong-coloured, wrong-shaped, un-Greek.

Siesta time. We're in a taverna. A notion of one, right on the waterfront; for a wide tarred road splits us from the owner's forecourt, and a low iron rail—it runs the length of the sea wall between squat, red-topped concrete posts—separates us from the bay. Such expanse: pavement, tarmac, the freakish 'architecture', the broad inlet with its infinite sparkle of waves. Hardly a soul, except for two Italians, oddly appropriate, at the next table. They have designer sunglasses, designer hair; we hear their lingo from beyond the trident lamppost.

The waiter visits us under our canvas parasol. Its shadow pinpoints us. The hot Sirocco gasps at us from brown hills opposite.

Café: Greek for brown. Fear's a taste.

'Julia.'

Sunglasses hide her eyes, too. She seems to stare at a yacht, but I can't be sure. 'Mm?'

'I need to run something by you.' The wind gusts, the parasol flaps. 'I told you I got married again,' I say. 'A year or so after I came back from Paris.'

'Yes.'

'Her name was Lily. She was my student.'

Student. The word's out. My heart thumps.

Her expression's unchanged: 'Was she?'

'Nineteen. Pregnant. By me.'

'Right.'

I feel my weak lips move. The blinding white tabletop. 'Lily. She was, is… almost a refugee. From life, as it were.'

'Okay.'

'She'd had a hellish time; I mean really bad. And was building a new life, with new people. A new start.'

Julia turns to me. The corners of her mouth curve neither down nor up; her black, reflective lenses give nothing away. 'Well?' she says at last. 'What was it you wanted to run by me?'

There's a movement in my jaw, a breathy sound. I'm like a boat failing its tack and losing headway. 'Julia. That was it! The marriage!'

'Oh.'

'I've felt very guilty about it. So guilty, I've… Intensely guilty.'

'Didn't you *want* to marry her?'

'Yes.'

'She didn't want to marry you?'

'She did.'

'So you both got what you wanted?'

'Yes. But…'

'The baby,' she says. 'You didn't want that?'

'We did. We were thrilled. Both of us. It's my daughter. It's Chloe.'

I fall away again from the conversation. In irons, the old sailors used to call it, when the ship's bow points dead into the wind, and the whole show starts to move backwards.

'How long were you married to her?'

'We still are. We parted years ago, but I couldn't afford a divorce at the time. Just some deed of separation. That set out the money and the children's residence. With me; I was ill. So I could be at home to look after them. Thirteen years we were actually together.'

'Quite a success, then.'

'You haven't got the point.'

'The point of what?' She tilts her head.

'Julia! I breached professional ethics. Massively! I got hauled up in front of the governors.'

'Okay. So they sacked you.'

The waiter brings our coffees, unloads the tray: the diminutive cups with paper napkins on their saucers, tumblers of water, the bill curled like a little paper foetus in a glass against the wind.

'*Evcharistó.*'

'*Parakaló.*'

'They didn't sack me.'

She laughs.

'So long as she went elsewhere. I mean to finish her course. A school, it was, they found her. Julia, I got a schoolgirl pregnant!' Half my face is burning; we shuffle the chairs round into the shadow again. 'I'd almost hoped they would.'

'What?'

'Sack me.' I mop my brow with a napkin. 'I was only part time. It was a tech college. Hammersmith. I loathed being back in teaching.

When I'd arrived back in London, you see, I'd found a bedsit and gone on the dole. I needed a zero job, anything. But I couldn't place myself. You see,' I say again and give an involuntary smile. 'A little English theatre group offered me a chance as an ASM.'

She raises her eyebrows.

'Assistant Stage Manager—a sort of dogsbody. I turned it down; not because I didn't want it, but because suddenly I was too frightened to move, scared I wouldn't have time to paint, scared of everything. It was bizarre. I tried to last it out.' I puff the air out through my nose. 'As the winter came on. But I had no telephone, no TV: just a one bar fire. Some money in the bank—you remember—but I didn't dare spend it.' My hands spread either side of the cup. 'I couldn't go anywhere or meet anyone. I couldn't do anything except sit in my room. Eventually I admitted defeat. Put my name down on some GLC list and was snapped up for the tech—virtually at once.'

Her eyes are invisible, her lips motionless.

'Teaching,' I say. 'Bloody prison.'

'You always seemed so dedicated, worked so hard.'

'Marriage. Teaching. Completely powerless. You know that. I couldn't paint.'

A lone car accelerates in the wide road behind us. Three hatted, booted walkers stride out of a gust. They speak Dutch, sport packs and trekking poles: their cheeks, hands, calves are all tanned to shoe-leather.

Julia dabs her face. She tries to fan herself. 'So all you did was get married to some nineteen year old.'

Theo, I've psyched myself up for this conversation. My tentacled sin seems still to pulse, far down, with passionate sea colours. Julia doesn't condemn; I can't trust her judgment. And the more I appear to extenuate myself, the more I blur what should be stark and plain.

So I describe to her how, before Lily, I still dressed unconventionally, even though I was back in the classroom, so to speak; saw myself as bohemian, hung out alone in London, galleries, the fringe. Took forlorn class in Floral Street.

'Class?' She jerks her head.

'In dance you feel clean.' I catch myself. 'I mean you disappear into technique. You escape. You watch yourself in mirrors, Julia, not even sure which one's you. Girl, girl, boy, girl. Even slept with a couple—women, that is.' An awkward laugh. 'Except nothing made sense. Love!'

335

The word hangs softly between us.

'And then?'

Therapy, Theo. The alternative therapy scene. The weird, the wacko, the fraudulent, the magnificent. My first venture into healing. It was as though, courtesy of the "Therapy & Growth" pages of Seventies *Time Out*, long before Mitchell and the proper thing, my poor, thwarted muscles might even then have been beginning to communicate. Yes, of course they were.

'But all that's beside the point.' I hurry on. 'The bare fact is that after about a year and a half,' another nervous laugh, 'there was this very attractive student at the tech who made no secret of her interest in me. Who was in my face with it, as it were. Which is no excuse at all. Because I responded. And it was entirely unprofessional and inappropriate. I abused her trust. Abused, Julia.'

There!

But she's shaking her head. 'Owen, you've brought me here on the hottest afternoon of the summer, when every sane person is asleep, or making love, just to tell me about screwing your nineteen year old student—or let's imagine she was eighteen when it happened, am I right? And a couple of other women besides.'

I make a sound.

'How long ago?'

'Nearly thirty years; but the time doesn't signify.'

'For God's sake! Girls I knew went out with teachers. It wasn't unusual.' She perches her sunglasses on her hair to dab the sweat, and at last I can see her eyes.

'They got pregnant?'

She turns to me, blinking. 'Not usually.'

'Exactly!'

'Oh, please!' She throws the crumpled napkin at me. 'Alright, you were out of order. You should have been more careful. Ineptitude isn't criminal. And it takes two, you know.'

'The girl is *always* the innocent party. It's *always* an abuse of power. It *is*, Julia. That's why it's so frowned on. That's why it's serious.'

She throws up her hands. 'Okay! It's sleazy! It's wrong, disgraceful, weak and pathetic, and that's men for you! Is that what you want me to say? You'd call it *transgressive*, I expect!' She sips triumphantly from her glass of water. 'But was it illegal?'

'No. And, to be fair, I suppose we did actually ask permission to go out with each other in the first place. From the family she was living with. But...'

'And even the governors didn't kick you out.'

'You see, I half wanted a public punishment.'

'You wanted to be punished?'

'To get it out in the open; and get me right out of the job. A spectacle. Foucault.'

No reply.

'Then it would have been over with, and we could have started clean, and I could paint; and Lily would have helped me.'

She compresses her lips.

'What I got instead was an official reprimand, and they kept me on. Amazingly.'

'Maybe they valued you.'

'They said we needed an income. So everything I'd thought was my decision and in my control – I mean, for example, the choice I made to have sex with her in the first place – was taken out of my hands. And I was chained back into the job, this time for good. Even got promotion after a while, and a permanent contract. It left me in their debt.'

'To tell the truth, Owen – and of course I've never spoken about this to anyone – I went out with one of my college lecturers.'

'And?'

'And nothing. We slept together – since we're on the subject. It ended.'

'But...'

'But nothing.'

Theo, I'm as nonplussed as I was at the start. What I've seen for so long as an inexpiable crime – one which puts me far beyond the pale and which was bound to come back to destroy me someday, no matter how far I ran or how deeply I hid myself away... She almost overlooks it. On the back of her responses, I am innocent. I should be ecstatic!

'Can we go now?' She finishes her coffee and stands up, smiling. 'I don't think I can bear this place any longer. And I really don't see why you're so hung up about this. You, who're normally so clear in your thinking – annoyingly so, Owen. Normally.'

She takes my hand. I leave coins on the table. We make our way along the sea front. We're just lovers. And half way to the Plátanos signpost, she asks the obvious question, the one I've never thought of.

'Didn't all this awful guilt get resolved in the marriage? Once it was all done and dusted? You had your telling off, the scandal, the governors, the gossip, I expect, and so on. But after the wedding you were legitimate. Weren't you? With a family and everything? Like you said, you got promotion. What was the problem?'

I'm so confused.

'She didn't help you paint?'

'Not really.'

'I see.' She turns to me. We kiss, briefly, on the lips. 'Sorry to be short with you,' she says. 'I know it bothers you, all this.'

'Where's Miles?'

'He's on another fishing trip. Won't be back until later.'

In the street between the fruit warehouse and the supermarket there are people. We drop all contact and walk slightly apart. But back in my studio, which is like a kiln, we share the heady sweat of flesh on flesh. Afterwards, I lie amazed at her again: the delicate female cartilage of her ear, the wisps of her hair, her profile. And then we snatch a quick, simple meal and talk of other things.

Subject: Fishermen at Pandéli

Miles caught us together. It was this morning. It was by the Pandéli quay. His boat came in a little earlier than we'd expected. We were gazing over the beach, preparing to part for the day; it wasn't far from her hotel. I heard a voice, 'Julia! Julia, look!' and we both turned abruptly round.

There he was, appearing incredibly pleased with himself and holding a substantial tuna across his outstretched arms. The fish was on its side, still twitching every now and then, and he was awkward with the weight of it. 'What do you think?' he said.

'Oh!' she said. She went to meet him. 'Miles! Well done! Darling. So that's one of them at last, is it. That's a tuna.'

'Not easy,' said Miles. 'Not so many left, now. In the Med,' he said to me by way of explanation, as I came up.

I raised my eyebrows and smiled stupidly, uncertain, of course, how to proceed. Then there was a hiatus as he looked from one of us to the other. His expression changed from childlike elation to something more quizzical.

I was all set to blurt a remark about the fish, but Julia took lightning control. 'Oh, I'm sorry. Introductions. Miles, this gentleman speaks no English. He paints. He lives here. I happened to bump into him.' She made a little laugh. 'Spíros, Miles. Miles, Spíros.'

'Miles,' I said, sounding the 's' hard. '*Chéro polý*.' I advanced my hand. He had to take it from under his fish and I made him shake it, with the poor dying creature's round eye and open mouth jigging up and down as he did so. '*Kalós ílthate sti Léro, kýrie* Miles. *Avtó íne éna polý oréo psári. Énas tónos, nomízo*.' So I flooded him with my rudimentary Greek: Welcome to Léros, nice fish, tuna, I believe.

Miles stood, bewildered, until I eventually let go of his hand.

Then I pressed home my advantage, smiling. '*Na sas voithíso me avtó? Ísos an egó*...?—Can I help you with it? Perhaps if I...?' I moved suddenly as if to seize the fish, and he backed away, protective, looking to Julia.

But she was smiling, too. 'I think Spíros means...'

'It's okay,' Miles said. 'I'll just get it back to them. They told me they'd do all the... I wanted... I just brought it to show you.' He turned away towards the fishing boat, where two guys I recognised were presently weighing someone else's tuna by the tail, dorsal spike held proud, in front of a girlfriend with a camera. The array of stout fishing rods was still propped up in the stern.

But Miles's shoe touched en route some fault in the concrete and he stumbled for a second, his slippery prize seeming at once to leap this way and that in his arms as he grappled it clumsily to his chest. Then he had to stop to collect himself, his whole body seeming to lack both strength and decision. From behind, I could see his heaving breaths.

I hurried to his shoulder, wondering why I'd ever felt threatened by him. '*Íste sígouros óti then boró na sas voithíse, kýrie?*—Are you sure I can't help you, sir. *Parakaló, epitrépste mou*...—I beg you, let me...' Again I made to take the fish.

'No. No. What the...! It's alright. I'm fine.' But he was not. 'Thanks very much. Look, I'm quite okay.' He turned his head to me and we stared directly at each other. I saw in his eyes a kind of watery fear—not unlike the expression of the tuna itself.

I confess it, Theo, revenge had begun to take on a certain fishy sweetness, a holiday from my late panic and all this constant overwhelm by the past. And so, still smiling and playing the Greek, I began congratulating him on his hunter-gathering: '*Kalá, kýrie, brávo yia éna tétio thriámvo*—Well, sir, bravo for such a triumph.' I clapped my hands, just as I had for Julia's picture. An artistic touch, that led me on to point out and admire the fish's features and qualities, its athletic shape, the shine of its skin, all the while keeping him sagging under its weight. A few choice and obscene Greek expressions formed in my head—a little thought-curse, made out of swear-words I'd learnt on this same quayside: '*Ánde gamísou. Phíla mou to kólo, maláka. Ke tóte, ánde, mouní, pháe skatá stin chóra sou ke psophá.*'

But I refrained, Theo, because it occurred to me that I already had him exactly where I wanted him. I had him *framed*, so to speak, in a very pleasing little portrait. For he was beginning to buckle, to stagger, almost, and I forced him to shake hands once more under the weight of his catch while his knees were clearly giving way. And so I left him. I gave Julia a grin as I passed her and came home, feeling that I'd maybe found my alternative occupation for the Father at last, as a humble carpenter of borders, edges, mounts and carved surrounds; perhaps even a maker of beehive frames—something I could do when I wasn't actually painting, say. Yes, I could perhaps set myself up with saw, mitre and chisel as my own framer, a determiner of boundaries!

Subject: The magistrates

I asked her to marry me.

But Miles is ill, Theo. Jesus, it almost made me regret my performance with the fish. Almost, I said. But it's not at all these days what I thought between him and Julia, which explains a number of things. Miles has cancer—the real sort as opposed to Nasir's storybook variety—of some vile organ or another. And so the roles are reversed, and he's suddenly entirely dependent on Julia's good offices. Prognosis uncertain. He's had chemo. This holiday is for his convalescence—genuinely. 'My children, Owen... He's their father. I can't abandon him now. He needs me. It's just something I have to do.'

And then Arun... the police, the magistrates. I don't understand, Theo. I don't understand why God, the universe, destiny, kismet—or whatever else you want to call it—ever allowed Julia to come here, to take part in... to play her part in what we've just been through together, when in a few days' time she'll simply pack up and leave. To remain with her husband. It's meaningless. It's unbearable, actually.

Subject: **Woman crying**

We had a row. It was evening. We were a little upward from our gully; someone's beehives stood in a bit of field not far away.

'You traded love for art,' she said.

'No,' I said.

'Didn't you?'

'I believed you'd betrayed me. I told you. I was sure of it.'

'Yes, but you couldn't paint in England. You were stuck, you said.'

'I painted you!'

'Even with me. I just couldn't make things work for you, could I. You couldn't find a way forward. You weren't... you weren't your*self*. You weren't the artist you wanted to be. Admit it, Owen!'

'To an extent.'

'Whereas in Paris...'

'I didn't paint a thing in Paris. Except some masks for Félix.'

'But you *would* have painted, surely. With Félix. You'd have painted if you'd stayed there. So why did you come back? Because it wasn't to look for me! Was it, Owen!'

'I thought...'

She looked at me, expectantly.

I was stumped. 'Félix was... I wrote a play.'

'What was it?'

'Just a dark farce.'

'And then?'

'I went to live with the two girls, Marie-José and Minalouche. We became inseparable, ate together, slept all in the same bed. We loved each other.'

'Of course you bloody did. And then?'

'Then no rain, no break in that endless heat, even after months. You remember how it was that year? And I left. Because my passport came through at last.'

'You left, just when you'd found yourself? Found yourself in girl's clothes, Owen. With girls. As actor, artist, dancer.'

'I left. Yes, just when I'd found myself. Because... Because I *had*n't found myself. Because I'm a man, Julia. Because art was death. Is death. I don't know.'

A bee settled on her hand. It traversed the ridges of her knuckles, and she looked down at it. I wanted to paint the beautiful angle of her head, the shaft of sunlight just catching her facial bones, the illuminated arm and the insect briefly incandescent before it sped away.

Then *I* grew angry—about Miles—and a flowering shrub beside us was suddenly alive with bees, some twilight pheromone bringing them... She said Miles loved her in his own way, and she just couldn't do it to him. Not now he was ill. Because of the children.

'Your children are grown up!'

'They'd think...'

'What?'

'They'd think I was... what Miles says I am. Sometimes.'

'For God's sake! What does it matter what they think! What about Stefan?'

'Oh, Stefan,' she said. 'You see? It's true. If we're talking betrayal, I'm betraying Miles. I'm betraying him here again, right now, with you.'

'He deserves it.'

'No, Owen. He doesn't. It makes me feel so bad. Terrible.'

'You mean it doesn't feel good to be here with me?'

'You know it does. Us. I'd like it, too, Owen. More than anything. Really I would. But...'

I was lost for words. I cast about for some weakness in her argument, her shield. These so judgmental children, did *they* have opinions about Stefan, I wondered?

No one knew about Stefan. He'd just... swept her off her feet. He'd aroused feelings... And there'd been a woman before that.'

'A woman!'

'Yes, a woman. You see?'

'No. I don't.'

'Between Myra and Stefan came depression.'

'But now Stefan won't leave *his* wife, it seems. And would you have left Miles for him? Or was Stefan also to be a perpetual hole-and-corner affair, your sexuality—your feelings—only getting turned on in some *illicit* fashion. Some betrayal. *It seems!*'

'Don't, Owen! Don't! I just don't know!'

'Well think about it! Think, Julia, for Christ's sake! Put it together. Humans are sexual creatures. We're *made* to live together. Openly! Happily! Not wretchedly! Why not *us*? You owe Miles nothing. I don't understand how you can be so inhibited and so sexual at the same time! Miles is controlling. He always was. He's kept you locked up, and now he's doing it another way. Through *your* guilt. Through pity. Let Miles die. What about us?! Think!'

And then she was tearful. Because, she said, she *couldn't* think. She'd never known how to think. Because, with her blustering, bullying dad, whatever she'd said had been criticised, so it was better to have no opinions about anything. She'd never known who she was. She'd never done anything with her life. She'd never known what she wanted.

She turned, Theo, from an acute observer of character — mine — to a woman entirely confused. And it was my fault, because here I was bullying and blustering with the best of them.

'If there's one worthwhile thing I can do, Owen, it's to look after him, now, when he's suffering so much.'

'Fucking Saint Julia!' I couldn't stop, because everything was slipping away. 'Not because you love him, but because you want to feel good. Like a good little girl. In front of your children. This so Christian act of renunciation, it's childish in itself. It's *from* childhood, can't you see? Because what happened in your childhood — I mean the molestation, the damned cousin — it made you feel *bad*. He made you feel bad, but that wasn't your fault. You don't have to spend your whole life atoning for it!' Rich, Theo, coming from me!

She was about to reply when her phone went. Relapsing Miles required her. 'Where are you?' I heard his crackly voice, and she was frightened. Not of his weakness, but of his old strength. I knew it. I saw the panic build up in her breathing as she gasped for air — panic clearly a commodity we share, my friend. Yet she hadn't even noticed it, she said, a moment later.

She had to go. We clung together and wept, and then she gathered up her things.

'Are you going to paint,' I said, 'when you get back?'

'I doubt it,' she said.

'Will I see you tomorrow?'

'I don't know, Owen. I can't say.'

Theo, her flight's next Wednesday. We've five days left. I went and stood in the town, looking up at the castle and contemplating the impregnable fortress into which her heart has been forced to retreat, and how its stiff walls cripple adult passion. I can't break through, even as I see exactly how these bids for love in people like us are always doomed to failure. I see it in myself. I see exactly how it always works, the internalised autocracy, formed during the abuse but then in adulthood still desperate to repel boarders and stop us *being with other people* — all for the sake of a false, outdated security. I see the

343

consequent affairs, the disasters, inevitable, half hidden, even from herself. I know the remedy, and curse myself for having berated the very quality in her I must own equally in me: the utter inability to take seriously the ills done by people we swear blind we 'love'—bastards to whom we still cling, emotionally, against all the evidence! Would it have made any difference if I'd told her about my dad? I doubt it.

Comédie? Now it seems that only low, populist art can ever bring the image of man and woman together. And that only as a kind of disgusting, sentimental voyeurism.

Subject: **Telemachus—Tireur isolé—The long shot**

Arun? Not good news. He and I spoke by phone at the weekend, but it was inconclusive. I dreamt about him: I dreamt that I was looking for him in a seedy night club. Desperately anxious, I went deeper, and deeper still, down twisted staircases, past narrow, rotting doorways into the sordid underworld of the place. I found him unconscious at last in the filth of a basement toilet, lying stretched out on the floor. The only good thing was that he wasn't dead. Surely it won't come to that, Theo, now I'm far away and fathers are out of fashion. I long to find him again and bestow the embrace: *But when he was yet a great way off, his father saw him, and had compassion, and ran, and fell on his neck, and kissed him*—ἔτι δὲ αὐτοῦ μακρὰν ἀπέχοντος εἶδεν αὐτὸν ὁ πατὴρ αὐτοῦ καὶ *ἐσπλαγχνίσθη*, καὶ δραμὼν ἐπέπεσεν ἐπὶ τὸν τράχηλον αὐτοῦ καὶ κατεφίλησεν αὐτόν. This 'compassion' is in the Greek 'a great yearning of emotion from the gut'. My son!

But St John makes 'Father' the toughest of the tough: either get the message, or take the consequences.

For God ... gave His only begotten son—τὸν Υἱὸν τὸν μονογενῆ ἔδωκεν.

Or did the adult Jesus of his own accord, *in certainty of his true father and in firm conviction of what unspeakable evil had gone before*, choose *himself* to bear the agony of it, rather than let any act of his, coerced by corrupt family, state, occupying power or lynch mob, pass it on? So the same crucifixion that once seemed to question the family, now redeems it.

344

28

Subject: Archangel *ex machina*

It looked very trite: the archangel's flat, silly face, the circular golden halo echoed by two rounded gold wings tacked either side—all against a glittery blue background. The breastplate had the childish shape you find in the oldest versions of the subject, and the legs below their military skirt were in that puppet-like articulation hallowed by tedious centuries.

St Michael, Supreme Commander of the Bodiless Hosts, here in the harbour church of Áyia Marína! I had to hover on the edge of matters, craning my neck now this way, now that, uncertain where to stand in all the holy fuss.

At least he'd made an effort with the armour. And at least metallic complexity would be the one thing to redeem this composition. Nevertheless, I felt mounting disappointment, Theo, as I stood beside Julia during that interminable, incomprehensible service. I'd been hoping too much: oh, how return fixtures always solicit anti-climax!

Spíros was at the other side of the church. I pointed him out to Julia, while priest and bishop swayed back and forth across the line of sight. Spíros had a woman with him. Children came and went. 'What am I going to say if I don't like it?' I whispered. 'Which I don't.'

'You'll think of something.' She touched my arm.

I nodded, but my spirit sank. She'd contrived to get away from Miles, but for all I knew this might be our last meeting. The dim interior, the emotional ambience, the druid bishop… I felt already a growing unease about my 'iconostasis' format for my commission—my double row. There was a kind of shadow here that no amount of sparkle from hanging candles, crystal-beaded lamps, no lovingly arranged flowers and bright, white ribbons, no quantity of silver fittings or gold seemed able to dispel.

A shadow on my heart. The liturgy ran on. The congregation sang. Between pillars and heavy, carved furnishings, the bearded bishop censed the icon, the bearded priest mumbled into his thick, embroidered robes. Unbearded acolytes materialised and dematerialised through angel doors in the screen. Theo, I wanted to be impressed, but the skeins of incense drifting about us turned even sweat sickly. Disapproving saints eyed me from the big wooden array, the stale apotheosis of stale portraiture.

Think of Italy. Think of that gorgeous painted physicality catalysed five and half centuries ago. Catalysed by Greeks, Theo, by Greeks fleeing invasion. Greeks, folk from time immemorial a byword for creativity, technical virtuosity and the installation of desire! But not here at home. Not for millennia. The Eastern Empire went inexplicably blind to the body with the start of the Christian era. The defeat of art! No renaissance could have happened in Byzantium, never mind the Turks. Even here, in the islands... even El Greco, if he hadn't left Crete for Venice, would have remained a mere copyist—of sexless, imagined death masks. In other words, of icons!

Julia and I only got really near Spíros's archangel at the close of the ceremony. The singing had stopped, but the smell of incense was still overpowering, and there were still people kissing the image and touching it. They kissed everything. They kissed us, greeted us like long lost friends, even though they'd never met us.

Right up close, the panel did even less for me. I admired the application of colour: so profound an effacement of brushstroke or mark—once again, it left virtually no trace of the artist. But I got no joy from it. Only imagine by contrast that electrifying Della Francesca in the National, or that wonderfully loony Spanish thing they've got— Bermejo, isn't it? While here: a stupid, formulaic, girl-faced knight holding his sword in one hand, his scroll in the other, just standing— in that mistaken pose—on some miniaturised and broken city of the damned.

The cryptic lettering was at least intriguing. I was trying to decipher it when Julia nudged me. 'What are these?' She pointed towards the stylised city.

'There's usually Satan there, or a dragon, I think. St Michael defeats him.'

'I could work that out myself, Owen, thanks very much. But these, here?'

I followed the direction of her hand. A few small figures were both displayed, and yet at the same time partly concealed, inside the symbolic ring of dilapidated buildings. Not so surprising, I thought.

And I was about to explain them as stock iconography—fallen angels turning to devils—when something about them struck me as familiar. I stared. And then I stared again.

'Christ Almighty!' I snatched my glasses from my jacket, wrestled them on and bent close. The detail came sharp. It was undeniable: the dark of an unroofed house in Spíros's symbolic little city enclosed nothing less than an intensely scaled down scene from one of my own left hand paintings.

That was impossible.

I put my hand to my head, blinked hard and stared yet again. 'How on earth...?' Not just the design but the colours: my own demonic blues touched with yellow—bottled acrylics they gave us in the Clinic—the Child so pallid, manhandled by malevolence, his just visible arms flung wide.

I looked wildly around me for Spíros. The church was emptying.

'What, Owen?' Julia tugged at my jacket. 'What is it?'

I turned back to her, lost for words. The bishop, the priest and their acolytes swept suddenly towards us in formation, their heavy vestments brushing us aside as they passed. One of the remaining families from the congregation swooped in to monopolise the picture. Their little girl bobbed down in front of it. Their son touched the frame. Both children crossed themselves and kissed the gold leaf. Another couple pressed in with another child while the first parents lingered. They kissed the angel's sword hand and smiled round at me, saying something in Greek.

Then I pushed rudely back through them all. '*Lipáme*—sorry. *Signómi*—excuse me.' I, too, touched the frame, kissed this, kissed that, stood back to command the space again. Spíros had poised his circle of masonry on some fanciful island. I crossed myself and squatted down. Typical stylised crags enlisted the bottom edge of the frame, before rising up under the angel's golden boots. Yet the precise orientation of the walls, their placement on the mounding rock... My God! I'd seen them. I'd been there. What I'd dismissed as stylised was nothing of the kind. Spíros's ruined mediaeval city was simply a cunning evocation of the old Chóra on Kálymnos, where he had his workshop. I followed my eye, and there, just camouflaged by an archway, was a tiny horned Satan. But not just any Satan; it was the exact fellow I'd let Spíros see, the Dad figure, his arms in turn stretched high before furnaces and engines of torment.

I stood up and looked frantically for him again. I grabbed Julia's hand.

'What is it, Owen? What's going on?'

There was no time to answer. I hurried her directly through the emptying church towards the door. We pushed through and out. For a

347

second, the sunlight was intolerable. Then the street was blocked in all directions; the clergy, their wives, the entire congregation, so it seemed, were busy socialising. Only children were on the move, darting here and there between the knots and clumps of their elders. We tried the same, merely to emerge, after halts and diversions, down among the taverna tables at the harbour's edge.

'Can you see him?' I said, glancing constantly about.

'Who, Owen?'

'Spíros, of course.'

But there were just the tourists sipping their coffees or beers under the parasols, and beyond them the usual waterfront idlers and a couple of moped riders.

Yanking Julia after me, I dived back into the crowd. A car was edging through towards us, leaving a slim channel in its wake. We took the opportunity and got to the town side of things just in time to see Spíros and family, and, yes, Marta walking well ahead of us up the slope between the picturesque old houses and the official buildings.

'There! Come on!'

'Why?'

'I have to speak to him.'

'Why?'

But I was striding on as fast as I could in my hot, dark suit. 'Come *on*!' I called over my shoulder.

'Give me a chance!' She had to run to keep up.

'That must be Marta's husband.'

'Who?'

'The tall man with Spíros.'

'How should I know?'

We were at the town museum and gaining on them.

But they'd reached the top of the street. And as they drew level with Marta's house, they turned straight in at the entrance where, followed by a cluster of people just behind them, they disappeared from view. By the time Julia and I came up to it, Marta's door was firmly shut. A hubbub of voices began to leak down from the open first floor windows.

'Ring,' she said.

I hesitated.

She made towards the bell push. 'I'll do it, if you won't.'

'No.'

'She's your friend.'

'Yes. She is.' But I pictured going up to gate-crash the party with Julia in tow. I imagined the conversation. Or rather I couldn't. For what would I say, amongst them all, and to whom, and in what language?

'Forget it.' I shook my head.

'She'll be pleased. Surely?'

I turned away. 'Let's get a drink.'

'If you'll just tell me what's going on.'

We found an air-conditioned bar in Plátanos. Over coffee, I tried to explain. 'They were from some of my pictures. In his painting.'

'Yours?'

'About forty of them, on paper. From one or two I showed him. Done years ago, with my left hand – when I was ill.'

'You were ill? You did icons?'

'No. Those little scenes you were pointing to. They're some of mine. I took them with me. To see him. In the stone town under the angel's feet. That was the place.' Sweat was still pouring off me. I dabbed at my brow with a paper napkin. 'That was where I... He must have memorised them. There's no other explanation. So talented. So bloody talented, Julia. He must have made copies straight away, as soon as I'd left. Incredible – the visual memory. His, I mean. Copying.' I put my hand on hers. 'But then icons are eternal copying. He called them something at the time, I remember now: "Icons of hell – *ikónes tis kólasis*".'

'Can you please just stop talking in riddles. Spíros stole your pictures? Is that what you're so upset about?'

'I'm not upset. I'm thrilled. He didn't steal them. He gave them a home; and so brilliantly. When I saw them there in the painting... Julia, I couldn't believe it. Do you see? If you hadn't pointed them out...' I took a breath. 'He did it for *me*. He must have. Who else? Do you *see*?' Completely spontaneously in the act of breathing my throat choked up, and for a moment I couldn't speak at all.

Julia freed her hand and put it on my shoulder. I turned and clung on to her beside the table, leaning my head softly against hers.

Once I'd realised quite what I was doing in public – and once I'd acclimatised myself again to the tantalising smell of her hair, the peculiar sexual intimacy of bone touching bone – I chanced to look up. Theo, there was a large advertising mirror on the wall next to us. I thought for a split second it was a window on to some couple next door, obvious lovers. Then I saw the Mythos Beer logo in its corner and realised it was all just a reflection of us.

349

Subject: The critical eye

I think of fresh gold leaf—or a saddlebag of pure lapis: true colour appears! So it's proved as I implement your suggestions. A skimp and a failure of texture here, a whole wasted painting there—as you spot them and point them out. At last, my doubtful surface begins to make sense.

I do live with other criticisms though, personal rather than artistic. Less friendly. Eléni gives tongue to some. Others, I hear not exactly as 'voices' but half-articulated convictions: 'locked up'; 'liar'; 'unforgivable'; 'beast'; 'parasite'... These are examples. There is also, at times, a hue and cry, hounds, a mob, the Greek Special Forces. Death, smiling, opens his door. To label all this symptom, and not fact, is hard. You say again it's the Father. Your kind concerns, Theo, almost convince me of an antidote. For a moment or two.

But yesterday evening there were vehicles outside the house, and voices. I froze at the knock on the door. I looked at Eléni. Her eyes widened, her face turned visibly pale and the book she was reading snapped shut. Nasir was watching TV. She rushed to hide him upstairs. I saw the coffee cup shake in her hand as she went, the liquid slopping over the edge on to the bare floor.

Knock, knock, knock!

Then from outside: 'Owen! Hurry up! This is heavy! Owen!'

I opened the door to find Marta, holding a large cardboard box.

She had helpers, Níkos and Irína from the lower road supermarket. And there was Andónis who drives a taxi, and some Pandéli fishermen—and others I'd never seen before. I went to the front window. Sunset silhouetted the cars. Two pick-up trucks were parked at our wall.

'Surprised?' Marta put the box on our table.

'We weren't expecting...'

'Spíros is on his way. We saw you at the church. But afterwards? Where did you get to? Help me unpack.' She began taking out bottles of local retsina, wine, lemonade, beer.

More people arrived, old ones, couples with children, unattached young men and women. And they brought more boxes. The house filled up. The party moved out into the dark. There were suddenly candles and lamps and light bulbs suspended on a cable. And we suddenly came alive with chatter and laughter, as though some curtain had risen abruptly upon a bustling scene. Pános from the fish boat held up an amplifier cable and searched for a socket inside the house. Soon, music blared outside from speakers on stands: it was at once those popular Greek songs which sound, yes, like amplified bees, and which, yes, I do love, Theo. Then Spíros came, and we shook hands.

But first there were introductions: Evangelía, his wife, and the two children. Eléni as *my* wife, though she declined any Greek, pretending only to *merikés léxis*—a few words. And someone found Nasir, who just smiled and shook people's hands, because I guess Marta had thoughtfully told them about his throat! Níkos at the shop has since taken a shine to him and found him a bit of a job. Theo, I have to admit his true status seems virtually an open secret, but the Greeks are being very generous, even in these times. So for all our great plan, it served more to bring Julia and me together than to do any great favours for Nasir. Anyway, Evangelía helped the other women put out food. And then, in the midst of all that bustle, Marta, Spíros and I remained alone.

He stood smiling at me, holding his glass.

'His picture,' I said to Marta. 'The new Archangel in the church. Will you tell him how profoundly it moved me?'

She did so.

'*Evcharistó polí.*' He took a good swig at his drink and smiled again.

'*Óchi.* It is I—*egó*—who should thank *you.*' The music strummed in through the open windows, the male singer relishing those exotic half and quarter tones. Marta translated. 'Mine is a different tradition,' I went on. 'To look at an icon... Physically, I have the same eyes as you, but... Your picture, I admire it. Very much. When I came first to it, I didn't see. Only after a change.' I pointed to my head, and then to my heart.

Again, Marta explained. And again Spíros simply thanked me. I tried 'The western vision... What we think of as art... My training...' Even with an interpreter, my speech proved halting and unpropitious.

And then at last I knew what to do. We should get tipsy together. I shook Spíros once more by the hand, kissed Marta on the cheek and dashed off my drink. I went in search of a bottle and re-filled us all. Then I swept us outside. There was no moon yet, and the constellations almost jumped down at me.

'*Éla*—Come on,' I said to Spíros, clapping him on his tall shoulder as though I were the provider of all this. '*As fáme*—Let's eat.'

Our own dining table was out, and there were folding ones, too, hastily set up, on which lay starlit dishes: courgettes, aubergines,

351

tomatoes, beans in oil. There were Greek breads, fruit, salads, moist cheeses, *tzatzíki*. Another had grilled cold chicken, olives, sardines, lamb *souvlákia*. We took plates and piled them up, and I stood smiling beside the icon painter, surrounded by chattering neighbours, glancing out every now and then at the dark glittering sea in the bay and wondering quite how all this could have come about. I looked Spíros in the eye and pointed to the horizon, which glinted with the lights of two ships. We smiled, both entirely ignorant, I believe, of the gesture's meaning. I refilled our glasses. We smiled again, and it didn't matter.

Then I drank seriously and with intent. Soon enough, in the swirl of new faces, there were conversations on every front: the house was very nice — *polý kaló*; the view was wonderful — *ipérochi*; my wife was pretty — *ómorphi*. My ears attuned and my tongue loosened. 'From whom was all this — *apó pión*?' 'From Marta, naturally — *physicá*.' 'I had no idea — *kamía ithéa*. Me? Yes, a boy and a girl — *éna agóri ke éna korítsi*; the weather — *o kerós* — unusual even for the islands, this heat so oppressive — *katathliptikí*; say that again — *ksaná*; on Kos there were fires, and on the mainland, so it said on TV — *stin tileórasi*; these *tiropitákia* are so good, *kiría Kateerína*; how beautiful the sky, magnificent the sea; the grapes this year; pomegranates, figs, olives, the water supply; the live ships map; the island mayor; the honey. The economy: ah, terrible — *katastrophikí*. Don't speak of it! Not tonight!'

Then I saw Elpítha, sitting alone on a plastic chair at the foot of the garden and staring out to sea just as Spíros and I had done.

'*Kalispéra, kiría Elpítha. Kalós ílthate sto spíti mou* — welcome to my house.' She made no acknowledgement of my presence.

Holding my re-charged plate in one hand, my fork in the other and my drink somehow between the two, I peered discreetly at her small face and just made out her line of sight. It was fixed on a patch of starlit sea beyond the bluff. I stared in turn. Were those the very faintest crests of foam shining out there? Was it dolphins, perhaps, or just the wind getting up? Yes, there was a hot gust here, too, behind my back, but nothing to trouble the party. I looked again.

All at once, and without shifting her gaze, she spoke. I was startled. I couldn't tell whether she was answering me, or whether I might be intruding on some stream of consciousness she was voicing spontaneously into the dark. And though I listened intently for words or phrases I could cling to, I made out not one. Either her accent and soft pronunciation, or the entirely recondite nature of her subject matter made her utterance more like a pure intonation, I don't know, like a song without tune, some inscrutable lament.

Now a woman stood with us, glass in one hand and cigarette in the other. She bent down to the old lady. '*Pou?*' she said. 'Where?'

Elpítha slowly raised her arm and pointed.

I looked, straining my vision again out into the night. The foam patch—if patch it was—had moved. Then, some way to the left of where I'd focused before, I thought I saw the sea churning as though upon rocks; though I knew for a certainty there were none in the bay and that the passage was as deep and unencumbered as any navigator might wish.

'*Thelphíniá?*' I ventured my theory. 'Dolphins?'

Elpítha gave an emphatic lift of the chin in the old Greek manner, as if to say, 'How can you strangers be so ridiculous, so blind?'

I wanted to kiss her cheek, but I'm glad, my friend, that I didn't. I only lowered my head a little nearer hers and followed once more her gaze out to sea. But this time I could see nothing, and so I left the two women together and walked, I confess with some detectable imprecision, back to the crowd...

Where, of course, there was more eating, more drinking, more chatter. And then the music changed. Pános put on a strong bouzouki beat, and a circle was forming. People linked hands, and it was at once the cliché we think of, tourist Greece, film Greece. Yet I sensed an edge to it, like a political gesture. The ancient circle dance was a microcosmic statement against the whole unseen host of shysters, gamblers, home grown and international conmen who'd pulled out the mat so disastrously from under Greece and her people.

Around and around we went with the intricate little step, track after track, the air lubricated, the stars jolting in rhythm. My guests loved to dance at my house—but truly I was the guest. England had lost this; nor had its inhabitants such a generality of grace, of dignity, the community joined against the persistence of evil, each individual spine, young or old, held upright and defiant without effort. I thought, too, of the circle dances we'd done in the Clinic—Lisa the nurse leading, once a week, a ring of reluctant bodies, each one speaking, in its frozen, awkward muscles, of solidified sorrow.

At least, Theo, I thought of the Clinic until I caught the eye of Julia on the other side of the circle. Then I could hardly think at all. For she was lost in the rhythm, impassioned, and I'd no idea how she'd come there or who might have thought to invite her.

Was it at that point Marta came with Spíros?

'Of course. Of course.' I broke off and led the way to the outbuilding. I let them in, turned on the lights. The bright 'full spectrum' bulbs and halogens blew night away, leaving only the hard outlines of my labour and my improvised bed in the corner.

I hastily pulled up this canvas or that from the assortment of sketches and half-finished surfaces. Something of Félix and Cécile? A street scene? I rummaged, bumping unsteadily into the bench, overbalancing slightly and nearly putting my foot through that brothel, and all the while glancing apologetically at my visitors; at once more nervous, to tell the truth, Theo, than I might have been before some high powered London show. Because a religious craftsman from an extinct volcano in the Aegean had done me the great honour of visiting!

The vast Bledlow piece leaned against the far wall. I put that up on the easel, of course. Spíros and Marta peered at it with interest. Then Spíros turned to me and nodded. More, he put his hand on my shoulder, almost embracing me, and I felt myself relax a little. I tried to explain what it showed; Marta relayed something of my words. He studied it in closer detail.

I said it meant nothing much out of its context. I wasn't interested in landscapes for their own sake, I explained, or portraits for that matter.

'*Piá íne aftí?*' Spíros interrupted, pointing.

'*Tin léne Julia,*' I replied. '*Ítan i phíli mou. I philenátha* — she was my girlfriend. *Íne* — she is. *Ethó íne, tóra* — She's here, now.'

He smiled uncertainly, but lingered, as I knew he must, over the few almost imperceptible winged forms that streaked the picture's sky. Then he looked up at me, just chewing his lip, and turned to rummage among my paintings for himself — a liberty I'd gladly permitted Marta, but would never have tolerated from anyone else — until him, I mean. In fact, it pleased me enormously. It released me; for now he made the choices, and I, through Marta, answered the questions.

So he teased out my scheme for the commission. Less drunk than I'd thought I was, I took paper and a pencil and sketched the grand design. He seemed to comprehend, while Marta watched over our shoulders. I indicated how, once they were *in situ*, the sequential images would occupy that central archway. Then I stood back.

Spíros took the pencil from me and identified a vacancy. He drew in deftly – effortlessly – the miniaturised scene from his icon of Michael. I drew breath, and I heard Marta, too, make a sound. It was confirmed; the reference to my left hand paintings had indeed been deliberate.

Then he picked out a fine brush I'd left soaking in oil and handed it to me. I understood. I put up a canvas of Cécile as the miraculous child and took the cling-film off my colours. I began where I'd left off, edging in a detailed blue-grey tone to the shadowed flesh of her neck. I handed him back the brush.

Momentarily, he was hesitant. I remembered the equivalent moment on Kálymnos when I'd paused in front of his Virgin and Child. I saw him feel the minute weight of the pigment at his fibres' tip, savour the almost imperceptible resistance before pushing the substance gingerly into the ground I'd made. He looked at me, then laid on the delicate strokes of a glaze. I turned to Marta. She was intent.

Using a slightly thicker brush, I laid on paler tints. I showed him how the colours might mix themselves on both canvas or brush – tricks foreign to his purer technique. His eyes lit up. I could see him playing, even in so limited a sample, with notions of depth and impasto. Yet I saw, too, how different was his signature from mine: how extraordinarily smooth he was able to leave the finish, even in these unfamiliar materials – and how some equally extraordinary fluid brilliance always seemed to glow from the result.

So we went on for some minutes, swapping possession, as it were; sharing the field. Theo, I've never experienced communication entirely through the medium before. The nearest was at Hornsey, in a class with Hendrik Thijssen, whose work you know I adore, during a residency. But even that paled compared to this, and what emerged was some inkling of an altered style, though I couldn't quite grasp it there and then. I was seeing my own work differently. It both puzzled and pleased me.

We were interrupted by Eléni, appearing suddenly in the doorway to the studio. She'd put on heels and a slinky dress and was holding a glass. 'Oh, there you are, Owen.' She made her way over to join us, smiling a shiny greeting to my guests. She had no difficulty walking, nor showed any overt signs of being drunk. 'So this is what you're up to. I thought you might be entertaining someone alone. Though of course it's none of my business whom you see or what you get up to. None of my concern, any more, thank God! To be perfectly frank,' she

355

addressed Marta and Spíros, 'I'd be pleased for him. It would do something for the burden of guilt he's so keen for me to feel. But nothing doing here, so it seems. All above board. Everything simply…' she looked inclusively around the studio '…hunky dory.'

'Spíros wanted to see my work.'

'Did you, Spíro?' She fixed him brightly. 'And you, Marta.' She took a pull at her drink.

'Eléni…'

'Some guys it's fast cars. Some just who can piss highest up a wall.' The sweep of her hand included all my paintings.

'Surely art is…' Marta tried saying.

'I used to think art,' said Eléni. 'I used to think artists. Did you know I'm here under duress? Has he told you that? Abject,' she said. 'What woman can respect a man who's *abject*,' she spat the word out. 'Sanctimonious. Self-righteous. You want my help, do you?'

I looked from one to the other of my guests. They stood, awkwardly silent.

She continued, returning to the easel. 'Here are a few pointers, if I must.' She jabbed a finger, smudging an outline with her polished nail. 'A few pointers. Because, you know, I have such a fucking great critical eye.'

'Don't,' I said. 'Please don't touch my picture.'

'But you begged me. You wanted me to hang on here on this son-of-a-bitch rock, even though it's over. It's over. Over! You wanted me to hang on because you were "painting for your life".'

'I am.'

'Oh, he *is*!' She stood back, squinting at the canvas. 'Seven hundred years out of date, and counting.' She turned to Marta, 'Or is it something more dilute, more PRB?'

'What?'

'Pre-Raphaelite Brotherhood,' I explained, before Eléni herself elaborated:

'Spoilt Englishmen with beards. Keen on turning back the clock. Keener still on younger women.' She eyed me pointedly.

But she was drawn back into the picture, despite herself, Theo, because for all the drunken bluster she really does understand them, and she does respond both to the pleasure of medium and the joy of representation. And she did grasp, I believe, the clear knowing gestures I'd made towards the extreme contemporary. I could feel her emotions fighting inside her. 'Okay, it's just fine,' she said at length. 'Classic Owen Davy. What more did you want?'

356

'Just your honest opinion,' I said.

'I've given it, haven't I? Look, I've been too generous. That's the trouble.'

'Sure. I respect that. But...'

'I've said. Alright?! Just what is it you want to know?' She took in the expanse of canvas again, the young woman in my 'dark farce' stepping out of her casket in a kind of resurrection, the mystified 'parents' still mostly outlines, with just a few areas of their modern dress painted in. She scrutinised where I'd begun to suggest an audience. She switched back to the detail of the witch's dress with its spiral designs. 'This work is crude.' She pointed to a patch I'd felt uncomfortable about myself. 'Those colour values by the side are confident, but these aren't.'

'Yeah?' I said.

'Hard to describe. It's like it's not quite... It's like it lacks a steady hand.'

A sound in my throat.

'What's that?' she eyed me suspiciously. 'Did I say something? You wanted my opinion; I've given it.'

Then she saw my nude of Julia, balanced by Spíros against a table leg.

She seemed unable to take her eyes off it. 'I don't know, do I,' she said. Her speech was abruptly disconnected. 'I'm not the fucking painter. You'll have to sort it out. Now, can I go, please? I've got things to do.' She began to sway.

'Maybe we should get you out of here. Maybe you'd be better sitting down.'

'You think so?' She said it to Spíros, acknowledging him suddenly again like a child.

'Yes. I really do think so,' Marta replied.

We steered her back out into the night and found her a plastic chair.'

'These heels,' she said, placidly. 'I guess I'm not used to them.' She laughed, then got up again and went towards the table with the bottles on it.

Theo, a moon came up, with new stars. There was more dancing, and the night reeled on. I did end up alone with Julia; it was down on the shore, where we found the sea boy. What can I say? I kissed her over again and held her in my arms; it ran through my limbs like honey.

357

Part IV

Unconditional Love

29

Subject: Athene's bird

She's gone. Another furnace of a day—another sweating race with paint, rags, brushes and the wads of foil, cling-film or the like. Julia in modern dress. The Child, half male, half female. The hero, Llew. The witch Arianhrod—Silver Wheel. The lanced sacrifice, neither on land nor water, walking nor riding, naked nor clothed, indoors nor out, neither by day nor night.

Just a dark farce.

Out in my bay, a lone yacht toils on a broad reach, standing for Áyia Marína before nightfall. And now the little owl, Athene's bird, that waits long sessions on the electricity pole behind my neighbour's fence, is beginning to twitch.

It's flown. I cannot tell you my feelings.

Two lights are on the hill. Four! And now they appear in a sudden spatter from the new houses over Pandéli quay. Soon the bright castle floods will come on, which is the moment I wait for every evening. Just after dark, the air continues to distort in this outrageous heat, and those faraway stone walls, solid as centuries, waver crazily before they settle. Look there! Do you see?

Subject: Ambrosia

We work from first light. The old van bumps, lurches endlessly over ruts and rocks. Here are Andónis' bees, here those of Oréstis. Here's the smell of burning pine needles on another sweltering hillside: the many hives of Yórgos, the few of Páris and Manólis. Their wooden lids come off: three, four frames at a time taken out from the ten in each box. Again and again, clad in our thickest clothing, we brush off the smoke-drowsed insects, who regroup and come at us, enraged. Too late: their combs are stacked safe in our own boxes, waiting ready. We load them and drive off singing, so elated at the great weight of our prize—kilos of the divine substance—that we can hardly feel our stings. Yes, even through jeans, through thick, sweat-soaked shirts and

361

clinging bee smocks, through tied leggings and long gloves, the desperate barbs have gone in.

Salute the first day of the honey harvest, Theo! Shades of some old rustic festival indeed, but the government's savage austerity cuts threaten everything, and this is raw survival. In the clean room back at the hospital, Cóstas runs the centrifuge, shining industrial steel. Yánnis hovers behind him. Women at the scrubbed pine table, their hair pinned under white, hygienic bonnets, collect each honeycombed frame as it arrives. An inspector from the mainland stands with his clipboard.

Next to Marta and Elpítha, I take my turn. We've shed our thicker clothes. Now we wield broad heated knives and uncap the waxen clag from row upon row of neat hexagonal cells. Honey drips; everything glazes, sticky and sweet.

Another batch spins. White-coated, white-bonneted male patients stand at the taps, where warm, semi-viscous amber flows once again down flexible pipes. Into jars on the circular tray it runs translucent. It oozes golden, again and again.

And we fight exhaustion as the hours tick on. Come siesta time, full hundreds of our jars stand stacked upon tables in the neighbouring rooms, each fat pot lidded and labelled, a prime elixir: ΘΥΜΑΡΙΣΙΟ ΜΕΛΙ "ΑΡΤΕΜΙΣ" – THYME HONEY "ARTEMIS".

Marta and I sit under tamarisk trees. The hospital unit's in the southern hills; it's the brown land that Julia and I scanned from across the inlet at Lakkí. Somewhere in the crag above us shimmers the Paleókastro, the island's oldest castle, crowning an ancient acropolis. Marta talks of Cóstas, of how proud she is, how moved. My own thoughts wander.

She calls me out on it. 'What is it, Owen? Your eyes are clouded… Before, in the van, you sang with us as we brought in the harvest. Now you're troubled.'

I laugh it away. 'It's nothing. My painting; it's good to have a day off, once in a while.'

'There's something. I know it.'

'Aren't you tired, Marta? Like the others?' I turn my head. For, here and there beneath the trees, small groups of white clad folk lie, worked out and at rest. And close around Marta, like blanch puppies with their dam, are particular friends – as if hard concrete, hard beds or hard ground were all one to them: Elpítha, neat and abstracted even in sleep, with the bib of her unstained gown lifting and falling almost

362

imperceptibly; gnarled Phílippos in his smock; portly Aristotélis, snoring on his back, his jeans sticking out at odd angles from his coat; Ariáthne with the grey curls; old Vangelíta and Evthímios who are in love—these I've met just today. Only Cóstas is awake, with Yánnis. They sit back to back a yard or two further off, smoking under their bee hoods, saying nothing—as always. I remember that first time in Manólis' glade, the hum of his bees, the white shapes.

'Me? Not so tired,' she says. 'Too pleased to sleep.'

'It's wonderful, all you're doing.' I wave my hand at the unit, the low, functional building, the few cars parked outside. 'All of you. It *must* succeed.'

'I *am* happy, Owen.' She scratches a twig idly at the dry earth. She laughs. 'I am happy, if somewhat stung! And I've never given so many anti-histamine shots—to so many people! But there is something you want very much to ask me, and you don't know if you should. Or you don't wish to burden me with it.'

Theo, am I so transparent?

'And,' she continues, 'I tell you I'm not sleepy. So you can burden me if you like.'

'You amaze me.' I smile. For she's right, Theo. The question that still torments me—how to ask it? Words, so long denied, do queue up at my throat. Because it's *the* question, the almost unspeakable, unaskable question of my guilt that seems fused into everything: to Julia's absence, to painting, to Eléni, to the future, to the deepest fibres in my body. 'But I don't know where to begin,' I tell her.

She surprises me. 'Begin, if you like, where it all starts: with the woman. Maybe with the English lady in your picture. What was her name again?' She pretends to look puzzled.

'You're very sharp, Marta, very acute. Yes, Julia's on my mind. As she is always. But just now it's not Julia I need to talk about. Though it concerns her—and her leaving.'

Marta murmurs in a throaty, Russian sound, drops her tamarisk stick and gestures out over the open space. 'Very well.'

'Could you bear to walk a bit? I don't think, in front of... even in English.'

'Walk? At this time of day?'

I get up.

She affects crossness, fusses to pull on her wide straw hat, stands, slings her bag over her shoulder. 'Well, if you must.'

She nods to Cóstas, and we leave the sleepers. We amble down the driveway, so slowly, because the heat is intense and our clothes already chafe and fret us. We pass the small concrete pillars at the end and turn right towards that old castle, towards the hamlet of Skáfia, where white houses range on sloping land above us and the plants wreathing from their balconies splash green with electric red, pink, blue.

I think how to start. By *indirections*?

'Misery memoirs,' I say. 'I wonder, have you heard of them?'

'Mis… What is that?'

'Books. A genre. White covers, tragic kids.'

'Oh, those. Yes, where I buy left-behind English books. Left-behind books. That shop by the harbour.'

'They sell in millions, Marta. At least they did. Before the fashion moved on. Because cruelty to children is very moving, very harrowing. And maybe these books strike chords—with so many victims.'

'Yes.'

'A new thing, Marta, to tell such stories in public. Or at all. A latter day phenomenon. Except perhaps for Charles Dickens—a little. And old pictures of saints, I guess—mostly female. Grievously abused girls turned into mini-goddesses by the church.'

There's a spot of cover from an oleander in one of the gardens. We stop a moment or two. She shifts her weight, transfers her bag from one shoulder to the other.

'Benvenuto Cellini,' I say. 'You know who I mean—great artist in bronze and precious metals.' That great blade for the beeswax, Theo, and the gorgon's severed head.

She nods. 'I've heard the name.'

'Cellini boasts, in his autobiography, of the rape of a young girl. A demonstration of manhood? An attempt to shock? Was he proud?'

'Who knows?' She adjusts her hat, rummages in her bag for a tissue, pats her hairline. We walk on.

'But, Marta, hasn't art always seen sexual transgression as one in the eye for the bourgeoisie.'

'In the eye? One? You make no sense to me with your English.'

'It means defiance. For years it was almost the artist's *duty* to offend, wasn't it, even to the limit. Yes, to shock, even in very recent times. By his life, his work.'

'Artists and soldiers. Always bad boys.' She sniffs. 'Lock up wives. Daughters. Sons, too, maybe!'

'Until, at last, society learnt the horror of violation, learnt it from women themselves. The horror—at all ages. And suddenly then, you see, pushing the limit is no longer something to boast about, in art or anywhere. It's merely disgusting and cruel.'

'Owen, where do you go with this?'

'Bear with me just a little. Because, if all goes well, I shall have my own work on display again soon enough. And this is what's on my mind.' I hold up my hand. 'You agree that the artist as sexual provocateur has had the wind taken out of his sails. Yes, rightly, very rightly. Because no one wants to play screw-everything ancient Greeks again. Or rapist Italians.

She looks at me and nods, humouring, indulgent.

'But you can see as well as I the flip side: that every contemporary artist now knows that to depict the human form at all puts his or her sexuality *on show*. That visual lust of the old days… what shall we call it: a kind of naivety. Because any serious male artist nowadays showing erotic relish is condemned at once, as a sell-out, or as a pervert—paradoxically, at a time when advertising and the internet heave with erotic iconography; when all shapes and species of actual sex between consenting adults, straight, gay, S & M, anything, are positively recommended to the public, as a medical issue, even, for the health! When every women's magazine has the word sex or orgasm on its cover.'

'Even in Greece!' she smiles.

'When even Christianity, that along with Judaism and Islam was once so set against sculpted shapes and the god's arousal—why, these days even churches offer sex counselling. At least, they do in America, so I read. Sex is taught in schools, isn't it. Eros, instead of being a threat to society, becomes the grin on its consumerist face…'

She has to laugh.

'But, Marta, I come back to that one exception in all this. Why, it's me. It's the artist. It's the serious male painter who must be most chary of showing any passionate interest whatsoever in the human form. And though this stance is all dressed up in intellectual or aesthetic scruples: that the camera frees us from it; that it's anti-feminist; that it's all been done before; that it's politically regressive, colonialist; that art is more about medium, space and materials—those are really just excuses. The actual reason is that male desire itself has lately become deeply suspect, and a prurient populist culture sets all men under suspicion, even as it ruthlessly peddles the sexual image.'

She laughs again. 'Okay, okay.'

'Marta, on the canvas everyone can see into your mind. So the male artist—like me—had better make sure he's got nothing creepy left in the closet. Even things he's not aware of. Especially those, eh! You're the psychiatrist! Safer, much safer, surely, to stay in the clouds.'

'Ah, but you know this better than I do, O Socrates,' still chuckling. 'Yet aren't there serious artists now who deliberately paint... what do you call them, pornographic scenes? Haven't I seen something like that, somewhere?'

'Exactly. But for them desire is both intellectualised and ironized. The artist parodies his own interest in the subject—or hers—and in that way disowns it. You see? So while it looks as though everything personal *might* be revealed, nothing is. But imagine, Marta, painting desire again from the heart, candidly...' I pause. The ruined castle's visible now on the leftward crest above us. Its Cyclopean foundations vibrate, and the wind scorches. 'Can you bear this temperature? Can you bear me to speak of all this?'

The risk of speech, Theo. So much to say, but the throat so long blocked, violated. And I think of her joke that I'm as disputative as Socrates.

'Let's sit under those trees.' She points to a wall overhung by stubby pines. The drop of the land makes the place a little amphitheatre, and the trees have a small patch of shade. 'You want to bring back desire, Owen? My surgery—I have Viagra. Is that what all this is about?'

'Don't mock. I want to paint... I want at last to dare to take as my subject the woman... Julia.'

She smiles. 'Yes, Julia. Of course.'

I look down, tactically, to attend to my stings. There's a hiatus.

'These matters,' she says at last, composed, her bag in her lap. 'They are touching you deeply.'

'These matters touch us all. At the deepest level.' I take a breath. 'Ach, I'm not making myself clear! These things are so difficult. And people *find* them so difficult. Surely that's why so few male survivors dare put their hands up—certainly not where it's a blood father involved. Survivors of incest...'

'It's okay, Owen,' she says, quietly. 'It's okay.'

'The misery memoirs... Marta, it's a very dubious business stirring up... stirring up pity and terror—just for their own sake. And revenge.' I look at her earnestly. 'Because these books aren't proper tragedies. They're melodrama, good and evil portrayed as absolutes. It's sheer exploitation, schlock. Yet some of the stories are true. And, God, they are heart-breaking. And I ask myself, shouldn't they be told? Don't the victims have that right?'

Now a bee sting on my leg throbs and burns, and I try to pat it through my jeans.

Socratic, obsessive, if you like, I continue. 'Hasn't high art gone to the other extreme?' I dash sweat from my eyes. 'My world, Marta. As I say, high art deals today only with intellect, with aesthetics, resonance, perception, with philosophical in-jokes—it all turns conceptual.' But I'm struggling. 'This business of my father, you know... It's hardly unique. If it's true...'

'But of course,' she says, softly. 'We know, yes, we know it does happen to boys as well as to girls. And we know these days that it is all too common for both boys and girls. Very sadly.'

'But very few *men* will speak about it. You see, Marta? You see what I'm trying to get at?'

She looks puzzled, then catches on. 'Oh, you mean...?'

'Exactly. Boys turn into men. A *number* will be abusers in turn. Most, of course, will not. But *all* of us, yes, of *us*, will have some weird distortions of sexuality, some problems of relationship, confusion over boundaries. It's unavoidable. Oh, God, Marta, you must know the maelstrom that surrounds this subject, the violent public oscillation of grief and fury. It's understandable.' The words spill suddenly out of me. 'Horrified society weeps for the innocent and burns for revenge. But no one can bear for it to touch *them*, can they. Because people want it simple. They don't care to think about families, especially not their own. So *men* become the problem—identifiable men. Men, named and shamed in the newspapers. Monsters, they call them, men listed on a register, or not yet listed, lurking. And, of course, there are such men. And that chimes with the feminist equation. But the real case... You see the real case isn't simple. Men! Men bring in complexity, precisely because some of them are likely to have been both innocent children *and* guilty adults. Marta, I once saw for myself a professional female teacher show such hatred for a boy caught interfering with his sister that I almost wouldn't have known her. Her face—I can still see it: contorted with rage, even though the kid was young and had to be acting out what older kids or adults had foisted upon him, one way or another. What he did was vile, and will have damaged the girl; but he was barely over the age of responsibility—about twelve. And yet the teacher could find in her heart neither understanding nor compassion for this shunned, neglected, unprepossessing lad — the kind no picture editor would want on a book cover, by the way. He was at once the monster in the case, and no one dared challenge her attitude: of blaming the child. My God, we hold up our hands at old time schoolteachers hanging placards round children's necks; we shudder at it from our enlightenment. Yet here it was exactly: a boy labelled "nonce", the worst prison slang in English, just so that his teachers could wash their hands of the bigger problem, the adults in the family.'

'It's alright, Owen.'

'It's not alright, Marta! Because all of us men are likely to be tarred with the same brush!' I pause. 'And that's why these books, these "misery memoirs", remain — what shall we call it — low art. Not because they're only about women...

'Surely not just women,' she interrupts.

'I've kept an eye on them, Marta. Believe me, and believe it or not, there's nothing from male survivors. I tell you, nothing at all in all those titles. Not of sexual abuse, incest.'

'Surely that's where it all started. The one about the boy...'

'Appalling violence, yes. Neglect, yes. But not sexual. And definitely not incestuous. Not with male victims. No one wants to know. And so society keeps the subject safely as a kind of ghetto of female suffering. Which can be set aside, as women themselves are set aside.'

'Are you sure of this?'

'Pretty much. I say, it's not just because the books are only about women. But because they ignore half the picture — the same half that high art fights shy of.'

'What? Men again?'

'No. Complexity.'

'What is it you want from me, Owen? Here, now.'

'Guilt torments me.'

'Is it that you yourself have something... something creepy in the closet?' She speaks very gently, wrapping her tongue around the words.

'There's a canzone of Dante's, so beautiful, when he was desperate to speak about Beatrice to a group of her friends:

> *Donne ch'avete intelletto d'amore,*
> *I' vo' con voi de la mia donna dire*

'And whatever does that mean?'

368

'It means, Ladies who have understanding of love, I want to speak with you about my lady.'

'Julia?'

'Yes. I don't know. More than one of my ladies, Marta. Before Julia and after. Not desire but *guilt* of desire, and of commission. Is it genuine, this guilt; or is it some cruel symptom... like a growth, some nasty tumour of my behaviour, of my own behaviour, confusion over boundaries... A growth lying concealed and radiating harm, which could in fact be exposed to someone and cut out? Could be scrutinised indeed — as in some novel, you know — one seemingly inconsequential detail of a life, perhaps trivial, perhaps momentous, set under a microscope and magnified for forensic examination. Marta, when I think of it, my whole life has been shaped by this terrible guilt. My whole life — I see that now, right down to here and now, and Julia. Because the worst thing is that for so many years I never even noticed. I just knew I *was* guilty, do you see? I believed it was 'real'; that guilt was the real, the true, and therefore unacceptable, unbearable portrait of myself, that could never even be shown, let alone painted. The portrait, Marta. But lately I have the faintest glimmer of an idea — suddenly, from Julia, I have to say, and from Theo in England — that there's a hope, the most fragile hope... You see, this endless inner accusation that I'm a... that I'm a... When it might be just a 'voice', Marta, a Part, the Father, something in my head, some kind of madness, paranoiac, buzzing, flapping, hissing at me — that also makes me so perpetually *confused*. You know? And now I think only if I dare speak about it will I ever find out the truth, to test it against you, an impartial judge — if you'll listen.'

'Because I have such an understanding, you imagine? Of love?'

'I believe so, Doctor.'

'Tomorrow, Owen. Here, at this same hour.' Abruptly, she looks back the way we've come. I turn to follow her gaze. Out in Lakkí Bay, the sea is creased and white-streaked with the wind. And now we're Aegean figures on a black background: a woman in a straw hat, a man. Ancient stones beneath a pine.

369

30

Subject: Arraignment

It's dawn. The van takes us to the island's northern segment, to the hills before the temple of Artemis and the military base. We collect honey frames on grey wakening slopes, amongst dried growths of herbs and scrub. Already, we've made three laden trips back to base. And we've been stung again, Theo — even though I've put on two pairs of jeans and taped them up at the ankles!

But the sun soon burns still hotter, and the talk, when talk there is, concerns the fires: few yet on Léros or Kálymnos, though serious blazes on Kos and Rhodes. Most troubling, the menace to Athens: now every TV news shows clips of distraught citizens against a backdrop of flames, fanned by the ever treacherous wind.

But we have our task. And so for the last time we lurch and bump singing down the hill tracks, back on to the long tarmac road and through town to the unit.

There we help once again at the processing, until, dog-tired and with some of us dosed-up with shots, we throw ourselves under the tamarisks to rest.

But Marta's as good as her word. No more than a token break and she nods to me. And we take ourselves off again along the hospital drive and up to that curious little amphitheatre about a mile off. What shall I call it, our debate: a struggle, an *agon*? Yes, Theo, we need the landscape.

So now, my friend, I must plunge you back into the heat beneath those pines. To confess this time to Marta the details of my marriage to Lily. Why, yes, to relate over again what I told Julia.

And does she recoil in horror, cross herself in agitation?

She remains silent. Seconds? A minute? Asks simply, 'Are you relieved to have told me?'

Adrenalin, the stomach, the heart. I explain about when I told Julia. How I suspected... how I *knew* she was too lenient.

'And the guilt?'

'It's returned — redoubled. That I should have dared to reach out for love. Julia's. All we've done here yesterday and today, the harvest... I sang, but I couldn't share your happiness. Because I interfered in someone else's life—Lily's. I changed its course. I shouldn't have.'

'What do you want me to do? Whip you? Abandon you? Yes, Owen, you *were* of the age of criminal responsibility. And you did something. Was it criminal?'

'No. She was nineteen.'

'Has she complained of it? Lily?'

'No.'

'Then am I supposed to call the police? On no grounds at all? Do the KGB have to come for your suspect male desire? And take you to the gulag?' Her accent heightens the sound.

'Or the British equivalent, Marta. Or the Greek—these old hospitals and prison camps right here.' I spread my hands to the island's history. Theo, these were my words to her and my gesture, though it's hard to believe now that I even said them, or could still present an aspect of myself so stricken, because tonight I'm rushing between canvas and keyboard, and everything seems changing around me. My head's awhirl.

Neither has she any patience with it. 'Tcha! You yourself call it paranoia. Yet still you let it rule you. No crime was committed. You got married. You had a family. This guilt…'

I say, my mind's racing. But I must take you step by step. Paranoia. Even to apply that label, Theo—even to begin to agree that this overwhelming guilt might be somehow inauthentic, that it might instead be just a *disorder*, a *delusion* with a proper Greek name… Just 'paranoia'. That's progress in itself.

'Yet still it comes after me, Marta, still attacks, as though—forgive me—with those beating wings and hissing snakes; and I can't rid myself of it. This business of painting, that springs from… this thing I have to do to get myself out… out of the pit… it's so public. Marta, there's a limit to pretending I'm someone else, a woman, whatever, disowning my own work, hiding from it, even, do you see, the Parts… that's what I've always done. Because the truth *will* come out; it's bound to: *what* I am, *who* I am. This commission… I almost cancelled it.'

'No one is coming for you, Owen,' she says quietly. 'No one will come for you just for putting brush to canvas.'

She forgets Stalin, of course. But I *have* to gamble. If I speak more to Marta and she listens, there's a chance that I'll listen, too. This is my reasoning; because, whenever I do get my head above it, I do admit I can actually recall the same crippling guilt in my childhood. I said so. I think so. And if I can establish that it's just a voice, a hateful symptom, then there's a hope, the elusive hope that I can put it aside, become visible at last…

'Then tell me,' she says. 'All of it.'

'I've bothered you enough.'

'Let me be judge of that, if judge I am to be. Tell me!'

So I begin, my dear friend, and the heat fires us, alternately blowing and broiling. And now, as the truth of the body begins to dawn, and though I've turned abruptly, here, in the crisis of my case, to this other confidante, yet you, too, must know these things, these memoirs, yes, of misery; firstly out of love, but also lest you, despite your immense generosity right down to this point, for which I remain so grateful… lest you also feel that same ambivalence I spoke of earlier, and hold, deep down, your own doubts and suspicions of my character and past conduct.

And to write does free me, for, believe it or not, this is the first time I've ever actually marshalled the evidence — at least in such a way that no one in my head can move in to scramble it or mysteriously 'forget' key information. If that sounds strange, almost incredible, then I assure you it's the way of it. And maybe writing lets the Parts read their own story, too, for the first time through my eyes — things they otherwise couldn't know. Maybe. Which helps… if you'll not be offended; though I shall need to be candid — as if I haven't been already!

So I tell Marta what I recorded once I'd left my first wife, back then in the seventies. How, simply to assuage a bedsit loneliness, I set down everything I could remember. How forgotten curiosities emerged almost at once, which otherwise by now would be lying eternally forgotten: how at five or six I routinely exposed myself to other children — lonely then, too, perhaps — in order to make friends. Yes, I admit it, a secret thing I would do, given the chance. And I played elaborate sexual 'games' with a boy over the road; not play at all, but a secret, shame-filled intimacy for which I made specially darkened corners in his house and mine. And I wore my mother's clothes with him, not by way of 'dressing up', but because it aroused me still further.

I search Marta's face for reaction. Like Julia the other day, she gives none.

Theo, I believed even then I was possessed by the devil. Well under the age of responsibility, I knew it was all wrong. Yet I couldn't stop.

372

Nor in those days could I connect these juvenile practices, of course, with bedwetting, or sometimes soiling myself on the way home from school, nor with other desperate muscular efforts to keep control. But how good it would have been had someone intervened, had found the cause and simply put a stop to it. No fuss. Just a stop. 'Someone who understood, Marta. How happy I'd have been.'

She nods.

'Instead, I became an actor just to appear normal. And, ironically, it was my most conventional intimacy—harmless show and touch with my playmate Bernadette—that left me most guilty. Because she was a girl. I was six and I thought for months I'd ruined her life. That's guilt, isn't it? Shame for boys, but a desperate guilt for anything to do with a girl.'

Marta's eyebrows lift momentarily. Still she offers no opinion.

There were complaints—from Bernie's mother. From someone's mother at the next place we lived... we moved and moved. Alarm bells should have been ringing—a problematic child. But even when, as I say, I first recalled these child behaviours and, having left my first wife, noted them down, I took no particular heed: because Freud was all we had, and whatever some kid might do in distress was just Freud's "infant sexuality". Grotesque phrase! For how worried I'd have been, as a parent myself, had my own kids shown the same tendencies. 'Wouldn't you?'

'Yes,' she says, at last. 'I'd have been concerned.' From her not-so-capacious bag, she produces a plastic water bottle. She opens it and drinks.

A good man once stayed with us, Jim Cole, a colleague of my father's—I was seven. He might have been that person to intervene. But we moved house, of course, hurriedly, to the far side of London. Where there was more I was ashamed of. Was that the reason I was packed off to boarding school after another few months? Did it feel like a prison, that grey Victorian building, still further off? I'd just turned eight.

She passes me the water bottle. 'Go on.'

Theo, I'm trying to lay out fully for you—to expose, if you will—a sexual history that must either convict or release me. I'd mentioned it to Mitchell, of course, but I was always too ill to hold it forensically in mind. And ever since... But now you and Marta and the accusing Parts... and exhibits, A, B, C, above, do show indeed how my sense of guilt goes right back—and would seem to be excessive.

373

Yes, in telling and writing this, I see clearly at last how something *must* have been wrong in that family. Mine. How, yes indeed, my paranoia may just possibly begin to qualify as a symptom.

Rushing between canvas and keyboard, I said. But I hesitate to paint again at once, for what of adolescence? Male hormones? Adulthood?

Yet I do maybe feel that feather touch of hope even as I continue: that the little boarding school I went to for a couple of years — well beyond our means and class, but well away from home, too — might just have taught me right enough from wrong.

Marta shifts on the stone wall. I sip the warm water from the bottle. I tell her rapidly of the horrors of torture that so preoccupied me night after night; and of the constant fear, when I was ten and back in a state school, of being held up publicly by the headmaster as an obscenity. Of the discovery of orgasm at twelve — courtesy of a boy in Australia for whom I dressed, once again, in my mother's clothes.

I tell her how, soon back in England again, I felt depraved like a sex addict, because I couldn't stop hiding and masturbating and drawing naked women — learning the artist's anatomy, you might say. Though this facility, if you think about it...

'Anatomy? Or masturbation?'

She extracts a jar of honey from her surprising bag, unscrews the lid. She places it between us, dips her finger, licks it.

I take my scoop in turn. Orgasm, Theo; it allowed me to *manage* myself at last. You see? Get the thing over with. So my out-of-control behaviours were internalised, myself my own sex-doll, a hermaphrodite, a base mixture, a sort of Jungian *prima materia*. I felt safer, if dirtier. Safe from relationship. Another school and then another. I became an atheist, like my father. At thirteen, first love: a girl in my class. Which was the true birth of art.

Hornets join us. They manoeuvre clumsily, yellow with red insignia like big insect bombers, legs a lowered undercarriage.

'You painted this girl?'

I remember, Theo, the line of her back. It just struck me one morning, my desk a couple of rows behind hers, like a thunder-stroke. And then, as she turned round to look — not at me, but at some friend at the far side of the classroom — I saw the female perfection of her shape! An epiphany!

'*Phóta!*'

Yes. Lights all around her. Radiance. A renaissance — Aphrodite rising.

Far in the past it seems, dear friend, when a boy could recognise first love from old stories and paintings, and not think himself so very out of step! I mean before the internet, when even rock and roll wasn't quite about raw sex. And so it never seemed so very odd that I couldn't imagine sex with Jennifer Mills. With any other girl, yes — but this was *love*, like my father's for my mother. I should marry her and be sanctified, clear of my sin... were it not that I had syphilis.

Marta invites me again to the jar, and honey enraptures my tongue.

Masturbation contracted syphilis, I was convinced. My face gave it away; no, but I'd read that syphilis could exist even without symptoms, and so I lived for some adolescent years in a half world where I ought never to approach any girl, nor dream of a family, because of my delusion of fatal contamination. From my filthy, incurable disease.

'Owen. You want to tell me all this? Even if it upsets you?'

'I must. I must come *clean* with it. Everything. You have to hear the details, how it works, so you can...' I remember myself and look up. 'If you don't mind.'

'I've said.'

'Because if ever I did find love, a girl, do you see — I've thought about this, in the light of what Josh Levinson said — Beauty and the Beast... a girl who was kind, whom I loved, who might take me on sexually, me, as a male, history and all, but who might also do as you're doing at this moment, Marta, or Julia...' I rush, embarrassed. 'I mean who might listen to this account and *not* conclude I was vile beyond hope... If someone balanced and generous ever heard me... Why, they might come to believe — as you just did — I might even come to believe myself... that these behaviours were...' I pause. 'That my family...'

But then I lose faith, because I'm making something out of nothing. I forget, too, the hope of the little boarding school away from the family, learning right from wrong. A dark mood engulfs me. 'What are you doing?'

She folds down a finger of her left hand. 'I'm counting the Parts, Owen. And if — just perhaps — it is not as trivial as you suggest, and maybe not all masturbating teenagers sustain long term delusions of public humiliation and venereal disease... And your face, the human identity, the persona, the mask we present to the world, the gateway, possibly, to mental health, the face, of all things the most important to an artist, I imagine: as the essence of the portrait... Should I have to tell you this?'

Theo, I attacked my face with a needle from twelve until thirty. But I make a joke of it; my skin fought back, and my first love was requited. Jennifer and I dated. We kissed chastely, even on the mouth.

Hornets buzz us with real intent. I brush them away. And I find I have, indeed, entered upon a kind of Platonic dialogue—perhaps a little akin to the trial scenes of Socrates—though Marta seems by far the wiser of us two... But I mean in the flavour of the writing: cool, forensic, adversarial, and needing baldly and scrupulously to follow the details. It is as though, Theo, the artist had reached the problem of the sitter's eyes, reached all the subtle miniature folds and tints around those eyes, and, as with Rembrandt, say, the delineation of the entire nature finds itself at stake—perhaps for several days. Bear with me, I implore you.

I tell Marta of another girl in the year below me, Lydia, to whom I never spoke at all. Cruel joy, divine pain—and how I began drawing in earnest, and painting, painting her face from memory as the Italians did. Months passed. I was so reserved around girls, so ruthlessly scientific, yet held the Faustian delusion I could have any one I wanted.

'Another devil, another delusion.'

I tell her, Theo, of my first diagnosable depression when Lydia turned me down—though what must we also say of an early childhood spent thinking of ways to die? That's a sad fact.

My adolescent depression lasted that winter.

We look at each other, Marta and I. I tell you, this is no casual meeting. Here, approaching—despite my florid panic at Eléni's doings and despite Julia's departure—is the prospect of birth out of some seemingly endless labour, the appearance of... a face.

Ah, but what face? There's the catch. And again I poise, here at the keyboard, before dashing off for my brushes; because the more Dad looks guilty, the more likely it makes me to have repeated...

That is the cruel, cruel Catch 22 that stops me always in my tracks. Can you conceive, Theo, how matters that may sound so remote and inconsequential to you can yet be so crucial to me? The portrait, the *pharmakon*: time's ripe for a cure, and this account, this declaration of things...

I'm sixteen, a premature, prudish, secretly cross-dressing head prefect, marked for art, not life. I run a severe police regime over twelve hundred comprehensive school kids—and over myself. I long to die.

Her left hand counts off another finger. I think of my many

headmasters: the sadist in Australia who caned and groomed me before he got removed, the humanist who giggled as he slippered me when I was eight—who also got removed, the one I worked for who spent his hours detaining the pretty sixth form girls. And there were good ones, too, of course. The war hero, the caring, inspirational ones. Headmaster and Father: two sides of the same coin, Janus, looking out, or menacing in.

That sixteen year old Spring I hardened myself, like an armoured knight. I'd have no more love, no more depression; I'd never again let my feelings wrap so comprehensively around a dream. For what else had Jennifer been, what Lydia, but incursions of unreality. And from where? Why, from my own imagination. How cocksure was I suddenly at beating the mind. Oh, yes, I passed my advanced maths and sciences and switched sides. I demanded peremptorily they teach me Art—it was to master these same foxing illusions.

And then I was born to paint; that was obvious, even to me. How I took up with a friend of Lydia's—her name was Anne—asked her to marry me and felt violence all around me, my own, for she agreed. I went to art school, grew my hair like a girl's, my beard like a man's—hermaphrodite. And how should I know, my friend, in my ridiculous condition, that I kept George Brede, my tutor, dangling sexually on a string. People hinted, but I was deaf to it. All through the political action, the famous Hornsey Sit-in—we spent it together, George and I, and talked for hours—I never once realised.

'Never?'

'He was difficult, tetchy. I could deal with him.'

'As a woman does.'

The wind gusts. Pine needles patter, the same long, paired spills we've been lighting during our harvest to smoke the bees.

'And—let me ask you this as a psychiatrist, Owen,' she says, 'your own sexual fantasies?'

Stubbornly female, Theo—including where I was female myself: older women, younger women, female fellow students, shop assistants, anyone and everyone.

'Like any man! But for the missing male. You were still cross-dressing?'

I turn away. 'Only in my head.'

Theo, there were more depressive episodes, but my sexuality was sewn up, wasn't it—by my engagement to Anne. I was safe. From myself. For life! But when we did get married, her unsatisfied arousal... We were both virgins, after a fashion. Both twenty-two. I couldn't paint. I hated my job. I told myself I had what I wanted.

'You didn't like her?'

'She punished me. For wanting sex and for having it. She'd blow up any time—a minefield, walking on eggshells. And I didn't fancy her that much. But I couldn't leave her.'

'No?'

'I was afraid.'

'Of?'

'Afraid she'd do something unstable, put herself at risk. Kill herself—she seemed to imply it.'

'And still you married her.'

'Precisely because I could *deal* with her... her antipathy. I *knew* it somehow. I *didn't* see all those tricksy lights around her: no *phóta*, therefore not a dream, not cursed imagination, but something more *manageable*, duller, more real, so I thought. Yes, her consistent inconsistency.'

'Like your father's?'

'And because I was looking for punishment? I could deal with that, too. Because I was guilty? Because I had no idea how to find anyone else? It's a terrible thing to do. Don't you think?

'Did she love you?'

'So she said. But then I said I loved *her*. I told myself I *would* love her, if only I could get her to stop... being so punitive. I tried. And then I fell in love with a student.'

'This Lily.' She looks at me piercingly.

'Before Lily, Marta.' And now I truly shake my head. 'You see? I *am* guilty. I *am* a... Because I had *form*. Never mind the one I married, I'd done it before. Before Lily, I mean. Evil, it's ingrained; and this is just what I meant, this... This is exactly the point at which the boy, the victim turns into the man; the former excusable, the latter unforgivable.'

She hesitates. 'Tell me then.'

Yes, tell. *Face* it. Not so easy, though—now we've got there. But I've taken the wager. And so, resigned, I begin disclosing an episode I've kept tight and never un-scrolled.

But then a strange thing happens, Theo—a phenomenon indeed. For as I open the tale of this, my first, and, as I'd always thought, clearly illicit adult relationship, that must, you'd have imagined, brand me *unsavoury* to say the least... My God, if the complete reverse doesn't happen even as I recount it! For, in the bright light of day, the whole affair quite changes shape, loses even the force of an 'affair'. In fact, the more I own up about this new Anne—her name intriguingly the same as my first wife's, her style incomparably different... I say, the more I reprise in front of Marta these feelings and events I've believed to be so culpable, and that I've never dared tell to anyone before... the less I can find wrong with them. I'm incredulous!

In brief, Theo, I began by thinking she was an infatuation: like Jennifer, Lydia, because, once again there were those lights, and I couldn't imagine sex with her—though she was reputedly sexually active... No, the plain truth was, I didn't want anything from her at all.

'Nothing?'

'No.'

'Not in your heart of hearts?' The hornets are round her, inquisitive. They nudge at me. I blink and flinch away. 'They hunt live bees, Owen, not honey.' She dips her finger again and licks it. 'She was how old?'

I follow suit with the honey as a heavy, droning creature flies almost into my mouth. I hold my nerve. It swerves aside, and I close my lips, chase the intense sugar hit with my tongue, swallow.

'She was eighteen, nineteen. I don't know.' The truth in painting; all I wanted was to paint. All I wanted from this Anne... I explain to Marta about Hendrik Thijssen's *Klaartje Van der Laar*, a woman who inspired some of his early work. How this forbidden Anne is somehow all about painting. How I tell myself this is Jung's *anima*, the painter's dangerous inspiration, and I said I'd never fall for it again. But I'm twenty-three; I can deal with it, because it's only in my head, and she's a key, the missing key, handed to me to unlock my art. She doesn't even need to know.

'A key? An imaginative phenomenon and absolutely nothing else?'

'You think I'm bending the facts.'

'Are you?'

'What would be the point? We both know I *have* to tell you the truth. Blurring it would defeat the purpose, because *I*'d know, and the guilt is what *I* feel.'

If I did want something from her, Theo, it was to talk. But I couldn't. She wasn't under age or anything—but she was my student. *And* I was married. A substantial breach of boundaries. But how much more did it feel than that. For she wasn't just off limits, she felt *categorically* forbidden—almost by divine injunction, like knowledge itself. I could sense, yes, real peril; it was something fearful, like a pact with the devil.'

'That fellow again.' Marta looks puzzled. 'You only wanted to talk, and yet you felt possessed by the devil?'

'In whom I didn't believe. Or did I?'

'Did you?'

'I said to myself, what could be the harm of something confined hermetically to my own mind?'

I look down and then off towards the distant bay. 'That's what offenders do, isn't it, Marta. They try to justify themselves.'

'Owen…'

'What?'

She checks herself. 'No. I want to hear this. Of how wicked you are. The first artist not to want sex with a muse!' Her eyes sparkle, her smile's mischievous. The hornets are gone, but the rasp of other insects steals from the trees and my stomach's tight, my breathing shallow.

Yet I can't uncover any wickedness, Theo, no matter how much I tell: of Anne's obvious feelings for me—yes, hers for me. And of my hopeless failure to believe in them… Of my scrupulous professionalism, my iron insistence that true love was for my wife and this was just a secret phantasm… Of our one brief conversation months later after she wrote to me and we were both free agents…

'You never even held hands?'

'We hardly knew each other. Did I like her? Did she like me? What on earth had she ever seen in conventional, uptight, still-face-attacking, still-sexually-self-compulsive me in the first place?'

'Oh, Quasimodo, without a doubt. For heaven's sake, she saw someone kind, and different, perhaps from other young men she'd known. Someone maybe charismatic…' She registers my expression. 'Well, there must be something! These beautiful, traumatised women throwing themselves at you!' Now she fixes me with her gaze. 'And even I, too, a happily married lady doctor, letting myself spend these hours with you, a little entranced, yes—if just for the moment—as you spin these stories of your life. She saw what you saw in her, a kindred soul. And maybe on some level she saw that you, too, were hurt.' Then she laughs, '*Ai*, Owen, take away the paranoid guilt and it's Jane Austen, so English, so genteel, these young people, a dance of manners: their eyes meet, they languish, they write letters.' She has her head in her hands, shaking with laughter. The hornets are back.

'I felt guilty, Marta. I don't know. "Love?" she'd said. "You mean intimacy?" she'd said. "Yes," I'd said. It ruined everything, mentioning sex.'

'You *didn't* mention sex!'

'A swine. A pervert. I'd already virtually described myself to her as one. Yes, I believe I sabotaged myself to her fairly comprehensively. *And* I told her I'd felt possessed by the devil. Because of her!'

'How could she resist you?! But you didn't do anything *wrong*! You just ruined your chances by being so… girlish!' She clenches her fists, '…by being, *da*, in your anxiety… *da*, *distvitlna*, you do shift strangely from role to stupid role—look at all the contradictions—and you must indeed have seemed to her, even as you burned with love, a soul so… cold!'

—which our cold maids

She straightens up. 'It's alright. I'm not cross with *you*. I am cross with… with what was done to you. That it left you like this. Oh, when you began telling, I thought, poor boy, he must have committed something, like when he was a child—he must have done in turn something that had been done to him. But not even holding hands! And you've been tormented by this and kept it a secret. For how long? For years and years. A tamer saga it would be hard to imagine. *Ach*, you were *both* such babies, only a few years of each other. You were *both* troubled. You fell in love a little. Or maybe it was just the symptom of an unhappy marriage, too soon, too young. That's all. Don't you think? And neither of you knew how to manage it. You, least of all, with your self-hatred, your dissociated sexuality. But you behaved impeccably, Owen. *Impeccably*! Do you see that? Do you know that? Can you understand it? Listen to me!' She holds my shoulders a second before turning away to mime comically banging her head against a pine tree.

'But then I did it again, didn't I. Don't you see? With Lily.'

'Oh, he's a tough one! He really doesn't want to give up! Alright. And you went straight from one to the other, did you?'

'No.'

'Well, then. We've heard enough for one day. The court rises. You shall tell me tomorrow.'

And still, Theo, excitement impels me, and I can't conceive of sleep. There's a physical pain, as though some tectonic plate were about to shift, my back, my neck—my stiff, amnesiac neck—the head prohibiting the body, the muscles shaking loose then clamping excruciatingly tight, then momentarily freeing themselves, only to lock up again. But I can't wait until morning. Even after this prodigious labour at the keyboard, text on image, you might say, and though it's well past midnight, I must go immediately and paint. The portrait, it's here. I think I can do it at last.

31

Subject: **Seascape — with cephalopod**

Neither can I wait for dawn. I'm up and working — studio lights full on against the dark outside — on three portraits at once, three wooden stands beside each other. My Bledlow face is taking flesh, my young man's bone structure and preliminary layers of colour. In the nude of Julia, I begin to appear, implicitly nude myself and lying close behind her, my hand smoothing her hip. And on the right hand easel, which solves, I realise, the anchor piece on the far right side of the commission, I've begun a close up of my face as it is now. Oh, for that hand of Rembrandt, who could relish these lines of age!

Yet, to tell the truth, each of these three images has something still stubbornly imprecise and undefined about it. At this stage, I can't clearly see my way with them, the medium sticky and uncooperative, still fighting back — reflecting the uncertainty in which Marta has left me; or rather my own sticky, melancholic layer of doubt regarding the outcome of all this.

Marta has surgery this morning. She'll pick me up at twelve.

For my part, I have Eléni's departure. The hired Toyota truck arrives at nine. It's driven by a full moustache called Themistoclís. The sign on his vehicle spells out, typically, fittingly, '*Metaphorés* — Removals', and I begin helping Eléni with her things — her *prágmata*.

'There's absolutely no need, Owen; I can manage, thanks.'

'It's alright, I'd like to. It's the least I can do.'

'Christ Jesus!'

'What's the problem?'

'If you must, then.' She clicks her tongue.

Most of her clothes and personal effects are in a large cabin trunk. The rest is an accumulation of boxes, canvas bags, rucksacks and suitcases. And her computer. We stow these smaller things in silence. Now the driver and I hoist the cabin trunk on to the Toyota's flatbed. It's a substantial weight. 'Maybe I'd better come down with you. You'll never lift that off again, much less get it on to the boat.'

'He'll *drive* on, won't he.' She indicates Themistoclís and regards me pityingly. 'Or whatever. Nasir will help us unload. Or someone on board. That's all it needs. The Athens end is taken care of.'

'I guessed it would be.'

'And what's that supposed to mean?'

'What it says, that's all. I was assuming you'd be met.'

'I shall be.'

Themistoclís slams up the tailgate. '*Endáxi?*'

'*Ne. Evcharistó.*'

'Well, that's it, I guess,' I say. 'I'm sorry it had to be like this, Eléni.'

'Are you?'

'Of course.'

'Even though you didn't waste any time finding my replacement?'

'Pardon me?'

'I knew it, Owen. From the moment you turned up at the door with her. The three of you.' She glances at Nasir. 'So all that fuss…'

'Fuss!'

'Yes, fuss. And the so desperate need for help. Two months!' She looks stonily at me.

'Out of seven years,' I say again.

'Where is she now?'

I'm taken off guard. 'Gone. With her husband.'

Eléni checks for a moment. 'Oh, really?' Her voice carries genuine surprise. Then she picks up her handbag. 'Well, I must be going, too. Ready, Nasir?' She calls out to him.

I should explain, he's coming back with Themistoclís when they've unloaded at the quayside and got Eléni installed. He speaks to her in his own language.

'Don't mention it. The least we could do. Wasn't it, Owen?'

I lean to kiss her cheek. 'Goodbye, Eléni.' Her skin's soft and cool. I've forgotten the feel of it.

Themistoclís sees her into the cab. He and Nasir squash in, and the door slams shut. The engine growls into life.

I wave until the truck turns out on to the roadway. Eléni waves back without smiling. Her face betrays no emotion.

I return to my studio, but now my thoughts turn constantly to yesterday's extraordinary shift in my perception, and, with mingled excitement and apprehension, to the coming appointment with Marta. 'Impeccably', she'd said. I behaved 'impeccably' with Anne. But then there's Lily, and that, to me, remains damning. And so the two student cases, Anne and Lily, which have flashed back and forth in my head for most of the night—now innocence, now guilt, goodness, evil, like an incandescent strobe-conscience—are brought centre stage in my head.

I leave the portraits and go down to the cove. There, on a rock, not far from where Nasir was first washed up, I sit in my sun hat and stare out to sea. I have in my hand Nasir's first few drawings. They show his boat—overcrowded, out of Smyrna, probably—chased by a Greek patrol. Searchlights, gunshots, the capsizing, the heads of drowning people. I admire the crude little scenes that I'd like to imagine as Islamic miniatures, subtly forbidden—but which in fact owe most to some American comics we bought him.

I look up from his work. In the distant haze, a heavy freighter ploughs northward. Nearer at hand, one of those hired Turkish pirate schooners emerges from Vromólithos Bay.

Nearer still, a snorkeler: I notice the lazy beat of his fins, little splashes of foam as he rounds the jut of the coast. He turns his course towards me. Now his breathing tube cuts the water just a few yards out from my rocky edge, and he enters the shallows, stands suddenly dripping, ungainly in his huge flippers. He carries a spear-gun in one hand and, in the other, an octopus still impaled on the harpoon shaft.

'*Yiássas*.' He lifts his face mask and glances up at the sun.

'*Yiássas. Káni zésti, étsi then ine*—hot, isn't it!'

'*Ne. Zésti*.' Holding the octopus by its tentacles, he pulls it off the little trident spear and smashes it five or six times against a rock. Then he takes off his fins and makes his way on up, turning in the direction of my neighbour. I, too, return up the path.

I can't settle, of course. I catch, midway, the smell of goats and wild sage, borne on a languid gust across the bluff's spiky growth. It's a smell that moves me, but I scuttle indoors to write this to you, Theo, because I'm on tenterhooks until Marta comes.

32

Subject: Lily

We drive straight down to Ksirókambos, the village in the southern segment, whose narrow bay, I've heard, is guarded by miniature islands, and whose little shrine to the Virgin is wedged into rocks: where a fisherman once found her icon lying—and got bitten by a crab into the bargain. *I Panaghía kavouráthena*—the Virgin of the Crab.

We've no time for that. Just before the village, the one road has improbably split, and Marta's uncertain which route to take. She phones the honey team, but no reception, or they're all too sticky to hold a phone. She asks instead at a nearby house.

Meanwhile, I shelter from the sun in a roadside church so small I have to stoop to enter. A brass lamp bracket hangs from the ceiling, two silver candlesticks rise from the floor; a tiny square of light blazes from a window in the thick wall above the altar table. The hint of incense drifts over a miniature iconostasis, with an array of little religious pictures.

I'm as uneasy with these as ever. But there's a subject I've never seen before. Quickly, I dart my head back out of the open door; and it's as well, for Marta's already beside the car, looking about for me. I beckon her and return to my diminutive picture, pulling out my glasses to examine it.

It shows a rocky defile: there are those random symbolic cliffs and crags, of course. Then a bearded man in a gold halo—Jesus, surely. Yet I'm still puzzled, Theo, because his hands and feet are pierced, while he wears an earth-coloured robe and holds by the hand an old woman and an old man. And he's lifting them—as in a kind of double Lazarus event—out of tomb-like boxes. There's an extra detail, too, bizarre: his feet are on small floating planks in the manner of snowshoes, angled wildly, as though he's just failing to walk, or surf, across dirty water. A whole crowd gazes on: even John the Baptist among them, apparently, and some kings.

'Owen, we'll miss them!' She must duck inside the church with me.
I point. 'What is it?'
She straightens cautiously. '*Íne i Anástasi*—it's the Resurrection!' She looks at me as though I'm as dim as the quiet light. Her finger

indicates the stylised red lettering above the central figure.

'What resurrection, though? Surely it's Christ who should rise from the tomb. For that, we need a garden, sleeping soldiers. As in Piero della Francesca, Tintoretto, Perugino—anything you like. And Rembrandt, didn't he…? Or there should be Mary Magdalen and the stone. So what on earth's all this?'

'All this,' she says pointedly, 'is not *on earth*. All this is… what should I say, Owen, the central moment. Don't you know it? Of our Orthodox belief, Owen. If you're Greek—or Russian—Owen, this is why Easter is the greatest and most important of our festivals.'

'I know what Easter is, Marta,' I spike back, nearly banging my head on the way out against a naïve *Last Judgement* painted on the wall over the doorway. 'What I don't understand is what it's got to do with floating shoes and a man and a woman in boxes.'

She explains as we drive. It's remarkable, Theo. Western iconography has no idea of this image. In fact, it's astonishing: a manifest of the invisible. It's one split grain of time, the precise unseen historical moment of transformation—of history itself. Look it up. Google it. Jesus is in the underworld, and the rocks show the valley of the dead. That's because he both *is* dead—and *isn't*. He's *in* death, Theo, in a cave—hence the marks of the crucifixion. But those snowshoes on his feet are actually the gates of hell, which he's trampling.

And what I took for some sort of decorative device, a blue shape, a womb or shell that surrounds him—Marta calls it a 'mandorla', the symbol of heaven itself, she says—at once separates him from the underworld and makes him available to it. And the folk rising from boxes are Adam and Eve, having died in due course of nature and long gone into their own tombs.

I'm fascinated, Theo, by this underworld, offstage moment of the *Anástasi*. It's when he's suddenly not dead any more. It's when Jesus can now stand up and reach out to them—to Adam and Eve—across the boundary of the mandorla. And they can reach out to him; their hands pierce it. So they suddenly emerge into life, too.

Our art knows nothing of this moment. Am I right?

But how pregnant that it should turn up just now. I've had time to think about it, of course. Do you see? Everything about the world suddenly changed. It's the historical point from which *recovery* became possible: Adam's, Eve's, everyone's! I mean, of course, recovery from 'character'. Theo, before the split second shown here, you were always who you were born to be. But after... Can you see? After this, it became at least *theoretically* possible to throw off our entombment as literary 'types', our burial in stock family roles. For surely all the roles of theatre are imprisoning and sad, the masks of mental disorder, no matter for their grins or antic clowning...

I mean how, instantly, discontinuously, suddenly, it became possible for us all to emerge from our 'fallen' families. Theo, listen! Before this moment, I'm obviously a chronic depressive and paranoiac—and that's that. That's my diagnosis. I have permanent doubtful gender identity and once during a bout of mental illness brought forth a few vile and slanderous mid-life accusations about incestuous abuse, unfairly incriminating my blameless father. Apart from that, I remain for ever a kind of Paris fool or would-be Pagliaccio still ridiculously pining for a lover lost thirty years ago. That, Theo, was my 'genetic' destiny. Bio-medically, conventionally, I'd have been stuck with it, quite incurable.

But, Theo, *but*, after the recovery of just this *one* body—I mean Jesus—from overwhelming *evil*, from extreme cruelty inflicted, historically, wounded observably, I mean recovery in this moment, as a real time event. This man, tortured, potentially verifiably, until he died...

Soon enough, we spot the van. It's on the hillside above terraced fields. But the team wave to us that we're too late and should stay put. They jolt the vehicle down over the rutted track, and Marta turns the car around. We all follow the road back to the unit, where everything is as yesterday: the tedious uncapping of the honey cells in their frames, the sudden whirr of the steel centrifuge and the hygienic bottling, over and again, of a flow that seems never to run dry. The women chatter; the men joke or look disapproving, the official inspector takes notes on his clipboard, and Marta, with her doctor's bag from her car, injects those who have stings. I, in cap and white apron, take my turn with the heated blade, or help swab the floor, or carry out jars on pallets to be labelled.

And I'm five or six. It's morning. Ah, God, the flashback comes authentically, as though I've known all along and merely misplaced the memory—for a season, for a lifetime! I'm on my parents' stripped bed, alone, in pyjamas—or not. My father has just gone downstairs. My mother, of course, is in the kitchen, has been there for some time, making our cooked breakfast. I, in the white, unmade centre of the sheet, am shaping my parents' bolster and pillows into a tight ring.

Sexually charged, I'm hurling myself, wolf-like, again and again upon the symbolised orifice.

Here and now, Theo, my eyes fill with tears, because — except to a dyed-in-the-wool Freudian — this is so wrong for a child of that age. And the next minute I'm sitting right inside this pillow-sculpted shape, this anus, this ring, saying the Lord's Prayer, as though somehow to seal off my erection and make it subside, along with all the tumultuous accompanying feelings. That was my first installation, Theo, my first and only: a toroid. My God, *the* toroid!

For when my mother suddenly appears at the door and catches me at it — which must be the reason I remember this scene at all — she's taken aback, and asks what I'm doing.

'Nothing.'

'What's that shape you've made on the bed?'

I tell her it's a 'medium hole'; for I know the controls on our cooker, and 'medium' means 'middle': not 'top', and certainly not 'bottom'. So I explain away my creation. And she tells me to hurry up and get dressed, because breakfast is ready.

Yes, I recall I needed often to build a 'medium hole' in the centre of my parents' bed, ah, quite often enough in the mornings of those days, after my father had left to go downstairs. And surely we must note how readily the family contrives not to ask, 'Why?'

For the medium hole becomes almost a family joke, a kind of amused acknowledgement from all concerned, Mum, Dad, me, that I require a certain time on my own some mornings, before I, too, can come down to breakfast. I needed it, Theo.

For the medium hole, this flashback I've held flashing in my mind all day until I can secure it in writing to you, I believe is even the very act of my amnesia. Beyond doubt, almost, the desperate, physical and material invention of a clever kid to blot out and encircle — with a secret religious magic and blind artistry of pillows — what has just happened, so that it all seals and goes away into another realm altogether. This structure that symbolically reveals and re-enacts the assault becomes a mere 'objective correlative', that in the process of its making seems to cast violation away from the self, from the mind, and into art, into the formal beauty, you might say, of a pure shape, an attitude, an urn.

Theo, in my central nude of Julia in my studio, I made perspective room for love, a space for memory. I began to paint myself in, and now here's a fragment of recall come in to my mind, too, clear as day.

Did that astonishing little icon back there in the church spark it?

I've brought fruit for Marta. We sit and eat before the others finish their work — because the only hives left are her own, and she's arranged to meet Cóstas there after siesta. For a private harvest, so to speak. And so this time we drive to the little amphitheatre instead of walking, both to fit her schedule and because she's exhausted. Yet she insists we go. We park the car on the downward slope.

And we leave behind its air conditioning in order to thrust ourselves a third time into that semi-shaded furnace on the wall under the pines. Yet my heart's sinking, Theo, and I'm sure things will go against me, because the excitement of the flashback has cruelly given way to an inexplicable self-hatred far heavier and more condemnatory than before.

She sets the honey jar between us. 'So what happened, Owen, between the one student and the next?'

My mood is so low, indeed, I can hardly bring myself to speak, much less to recall. 'Between Anne and Lily. Anne... the experience changed things, I suppose.'

'Your feelings. You discovered you had them.'

'Well...' It's suddenly all such an effort. 'She wasn't pusillanimous, like me.'

'And?'

'I guess I was motivated by the experience. Once my first marriage had gone down. To get out and start living.' My voice sounds drained and far off, at odds with anything I'm saying. I make myself continue. 'To meet people, go places. For years I'd been hiding, afraid of everything, violence, other people. Suddenly, because of Anne, I could *aspire*, artistically, politically. And imaginatively: I began the inner exploration which seemed so perilous at the time: to travel down into the unconscious, to find... yes, I did find the first inklings of memory stored in the body. But I didn't understand them.'

'You identified with Anne. You became her.'

'Maybe that led me to Julia,' I said. 'But Marta...' The truth is, I can barely open my lips.

'Very well. Then Julia.'

It's the heat, maybe. It's too much. 'Marta, we... Can't we give it up? I'm not worth it. Why are we doing this, anyway? It's obvious I'm guilty. And that's why she's gone. I'm merely wasting your time.'

But why, Owen? Why? Why do you still insist on casting yourself as the villain?'

'I've told you. Because I did it again.' I say. 'Because... because I found other girls attractive. Because, now that I think of it, I went out a couple of times with another former student. You see?'

'Former. You said former.'

'I bumped into her somewhere.'

'How old was she?'

'Twenty, twenty-one.'

'Bah! It shows nothing—except limited horizons! Please! You're a man. You find girls attractive. And they you. It's the way of the world.'

'A serial offender.' Dry, grating words. 'Like when I was a child!'

'Owen!' Marta swears in Russian. We face one another. Now she brings the jar from its place on the wall. She stands in front of me and makes me take a scoop. She takes one herself, and we feast on the stuff, and I can't concentrate, can't make out why I'm still so seemingly ungrateful or even doggedly oblivious to the fight she's putting up, prepared as she is—through heat and extreme tiredness, and even in the midst of fighting tooth and nail for everything she's doing here—to go the distance for me.

'Very well,' she says again. 'So we come to Lily. But first I tell you again there was no repeating pattern, because there was no pattern between the two, Anne and Lily. Only a twenty-something girlfriend and *that's-another-story* Julia.'

'Julia and I. I really thought we'd succeeded back then, Marta. But forces I hadn't bargained for... I thought she'd betrayed me.'

'Yes?'

I came back from Paris, Theo. And of course Julia was out of the question. I was still angry and disillusioned, and so I just tried to blank her out. I fell straight back down into another teaching job. Then there were various women. But either they weren't interested, or I wasn't, and I was stuck, and every bid to be myself now seemed to have failed, and the hippy-style therapy I was doing in London led precisely nowhere, and all I could see was a charmed upbringing full of golden opportunities that I'd simply squandered through weakness of character. I was as Dad had always implied: no fibre, backbone. I guess I must have been cripplingly lonely. And then I looked around me, I suppose, and saw Lily.'

'Lily.'

'She was very public about it. That she fancied me. She even got warned off—she told me later—in case she wrecked my career. But bad men always say they were led on, don't they.'

'Are you saying you were led on?'

'No.'

'Well then.'

'I talked to her a little about painting. She had a certain insight, and I persuaded myself. *Why* is this happening here, I reasoned, like this — *as if* in a pattern — with this second student? Is it a *real* Faustian bargain this time? Or simply the artistic choice of Dionysus over Apollo.'

Insects in the dusty vegetation contrive a lull. Mocking sounds fill it from further off: a truck cornering in the village of Lépitha below, even the rattle of a yacht's anchor chain far out in Lakkí Bay. My old stings throb.

Marta sighs and perches on the wall. She dabs her brow. She's weary, Theo, and exasperated. She looks into the distance. 'I don't know anything of this Apollo and Dionysus,' she says. 'I don't know what you're talking about. Right now you're on Léros, with me. *Ímaste káto apó ta tíchi tou palioú kástrou,*' she slips into Greek — 'we're beneath the walls of the old castle, somewhere up there, and it's our honey harvest. And once upon a time, just once, Owen, you behaved unprofessionally. You breached a code and you took the consequences. Did you break any laws?'

'No.'

'Then what on earth...? Have you broken *any* laws, *ever*?' She eyes me cannily. 'We shall exempt Eléni's illegal cousin, of course just lately. What was his name again? Billy...? Perry...?'

I catch on. 'Oh, Paddy.' We stare at each other, and I feel my own eyes widen. Then she smiles, and an unspoken agreement hangs between us. 'Nasir, actually.'

'Ah, yes. Apart from Nasir, then.'

'I've always had to be *good*, Marta. The family stakes were so high. I've broken the English speed limit now and then, but not by much. And I once shot out a couple of street lamps with an airgun; but I was only a kid.'

'Then you've become an exemplary citizen — tediously so. And yet you feel so guilty you can hardly show your face in England.'

'Yes.'

'And you came here to this island where no one would find you.'

> — *A goodly one, in which there are many confines, wards, and dungeons*

'Yes.'

'With someone who — like your first wife — discovers a way to

392

punish you.'

'Eléni, She's so young. She looks young. Surely, I've done it again. Did it, actually. She's just gone.'

Her eyes widen, her nostrils flare. 'Do you know what most men would call you, as to these younger women?'

I'm blank, so confused, still convinced my crimes will rise up and condemn me.

'Lucky!'

The wind gusts, and pine needles rain down around us. But she can't convince me. Guilt won't, it can't, let go. 'Any sexual approach to a woman... Something wolfish takes me over, and then I start telling myself the artist must break convention, man must seize the fire, or he's nothing. But later, when I open my eyes in the light of day, I'm horrified...'

'Owen! That feeling *is* desire! That's all. It's you, only you were so sexualised that now you don't recognise it. You're a man; you feel desire. You attract women. What's wrong with that? Listen! Eléni's an adult, a grown-up. It's normal. I have to be blunt, do I? To spell it out. Do you find yourself drawn to minors? Do you fantasise about children?'

'Good God, no.'

'Do you haunt school playgrounds? Download child pornography?'

'Of course not.'

'Then I repeat, where is the problem?'

Surely, we're talked to a standstill. I should go home. No sane man would force the issue further.

Yet Marta makes no move, and I feel compelled to fill the vacuum, though my words are directionless as the broiling hour itself. 'Mitchell tried to get me to reach out,' I say. 'He said adults should aim to use words to manage their relationships, not body language. You can be close to people if you know that: if you give clear statements yourself and if you respect theirs. He encouraged me to go ahead with Eléni.'

'Of course,' she snaps. 'Why not? But when *you* get close to someone, it's suddenly not Apollo and Dionysus but God and the devil. You think you're damned!'

I blunder on. 'I'm not a moral relativist, Marta. I believe in the law. The law is to stop us hurting and causing harm to others. Well, there are wicked, bigoted laws, like those against homosexuality, like the old American race laws.'

393

'And like laws made by horrible mad dictators. Yes, yes, yes. Those excepted, of course. And stupid censorship laws. And vicious, crazy patriotism laws. And laws to keep the poor enslaved. Putting those aside, too, I suppose. And laws to watch everyone and monitor every email and store everyone's DNA—I may live on an island of no account, but I can read the news online, Owen. And your point is...?'

'My point is that generally, Marta, generally in a healthy society, the law is positive. And, alright, taking up with Lily wasn't against the law. I'd lost Julia for good. I was surrounded by attractive young women. I remembered my guilt and hypercorrectness over Anne. I said to myself, I'm not going to let that happen again...'

'Sure. You... fancied Lily. Forget all that intellectual talk—you were just horny. And angry!'

'I may have been. So there we are: I *am* corrupt. Not passion at all but some other warped emotion.'

'Damn you, you're *allowed* to be horny. And angry. To make mistakes. You're *expected* to misspend your youth—an artist! That's what you're saying, isn't it? Your painting—so Lily unlocked it. And all went on from there. End of story, Owen. I assume the marriage broke down at some stage—but so do many marriages. What else do I have to say to convince you? Why do you still feel so bad about it? *Why*?' She grapples a fistful of loose stones from beside the wall and flings them at the ground.

Then her face changes, her gaze becomes abstracted. 'Wait!' She turns back to me, eyes suddenly wide. 'Faustian bargain, you said. A real Faustian bargain. There's something you have not told me. Isn't there, Owen. Something about Lily.' She eyes me sharply. 'I am right, aren't I. Admit it!'

'Admit what? I don't see... There's nothing I can think of. As far as I know, I've told you everything. We got together. We conceived Chloe. We got married.'

'And then you could paint. You painted Lily. She became your muse in turn.'

'No.'

'She didn't?'

'It didn't happen that way.'

'No. It didn't, Owen, did it.'

I seek to defend myself. 'Well, she was nothing like Anne, as it turned out. Certainly not like Julia. And no, there was no meeting of minds; quite the reverse. Don't get me wrong. I don't for a minute step back from what I did. I chose Lily, and she chose me. And as for becoming an artist; it could never have happened without her. We needed one another. We were somehow marked for each other—at that time. I believe that absolutely; but it wasn't how anyone could have imagined. Certainly not me. As soon as we started, I was all the more trapped. I couldn't paint a thing. I was too busy being... punished, as a matter of fact. So there we are.'

'You said nothing much happened at work.'

'Not punished by the college. By her. By Lily.'

'You said she wanted you.'

'She did. But... She was very damaged, terribly abused as a child; it wasn't her fault.' I hesitate.

Marta insists. 'Yes?'

'Okay. If you must know, she split dramatically. Lily did. None of it was her fault.'

You see, Theo, I hadn't intended to go here. Really, I hadn't. It's just Marta worms the truth out of me.

'You knew this history of hers?' she says.

'She told me. The first time we went out together. I think I'd heard something before anyway, and then forgotten. You see? What does that make me?'

'Human. What did she do?'

'Things. It doesn't matter.'

'What things?'

'She couldn't help it.'

'Couldn't help what? Are you protecting her?'

'No.'

'I say you are.'

We stand off, like two prize-fighters, who, bloodied nearly to a standstill, sense the next exchange will be decisive. I heave a sigh. 'Alright, Marta, she broke me down. We lived together from the start; we kind of had to. That's when it began. Every night, she kept telling me how I hated her and wanted her dead. Over and over. For hours. She tried to force me to murder her. It was like some demon had hold of her, and of me. She'd kill herself, she said, if I wouldn't do it. And she kept going to the window, to jump out—or whatever. Because that was what I wanted. She done it before, she said. Jumped. She insisted over and over that her death would be to please me. She would have made me her killer—and the baby's. And I kept holding her back, physically. I could only try to keep assuring her I didn't want her dead. And that I loved her. And, yes, it would go on for hours, after midnight, back and forth from the window—we were three storeys up—until I cracked.'

'Cracked?' Her eyes are stony.

'Became desperate, broke down. Wept. I don't cry easily, but there had to be tears, forced out of me, and they had to be genuine. Then at last she'd tell me she didn't mean it. She'd tell me I knew she'd never meant a word of it, and it was alright. She'd laugh and embrace me. And then I'd be so grateful, and so fond of her. Except if I recovered too soon she'd start all over again. And only when I'd been truly driven to the limit could we go to sleep. But, you see, if someone hadn't broken me down... I'm so well-armoured, you know. If she hadn't done it... then I'd never have met Mitchell. I'd never have discovered...'

'For God's sake!' She's furious.

'Marta, it was obvious what it was.'

'*Alíthiá*—really?!'

'It was her own grief. I could see that. I thought at first she was genuinely suicidal. Then I realised at last after many repetitions that it was a kind of unconscious ploy. To make me cry the tears she couldn't shed herself. But I could never be quite sure, of course. So I always had to... to take the threat seriously. Always. Night after night. And it was complex, too. Her stepfather had done such wicked things to her; so now she could turn the tables on another man, one she had at her mercy. She wanted revenge, it's completely understandable. Understandable, that then and throughout our marriage she did everything she could to destroy me. Abuse—no one spoke about it back then. But I... I learnt at first hand through Lily right from the start—years before the whole business came to public notice, before Freud was exposed, even—just how devastating it could be to a child. To her. What that bastard did to her! It made me try above all to guard my own children—from men, from anything like that. And from her, of course. But she was also testing, wasn't she. To see if I could really love her. She couldn't help it, Marta.'

Marta remains silent, her pressed lips barely containing the emotion. She looks piercingly out towards Lakkí, taps one foot.

'And, you know, in the mornings I was almost glad, a little light-headed. All my childhood I'd had this conviction I'd grow up to be tortured, and was afraid that when it came to it I wouldn't be able to... to behave honourably under duress. I mean while it was going on.

And now, I thought, it's come true, it's happening. Melodramatic, I know, because there was no physical pain; it wasn't real torture. Of course not. But it did at least add up to an image of it: the constant sleep deprivation, night after night, the emotional, psychological stuff, to be brought again and again really to the edge of despair. And I thought, this must be it, the torture; here at last is the future I've been psychically foreseeing all this time. And look, I'm functioning, I'm coping, I'm going into work as though things are just fine, doing my job, earning money and fixing up a home for us. It *is* a test. Of course she's testing me, breaking me, trying to make me retaliate and beat her up, murder her—and I just have to bear it and survive, for her sake. And in due course, for the children's.' I wave my hands as if to include the bleached, oracular land. 'Because I knew then, and ever after, that she was trying to destroy me. Yes, she really was, in every possible way. In truth, I've never felt so hated.' I stare into the distance. 'But I can't expect you to believe me. Domestic… That's the kind of thing men say to try to excuse themselves, isn't it. It's women need our sympathy in these issues, not men. So you must think I'm twisting things, or—even if you do believe me—that I deserved all I got.'

Her brow's thunderous. 'You were bathed in guilt, I suppose—now your expectations had all gone wrong.'

'Expectations?'

'Of the marriage, of course. Your artistic gesture. It had backfired, and you were "all the more trapped". You say. Carrying on at work in a climate of disapproval, I'd imagine.'

'Pretty much. Yes. That's what I mean. In the cold light of day…'

'And this… punishment. Perhaps you enjoyed it?'

Now it's my turn to bridle. 'It wasn't some game. There was nothing the least arousing in it. She played for real; it was life and death. I loathed it. Her face would change, her voice.'

'The splitting you spoke of.'

'Yes, as if that bastard would speak through her. A he-devil, I thought.'

'That again!'

'Yes!' I'm really cross. 'Possession! Evil! Whatever it was that *had* used her; whoever *now* worked through her!'

'But splitting at will? Just, like that? Dissociating in the middle of the night just because she felt like it?'

'Yes! No. What do you mean?' And at once the answer to my own question is like a bolt between the eyes: the logical detail I've conveniently forgotten, or not quite added in, until this moment, the detail that makes sense of it all. What can I say, Theo? What can I do but own up, cough up the accusing fact of it, with my own anger suddenly drained away. 'No, Marta. Not because she felt like it. Not that at all. It was because we'd had sex, of course. She was split by sex. By me, Marta. Don't you see? I was re-traumatising her. She was responding to it *as if* to abuse.'

And yes, Theo, I remember how even at the time I *did* put the simple two and two together to make four. What was it but her violent dissociations right back then that ended any excuse of an "artistic gesture"? What else was it but the all too obvious connection between our intimacy and her nightly episodes that proved I was no better than the original perpetrator. Because I'd conformed exactly to the former pattern of her life: the betrayal by an authority figure. That was why her whole schizoid defence system had mobilised to attack and subdue me — because *it* recognised me for what I was.

And that, I believe, Theo, is why Marta's now so angry with me. She's fished out the unappealing admission and finally sees the truth.

She's beside herself, it's true; anyone can see that: 'A man spoke through her, you say.' Her tone is icy, even in this heat.

'Yes. That's what it felt like. When she kept threatening suicide, I felt I was dealing directly with him, the man, her stepfather. It was like he — the fiend, the abuser — was threatening to kill her if I didn't...'

'Didn't what?' Her tone is abrupt.

'If I didn't give in. If I didn't start to hate her, hit her, abandon her.'
'Did you?'

'No. I wanted to, often enough. Look, I'm trying to be honest. She got so beyond reach. Nothing I said could make her stop. But if I'd done any of those violent things, it was obvious we'd both be lost. Do you see? Forever. The world would be lost. So she, and my struggle with her, were suddenly the spiritual dimensions to my life. Finally I had a purpose: I could do this for her — to pay off the harm I'd caused.'

'Do this? Do what?'

'Endure. Love. Take it. Soak it all up. I set myself to bear it, to survive. For her sake.' I hear my weak justification. I remember the window with its difficult starlight, the darkened bedroom, the single bed. And I remember the invisible made manifest in Lily's horrifying transformation. Greece, India, every culture has its demons, in art or drama. Lily and I, Theo, were as in some Christian 'interlude'. We were maybe as in some folk memory still infused with hook-toting, fire-crackling agents of the underworld leaping up from below stage to where the fraught soul can't see God, nor his angels, for smoke. And here in my extremity of writing I can no longer for the life of me unpick true devils from Parts dressed as devils, dressed as Flea. I can hardly tell one Father from another...

'Arrgch!' Marta stands up, incensed. She stamps her sandaled foot and yells some Russian curse that ends in '...*blya*!'

'Thank you,' I say. 'I wanted your judgement; now I've got it. You've reached very patiently like a surgeon into the heart of the matter, and there's no way I can pretend otherwise. My self-disgust springs from here, Marta, and it's entirely justified. I *am* guilty, and you've done an amazing job to keep me reminded of it. Just for a while, I'd hoped things might be different. Clearly, since the event, I've succeeding in fudging the evidence, probably deliberately. If I'd kept matters in focus, I needn't have bothered you with all this. I really have wasted your time, Marta—three days of it—with such an inordinate rigmarole of a confession. It's served only to muddy waters that are, in reality, perfectly transparent. You're right to be angry; there *is* no way out for me, no *anástasi*, no resurrection. I am what I am and had just better live with it.'

She faces me. 'No, Owen! No!' She turns away, stamping again. '*Ai*, you pair of babies. That's the tragedy of it, *schízate o énas ton állon. Chorízate o énas ton állon se komátia!*'

33

Subject: An unknown saint

Theo, twenty minutes ago I could write no more. I clicked 'Send' and went upstairs to bed—now that Eléni's gone. But, weary as I am from the three days of honey harvest, from intensive painting and from writing so, so much, and so furiously, sleep still eluded me. For the shocks of what transpired in this conversation with Marta have turned me this way and that. My sheet's soaked with sweat, because everything really has changed.

Or has it? I can't tell. My head's a-whirl. What could I do but restart my machine and look up that enigmatic pronouncement of hers—in a difficult language. *Schízate*—past tense: 'you (plural) split'. *O énas*—nominative: 'the one'. *Ton állon*—accusative: 'the other'. *Chorízate*? Had I heard it correctly? Another word for split?—past tense: 'you (plural) put space between'—space as in *chóra*, I suppose. But then *komátia*…?

'Parts, you fool. You split *each other*. She split you as you split her.' Her voice, almost a whisper. 'An adult would have told someone. You could have got help.'

'And who would have believed me? *Me!*' I point hotly to my chest as a gust of wind brings pine needles pattering all around us.

'She, Lily, was crying out to be stopped. This dreadful cruelty of hers—oh, yes, it is profound, prolonged violence, if not of the physical kind… She needed help. She saw in you… She heard… Something in her saw that you had the… the potential to help her through her wretchedness. But you felt too guilty—you know it, Owen. You felt too guilty to open it up. Don't deny it. I *see* it! You and your damned paranoid guilt!'

I'm blinking at her.

'This Christ-like suffering of yours. You didn't have to do it. If you want the theology… Oh, for pity's sake, *he* did it, Jesus, so you don't have to.'

We stare at each other, and the wind gusts again.

'Your horrible endurance, Owen. It's not adult, it's the Child.' She groans, looks away and puts her face in her hands. 'And so Lily: she saw in you, too, the perfect victim.'

An image flashes into my mind from the left hand pictures. Yes, in their whole gamut, the Child, where he appears, is always grey-white with his arms outstretched, like some figurine from a crucifix. I recall watching myself paint him, the motif constantly suggesting itself in the process, the artist—myself—half aware, half not, in some kind of trance.

'Marta?'

She lifts her head only to glare at me.

'I'm sorry. I'm confused. I'm the bad guy. Is that what you think?'

'Oh, stop, for God's sake! Stop going on about it! Forget the guilt! Forget the sex! Who gives a damn what consenting adults do in private?'

I draw breath.

'Well, that's what you both were,' she says. 'Wasn't it? So you got her pregnant, so you got married. Good! Or whatever. Who cares? I tell you the sex is irrelevant, Owen. What you did *wasn't* abuse, no matter what you say. It was professionally "out of order", and then you got married. Lots of things are "out of order". People aren't saints. But you! You come here to tell me about your women, your life, and then your noble suffering, like some dark age hermit. And why? Because you hope I will set it in the balance against your oh-my-God wickedness. Because you think it redeems you. It's nothing but pride, Owen, spiritual pride. And it covers up what? Cowardice! Think about it! Your children! Yes, think of them, damn you! You should have told someone. About Lily. Alright, there were no bruises to show, but you should have got help. Except that you were *afraid*.'

I nod.

'Don't just agree with me!'

'What, then? What are you saying?'

'Owen.' Marta stands up. She finds her bag and picks it up, packs away the water bottle and the honey. 'It is late. Cóstas will be waiting.'

'I'm sorry. I'm really sorry.'

'No. It's okay. It's fine. Understand? Fine. Stop apologising. Remember, I'm your *friend*, not some therapist. There's no time limit, except we might now and then have other things to do.'

'I'm very grateful.'

'Owen. Look at me. It's okay. I'm not angry with *you*. Just… just the *bloody* tragedy of it makes me so mad.' She rolls the English swearword on her Eastern tongue. 'Did it ever occur to you she saw you coming? Did it? Not all maidens in distress wait chained to rocks, you know; some walk their dragon on a lead. You were being re-traumatised as much as anyone, Owen. She was splitting *you* by this ferocious... onslaught! And you let her!'

We get into the car and begin the drive back, the seats intolerable, the sun not a whit less savage for the hour just passed. The aircon hisses, the afternoon re-embraces us in its extremity, and I'm dazed. She coasts, her feet on the pedals, slowly down the hill towards the village, as though reluctant to conclude matters. Yet the silence between us is a membrane.

She breaks it. 'We have a great painter in Russia: Rublyev, his name. Andrei Rublyev, an icon painter. *The* icon painter. He was from hundreds of years ago. A monk; they've made him a saint, I think. You in the West have your bad boy artists; we Russians look for hermits, yes, madmen, monks. We always have. Maybe that's why I got angry. This grim endurance of yours; so very familiar, so very Russian. We're soaked in our suffering—and my God, how we've suffered, it's true. But then I'm a doctor.'

'A remarkable one, I should think.'

'Maybe. And maybe it's my Soviet training; at least that was good. Maybe it's my... Whatever, I'm not pleased with suffering. And I think this is why I'm happy in Greece; though I think we're now about to suffer very much—economically, and in every other way.' She turns to me and laughs suddenly. 'Listen. Your Lily. She must have experienced something very bad indeed.'

'Yes. She told me everything, and it truly was terrible. Sometimes, she *could* weep. I tried to help her; help her to feel better about herself. We went through it all together.'

'Poor girl. At least you were kind to her.'

'I guess I'm probably making my stuff with her sound worse than it was. Just to let myself off the hook.'

'No, you stupid man. I don't think so for a minute.'

There's a hold-up in a narrow cutting between two houses on the rough slope—the school bus in dispute with a bin lorry. We have to wait, and it feels to me one of those times when everything is perpetually shaken and turned upside down. At last, the bus moves on ahead of us, and we, too, squeeze past the bin lorry.

'Did she change?' Marta shifted gear. 'Did the punishment decrease? No. You said she broke you down.'

'It slackened off a little after our daughter was born. It was no longer every night.'

'Once she had complete control over you.' Now the bus stops again to let a child off at another house.

'Not *complete* control. I tried to keep standing up for what I thought was right, especially over the children—even if it meant taking a beating, emotionally. I didn't always succeed, but I honestly didn't see what other options I had. There was an incident, five years down the line—it doesn't matter what: she was ordered to have psychotherapy as part of her sentence. But that all fizzled out.'

'You let *yourself* be broken down.'

I rehearse for her the rest of the details, Theo. How she'd keep threatening to endanger herself, and the children. How for years I had no money in the relationship—I was earning it, but had none. How I quit the college job to try selling insurance, hoping that if I showed myself ruthless enough, she'd come to respect and love me.

'The Stockholm syndrome.'

'It was a fiasco.' How I just scraped back into a temporary teaching post; of all the possible places in South London the one where I'd first been so troubled by Anne. How Iraq invaded Kuwait, and I kept having to get signed off work. Then more strange coincidences, until an angel pointed to darkness in the East. How at the worst point, I gave Lily an ultimatum just hours before Bush senior gave his ultimatum to Saddam. Messages from the TV—how I was glued to the war, and when she went for me, I'd only give name, rank and number. 'It was delusion. Or perhaps not.'

'And that was when they took you into the clinic.'

'No. I still didn't cave in. There came a time when I judged both children were just about old enough to hear that things were wrong. It forced the issue, and Lily had to agree to see someone with me—because the children thought we should try. She was hopping mad. We had meetings with marital therapists, and I thought then, Marta, that now at last I did have an opportunity to tell someone what had been happening. But even as I told, they didn't believe me. You see? Nobody knew much in those days what abuse can do to people.'

'Of whom are you speaking?'

'Lily, of course. It wasn't her fault. None of it was her fault.'

She doesn't answer. We're nearing the hospital. In the distance, a giant ferry boat enters the mouth of the bay. Dwarfing everything, it glows, glints and disrupts the proportions of the landscape. She stops the car to look at it, then rubs her stings through her jeans. She sits beside me on our narrow stretch of road, frowning down her straight nose, her regular, slightly heavy features wincing a little. Her brown hair falls from her straw hat and lies upon the collar of the man's checked flannel shirt she wears. Its tails are tucked in at her belt—as though the bees are still a threat—her waist cinched in. The jeans, the trainers—the whole ensemble is highly inappropriate for the sweltering afternoons I've subjected her to these last three days.

But she's never complained. And though her anger seems past, yet I'm as anxious as I'm befuddled and believe the verdict could still go either way. So now, cocooned from an atmosphere almost too oppressive to breathe, I wait to know my fate; for surely some pronouncement, some adjudication must come at the end of all this.

Yet we drive on again, and a little further, and the wartime crane that marks the region of the hospital looms into view, and still she says nothing more; and I begin to wonder whether the great risk of these afternoons—I feel it as such—with their potentially life-changing gyrations of perception, will simply fade without consequence into an image as small and inconsequential as that little icon in its little shrine down at Ksirókambos; and will, after the dust settles, resolve nothing.

For now there's a call on her mobile. She takes it, her other hand on the wheel. She speaks quickly in Greek. Something's wrong. She signs off the call, throws the phone at my lap and accelerates. I'm pressed back into my seat as the car shoots forward between the white houses of Skáfia.

Subject: **An apparent corpse**

Emergency it really was, Theo. We're careering up the track towards her hives. They're above the town, you remember. We've raced—if not at breakneck speed, then with all dust and precipitousness—along the narrow main street, through the square with its cyclists, tourists, shopkeepers, around the tight, blind corner that leads on up to that magical nook where she keeps her bees, only to see ominous clouds of black smoke over the hill before us.

Look! Our honey van is tucked under the tree at the entrance to the dell. But blocking it in are two other vehicles: a municipal fire truck and a military pick-up—the on-board water tank marked with camouflage. Marta gives a cry, and I sense the air troubled and unstable even from a distance. Certainly, we meet jags and sudden, incomprehensible lines like one diagram of rage as we draw up. It's bees, flying in thousands

We get out and brave them past the fire wagons. The honey van's windows are tight sealed. Sweltering in the passenger seat is veiled Ylka — the amnestied Albanian who works at the hospital. She mouths at us incomprehensibly. Enver, her husband, gestures from the wheel. Behind them, in the back of the van, white-clad figures crouch. But insects buzz us, hit us, land on us. I twist away, glance through the bee storm to the hives. Two are toppled. Water hoses run across the boxes and on up the slope. At the ridge crest, I make out uniformed figures against the blown smoke clouds. And now a fire-fighter stumbles back heavily towards us out of the nearest scrub, holding his long handled beater like a weapon. He shouts, points accusingly at the van. Then he yells and thrashes one-handed at his arms, his thighs, his face, panic-dancing to sudden stings.

I guess at the causes of all this. Nothing so very terrible: our team simply caught up and delayed in a fire action. But it's enough. The bees are disturbed. For how should firemen know that their heavy hoses, laid hurriedly through the dell — along with all the booted coming and going — would create such havoc.

Marta calls to me. The van's back doors are suddenly open. Someone is helped out of it, down past the fire tender. It's Cóstas; I know the suit. Yánnis is on his left, bearing his weight. Enver steadies his right. The heat's suddenly intolerable, as though tongues of flame from the still distant blaze lick all around us, about to engulf. But this is illusion. The nurse, Iríni, panicking, protects her face. Bees, concentrating, streak and hum, seemingly from all directions. I bat them with my hands — until we stow Cóstas in the back of Marta's car. Yánnis and Iríni get in on either side to prop him up. I slam myself into the front seat as Marta shunts the vehicle round in the tight space. Now we jolt urgently, crazily down the track, tyres skidding in potholes, windows wide open to clear the bees.

Now Cóstas shivers on her surgery couch. His right arm shakes. His hand clenches and unclenches. Heaters go on, even in this temperature. Great globes of sweat show on his brow, his cheeks. Then his chest locks up; he breathes in gasps; he starts to convulse. Marta cuts and rips away the bee suit, his jeans, his shirt. The damage is lurid, appalling: stings have gone in around the tops of the thighs, around the eyes, the neck, in the ankles, the wrists, all swollen and inflamed. The rest of the skin is deathly pale. Poor Yánnis is beside himself. Marta has him stand ready with blankets. Iríni monitors the

405

blood pressure. I, supernumerary, hold the temperature strip across his forehead. Now Marta injects into the exposed buttock: adrenaline, cortisone, anti-histamine. Yánnis covers his friend with blankets. We can only stand to our posts, like guards beside a bier, alert in our own sweat. And wait, our attention glued to our readings. We pray we're in time, for he's inert, almost a corpse, the shape on the surgical couch afloat on death.

Theo, it takes a full forty-five minutes before the reaction subsides — anaphylactic shock. For, when one bee stings and dies, a pheromone coordinates others, and so the attack grows stronger and more determined. Even an experienced bee-keeper, who might normally think nothing of a few stings...

Apis mellifera is no Hollywood killer bee. Cóstas would never have flailed to earth under a carpet of swarming, clinging bodies. Something less graphic; but no less deadly. The body's immune system simply overwhelms itself — catastrophically.

So how relieved we are to find him come back, stir and move his head. Come back from death. Rise again.

Another minute, he sits up, nods to Yánnis. He reaches for a cigarette. He shrugs. He lives, and the scene humbles me. What are my preoccupations compared to this battle for our friend. Indeed, I might have caused it — delaying Marta with my vast and selfish tale, making her miss her own harvest.

But perhaps, my friend, that's just the habit of blame. For who could have predicted this concatenation of events. And Marta herself is remarkably matter of fact, now Cóstas is out of danger. 'The harvest is in. *Íne kalí* — It's good. Whether it is enough, we can only hope.' It's she, would you believe, who insists we carry on.

'What? Are you serious?'

'Quite serious.' Her face is set. 'We made a deal, I thought. You're not shirking, are you?'

She fixes strong coffee. We sit out in the little town garden behind her house, under the fig tree — the scene, almost, where I first met Spíros at her party.

But, for a long time, we say nothing. And though the fig tree shades us, my doubts resurface. I fear her eye. No smile, no clue, no slip of comfort in her face. And yes, it's hubris — mine — to elevate mere qualms to life or death. To take up her time, her attention, her manifest powers of healing with my paltry metaphysics. I must prepare to take my own medicine.

Now, at this time of day, heat merely irritates; yet we court discomfort, perhaps for Cóstas' sake. Sweat stings the eyes, but what's that beside his swollen sockets, red, envenomed lids. Did he complain?

At last, as though reading my thoughts, she begins. 'Yes, very well, my dear Owen...' She pauses, only to start again. 'But you must remember I speak only for myself and as your friend. I'm well out of the current of these cases, only a woman on an island, trying to pick my way through information you have yourself so kindly given me.'

'I know that.' At once I'm on hot bricks, keyed up.

She shakes her head. 'An odd kind of healing, that turns my surgery into a courtroom. 'Well, so be it,' she says. And at the commitment, her voice heightens and her speech begins to broaden. 'But this is between ourselves, Owen, here, isn't it—*étsi then íne*—far from anywhere, and is life and death, so to speak, only to you. The wider world will never hear what *we* say. *Ai*, to be human—and isn't that to be split at least in some degree from how things are. This interests me, as a woman, as a psychiatrist. Both Freud and Jung spoke of the unconscious. But the honest study of abuse rewrites the notion of character: the identity, the overall *presentation* of the person—say to a clinician. Do you see? To speak of character not as a given, but as a hard shell, perhaps. Character as a kind of mask, through which various voices might speak...' She smiles. 'You might call it cognitive behavioural therapy taken to the extreme: about how we think, but also about the *family* of our attitudes. That's one reason why I listen closely to what you say. My dear.'

She eyes me, meaningfully, Theo, and slips, softly and almost without appearing to do more than muse to herself, into the great speech with which she has now left me to digest, and left me also amazed both by her reach and her grasp. Yes, *character*, Theo: to speak no longer of *traits* or *contradictions* within the *nature* so much as conflicting *voices* within the *being*. No more of inanimate forces and drives, as in the quasi-biological world of Psychoanalysis, but as of *sentient players*, or *actors*. No more of repressed mechanical urges and hidden desires or drives. Indeed, no more of that nonsense. Henceforth we return to judging people by what they *do* and leave off that fascist practice of trying to label what they *are*.

Here, under her fig tree's fat leaves, I sense the heat just slacken. The air may have changed, and the shade is suddenly delicious. I notice how shrubs in containers drop their flowers, yellow, blue and

407

pink, over the coping of a wall.

'Do you remember,' she says, 'that moment yesterday when I felt there was something you weren't telling me, about Lily: the Faustian bargain. I felt, in that instant, an inward joy, Owen. Because it wasn't simply a flash of intuition—I mean like that sense we sometimes get from just listening very closely to a patient's speech. No, it was more. I think I could *see* your condition as I did when I was a girl in Russia— the little 'talent' I had that made me sure I should be a doctor. The one I later lost, by the time I'd finished my training and was married... Yes, Owen, it was as though—it sounds strange and foolish, I know, even a little romantic... as though virginity, that mysterious quality... I glimpsed it somehow restored to me, and I felt as though my own dear father was present, standing just behind, looking after me.'

She smiles; there's a certain embarrassment in her eye. She looks down a moment before continuing. 'It would make sense, eh? That to speak to your lost self, I should need to mobilise mine! For we see now, don't we, that if you and Lily had lived happily and "normally", then you would have felt no guilt, because the matter would have been in adult proportion. Isn't that right, Owen? Don't you have to agree? With Lily's encouragement, you'd most certainly have left a job in which you'd felt so trapped. You'd have flourished and become yourself—no doubt as an artist. And she'd have flourished, too, even if the marriage had not survived, because everyone would have been themselves and free to choose.

'Why, this is the picture of love,' Marta went on. 'You wouldn't have felt guilty at all, I think, even if the sequence of events that led up to your marriage might have been exactly the same. There are plenty of oh-so-similar marriages between teacher and student to prove it. And therefore we agree now, I hope—surely we do agree, Owen—that it was far more likely to have been Lily's treatment of you in your, what shall we call it, agoraphobic complicity, that mobilised your childhood sense of guilt, rather than your original behaviour to her. Or your previous involvement with another student, which was all along quite different and so ultra-prim and correct that absolutely nothing happened at all!'

'Yes, but...' I look at her, shaking my head. 'Marta, was I right or wrong?'

'It's clear you were confused. You are still. You acted improperly with Lily. But you didn't do so in a secret or guilty way, and were quite prepared at the time to face the consequences. Well then!

Engendering guilt for sins uncommitted or for sins that are not sinful we leave to the Western churches, don't we? Yes, I'm speaking to your deepest self. I'm speaking to the you that wants to recover, which is the true self, in your case buried beneath the chalk of Bledlow, the absent ego you once spoke of...'

Theo, are these her words, or mine? How could she know anything of Bledlow? The voice I'm creating in order to transcribe her words... Yes, of course she speaks now through my typing hands, and bids to appear in my internal gallery, like a missing corrective, a bright figure high in the iconostasis, seeking to appear—no, now clearly visible above the field and already lending strength to the embattled arm...

'...not those who have some other agenda, like the Father. No, he can simply be quiet and listen. Maybe I was aware you were speaking with two tongues from the moment I realised I was doing the same: my scientific self and my virginal magical self!' She laughs. 'Nevertheless, the scientist must be satisfied. I'm an advocate of rigour. Exposure to sunlight is most healing!' She laughs again, and a sudden hot gust stirs all the stems, the breeze with its fiery fingers... 'Well,' she says, 'it's always the crucial medical decision, to intervene or not to intervene, and when. You've told me things. You felt at such a young age so sexually wicked. Is it helpful to say it back to you?'

'Very much.'

'Your guilt over Lily has kept you locked in the past, has kept your art, too, locked in the past—along with its "Parts". So your face, covered in isolation and shame, was unable to appear in the contemporary world.'

She looks directly at me, the figure in the icon with the sword arm raised, the poised weapon glinting in divine, shadowless light. 'But, Owen, speaking entirely for myself, you understand, I can't see so very much to condemn you for, certainly not the kind of thing that could put a brand upon you, as you tend to do for yourself. No, you seem to me much like any man or woman, neither walking saint nor abysmal sinner, but in between. And that's my verdict. I say this even though you do seem still to shake your head and struggle with what I tell you. Why, you're almost like one of those who'd confess to any crime they come to hear of. Perhaps you have. But what do we find in your so-damning confession? I repeat, nothing so very terrible. The self-exposing, cross-dressing boy and the guilty, self-punishing man merely show someone very unhappy. And someone who wanted to talk. With Anne, say. Ah, with Julia. With Lily, even. That you should

409

have thought it so wicked to want to talk—that speaks volumes, don't you think?

'And love, Owen. I've been listening to what you say. Syphilis. Depression. Possession. It's *love* that's forbidden you. Isn't it? Perhaps at your little Spartan school they showed you love by their firmness and security. Perhaps that did save you. Maybe your father saved you from himself—for a crucial time—by sending you there. We cannot know. But, Owen, I believe this meeting is why you made this journey and came here to this island. Yes, I do believe it, even though everything about your case—your X-ray picture, portrait, call it what you like—appears problematic, ambiguous. It could be this; it could be that. Everything is not as we expect to see it, or have been taught. You throw a spanner in many works, Owen, and that *is* a heavy fate. And I see, too, your perpetual confusion, as the Parts have been a chaotic alchemical mixture, tangled together and occupying only the left hand, while the right looks for an absolute determinant. Where shall we find it? Nowhere, I think, except in the love of self that enables the love of our neighbour. But enough of this. You can paint desire. You can approach the woman who will love and not punish you. I find you guilty—yes, but not of the beast you thought you were. You once disobeyed and stole knowledge. You have paid the price. For your cowardice and complicity in the matter of Lily, you must make reparation; say, to your children. Beyond that, you're free to go.'

Theo, the night's almost over. The house still throbs with heat. Eléni's noisy fan, the machine we bought to give Nasir a chance of sleeping—though in truth it makes little difference—is humming at my shoulder. Our whitewashed walls seem almost to sweat: my forehead drips, my tired eyes sting, my blue-white screen is almost soft to the touch and my fingers skid and stick on the plastic keys beneath it. Soon the sun will rise again, and the temperature, I don't doubt, will be notched still higher.

Yet I'm exalted. Dare one speak, yes, of a cure? A cure of the seemingly incurable? The paranoia has gone. A miracle? I chose, I threw the die, to slip out of these shades into a different world—in which I no longer feel under eternal durance, but catch a glimpse instead, the faintest glimpse, of innocence. Have I wrestled for and installed Marta's voice? The notion of innocence, an almost blindingly joyous possibility…

My friend, I've recorded our conversation in all its detail—and by that become its author. And there, not so far above the line you're scanning now — if indeed I've not exhausted you, too, along with your patience — her words persist. They persist in an English she couldn't possibly have spoken. Why was I so urgent to reach this place in the account where, after everything, they could be set down? Because now, in front of both of us and in order to face down the constant vile insinuations of the Part called the Father, I've transcribed the first speech of the Angel.

34

Subject: **The card players**

Lily phoned. My father's dead. She told me while we were discussing Arun. Had I heard, she asked?

'How should I hear?'

'Oh, I don't know... How do you feel?' Her voice over the airwaves.

'I'll have to wait and see.'

'Only I thought you might have been sad he wasn't in touch with you all this time. That he hadn't been there for you.'

Sad? *There for me*? I'd told her all the clinic details, Theo, right at the time. So why on earth should she suddenly think I wanted him to be *there for me*? Odious phrase! I didn't want anything to do with him.

'I just thought... Do you think your mother knows? Do you want to tell her? Or shall I?'

'But I'm not in touch with her, either. You *know* the score, Lily. If you're in touch with her, that's your business. You can tell her what you like.'

Theo, it turns out Lily's been in the habit of sending Dad birthday cards: 'Only to keep him up to date with his grandchildren'. She's been sending birthday cards, Christmas cards to him, all these years! And he's been sending her money. The latest of these... communications prompted a reply from Dad's poor wife: No more birthdays; dead two months.

Subject: **A letter**

No, exactly. A league, you think? Anyway, I walked into town, and there was a letter in the post. I took it up to the castle. The sun already had desert breath off the Sahara, and it made me look North-West, as if for the flames of Athens, or at least smoke plumes in the haze. Hardly — they're a couple of hundred miles away.

The letter was from Arun, Theo, and nothing could have been more strange or welcome — his sincere self-appraisal, his genuine desire for rapprochement.

412

I hurried home. I've worked hard all day on the self-portraits, and the matter holds, the man emerges. It's a joy! I can do it! Nothing is finished, of course. But the overall design; believe me, it's almost there. My head's aflame with ideas; the floor's all messed up with spilt primer! Now every second counts, it seems—and this urgent writing, too, once maybe as I said just a species of supplement, becomes integral to the paintwork: as in the tale of Minalouche and Marie-José, destined for the right side of the project, where the Point of View hangs beside the great bed of us three.

What shall I say of this *ménage*, Theo? Our room without furniture near the Gare de Lyon; it had a desperate grandeur, a tall ceiling with two long sets of casement windows, through which the dawn struck like a brand. Waking, the one of us nearest would reach to throw the long casements wide, and we'd savour, like absinthe drinkers, the sun's now familiar burn on our green walls, the churn of the traffic outside, the nose of its unwashed gutters.

35

Subject: Gilles the Pierrot—after Watteau

Very well. Our great double bed was in point of fact an old Parisian bourgeois item of such iron and wooden construction I imagine the owner balked at ever getting it out of there. It had a huge stained mattress but no bed linen. When we'd viewed the room, you see, I and the two girls, the question of *who* and *where* wasn't even discussed. We were *friends*, Theo. We loved one another chastely across the sexes. I'd borrowed a sleeping bag, and the girls had their duvets. Where was the problem?

In retrospect, *mon ami*, I see it was I who set up and maintained this fable of innocence. I kept myself packaged, despite the heat. And Minalouche and Marie-José, in their bras and knickers, divided themselves with their quilts. We took turn and turn about for the sides and middle. For my heart was with Julia, and my continuing lusts I kept secret. And so we lived out my abstinence.

Here, in one dawn among many, Minalouche lies closest to the windows, eyes closed, mouth slightly open, her cap of brown hair on the grey-white pillow. See there her pale throat, her delicate collar bones, her discreet white straps on each shoulder holding the modesty of small breasts in lacy cups—and the rest of her nakedness draped in some faded Indian patchwork, because the small hours turned just cool enough for a cocoon. But now the sun inches over the rooftops opposite. It blazes on her faint snoring; and on Marie-José, next to her, who faces this way, her fine features occupying, with dark strands of tousled hair, the gap between the pillows. Look: the soft rise and fall of the cover. She breathes, and I, on the near edge, am zipped at least to the waist in my cheap brown bag. I loll out sideways.

Fiercer shadows: the straight line from the window frame cuts a wayward lilt over us all, and now the foreground floorboards glow in varnished perspective, and the right hand wall, that spiritous green, vibrates around the empty fireplace.

Sleep at once impossible. Windows flung wide, we're at bright ablutions. Sun here on Minalouche drying between her toes, on Marie-José soaping her armpit—the raised female limb wet and gleaming at the old fashioned sink by the door. I pull on my resolute cotton

414

trousers over the tights I shall wear to rehearse. We face away from each other. We wrap a towel around, as on any beach in England.

Stale bread and coffee. Minalouche smokes tobacco from her tin with the potato slice in it. I sketch her. I sketch Marie-José fussing, a little on edge, with her rinsed underwear. She hangs them out on a string.

Naïve, and controlling... Yes, I must have been; for, as I've said, this is a purity I've imposed on them—not wittingly, but perhaps insistently for all that. I was deceiving myself.

For there came a day where all surfaces turned sticky. Even the lightest cloth clung damply to the skin, and every movement was an effort.

Nevertheless, the company performed that evening, and we all ate afterwards at Cécile and Félix's—a cheap pasta meal from the great saucepan, whose steam virtually peeled the walls of their floral paper, almost blistered the paintwork on the sills and ledges. Gasping, listless, we sat with our plates. Spuriously, we quenched our thirsts with cheap wine. My two girls and I crossed at last the Pont d'Austerlitz and waded home through air so stale we could only look at one another, sigh and laugh.

More wine, Theo, up in our room with the windows tied open. Minalouche and I rolling a cigarette each. Then we took turns to brush our teeth, splash off the sweat and prepare to sleep—in the same configuration, as it happens, that I described to you above.

Dutifully on my near edge, I pulled up my sleeping bag, but sweat dripped from my brow, and I groaned as I tugged at the zip.

'Owen!' It was Marie-José, nearly naked next to me. 'You'll kill yourself with heat—and kill me, too!'

I stared dumbly at my kapok and got rid of it. She threw her corner of duvet over my legs, and I lay beside her bare limbs for the first time.

All perfectly reasonable. But it was our custom to kiss each other before sleep: the peck of brotherhood, sisterhood, friendship. In the dark that evening, my kiss with Marie-José lingered on the cheek. Her hand smoothed my arm; her naked knee chanced against mine. No help for it: I slipped my arm under her, pulled her to me and kissed her lips, and in a moment we were greedily at each other's mouths.

Ah, my friend, the bee with the flower, the bear that breaks into the comb, the gods at eternal banquet: divine food and sweet medicament, too, alexipharmic balm for cares and all bodily ills—we lingered in our

415

kiss. And kissed again. And more. Oh, what it is to touch, be touched: her waist, her hips, her back under my fingertips — the wine — her thigh pressed to my own, and the heat, lately so debilitating, now an active flame. Salt, wine, ambrosial her breath, sensuous her hair, amorous that clasp of her straying hand.

What is it, Theo, this heavenly disposition of shapes and textures? The draughtsman's question: what's a woman's shoulder but a compact hemisphere, her ribcage bony bands, her buttock the swell of stearic tissue? Yet rightly assembled into one yielding, callipygous form — and with almost no latitude for error in line or shading — these elements possess such power to arouse. The desert blooms, the wilderness turns paradise, when, out of solitude, we meet another.

Two anothers. It might have come from one of our own comic scenes: for there, of course, only inches beyond Marie-José, lay Minalouche.

But we were quiet. So Harlequin fumbles Columbine beside her snoring father; so Valentine woos Eugenie under the nose of her drunken duenna. And, for a moment, I kidded myself Minalouche might have tumbled straight to sleep.

'Ah,' muttered Marie-José, her whole body suddenly flinching towards me. 'Owen, you'd better come in the middle.'

So I did. And found myself kissing Minalouche. Then returned to Marie-José. And then simply back, and forth, and back, and forth. And so I ended up — how shall I put this delicately — a woman on each leg!

36

Yes, and energy drives colour beyond boundaries, thrusts line across space. Well, I was in the great city of Art, perfectly placed, at last, to *come into my own*. It was the very career opportunity, perhaps, that I'd envisaged when I left England. Why, I could *launch*!

I had only to choose which girl.

A judgment of Paris indeed! To my left, compliant Minalouche, to my right, assertive Marie-José, each, as my fingers told me, in equal readiness. Theo, I was staunchly erect, but paralysed in my tongue, that cognate member, because I couldn't say which one I wanted. I simply couldn't become the decisive man in the case, and turned neither to this opening, nor that. Which is why I include this scene.

For so our summer entered that dumb, entranced and imprisoning sweetness, when, for a few hectic nights, we stoked our passions, but left them un-slaked—as vain and decorative as the scenes, indeed, upon that Grecian urn.

Fear, scruple, 'delicacy', shame? Our ludicrous little satyr play has lain in the back of my mind, Theo, full of youthful bewilderment.

Naturally, I've told no one about it—at least, not in detail. Why bother? In the Courts of Contemporary Art, against embroidered sexual history, polymorphously fucking plastic figurines and transgendered prizewinning pots, my tame phallic dilemma boasts a shock rating of less than zero!

Yet I've decided to use it: yes, I've done most of it with my left, a small panel—you'll see from the attached—which hints at maybe Currin or Jeff Koons. And I feel in it now what I should have felt then: blinding, all-consuming rage. Rage at being ruined, crippled from the start; rage at seeing my every enterprise lose the name of action; rage at finding myself humiliated and punished if ever I did 'let go a bit', throw over the traces; rage at having to 'hold my tongue', trapped in my pre-linguistic *chóra*; rage at ending up tied, sirens and mermaids singing, to my own fucking mast.

Subject: **The king of the winds**

I know. But Marta's honey harvest! Athene's casting vote, her pebble thrown in! Just innocent enough, Theo, to show my face — no longer phobic — in the *agorá*. My friend, I'll need to get used to it — and to the notion that with me it really does end, this horrid vampirism, this behavioural disease, passed down in my family for... how long? Generations? Millenia? Or did it simply kick off with Dad's old man? What do I know, except *suddenly* my father's dead, and my son's back in touch. And *suddenly* I'm free!

I forget myself. The room with the bed — my final Paris night with the girls. For it couldn't last. We had a saint's day, I remember, good for audiences. But the company couldn't perform, as both Cécile and Dmitri had what looked like heat exhaustion.

So we'd been to church, Marie-José, Minalouche and I. We'd heard evening mass at the Sacré Coeur, and my thoughts retained that ivory and golden interior even when we stopped afterwards at a bar, where people danced outside, so heady the night air. I danced with Minalouche, she awkward with me and tentative. I danced with Marie-José, thrilled as always by the way she moulded into me, yet half-irritated with her, too. We danced together, and with others. And the soft evening wore away.

We dined in late: heating something from a tin on the gas ring by our fireplace. Then we talked and drank what was left of our whisky — while Minalouche and I smoked the roll-ups she made. Insouciant, as though butter wouldn't melt and nothing could have been further from our minds than the intimacy always to come, we prepared for bed; and Marie-José took longest, as usual.

It was only with three of us that the spell worked. For, once Marie-José responded to me, so could Minalouche. Heat flung the covers back; kisses and unfulfilling caresses grew more fervent. We kindled and stroked as though the night should never end, and we should become... what? The three Graces, three erotic Gorgons, three Graeae, still passing between them the eye of pleasure, the tooth of desire. We were a legend of intent.

But, oh! The vase broke. The dream shattered. How should I render it, Theo; what shall I say? Without warning and under my attentions Marie-José gave out a yelp: of surprise, we first thought. Then next she shuddered, relaxed and rolled away. Ah, then we knew, all of us.

Dream, perpetual arousal — Paris, precisely that drowsy, feminine state Blake named Beulah, that Palmer longed to capture in his moonlit, breezeless scenes of gum and sepia. A kind of transcendent, between-lives, Elysian, out-of-the-body time. Yes, so Paris had become at last. But it was in Paris at last that I met Marie-José, a sweet woman who was willing to have an orgasm with me, and I scampered away. Bolted.

I arranged to sleep on Dmitri's floor. Yes, she spoke to me the following week, Theo, after rehearsal, and I was still dossing at the still feverish Dmitri's; he and I getting on each other's nerves. And she asked me to go for a walk with her. Beside the river.

And we went to the languid Seine. We strolled around *l'Île de la Cité* under the eye of the cathedral—as I'd done with Cécile—and she told me how deep she was enthralled to these feelings I'd happened to set loose in her. 'Sometimes, Owen, I repeat them with myself thirty or forty times. In one session! This morning, even, in the little storeroom at the warehouse, lying across two sacks of lentils. I prayed no one would come in. Can you believe it? I'm abandoned! I'm such a scarlet woman! And grateful to you, Owen, for that, for showing me myself.'

The copper-coloured river hunkered down under the heat. What was I intending, she asked, earnestly.

'Carry on as now, I suppose. Shan't we all? Once Dmitri gets over his bug or whatever it is.' I was noncommittal and offhand, without touching her, of course.

'Ah, yes,' she said. 'Carry on as now. The show must go on.' She stopped. Looked down, the water oily and flat, hardly moving. 'How *is* Dmitri?'

'*Comme ci, comme ça.* He feels better.'

'And you've looked after him.'

I met her eye. I was struck by her expression—so struck, in fact, that it comes back now with full force, as poignant and full of hurt as then. 'It's the least I can do.'

'*D'accord.*' Still she held that gaze, until I looked away, abashed.

We walked on, and I held myself distant, trying to insist to myself nothing had happened. So we crossed the bridge and came in due course to Dmitri's, who was out, for once. I remember the sun streaming in through his window, and nowhere for us to sit but on his bed. I remember how Marie-José curled up those beautiful, supple legs and spread her skirt over them in a muslin circle. Yes, she was so glad, she said: twenty-eight, and the secret of her body… *Alors*, it had lain undiscovered, this elusive capacity for orgasm, even in her previous long affair with a set designer called Patrice. So grateful; her wide eyes flashed at me.

And, shamefully, I was neither warm, nor cold, nor amorous, nor disappointed. I was embarrassed. And so she went away.

And so, along with Minalouche, I faded, tongue-tied, into the scenery. No, that's even unfair on Minalouche; for she, too, spoke to me and tried to tell me something of her lesbian self, and I was unable to listen. Nor had I any idea who I was or what I wanted. I remained a blank, and so I blighted our scene with my ghostly note.

Except one incident, though—and that was indeed a flash, a profitable one that also explains these last quick sketches. For Dmitri had a liaison with some girl at the Sorbonne, and it was the same day I rejected Marie-José, yes, that he dragged us to a lecture at the École Normale.

'She tells me it'll be packed. But she can get us in. You must come. He's a genius, so they say. You must.'

And so we went, the five of us, not-well Dmitri and the student girl, and Marie-José, Minalouche and I, up to the Panthéon and the Rue D'Ulm. And there we saw him—with his compelling looks and shock of whitening hair that stood in waves upon his crown as though the wind still rippled it—and heard him speak. And I confess, Theo, I understood not a word, so abstruse were his concepts, so arcane his terms, so recondite the text—a dialogue of Plato's—that he invited us to share; to read so closely, with such attention, that no nuance of interpretation could escape him, no assumption in the world pass unchallenged. And I? Not one word did I grasp, I insist, though my French by this time was becoming passable for most occasions. For he seemed to spin new language out of old, broke apart its skeins and re-plaited them. Or melted them to phonemes, only to reconstitute some seemingly impossible substance, as though he were the very alchemist or high priest of lexis.

With the result that in my bafflement I promptly forgot him— forgot him almost the instant we came out into the City air.

Sure, I went back with Dmitri, because the girls scattered to this or that prior engagement. So we picked up bread and wine, *nous gamins*, and now Dmitri sat beside me on his own bed and sniffed the air.

'Who's been here?'

'Marie-José.'

'Thought there was scent. Why?'

'To see me.'

'Why?'

'Because I was sleeping with her and Minalouche. You know that.'

'All I know is you three got kicked out of somewhere. Sleeping with them both?'

'Only literally.'

'Did you fuck her today? Here, in my bed?' He felt under the cover. 'No.'

He made doubly sure, and then stood up, tall, a little wasted, still pale from his illness. 'More fool you.'

'It's not so easy.'

'*Quoi?*'

'The body has its own...'

'You couldn't do it?'

'No! I mean yes. I just didn't love her. Someone in England,' I said, lamely. 'Someone I'm still involved with. My heart...'

'You don't believe that shit of Félix's, do you? You talk like a girl.'

'What shit?'

'All that's over, Owen. Don't you get it? We're just skin and bone worked by pulleys, and what we do is entirely abstract.' He flicked up a silvery ten new franc coin from his pocket and caught it. 'This says you're soft left.'

And he began a bizarre doctrinal questionnaire—about what I'd be prepared to do in the cause of the revolution, and there was no stopping him. He was mad, I think; or maybe still delirious.

But I wouldn't be called soft, so made my answers as ruthless and radical as he seemed to want: bombs, killing—everything the Red Brigade or Baader Meinhof could do. And so he lost the bet, and the sad truth is I half believed it. I was angry and murderous—like a coil of hatred inside me. And it was suddenly like George all over again, or that woman I worked with, Rosemary Boyle, scooping me along on a breath of agitprop and a promise of masculinity that was never going to stand up. And here I was, telling myself once more that the age was modern, that Freud and Sartre were its prophets, and anything less would be to play into the hands of the reactionary torturers and neo-fascists behind the billboards of commerce. Which does have its points, I grant.

So we went out and got kippered together, Dmitri and I, on my 10 NF winnings—which you almost could, then.

And we drank because we were mad together, and because '68 was almost still in the air. *Liberté, Egalité, Fraternité*, I shouted. *Le patron a besoin de toi, tu n'as pas besoin de lui!* cried Dmitri. *Allons enfants de la*

Patrie, we both roared quite tipsily. And I was happy and made a night speech to the Seine about the colour wheel, the tone row in music, and the death of Painting. And the only person who heard it was the American, Dave, blown back by chance from wherever he'd been in the interim—India, or the Rue Mouffetarde. 'Do you guys have any grass?' Which was where I came in.

But now, Theo, now that I'm older and maybe wiser and realise just who it was I saw lecture at the Rue D'Ulm, I make amid these flames—my fires on Rhodes and Kos, on the hills around Athens—a last memorial, not of Dave or Dmitri and certainly not Dad... but of another D, a warrior of the intellect. Theo, I called him our Agamemnon. There, in that underworld babble of shades, amid the darkness, the arts nonsense, the gibber for blood, I looked for a father and found one—a man to admire. See! I've begun him in the style of the icon painter: script on image *Jacques Derrida*. His stance is in mid-sentence; his gesture passionate, photorealistic, yet stilled somehow into shadowless serenity. He is not, as in his later, obscurantist form, infected to the fingertips, if you will, with Freud. He holds, as befits a saint of letters, two scrolls. We'd say documents: *De la Grammatologie*, and *La Pharmacie de Platon*.

He, as the hero should be, and as my father was not, is gateway to my art, door to my faith. Forget his more idiotic pronouncements, the burden of his times. See only his linguistic demonstrations, pictured here: that the assumed hierarchy of speech over writing—upon which every philosophic project still rests—is a hypnotic sleight of hand; that writing precedes speech; that intentionality necessarily undoes its own text. Bear with this, Theo, for just as Marta collapsed for me decades of delusion and thus set free joy and rage, so Derrida, by hauling those most secret assumptions of reading out into the sun, collapses philosophy, collapses, too, the depressive graveyard philosophy always digs for itself.

And if that goes, then a new world springs up, that's also the ancient world, where choice—as in my choice to risk and declare all— changes not only my self-perception, but alters, too, the universe, at a stroke, and God is with us. And my rage is with artists who, finding Derrida hard, pretend he never happened, and with academics who, worshipping him, follow him up Freud's arse. Both betray art's religious function, which was, and is, to make us a doorway to the real world—not Science's world, not Plato's metaphysical ideal, but the living miracle of love and of the risen body.

I accept Marta's judgement. I'll act on her criticism and hold my head up.

Now, consider the neck, gateway to the missing loves, loves which should rise through spine, musculature, throat, blood vessels to enthuse the intellect, that lone attachment to a floating spar, amid all the pull and slide of our linguistic waves. The loves, including desire... I laugh, remembering Derrida on Rousseau's *Confessions*. Very candid *Confessions*. *Confessions*, Theo, in which the great Genevan places masturbation as a supplement to sex, *ce dangereux supplément qui trompe la nature*, until Derrida overturns his hierarchy from the text's own logic; and makes sex, hilariously but legitimately, supplement to masturbation! Yet, in the process, he treats seriously our whole question of writing, writing, writing—as a substitute for the *presence*, yes, of the beloved.

But, oh, that he hadn't still violated the beauty of his own case, seeing the beloved only through Freud's eyes and with Freud's nasty rubber stamp. Bastard! Bastard! Bastard F for both Fucking Freud and Father! Theo, this was Derrida's fatal error: that wickedly, horribly, like my own Dad, he ignored the sentient body. And that's why I insist on the four Greek loves—arising, I say now, each from *discrete* regions of our frame and *not* all from the sexual organs, as Psychoanalysis would teach. No, love is a holier, more originary spirit, that only makes Éros through the genitals, as Aphrodite was foam born; but, through the heart and guts, Stórge, our love of family; through heart and voice, Philía, friendship; and, in the noble head, Agápe.

Now when I could work no longer, Theo, I thought to find Nasir. But he'd gone, along with his few belongings and the little wad of money we'd agreed. And that explained why he'd touched his heart and nodded to me the previous night. And I was glad for him and thought of my son. And I went out past the pines to the road and then turned, following my intuition, down towards the port; and saw, between the twin heads of the inlet—its stern windows glinting in the low evening rays—the vast hull of the Blue Star ferry bound for Piraeus.

37

Subject: Icon

My canvases are crated, ready to ship. I'm attaching here detailed drawings and indications of the whole projected design, including the special homage to Spíros, and the 'Archangel Michael' image I spoke about some time ago. The painting of the first I've just worked up quickly for now; the other, you remember, is to appear over the whole construct, as if in the central raised section of an altarpiece. The under-work of it — the background of island hills and the rather earnest half-finished 'devil' figure — is perfectly safe to the touch.

But the detail on my current self-portraits, over which I confess I've spent most of the last two weeks — simply because I couldn't resist bringing them more or less to completion — will just have to dry off in transit.

That shouldn't be a problem, so don't worry: I've left plenty of space between the painted surfaces and the box, and fastened the images very securely to the woodwork behind them. They'll all be fine when they reach you, I'm sure of it.

As for the finished Bledlow portrait, you'll just have to wait until it arrives to see it. The artist as a young man, done 'warts and all', I believe: neither saint nor unpardonable sinner, but finally assuming his place in the canvas, and, by that, we must hope, in the world.

What can I say? I'm so relieved and encouraged by the feedback you forwarded from the buyers. They do seem genuinely keen. Tell them six months from contract and they can have the finished product, all done and dusted. It'll do just what they want — fill up the space, provide a big splash of colour and furnish something of a talking point. As to the meanings, hidden intricacies and shared crises by which the thing came into being and got itself done, well, nobody need concern themselves one jot about all that. Nor will they, I'm sure!

Theo, I can't thank you enough for all your hard work. Dear friend, I'll see you very soon on my visit, for now Chloe helps me pack. Yes, indeed — she arrived yesterday by plane. Right now, as I write, she's holding up one of Elpítha's four pretty gift-stones and wondering where she should stow them. 'Hand luggage,' I say, without hesitation. 'I want them with me.'

I still can't quite believe she's here. I beam, as I type, with delight. She and Matthew, they move into their London home in the Autumn. I'm glad. A provincial bind had once held her captive, she says, and I hadn't known, thinking all well.

Today, we've been to Kálymnos; I wanted to surprise her. The local boat carried us choppily to Myrtiés, where this time I made sure of a taxi—rather than subject her to any crazy walk across the hills! 'Póthia,' I said to the driver. 'The principal harbour of Kálymnos,' I explained to Chloe, 'on the island's southern side. I've never been; it'll be an adventure for us both. We'll have lunch there, shall we? And maybe something interesting will turn up.'

Thus I hid my extra intelligence, gleaned from an email which arrived this morning. And so we set off along the coast road under a bronze-bright sky, the abnormal heat slackening, the season restored—even a shower of rain last night, I believe—with rocky Télenthos jutting sharply out of the water to our right. The sunlight, the taxi radio's Greek phone-in, the popular songs and the road soon snaking inland and upward, between the volcanic masses: the same that on my former trip made me late for my appointment... all of these brought us swiftly enough to the head of the central populated valley that descends slowly again towards the port of Póthia.

But at the sign of Chorió, or Chóra, as they may sometimes call it, I couldn't resist asking the driver to stop. Land, space, the country... it occurred to me suddenly that I ought to call in on Spíros—a last chance to thank him, you see, before I left; to introduce my beloved daughter as a way of saying, perhaps, as my still limited Greek never could, how grateful I was. For what? Indeed for nothing I could ever put into words, Theo, even in English. For everything, I suppose, in a way. And I'd been so preoccupied lately that I'd given virtually no consideration to these matters. Nor, on his own different island, to the hazy, undefined, and... what shall I say: the very technical nature of our... friendship.

Yes, Theo, I thought, as I got out of the taxi and began searching about for the house—the street would have been a good start—of a bond defined almost entirely physically, through shared brushstrokes, and yet by those strokes rendered somehow transcendent of the physical altogether.

'Where is it you're looking for, Daddy?'

'It's here on the right. At least, I think it is. Someone I'd like you to meet. Or maybe it was the next turning. Is that the shop?'

'How should I know?' she shrugs. 'It doesn't look like one.'

'I could have sworn there was a shop here. It's the grid layout. So many white houses, and one corner looks very much like another.'

'Maybe the driver…?'

'I think it's just down here.'

But it wasn't, Theo. And with the visit such a spur-of-the-moment decision, I hadn't taken the trouble to look up the address again beforehand or bothered to get directions.

'Could you ring his mobile? Your friend?'

'Not and make any sense. My Greek… Even if I had the number.' I was hurrying on to a further corner; but stopped soon enough, because still no point of reference suggested itself, or any prompt of recognition. All remained stubbornly unfamiliar; and yet the old, broken citadel loomed over us from the mountain slope, just as it had when I'd first come calling. The turn, the house, it had been just hereabouts, surely.

I made a further attempt—in the other direction. But no luck there, either, and I looked foolishly all about me. It was puzzling. Theo, if I hadn't once genuinely lost my bearings only yards from the entrance to Paddington Station, I might have suspected some fairytale trope to be in operation: of the kind that casts linear narrative into circular question!

Somewhat disconsolately, I led Chloe back to the taxi. And now our driver had gone.

She laughed. 'At least *he* knows where the shop is.'

'Just when we can't ask him,' I said. But I wasn't to be daunted. 'Maybe he's in his workshop, anyway.'

'The driver?'

'No, Spíros. Spíros Apostolíthis, the icon painter.' I looked up. 'Come on!'

'Where?'

'Up there.' I pointed.

'Okay,' she said.

We crossed the road and set off up the track.

And gained, breathless but before too long, those ruined heights. We stopped to rest.

'It's magnificent,' she said. 'All of it. I do know why you came, Dad. To Greece, I mean. I can see why you love it.'

'Yes. But not to hide in, eh?'

'No. Not to hide in any more.'

426

We looked at each other and smiled. And here, high up in the heated air and with that gull hanging over me, perhaps the same one I saw before, I had no difficulty at all finding my bearings. Across the old square, along the rutted shapes of streets, beside long fallen stone houses, no, it took hardly any time to find first the signs of recent activity — attempts to mend, paint, rebuild and so on — and then soon, via that concealed twist of the route, the open stone steps up to his wooden door.

It was locked.

I tried again. I knocked hard at the heavy, studded timber. It merely hurt my knuckles. And so we stood together, nonplussed, turning this way and that on the step. 'Oh, well. That's it, then. Never mind.'

'Perhaps he's on holiday,' she said. 'It's August, after all.'

'Yes,' I said. 'Perhaps even Greeks go somewhere else. In August.' My thoughts were darker, though. That the ruin of Greece had reached him, too, and he'd suddenly lost everything and had to leave.

I gave the handle just one more futile twist. There was nothing for it but to give up and go down again. Theo, in our condition of lack... Theo, all the textbooks say absence is the eternal price of our entry into language. I make light of this. But the un-shadowed icon... 'I wish you could have seen them, Chlo. St George, he had that down there in the house. It was stunning, just this size: the horse, the dragon, the knight among the rocks. And then his Mary, *I Megáli Mitéra* — the Great Mother. He was in the middle of painting it when I...' I gestured upward at the locked door. 'A genuine master. Really. I wish you could have met him. At least I can show you the one he did for the church before we go. On Léros, I mean. The Angel. Archangel, I should say: Michael *Taxiárchis*. A perpetual fight, but at the same time perpetual victory. For reality. At least, so I say.'

'Yes, I know you do.'

We reached the foot of the workshop steps. In what had once been a little courtyard, I stared about. I remembered all too clearly sitting on that crumbling wall, weeping, so ashamed, holding my head in my hands. Now I climbed it boldly. Below was our taxi driver, returned, standing beside his car. I waved and shouted as loudly as I could. '*Periménete*! *Erchómaste*! — Wait! We're coming!'

'*Endáxi*! — Okay!' His voice echoed and dispersed itself, like mine, among the high crags.

Jumping down, I motioned Chloe to go. Theo, it was then I noticed a sheet of paper trapped not far off between some stones, where a tree grew out of another wall. At first I was inclined to dismiss it. One becomes used here to bits of detritus, even in the remotest, most charmed spots. With little rain, the sun preserves, and most modern materials stubbornly refuse to break down. Besides, the modern Greeks see their landscape more as a place of work than as our classical ideal; they're not much inclined to tidy — why should they?

The paper, however, struck me because of its large size and distinctive shape. And then I recognised it. You will have guessed, my friend, even as you shake your head, that it was one of mine. I must simply have failed to gather it up, that time so many weeks ago, when the roll of them fell from above and was scattered all over the rocks. And, with the winds, it had swept itself into a corner and became lodged.

Of course, I rescued it. I turned it up, smoothed it out on a flat rock. There it lay, in front of Chloe, a terrible darkness in cheap acrylics, damaged just a little by our one great storm. It showed a wolf and a boy — I say no more than that. I'd forgotten it, Theo, in all senses of the word. Just as I can't really now remember painting it, even so I hadn't remembered losing it. And no, I'm not implying anything miraculous about this particular case. No miracle is needed. If ever I'd glanced through my pile of left hand paintings before coming to Greece, I'd simply skipped over this one, or had failed to note it — so ambivalent I've always been about these pieces, so reluctant to see and so ready to disown — trance is our constant companion. But here, I guess, the page had simply tried to expose itself to the world. Of course it had; except no one had noticed — not me, not Spíros, nor even the patrolling birds and goats. Until now.

There could be absolutely no doubt I'd painted it. No one else would have, and it was truly part of the set. It had my left hand all over it. But, Theo, the Child, the poor Child. I looked at it again.

'It's okay, Dad.'

'Yeah,' I said. 'It's okay. It probably means nothing. Come on. Let's go.' I rolled the painting tight enough to hold, and we trekked down the hill.

At Póthia we had lunch on the waterfront. Then the big ferry came in, and the surprise I'd held in store was Arun, walking down the stern ramp, tall, upright, fashionably bearded, smiling and waving a greeting. What was that term: ἐσπλαγχνίσθη — a great yearning of emotion from the gut? So it was when the father in the story saw his son from afar and ran to embrace him. I ran, Theo. The love of family, exactly so it is.

I brought him to our table. He and Chloe embraced while I went to find the waiter — whom I'd seen bringing up crates and boxes from the ship. Inside at the bar, I watched with beating heart my children at their sunlit table. They talked and laughed. I was a father, flawed, human but not beyond hope, not beyond redemption; and there behind them the ferry's vast blue hull swallowed up lorries and cars and the island-hopping travellers on the harbour side with their back packs and suitcases. I saw the water churn blue-green and white as the hawsers slipped, and the huge vessel, delaying its turnaround not a moment longer, gathered pace, its funnels smoking black diesel exhaust, its aft ramp clanking and winding up as it headed off into the bay, to the horizon.

But even as I stepped out again from the bar and into the daylight, there was another ship in the offing, looming workmanlike round the Póthia headland — a ship a degree smaller, with an older, shabbier superstructure and a hull of rusty beige. I saw the Greek letters of its name, and it reminded me of the jaunty Pegasus, that had used to ply into Lakkí until the debt crisis forced that whole line out of business.

In fact the waiter came with our beers just as it swung around to dock, tail first; just as its anchor ran down with a rattle, and the chains of its winding gear began lowering the ramp.

But, Theo, my children were here, and, of course, we began at once an animated chattering — so animated, in fact, that I wouldn't have given a second thought to the new ship; had I not happened to brush away a visiting hornet and in the process glance around to where the passengers were just about starting to stream off.

My friend, if I'd kept a surprise for Chloe up my sleeve, it was nothing to the convergence of improbabilities that had arranged to beset me, and one other. I tell you, I'd thought I'd truly lost her. Sure, you've seen me quietly resigned to it; my feelings in that respect have been, maybe, too deep to articulate. Let's just say I believed her quite gone this time, and for good.

So to see her standing there on the lip of the ramp, waving suddenly, excitedly, as she saw me, waving as though she'd known all along that somehow we'd be here — though she tells me she was as astonished as I — now coming towards me, the breeze at last changed around, at last a cooler breath from the north gently tugging at the fabric of her blouse… My friend, it was a blessing, it was Julia: Julia, all at once and finally, the gift of the Aegean.

Author's Postscript & Discussion

My books take a long time to write. I like to work over the material a great deal, getting both hands into the keyboard (like Owen in the story) and feeling the substance of the language develop and mould as if it were a variety of clay. Even so, *The Icon Painter* surprised me, demanding a prodigious eight years in all. And it wasn't for want of application: the work was 'full on', only excepting the time I had to take out for my part time job. Quite why the book claimed so many hours, I don't know. I kept apologising to my agent, but, in the end, I just had to resign myself to the fact that each novel has its own rhythm.

During those eight years, however, the publishing landscape changed volcanically (and fundamentally). At the centre of it all came the financial crash, and one consequence was that the trade's appetite for so-called 'literary' fiction, already dwindling, withered to near zero. I should describe Literary Fiction (this time in capitals). It's a bookselling category to mop up novels that don't fit into an accepted genre but which are thought to exhibit 'literary' aspirations. Needless to say, such books don't usually make money, and the question arises as to why any commercial outfit would ever publish them in the first place.

The answer is, of course, that publishers like to publish—and to be seen to publish—authors whom the critics rate. It brings them kudos. They also like to gamble, for the industry is all about chance and speculation: where's the next bestseller coming from; who can spot the next J. K. Rowling; and so on. In good times, publishers gamble with a stable of 'literary' authors. They hope that at least one such writer will produce a runaway success, perhaps by winning a major prize, or having a novel made into a film, or turning out that magical book everyone's suddenly talking about. Publishers gamble on one big seller paying for the outlay on all the others! And there's nothing wrong with that; it's all part of the thrill. In hard times, though, the 'literary' list is the first to be axed. My books fulfil the trade definition of 'literary' on at least two counts: they elude recognised genres, and they haven't yet made my publishers any money!

But I'd like to come back about the literary aspirations. It's an unspoken given, both inside and out of publishing, that what makes a book 'literary' is some notion of 'good writing'. It's also widely assumed that 'good writing' is plain to detect and will somehow stand up on its own for all to see. It isn't, and it won't. Good writing is never an absolute, and the whole subject is, perhaps wilfully, shrouded in mystification.

Try this. Get hold of any Mills & Boon romance from the library and look at a paragraph or so. I defy you not to find the writing polished, effective, pacey and grammatically secure. If you read the whole book, you'll find that the construction, too, is tight and assured — probably tighter than in most other books. In particular, the sex scenes will occur on exactly the correct pages to bring off the desired effect. And yet so many people condemn these novels as 'bad' — more specifically as 'bad writing'. On the contrary, for their function, they're spectacularly well written, if somewhat mechanical. They have to be well crafted, or their customers wouldn't buy them in such vast quantities.

And that's the point, isn't it? In order to call writing 'good' or not, we have to assess it against its function. Does it do the job? Does it deliver the buzz the reader bought it for? Writing for Mills & Boon is such a precise art and so difficult a skill simply because the readership for those novels is extremely exacting. The stories have to deliver precisely the fantasy the reader expects — but deliver it as though it were freshly imagined each time. The writing must also draw so little attention to itself, by being so 'normal', so 'good' and so technically, grammatically and syntactically 'correct' that the reader forgets the reading process and becomes lost in the emotional trance of the plot — as if in a film.

* * * *

Novels as a form of literature haven't been around for long — compared, say, to Poetry or Histories. There's a debate about this terminology, but for all intents and purposes the idea of selling fiction — that is to say lies, made-up stories — first became acceptable in the early eighteenth century. One sometimes hears complaints that writers who lived before that turning point, e.g. Shakespeare, didn't make up their own plots. Indeed, inventing storylines is today taken so much to be an author's overwhelming preoccupation that the actual writing process is frequently spoken of as a mere chore to be slogged through.

Such a view is modern. For Shakespeare and his sixteenth/seventeenth century contemporaries, making up stories was never paramount. Apart from the fact that it ran the religious risk of contravening the Ninth Commandment (about bearing false witness), invention made the authorities wary that they might be satirised in the process. And although some plots *were* fabricated, often for that very reason, composition in general was far less about fantasising plots than delivering rhetorical colour to material already firmly 'in the public domain'. In other words, writing was for bringing known stories to life. And the playwrights were called 'poets'; they definitely weren't 'authors'. It would take a revolution, a regicide and the first signs of a middle class democracy before the profitability of lying in prose began regularly to catch on with both writers and printers.

Once cooked up, though, the Novel was just another commodity: to be marketed along with sugar, coffee, tea, clothing, the news media and all the other tempting luxuries and lies of an emerging global mercantile environment. And so for its first forty or fifty years the upstart Novel's fake life-histories, startling voyages, candid sexual confessionals, forged letters and mock epics dangled titillating questions of true or false over the public—until the form eventually began to settle down into certain recognisable *genres*.

To cut a long story short, these genres have kept pace with fashion and technology over the succeeding three centuries. And now we have all the well known labels: Romance, War, Action, Crime, Gay, Sci-Fi, Fantasy, Chick Lit, Historical, Thriller, Horror, Family Stories, Aga Saga and so on, each with its intricately worked out sub-categories. In all of them, the Novel continues to deliver a cleverly contrived escape: it takes the reader to another world, into someone else's life and adventures—the more stimulating and exotic the better. Long before the invention of film, the Novel could arouse the sensibilities, the sympathies and the passions. Hence the numerous prohibitions and dire warnings aimed down the years at those (especially females!) who would read them.

The novel came at an 'affordable' price. Like sugar, gin, and, in time, the opium derivatives, it provided a readily attainable kick of 'forbidden fruit'. In moderate doses, it could simply ease the tedium of the everyday. But, like all such items, each novel is an escape to be used just the once—for the hit of the plot—and then discarded. As soon as we 'know what happens' the pleasure is over.

It's precisely this throwaway characteristic of the form, its pre-installed obsolescence, that makes it such an ideal vehicle for generating a fast buck. 'Good writing', for such a purpose, should therefore seek to efface itself. 'Good writing' should aim to get out of the way — to be, as I said of Mills & Boon, so skilled, so grammatical, so very orthodox and 'ordinary' that the reader never notices it at all, but instead takes it as 'reality'. Writing as transparent, photographic 'reality' is the requirement of the marketplace. Constantly being distracted by quirks, oddities and imperfections in the style simply spoils the film-like trance of an un-put-down-able plot.

* * * *

So wherever did the idea of the 'literary' novel first creep in? If mass popularity determines quality, and 'bestseller' is the highest accolade, how can a not-for-profit form ever have arisen?

Right from the start, the Novel did have another kind of incarnation. It wasn't so much a genre as a *version* of itself. Jonathan Swift's tale of *Gulliver's Travels* (1726) is an early example. That book fed parasitically upon a contemporary vogue for travellers' tales, both true and falsified. Its primary purpose, nevertheless, was antithetical to the key idea of 'the Novel'; it was, in a sense, an *anti*-novel, and to miss this point is to miss the dialectics by which the novel form has continued to generate itself right down to the present. In fact, *Gulliver's Travels* took fiction — making things up — to the point of absurdity, with just enough of a straight face to bring off a blistering satire on the human race.

You might say, then, that it attempted to tell a kind of moral *truth*. That, surely, is the crucial difference. Never mind the modern book trade's Literary Fiction category, it was Swift's outraged attempt to subvert the Novel *as a form* that makes *Gulliver's Travels*, at least to my mind, a 'literary' work as opposed to a 'genre' one.

Yes, the genuinely 'literary' novel does *masquerade* as the genre item, but it is actually designed to fulfil some other purpose. It stands *against* the commercial promulgation of fantasies and myths. It hopes to disrupt the falsehoods upon which, it implies, mercantile society is founded. You'll see at once why the genuinely 'literary' novel is at heart no friend to the book trade. It is an intruder, an *agent provocateur*, a parasite, a stirrer, a dissenter. Publishers and booksellers are right to view it askance.

But the trade can't ignore it. The genuinely 'literary' novel has its occasional dramatic commercial successes, as I mentioned, and publishers have to keep an eye on that chance. *Gulliver's Travels* has never been out of print. That isn't because of its intrinsic commercial viability, of course; we don't buy it to throw it away. Its preservation (setting aside its neutered 'afterlife' as a nursery story) is owing to its academic designation as *Literature*.

Literature is writing we might need to read more than once. Literature is artificially removed from the Darwinist imperatives of the marketplace. Literature is deliberately held aloof from the forces of time. It suggests *personal* struggles with spirituality and relationship rather than generic ones. It occupies a 'sacred space'. As Literature, *Gulliver's Travels* remains persistently *in* the marketplace but not *of* it.

Unsurprisingly, most of Swift's contemporary rivals and novelistic models have long since died out of publication and been forgotten. What does still survive of them, paradoxically perhaps, is the entire *genre* he originally hijacked and then refuelled. We can recognise it today. It's the genre of exotic travellers' tales, now morphed into Fantasy, Speculative Fiction and Sci-Fi. It marches on totally innocent (with a few honourable dystopian exceptions) of Swift's original comedic and satirical fury. Effectively, it was the *genre* — the 'species' rather than its members — that continued to evolve in time, down to the present, while the individual 'literary' parasite that first preyed upon it still hangs in suspended animation, a little like those insects that can lie quite dormant until the next passing animal triggers them into action. Or maybe like some famous relic in its shrine… Whatever, *Gulliver's Travels* illustrates very well the *dual nature* of the form and the parasitic action of the 'literary' novel upon the genres. Or perhaps I should call it symbiotic. Yes, the more you think it through, the relationship is definitely symbiotic. I mentioned dialectics: 'genre' and 'literary' are bound together forever!

* * * *

Let me clarify just a little further. 'Literary' fiction could never exist of itself. Without the nourishment of the genres, the 'great' novels of Literature could never have sprung up out of nothing through any intrinsic notion of their 'good' or 'literary' writing. And every aspirational 'literary' novel today can only build upon, react against or modify genre fiction. In almost the same symbiotic instant, the genre novels are all responses to successful literary works, through imitations, sequels, prequels, spin-offs, developments and sheer naked attempts to cash in by association: for what appears at first provocative and threatening quickly becomes mainstream, once the readership grows accustomed to the new terms and conditions of the reading environment. In examining the history of the Novel, we constantly find ourselves in chicken and egg territory; 'literary' and 'genre' share this strange indeterminacy — it always looks as though the one were there before the other.

James Joyce's *Ulysses* was first 'published' in 1922. I set 'published' in quotes because *Ulysses* was originally printed in only a very limited edition by Sylvia Beach's ironically named 'Shakespeare and Company' in Paris. Beach effectively bankrolled the book for 'artistic' rather than commercial reasons. In any English speaking country of the time, Ulysses was totally *un*publishable, not only because it was explicit both in sexual and scatological terms, but also because it was written in no 'good' style. In fact, Joyce deliberately wrote its various sections in a plethora of styles — including popular newsprint journalese, coy romance and several completely experimental stream-of-consciousness techniques — in order to subvert the entire concept of a 'good' style.

Ulysses aimed to tell the truth about everyday life and its raw bodily functions rather than offer an escape from them. It defied the induction of trance; the reader certainly *could* put it down. More, as I've just noted, it was parasitic upon, or symbiotic with, not just one genre but the whole gamut of them. Its writing drew particular attention to itself *as writing*; it didn't seek to pretend it wasn't a construct. By all the publishing criteria of its day, *Ulysses* was stunningly 'bad' writing, and its impenetrability made its obscenity uncommercial even on the under-the-counter market.

Somewhere between 1930 and 1950, however, Joyce's *Ulysses* came to be acknowledged as Literature with a capital 'L' and was made properly available to the Anglo-Saxon world. What had previously been such 'bad' writing then, of course, became — by definition — 'good'. Imitators multiplied, and once again the literary exemplar caused genre fiction to mutate in turn. One of Joyce's most originally 'abhorrent' stylistic inventions — the abbreviated and anatomically candid interior monologue of his character Leopold Bloom — began to appear as the style of choice for a substantial amount of leading edge fiction, both genre and literary. It's a spare, minimal style, often in incomplete sentences, with observed facts and features presented next to each other, interspersed with snatches of thought and spontaneous expostulations. We now find it in all sorts of places, maybe crossed with Ernest Hemingway's gritty realism for novels of Action, Crime and War; or softened and feminised via influences from Virginia Woolf for Chick Lit, Celebrity or Shopping fiction. It has also penetrated the substantial and growing Teenage Fiction and Children's markets. Not only that, but the trade's current model of 'good writing' for the so-called Literary section of today's output (whatever of this remains) is also derived from it. Spare, terse, chopped and minimal styles are highly prized. Editors, like great surgeons or sculptors in marble, love creative cutting; and there exists a horror of amplification—for fear of losing the reader and surrendering the trance.

Thus in the market today a fast, write-as-you-speak, write-as-you-think style passes largely unquestioned and unremarked upon, even though it is still rhetorically distinctive. That said, it does retain at least some capacity to offend, or annoy, and so isn't *quite* the most currently employed technique of 'good-for-its-purpose' genre writing.

Which is, then? Well, the ideal market requirement, if you remember, is that there should be the least possible sense of interface between reader and narrative. As a result, the market actually prizes most of all a style that steers a safe middle course between the rather stilted correctness of Mills & Boon and the slightly too streetwise post-Joycean stream of consciousness. It prefers proper sentences, but short and pithy ones. It privileges dialogue over description, but still likes the narrative room for sex, movement, drama and so on. The market looks, in sum, for a rhetoric of non-rhetoric, a kind of deliberate self-effacement of 'writing'.

Where, historically, would it have discovered such a style?

* * * *

Jane Austen is not and was not a genre novelist. Despite what many would like to think, the literary status of Austen's work is not the result of her skill at telling love stories. Two of her books, *Northanger Abbey* and *Emma*, are quite explicitly *predatory* upon genre fiction. In the first case, she mocks the Gothic Romance, and, in the second, she clearly satirises Romantic Fiction *per se*. That she manages to pull positive love stories out of the satire every time she writes is a testament to her creative achievement and optimistic religious beliefs rather than evidence of any enslavement to the genre. No, her work is anti-commercial as a premise, and whatever rewards her writing gained her in her own lifetime were not the result of her fulfilling book trade expectations. If she'd wanted to make a fast buck, she could have hooked up with the genre publishers operating at the time. What turns genre conventions into a vehicle for her personal revenges—upon the thwarting moral weakness and hypocrisy she finds around her—is her *anger*.

Her work became Literature with a capital 'L' because academia gradually recognised the great technical leaps and supreme narrative achievements this anger drove. Academia now acknowledges that a century before Joyce's experiments it was Austen who virtually invented—or at least fully assembled and developed—the over-the-shoulder third person narrative. It's a kind of camera angle whereby the third person narrator sits so close to the head of the central character that we find it hard to distinguish the one from the other. As a result, we're constantly sucked into the central character's mind without quite realising it. At the same time, the authorial voice always retains the ability—as with any camera—to detach and provide those more dispassionate observations by which a corrective reality can be conveyed. It was the great and literary Jane Austen who discovered how to hold the novel reader firmly in both an intellectual and an emotional grip!

What happened subsequently, of course, involved the usual pattern of imitation and assimilation. Austen's striking technical advances somehow fed into and enriched the English and European *literary* traditions of the nineteenth century. There we begin to find the narrator assuming godlike insight into a variety of characters by sitting on *several* shoulders rather than just the one—perhaps a dangerous kind of hubris! It is these techniques that have contributed crucially, if in a very simplified form, to the *genre* style most dominant now. Sit the narrator right by a character's head, record a great deal of conversation, pare the description down to the bare essentials, and you have the most popular genre style. Browse in any bookshop or library and you find it everywhere on the shelves. And its other great advantage is that it comes 'camera ready': this writing style is instantly translatable into TV or film. It's the genre fiction gold standard: quintessentially 'good' writing—for that purpose.

* * * *

To sum up, the genre novel, with its self-effacing and 'transparent' mainstream writing style aims to evoke emotions in the reader principally via the workings of the plot. The author of the genre novel is a highly skilled manipulator of events, a puppet master or mistress, who pulls the strings to jerk the feelings (or laughs) which can only really be generated once per story. Neither do we expect the storyteller to be affected by the material. Not on the page, at least. We demand a professional detachment. We don't want the author's burning passions and crippling neuroses upstaging our own responses, or those of the characters! Nor must there be any expectation of effort on the part of the reader. In the world of the genre novel, which is increasingly the entire world of modern commercial publishing of fiction, the readers are customers, and the last thing they want after a hard day at work is to be distracted by heavy philosophical demands, quirks or 'errors' in the writing.

In the 'literary' novel, on the other hand, the reader's feelings are often secondary to those of the writer, and the emotional content of the story is at least to some extent taken over by authorial preoccupations. In that respect, the literary novel is more like poetry (as the term 'literary' implies); the customer is not king, and there's a sense of a 'voice' behind the writing. Very often in the literary novel, though not always, that voice is motivated by anger or outrage.

What we have to come to terms with is that 'literary' fiction is writing that tries to refuse its reader an entirely unconditional experience. Rather than hide its own artifice in 'transparency', it likes to insist, at least to some extent, upon its writing *as writing*. It makes some show of it. It also looks to take responsibility for what it's doing, perhaps by varying styles, perhaps even by making overt its status as a forgery of events. And because it resists, at least partially, the induction of trance, the reader, as I suggested, *can* put it down. The pleasure is less in the escape of pursuing 'what happens next' than in the text *as text*. The writing will not be uniform and self-effacing. It may be experimental, it may be multifarious; it may well have all the idiosyncrasies associated with any individual voice, or voices. It's less winning and professional than the market novel, perhaps, because there's a purpose to it overriding (at least slightly!) the aim to make money.

And, because its ultimate justification rests not on the measurable index of a sales spreadsheet but only upon academic or 'Arts Pages' esteem, the literary novel is far more vulnerable to criticism. Rightly so, for while the genre item is straightforwardly for recreational use and can be judged as such, the literary novel would — sometimes pompously—seek to package almost the same 'drug' as a moral corrective or social 'medicine'.

Such a prescription was very aptly summed up by the early twentieth century Russian theorist Viktor Shklovsky. Art, he suggested, should aim to 'de-familiarise', to 'alienate' or 'make strange' the world as we think we know it. Art should not make things easy for the viewer or the reader. Art should be difficult. Art should confront the viewer/reader's preconceptions and seek to disrupt them. Only in this way is the body of the creative tradition re-energised.

Difficult art obviously includes difficult novels. But they need not be abstract in their difficulty. Mikhail Bakhtin, a contemporary of Shklovsky, argued further that the corrective or even purgative duty of the novel was the duty of 'carnival'—to turn upside down the normal order of things, to insist, sometimes riotously, on disclosing those parts of the body or aspects of life that society for the rest of the year insists on covering up. Both of these Russian scholars are little known nowadays outside of academic circles, but it would be hard, I think, to formulate more succinctly than in their terms the pretty much universal 'project' of the 'literary' novel: to write so as to interrupt the complacent flow of normality and, with some gusto, to make strange the everyday. It was a project fully in play even as Shklovsky and Bakhtin were formulating it, as we've seen from Joyce. And then many subsequent twentieth century novelists persisted quite literally with the body parts and carnival until the usual thing happened: the formerly shocking became completely commonplace. Today, riotous impropriety is everywhere in genre fiction. But that's beside the key point. To my mind, it's still those two active *principles*—de-familiarisation and carnival*esque* disruption—that perfectly encapsulate the aims of the genuinely literary novelist.

And so marking literary novels for 'good' writing is impossible. To demonstrate that really starkly just have a look at *Last Exit to Brooklyn*—there simply isn't a clear and obvious *function* to assess the writing against. Nevertheless, its denotation as literary is secure.

To appear in the marketplace at all, any novel with genuinely 'literary' aspirations will most likely have to smuggle itself in, under the noses, as it were, of the accountants and sales directors. It will have to convince a risk-taking commissioning editor that what might even appear to be 'bad' writing might one day turn out to be 'good'. 'Good writing'/'bad writing'—I hope by now I've established how very slippery are these terms.

I remember how, when I was a student, I saw *Wuthering Heights* on a list of 'The 100 worst novels ever written'. I was a student when The Novel as a form was still only rather grudgingly accepted as worth serious academic attention, and the revolution in critical thought that had its roots in Shklovsky and Bakhtin hadn't yet happened to England. Novels in those days, apart from some obvious literary 'heavies', were assumed to be straightforward enough—what was there to be said about them? *Wuthering Heights* was clearly overemotional teenage stuff for girls.

Following the great shifts of the seventies and eighties in the theoretics of criticism, however, *Wuthering Heights* became a prime subject for 're-reading', as in re-evaluation. Its unusual construction, its unexpected narrative techniques and its wholly unconventional levels of violence all made it an ideal site for the deployment of experimental critical approaches. As a result (although the habit of 're-reading' texts has dwindled somewhat in academic prominence), the book has now been firmly established as potential Literature.

* * * *

It was about ten years ago that the publishing industry invented a new category. The aim was to wrest back control over so unpredictable a business and, it goes without saying, to boost profits—particularly since a big new group of more sophisticated readers was just opening up in the mass market. The new category was to be called Accessible Literary Fiction. Maybe, its inventors reasoned, the hard distinctions between 'literary' and 'genre' could be blurred, and then we should have no more of those unreadable Modernist or dialect novels that twentieth century academics professed to admire so much, no more difficult and unsaleable books influenced by Europeans, no more artsy Post-Modernist stuff.

And academics themselves, those souls with the 'priestly' function of determining what is and what isn't Literature, seem to have turned a blind eye to the move. Perhaps they, too, saw the advantages of 'accessibility', pressed as they were to cope with a sudden vast expansion in student numbers. Perhaps they, too, were weary of the seeming dead end of Post-Structuralism. Perhaps their attention was merely diverted by the constant fight against government cuts and ever increasing personal duties. Whatever, Accessible Literary Fiction succeeded in establishing itself without a whisper and without hardly mentioning its name. And it began generating a great many books. As the new space opened up in the market, new writers rushed in to fill it.

The result was a change in perspective. 'The book' as sales success became more relevant than 'the author' as artist. It took us all by surprise. Even before the great financial crash of 2008, pressure fell quite suddenly upon previously 'literary' authors to change stance, to adapt to the new 'accessible' terms of reference. And the great drive to expand reading as 'a leisure experience' had wider consequences, too. Never mind the paperbacks, I'd been accustomed to see my new *hardbacks* in the bookshops at least on publication day. But when my fourth novel came out and was nowhere to be found, I was flummoxed. I walked from big London bookstore to big London bookstore until I noticed it wasn't just mine that was missing. *All* hardback fiction had completely disappeared from view—with the exception of a few huge genre bestsellers. The bookshops, as though at some prearranged signal, had abruptly ceased to stock any, and all the publishers were caught out. What was the point, suddenly, of my artsy radio appearances and my 'so important' press reviews if the book itself was invisible? What was the point of anybody's? 'Sorry, Derek, it's the discount sales effect, the Tesco effect, the media moguls...' There were all sorts of explanations; but the message, at first so bewildering, soon became starkly clear. Paperback volume sales were the future. Become More Accessible. Or—in a very polite, English manner of speaking—Else.

Shouldn't books be accessible? Where was the problem? Who the heck did we think we were?

Fair questions; but the discerning reader of this article will see that the introduction of a sliding scale between 'literary' and 'genre' and the discreet yet all-pervasive brutality of simply comparing sales figures threatens at root what I've described as a creative tension between these two *versions* of the novel. It fudges that interaction between the individual and the generic that I've tried to suggest is crucial to the form. To put it bluntly, it destroys the vital dialogue between the imperfect, experimental artist and the skilled, polished craftsperson.

Yes, it's right to debunk the mystique of the artist. The twentieth century critical tradition I've already alluded to ended up by pulling 'The Author' completely off his pedestal. Who needs artists? Who needs 'authors', with all their airs and angst and self-absorption?

Yes, I'd agree; but for the fact that when the 'literary' novelists are kicked out of the city, the preoccupations of *all* novels become gradually dragged into the preoccupations of the market. Everything has to become market friendly. Even if someone here or there does stretch genre boundaries a little the product must ultimately be *designed* to sell.

The form loses its dynamism. For all the deluge of books published, many of them very 'good' and very skilled, fewer boats are actually rocked, fewer perceptions or preconceptions really challenged, fewer awkward artistic questions posed. Connoisseurship returns. Taste rules. Entertainment triumphs. The art ossifies. And for all the labels of 'good writing' generously applied to jackets or lavished in reviews, we often discover nothing more inside the text than a slight conservative rowing back in style towards those modes of expression orthodox before the impact of the twentieth century. Or we find some slightly more demanding or 'poetic' register that simply offers to a more sophisticated readership the same escapism, the same delicious one-hit trance of a damned good story! I say again, that for this precise purpose, many 'accessible literary novels' are indeed very 'well written' and extremely well crafted: many are very 'good' books. But, on my definition, they're rarely in any necessary sense 'literary'.

* * * *

The discerning reader will also note that in all this talk of writing, I've so far implied reading as a given. Everyone knows what reading is, don't they? The writer writes and the reader reads—it's as simple as that. Isn't it?

Well, no, it isn't. I'm aware that much of the public conversation about books and their reception today *does* see reading as wonderfully unproblematic. But it simply is not. Precisely what we're doing when we read a book—or a film, for that matter—was a key subject in all that academic analysis during the last century. Ah, how much important radical thought appears to have been just swept up and junked into skips by the new globalised economy!

For, when I mentioned the opposing types of pleasure available to the reader, I had in mind *Le Plaisir du Texte*, by the French academic Roland Barthes, one of the most influential of all those late theorists of literary reception. In his studies we find outlined another kind of reading than the everyday, just as the 'literary' novel seems to ask for another kind of writing. Barthes always challenges us to resist the passive trance induced, say, by the genre novel. He suggests a notion of reading both active and constructive: what can we make out of this text; in what unexpected ways can we enter it; how can we break out of the special trap the author has set? Reading in this assertive, profoundly attentive way snatches control away from 'the author', and, by implication, from the commercial interests behind publication. Such reading offers the pleasure of liberation—Barthes uses the word *jouissance*, with all its connotations. This is essentially a *creative* pleasure within which the reader may potentially make the text in question sing to a different tune.

Now, a moment's reflection reveals that there's not so very much difference between reading in the way Barthes demands and the writing of a 'literary' novel. This is because, on the definition I've made, the genuinely literary novel is nothing if not a creative 'reading' of other texts. It acknowledges its sources in a way the genre novel never does; the genuinely literary novel inserts itself into a tradition of *reading*, so that its content appears to ripple back and forth across the history of literary production.

Of course, the genre novel also makes readings—of literary texts— as we've seen. Yes, indeed, but its readings are unacknowledged, implicit or hidden, in order that the story should remain crucially one-directional. This is not a criticism of the genre novel or of genre novelists. I admire many and wouldn't dream of denigrating them. What I'm trying to hold on to is that there really are two distinct versions of the Novel as a form, and that they really do play off, one against the other, in that tantalising, dialectical, chicken and egg way. I'm arguing, once again, that the notion of a middle ground between them—Accessible Literary Fiction—is a superbly fraudulent construct designed to neutralise the threat to business ideology posed by the genuinely literary novel and those texts marked out by academia as Literature. If we're not mindful of this we shall effectively 'misread' what novels are and how they work. And we shall surrender total control of the reception of text to powerful market interests.

For reading today is big business; almost as many people are reading novels as writing them! On book websites, readers are given stars to award and a little space to write a comment. This offers a sense of community—a social democracy of reading—and must be accounted a 'good thing'; but it has little to do with what Barthes envisaged. In truth, matters are neatly contrived so that the terms of the marketplace and the values of genre fiction are yet again always privileged, and the reader is only really encouraged to evaluate the degree of passive buzz s/he has been exposed to. Every book, whether Literature, 'literary' or 'genre' is subject to the same consumerist appraisal. On the Goodreads website, Joyce's *Ulysses* – probably the most influential novel of the twentieth century – is awarded only a hilarious 3.7 stars out of a potential five.

If we're to reclaim from the current undifferentiated flood of novels some sense of what Fiction is and what it might become, and if the bookselling category Literary Fiction is to mean anything at all, then we must surely challenge the easy falsehoods of 'accessibility'. It's time to resurrect in the public arena that fading idea of another kind of reading: reading that requires a willingness to engage with the challenges of the difficult text; reading with the humility to accept that all may not reveal itself in one breath; reading for the pleasure to be gained specifically from the writing *as writing*, and not from writing's self-effacement. Isn't it a duty to question the thrust of the marketplace and reapportion some value to 'literary' as distinct from 'genre'? And, with no disrespect to those great critics who did us such a service in killing off the former unexamined concept of 'The Author', isn't it now also a duty, by wrestling through all that, to breathe a bit of life back into the corpse?

* * * *

I began by mentioning my own books. I have tried to challenge the genre setup in all of them. Whether or not I've succeeded isn't for me to say. I've already acknowledged that they don't fit into the marketplace very well. But it was only after the threat to the Literary Fiction category became clear, that I really had to make a choice. Should I give up on the uncomfortable material I seemed to be saddled with and learn to write more accessible stories, or should I kick against the pricks and go in the opposite direction?

I guess I never particularly wanted to spin yarns. My writing springs from a sort of physical compulsion: it comes more from my hands than from my head, and maybe that's why the books take so long. For it's often as though the head actively resists them, and the angry hands, at work on the keyboard, are left to drive the composition forward.

There we have it. If anger and outrage are the spurs to the genre-hijacking operation I've been describing as 'literary', then my books do at least qualify on that front. It's a bodily anger that can find no other outlet, apparently, than forcing experience into the novelistic form.

Newton's Niece, my first, fed clearly upon the Historical genre. Every detail in it that could be researched was researched, and I made it a matter of conscience not to invent or rearrange any known historical fact or document. It certainly isn't a Historical Novel, though; I mean in the genre sense of the word (although critics seemed to struggle with this when the book came out). Careful reading shows that it's simply an act of memory modelled on the eighteenth century *Female Picaresque*. Of course, for anyone's memory to stretch back three centuries to the origins both of the Novel and of modern Science must surely require a little 'Science Fiction' input—but I used it for that purpose and that purpose only. So it's not a Sci-Fi novel either. I wanted to write an account of real historical events that would fit all the known details but none of the dominant 'male' interpretations of them. By taking the astonishing historical fact that Isaac Newton really did have with him in London a figure as potentially disruptive to his hard-line all-male intellectual project as his pretty niece, Catherine Barton, I wanted to show that the Novel (Fiction) could challenge Science (Fact) on its own terms. (That was one of the purposes of the book, at least.) So *Newton's Niece* is a novel that seeks to *read* Science's foundation myth 'against the grain'.

Acts of Mutiny is a Sea Story, a Love Story, a Comedy of Manners and a tragic Political Thriller (I capitalise the genre categories). But it's also none of these, being simply another document of memory. This one includes the imagined reconstructions of its narrator and therefore confesses to certain 'fictions'. I thought of it as a fugue in five voices, three of them in the third person and two in the first. If *Newton's Niece* harks back to early eighteenth century texts, *Acts of Mutiny* pays homage to Conrad and Melville, those nineteenth century masters of the sea. Its style is consequently a little more formal, a touch more reflective. Its purpose is not primarily to entertain.

If the Invader Comes smuggles itself through as an out-and-out Second World War story, and yet we stay away from the typical scenes of the war itself and look instead at parallel kinds of invaders, domestic battles and 'war crimes' that are personal; at least until the last part. There's also a broad organising structure based on the Indonesian shadow play mentioned early in the book, but so far no reader has noticed this, I think. This book, too, acknowledges itself as a construct, if you read carefully.

446

His Coldest Winter is the book of mine so far that *doesn't* seek to account for itself as a document. In one sense, it's a straight third person Cold War Spy Thriller. And yet, in another, it's a teenage Love Story structured closely on *Romeo and Juliet*. It also has a small Science Fiction element that attempts to read outwards from some visions under an electron microscope in order to re-form the whole plot on a kind of quantum theory of events; though, again, I don't think anyone has particularly noticed. Of course they haven't. Heavens! Why should they! Anyway, all my work to date does have enough 'literary aspirations', I'd have thought, to annihilate all chance of royalties for me or profit for the publishers. Case proven, at least on that ground! Anything beyond aspiration to the literary is, as I've said, not up to me to judge.

Perhaps I've already gone too far; because I've observed that, as an author, it's considered unseemly to discuss the technicalities of writing. Other matters are very much up for grabs: such as how many hours a day one spends at the computer, or how one goes about research, or who one admires, or whether one waits for inspiration to arrive or just slogs away at it, day in, day out. But not the structural matters; and this is the case even within the trade—perhaps especially within the trade. It's true: no one in publishing ever talks about such things. When I first discovered this, I was amazed. I'd expected the industry's whole conversation to be about the mechanism of plots, the intricacies of character, the impact of Deconstruction and the theoretics of Reader Response. On the contrary, publishing knows nothing of these things; and what it did know it has laboured to forget. Publishing runs on feelings, on gut intuition, and on that elusive experience they call 'falling in love' with a book. Any analysis, it's said, is to be left to 'the critics'.

There's a reason for this which I've already given. Publishing is always such a scary risk, even with potentially 'sure fire' bestsellers. Everything is at stake with a book: careers, status, money—and the market is very, very fickle. There's just no room for complications.

Unfortunately, though, 'the critics' don't want to discuss the technicalities either, being themselves mostly part of the trade. And academics really only analyse the dead. You will see from this article how sad I feel that fiction is now taken as so obvious and self-explanatory that anyone's opinion is as good as anyone else's. On review sites it all pretty much comes down to whether a reader 'liked' it or not. Yes, I know, that is laudably democratic and flips the bird at the elite who previously controlled what we read and what we thought, but it does little for genuine understanding of fiction as a medium. I think we can see how maintaining the mystique and the mystery about 'good writing' has effectively sabotaged informed discussion. At the same time, it has neatly defused at source any threat to the market proposed by the 'literary'.

* * * *

So *The Icon Painter* is the product of my conscious choice to go my own way and not the way of the market. When I began it, I knew in my heart there would be little chance of it ever seeing the light. The very strange thing about its long gestation, however, is that electronic publishing has — astonishingly — come along. And that gives someone like me the extraordinary chance to publish the book he wants to and the chance also to talk a little about what he's actually been trying to do — a freedom, as I suggested, mostly unavailable under previous conditions.

Let's come to the book, then. Although it's set resolutely in 2012 (effectively, 'The Present'), it returns to an eighteenth century technique, where my career began, by echoing the epistolary, or Letter Novel; or echoing, indeed, that strange one-way (as we receive it) 'journal' also written by Jonathan Swift: the *Journal to Stella*. I've done mine via emails, although they're not in the hasty convention of email-*ese* but rather in normal sentences. It's already been objected to me that no one writes long emails in this fashion. But that's precisely the point of the story. Owen Davy, the painter, the artist, discovers how emails can in fact expand to any length their writer wishes. I don't think he's alone in this: I've certainly written long emails at times and been involved in correspondences where the luxury and speed of the keyboard meant that the word count far exceeded anything I'd ever have done using pen and paper. I had in mind, too, the enormous and strange expansion of material in Samuel Richardson's letter novels *Pamela* (1740) and *Clarissa* (1748), both of which I very much admire, particularly because they study accurately, and from so early a perspective, the horrible consequences of sexual assault.

The Icon Painter is also explicitly built on a number of Greek myths and Greek plays, and modelled to some extent on *Hamlet*. But none of these sources and structuring narratives could be called genre fiction, and they're really just the means of anchoring the novel into a 'tradition'. The true genre that organises my book is simply that of the Love Story, that most fundamental of all literary forms. I hope you'll enjoy it.

Previous Novels, Prizes, Shortlists and Reviews

Derek Beaven's first novel, *Newton's Niece* (1994), won a Commonwealth Writers Prize and was shortlisted for the Writers' Guild 'Best Fiction Book' 1994 award. *Acts of Mutiny* (1998) was shortlisted for the Guardian Fiction Prize and the Encore Prize; the American edition was listed as one of the *Los Angeles Times* Best Books of the Year (2000). *If the Invader Comes* (2001) was long-listed for the Man Booker Prize. *His Coldest Winter* was published in 2005.

Samples from Reviews

Newton's Niece

'Magnificent set pieces, a richness of thought, a prodigal and original talent make this a novel worth reading from a writer worth watching.' *Time Out*

'An exuberant debut, ambitious and questing.' *Observer*

'One is in no doubt that one is in the hands of a truly remarkable and gifted writer ... This endlessly fascinating and inventive novel is funny and profound by turns.' *Hampstead & Highgate Express*

'An important and original writer' Hilary Mantel

Acts of Mutiny

'An extraordinary novel.' *Sunday Times*

'In its method, slowly pulling the whole into focus, Beaven is reminiscent of William Faulkner ... But the strength of his novel, its confident eloquence and menace are distinctive and unforgettable.' David Horspool *Daily Telegraph*

'Arresting ... [Beaven] displays an impressive and wholly distinctive grip on both language and form.' Eve Claxton *Time Out* (New York)

'Ambitious, relentlessly ominous ... Mark Rozzo *Los Angeles Times*

'You'll be lulled by Beaven's descriptive talent and transported by the novel's more conventional pleasures — sympathetic characters and an exciting, geopolitical plot.' Mark Schone *New York Times Book Review*

'The psychological accuracy with which Beaven describes character, and the truthfulness of his observation of childhood, is matched by the enjoyable precision with which he evokes time and place ... a beautifully written book.' Christina Koning *The Times*

If the Invader Comes

'Large, deft, prickly and ambitious. His work practically explodes with narrative assurance.' Julie Myerson *Guardian*

'A remarkable feat of the imagination.' *Literary Review*

'Vic and Clarice are not asking for much, simply to be together. Yet with the intensifying horror around them, plus the burden of their own secrets and deceits, that simple ambition tests them both in this powerful, sharply conceived novel.' Dominic Bradbury *The Times*

A grand love story, tenderly written, that does justice to the huge subject of war by showing us the often terrible, sometimes magnificent effects it has on small lives.' Alison Rowatt, *Herald*

'Beaven has a gift for creating insistently human individuals who prove to be illuminating under pressure ... a fine engagement with the largest and smallest details of what it is to be English.' Lavinia Greenlaw *Times Literary Supplement*

His Coldest Winter

'With wonderful imaginative intensity, expressed in an original style of elliptical impressionism galvanised by sudden realistic shocks, Derek Beaven uses an austere background to dramatize a story of the rivalry of young love, the rivalry of ton-up motorcycle gangs, and the rivalry of international industrial espionage of military urgency ... An ingenious, multi-layered novel.' *Sunday Telegraph*

'An oblique, suggestive, estranging book that knits together sex, treachery, Cold War politics and hard science.' *Literary Review*

'Gripping' *Sunday Express*

'A wonderful book ... very moving' Rosie Boycott on BBC Radio 4

'A master of evoking atmosphere ... Beaven writes about physical surroundings and physical sensations with absolute clarity and a poetically oblique manner.' *Sunday Business Post*

'One of our most uncompromisingly individual novelists' *Guardian*

'This is a fine novel that achieves an extraordinary exactitude of feeling matched by a perfect sense of place.' Jane Housham *Guardian*

'A cold weather, Cold War thriller' *Telegraph*

About the Author

Printed in Great Britain
by Amazon.co.uk, Ltd.,
Marston Gate.